Praise for Michael Connelly

'Connelly is one of the great crime writers, a novelist who creates a fictional world so succinctly, and inhabits it so purposefully, that you are convinced it must be real. His mastery of place and character, his ease with dialogue, his control of plot gives his books a subtlety that is irresistible'
Daily Mail

'A clever plot, full of twists, to make a first-rate legal thriller'
Sunday Telegraph

'Connelly's fifth novel to feature roguish defence lawyer Mickey Haller is even better than last year's *The Black Box*'
Mail on Sunday

'Expect surprises and plenty of dark moments in this punchy legal drama from an ever-reliable writer' *Financial Times*

'Connelly is superb at building suspense' *Wall Street Journal*

'In the crime fiction stakes Connelly is comfortably in the upper bracket' *Daily Express*

'A clever thriller with a brilliant double twist but also a heartfelt examination of the difference between natural justice and the law' *Evening Standard*

'Connelly masterfully manages to marry an absorbing courtroom drama with a tense and exciting thriller of detection'
The Times

'While the themes of Connelly's LA crime novels are familiar (power, envy, corruption), his plotting is anything but' *Esquire*

'A story that's as old as the genre itself but Connelly's skill is such that it all feels entirely fresh and vibrant, but heartbreakingly poignant too' *Irish Sunday Independent*

By Michael Connelly

A former police reporter for the *Los Angeles Times*, Michael Connelly is the author of the Harry Bosch thriller series as well as several other bestsellers, including the highly acclaimed legal thriller, *The Lincoln Lawyer*, selected for the Richard and Judy Book Club. Michael Connelly has been President of the Mystery Writers of America. His books have been translated into 31 languages and have won awards all over the world, including the Edgar and Anthony Awards. He lives in Tampa, Florida, with his family. Visit his website at www.michaelconnelly.com

MICHAEL CONNELLY
THE REVERSAL

An Orion paperback

First published in Great Britain in 2010
by Orion Books
This paperback edition published in 2011
by Orion Books
and imprint of The Orion Publishing Group Ltd,
Orion House, 5 Upper St Martin's Lane,
London WC2H 9EA

An Hachette UK company

Reissued 2015

A CIP catalogue record for this book
is available from the British Library.

ISBN 978-1-4091-5740-3

Printed and bound in Great Britain by Clays Ltd, St Ives plc

The Orion Publishing Group's policy is to use papers that
are natural, renewable and recyclable products and
made from wood grown in sustainable forests. The logging
and manufacturing processes are expected to conform to
the environmental regulations of the country of origin.

www.orionbooks.co.uk

To Shannon Byrne with many thanks

PART ONE
–The Perp Walk

1

The last time I'd eaten at the Water Grill I sat across the table from a client who had coldly and calculatedly murdered his wife and her lover, shooting both of them in the face. He had engaged my services to not only defend him at trial but fully exonerate him and restore his good name in the public eye. This time I was sitting with someone with whom I needed to be even more careful. I was dining with Gabriel Williams, the district attorney of Los Angeles County.

It was a crisp afternoon in midwinter. I sat with Williams and his trusted chief of staff—read political advisor—Joe Ridell. The meal had been set for 1:30 P.M., when most courthouse lawyers would be safely back in the CCB, and the DA would not be advertising his dalliance with a member of the dark side. Meaning me, Mickey Haller, defender of the damned.

The Water Grill was a nice place for a downtown lunch. Good food and atmosphere, good separation between tables for private conversation, and a wine list hard to top in all of downtown. It was the kind of place where you kept your suit jacket on and the waiter put a black napkin across your lap so you needn't be bothered

3

with doing it yourself. The prosecution team ordered martinis at the county taxpayers' expense and I stuck with the free water the restaurant was pouring. It took Williams two gulps of gin and one olive before he got to the reason we were hiding in plain sight.

'Mickey, I have a proposition for you.'

I nodded. Ridell had already said as much when he had called that morning to set up the lunch. I had agreed to the meet and then had gone to work on the phone myself, trying to gather any inside information I could on what the proposition would be. Not even my first ex-wife, who worked in the district attorney's employ, knew what was up.

'I'm all ears,' I said. 'It's not every day that the DA himself wants to give you a proposition. I know it can't be in regard to any of my clients — they wouldn't merit much attention from the guy at the top. And at the moment I'm only carrying a few cases anyway. Times are slow.'

'Well, you're right,' Williams said. 'This is not about any of your clients. I have a case I would like you to take on.'

I nodded again. I understood now. They all hate the defense attorney until they need the defense attorney. I didn't know if Williams had any children but he would have known through due diligence that I didn't do juvy work. So I was guessing it had to be his wife. Probably a shoplifting grab or a DUI he was trying to keep under wraps.

'Who got popped?' I asked.

Williams looked at Ridell and they shared a smile.

'No, nothing like that,' Williams said. 'My proposition is this. I would like to hire you, Mickey. I want you to come work at the DA's office.'

Of all the ideas that had been rattling around in my head since I had taken Ridell's call, being hired as a prosecutor wasn't one of them. I'd been a card-carrying member of the criminal defense bar for more than twenty years. During that time I'd grown a suspicion and distrust of prosecutors and police that might not have equaled that of the gangbangers down in Nickerson Gardens but was at least at a level that would seem to exclude me from ever joining their ranks. Plain and simple, they wouldn't want me and I wouldn't want them. Except for that ex-wife I mentioned and a half brother who was an LAPD detective, I wouldn't turn my back on any of them. Especially Williams. He was a politician first and a prosecutor second. That made him even more dangerous. Though briefly a prosecutor early in his legal career, he spent two decades as a civil rights attorney before running for the DA post as an outsider and riding into office on a tide of anti-police and -prosecutor sentiment. I was employing full caution at the fancy lunch from the moment the napkin went across my lap.

'Work for you?' I asked. 'Doing what exactly?'

'As a special prosecutor. A onetime deal. I want you to handle the Jason Jessup case.'

I looked at him for a long moment. First I thought I would laugh out loud. This was some sort of cleverly orchestrated joke. But then I understood that couldn't be the case. They don't take you out to the Water Grill just to make a joke.

'You want me to prosecute Jessup? From what I hear there's nothing to prosecute. That case is a duck without wings. The only thing left to do is shoot it and eat it.'

Williams shook his head in a manner that seemed intended to convince himself of something, not me.

'Next Tuesday is the anniversary of the murder,' he said. 'I'm going to announce that we intend to retry Jessup. And I would like you standing next to me at the press conference.'

I leaned back in my seat and looked at them. I've spent a good part of my adult life looking across courtrooms and trying to read juries, judges, witnesses and prosecutors. I think I've gotten pretty good at it. But at that table I couldn't read Williams or his sidekick sitting three feet away from me.

Jason Jessup was a convicted child killer who had spent nearly twenty-four years in prison until a month earlier, when the California Supreme Court reversed his conviction and sent the case back to Los Angeles County for either retrial or a dismissal of the charges. The reversal came after a two-decade-long legal battle staged primarily from Jessup's cell and with his own pen. Authoring appeals, motions, complaints and whatever legal challenges he could research, the self-styled lawyer made no headway with state and federal courts but did finally win the attention of an organization of lawyers known as the Genetic Justice Project. They took over his cause and his case and eventually won an order for genetic testing of semen found on the dress of the child Jessup had been convicted of strangling.

Jessup had been convicted before DNA analysis was used in criminal trials. The analysis performed these many years later determined that the semen found on the dress had not come from Jessup but from another unknown individual. Though the courts had repeatedly upheld Jessup's conviction, this new information tipped the scales in Jessup's favor. The state's supreme court cited the DNA findings and other inconsistencies in the evidence and trial record and reversed the case.

This was pretty much the extent of my knowledge of the Jessup case, and it was largely information gathered from newspaper stories and courthouse scuttlebutt. While I had not read the court's complete order, I had read parts of it in the *Los Angeles Times* and knew it was a blistering decision that echoed many of Jessup's long-held claims of innocence as well as police and prosecutorial misconduct in the case. As a defense attorney, I can't say I wasn't pleased to see the DA's office raked over the media coals with the ruling. Call it underdog schadenfreude. It didn't really matter that it wasn't my case or that the current regime in the DA's office had nothing to do with the case back in 1986, there are so few victories from the defense side of the bar that there is always a sense of communal joy in the success of others and the defeat of the establishment.

The supreme court's ruling was announced the week

before, starting a sixty-day clock during which the DA would have to retry or discharge Jessup. It seemed that not a day had gone by since the ruling that Jessup was not in the news. He gave multiple interviews by phone and in person at San Quentin, proclaiming his innocence and potshotting the police and prosecutors who put him there. In his plight, he had garnered the support of several Hollywood celebrities and professional athletes and had already launched a civil claim against both the city and county, seeking millions of dollars in damages for the many long years during which he was falsely incarcerated. In this day of nonstop media cycles, he had a never-ending forum and was using it to elevate himself to folk hero status. When he finally walked out of prison, he, too, would be a celebrity.

Knowing as little as I did about the case in the details, I was of the impression that he was an innocent man who had been subjected to a quarter century of torture and that he deserved whatever he could get for it. I did, however, know enough about the case to understand that with the DNA evidence cutting Jessup's way, the case was a loser and the idea of retrying Jessup seemed to be an exercise in political masochism unlikely to come from the brain trust of Williams and Ridell.

Unless…

'What do you know that I don't know?' I asked. 'And that the *Los Angeles Times* doesn't know.'

Williams smiled smugly and leaned forward across the table to deliver his answer.

'All Jessup established with the help of the GJP is

that his DNA was not on the victim's dress,' he said. 'As the petitioner, it was not up to him to establish who it did come from.'

'So you ran it through the data banks.'

Williams nodded.

'We did. And we got a hit.'

He offered nothing else.

'Well, who was it?'

'I'm not going to reveal that to you unless you come aboard on the case. Otherwise, I need to keep it confidential. But I will say that I believe our findings lead to a trial tactic that could neutralize the DNA question, leaving the rest of the case—and the evidence—pretty much intact. DNA was not needed to convict him the first time. We won't need it now. As in nineteen eighty-six, we believe Jessup is guilty of this crime and I would be delinquent in my duties if I did not attempt to prosecute him, no matter the chances of conviction, the potential political fallout and the public perception of the case.'

Spoken as if he were looking at the cameras and not at me.

'Then why don't you prosecute him?' I asked. 'Why come to me? You have three hundred able lawyers working for you. I can think of one you've got stuck up in the Van Nuys office who would take this case in a heartbeat. Why come to me?'

'Because this prosecution can't come from within the DA's office. I am sure you have read or heard the allegations. There's a taint on this case and it doesn't matter

9

that there isn't one goddamn lawyer working for me who was around back then. I still need to bring in an outsider, an independent to take it to court. Somebody—'

'That's what the attorney general's office is for,' I said. 'You need an independent counsel, you go to him.'

Now I was just poking him in the eye and everybody at the table knew it. There was no way Gabriel Williams was going to ask the state AG to come in on the case. That would cross the razor-wire line of politics. The AG post was an elected office in California and was seen by every political pundit in town as Williams's next stop on his way to the governor's mansion or some other lofty political plateau. The last thing Williams would be willing to do was hand a potential political rival a case that could be used against him, no matter how old it was. In politics, in the courtroom, in life, you don't give your opponent the club with which he can turn around and clobber you.

'We're not going to the AG with this one,' Williams said in a matter-of-fact manner. 'That's why I want you, Mickey. You're a well-known and respected criminal defense attorney. I think the public will trust you to be independent in this matter and will therefore trust and accept the conviction you'll win in this case.'

While I was staring at Williams a waiter came to the table to take our order. Without ever breaking eye contact with me, Williams told him to go away.

'I haven't been paying a lot of attention to this,' I said. 'Who's Jessup's defense attorney? I would find it difficult to go up against a colleague I know well.'

'Right now all he's got is the GJP lawyer and his civil litigator. He hasn't hired defense counsel because quite frankly he's expecting us to drop this whole thing.'

I nodded, another hurdle cleared for the moment.

'But he's got a surprise coming,' Williams said. 'We're going to bring him down here and retry him. He did it, Mickey, and that's all you really need to know. There's a little girl who's still dead, and that's all any prosecutor needs to know. Take the case. Do something for your community and for yourself. Who knows, you might even like it and want to stay on. If so, we'll definitely entertain the possibility.'

I dropped my eyes to the linen tablecloth and thought about his last words. For a moment, I involuntarily conjured the image of my daughter sitting in a courtroom and watching me stand for the People instead of the accused. Williams kept talking, unaware that I had already come to a decision.

'Obviously, I can't pay you your rate, but if you take this on, I don't think you'll be doing it for the money anyway. I can give you an office and a secretary. And I can give you whatever science and forensics you need. The very best of every—'

'I don't want an office in the DA's office. I would need to be independent of that. I have to be completely autonomous. No more lunches. We make the announcement and then you leave me alone. I decide how to proceed with the case.'

'Fine. Use your own office, just as long as you don't

store evidence there. And, of course, you make your own decisions.'

'And if I do this, I pick second chair and my own investigator out of the LAPD. People I can trust.'

'In or outside my office for your second?'

'I would need someone inside.'

'Then I assume we're talking about your ex-wife.'

'That's right—if she'll take it. And if somehow we get a conviction out of this thing, you pull her out of Van Nuys and put her downtown in Major Crimes, where she belongs.'

'That's easier said than—'

'That's the deal. Take it or leave it.'

Williams glanced at Ridell and I saw the supposed sidekick give an almost imperceptible nod of approval.

'All right,' Williams said, turning back to me. 'Then I guess I'll take it. You win and she's in. We have a deal.'

He reached his hand across the table and I shook it. He smiled but I didn't.

'Mickey Haller for the People,' he said. 'Has a nice ring to it.'

For the People. It should have made me feel good. It should have made me feel like I was part of something that was noble and right. But all I had was the bad feeling that I had crossed some sort of line within myself.

'Wonderful,' I said.

2

Harry Bosch stepped up to the front counter of the District Attorney's Office on the eighteenth floor of the Criminal Courts Building. He gave his name and said he had a ten A.M. appointment with District Attorney Gabriel Williams.

'Actually, your meeting is in conference room A,' said the receptionist after checking a computer screen in front of her. 'You go through the door, turn right and go to the end of the hall. Right again and conference room A is on the left. It's marked on the door. They're expecting you.'

The door in the paneled-wood wall behind her buzzed free and Bosch went through, wondering about the fact that *they* were waiting for him. Since he had received the summons from the DA's secretary the afternoon before, Bosch had been unable to determine what it was about. Secrecy was expected from the DA's Office but usually some information trickled out. He hadn't even known he would be meeting with more than one person until now.

Following the prescribed trail, Bosch came to the door marked CONFERENCE ROOM A, knocked once and heard a female voice say, 'Come in.'

He entered and saw a woman seated by herself at an eight-chaired table, a spread of documents, files, photos and a laptop computer in front of her. She looked vaguely familiar but he could not place her. She was attractive with dark, curling hair framing her face. She had sharp eyes that followed him as he entered, and a pleasant, almost curious smile. Like she knew something he didn't. She wore the standard female prosecutor's power suit in navy blue. Harry might not have been able to place her but he assumed she was a DDA.

'Detective Bosch?'

'That's me.'

'Come in, have a seat.'

Bosch pulled out a chair and sat across from her. On the table he saw a crime scene photograph of a child's body in an open Dumpster. It was a girl and she was wearing a blue dress with long sleeves. Her feet were bare and she was lying on a pile of construction debris and other trash. The white edges of the photo were yellowed. It was an old print.

The woman moved a file over the picture and then offered her hand across the table.

'I don't think we've ever met,' she said. 'My name is Maggie McPherson.'

Bosch recognized the name but he couldn't remember from where or what case.

'I'm a deputy district attorney,' she continued, 'and I'm going to be second chair on the Jason Jessup prosecution. First chair—'

'Jason Jessup?' Bosch asked. 'You're going to take it to trial?'

'Yes, we are. We'll be announcing it next week and I need to ask you to keep it confidential until then. I am sorry that our first chair is late coming to our meet—'

The door opened and Bosch turned. Mickey Haller stepped into the room. Bosch did a double take. Not because he didn't recognize Haller. They were half brothers and he easily knew him on sight. But seeing Haller in the DA's office was one of those images that didn't quite make sense. Haller was a criminal defense attorney. He fit in at the DA's office about as well as a cat did at the dog pound.

'I know,' Haller said. 'You're thinking, What in the hell is this?'

Smiling, Haller moved to McPherson's side of the table and started pulling out a chair. Then Bosch remembered how he knew McPherson's name.

'You two...' Bosch said. 'You were married, right?'

'That's right,' Haller said. 'Eight wonderful years.'

'And what, she's prosecuting Jessup and you're defending him? Isn't that a conflict of interest?'

Haller's smile became a broad grin.

'It would only be a conflict if we were opposing each other, Harry. But we're not. We're prosecuting him. Together. I'm first chair. Maggie's second. And we want you to be our investigator.'

Bosch was completely confused.

'Wait a minute. You're not a prosecutor. This doesn't—'

'I'm an appointed independent prosecutor, Harry.

It's all legit. I wouldn't be sitting here if it weren't. We're going after Jessup and we want you to help us.'

'From what I heard, this case is beyond help. Unless you're telling me Jessup rigged the DNA test.'

'No, we're not telling you that,' McPherson said. 'We did our own testing and matching. His results were correct. It wasn't his DNA on the victim's dress.'

'But that doesn't mean we've lost the case,' Haller quickly added.

Bosch looked from McPherson to Haller and then back again. He was clearly missing something.

'Then whose DNA was it?' he asked.

McPherson glanced sideways at Haller before answering.

'Her stepfather's,' she said. 'He's dead now but we believe there is an explanation for why his semen was found on his stepdaughter's dress.'

Haller leaned urgently across the table.

'An explanation that still leaves room to reconvict Jessup of the girl's murder.'

Bosch thought for a moment and the image of his own daughter flashed in his mind. He knew there were certain kinds of evil in the world that had to be contained, no matter the hardship. A child killer was at the top of that list.

'Okay,' he said. 'I'm in.'

3

Tuesday, February 16, 1:00 P.M.

The DA's Office had a press conference room that had not been updated since the days they'd used it to hold briefings on the Charles Manson case. Its faded wood-paneled walls and drooping flags in the corner had been the backdrop of a thousand press briefings and they gave all proceedings there a threadbare appearance that belied the true power and might of the office. The state prosecutor was never the underdog in any undertaking, yet it appeared that the office did not have the money for even a fresh coat of paint.

The setting, however, served the announcement on the Jessup decision well. For possibly the first time in these hallowed halls of justice, the prosecution would indeed be the underdog. The decision to retry Jason Jessup was fraught with peril and the realistic likelihood of failure. As I stood at the front of the room next to Gabriel Williams and before a phalanx of video cameras, bright lights and reporters, it finally dawned on me what a terrible mistake I had made. My decision to take on the case in hopes of currying favor with my daughter, ex-wife and myself was going to be met with disastrous consequences. I was going to go down in flames.

It was a rare moment to witness firsthand. The media had gathered to report the end of the story. The DA's Office would assuredly announce that Jason Jessup would not be subjected to a retrial. The DA might not offer an apology but would at the very least say the evidence was not there. That there was no case against this man who had been incarcerated for so long. The case would be closed and in the eyes of the law as well as the public Jessup would finally be a free and innocent man.

The media is rarely fooled in complete numbers and usually doesn't react well when it happens. But there was no doubt that Williams had punked them all. We had moved stealthily in the last week, putting together the team and reviewing the evidence that was still available. Not a word had leaked, which must've been a first in the halls of the CCB. While I could see the first inkling of suspicion creasing the brows of the reporters who recognized me as we entered, it was Williams who delivered the knockout punch when he wasted no time in stepping before a lectern festooned with microphones and digital recorders.

'On a Sunday morning twenty-four years ago today, twelve-year-old Melissa Landy was taken from her yard in Hancock Park and brutally murdered. An investigation quickly led to a suspect named Jason Jessup. He was arrested, convicted at trial and sentenced to life in prison without parole. That conviction was reversed two weeks ago by the state supreme court and remanded to my office. I am here to announce that the Los Angeles

County District Attorney's Office will retry Jason Jessup in the death of Melissa Landy. The charges of abduction and murder stand. This office intends once again to prosecute Mr. Jessup to the fullest extent of the law.'

He paused to add appropriate gravity to the announcement.

'As you know, the supreme court found that irregularities occurred during the first prosecution—which, of course, occurred more than two decades before the current administration. To avoid political conflicts and any future appearance of impropriety on the part of this office, I have appointed an independent special prosecutor to handle the case. Many of you know of the man standing here to my right. Michael Haller has been a defense counselor of some note in Los Angeles for two decades. He is a fair-minded and respected member of the bar. He has accepted the appointment and has assumed responsibility for the case as of today. It has been the policy of this department not to try cases in the media. However, Mr. Haller and I are willing to answer a few questions as long as they don't tread on the specifics and evidence of the case.'

There was a booming chorus of voices calling questions out at us. Williams raised his hands for calm in the room.

'One at a time, people. Let's start with you.'

He pointed to a woman sitting in the first row. I could not remember her name but I knew she worked for the *Times*. Williams knew his priorities.

'Kate Salters from the *Times*,' she said helpfully.

'Can you tell us how you came to the decision to pro-secute Jason Jessup again after DNA evidence cleared him of the crime?'

Before coming into the room, Williams had told me that he would handle the announcement and all questions unless specifically addressed to me. He made it clear that this was going to be his show. But I decided to make it clear from the outset that it was going to be my case.

'I'll answer that,' I said as I leaned toward the lectern and the microphones. 'The DNA test conducted by the Genetic Justice Project only concluded that the bodily fluid found on the victim's clothing did not come from Jason Jessup. It did not clear him of involvement in the crime. There is a difference. The DNA test only provides additional information for a jury to consider.'

I straightened back up and caught Williams giving me a don't-fuck-with-me stare.

'Whose DNA was it?' someone called out.

Williams quickly leaned forward to answer.

'We're not answering questions about evidence at this time.'

'Mickey, why are you taking the case?'

The question came from the back of the room, from behind the lights, and I could not see the owner of the voice. I moved back to the microphones, angling my body so Williams had to step back.

'Good question,' I said. 'It's certainly unusual for me to be on the other side of the aisle, so to speak. But I think this is the case to cross over for. I'm an officer of the court and a proud member of the California bar. We take an oath to seek justice and fairness while upholding the Constitution and laws of this nation and state. One of the duties of a lawyer is to take a just cause without personal consideration to himself. This is such a cause. Someone has to speak for Melissa Landy. I have reviewed the evidence in this case and I think I'm on the right side of this one. The measure is proof beyond a reasonable doubt. I think that such proof exists here.'

Williams moved in and put a hand on my arm to gently move me off the microphone stand.

'We do not want to go any further than that in regard to the evidence,' he said quickly.

'Jessup's already spent twenty-four years in prison,' Salters said. 'Anything less than a conviction for first-degree murder and he will probably walk on time served. Mr. Williams, is it really worth the expense and effort of retrying this man?'

Before she was finished asking the question, I knew she and Williams had a deal working. She lobbed softballs and he hit them out of the park, looking good and righteous on the eleven o'clock news and in the morning paper. Her end of the deal would come with inside scoops on the evidence and trial strategy. I decided in that moment that it was *my case, my trial, my deal*.

'None of that matters,' I said loudly from my position to the side.

All eyes turned to me. Even Williams turned.

'Can you talk into the microphones, Mickey?'

It was the same voice from behind the line of lights. He knew to call me Mickey. I once again moved to the microphones, boxing Williams out like a power forward going for the rebound.

'The murder of a child is a crime that must be prosecuted to the full extent of the law, no matter what the possibilities or risks are. There is no guarantee of victory here. But that was not part of the decision. The measure is reasonable doubt and I believe we surpass that. We believe that the totality of evidence shows that this man committed this horrible crime and it doesn't matter how much time has gone by or how long he has been incarcerated. He must be prosecuted.

'I have a daughter only a little older than Melissa was.... You know, people forget that in the original trial, the state sought the death penalty but the jury recommended against it and the judge imposed a life sentence. That was then and this is now. We will once again be seeking the death penalty on this case.'

Williams put his hand on my shoulder and pulled me away from the microphones.

'Uh, let's not get ahead of ourselves here,' he said quickly. 'My office has not yet made a determination in regard to whether we will be seeking the death penalty. That will come at a later time. But Mr. Haller makes a very valid and sad point. There can be no worse crime in our society than the murder of a child. We must do all that is within our power and our reach to seek justice for Melissa Landy. Thank you for being here today.'

'Wait a minute,' called a reporter from one of the

middle seats. 'What about Jessup? When will he be brought here for trial?'

Williams put his hands on both sides of the lectern in a casual move designed to keep me from the microphones.

'Earlier this morning Mr. Jessup was taken into custody by the Los Angeles police and is being transported from San Quentin. He will be booked into the downtown jail and the case will proceed. His conviction was reversed but the charges against him remain in place. We have nothing further at this time.'

Williams stepped back and signaled me toward the door. He waited until I started moving and was clear of the microphones. He then followed, coming up behind me and whispering into my ear as we went through the door.

'You do that again and I'll fire you on the spot.'

I turned to look back at him while I walked.

'Do what? Answer one of your setup questions?'

We moved into the hallway. Ridell was waiting there with the office's media spokesman, a guy named Fernandez. But Williams turned me down the hall away from them. He was still whispering when he spoke.

'You went off the script. Do it again and we're done.'

I stopped and turned and Williams almost walked into me.

'Look, I'm not your puppet,' I said. 'I'm an independent contractor, remember? You treat me otherwise and you're going to be holding this hot potato without an oven mitt.'

Williams just glared at me. I obviously wasn't getting through.

'And what was this shit about the death penalty?' he asked. 'We haven't even gotten there and you didn't have the go-ahead to say it.'

He was bigger than me, taller. He had used his body to crowd my space and back me up against the wall.

'It will get back to Jessup and keep him thinking,' I said. 'And if we're lucky, he comes in for a deal and this whole thing goes away, including the civil action. It'll save you all that money. That's really what this is about, right? The money. We get a conviction and he's got no civil case. You and the city save a few million bucks.'

'That's got nothing to do with this. This is about justice and you still should have told me what you were doing. You don't sandbag your own boss.'

The physical intimidation got old real fast. I put my palm on his chest and backed him off me.

'Yeah, well, you're not my boss. I don't have a boss.'

'Is that right? Like I said, I could fire your ass right here right now.'

I pointed down the hall to the door to the press conference room.

'Yeah, that'll look good. Firing the independent prosecutor *you* just hired. Didn't Nixon do that during the Watergate mess? Worked real well for him. Why don't we go back in and tell them? I'm sure there are still a few cameras in there.'

Williams hesitated, realizing his predicament. I had backed him against the wall without even moving. He would look like a complete and unelectable fool if he fired me, and he knew it. He leaned in closer and his whisper dropped lower as he used the oldest threat in the mano a mano handbook. I was ready for it.

'Do not fuck with me, Haller.'

'Then don't fuck with my case. This isn't a campaign stop and it's not about money. This is murder, boss. You want me to get a conviction, then get out of my way.'

I threw him the bone of calling him boss. Williams pressed his mouth into a tight line and stared at me for a long moment.

'Just so we understand each other,' he finally said.

I nodded.

'Yeah, I think we do.'

'Before you talk to the media about this case, you get it approved by my office first. Understand?'

'Got it.'

He turned and headed down the hall. His entourage followed. I remained in the hallway and watched them go. The truth was, there was nothing in the law that I objected to more than the death penalty. It was not that I had ever had a client executed or even tried such a case. It was simply a belief in the idea that an enlightened society did not kill its own.

But somehow that didn't stop me from using the threat of the death penalty as an edge in the case. As I stood there alone in the hallway, I thought that maybe that made me a better prosecutor than I had imagined I could be.

4

It usually was the best moment of a case. The drive downtown with a suspect handcuffed in the backseat. There was nothing better. Sure there was the eventual payoff of a conviction down the line. Being in the courtroom when the verdict is read—watching the reality shock and then deaden the eyes of the convicted. But the drive in was always better, more immediate and personal. It was always the moment Bosch savored. The chase was over and the case was about to morph from the relentless momentum of the investigation to the measured pace of the prosecution.

But this time was different. It had been a long two days and Bosch wasn't savoring anything. He and his partner, David Chu, had driven up to Corta Madera the day before, checking into a motel off the 101 and spending the night. In the morning they drove over to San Quentin, presented a court order that transferred custody of Jason Jessup to them, and then collected their prisoner for the drive back to Los Angeles. Seven hours each way with a partner who talked too much. Seven hours on the return with a suspect who didn't talk enough.

They were now at the top of the San Fernando Valley and an hour from the City Jail in downtown L.A. Bosch's back hurt from so many hours behind the wheel. His right calf muscle ached from applying pressure to the gas pedal. The city car did not have cruise control.

Chu had offered to drive but Bosch had said no. Chu religiously stuck to the speed limit, even on the freeway. Bosch would take the backache over an extra hour on the freeway and the anxiety it would create.

All of this aside, he drove in uneasy silence, brooding about a case that seemed to be proceeding backwards. He had been on it for only a few days, hadn't had the opportunity to even become acquainted with all the facts, and here he was with the suspect hooked up and in the backseat. To Bosch it felt like the arrest was coming first and the investigation wouldn't really start until after Jessup was booked.

He checked his watch and knew the scheduled press conference must be over by now. The plan was for him to meet with Haller and McPherson at four to continue kicking around the case. But by the time Jessup was booked he would be late. He also needed to go by LAPD archives to pick up two boxes that were waiting for him.

'Harry, what's wrong?'

Bosch glanced at Chu.

'Nothing's wrong.'

He wasn't going to talk in front of the suspect. Besides, he and Chu had been partnered for less than a year. It was a little soon for Chu to be making reads off of Bosch's demeanor. Harry didn't want him to know that he had accurately deduced that he was uncomfortable.

Jessup spoke from the backseat, his first words since asking for a bathroom break outside of Stockton.

'What's wrong is that he doesn't have a case. What's wrong is that he knows this whole thing is bullshit and he doesn't want to be part of it.'

Bosch checked Jessup in the rearview mirror. He was slightly hunched forward because his hands were cuffed and locked to a chain that went to a set of shackles around his ankles. His head was shaved, a routine prison practice among men hoping to intimidate others. Bosch guessed that with Jessup it had probably worked.

'I thought you didn't want to talk, Jessup. You invoked.'

'Yeah, that's right. I'll just shut the fuck up and wait for my lawyer.'

'He's in San Francisco, I wouldn't hold my breath.'

'He's calling somebody. The GJP's got people all over the country. We were ready for this.'

'Really? You were ready? You mean you packed your cell up because you thought you were being transferred? Or was it because you thought you were going home?'

Jessup didn't have an answer for that one.

Bosch merged onto the 101, which would take them through the Cahuenga Pass and into Hollywood before they reached downtown.

'How'd you get hooked up with the Genetic Justice Project, Jessup?' he asked, trying once again to get something going. 'You go to them or they come to you?'

'Website, man. I sent in my appeal and they saw the bullshit going on in my case. They took it over and here I am. You people are totally fucked if you think you're going to win this. I was railroaded by you motherfuckers once before. Ain't gonna happen again. In two months, this'll all be over. I've been in twenty-four years. What's two more months? Just makes my book rights more valuable. I guess I should be thanking you and the district attorney for that.'

Bosch glanced at the mirror again. Normally, he would love a talkative suspect. Most times they talked themselves right into prison. But Jessup was too smart and too cagey. He chose his words carefully, stayed away from talking about the crime itself, and wouldn't be making a mistake that Bosch could use.

In the mirror now, Bosch could see Jessup staring out the window. No telling what he was thinking about. His eyes looked dead. Bosch could see the top of a prison ink tattoo on his neck, just breaking the collar line. It looked like part of a word but he couldn't tell for sure.

'Welcome to L.A., Jessup,' Chu said without turning around. 'Guess it's been a while, huh?'

'Fuck you, you chink motherfucker,' Jessup retorted. 'This'll all be over soon and then I'll be out and on the beach. I'm going to get a longboard and ride some tasty waves.'

'Don't count on it, killer,' Chu said. 'You're going down. We got you by the balls.'

Bosch knew Chu was trying to provoke a response,

a slip of the tongue. But he was coming off as an amateur and Jessup was too wise for him.

Harry grew tired of the back-and-forth, even after six hours of almost complete silence. He turned on the car's radio and caught the tail end of a report on the DA's press conference. He turned it up so Jessup would hear, and Chu would keep quiet.

'Williams and Haller refused to comment on the evidence but indicated they were not as impressed with the DNA analysis as the state's supreme court was. Haller acknowledged that the DNA found on the victim's dress did not come from Jessup. But he said the findings did not clear him of involvement in the crime. Haller is a well-known defense attorney and will be prosecuting a murder case for the first time. It did not sound this morning as though he has any hesitation. "We will once again be seeking the death penalty on this case."'

Bosch flicked the volume down and checked the mirror. Jessup was still looking out the window.

'How about that, Jessup? He's going for the Jesus juice.'

Jessup responded tiredly.

'Asshole's posturing. Besides, they don't execute anybody in this state anymore. You know what *death row* means? It means you get a cell all to yourself and you control what's on the TV. It means better access to phone, food and visitors. Fuck it, I hope he does go for it, man. But it won't matter. This is bullshit. This whole thing is bullshit. It's all about the money.'

The last line floated out there for a long moment before Bosch finally bit.

'What money?'

'My money. You watch, man, they'll come at me with a deal. My lawyer told me. They'll want me to take a deal and plead to time served so they don't have to pay me the money. That's all this fucking is and you two are just the deliverymen. Fuckin' FedEx.'

Bosch was silent. He wondered if it could be true. Jessup was suing the city and county for millions. Could it be that the retrial was simply a political move designed to save money? Both government entities were self-insured. Juries loved hitting faceless corporations and bureaucracies with obscenely large judgments. A jury believing prosecutors and police had corruptly imprisoned an innocent man for twenty-four years would be beyond generous. A hit from an eight-figure judgment could be devastating to both city and county coffers, even if they were splitting the bill.

But if they jammed Jessup and maneuvered him into a deal in which he acknowledged guilt to gain his freedom, then the lawsuit would go away. So would all the book and movie money he was counting on.

'Makes a lot of sense, doesn't it?' Jessup said.

Bosch checked the mirror and realized that now Jessup was studying him. He turned his eyes back to the road. He felt his phone vibrate and pulled it out of his jacket.

'You want me to take it, Harry?' Chu asked.

A reminder that it was illegal to talk on a phone while driving an automobile. Bosch ignored him and took the call. It was Lieutenant Gandle.

'Harry, you close?'

'Getting off the one-oh-one.'

'Good. I just wanted to give you a heads-up. They're lining up at intake. Comb your hair.'

'Got it, but maybe I'll give my partner the airtime.'

Bosch glanced over at Chu but didn't explain.

'Either way,' Gandle said. 'What's next?'

'He invoked so we just book him. Then I have to go back to the war room and meet with the prosecutors. I've got questions.'

'Harry, do they have this guy or not?'

Bosch checked Jessup in the mirror. He was back to looking out the window.

'I don't know, Lieutenant. When I know, you'll know.'

A few minutes later they pulled into the rear lot of the jail. There were several television cameras and their operators lined up on a ramp leading to the intake door. Chu sat up straight.

'Perp walk, Harry.'

'Yeah. You take him in.'

'Let's both do it.'

'Nah, I'll hang back.'

'You sure?'

'I'm sure. Just don't forget my cuffs.'

'Okay, Harry.'

The lot was clogged with media vans with their transmitters cranked to full height. But they had left the space in front of the ramp open. Bosch pulled in and parked.

'Okay, you ready back there, Jessup?' Chu asked. 'Time to sell tickets.'

Jessup didn't respond. Chu opened the door and got out, then opened the rear door for Jessup.

Bosch watched the ensuing spectacle from the confines of the car.

5

One of the very best things about having previously been married to Maggie McPherson was that I never had to face her in court. The marital split created a conflict of interest that saved me professional defeat and humiliation at her hands on more than one occasion. She was truly the best prosecutor I'd ever seen step into the well and they didn't call her Maggie McFierce for no reason.

Now, for the first time, we would be on the same team in court, sitting side by side at the same table. But what had seemed like such a good idea—not to mention such a positive potential payoff for Maggie—was already manifesting itself as something jagged and rusty. Maggie was having issues with being second chair. And for good reason. She was a professional prosecutor. From drug dealers and petty thieves to rapists and murderers, she had put dozens of criminals behind bars. I had appeared in dozens of trials myself but never as a prosecutor. Maggie would have to play backup to a novice and that realization wasn't sitting well with her.

We sat in conference room A with the case files spread out before us on the big table. Though Williams had said I could run the case from my own independent office, the truth was, that wasn't practical at the moment. I didn't have an office outside my home. I primarily used the backseat of my Lincoln Town Car as my office and that wouldn't do for *The People versus Jason Jessup*. I had my case manager setting up a temporary office in downtown but we were at least a few days away from that. So temporarily there we sat, eyes down and tensions up.

'Maggie,' I said, 'when it comes to prosecuting bad guys, I will readily admit that I couldn't carry your lunch. But the thing is, when it comes to politics *and* prosecuting bad guys, the powers that be have put me in the first chair. That's the way it is and we can either accept it or not. I took this job and asked for you. If you don't think we—'

'I just don't like the idea of carrying your briefcase through this whole thing,' Maggie said.

'You won't be. Look, press conferences and outward appearances are one thing, but I fully assume that we'll be working as a tag team. You'll be conducting just as much of the investigation as I will be, probably more. The trial should be no different. We'll come up with a strategy and choreograph it together. But you have to give me a little credit. I know my way around a courtroom. I'll just be sitting at the other table this time.'

'That's where you're wrong, Mickey. On the defense side you have a responsibility to one person. Your client. When you are a prosecutor, you represent the people and that is a lot more responsibility. That's why they call it the *burden of proof*.'

'Whatever. If you're saying I shouldn't be doing this, then I'm not the guy you should be complaining to. Go down the hall and talk to your boss. But if he kicks me off the case, you get kicked as well, and then you go back to Van Nuys for the rest of your career. Is that what you want?'

She didn't answer and that was an answer in itself.

'Okay, then,' I said. 'Let's just try to get through this without pulling each other's hair out, okay? Remember, I'm not here to count convictions and advance my career. For me, it's one and done. So we both want the same thing. Yes, you will have to help me. But you will also be helping—'

My phone started vibrating. I had left it out on the table. I didn't recognize the number on the screen but took the call, just to get away from the conversation with Maggie.

'Haller.'

'Hey, Mick, how'd I do?'

'Who is this?'

'Sticks.'

Sticks was a freelance videographer who fed footage to the local news channels and sometimes even the bigs. I had known him so long I didn't even remember his real name.

'How'd you do at what, Sticks? I'm busy here.'

'At the press conference. I set you up, man.'

I realized that it had been Sticks behind the lights, throwing the questions to me.

'Oh, yeah, yeah, you did good. Thanks for that.'

'Now you're going to take care of me on the case, right? Give me the heads-up if there's something for me, right? Something exclusive.'

'Yeah, no need to worry, Sticks. I got you covered. But I gotta go.'

I ended the call and put the phone back on the table. Maggie was typing something into her laptop. It looked like the momentary discontent had passed and I was hesitant to touch it again.

'That was a guy who works for the news stations. He might be useful to us at some point.'

'We don't want to do anything underhanded. The prosecution is held to a much higher standard of ethics than the defense.'

I shook my head. I couldn't win.

'That's bullshit and I am not talking about doing anything un—'

The door opened and Harry Bosch stepped in, push-ing the door with his back because he was carrying two large boxes in his hands.

'Sorry, I'm late,' he said.

He put the boxes down on the table. I could tell the larger one was a carton from evidence archives. I guessed that the smaller one contained the police file on the original investigation.

'It took them three days to find the murder box. It was on the 'eighty-five aisle instead of 'eighty-six.'

He looked at me and then at Maggie and then back at me.

'So what'd I miss? War break out in the war room?'

'We were talking about prosecutorial tactics and it turns out we have opposing views.'

'Imagine that.'

He took the chair at the end of the table. I could tell he was going to have more to say. He lifted the top off the murder box and pulled out three accordion files and put them on the table. He then moved the box to the floor.

'You know, Mick, while we're airing out our differences...I think before you pulled me into this little soap opera, you should've told me a few things up front.'

'Like what, Harry?'

'Like that this whole goddamn thing is about money and not murder.'

'What are you talking about? What money?'

Bosch just stared at me without responding.

'You're talking about Jessup's lawsuit?' I asked.

'That's right,' he said. 'I had an interesting discussion with Jessup today on the drive down. Got me thinking and it crossed my mind that if we jam this guy into a deal, the lawsuit against the city and county goes away because a guy who admits to murder isn't going to be able to sue and claim he was railroaded. So I guess what I want to know is what we're really doing here. Are we trying to put a murder suspect on trial or are we just trying to save the city and county a few million bucks?'

I noticed Maggie's posture straighten as she considered the same thing.

'You gotta be kidding me,' she said. 'If that—'

38

'Hold on, hold on,' I interjected. 'Let's be cool about this. I don't think that's the case here, okay? It's not that I haven't thought about it but Williams didn't say one word about going for a dispo on this case. He told me to take it to trial. In fact, he assumes it will go to trial for the same reason you just mentioned. Jessup will never take a dispo for time served or anything else because there is no pot of gold in that. No book, no movie, no payout from the city. If he wants the money, he's got to go to trial and win.'

Maggie nodded slowly as if weighing a valid supposition. Bosch didn't seem appeased at all.

'But how would you know what Williams is up to?' he asked. 'You're an outsider. They could've brought you in, wound you up and pointed you in the right direction and then sat back to watch you go.'

'He's right,' Maggie added. 'Jessup doesn't even have a defense attorney. As soon as he does he'll start talking deal.'

I raised my hands in a calming gesture.

'Look, at the press conference today. I threw out that we were going for the death penalty. I just did that to see how Williams would react. He didn't expect it and afterward he pressed me in the hallway. He told me that it wasn't a decision I got to make. I told him it was just strategy, that I wanted Jessup to start thinking about a deal. And it gave Williams pause. He didn't see it. If he was thinking of a deal just to blow up the civil action, I would have been able to read it. I'm good at reading people.'

I could tell I still hadn't quite won Bosch over.

'Remember last year, with the two men from Hong Kong who wanted your ass on the next plane to China? I read them right and I played them right.'

In his eyes I saw Bosch relent. That China story was a reminder that he owed me one and I was collecting.

'Okay,' he said. 'So what do we do?'

'We assume Jessup's going to go to trial. As soon as he lawyers up, we'll know for sure. But we start preparing for it now, because if I was going to represent him, I would refuse to waive speedy trial. I would try to jam the prosecution on time to prepare and make the people put up or shut up.'

I checked the date on my watch.

'If I'm right, that gives us forty-eight days till trial. We've got a lot of work to do between now and then.'

We looked at one another and sat in silence for a few moments before I threw the lead to Maggie.

'Maggie has spent the better part of the last week with the prosecution file on this. Harry, I know what you just brought in will have a lot of overlap. But why don't we start here by having Mags go through the case as presented at trial in 'eighty-six? I think that will give us a good starting point of looking at what we need to do this time out.'

Bosch nodded his approval and I signaled for Maggie to begin. She pulled her laptop over in front of her.

'Okay, a couple of basics first. Because it was a death penalty case, jury selection was the longest part of the trial. Almost three weeks. The trial itself lasted seven days and then there were three days of deliberation on the initial verdicts, then the death penalty phase went another two weeks. But seven days of testimony and arguments—that to me is fast for a capital murder case. It was pretty cut-and-dried. And the defense... well, there wasn't much of a defense.'

She looked at me as if I were responsible for the poor defense of the accused, even though I hadn't even gotten out of law school by 'eighty-six.

'Who was his lawyer?' I asked.

'Charles Barnard,' she said. 'I checked with the California bar. He won't be handling the retrial. He's listed as deceased as of 'ninety-four. The prosecutor, Gary Lintz, is also long gone.'

'Don't remember either of them. Who was the judge?'

'Walter Sackville. He's long retired but I do remember him. He was tough.'

'I had a few cases with him,' Bosch added. 'He wouldn't take any shit from either side.'

'Go on,' I said.

'Okay, so the prosecution's story was this. The Landy family—that was our victim, Melissa, who was twelve, her thirteen-year-old sister, Sarah, mother, Regina, and stepfather, Kensington—lived on Windsor Boulevard in Hancock Park. The home was about a block north of Wilshire and in the vicinity of the Trinity United Church of God, which on Sundays back then drew about six thousand people to its two morning services. People parked their cars all over Hancock

Park to go to the church. That is, until the residents there got tired of their neighborhood being overrun every Sunday with traffic and parking issues and went to City Hall about it. They got the neighborhood turned into a residential parking zone during weekend hours. You had to have a sticker to park on the streets, including Windsor. This opened the door to city-contracted tow truck operators patrolling the neighborhood like sharks on Sunday morning. Any cars without the proper resident sticker on the windshield were fair game. They got towed. Which finally brings us to Jason Jessup, our suspect.'

'He drove a tow truck,' I said.

'Exactly. He was a driver for a city contractor named Aardvark Towing. Cute name, got them to the front of the listings in the phone book back when people still used phone books.'

I glanced at Bosch and could tell by his reaction that he was somebody who still used the phone book instead of the Internet. Maggie didn't notice and continued.

'On the morning in question Jessup was working the Hancock Park patrol. At the Landy house, the family happened to be putting a pool in the backyard. Kensington Landy was a musician who scored films and was doing quite well at the time. So they were putting in a pool and there was a large open hole and giant piles of dirt in the backyard. The parents didn't want the girls playing back there. Thought it was dangerous, plus on this morning the girls were in their church dresses. The house has a large front yard. The stepfather told the girls to play outside for a few minutes before the family was planning to go off to church themselves. The older one, Sarah, was told to watch over Melissa.'

'Did they go to Trinity United?' I asked.

'No, they went to Sacred Heart in Beverly Hills. Anyway, the kids were only out there about fifteen minutes. Mother was still upstairs getting ready and the stepfather, who was also supposed to be keeping an eye on the girls, was watching television inside. An overnight sports report on ESPN or whatever they had back then. He forgot about the girls.'

Bosch shook his head, and I knew exactly how he felt. It was not in judgment of the father but in understanding of how it could have happened and in the dread of any parent who knows how a small mistake could be so costly.

'At some point, he heard screaming,' Maggie continued. 'He ran out the front door and found the older girl, Sarah, in the yard. She was screaming that a man took Melissa. The stepfather ran up the street looking for her but there was no sign. Like that, she was gone.'

My ex-wife stopped there for a moment to compose herself. Everyone in the room had a young daughter and could understand the shearing of life that happened at that moment for every person in the Landy family.

'Police were called and the response was quick,' she continued. 'This was Hancock Park, after all. The first bulletins were out in a matter of minutes. Detectives were dispatched right away.'

'So this whole thing went down in broad daylight?' Bosch asked.

Maggie nodded.

'It happened about ten-forty. The Landys were going to an eleven o'clock service.'

'And nobody else saw this?'

'You gotta remember, this was Hancock Park. A lot of tall hedges, a lot of walls, a lot of privacy. People there are good at keeping the world out. Nobody saw anything. Nobody heard anything until Sarah started screaming, and by then it was too late.'

'Was there a wall or a hedge at the Landy house?'

'Six-foot hedges down the north and south property lines but not on the street side. It was theorized at the time that Jessup drove by in his tow truck and saw the girl alone in the yard. Then he acted impulsively.'

We sat in silence for a few moments as we thought about the wrenching serendipity of fate. A tow truck goes by a house. The driver sees a girl, alone and vulnerable. All in a moment he figures he can grab her and get away with it.

'So,' Bosch finally said, 'how did they get him?'

'The responding detectives were on the scene in less than an hour. The lead was named Doral Kloster and his partner was Chad Steiner. I checked. Steiner is dead and Kloster is retired and has late-stage Alzheimer's. He's no use to us now.'

'Damn,' Bosch said.

'Anyway, they got there quickly and moved quickly. They interviewed Sarah and she described the abductor

44

as being dressed like a garbage man. Further questioning revealed this to mean that he was wearing dirty coveralls like the city garbage crews used. She said she heard the garbage truck in the street but couldn't see it through a bush where she had hidden from her sister during a game of hide-and-seek. Problem is that it was a Sunday. There was no garbage pickup on Sundays. But the stepfather hears this and puts it together, mentions the tow trucks that run up and down the street on Sunday mornings. That becomes their best lead. The detectives get the list of city contractors and they start visiting tow yards.

'There were three contractors who worked the Wilshire corridor. One of them is Aardvark, where they go and are told they have three trucks working in the field. The drivers are called in and Jessup is one of them. The other two guys are named Derek Wilbern and William Clinton—really. They're separated and questioned but nothing comes up suspicious. They run 'em through the box and Jessup and Clinton are clean but Wilbern has an arrest but no conviction on an attempted rape two years before. That would be good enough to get him a ride downtown for a lineup, but the girl is still missing and there's no time for formalities, no time to put together a lineup.'

'They probably took him back to the house,' Bosch said. 'They had no choice. They had to keep things moving.'

'That's right. But Kloster knew he was on thin ice. He might get the girl to ID Wilbern but then he'd lose it in court for being unduly suggestive—you know, "Is this the guy?" So he did the next best thing he could. He took all three drivers in their overalls back to the Landy house. Each was a white man in his twenties. They all wore the company overalls. Kloster broke procedure for the sake of speed, hoping to have a chance to find the girl alive. Sarah Landy's bedroom was on the second floor in the front of the house. Kloster takes the girl up to her room and has her look out the window to the street. Through the venetian blinds. He radios his partner, who has the three guys get out of two patrol cars and stand in the street. But Sarah doesn't ID Wilbern. She points to Jessup and says that's the guy.'

Maggie looked through the documents in front of her and checked an investigative chronology before continuing.

'The ID is made at one o'clock. That is really quick work. The girl's only been gone a little over two hours. They start sweating Jessup but he doesn't give up a thing. Denies it all. They are working on him and getting nowhere when the call comes in. A girl's body has been found in a Dumpster behind the El Rey Theatre on Wilshire. That was about ten blocks from Windsor and the Landy house. Cause of death would later be determined to be manual strangulation. She was not raped and there was no semen in the mouth or throat.'

Maggie stopped her summary there. She looked at Bosch and then me and solemnly nodded, giving the dead her moment.

6

Bosch liked watching her and listening to the way she talked. He could tell the case was already under her skin. Maggie McFierce. Of course that was what they called her. More important, it was what she thought about herself. He had been on the case with her for less than a week but he understood this within the first hour of meeting her. She knew the secret. That it wasn't about code and procedure. It wasn't about jurisprudence and strategy. It was about taking that dark thing that you knew was out there in the world and bringing it inside. Making it yours. Forging it over an internal fire into something sharp and strong that you could hold in your hands and fight back with.

Relentlessly.

'Jessup asked for a lawyer and gave no further statement,' McPherson said, continuing her summary. 'The case was initially built around the older sister's identification and evidence found in Jessup's tow truck. Three strands of the victim's hair found in the seat crack. It was probably where he strangled her.'

'There was nothing on the girl?' Bosch asked. 'Nothing from Jessup or the truck?'

47

'Nothing usable in court. The DNA was found on her dress while it was being examined two days later. It was actually the older girl's dress. The younger girl borrowed it that day. One small deposit of semen was found on the front hem. It was typed but of course there was no DNA in criminal prosecutions back then. A blood type was determined and it was A-positive, the second-most popular type among humans, accounting for thirty-four percent of the population. Jessup matched but all it did was include him in the suspect pool. The prosecutor decided not to introduce it at trial because it would've just given the defense the ability to point out to the jury that the donor pool was more than a million men in Los Angeles County alone.'

Bosch saw her throw another look at her ex-husband. As if he were responsible for the courtroom obfuscations of all defense attorneys everywhere. Harry was starting to get an idea about why their marriage didn't work out.

'It's amazing how far we've come,' Haller said. 'Now they make and break cases on the DNA alone.'

'Moving on,' McPherson said. 'The prosecution had the hair evidence and the eyewitness. It also had opportunity—Jessup knew the neighborhood and was working there the morning of the murder. As far as motivation went, their backgrounding of Jessup produced a history of physical abuse by his father and psychopathic behavior. A lot of this came out on the record during the death penalty phase, too. But—and I will say this before you jump on it, Haller—no criminal convictions.'

'And you said no sexual assault?' Bosch asked.

'No evidence of penetration or sexual assault. But this was no doubt a sexually motivated crime. The semen aside, it was a classic control crime. The perpetrator seizing momentary control in a world where he felt he controlled very little. He acted impulsively. At the time, the semen found on her dress was a piece of the same puzzle. It was theorized that he killed the girl and then masturbated, cleaning up after himself but leaving one small deposit of semen on the dress by mistake. The stain had the appearance of a transfer deposit. It wasn't a drop. It was a smear.'

'The hit we just got on the DNA helps explain that,' Haller said.

'Possibly,' McPherson responded. 'But let's discuss new evidence later. Right now, I'm talking about what they had and what they knew in nineteen eighty-six.'

'Fine. Go on.'

'That's it on the evidence but not on the prosecution's case. Two months before trial they get a call from the guy who's in the cell next to Jessup at County. He—'

'Jailhouse snitches,' Haller said, interrupting. 'Never met one who told the truth, never met a prosecutor who didn't use them anyway.'

'Can I continue?' McPherson asked indignantly.

'Please do,' Haller responded.

'Felix Turner, a repeat drug offender who was in and out of County so often that they made him a jail orderly because he knew the day-to-day operations as well as the deputies. He delivered meals to inmates in high-power lockdown. He tells investigators that Jessup provided him with details that only the killer would know. He was interviewed and he did indeed have details of the crime that were not made public. Like that the victim's shoes were removed, that she was not sexually assaulted, that he had wiped himself off on her dress.'

'And so they believed him and made him the star witness,' Haller said.

'They believed him and put him on the stand at trial. Not as a star witness. But his testimony was significant. Nevertheless, four years later, the *Times* comes out with a front-page exposé on Felix "The Burner" Turner, professional jailhouse snitch who had testified for the prosecution in sixteen different cases over a seven-year period, garnering significant reductions in charges and jail time, and other perks like private cells, good jobs and large quantities of cigarettes.'

Bosch remembered the scandal. It rocked the DA's office in the early nineties and resulted in changes in the use of jailhouse informants as trial witnesses. It was one of many black eyes local law enforcement suffered in the decade.

'Turner was discredited in the newspaper investigation. It said he used a private investigator on the outside to gather information on crimes and then to feed it to him. As you may remember, it changed how we used information that comes to us through the jails.'

'Not enough,' Haller said. 'It didn't end the entire use of jailhouse snitches and it should have.'

'Can we just focus on our case here?' McPherson said, obviously tired of Haller's posturing.

'Sure,' Haller said. 'Let's focus.'

'Okay, well, by the time the *Times* came out with all of this, Jessup had long been convicted and was sitting in San Quentin. He of course launched an appeal citing police and prosecutorial misconduct. It went nowhere fast, with every appellate panel agreeing that while the use of Turner as a witness was egregious, his impact on the jury was not enough to have changed the verdict. The rest of the evidence was more than enough to convict.'

'And that was that,' Haller said. 'They rubber-stamped it.'

'An interesting note is that Felix Turner was found murdered in West Hollywood a year after the *Times* exposé,' McPherson said. 'The case was never solved.'

'Had it coming as far as I'm concerned,' Haller added.

That brought a pause to the discussion. Bosch used it to steer the meeting back to the evidence and to step in with some questions he had been considering.

'Is the hair evidence still available?'

It took McPherson a moment to drop Felix Turner and go back to the evidence.

'Yes, we still have it,' she said. 'This case is twenty-four years old but it was always under challenge. That's where Jessup and his jailhouse lawyering actually helped us. He was constantly filing writs and appeals. So the trial evidence was never destroyed. Of course, that eventually allowed him to get the DNA analysis off the swatch cut from the dress, but we still have all trial evidence and will be able to use it. He has claimed since day one that the hair in the truck was planted by the police.'

'I don't think his defense at retrial will be much different from what was presented at his first trial and in his appeals,' Haller said. 'The girl made the wrong ID in a prejudicial setting, and from then on it was a rush to judgment. Facing a monumental lack of physical evidence, the police planted hair from the victim in his tow truck. It didn't play so well before a jury in 'eighty-six, but that was before Rodney King and the riots in 'ninety-two, the O.J. Simpson case, the Rampart scandal and all the other controversies that have engulfed the police department since. It's probably going to play really well now.'

'So then, what are our chances?' Bosch asked.

Haller looked across the table at McPherson before answering.

'Based on what we know so far,' he said, 'I think I'd have a better chance if I were on the other side of the aisle on this one.'

Bosch saw McPherson's eyes grow dark.

'Well then, maybe you should cross back over.'

Haller shook his head.

'No, I made a deal. It may have been a bad deal but I'm sticking to it. Besides, it's not often I get to be on the side of might and right. I could get used to that—even in a losing cause.'

He smiled at his ex-wife but she didn't return the sentiment.

'What about the sister?' Bosch asked.

McPherson swung her gaze toward him.

'The witness? That's our second problem. If she's alive, then she's thirty-seven now. Finding her is the problem. No help from the parents. Her real father died when she was seven. Her mother committed suicide on her sister's grave three years after the murder. And the stepfather drank himself into liver failure and died while waiting for a transplant six years ago. I had one of the investigators here do a quick rundown on her on the computer and Sarah Landy's trail drops off in San Francisco about the same time her stepfather died. That same year she also cleared a probation tail for a controlled substance conviction. Records show she's been married and divorced twice, arrested multiple times for drugs and petty crimes. And then, like I said, she dropped off the grid. She either died or cleaned up her act. Even if she changed names, her prints would have left a trail if she'd been popped again in the past six years. But there's nothing.'

'I don't think we have much of a case if we don't have her,' Haller said. 'We're going to need a real live person to point the finger across twenty-four years and say he did it.'

'I agree,' McPherson said. 'She's key. The jury will need to hear the woman tell them that as a girl she did not make a mistake. That she was sure then and she is sure now. If we can't find her and get her to do that, then we have the victim's hair to go with and that's about it. They'll have the DNA and that will trump everything.'

'And we will go down in flames,' Haller said.

McPherson didn't respond, but she didn't have to.

'Don't worry,' Bosch said. 'I'll find her.'

The two lawyers looked at him. It wasn't a time for empty rah-rah speeches. He meant it.

'If she's alive,' he said, 'I'll find her.'

'Good,' Haller said. 'That'll be your first priority.'

Bosch took out his key chain and opened the small penknife attached to it. He used it to cut the red seal on the evidence box. He had no idea what would be in the box. The evidence that had been introduced at trial twenty-four years earlier was still in the possession of the DA's Office. This box would contain other evidence that was gathered but not presented at trial.

Bosch put on a set of latex gloves from his pocket and then opened the box. On top was a paper bag that contained the victim's dress. It was a surprise. He had assumed that the dress had been introduced at trial, if only for the sympathetic response it would get from the jurors.

Opening the bag brought a musty smell to the room. He lifted the dress out, holding it up by the shoulders. All three of them were silent. Bosch was holding up a dress that a little girl had been wearing when she was murdered. It was blue with a darker blue bow in the front. A six-inch square had been cut out of the front hem, the location of the semen stain.

'Why is this here?' Bosch asked. 'Wouldn't they have presented this at trial?'

Haller said nothing. McPherson leaned forward and looked closely at the dress as she considered a response.

'I think...they didn't show it because of the cutout. Showing the dress would let the defense ask about the cutout. That would lead to the blood-typing. The prosecution chose not to get into it during the presentation of the evidence. They probably relied on crime scene photos that showed the girl in the dress. They left it to the defense to introduce it and they never did.'

Bosch folded the dress and put it down on the table. Also in the box was a pair of black patent leather shoes. They seemed very small and sad to him. There was a second paper bag, which contained the victim's underwear and socks. An accompanying lab report stated that the items had been checked for bodily fluids as well as hair and fiber evidence but no such evidence had been found.

At the bottom of the box was a plastic bag containing a silver necklace with a charm on it. He looked at it through the plastic and identified the figure on the charm as Winnie the Pooh. There was also a bag containing a bracelet of aqua-blue beads on an elastic string.

'That's it,' he said.

'We should have forensics take a fresh look at it all,' McPherson said. 'You never know. Technology has advanced quite a bit in twenty-four years.'

'I'll get it done,' Bosch said.

'By the way,' McPherson asked, 'where were the shoes found? They're not on the victim's feet in the crime scene photos.'

Bosch looked at the property report that was taped to the inside of the box's top.

'According to this they were found underneath the body. They must've come off in the truck, maybe when she was strangled. The killer threw them into the Dumpster first, then dropped in her body.'

The images conjured by the items in the box had brought a decidedly somber mood to the prosecution team. Bosch started to carefully return everything to the box. He put the envelope containing the necklace in last.

'How old was your daughter when she left Winnie the Pooh behind?' he asked.

Haller and McPherson looked at each other. Haller deferred.

'Five or six,' McPherson said. 'Why?'

'Mine, too, I think. But this twelve-year-old had it on her necklace. I wonder why.'

'Maybe because of where it came from,' Haller said. 'Hayley—our daughter—still wears a bracelet I got for her about five years ago.'

McPherson looked at him as if challenging the assertion.

'Not all the time,' Haller said quickly. 'But on occasion. Sometimes when I pick her up. Maybe the necklace came from her real father before he died.'

A low chime came from McPherson's computer and

she checked her e-mail. She studied the screen for a few moments before speaking.

'This is from John Rivas, who handles afternoon arraignments in Department one hundred. Jessup's now got a criminal defense attorney and John's working on getting Jessup on the docket for a bail hearing. He's coming over on the last bus from City Jail.'

'Who's the lawyer?' Haller asked.

'You'll love this. Clever Clive Royce is taking the case pro bono. It's a referral from the GJP.'

Bosch knew the name. Royce was a high-profile guy who was a media darling who never missed a chance to stand in front of a camera and say all the things he wasn't allowed to say in court.

'Of course he's taking it pro bono,' Haller said. 'He'll make it up on the back end. Sound bites and headlines, that's all Clive cares about.'

'I've never gone up against him,' McPherson said. 'I can't wait.'

'Is Jessup actually on the docket?'

'Not yet. But Royce is talking to the clerk. Rivas wants to know if we want him to handle it. He'll oppose bail.'

'No, we'll take it,' Haller said. 'Let's go.'

McPherson closed her computer at the same time Bosch put the top back on the evidence box.

'You want to come?' Haller asked him. 'Get a look at the enemy?'

'I just spent seven hours with him, remember?'

'I don't think he was talking about Jessup,' McPherson said.

Bosch nodded.

'No, I'll pass,' he said. 'I'm going to take this stuff over to SID and get to work on tracking down our witness. I'll let you know when I find her.'

7

Tuesday, February 16, 5:30 P.M.

Department 100 was the largest courtroom in the CCB and reserved for morning and evening arraignment court, the twin intake points of the local justice system. All those charged with crimes had to be brought before a judge within twenty-four hours, and in the CCB this required a large courtroom with a large gallery section where the families and friends of the accused could sit. The courtroom was used for first appearances after arrest, when the loved ones were still naive about the lengthy, devastating and difficult journey the defendant was embarking upon. At arraignment, it was not unusual to have mom, dad, wife, sister-in-law, aunt, uncle and even a neighbor or two in the courtroom in a show of support for the defendant and outrage at his arrest. In another eighteen months, when the case would grind to a finale at sentencing, the defendant would be lucky to have even dear old mom still in attendance.

The other side of the gate was usually just as crowded, with lawyers of all stripes. Grizzled veterans, bored public defenders, slick cartel reps, wary prosecutors and media hounds all mingled in the well or stood against the glass partition surrounding the prisoner pen and whispered to their clients.

Presiding over this anthill was Judge Malcolm Firestone, who sat with his head down and his sharp shoulders jutting up and closer to his ears with each passing year. His black robe gave them the appearance of folded wings and the overall image was one of Firestone as a vulture waiting impatiently to dine on the bloody detritus of the justice system.

Firestone handled the evening arraignment docket, which started at three P.M. and went as far into the night as the list of detainees required. Consequently, he was a jurist who liked to keep things moving. You had to act fast in one hundred or risk being run over and left behind. In here, justice was an assembly line with a conveyor belt that never stopped turning. Firestone wanted to get home. The lawyers wanted to get home. Everybody wanted to get home.

I entered the courtroom with Maggie and immediately saw the cameras being set up in a six-foot corral to the left side, across the courtroom from the glass pen that housed defendants brought in six at a time. Without the glare of spotlights this time, I saw my friend Sticks setting the legs of the tool that provided his nickname, his tripod. He saw me and gave me a nod and I returned it.

Maggie tapped me on the arm and pointed toward a man seated at the prosecution table with three other lawyers.

'That's Rivas on the end.'

'Okay. You go talk to him while I check in with the clerk.'

'You don't have to check in, Haller. You're a prosecutor, remember?'

'Oh, cool. I forgot.'

We headed over to the prosecution table and Maggie introduced me to Rivas. The prosecutor was a baby lawyer, probably no more than a few years out of a top-ranked law school. My guess was that he was biding his time, playing office politics and waiting to make a move up the ladder and out of the hellhole of arraignment court. It didn't help that I had come from across the aisle to grab the golden ring of the office's current caseload. By his body language I registered his wariness. I was at the wrong table. I was the fox in the henhouse. And I knew that before the hearing was over, I was going to confirm his suspicions.

After the perfunctory handshake, I looked around for Clive Royce and found him seated against the railing, conferring with a young woman who was probably his associate. They were leaning toward each other, looking into an open folder with a thick sheaf of documents in it. I approached with my hand out.

'Clive "The Barrister" Royce, how's it hanging, old chap?'

He looked up and a smile immediately creased his well-tanned face. Like a perfect gentleman, he stood up before accepting my hand.

'Mickey, how are you? I'm sorry it looks like we're going to be opposing counsel on this one.'

I knew he was sorry but not too sorry. Royce had built his career on picking winners. He would not risk going pro bono and stepping into a heavy media case if he didn't think it would amount to free advertising and another victory. He was in it to win it and behind the smile was a set of sharp teeth.

'Me, too. And I am sure you will make me regret the day I crossed the aisle.'

'Well, I guess we're both fulfilling our public duty, yes? You helping out the district attorney and me taking on Jessup on the cuff.'

Royce still carried an English accent even though he had lived more than half his fifty years in the United States. It gave him an aura of culture and distinction that belied his practice of defending people accused of heinous crimes. He wore a three-piece suit with a barely discernible chalk line in the gabardine. His bald pate was well tanned and smooth, his beard dyed black and groomed to the very last hair.

'That's one way of looking at it,' I said.

'Oh, where are my manners? Mickey, this is my associate Denise Graydon. She'll be assisting me in the defense of Mr. Jessup.'

Graydon stood up and shook my hand firmly.

'Nice to meet you,' I said.

I looked around to see if Maggie was standing nearby and could be introduced but she was huddled with Rivas at the prosecution table.

'Well,' I said to Royce. 'Did you get your client on the docket?'

'I did indeed. He'll be first in the group after this one. I've already gone back and visited and we'll be ready to make a motion for bail. I was wondering, though, since we have a few minutes, could we step out into the corridor for a word?'

'Sure, Clive. Let's do it now.'

Royce told his associate to wait in the courtroom and retrieve us when the next group of defendants was brought into the glass cage. I followed Royce through the gate and down the aisle between the crowded rows of the gallery. We went through the mantrap and into the hallway.

'You want to get a cup of tea?' Royce asked.

'I don't think there's time. What's up, Clive?'

Royce folded his arms and got serious.

'I must tell you, Mick, that I am not out to embarrass you. You are a friend and colleague in the defense bar. But you have gotten yourself into a no-win situation here, yes? What are we going to do about it?'

I smiled and glanced up and down the crowded hallway. Nobody was paying attention to us.

'Are you saying that your client wants to plead this out?'

'On the contrary. There will be no plea negotiation on this matter. The district attorney has made the wrong choice and it's very clear what maneuver he is undertaking here and how he is using you as a pawn in the process. I must put you on notice that if you insist on taking Jason Jessup to trial, then you are going to embarrass yourself. As a professional courtesy, I just thought I needed to tell you this.'

Before I could answer, Graydon came out of the courtroom and headed quickly toward us.

'Somebody in the first group is not ready, so Jessup's been moved up and was just brought out.'

'We'll be in straightaway,' Royce said.

She hesitated and then realized her boss wanted her to go back into the courtroom. She went back through the doors and Royce turned his attention back to me. I spoke before he could.

'I appreciate your courtesy and concern, Clive. But if your client wants a trial, he'll get a trial. We'll be ready and we'll see who gets embarrassed and who goes back to prison.'

'Brilliant, then. I look forward to the contest.'

I followed him back inside. Court was in session and on my way down the aisle I saw Lorna Taylor, my office manager and second ex-wife, sitting at the end of one of the crowded rows. I leaned over to whisper.

'Hey, what are you doing here?'

'I had to come see the big moment.'

'How did you even know? I just found out fifteen minutes ago.'

'I guess so did KNX. I was already down here to look at office space and heard it on the radio that Jessup was going to appear in court. So I came.'

'Well, thanks for being here, Lorna. How is the search going? I really need to get out of this building. Soon.'

'I have three more showings after this. That'll be enough. I'll let you know my final choices tomorrow, okay?'

'Yeah, that's—'

I heard Jessup's name called by the clerk.

'Look, I gotta get in there. We'll talk later.'

'Go get 'em, Mickey!'

I found an empty seat waiting for me next to Maggie at the prosecution table. Rivas had moved to the row of seats against the gate. Royce had moved to the glass cage, where he was whispering to his client. Jessup was wearing an orange jumpsuit—the jail uniform—and looked calm and subdued. He was nodding to everything Royce whispered in his ear. He somehow seemed younger than I had thought he would. I guess I expected all of those years in prison to have taken their toll. I knew he was forty-eight but he looked no older than forty. He didn't even have a jailhouse pallor. His skin was pale but it looked healthy, especially next to the overtanned Royce.

'Where did you go?' Maggie whispered to me. 'I thought I was going to have to handle this myself.'

'I was just outside conferring with defense counsel. Do you have the charges handy? In case I have to read them into the record.'

'You won't have to enter the charges. All you have to do is stand up and say that you believe Jessup is a flight risk and a danger to the community. He—'

'But I don't believe he's a flight risk. His lawyer just told me they're ready to go and that they're not interested in a disposition. He wants the money and the only way he'll get it is to stick around and go to trial—and win.'

'So?'

She seemed astonished and looked down at the files stacked in front of her.

'Mags, your philosophy is to argue everything and give no quarter. I don't think that's going to work here. I have a strategy and—'

She turned and leaned in closer to me.

'Then I'll just leave you and your strategy and your bald buddy from the defense bar to it.'

She pushed back her chair and got up, grabbing her briefcase from the floor.

'Maggie...'

She charged through the gate and headed toward the rear door of the courtroom. I watched her go, knowing that while I didn't like the result, I had needed to set the lines of our prosecutorial relationship.

Jessup's name was called and Royce identified himself for the record. I then stood and said the words I never expected I would say.

'Michael Haller for the People.'

Even Judge Firestone looked up from his perch, peering at me over a pair of reading glasses. Probably for the first time in weeks something out of the ordinary had occurred in his courtroom. A dyed-in-the-wool defense attorney had stood for the People.

'Well, gentlemen, this is an arraignment court and I have a note here saying you want to talk about bail.'

Jessup was charged twenty-four years ago with murder and abduction. When the supreme court reversed his conviction it did not throw out the charges. That had been left to the DA's Office. So he still stood accused of the crimes and his not-guilty plea of twenty-four years ago remained in place. The case now had to be assigned to a courtroom and a judge for trial. A motion to discuss bail would usually be delayed until that point, except that Jessup, through Royce, was pushing the issue forward by coming to Firestone.

'Your Honor,' Royce said, 'my client was already arraigned twenty-four years ago. What we would like to do today is discuss a motion for bail and to move this case along to trial. Mr. Jessup has waited a long time for his freedom and for justice. He has no intention of waiving his right to a speedy trial.'

I knew it was the move Royce would make, because it was the move I would have made. Every person accused of a crime is guaranteed a speedy trial. Most often trials are delayed at the defense's request or acquiescence as both sides want time to prepare. As a pressure tactic, Royce was not going to suspend the speedy-trial statute. With a case and evidence twenty-four years old, not to mention a primary witness whose whereabouts were at the moment unknown, it was not only prudent but a no-brainer to put the prosecution on the clock. When the supreme court reversed the conviction, that clock started ticking. The People had sixty days from that point to bring Jessup to trial. Twelve of them had already gone by.

'I can move the case to the clerk for assignment,' Firestone said. 'And I would prefer that the assigned judge handle the question of bail.'

Royce composed his thoughts for a moment before responding. In doing so he turned his body slightly so the cameras would have a better angle on him.

'Your Honor, my client has been falsely incarcerated for twenty-four years. And those aren't just my words, that's the opinion of the state supreme court. Now they have pulled him out of prison and brought him down here so he can face trial once again. This is all part of an ongoing scheme that has nothing to do with justice, and everything to do with money and politics. It's about avoiding responsibility for corruptly taking a man's freedom. To put this over until another hearing on another day would continue the travesty of justice that has beset Jason Jessup for more than two decades.'

'Very well.'

Firestone still seemed put out and annoyed. The assembly line had thrown a gear. He had a docket that had probably started with more than seventy-five names on it and a desire to get through them in time to get home for dinner before eight. Royce was going to slow things down immeasurably with his request for a full debate on whether Jessup should be allowed his release while awaiting trial. But Firestone, like Royce, was about to get the surprise of the day. If he didn't make it home in time for dinner, it wouldn't be because of me.

Royce asked the judge for an OR, meaning Jessup would have to put up no money as bail and simply be released on his own recognizance. This was just his opener. He fully expected there to be a financial figure attached to Jessup's freedom, if he was successful at all.

Murder suspects didn't get OR'ed. In the rare instance when bail was granted in a murder case, it usually came with a steep price tag. Whether Jessup could raise the money through his supporters or from the book and movie deals he was supposedly negotiating was not germane to the discussion.

Royce closed his request by arguing that Jessup should not be considered a flight risk for the very same reason I had outlined to Maggie. He had no interest in running. His only interest was in fighting to clear his name after twenty-four years of wrongful imprisonment.

'Mr. Jessup has no other purpose at this time than to stay put and prove once and for all that he is innocent and that he has paid a nightmarish price for the mistakes and misconduct of this District Attorney's Office.'

The whole time Royce spoke I watched Jessup in the glass cage. He knew the cameras were on him and he maintained a pose of rightful indignation. Despite his efforts, he could not disguise the anger and hate in his eyes. Twenty-four years in prison had made that permanent.

Firestone finished writing a note and then asked for my response. I stood and waited until the judge looked up at me.

'Go ahead, Mr. Haller,' he prompted.

'Judge, providing that Mr. Jessup can show documentation of residence, the state does not oppose bail at this time.'

Firestone stared at me for a long moment as he computed that my response was diametrically opposite to what he thought it would be. The hushed sounds of the courtroom seemed to get even lower as the impact of my response was understood by every lawyer in the room.

'Did I get that right, Mr. Haller?' Firestone said. 'You are not objecting to an OR release in a murder case?'

'That is correct, Your Honor. We are fully expecting Mr. Jessup to show for trial. There's no money in it for him if he doesn't.'

'Your Honor!' Royce cried. 'I object to Mr. Haller infecting the record with such prejudicial pap directed solely at the media in attendance. My client has no other purpose at this point than—'

'I understand, Mr. Royce,' Firestone interjected. 'But I think you did a fair amount of playing to the cameras yourself. Let's just leave it at that. Without objection from the prosecution, I am releasing Mr. Jessup on his own recognizance once he provides the clerk with documentation of residence. Mr. Jessup is not to leave Los Angeles County without permission of the court to which his case is assigned.'

Firestone then referred the case to the clerk of the court's office for reassignment to another department for trial. We were now finally out of Judge Firestone's orbit. He could restart the assembly line and get home for dinner. I picked up the files Maggie had left behind and left the table. Royce was back at the seat at the railing, dumping files into a leather briefcase. His young associate was helping him.

'How did it feel, Mick?' he asked me.

'What, being a prosecutor?'

'Yes, crossing the aisle.'

'Not too much different, to tell you the truth. It was all procedure today.'

'You will be raked over the coals for letting my client walk out of here.'

'Fuck 'em if they can't take a joke. Just make sure he stays clean, Clive. If he doesn't, then my ass really will be thrown on the fire. And so will his.'

'No problem there. We'll take care of him. He's the least of your worries, you know.'

'How's that, Clive?'

'You don't have much in the way of evidence, can't find your main witness, and the DNA is a case killer. You're captain of the *Titanic*, Mickey, and Gabriel Williams put you there. Makes me wonder what he's got on you.'

Out of all that he said, I only wondered about one thing. How did he know about the missing witness? I, of course, didn't ask him or respond to his jab about what the DA might have on me. I played it like all the overconfident prosecutors I had ever gone up against.

'Tell your client to enjoy himself while he's out there, Clive. Because as soon as the verdict comes in, he's going back inside.'

Royce smiled as he snapped his case closed. He changed the subject.

'When can we talk about discovery?'

'We can talk about it whenever you like. I'll start putting a file together in the morning.'

'Good. Let's talk soon, Mick, yes?'

'Like I said, anytime, Clive.'

He headed over to the court deputy's desk, most likely to see about his client's release. I pushed through the gate and connected with Lorna and we left the courtroom together. Waiting for me outside was a small gathering of reporters and cameras. The reporters shouted questions about my not objecting to bail and I told them no comment and walked on by. They waited in place for Royce to come out next.

'I don't know, Mickey,' Lorna confided. 'How do you think the DA is going to respond to the no bail?'

Just as she asked it my phone started beeping in my pocket. I realized I had forgotten to turn it off in the courtroom. That was an error that could have proven costly, depending on Firestone's view of electronic interruptions while court was in session.

Looking at the screen, I said to Lorna, 'I don't know but I think I'm about to find out.'

I held up the phone so she could see that the caller ID said LADA.

'You take it. I'm going to run. Be careful, Mickey.'

She kissed me on the cheek and headed off to the elevator alcove. I connected to the call. I had guessed right. It was Gabriel Williams.

'Haller, what the hell are you doing?'

'What do you mean?'

'One of my people said you allowed Jessup to walk on an OR.'

'That's right.'

'Then I'll ask again, What the hell are you doing?'

'Look, I—'

'No, you look. I don't know if you were just giving one of your buddies in the defense bar what he wanted or you are just stupid, but you *never* let a murderer walk. You understand me? Now, I want you to go back in there and ask for a new hearing on bail.'

'No, I'm not going to do that.'

There was a hard silence for at least ten seconds before Williams came back.

'Did I just hear you right, Haller?'

'I don't know what you heard, Williams, but I'm not going back for a rehearing. You have to understand something. You gave me a bag of shit for a case and I have to do the best I can with it. What evidence we do have is twenty-four years old. We have a big hole blown in the side of the case with the DNA and we have an eyewitness we can't find. So that tells me I have to do whatever I can do to make this case.'

'And what's that got to do with letting this man out of jail?'

'Don't you see, man? Jessup has been in prison for twenty-four years. It was no finishing school. Whatever he was when he went in? He's worse now. If he's on the outside, he'll fuck up. And if he fucks up, that only helps us.'

'So in other words, you are putting the general public at risk while this guy is out there.'

'No, because you are going to talk to the LAPD and get them to watch this guy. So nobody gets hurt and they are able to step in and grab him the minute he acts out.'

Another silence followed but this time I could hear muffled voices and I figured that Williams was talking it over with his advisor, Joe Ridell. When his voice came back to me, it was stern but had lost the tone of outrage.

'Okay, this is what I want you to do. When you want to make a move like this, you come to me first. You understand?'

'That's not going to happen. You wanted an independent prosecutor. That's what you've got. Take it or leave it.'

There was a pause and then he hung up without further word. I closed my phone and watched for a few moments as Clive Royce exited the courtroom and waded into the crowd of reporters and cameras. Like a seasoned expert, he waited a moment for everyone to get their positions set and their lenses focused. He then proceeded with the first of what would be many impromptu but carefully scripted press briefings.

'I think the District Attorney's Office is running scared,' he began.

It was what I knew he would say. I didn't need to listen to the rest. I walked away.

8

Some people don't want to be found. They take measures. They drag the branch behind them to confuse the trail. Some people are just running and they don't care what they leave in their wake. What's important is that the past is behind them and that they keep moving away from it.

Once he back-checked the DA investigator's work, it took Bosch only two hours to find a current name and address for their missing witness, Melissa Landy's older sister, Sarah. She hadn't dragged a branch. She had used the things that were close and just kept moving. The DA's investigator who lost the trail in San Francisco had not looked backwards for clues. That was his mistake. He had looked forward and he'd found an empty trail.

Bosch had started as his predecessor had, typing the name Sarah Landy and birth date April 14, 1972, into the computer. The department's various search engines provided myriad points of impact with law enforcement and society.

First there were arrests on drug charges in 1989 and 1990—handled discreetly and sympathetically by the

Division of Children's Services. But she was beyond the reach and understanding of DYS for similar charges in late 1991 and two more times in 1992. There was probation and a period of rehabilitation and this was followed by a few years during which she left no digital fingerprints at all. Another search site provided Bosch with a series of addresses for her in Los Angeles in the early nineties. Harry recognized these as marginal neighborhoods where rents were probably low and drugs close by and easy to acquire. Sarah's illegal substance of choice was crystal meth, a drug that burned away brain cells by the billions.

The trail on Sarah Landy, the girl who had hidden behind the bushes and watched her younger sister get taken by a killer, ended there.

Bosch opened the first file he had retrieved from the murder box and looked at the witness information sheet for Sarah. He found her Social Security number and fed that along with the DOB into the search engine. This gave him two new names: Sarah Edwards, beginning in 1991, and Sarah Witten in 1997. With women changes of last names only were usually an indicator of marriage, and the DA's investigator had reported finding records of two marriages.

Under the name Sarah Edwards, the arrests continued, including two pops for property crimes and a tag for soliciting for prostitution. But the arrests were spread far enough apart and perhaps her story was sad enough that once again she never saw any jail time.

Bosch clicked through the mug shots for these arrests.

They showed a young woman with changing hairstyles and colors but the unwavering look of hurt and defiance in her eyes. One mug shot showed a deep purple bruise under her left eye and open sores along her jawline. The photos seemed to tell the story best. A downward spiral of drugs and crime. An internal wound that never healed, a guilt never assuaged.

Under the name Sarah Witten, the arrests didn't change, only the location. She had probably realized she was wearing thin on the prosecutors and judges who had repeatedly given her breaks—most likely after reading the summary of her life contained in the presentencing investigations. She moved north to San Francisco and once again had frequent encounters with the law. Drugs and petty crime, charges that often go hand in hand. Bosch checked the mug shots and saw a woman who looked old beyond her years. She looked like she was forty before she was yet thirty.

In 2003 she did her first significant jail time when she was sentenced to six months in San Mateo County Jail after pleading guilty to a possession charge. The records showed that she served four months in jail followed by a lockdown rehab program. It was the last marker on the system for her. No one with any of her names or Social Security number had been arrested since or applied for a driver's license in any of the fifty states.

Bosch tried a few other digital maneuvers he had learned while working in the Open-Unsolved Unit, where Internet tracing was raised to an art form, but could not pick up the trail. Sarah was gone.

Putting the computer aside, Bosch took up the files from the murder box. He started scanning the documents, looking for clues that might help him track her. He got more than a clue when he found a photocopy of Sarah's birth certificate. It was then that he remembered that she had been living with her mother and stepfather at the time of her sister's murder.

The birth name on the certificate was Sarah Ann Gleason. He entered it into the computer along with her birth date. He found no criminal history under the name but he did find a Washington State driver's license that had been established six years earlier and renewed just two months before. He pulled up the photo and it was a match. But barely. Bosch studied it for a long time. He would have sworn that Sarah Ann Gleason was getting younger.

His guess was that she had left the hard life behind. She had found something that made her change. Maybe she had taken the cure. Maybe she had a child. But something had changed her life for the better.

Bosch next ran her name through another search engine and got utility and satellite hookups under her name. The addresses matched the one on her driver's license. Bosch was sure he had found her. Port Townsend. He went onto Google and typed it in. Soon he was looking at a map of the Olympic Peninsula in the northwest corner of Washington. Sarah Landy had changed her name three times and had run to the farthest tip of the continental United States, but he had found her.

The phone rang as he was reaching for it. It was Lieutenant Stephen Wright, commander of the LAPD's Special Investigation Section.

'I just wanted you to know that as of fifteen minutes ago we're fully deployed on Jessup. The full unit's involved and we'll get you surveillance logs each morning. If you need anything else or want to ride along at any point, you call me.'

'Thank you, Lieutenant. I will.'

'Let's hope something happens.'

'That would be nice.'

Bosch disconnected. And made the call to Maggie McPherson.

'Couple things. First, SIS is in place now on Jessup. You can let Gabriel Williams know.'

He thought he heard a small chuckle before she responded.

'Ironic, huh?'

'Yeah. Maybe they'll end up killing Jessup and we won't have to worry about a trial.'

The Special Investigation Section was an elite surveillance squad that had existed for more than forty years despite a kill rate higher than that of any other unit in the department, including SWAT. The SIS was used to clandestinely watch apex predators—individuals suspected in violent crimes who would not cease until caught in the act and stopped by the police. Masters of surveillance, SIS officers waited to observe suspects committing new crimes before moving in to make arrests, often with fatal consequences.

The irony McPherson mentioned was that Gabriel Williams was a civil rights attorney before running for and winning the DA's post. He had sued the department over SIS shootings on multiple occasions, claiming that the unit's strategies were designed to draw suspects into deadly confrontations with police. He had gone so far as to call the unit a 'death squad' while announcing a lawsuit over an SIS shooting that had left four robbers dead outside a Tommy's fast-food franchise. That same death squad was now being used in a gambit that might help win the case against Jessup and further Williams's political rise.

'You'll be informed of his activities?' McPherson asked.

'Every morning I'll get the surveillance log. And they'll call me out if anything good happens.'

'Perfect. Was there something else? I'm in a bit of a rush. I'm working on one of my preexisting cases and have a hearing about to start.'

'Yeah, I found our witness.'

'You're brilliant! Where is she?'

'Up in Washington on the northern tip of the Olympic Peninsula. A place called Port Townsend. She's using her birth name, Sarah Ann Gleason, and it appears that she's been living clean up there for about six years.'

'That's good for us.'

'Maybe not.'

'How so?'

'It looks to me like most of her life has been spent trying to get away from what happened that Sunday in

Hancock Park. If she's finally gotten past it and is living the clean life up there in Port Townsend, she might not be interested in picking at old scabs, if you know what I mean.'

'Not even for her sister?'

'Maybe not. We're talking about twenty-four years ago.'

McPherson was quiet for a long moment and then finally responded.

'That's a cynical view of the world, Harry. When are you planning on going up there?'

'As soon as I can. But I have to make arrangements for my daughter. She stayed with a friend when I went up to get Jessup at San Quentin. It didn't turn out so good and now I have to hit the road again.'

'Sorry to hear that. I want to go up with you.'

'I think I can handle it.'

'I know you can handle it. But it might be good to have a woman and a prosecutor with you. More and more, I think she's going to be the key to this whole thing and she's going to be my witness. Our approach to her will be very important.'

'I've been approaching witnesses for about thirty years. I think I—'

'Let me have the travel office here make the arrangements. That way we can go up together. Talk out the strategy.'

Bosch paused. He knew he wasn't going to be able to change her mind.

'Whatever you say.'

'Good. I'll tell Mickey and contact travel. We'll book a morning flight. I'm clear tomorrow. Is that too soon for you? I'd hate to wait on this till next week.'

'I'll make it work.'

Bosch had had a third reason to call her but now decided to hold back. Her taking over the trip to Washington made him gun-shy about discussing his investigative moves.

They hung up and he was left drumming his fingers on the edge of his desk as he contemplated what he would say to Rachel Walling.

After a few moments he pulled out his cell phone and used it to make the call. He had Walling's number in its memory. To his surprise, she answered right away. He had envisioned her seeing his name on the ID and letting him go to the message. They'd had a relationship that was long over but still left a trail of intense feelings.

'Hello, Harry.'

'Hello, Rachel. How are you?'

'I'm fine. And you?'

'Pretty good. I'm calling about a case.'

'Of course. Harry Bosch never goes through channels. He goes direct.'

'There are no channels for this. And you know I call you because I trust you and more than anything else respect your opinion. I go through channels and I get some profiler in Quantico who's just a voice on the phone. And not only that, he doesn't call me back with anything for two months. What would you do if you were me?'

'Oh...probably the same thing.'

'Besides that, I don't want the bureau's official involvement. I am just looking for your opinion and advice, Rachel.'

'What's the case?'

'I think you're going to like it. It's a twenty-four-year-old murder of a twelve-year-old girl. A guy went down for it back then and now we have to retry him. I was thinking a profile of the crime might be helpful to the prosecutor.'

'Is this that Jessup case that's in the news?'

'That's right.'

He knew she would be interested. He could hear it in her voice.

'All right, well, bring by whatever you've got. How much time are you giving me? I've got my regular job, you know.'

'No hurry this time. Not like with that Echo Park thing. I'll probably be out of town tomorrow. Maybe longer. I think you can have a few days with the file. You still in the same place above the Million Dollar Theater?'

'That's it.'

'Okay, I'll drop the box by.'

'I'll be here.'

9

The holding cell next to Department 124 on the thir-teenth floor of the CCB was empty except for my client Cassius Clay Montgomery. He sat morosely on the bench in the corner and didn't get up when he saw me come back.

'Sorry I'm late.'

He didn't say anything. He didn't acknowledge my presence.

'Come on, Cash. It's not like you'd be going any-where. What's it matter if you were waiting here or back in County?'

'They got TV in County, man,' he said, looking up at me.

'Okay, so you missed *Oprah*. Can you come over here so I don't have to shout our business across the room?'

He got up and came over to the bars. I stood on the other side, beyond the red line marking the three-foot threshold.

'Doesn't matter if you shout our business. There ain't nobody left to hear it.'

'I told you, I'm sorry. I've been having a busy day.'

'Yeah, and I guess I'm just a no-count nigger when it comes to being on TV and turnin' into the man.'

'What's that supposed to mean?'

'I saw you on the news, dog. Now you a prosecutor? What kinda shit is that?'

I nodded. Obviously, my client was more concerned with me being a turncoat than with waiting until the last hearing of the day.

'Look, all I can tell you is that I took the job reluctantly. I am not a prosecutor. I am a defense attorney. I'm your defense attorney. But every now and then they come to you and they want something. And it's hard to say no.'

'So what happens to me?'

'Nothing happens to you. I'm still your lawyer, Cash. And we have a big decision to make here. This hearing is going to be short and sweet. It's to set a trial date and that's it. But Mr. Hellman, the prosecutor, says the offer he made to you is good only until today. If we tell Judge Champagne we're ready to go to trial today, then the deal disappears and we go to trial. Have you thought about it some more?'

Montgomery leaned his head in between two bars and didn't speak. I realized he couldn't pull the trigger on a decision. He was forty-seven and had already spent nine years of his life in prison. He was charged with armed robbery and assault with great bodily injury and was looking at a big fall.

According to the police, Montgomery had posed as a buyer at a drive-through drug market in the Rodia

Gardens projects. But instead of paying, he pulled a gun and demanded the dealer's drugs and money roll. The dealer went for the gun and it went off. Now the dealer, a gang member named Darnell Hicks, was in a wheelchair for the rest of his life.

As is usual in the projects, no one cooperated with the investigation. Even the victim said he didn't remember what happened, choosing in his silence to trust that his fellow Crips would handle justice in the matter. But investigators made a case anyway. Picking up my client's car on a video camera at the entrance to the projects, they found the car and matched blood on the door to the victim.

It wasn't a strong case but it was solid enough for us to entertain an offer from the prosecution. If Montgomery took the deal he'd be sentenced to three years in prison and would likely serve two and a half. If he gambled and took a conviction at the end of a trial, then he'd be looking at a mandatory minimum of fifteen years inside. The add-on of GBI and use of a firearm in the commission of a robbery were the killers. And I knew firsthand that Judge Judith Champagne wasn't soft on gun crimes.

I had recommended to my client that he take the deal. It was a no-brainer to me but then I wasn't the one who had to do the time. Montgomery couldn't decide. It wasn't so much about the prison time. It was the fact that the victim, Hicks, was a Crip and the street gang had a long reach into every prison in the state. Even taking the three-year sentence could be a death penalty.

Montgomery wasn't sure he would make it.

'I don't know what to tell you,' I said. 'It's a good offer. The DA doesn't want to go to trial on this. He doesn't want to put a victim on the stand who doesn't want to be there and may hurt the case more than help it. So he's gone as low as he can go. But it's up to you. Your decision. You've had a couple weeks now and this is it. We have to go out there in a couple minutes.'

Montgomery tried to shake his head but his forehead was pressed between the two bars.

'What's that mean?' I asked.

'It means shit. Can't we win this case, man? I mean, you a prosecutor now. Can't you get a good word in for me on this?'

'They're two different matters, Cash. I can't do anything like that. You got your choice. Take the three or we go to trial. And like I told you before, we can certainly do some stuff at trial. They've got no weapon and a victim who won't tell the story, but they still got his blood on the door of your car and they got video of you driving it out of Rodia right after the shooting. We can try to play it the way you said it went down. Self-defense. You were there to buy a rock and he saw *your* roll and tried to rip *you* off. The jury might believe it, especially if he won't testify. And they might believe it even if he does testify because I'll make him take the fifth so many times they'll think he's Al Capone before he gets off the stand.'

'Who's Al Capone?'

'You're kidding me, right?'

'No, man, who is he?'

'Never mind, Cash. What do you want to do?'

'You're cool if we go to trial?'

'I'm cool with it. It's just that there is that gap, you know?'

'Gap?'

'There is a wide gap between what they're offering you right now and what you could get if we lose at trial. We're talking about a minimum twelve-year swing, Cash. That's a lot of time to gamble with.'

Montgomery backed away from the bars. They had left twin impressions on both sides of his forehead. He now gripped the bars in his hands.

'The thing is, three years, fifteen years, I ain't going to make it either way. They got hit men in every prison. But in County, they got the system and ev'rybody is separated and locked up tight. I'm okay there.'

I nodded. But the problem was that any sentence over a year had to be served in a state prison. The county system was a holding system for those awaiting trial or sentenced to short terms.

'Okay, then I guess we go to trial.'

'I guess we do.'

'Sit tight. They'll be coming back for you soon.'

I knocked quietly on the courtroom door and the deputy opened it. Court was in session and Judge Champagne was holding a status conference on another case. I saw my prosecutor sitting against the rail and went over to confer. This was the first case I'd had with Philip Hellman and I had found him to be extremely reasonable. I decided to test the limits of that reason one last time.

'So, Mickey, I hear we are now colleagues,' he said with a smile.

'Temporarily,' I said. 'I don't plan to make it a career.'

'Good, I don't need the competition. So what are we going to do here?'

'I think we are going to put it over one more time.'

'Mickey, come on, I've been very generous. I can't keep—'

'No, you're right. You've been completely generous, Phil, and I appreciate that. My client appreciates that. It's just that he can't take a deal because anything that puts him in a state prison is a death penalty. We both know that the Crips will get him.'

'First of all, I don't know that. And second of all, if that's what he thinks, then maybe he shouldn't have tried to rip off the Crips and shoot one of their guys.'

I nodded in agreement.

'That's a good point but my client maintains it was self-defense. Your vic drew first. So I guess we go to trial and you've got to ask a jury for justice for a victim who doesn't want it. Who will testify only if you force him to and will then claim he doesn't remember shit.'

'Maybe he doesn't. He did get shot, after all.'

'Yeah, and maybe the jury will buy that, especially when I bring out his pedigree. I'll ask him what he does for a living for starters. According to what Cisco, my investigator, has found out, he's been selling drugs since he was twelve years old and his mother put him on the street.'

'Mickey, we've already been down this road. What do you want? I'm getting ready to just say fuck it, let's go to trial.'

'What do I want? I want to make sure you don't fuck up the start of your brilliant career.'

'What?'

'Look, man, you are a young prosecutor. Remember what you just said about not wanting the competition? Well, another thing you don't want is to risk putting a loss on your ledger. Not this early in the game. You just want this to go away. So here's what I want. A year in County and restitution. You can name your price on restitution.'

'Are you kidding me?'

He said it too loud and drew a look from the judge. He then spoke very quietly.

'Are you fucking kidding me?'

'Not really. It's a good solution when you think about it, Phil. It works for everybody.'

'Yeah, and what's Judge Judy going to say when I present this? The victim is in a wheelchair for life. She won't sign off on this.'

'We ask to go back to chambers and we both sell it to her. We tell her that Montgomery wants to go to trial and claim self-defense and that the state has real reservations because of the victim's lack of cooperation and status as a high-ranking member of a criminal organization. She was a prosecutor before she was a judge.

She'll understand this. And she'll probably have more sympathy for Montgomery than she does for your drug-dealing victim.'

Hellman thought for a long moment. The hearing before Champagne ended and she instructed the court-room deputy to bring Montgomery out. It was the last case of the day.

'Now or never, Phil,' I prompted.

'Okay, let's do it,' he finally said.

Hellman stood up and moved to the prosecution table.

'Your Honor,' he intoned, 'before we bring the defendant out, could counsel discuss this case in chambers?'

Champagne, a veteran judge who had seen everything at least three times, creased her brow.

'On the record, gentlemen?'

'That's probably not necessary,' Hellman said. 'We would like to discuss the terms of a disposition in the case.'

'Then by all means. Let's go.'

The judge stepped down from the bench and headed back toward her chambers. Hellman and I started to follow. As we got to the gate next to the clerk's pod, I leaned forward to whisper to the young prosecutor.

'Montgomery gets credit for time served, right?'

Hellman stopped in his tracks and turned back to me.

'You've got to be—'

'Just kidding,' I quickly said.

I held my hands up in surrender. Hellman frowned and then turned back around and headed toward the judge's chambers. I had thought it was worth a try.

10

Thursday, February 18, 7:18 A.M.

It was a silent breakfast. Madeline Bosch poked at her cereal with her spoon but managed to put very little of it into her stomach. Bosch knew that his daughter wasn't upset because he was going away for the night. And she wasn't upset because she wasn't going. He believed she had come to enjoy the breaks his infrequent travels gave her. The reason she was upset was the arrangements he had made for her care while he was gone. She was fourteen going on twenty-four and her first choice would have been to simply be left alone to fend for herself. Her second choice would have been to stay with her best friend up the street, and her last choice would have been to have Mrs. Bambrough from the school stay at the house with her.

Bosch knew she was perfectly capable of fending for herself but he wasn't there yet. They had been living together for only a few months and it had been only those few months since she had lost her mother. He just wasn't ready to turn her loose, no matter how fervently she insisted she was ready.

He finally put down his spoon and spoke.

'Look, Maddie, it's a school night and last time when you stayed with Rory you both stayed up all night, slept through most of your classes and had your parents and all your teachers mad at both of you.'

'I told you we wouldn't do that again.'

'I just think we need to wait on that a little bit. I'll tell Mrs. Bambrough that it's all right if Rory comes over, just not till midnight. You guys can do your home-work together or something.'

'Like she's really going to want to come here when I'm being watched by the assistant principal. Thanks for that, Dad.'

Bosch had to concentrate on not laughing. This issue seemed so simple compared with what she had faced in October after coming to live with him. She still had regular therapy sessions and they seemed to go a long way toward helping her cope with her mother's death. Bosch would take a dispute over child care over those other deeper issues any day.

He checked his watch. It was time to go.

'If you're done playing with your food you can put your bowl in the sink. We have to get going.'

'*Finished*, Dad. You should use the correct word.'

'Sorry about that. Are you *finished* playing with your cereal?'

'Yes.'

'Good. Let's go.'

He got up from the table and went back to his room to grab his overnight bag off the bed. He was traveling light, expecting the trip to last one night at the most. If they got lucky, they might even catch a late flight home tonight.

When he came back out, Maddie was standing by the door, her backpack over one shoulder.

'Ready?'

'No, I'm just standing here for my health.'

He walked up to her and kissed the top of her head before she could move away from him. She tried, though.

'Gotcha.'

'Daaaad!'

He locked the door behind them and put his bag in the backseat of the Mustang.

'You have your key, right?'

'Yes!'

'Just making sure.'

'Can we go? I don't want to be late.'

They drove down the hill in silence after that. When they got to the school, he saw Sue Bambrough working the drop-off lane, getting the slow-moving kids out of the cars and into the school, keeping things moving.

'You know the routine, Mads. Call me, text me, vid me, let me know you're doing okay.'

'I'll get out here.'

She opened the door early, before they got to where the assistant principal was stationed. Maddie got out and then reached back in to grab her bag. Bosch waited for it, the sign that everything was really okay.

'Be safe, Dad.'

There it was.

'You, too, baby.'

She closed the door. He lowered the window and drove down to Sue Bambrough. She leaned into the open window.

'Hey, Sue. She's a little upset but she'll get over it by the end of the day. I told her that Aurora Smith could come by but not to make it late. Who knows, maybe they'll do some homework.'

'She'll be fine, Harry.'

'I left the check on the kitchen counter and there's some cash there for anything you guys'll need.'

'Thanks, Harry. Just let me know if you think it will be more than one night. No problem on my end.'

Bosch checked the rearview. He wanted to ask a question but didn't want to hold people up.

'What is it, Harry?'

'Uh, to say you're done doing something, is that wrong? You know, bad English?'

Sue tried to hide a smile.

'If she's correcting you, that's the natural course of things. Don't take it personally. We drill it into them here. They go home and want to drill somebody else. It would be proper to say you *finished* doing something. But I know what you meant.'

Bosch nodded. Somebody in the line behind him tapped the horn—Bosch assumed it was a man hurrying to make drop-off and then get to work. He waved his thanks to Sue and pulled out.

Maggie McFierce had called Bosch the night before and told him that there was nothing out of Burbank, so they were taking a direct flight out of LAX. That meant it would be a brutal drive in morning traffic. Bosch lived on a hillside right above the Hollywood Freeway but it was the one freeway that wouldn't help him get to the airport. Instead, he took Highland down into Hollywood and then cut over to La Cienega. It bottle-necked through the oil fields near Baldwin Hills and he lost his cushion of time. He took La Tijera from there and when he got to the airport he was forced to park in one of the expensive garages close in because he didn't have time to ride a shuttle bus in from an economy lot.

After filling out the Law Enforcement Officer forms at the counter and being walked through security by a TSA agent, he finally got to the gate while the plane was in the final stages of loading its passengers. He looked for McPherson but didn't see her and assumed she was already on the plane.

He boarded and went through the required meet-and-greet, stepping into the cockpit, showing his badge and shaking the hands of the flight crew. He then made his way toward the back of the plane. He and McPherson had exit-row seats across the aisle from each other. She was already in place, a tall Starbucks cup in hand. She had obviously arrived early for the flight.

'Thought you weren't going to make it,' she said.

'It was close. How'd you get here so early? You have a daughter just like me.'

'I dropped her with Mickey last night.'

Bosch nodded.

'Exit row, nice. Who's your travel agent?'

'We've got a good one. That's why I wanted to handle it. We'll send LAPD the bill for you.'

'Yeah, good luck with that.'

Bosch had put his bag in an overhead compartment so he would have room to extend his legs. After he sat down and buckled in, he saw that McPherson had shoved two thick files into the seat pocket in front of her. He had nothing out to prep with. His files were in his bag but he didn't feel like getting them out. He pulled his notebook out of his back pocket and was about to lean across the aisle to ask McPherson a question when a flight attendant came down the aisle and stooped down to whisper to him.

'You're the detective, right?'

'Uh, yes. Is there a—'

Before he could finish the Dirty Harry line, the flight attendant informed him that they were upgrading him to an unclaimed seat in the first-class section.

'Oh, that's nice of you and the captain, but I don't think I can do that.'

'There's no charge. It's—'

'No, it's not that. See, I'm with this lady here and she's my boss and I—I mean we—need to talk and go over our investigation. She's a prosecutor, actually.'

The attendant took a moment to track his explanation and then nodded and said she'd go back to the front of the plane and inform the powers that be.

'And I thought chivalry was dead,' McPherson said. 'You gave up a first-class seat to sit with me.'

'Actually, I should've told her to give it to you. That would have been real chivalry.'

'Uh-oh, here she comes back.'

Bosch looked up the aisle. The same smiling attendant was headed back to them.

'We're moving some people around and we have room for you both. Come on up.'

They got up and headed forward, Bosch grabbing his bag out of the overhead and following McPherson. She looked back at him, smiled and said, 'My tarnished knight.'

'Right,' Bosch said.

The seats were side by side in the first row. McPherson took the window. Soon after they were resituated, the plane took off for its three-hour flight to Seattle.

'So,' McPherson said, 'Mickey told me our daughter has never met your daughter.'

Bosch nodded.

'Yeah, I guess we need to change that.'

'Definitely. I hear they're the same age and you guys compared photos and they even look alike.'

'Well, her mother sort of looked like you. Same coloring.'

And fire, Bosch thought. He pulled out his phone and turned it on. He showed her a photo of Maddie.

'That's remarkable,' McPherson said. 'They could be sisters.'

Bosch looked at his daughter's photo as he spoke.

'It's just been a tough year for her. She lost her mother and moved across an ocean. Left all her friends behind.

I've been kind of letting her move at her own pace.'

'All the more reason she should know her family here.'

Bosch just nodded. In the past year he had fended off numerous calls from his half brother seeking to get their daughters together. He wasn't sure if his hesitation was about the potential relationship between the two cousins or the two half brothers.

Sensing that angle of conversation was at an end, McPherson unfolded her table and pulled out her files. Bosch turned his phone off and put it away.

'So we're going to work?' he asked.

'A little. I want to be prepared.'

'How much do you want to tell her up front? I was thinking we just talk about the ID. Confirm it and see if she's willing to testify again.'

'And not bring up the DNA?'

'Right. That could turn a yes into a no.'

'But shouldn't she know everything she's going to be getting into?'

'Eventually, yes. It's been a long time. I did the trace. She hit some hard times and rough spots but it looks like she might've come out okay. I guess we'll see when we get up there.'

'Let's play it by ear, then. I think if it feels right, we need to tell her everything.'

'You make the call.'

'The one thing that's good is that she'll only have to do it once. We don't have to go through a preliminary hearing or a grand jury. Jessup was held over for trial in 'eighty-six and that is not what the supreme court reversed. So we just go directly to trial. We'll need her one time and that will be it.'

'That's good. And you'll be handling her.'

'Yes.'

Bosch nodded. The assumption was that she was a better prosecutor than Haller. After all, it was Haller's first case. Harry was happy to hear she would be handling the most important witness at trial.

'What about me? Which one of you will take me?'

'I don't think that's been decided. Mickey anticipates that Jessup will actually testify. I know he's waiting for that. But we haven't talked about who will take you. My guess is that you'll be doing a lot of read-backs to the jury of sworn testimony from the first trial.'

She closed the file and it looked like that was it for work.

They spent the rest of the flight small-talking about their daughters and looking through the magazines in their seat pockets. The plane landed early at SeaTac and they picked up a rental car and started north. Bosch did the driving. The car came equipped with a GPS system but the DA travel assistant had also provided McPherson with a full package of directions to Port Townsend. They drove up to Seattle and then took a ferry across Puget Sound. They left the car and went up for coffee on the concessions deck, finding an open table next to a set of windows. Bosch was staring out the window when McPherson surprised him with an observation.

'You're not happy, are you, Harry?'

Bosch looked at her and shrugged.

'It's a weird case. Twenty-four years old and we start with the bad guy already in prison and we take him out. It doesn't make me unhappy, it's just kind of strange, you know?'

She had a half smile on her face.

'I wasn't talking about the case. I was talking about you. You're not a happy man.'

Bosch looked down at the coffee he held on the table with two hands. Not because of the ferry's movement, but because he was cold and the coffee was warming him inside and out.

'Oh,' he said.

A long silence opened up between them. He wasn't sure what he should reveal to this woman. He had known her for only a week and she was making observations about him.

'I don't really have time to be happy right now,' he finally said.

'Mickey told me what he felt he could about Hong Kong and what happened with your daughter.'

Bosch nodded. But he knew Maggie didn't know the whole story. Nobody did except for Madeline and him.

'Yeah,' he said. 'She caught some bad breaks there. That's the thing, I guess. I think if I can make my daughter happy, then I'll be happy. But I am not sure when that will be.'

He brought his eyes up to hers and saw only sympathy. He smiled.

'Yeah, we should get the two cousins together,' he said, moving on.

'Absolutely,' she said.

11

The *Los Angeles Times* carried a lengthy story on Jason Jessup's first day of freedom in twenty-four years. The reporter and photographer met him at dawn on Venice Beach, where the forty-eight-year-old tried his hand at his boyhood pastime of surfing. On the first few sets, he was shaky on a borrowed longboard but soon he was up and riding the break. A photo of Jessup standing upright on the board and riding a curl with his arms outstretched, his face turned up to the sky, was the centerpiece photo on the newspaper's front page. The photo showed off what two decades of lifting prison iron will do. Jessup's body was roped with muscle. He looked lean and mean.

From the beach the next stop was an In-N-Out franchise in Westwood for hamburgers and French fries with all the catsup he wanted. After lunch Jessup went to Clive Royce's storefront office in downtown, where he attended a two-hour meeting with the battery of attorneys representing him in both criminal and civil matters. This meeting was not open to the *Times*.

Jessup rounded out the afternoon by watching a movie called *Shutter Island* at the Chinese theater in

Hollywood. He bought a tub of buttered popcorn large enough to feed a family of four and ate every puffed kernel. He then returned to Venice, where he had a room in an apartment near the beach courtesy of a high-school surfing buddy. The day ended at a beach barbecue with a handful of supporters who had never wavered in their belief in his innocence.

I sat at my desk studying the color photos of Jessup that graced two inside pages of the A section. The paper was going all-out on the story, as it had all along, surely smelling the journalistic honors to be gathered at the end of Jessup's journey to complete freedom. Springing an innocent man from prison was the ultimate newspaper story and the *Times* was desperately trying to take credit for Jessup's release.

The largest photo showed Jessup's unabashed delight at the red plastic tray sitting in front of him at a table at In-N-Out. The tray contained a fully loaded double-double with fries smothered in catsup and melted cheese. The caption said

Why Is This Man Smiling? 12:05 — Jessup eats his first Double-Double in 24 years. 'I've been thinking about this forever!'

The other photos carried similarly lighthearted captions below shots of Jessup at the movies with his bucket of popcorn, hoisting a beer at the barbecue and hugging his high-school pal, walking through a glass door that said ROYCE AND ASSOCIATES, ATTORNEYS-

AT-LAW. There was no indication in the tone of the article or photos that Jason Jessup was a man who happened to still be accused of murdering a twelve-year-old girl.

The story was about Jessup relishing his freedom while being unable to plan his future until his 'legal issues' were resolved. It was a nice turn of phrase, I thought, calling abduction and murder charges and a pending trial merely legal issues.

I had the paper spread wide on the desk Lorna had rented for me in my new office on Broadway. We were on the second floor of the Bradbury Building and only three blocks from the CCB.

'I think you need to put something up on the walls.'

I looked up. It was Clive Royce. He had walked through the reception room unannounced because I had sent Lorna over to Philippe's to get us lunch. Royce gestured to the empty walls of the temporary office. I flipped the newspaper closed and held up the front page.

'I just ordered a twenty-by-twenty shot of Jesus on the surfboard here. I'm going to hang him on the wall.'

Royce stepped up to the desk and took the paper, studying the photo on the front as if for the first time, which we both knew was not the case. Royce had been deeply involved in the generation of the story, the payoff being the photo of the office door with his firm's name on the glass.

'Yes, they did a good job with it, didn't they?'

He handed it back.

'I guess so, if you like your killers happy-go-lucky.'

Royce didn't respond, so I continued.

'I know what you're doing, Clive, because I would do it, too. But as soon as we get a judge, I'm going to ask him to stop you. I'm not going to let you taint the jury pool.'

Royce frowned as if I had suggested something completely untoward.

'It's a free press, Mick. You can't control the media. The man just got out of prison, and like it or not, it's a news story.'

'Right, and you can give exclusives in exchange for display. Display that might plant a seed in a potential juror's mind. What do you have planned for today? Jessup co-hosting the morning show on Channel Five? Or is he judging the chili cook-off at the state fair?'

'As a matter of fact, NPR wanted to hang with him today but I showed restraint. I said no. Make sure you tell the judge that as well.'

'Wow, you actually said no to NPR? Was that because most people who listen to NPR are the kind of people who can get out of jury duty, or because you got something better lined up?'

Royce frowned again, looking as though I had impaled him with an integrity spear. He looked around, grabbed the chair from Maggie's desk and pulled it over so he could sit in front of mine. Once he was seated with his legs crossed and had arranged his suit properly he spoke.

'Now, tell me, Mick, does your boss think that housing

you in a separate building is really going to make people think you are acting independently of his direction? You're having us on, right?'

I smiled at him. His effort to get under my skin was not going to work.

'Let me state once again for the record, Clive, that I have no boss in this matter. I am working independently of Gabriel Williams.'

I gestured to the room.

'I'm here, not in the courthouse, and all decisions on this case will be made from this desk. But at the moment my decisions aren't that important. It's you who has the decision, Clive.'

'And what would that be? A disposition, Mick?'

'That's right. Today's special, good until five o'clock only. Your boy pleads guilty, I'll come down off the death penalty and we both roll the dice with the judge on sentencing. You never know, Jessup could walk away with time served.'

Royce smiled cordially and shook his head.

'I am sure that would make the powers that be in this town happy, but I'm afraid I must disappoint you, Mick. My client remains absolutely uninterested in a plea. And that is not going to change. I was actually hoping that by now you would have seen the uselessness of going to trial and would simply drop the charges. You can't win this thing, Mick. The state has to bend over on this one and you unfortunately are the fool who volunteered to take it in the arse.'

'Well, I guess we'll see, won't we?'

'We will indeed.'

I opened the desk's center drawer and removed a green plastic case containing a computer disc. I slid it across the desk to him.

'I wasn't expecting you to come by for it yourself, Clive. Thought you'd send an investigator or a clerk. You gotta bunch of them working for you, don't you? Along with that full-time publicist.'

Royce slowly collected the disc. The plastic case was marked DEFENSE DISCOVERY 1.

'Well, aren't we snarky today? Seems that only two weeks ago you were one of us, Mick. A lowly member of the defense bar.'

I nodded my contrition. He had nailed me there.

'Sorry, Clive. Perhaps the power of the office is getting to me.'

'Apology accepted.'

'And sorry to waste your time coming over here. As I told you on the phone, that's got everything we have up until this morning. Mostly the old files and reports. I won't play discovery games with you, Clive. I've been on the wrong end of that too many times to count. So when I get it, you get it. But right now that's all I've got.'

Royce tapped the disc case on the edge of the desk.

'No witness list?'

'There is but as of now it's essentially the same list from the trial in 'eighty-six. I've added my investigator and subtracted a few names—the parents, other people no longer alive.'

'No doubt Felix Turner has been redacted.'

I smiled like the Cheshire cat.

'Thankfully you won't get the chance to bring him up at trial.'

'Yes, a pity. I would have loved the opportunity to shove him up the state's ass.'

I nodded, noting that Royce had come off the English colloquialisms and was hitting me with pure Americana now. It was a symptom of his frustration over Turner, and as a longtime counsel for the defense I certainly felt it. In the retrial, there would be no mention of any aspect of the first trial. The new jurors would have no knowledge of what had transpired before. And that meant the state's use of the fraudulent jailhouse informant — no matter how grievous a prosecutorial sin — would not hurt the current prosecution.

I decided to move on.

'I should have another disc for you by the end of the week.'

'Yes, I can't wait to see what you come up with.'

Sarcasm noted.

'Just remember one thing, Clive. Discovery is a two-way street. You go beyond thirty days and we'll go see the judge.'

The rules of evidence required that each side complete its discovery exchange no later than thirty days before the start of trial. Missing this deadline could lead to sanctions and open the door to a trial delay as the judge would grant the offended party more time to prepare.

'Yes, well, as you can imagine, we weren't expecting the turn of events that has transpired here,' Royce said.

'Consequently, our defense is in its infancy. But I won't play games with you either, Mick. A disc will be along to you in short order—provided that we have any discovery to give.'

I knew that as a practical matter the defense usually had little in the way of discovery to give unless the plan was to mount an extensive defense. But I sounded the warning because I was leery of Royce. In a case this old, he might try to dig up an alibi witness or something else out of left field. I wanted to know about it before it came up in court.

'I appreciate that,' I said.

Over his shoulder I saw Lorna enter the office. She was carrying two brown bags, one of which contained my French dip sandwich.

'Oh, I didn't realize...'

Royce turned around in his seat.

'Ah, the lovely Lorna. How are you, my darling?'

'Hello, Clive. I see you got the disc.'

'Indeed. Thank you, Lorna.'

I had noticed that Royce's English accent and formal parlance became more pronounced at times, especially in front of attractive women. I wondered if that was a conscious thing or not.

'I have two sandwiches here, Clive,' Lorna said. 'Would you like one?'

It was the wrong time for Lorna to be magnanimous.

'I think he was just about to leave,' I said quickly.

'Yes, love, I must go. But thank you for the most gracious offer.'

'I'll be out here if you need me, Mickey.'

Lorna went back to the reception room, closing the door behind her. Royce turned back to me and spoke in a low voice.

'You know you should never have let that one go, Mick. She was the keeper. And now, joining forces with the first Mrs. Haller to deprive an innocent man of his long-deserved freedom, there is something incestuous about the whole thing, isn't there?'

I just looked at him for a long moment.

'Is there anything else, Clive?'

He held up the disc.

'I think this should do it for today.'

'Good. I have to get back to work.'

I walked him out through reception and closed the door after him. I turned and looked at Lorna.

'Feels weird, doesn't it?' she said. 'Being on this side of it—the prosecution side.'

'It does.'

She held up one of the sandwich bags.

'Can I ask you something?' I said. 'Whose sandwich were you going to give him, yours or mine?'

She looked at me with a straight face, then a smile of guilt leaked out.

'I was being polite, okay? I thought you and I could share.'

I shook my head.

'Don't be giving my French dip sandwich to anybody. Especially a defense lawyer.'

I snatched the bag from her hand.

'Thank you, love,' I said in my best British accent.

She laughed and I headed back into my office to eat.

12

After driving off the ferry at Port Townsend, Bosch and McPherson followed directions from the rental car's GPS to the address on Sarah Ann Gleason's driver's license. The trail led them through the small Victorian sea village and then out into a more rural area of large and isolated properties. Gleason's house was a small clapboard house that failed to keep the nearby town's Victorian theme. The detective and the prosecutor stood on the porch and knocked but got no response.

'Maybe she's at work or something,' McPherson said.

'Could be.'

'We could go back into town and get rooms, then come back after five.'

Bosch checked his watch. He realized that school was just over and Maddie was probably heading home with Sue Bambrough. He guessed that his daughter was giving the assistant principal the silent treatment.

He stepped off the porch and started walking toward the corner of the house.

'Where are you going?'

'To check the back. Hold on.'

But as soon as Bosch turned the corner he could see

that a hundred yards beyond the house there was another structure. It was a windowless barn or garage. What stood out was that it had a chimney. He could see heat waves but no smoke rising from the two black pipes that extended over the roofline. There were two cars and a van parked in front of the closed garage doors.

Bosch stood there watching for so long that McPherson finally came around the corner as well.

'What's taking—?'

Bosch held up his hand to silence her, then pointed toward the outbuilding.

'What is it?' McPherson whispered.

Before Bosch could answer, one of the garage doors slid open a few feet and a figure stepped out. It looked like a young man or a teenager. He was wearing a full-length black apron over his clothes. He took off heavy elbow-length gloves so he could light a cigarette.

'Shit,' McPherson whispered, answering her own question.

Bosch stepped back to the corner of the house to use it as a blind. He pulled McPherson with him.

'All her arrests—her drug of choice was meth,' he whispered.

'Great,' McPherson whispered back. 'Our main witness is a meth cook.'

The young smoker turned when apparently called from within the barn. He threw down his cigarette, stepped on it, and went back inside. He yanked the door closed behind him but it slid to a stop six inches before closing.

'Let's go,' Bosch said.

He started to move but McPherson put her hand on his arm.

'Wait, what are you talking about? We need to call Port Townsend police and get some backup, don't we?'

Bosch looked at her a moment without responding.

'I saw the police station when we went through town,' McPherson said, as if to assure him that backup was waiting and willing.

'If we call for backup they're not going to be very cooperative, since we didn't bother to check in when we got to town in the first place,' Bosch said. 'They'll arrest her and then we have a main witness awaiting trial on drug charges. How do you think that will work with Jessup's jury?'

She didn't answer.

'Tell you what,' he said. 'You hold back here and I'll go check it out. Three vehicles, probably three cooks. If I can't handle it, we call backup.'

'They're probably armed, Harry. You—'

'They're probably not armed. I'll check it out and if it looks like a situation we'll call Port Townsend.'

'I don't like this.'

'It could work to our favor.'

'What? How?'

'Think about it. Watch for my signal. If something goes wrong, get in the car and get out of here.'

He held up the car keys and she reluctantly took them. He could tell she was thinking about what he had said. The advantage. If they caught their witness in a compromising situation, it could give them the leverage they needed to ensure her cooperation and testimony.

Bosch left McPherson there and headed on foot down the crushed-shell drive to the barn. He didn't attempt to hide in case they had a lookout. He put his hands in his pockets to try to convey he was no threat, somebody just lost and looking for directions.

The crushed shell made it impossible for him to make a completely silent approach. But as he got closer he heard loud music coming from the barn. It was rock and roll but he could not identify it. Something heavy on the guitar and with a pounding beat. It had a retro feel to it, like he had heard the song a long time ago, maybe in Vietnam.

Bosch was twenty feet from the partially opened door when it moved open another two feet and the same young man stepped out again. Seeing him closer, Bosch pegged his age at twenty-one or so. In the moment he stepped out Bosch realized he should have expected that he'd be back out to finish his interrupted smoke. Now it was too late and the smoker saw him.

But the young man didn't hesitate or sound an alarm of any sort. He looked at Bosch curiously as he started tapping a cigarette out of a soft pack. He was sweating profusely.

'You parked up at the house?' he asked.

Bosch stopped ten feet from him and took his hands out of his pockets. He didn't look back toward the house, choosing instead to keep his eyes on the kid.

'Uh, yes, is that a problem?' he asked.

'No, but most people just drive on down to the barn. Sarah usually tells them to.'

'Oh, I didn't get that message. Is Sarah here?'

'Yeah, inside. Go on in.'

'You sure?'

'Yeah, we're almost done for the day.'

Bosch was getting the idea that he had walked into something that was not what he thought it was. He now glanced back and saw McPherson peering around the corner of the house. This wasn't the best way to do this but he turned and headed toward the open door.

The heat hit him the moment he entered. The inside of the barn was like an oven and for good reason. The first thing Bosch saw was the open door of a huge furnace that was glowing orange with flames.

Standing eight feet from the heat source was another young man and an older woman. They also wore full-length aprons and heavy gloves. The man was using a pair of iron tongs to hold steady a large piece of molten glass attached to the end of an iron pipe. The woman was shaping it with a wooden block and a pair of pliers.

They were glassmakers, not drug cooks. The woman wore a welder's mask over her face as protection. Bosch could not identify her but he was pretty sure he was looking at Sarah Ann Gleason.

Bosch stepped back through the door and signaled to McPherson. He gave the okay sign but was unsure she would be able to identify it from the distance. He waved her in.

'What's going on, man?' the smoker asked.

'That's Sarah Gleason in there, you said?' Bosch responded.

'Yeah, that's her.'

'I need to talk to her.'

'You're going to have to wait until she's set the piece. She can't stop while it's soft. We've been working it for almost four hours.'

'How much longer?'

'Maybe an hour. You can probably talk to her while she's working. You want a piece made?'

'That's okay, I think we can wait.'

McPherson drove up in the rental car and got out. Bosch opened the door for her and explained quietly that they had read wrong what they had seen. He told her the barn was a glassmaking studio. He told her how he wanted to play it until they could get Gleason into a private setting. McPherson shook her head and smiled.

'What if we had gone in there with backup?'

'I guess we would've broken some glass.'

'And had one pissed-off witness.'

She got out of the car and Bosch reached in for the file he had put on the dashboard. He put it inside his jacket and under his arm so he could carry it unseen.

They entered the studio and Gleason was waiting for them, with her gloves off and her mask folded up to reveal her face. She had obviously been told by the smoker that they were potential customers and Bosch initially did nothing to dissuade her of that interpretation. He didn't want to reveal their true business until they were alone with her.

'I'm Harry and this is Maggie. Sorry to barge in like this.'

'Oh, no problem. We like it when people get a chance to see what we do. In fact, we're right in the middle of a project right now and need to get back to it. You're welcome to stay and watch and I can tell you a little bit about what we're doing.'

'That would be great.'

'You just have to stay back. We're dealing with very hot material here.'

'Not a problem.'

'Where are you from? Seattle?'

'No, actually we're all the way up from California. We're pretty far from home.'

If the mention of her native state caused Gleason any concern, she didn't show it. She pulled the mask back down over a smile, put her gloves on and went back to work. Over the next forty minutes Bosch and McPherson watched Gleason and her two assistants finish the glass piece. Gleason provided a steady narration as she worked, explaining that the three members of her team had different duties. One of the young men was a blower and the other was a blocker. Gleason was the gaffer, the one in charge. The piece they were sculpting was a four-foot-long grape leaf that would be part of a larger piece commissioned to hang in the lobby of a business in Seattle called Rainier Wine.

Gleason also filled in some of her recent history. She said she started her own studio only two years ago after spending three years apprenticing with a glass artist in

Seattle. It was useful information to Bosch. Both hearing her talk about herself and watching her work the soft glass. *Gathering color,* as she called it. Using heavy tools to manipulate something beautiful and fragile and glowing with red-hot danger all at the same time.

The heat from the furnace was stifling and both Bosch and McPherson took off their jackets. Gleason said the oven burned at 2,300 degrees and Bosch marveled at how the artists could spend so many hours working so close to the source. The glory hole, the small opening into which they repeatedly passed the sculpture to reheat and add layers, glowed like the gateway to Hell.

When the day's work was completed and the piece was placed in the finishing kiln, Gleason asked the assistants to clean up the studio before heading home. She then invited Bosch and McPherson to wait for her in the office while she got cleaned up herself.

The office doubled as a break room. It was sparely furnished with a table and four chairs, a filing cabinet, a storage locker and a small kitchenette. There was a binder on the table containing plastic sleeves with photos of glass pieces made previously in the studio. McPherson studied these and seemed taken with several. Bosch took out the file he had been carrying inside his jacket and put it down on the table ready to go.

'It must be nice to be able to make something out of nothing,' McPherson said. 'I wish I could.'

Bosch tried to think of a response but before he could come up with anything the door opened and Sarah

Gleason entered. The bulky mask, apron and gloves were gone and she was smaller than Bosch had expected. She barely crested five feet and he doubted there were more than ninety pounds on her tiny frame. He knew that childhood trauma sometimes stunted growth. So it was no wonder Sarah Gleason looked like a woman in a child's body.

Her auburn hair was down now instead of tied into a knot behind her head. It framed a weary face with dark blue eyes. She wore blue jeans, clogs and a black T-shirt that said *Death Cab* on it. She headed directly to the refrigerator.

'Can I get you something? Don't have any alcohol in here but if you need something cold...'

Bosch and McPherson passed. Harry noticed she had left the door to the office open. He could hear someone sweeping in the studio. He stepped over and closed it.

Gleason turned from the refrigerator with a bottle of water. She saw Bosch closing the door and a look of apprehension immediately crossed her face. Bosch raised one hand in a calming gesture as he pulled his badge with the other.

'Ms. Gleason, everything is okay. We're from Los Angeles and just need to speak privately with you.'

He opened his badge wallet and held it up to her.

'What is this?'

'My name is Harry Bosch and this is Maggie McPherson. She is a prosecutor with the L.A. County District Attorney's Office.'

'Why did you lie?' she said angrily. 'You said you wanted a piece made.'

'No, actually we didn't. Your assistant, the blocker, just assumed that. We never said why we were here.'

Her guard was clearly up and Bosch thought they had blown their approach and with that the opportunity to secure her as a witness. But then Gleason stepped forward and grabbed the badge wallet out of his hand. She studied it and the facing ID card. It was an unusual move, taking the badge from him. No more than the fifth time that had ever happened to Bosch in his long career as a cop. He saw her eyes hold on the ID card and he knew she had noticed the discrepancy between what he had said his name was and what was on the ID.

'You said *Harry* Bosch?'

'Harry for short.'

'Hieronymus Bosch. You're named after the artist?'

Bosch nodded.

'My mother liked the paintings.'

'Well, I like them, too. I think he knew something about inner demons. Is that why your mother liked him?'

'I think so, yeah.'

She handed the badge wallet back to him and Bosch sensed a calmness come over her. The moment of anxiety and apprehension had passed, thanks to the painter whose name Bosch carried.

'What do you want with me? I haven't been to L.A. in more than ten years.'

Bosch noted that if she was telling the truth, then she

had not returned when her stepfather was ill and dying.

'We just want to talk,' he said. 'Can we sit down?'

'Talk about what?'

'Your sister.'

'My sister? I don't—look, you need to tell me what this is—'

'You don't know, do you?'

'Know what?'

'Sit down and we'll tell you.'

Finally, she moved to the lunch table and took a seat. She pulled a soft pack of cigarettes out of her pocket and lit one.

'Sorry,' she said. 'It's my one remaining addiction. And you two showing up like this—I need a smoke.'

For the next ten minutes Bosch and McPherson traded off the story and walked her through the short version of Jason Jessup's journey to freedom. Gleason showed almost no reaction to the news. No tears, no outrage. And she didn't ask questions about the DNA test that had sprung him from prison. She only explained that she had no contact with anyone in California, owned no television and never read newspapers. She said they were distractions from work as well as from her recovery from addiction.

'We're going to retry him, Sarah,' McPherson said. 'And we're here because we're going to need your help.'

Bosch could see Sarah turn inward, to start to measure the impact of what they were telling her.

'It was so long ago,' she finally responded. 'Can't you just use what I said from the first trial?'

McPherson shook her head.

'We can't, Sarah. The new jury can't even know there was an earlier trial because that could influence how they weigh the evidence. It would prejudice them against the defendant and a guilty verdict wouldn't stand. So in situations where witnesses from the first trial are dead or mentally incompetent, we read their earlier testimony into the trial record without telling the jury where it's from. But where that's not the case, like with you, we need the person to come to court and testify.'

It wasn't clear whether Gleason had even registered McPherson's response. She sat staring at something far away. Even as she spoke, her eyes didn't come off their distant focus.

'I've spent my whole life since then trying to forget about that day. I tried different things to make me forget. I used drugs to make a big bubble with me in the middle of it. I made... Never mind, the point is, I don't think I'm going to be much help to you.'

Before McPherson could respond, Bosch stepped in.

'I'll tell you what,' he said. 'Let's just talk here for a few minutes about what you can remember, okay? And if it's not going to work, then it won't work. You were a victim, Sarah, and we don't want to victimize you all over again.'

He waited a moment for Gleason to respond but she sat mute, staring at the water bottle in front of her on the table.

'Let's start with that day,' Bosch said. 'I don't need

you at this point to go through the horrible moments of your sister's abduction, but do you remember making the identification of Jason Jessup for the police?'

She slowly nodded.

'I remember looking through the window. Upstairs. They opened the blinds a little bit so I could look out. They weren't supposed to be able to see me. The men. He was the one with the hat. They made him take it off and that's when I saw it was him. I remember that.'

Bosch was encouraged by the detail of the hat. He didn't recall seeing that in the case records or hearing it in McPherson's summary but the fact that Gleason remembered it was a good sign.

'What kind of hat was he wearing?' he asked.

'A baseball cap,' Gleason said. 'It was blue.'

'A Dodgers cap?'

'I'm not sure. I don't think I knew back then either.'

Bosch nodded and moved in.

'Do you think if I showed you a photo lineup, you would be able to identify the man who took your sister?'

'You mean the way he looks now? I doubt it.'

'No, not now,' McPherson said. 'What we would need to do in trial is confirm the identification you made back then. We would show you photos from back then.'

Gleason hesitated and then nodded.

'Sure. Through everything I've done to myself over the years, I've never been able to forget that man's face.'

'Well, let's see.'

While Bosch opened the file on the table, Gleason lit a new cigarette off the end of her old one.

The file contained a lineup of six black-and-white booking photos of men of the same age, build and coloring. A 1986 photo of Jessup was included in the spread. Harry knew that this was the make-or-break moment of the case.

The photos were displayed in two rows of three. Jessup's shot was in the middle window on the bottom row. The five hole. It had always been the lucky spot for Bosch.

'Take your time,' he said.

Gleason drank some water and then put the bottle to the side. She leaned over the table, bringing her face within twelve inches of the photos. It didn't take her long. She pointed to the photo of Jessup without hesitation.

'I wish I could forget him,' she said. 'But I can't. He's always there in the back of my mind. In the shadows.'

'Do you have any doubt about the photo you have chosen?' Bosch asked.

Gleason leaned down and looked again, then shook her head.

'No. He was the man.'

Bosch glanced at McPherson, who made a slight nod. It was a good ID and they had handled it right. The only thing that was missing was a show of emotion on Gleason's part. But maybe twenty-four years had drained her of everything. Harry took out a pen and handed it to Gleason.

'Would you put your initials and the date below the photo you chose, please?'

'Why?'

'It confirms your ID. It just helps make it more solid when it comes up in court.'

Bosch noted that she had not asked if she had chosen the right photo. She didn't have to and that was a secondary confirmation of her recall. Another good sign. After she handed the pen back to Bosch he closed the file and slid it to the side. He glanced at McPherson again. Now came the hard part. By prior agreement, Maggie was going to make the call here on whether to bring up the DNA now or to wait until Gleason was more firmly onboard as a witness.

McPherson decided not to wait.

'Sarah, there is a second issue to discuss now. We told you about the DNA that allowed this man to get this new trial and what we hope is only his temporary freedom.'

'Yes.'

'We took the DNA profile and checked it against the California data bank. We got a match. The semen on the dress your sister was wearing came from your stepfather.'

Bosch watched Sarah closely. Not even a flicker of surprise showed on her face or in her eyes. This information was not news to her.

'In two thousand four the state started taking DNA swabs from all suspects in felony arrests. That same year your father was arrested for a felony hit-and-run with injuries. He ran a stop sign and hit—'

'Stepfather.'

'Excuse me?'

'You said "your father." He wasn't my father. He was my stepfather.'

'My mistake. I'm sorry. The bottom line is Kensington Landy's DNA was in the data bank and it's a match with the sample from the dress. What could not be determined is how long that sample was on the dress at the time of its discovery. It could have been deposited on the dress the day of the murder or the week before or maybe even a month before.'

Sarah started flying on autopilot. She was there but not there. Her eyes were fixed on a distance that was far beyond the room they were in.

'We have a theory, Sarah. The autopsy that was conducted on your sister determined that she had not been sexually abused by her killer or anyone else prior to that day. We also know the dress she wore happened to be yours and Melissa was borrowing it that morning because she liked it.'

McPherson paused but Sarah said nothing.

'When we get to trial we're going to have to explain the semen found on the dress. If we can't explain it, the assumption will be that it came from the killer and that killer was your stepfather. We will lose the case and Jessup, the real killer, will walk away free. I'm sure you don't want that, do you, Sarah? There are some people out there who think twenty-four years in prison is enough time served for the murder of a twelve-year-old girl. They don't know why we're doing this. But I want you to know that I don't think that, Sarah. Not by a long shot.'

Sarah Gleason didn't answer at first. Bosch expected tears but none came and he began to wonder if her emotions had been cauterized by the traumas and depravities of her life. Or maybe she simply had an internal toughness that her diminutive stature camouflaged. Either way, when she finally responded, it was in a flat, emotionless voice that belied the heartfelt words she spoke.

'You know what I always thought?' she said.

McPherson leaned forward.

'What, Sarah?'

'That that man killed three people that day. My sister, then my mother...and then me. None of us got away.'

There was a long moment of silence. McPherson slowly reached out and put her hand on Gleason's arm, a gesture of comfort where no comfort could exist.

'I'm sorry, Sarah,' McPherson whispered.

'Okay,' Gleason said. 'I'll tell you everything.'

13

My daughter was already missing her mother's cooking—and she'd only been gone one day. I was dropping
her half-eaten sandwich into the garbage and wondering how the hell I could've messed up a grilled cheese
when my cell phone's ring interrupted. It was Maggie
checking in from the road.

'Tell me something good,' I said by way of greeting.

'You get to spend the evening with our beautiful
daughter.'

'Yes, that's something good. Except she doesn't like
my cooking. Now tell me something else that's good.'

'Our primary witness is good to go. She'll testify.'

'She made the ID?'

'She did.'

'She told you about the DNA and it fits with our
theory?'

'She did and it does.'

'And she'll come down here and testify to all of it at
the trial?'

'She will.'

I felt a twelve-volt charge go through my body.

'That's actually a lot of good things, Maggie. Is there any downside?'

'Well...'

I felt the wind go out of the sails. I was about to learn that Sarah was still a drug addict or there was some other issue that would prevent me from using her at trial.

'Well, what?'

'Well, there are going to be challenges to her testimony, of course, but she's pretty solid. She's a survivor and it shows. There's really only one thing missing: emotions. She's been through a lot in her life and she basically seems to be a bit burned out—emotionally. No tears, no laughter, just straight down the middle.'

'We can work on that. We can coach her.'

'Yeah, well, we just have to be careful with that. I am not saying she isn't fine the way she is. I'm just saying that she's sort of a flat line. Everything else is good. I think you're going to like her and I think she'll help us put Jessup back in prison.'

'That's fantastic, Maggie. Really. And you're still all right handling her at trial, right?'

'I've got her.'

'Royce will attack her on the meth—memory loss and all of that. Her lifestyle...you'll have to be ready for anything and everything.'

'I will be. That leaves you with Bosch and Jessup. You still think he'll testify?'

'Jessup? Yes, he's got to. Clive knows he can't do that to a jury, not after twenty-four years. So, yes, I've got him and I've got Bosch.'

'At least with Harry you don't have to worry about any baggage.'

'That Clive knows about yet.'

'And what's that supposed to mean?'

'It means don't underestimate Clever Clive Royce. See, that's what you prosecutors always do. You get over-confident and it makes you vulnerable.'

'Thank you, F. Lee Bailey. I'll keep that in mind.'

'How was Bosch today?'

'He was Bosch. What happened on your end?'

I checked through the door of the kitchen. Hayley was sitting on the couch with her homework spread out on the coffee table.

'Well, for one thing, we've got a judge. Breitman, Department one-twelve.'

Maggie considered the case assignment for a moment before responding.

'I would call that a no-win for either side. She's straight down the middle. Never a prosecutor, never a defense attorney. Just a good, solid civil trial lawyer. I think neither side gets an advantage with her.'

'Wow, a judge who's going to be impartial and fair. Imagine that.'

She didn't respond.

'She set the first status conference in chambers. Wednesday morning at eight before court starts. You read anything into that?'

This meant the judge wanted to meet the lawyers and discuss the case in chambers, starting things off informally and away from the lens of the media.

'I think that's good. She's probably going to set the rules with media and procedure. It sounds to me like she's going to run a tight ship.'

'That was what I was thinking. You're free Wednesday to be there?'

'I'll have to check my calendar but I think so. I'm trying to clear everything except for this.'

'I gave Royce the first bit of discovery today. It was mostly composed of material from the first trial.'

'You know you could have held off on that until the thirty-day marker.'

'Yeah, but what's the point?'

'The point is strategy. The earlier you give it to him, the more time he has to be ready for it. He's trying to put the squeeze on us by not waiving speedy trial. You should put the squeeze right back on him by not showing our hand until we have to. Thirty days before trial.'

'I'll remember that with the next round. But this was pretty basic stuff.'

'Was Sarah Gleason on the witness list?'

'Yes, but under the name Sarah Landy—as it was in 'eighty-six. And I gave the office as the address. Clive doesn't know we found her.'

'We need to keep it that way until we have to reveal it. I don't want her harassed or feeling threatened.'

'What did you tell her about coming down for the trial?'

'I told her she would probably be needed for two days in trial. Plus the travel.'

'And that's not going to be a problem?'

'Well…she runs her own business and has been at it only a couple years. She has one big, ongoing project but otherwise said that things are slow. My guess is we can get her down when we need her.'

'Are you still in Port Townsend?'

'Yes, we just got finished with her about an hour ago. We grabbed dinner and checked in at a hotel. It's been a long day.'

'And you're coming back tomorrow?'

'We were planning on it. But our flight's not till two. We have to take a ferry—it's a journey just to the airport.'

'Okay, call me in the morning before you leave. Just in case I think of something involving the witness.'

'Okay.'

'Did either of you take notes?'

'No, we thought it might freeze her.'

'Did you record it?'

'No, same reason.'

'Good. I want to keep as much of this out of discovery as possible. Tell Bosch not to write anything up. We can copy Royce on the six-pack she made the ID off of, but that's it.'

'Right. I'll tell Harry.'

'When, tonight or tomorrow?'

'What's that supposed to mean?'

'Nothing, never mind. Anything else?'

'Yes.'

I braced for it. My petty jealousy had slipped out for one small moment.

'I would like to say good night to my daughter now.'

'Oh,' I said, relief bursting through my body. 'I'll put her on.'

I took the phone out to Hayley.

'It's your mother.'

PART TWO
–The Labyrinth

14

Each of them worked in silence. Bosch at one end of the dining room table, his daughter at the other. He with the first batch of SIS surveillance logs, she with her homework, her school books and laptop computer spread out in front of her. They were close in proximity but not in much else. The Jessup case had become all-encompassing with Bosch tracing old witnesses and trying to find new ones. He had spent little time with her in recent days. Like her parents, Maddie was good at holding grudges and had not let go of the perceived slight of having been left for a night in the care of an assistant school principal. She was giving Harry the silent treatment and already at fourteen she was an expert at it.

The SIS logs were another frustration to Bosch. Not because of what they contained but because of their delay in reaching him. They had been sent through bureaucratic channels, from the SIS office to the RHD office and then to Bosch's supervisor, where they had sat in an in basket for three days before finally being dropped on Bosch's desk. The result was he had logs from the first three days of the surveillance of Jason

Jessup and he was looking at them three to six days after the fact. That process was too slow and Bosch was going to have to do something about it.

The logs were terse accounts of the surveillance subject's movements by date, time and location. Most entries carried only a single line of description. The logs came with an accompanying set of photos as well, but most of the shots were taken at a significant distance so the followers could avoid detection. These were grainy images of Jessup as he moved about the city as a free man.

Bosch read through the reports and quickly surmised that Jessup was already leading separate public and private lives. By day his movements were in concert with the media as he very publicly reacquainted himself with life outside a prison cell. It was about learning to drive again, to choose off a menu, to go for a three-mile run without having to make a turn. But by night a different Jessup emerged. Unaware that he was still being watched by eyes and cameras, he went out cruising alone in his borrowed car. He went to all corners of the city. He went to bars, strip clubs, a prostitute's trick pad.

Of all his activities, one was most curious to Bosch. On his fourth night of freedom, Jessup had driven up to Mulholland Drive, the winding road atop the crest of the Santa Monica Mountains, which cut the city in half. Day or night, Mulholland offered some of the best views of the city. It was no surprise that Jessup would go up there. There were overlooks that offered north and south views of the shimmering lights of the city.

They could be invigorating and even majestic. Bosch had gone to these spots himself in the past.

But Jessup didn't go to any of the overlooks. He pulled his car off the road near the entrance to Franklin Canyon Park. He got out and then entered the closed park, sneaking around a gate.

This caused a surveillance issue for the SIS team because the park was empty and the watchers were at risk of being seen if they got too close. The report here was briefer than most entries in the log:

02/20/10 — 01:12. Subject entered Franklin Canyon Park. Observed at picnic table area, northeast corner, blind man trailhead.

02/20/10 — 02:34. Subject leaves park, proceeds west on Mulholland to 405 freeway and then south.

After that, Jessup returned to the apartment where he was living in Venice and stayed in for the rest of the night.

There was a printout of an infrared photograph taken of Jessup in the park. It showed him sitting at a picnic table in the dark. Just sitting there.

Bosch put the photo print down on the table and looked at his daughter. She was left-handed like he was. It looked like she was writing out a math problem on a work sheet.

'What?'

She had her mother's radar.

'Uh, are you online there?'

'Yes, what do you need?'

'Can you pull up a map of Franklin Canyon Park? It's off of Mulholland Drive.'

'Let me finish this.'

He waited patiently for her to complete her computations on a mathematical problem he knew would be light-years beyond his understanding. For the past four months he had lived in fear that his daughter would ask him for help with her homework. She had passed by his skills and knowledge long ago. He was useless in this area and had tried to concentrate on mentoring her in other areas, observation and self-protection chief among them.

'Okay.'

She put her pencil down and pulled her computer front and center. Bosch checked his watch. It was almost nine.

'Here.'

Maddie slid the computer down the table, turning the screen toward him.

The park was larger than Bosch had thought, running south of Mulholland and west of Coldwater Canyon Boulevard. A key in the corner of the map said it was 605 acres. Bosch hadn't realized that there was such a large public reserve in this prime section of the Hollywood Hills. He noticed that the map had several of the hiking trails and picnic areas marked. The picnic area in the northeast section was off of Blinderman Trail. He assumed it had been misspelled in the SIS log as 'blind man trailhead.'

'What is it?'

Harry looked at his daughter. It was her first attempt at conversation in two days. He decided not to miss it.

'Well, we've been watching this guy. The Special Investigations Section. They're the department's surveillance experts and they're watching this guy who just got out of prison. He killed a little girl a long time ago. And for some reason he went to this park and just sat there at a picnic table.'

'So? Isn't that what people do at parks?'

'Well, this was in the middle of the night. The park was closed and he snuck in...and then he sort of just sat there.'

'Did he grow up near the park? Maybe he's checking out the places where he grew up.'

'I don't think so. We have him growing up out in Riverside County. He used to come to L.A. to surf but I haven't found any connection to Mulholland.'

Bosch studied the map once more and noticed there was an upper and lower entrance to the park. Jessup had gone in through the upper entrance. This would have been out of his way unless that picnic area and Blinderman Trail were specific destinations for him.

He slid the computer back to his daughter. And checked his watch again.

'Are you almost done your work?'

'*Finished*, Dad. Are you almost finished? Or you could say "done *with*."'

'Sorry. Are you almost finished?'

'I have one more math problem.'

'Good. I have to make a quick call.'

Lieutenant Wright's cell number was on the surveillance log. Bosch expected him to be home and annoyed with the intrusion but decided to make the call anyway. He got up and walked into the living room so he would not disturb Maddie on her last problem. He punched the number into his cell.

'Wright, SIS.'

'Lieutenant, it's Harry Bosch.'

'What's up, Bosch?'

He didn't sound annoyed.

'Sorry to intrude on you at home. I just wanted—'

'I'm not at home, Bosch. I'm with your guy.'

Bosch was surprised.

'Is something wrong?'

'No, the night shift is just more interesting.'

'Where is he right now?'

'We're with him at a bar on Venice Beach called the Townhouse. You know it?'

'I've been there. Is he alone?'

'Yes and no. He came alone but he got recognized. He can't buy a drink in there and probably has his pick of the skanks. Like I said, more interesting at night. Are you calling to check up on us?'

'Not really. I just have a couple of things I need to ask. I'm looking at the logs and the first thing is, how can I get them sooner? I'm looking at stuff from three days ago or longer. The other thing is Franklin Canyon Park. What can you tell me about his stop there?'

'Which one?'

'He's been there twice?'

'Actually, three times. He's gone there the last two nights after the first stop four days ago.'

This information was very intriguing to Bosch, mostly because he had no idea what it meant.

'What did he do the last two times?'

Maddie got up from the dining room table and came into the living room. She sat on the couch and listened to Bosch's side of the conversation.

'The same thing he did the first night,' Wright said. 'He sneaks in there and goes to the same picnic area. He just sits there, like he's waiting for something.'

'For what?'

'You tell me, Bosch.'

'I wish I could. Did he go at the same time each night?'

'Give or take a half hour or so.'

'Does he go in through the Mulholland entrance each time?'

'That's right. He sneaks in and picks up the same trail that takes him to the picnic area.'

'I wonder why he doesn't go in the other entrance. It would be easier for him to get to.'

'Maybe he likes driving on Mulholland and seeing the lights.'

That was a good point and Bosch needed to consider it.

'Lieutenant, can you have your people call me the next time he goes there? I don't care what time it is.'

'I can have them call you but you're not going to be

able to get in there and get close. It's too risky. We don't want to expose the surveillance.'

'I understand, but have them call me. I just want to know. Now, what about these logs? Is there a way for me to get them a little quicker?'

'You can come by SIS and pick one up every morning if you want. As you probably noticed, the logs run six P.M. to six P.M. Each daily log is posted by seven the following morning.'

'Okay, LT, I'll do that. Thanks for the info.'

'Have a good one.'

Bosch closed the phone, wondering about Jessup in Franklin Canyon and what he was doing on his visits there.

'What did he say?' Maddie asked.

Bosch hesitated, wondering for the hundredth time whether he should be telling her as much as he did about his cases.

'He said my guy's gone back to that park the last two nights. Each time, he just sits there and waits.'

'For what?'

'Nobody knows.'

'Maybe he just wants to be somewhere where he's completely by himself and away from everybody.'

'Maybe.'

But Bosch doubted it. He believed there was a plan to almost everything Jessup did. Bosch just had to figure out what it was.

'I'm finished with my homework,' Maddie said. 'You want to watch *Lost*?'

They had been slowly going through the DVDs of the television show, catching up on five years' worth of episodes. The show was about several people who survived a plane crash on an uncharted island in the South Pacific. Bosch had trouble keeping track of things from show to show but watched because his daughter had been completely taken in by the story.

He had no time to watch television right now.

'Okay, one episode,' he said. 'Then you have to go to bed and I have to get back to work.'

She smiled. This made her happy and for the moment Bosch's grammatical and parental transgressions seemed forgotten.

'Set it up,' Bosch said. 'And be prepared to remind me what's happening.'

Five hours later, Bosch was on a jet that was shaking with wild turbulence. His daughter was sitting across the aisle from him rather than in the open seat next to him. They reached across the aisle to each other to hold hands but the bouncing of the plane kept knocking them apart. He couldn't grab her hand.

Just as he turned in his seat to see the tail section break off and fall away, he was awakened by a buzzing sound. He reached to the bed table and grabbed his phone. He struggled to find his voice as he answered.

'This is Bosch.'

'This is Shipley, SIS. I was told to call.'

'Jessup's at the park?'

'He's in a park, yeah, but tonight it's a different one.'

'Where?'

'Fryman Canyon off Mulholland.'

Bosch knew Fryman Canyon. It was about ten minutes away from Franklin Canyon.

'What's he doing?'

'He's just sort of walking on one of the trails. Just like at the other park. He walks the trail and then he sits down. He doesn't do anything after that. He just sits for a while and then leaves.'

'Okay.'

Bosch looked at the glowing numbers on the clock. It was two o'clock exactly.

'Are you coming out?' Shipley asked.

Bosch thought about his daughter asleep in her bedroom. He knew he could leave and be back before she woke up.

'Uh...no, I have my daughter here and I can't leave her.'

'Suit yourself.'

'When does your shift end?'

'About seven.'

'Can you call me then?'

'If you want.'

'I'd like you to call me every morning when you are getting off. To tell me where he's been.'

'Uh...all right, I guess. Can I ask you something? This guy killed a girl, right?'

'That's right.'

'And you're sure about that? I mean, no doubt, right?'

Bosch thought about the interview with Sarah Gleason.

'I have no doubt.'

'Okay, well, that's good to know.'

Bosch understood what he was saying. He was looking for assurance. If circumstances dictated the use of deadly force against Jessup, it was good to know who and what they would be shooting at. Nothing else needed to be said about it.

'Thanks, Shipley,' Bosch said. 'I'll talk to you later.'

Bosch disconnected and put his head back on the pillow. He remembered the dream about the plane. About reaching out to his daughter but being unable to grab her hand.

15

Judge Diane Breitman welcomed us into her chambers and offered a pot of coffee and a plate of shortbread cookies, an unusual move for a criminal courts judge. In attendance were myself and my second chair, Maggie McPherson, and Clive Royce, who was without his second but not without his temerity. He asked the judge if he could have hot tea instead.

'Well, this is nice,' the judge said once we were all seated in front of her desk, cups and saucers in hand. 'I have not had the opportunity to see any of you practice in my courtroom. So I thought it would be good for us to start out a bit informally in chambers. We can always step out into the courtroom to go on the record if necessary.'

She smiled and none of the rest of us responded.

'Let me start by saying that I have a deep respect for the decorum of the courtroom,' Breitman continued. 'And I insist that the lawyers who practice before me do as well. I am expecting this trial to be a spirited contest of the evidence and facts of the case. But I won't stand for any acting out or crossing of the lines of courtesy and jurisprudence. I hope that is clearly understood.'

'Yes, Your Honor,' Maggie responded while Royce and I nodded.

'Good, now let's talk about media coverage. The media is going to be hovering over this case like the helicopters that followed O.J. down the freeway. That is clearly a given. I have requests here from three local network affiliates, a documentary filmmaker and *Dateline NBC*. They all want to film the trial in its entirety. While I see no problem with that, as long as proper protections of the jury are put in place, my concern is in the extracurricular activity that is bound to occur outside the courtroom. Do any of you have any thoughts in this regard?'

I waited a beat and when no one spoke up, I did.

'Judge, I think because of the nature of this case—a retrial of a case twenty-four years old—there has already been too much media attention and we're going to have a difficult time seating twelve people and two alternates who aren't aware of the case through the filter of the media. I mean, we've had the accused surfing on the front page of the *Times* and sitting courtside at the Lakers. How are we going to get an impartial jury out of this? The media, with no lack of help from Mr. Royce, is presenting this guy as this poor, persecuted innocent man and they don't have the slightest idea what the evidence is against him.'

'Your Honor, I object,' Royce said.

'You can't object,' I said. 'This isn't a court hearing.'

'You *used* to be a defense attorney, Mick. Whatever happened to innocent until proven guilty?'

'He already has been.'

'In a trial the top court in this state termed a travesty. Is that what you want to stand on?'

'Listen, Clive, I'm an attorney and *innocent until proven guilty* is a measure you apply in court, not on *Larry King Live*.'

'We haven't been on *Larry King Live*—yet.'

'See what I mean, Judge? He wants to—'

'Gentlemen, please!' Breitman said.

She waited a moment until she was certain our debate had subsided.

'This is a classic situation where we need to balance the public's right to know with safeguards that will provide us an untainted jury, an unimpeded trial and a just result.'

'But, Your Honor,' Royce said quickly, 'we can't forbid the media to examine this case. Freedom of the press is the cornerstone of American democracy. And, further, I draw your attention to the very ruling that granted this retrial. The court found serious deficiencies in the evidence and castigated the District Attorney's Office for the corrupt manner in which it has prosecuted my client. Now you are going to prohibit the media from looking at this?'

'Oh, please,' Maggie said dismissively. 'We're not talking about prohibiting the media from looking at anything, and your lofty defense of the freedom of the press aside, that's not what this is about. You are clearly trying to influence voir dire with your pretrial manipulation of the media.'

'That is absolutely untrue!' Royce howled. 'I have responded to media requests, yes. But I am not trying to influence anything. Your Honor, this is an—'

There was a sharp crack from the judge's desk. She had grabbed a gavel from a decorative pen set and brought it down hard on the wood surface.

'Let's cool down here,' Breitman said. 'And let's hold off on the personal attacks. As I indicated before, there has to be a happy medium. I am not inclined to muzzle the press, but I will issue a gag order against the lawyers in my court if I believe they are not acting in a manner that is responsible to the case at hand. I am going to start off by leaving each of you to determine what is reasonable and responsible interaction with the media. But I will warn you now that the consequences for a transgression in this area will be swift and possibly detrimental to one's cause. No warnings. You cross the line and that's it.'

She paused and waited for a comeback. No one said anything. She placed the gavel back in its special holder next to the gold pen. Her voice returned to its friendly tone.

'Good,' she said. 'I think that's understood, then.'

She said she wanted to move on to other matters germane to the trial and her first stop was the trial date. She wanted to know if both sides would be ready to proceed to trial as scheduled, less than six weeks away. Royce said once again that his client would not waive the speedy trial statute.

'The defense will be ready to go on April fifth, provided

that the prosecution doesn't continue to play games with discovery.'

I shook my head. I couldn't win with this guy. I had gone out of my way to get the discovery pipeline going, but he had decided to take a shot at making me look like a cheater in front of the judge.

'Games?' I said. 'Judge, I've already turned over to Mr. Royce an initial discovery file. But as you know, it's a two-way street and the prosecution has received nothing in return from him.'

'He turned over the discovery file from the first trial, Judge Breitman, complete with a nineteen eighty-six witness list. It completely subverts the spirit and the rules of discovery.'

Breitman looked at me and I could see that Royce had successfully scored a hit.

'Is this true, Mr. Haller?' she asked.

'Hardly, Your Honor, the witness list was both subtracted from and added to. Additionally, I turned over—'

'One name,' Royce interjected. 'He added one name and it was his own investigator. Big deal, like I didn't know his investigator might be a witness.'

'Well, that's the only new name I have at the moment.'

Maggie jumped into the fray with both feet.

'Your Honor, the prosecution is duty-bound to turn over all discovery materials thirty days prior to trial. By my count we are still forty days out. Mr. Royce is complaining about a good-faith effort on the part of the prosecution to provide him with discovery material before it even has to. It seems that no good deed goes unpunished with Mr. Royce.'

The judge held up her hand to stop commentary while she looked at the calendar hanging on the wall to the left of her desk.

'I think Ms. McPherson makes a good point,' she said. 'Your complaint is premature, Mr. Royce. All discovery materials are due to both sides by this Friday, March fifth. If you have a problem then, we will take this up again.'

'Yes, Your Honor,' Royce said meekly.

I wanted to reach over, raise Maggie's hand in the air and shake it in victory but I didn't think that would be appropriate. Still, it felt good to win at least one point against Royce.

After discussion of a few more routine pretrial issues, the meeting ended and we walked out through the judge's courtroom. I stopped there to talk small talk with the judge's clerk. I didn't really know her that well but I didn't want to walk out of the courtroom with Royce. I was afraid I might lose my temper, which would be exactly what he'd want.

After he went through the double doors at the back of the courtroom I cut off the conversation and headed out with Maggie at my side.

'You kicked his ass, Maggie McFierce,' I said to her. 'Verbally.'

'Doesn't matter unless we kick it at trial.'

'Don't worry, we will. I want you to take over discovery fulfillment. Go ahead and do what you prosecutors do. Haystack everything. Give him so much material he'll never see what and who's important.'

She smiled as she turned and used her back to push through the door.

'Now you're getting it.'

'I hope so.'

'What about Sarah? He's got to figure we found her and if he's smart he won't wait for discovery. He probably has his own guy looking. She can be found. Harry proved that.'

'There's not a whole lot we can do about it. Speaking of Harry, where is he this morning?'

'He called me and said he had some things to check out. He'll be around later. You didn't really answer my question about Sarah. What should—?'

'Tell her that she might have another visitor, somebody working for the defense, but that she doesn't have to talk to anybody unless she wants to.'

We headed out into the hallway and then went left toward the elevator bank.

'If she doesn't talk to them, Royce will complain to the judge. She's the key witness, Mickey.'

'So? The judge won't be able to make her talk if she doesn't want to talk. Meantime, Royce loses prep time. He wants to play games like he did with the judge in there, then we'll play games, too. In fact, how about this? We put every convict Jessup ever shared a prison cell with on the witness list. That should keep his investigators out of the way for a while.'

A broad smile broke across Maggie's face.

'You really *are* getting it, aren't you?'

We squeezed onto the crowded elevator. Maggie and I were close enough to kiss. I looked down into her eyes as I spoke.

'That's because I don't want to lose.'

16

After school drop-off Bosch turned his car around and headed back up Woodrow Wilson, past his house, and to what those in the neighborhood called the upper crossing with Mulholland Drive. Both Mulholland and Woodrow Wilson were long and winding mountain roads. They intersected twice, at the bottom and top of the mountain, thus the local description of upper and lower crossings.

At the top of the mountain Bosch turned right onto Mulholland and followed it until it crossed Laurel Canyon Boulevard. He then pulled off the road to make a call on his cell. He punched in the number Shipley had given him for the SIS dispatch sergeant. His name was Willman and he would know the current status of any SIS surveillance. At any given time, SIS could be working four or five unrelated cases. Each was given a code name in order to keep them in order and so that the real names of suspects did not ever go out over the radio. Bosch knew that the Jessup surveillance had been termed Operation Retro because it involved an old case and a retrial.

'This is Bosch, RHD. I'm lead on the Retro case. I

158

want to get a location on the suspect because I'm about to pull into one of his favorite haunts. I want to make sure I don't run into him.'

'Hold one.'

Bosch could hear the phone being put down, then a radio conversation in which the duty sergeant asked for Jessup's location. The response was garbled with static by the time it reached Bosch over the phone. He waited for the sergeant's official response.

'Retro is in pocket right now,' he promptly reported to Bosch. 'They think he's catching Zs.'

In pocket meant he was at home.

'Then I'm clear,' Bosch said. 'Thank you, Sergeant.'

'Any time.'

Bosch closed the phone and pulled the car back onto Mulholland. A few curves later he reached Fryman Canyon Park and turned in. Bosch had talked to Shipley early that morning as he was passing surveillance off to the day team. He reported that Jessup had once again visited both Franklin and Fryman canyons. Bosch was becoming consumed with curiosity about what Jessup was up to and this was only increased by the report that Jessup had also driven by the house on Windsor where the Landy family had once lived.

Fryman was a rugged, inclined park with steep trails and a flat-surface parking and observation area on top and just off Mulholland. Bosch had been there before on cases and was familiar with its expanse. He pulled to a stop with his car pointing north and the view of the San Fernando Valley spread before him. The air was pretty clear and the vista stretched all the way across the valley to the San Gabriel Mountains. The brutal week of storms that had ended January had cleared the skies out and the smog was only now climbing back into the valley's bowl.

After a few minutes Bosch got out and walked over to the bench where Shipley had told him Jessup had sat for twenty minutes while looking out at the lights below. Bosch sat down and checked his watch. He had an eleven o'clock appointment with a witness. That gave him more than an hour.

Sitting where Jessup had sat brought no vibe or insight into what the suspect was doing on his frequent visits to the mountainside parks. Bosch decided to move on down Mulholland to Franklin Canyon.

But Franklin Canyon Park offered him the same thing, a large natural respite in the midst of a teeming city. Bosch found the picnic area Shipley and the SIS reports had described but once again didn't understand the pull the park had for Jessup. He found the terminus of Blinderman Trail and walked it until his legs started to hurt because of the incline. He turned around and headed back to the parking and picnic area, still puzzled by Jessup's activities.

On his return Bosch passed a large old sycamore that the trail had been routed around. He noticed a buildup of a grayish-white material at the base of the tree between two fingers of exposed roots. He looked closer and realized it was wax. Somebody had burned a candle.

There were signs all over the park warning against smoking or the use of matches, as fire was the park's greatest threat. But somebody had lit a candle at the base of the tree.

Bosch wanted to call Shipley to ask if Jessup could have lit a candle while in the park the night before, but knew it was the wrong move. Shipley had just come off a night of surveillance and was probably in his bed asleep. Harry would wait for the evening to make the call.

He looked around the tree for any other signs that Jessup had possibly been in the area. It looked like an animal had burrowed recently in a few spots under the tree. But otherwise there was no sign of activity.

As he came off the trail and into the clearing where the picnic area was located, Bosch saw a city parks ranger looking into a trash can from which he had removed the top. Harry approached him.

'Officer?'

The man whipped around, still holding the top of the trash can away from his body.

'Yes, sir!'

'Sorry, I didn't mean to sneak up on you. I was...I was walking up on that trail and there's a big tree there—I think a sycamore—and it looks like somebody burned a candle down at its base. I was wondering—'

'Where?'

'Up on Blinderman Trail.'

'Show me.'

'Actually, I'm not going to go all the way back up

there. I don't have the right shoes. It's the big tree in the middle of the trail. I'm sure you can find it.'

'You can't light fires in the park!'

The ranger put the top back on the trash can, banging it loudly to underline his statement.

'I know. That's why I was reporting it. But I wanted to ask you, is there anything special about that tree that would make somebody do that?'

'Every tree is special here. The whole park is special.'

'Yes, I get that. Can you just tell—'

'Can I see some ID, please?'

'Excuse me?'

'ID. I want to see some ID. A man in a shirt and tie walking the trails with "the wrong shoes" is a little bit suspicious to me.'

Bosch shook his head and pulled out his badge wallet.

'Yeah, here's my ID.'

He opened it and held it out and gave the ranger a few moments to study it. Bosch saw the nameplate on his uniform said Brorein.

'Okay?' Bosch said. 'Can we get to my questions now, Officer Brorein?'

'I'm a city ranger, not an officer,' Brorein said. 'Is this part of an investigation?'

'No, it's part of a situation where you just answer my questions about the tree up on that trail.'

Bosch pointed in the direction he had come from.

'You get it now?' he asked.

Brorein shook his head.

'I'm sorry but you're on my turf here and it's my obligation to—'

'No, pal, you're actually on my turf. But thanks for all the help. I'll make a note of it in the report.'

Bosch walked away from him and headed back toward the parking clearing. Brorein called after him.

'As far as I know, there's nothing special about that tree. It's just a tree, Detective Borsh.'

Bosch waved without looking back. He added poor reading skills to the list of things he didn't like about Brorein.

17

My successes as a defense attorney invariably came when the prosecution was unprepared for and surprised by my moves. The entire government grinds along on routine. Prosecuting violators of the government's laws is no different. As a newly minted prosecutor I took this to heart and vowed not to succumb to the comfort and dangers of routine. I promised myself that I would be more than ready for clever Clive Royce's moves. I would anticipate them. I would know them before Royce did. And I would be like a sniper in a tree, waiting to skillfully pick them off from a distance, one by one.

This promise brought Maggie McFierce and me together in my new office for frequent strategy sessions. And on this afternoon the discussion was focused on what would be the centerpiece of our opponent's pre-trial defense. We knew Royce would be filing a motion to dismiss the case. That was a given. What we were discussing were the grounds on which he would make the motion. I wanted to be ready for each one. It is said that in war the sniper ambushes an enemy patrol by first taking out the commander, the radioman and the medic. If he accomplishes this, the remaining members of the patrol panic and scatter. This was what I hoped to quickly do when Royce filed his motion. I wanted to move swiftly and thoroughly with demoralizing arguments and answers that would put the defendant on strong notice that he was in trouble. If I panicked Jessup, I might not even have to go to trial. I might get a disposition. A plea. And a plea was a conviction. That was as good as a win on this side of the aisle.

'I think one thing he's going to argue is that the charges are no longer valid without a preliminary hearing,' Maggie said. 'This will give him two bites out of the apple. He'll first ask the judge to dismiss but at the very least to order a new prelim.'

'But the verdict of the trial was what was reversed,' I said. 'It goes back to the trial and we have a new trial. The prelim is not what was challenged.'

'Well, that's what we'll argue.'

'Good, you get to handle that one. What else?'

'I'm not going to keep throwing out angles if you keep giving them back to me to be prepared for. That's the third one you've given me and by my scorecard you've only taken one.'

'Okay, I'll take the next one sight unseen. What do you have?'

Maggie smiled and I realized I had just walked into my own ambush. But before she could pull the trigger, the office door opened and Bosch entered without knocking.

'Saved by the bell,' I said. 'Harry, what's up?'

'I've got a witness I think you two should hear. I

think he's going to be good for us and they didn't use him in the first trial.'

'Who?' Maggie asked.

'Bill Clinton,' Bosch said.

I didn't recognize the name as belonging to anyone associated with the case. But Maggie, with her command of case detail, brought it together.

'One of the tow truck drivers who worked with Jessup.'

Bosch pointed at her.

'Right. He worked with Jessup back then at Aardvark Towing. Now he owns an auto repair shop on LaBrea near Olympic. It's called Presidential Motors.'

'Of course it is,' I said. 'What does he do for us as a witness?'

Bosch pointed toward the door.

'I got him sitting out there with Lorna. Why don't I bring him in and he can tell you himself?'

I looked at Maggie, and seeing no objection, I told Bosch to bring Clinton in. Before stepping out Bosch lowered his voice and reported that he had run Clinton through the crime databases and he had come up clean. He had no criminal record.

'Nothing,' Bosch said. 'Not even an unpaid parking ticket.'

'Good,' Maggie said. 'Now let's see what he has to say.'

Bosch went out to the reception room and came back with a short man in his midfifties who was wearing blue work pants and a shirt with an oval patch above the breast pocket. It said Bill. His hair was neatly combed and he didn't wear glasses. I saw grease under his fingernails but figured that could be remedied before he ever appeared in front of a jury.

Bosch pulled a chair away from the wall and placed it in the middle of the room and facing my desk.

'Why don't you sit down here, Mr. Clinton, and we'll ask you some questions,' he said.

Bosch then nodded to me, passing the lead.

'First of all, Mr. Clinton, thank you for agreeing to come in and talk to us today.'

Clinton nodded.

'That's okay. Things are kind of slow at the shop right now.'

'What kind of work do you do at the shop? Is there a specialty?'

'Yeah, we do restoration. Mostly British cars. Triumphs, MGs, Jags, collectibles like that.'

'I see. What's a Triumph TR Two-Fifty go for these days?'

Clinton looked up at me, surprised by my apparent knowledge of one of the cars he specialized in.

'Depends on the shape. I sold a beauty last year for twenty-five. I put almost twelve into the restoration. That and a lot of man-hours.'

I nodded.

'I had one in high school. Wish I'd never sold it.'

'They only made them for one year. 'Sixty-eight. Makes it one of the most collectible.'

I nodded. We had just covered everything I knew

about the car. I just liked it because of its wooden dash-board and the drop top. I used to cruise up to Malibu in it on weekends, hang out on the surf beaches even though I didn't know how to surf.

'Well, let's jump from 'sixty-eight to 'eighty-six, okay?'

Clinton shrugged.

'Fine by me.'

'If you don't mind, Ms. McPherson is going to take notes.'

Clinton shrugged again.

'So then, let's start. How well do you remember the day that Melissa Landy was murdered?'

Clinton spread his hands.

'Well, see, I remember it real well because of what happened. That little girl getting killed and it turning out I was working with the guy who did it.'

'Must've been pretty traumatic.'

'Yeah, it was for a while there.'

'And then you put it out of your mind?'

'No, not exactly . . . but I stopped thinking about it all the time. I started my business and everything.'

I nodded. Clinton seemed genuine enough and hon-est. It was a start. I looked at Bosch. I knew he had pulled some nugget from Clinton that he believed was gold. I wanted him to take over.

'Bill,' Bosch said. 'Tell them a little about what was going on with Aardvark at the time. About how busi-ness was bad.'

Clinton nodded.

'Yeah, well, back then we weren't doing so hot. What

happened was they passed a law that nobody could park on the side streets off of Wilshire without a resident sticker, you know? Anybody else, we got to tow. So we would go in the neighborhoods on a Sunday morning and hook up cars right and left on account of the church services. In the beginning. Mr. Korish was the owner and we were getting so many cars that he hired another driver and even started paying us for our overtime. It was fun because there were a couple other companies with the same contract, so we were all competing for tows. It was like keeping score and we were a team.'

Clinton looked at Bosch to see if he was telling the right story. Harry nodded and told him to keep going.

'So then it all kind of went bad. The people started getting wise and they stopped parking over there. Somebody said the church was even making announcements: "Don't park north of Wilshire." So we went from having too much to do to not enough. So Mr. Korish said he had to cut back on costs and one of us was going to have to go, and maybe even two of us. He said he was going to watch our performance levels and make his decision based on that.'

'When did he tell you this in relation to the day of the murder?' Bosch asked.

'It was right before. Because all three of us were still there. See, he didn't fire anybody yet.'

Taking over the questioning, I asked him what the new edict did to the competition among tow truck drivers.

'Well, it made it rough, you know. We were all friends

and then all of a sudden we didn't like each other because we wanted to keep our jobs.'

'How was Jason Jessup to work with then?'

'Well, Jason was real cutthroat.'

'The pressure got to him?'

'Yeah, because he was in last place. Mr. Korish put up a tote board to keep track of the tows and he was last place.'

'And he wasn't happy about it?'

'No, not happy. He became a real prick to work with, excuse my French.'

'Do you remember how he acted on the day of the murder?'

'A little bit. Like I told Detective Bosch, he started claiming streets. Like saying Windsor was all his. And Las Palmas and Lucerne. Like that. And me and Derek—he was the other driver—we told him there were no rules like that. And he said, "Fine, try hooking a car on one of those streets and see what happens."'

'He threatened you.'

'Yeah, you could say that. Definitely.'

'Do you remember specifically that Windsor was one of the streets he claimed was his?'

'Yes, I do. He claimed Windsor.'

This was all good information. It would go to the state of mind of the defendant. It would be a challenge getting it on the record if there wasn't additional corroboration from Wilbern or Korish, if either was still alive and available.

'Did he ever act on that threat in any way?' Maggie asked.

'No,' Clinton said. 'But that was the same day as the girl. So he got arrested and that was that. I can't say I was too upset about seeing him go. Turned out Mr. Korish then laid off Derek 'cause he lied about not having a record. I was the last man standing. I worked there another four years—till I saved up the money to start my place.'

A regular American success story. I waited to see if Maggie had a follow but she didn't. I did.

'Mr. Clinton, did you ever talk about any of this with the police or prosecutors twenty-four years ago?'

Clinton shook his head.

'Not really. I mean I spoke to the detective who was in charge back then. He asked me questions. But I wasn't ever brought to court or anything like that.'

Because they didn't need you back then, I thought. But I'm going to need you now.

'What makes you so sure that this threat from Jessup occurred on the day of the murder?'

'I just know it was that day. I remember that day because it's not every day that a guy you're working with gets arrested for murder.'

He nodded as if to underscore the point.

I looked at Bosch to see if we had missed anything. Bosch took the cue and took back the lead.

'Bill, tell them what you told me about being in the police car with Jessup. On the way to Windsor.'

Clinton nodded. He could be led easily and I took that as another good sign.

'Well, what happened was they really thought that

Derek was the guy. The police did. He had a criminal record and lied about it and they found out. So that made him suspect numero uno. So they put Derek in the back of one patrol car and then me and Jason in another.'

'Did they say where they were taking you?'

'They said they had additional questions, so we thought we were going to the police station. There were two officers in the car with us and we heard them talking about all of us being in a lineup. Jason asked them about it and they said it was no big thing, they just wanted guys in overalls because they wanted to see if a witness could pick out Derek.'

Clinton stopped there and looked expectantly from Bosch to me and then to Maggie.

'So what happened?' I asked.

'Well, first Jason told the two cops that they couldn't just take us and put us in a lineup like that. They just said that they were following orders. So we go over to Windsor and pull up in front of a house. The cops got out and went and talked to the lead detective, who was standing there with some other detectives. Jason and I were watching out the windows but didn't see any witness or anything. Then the detective in charge goes inside the house and doesn't come back out. We don't know what's going on, and then Jason says to me he wants to borrow my hat.'

'Your hat?' Maggie asked.

'Yeah, my Dodgers hat. I was wearing it like I always did and Jason said he needed to borrow it because he recognizes one of the other cops that was already standing there at the house when we pulled up. He said that he got in a fight with the guy over a tow and if he sees him there's going to be trouble. He goes on like that and says, let me have your hat.'

'What did you do?' I asked.

'Well, I didn't think it was a big deal on account of I didn't know what I knew later, you know what I mean? So I gave him my hat and he put it on. Then when the cops came back to get us out of the car, they didn't seem to notice that the hat was switched. They made us get out of the car and we had to go over and stand next to Derek. We were standing there and then one of the cops gets a call on the radio—I remember that—and he turns and tells Jason to take off the hat. He did and then a few minutes later they're all of a sudden surrounding Jason and putting the cuffs on him, and it wasn't Derek, it was him.'

I looked from Clinton to Bosch and then to Maggie. I could see in her expression that the hat story was significant.

'You know the funny thing?' Clinton asked.

'No, what?' I said.

'I never got that hat back.'

He smiled and I smiled back.

'Well, we'll have to get you a new hat when this is all said and done. Now let me ask you the key question. What you have told us here, are you willing to testify to all of it at Jason Jessup's trial?'

Clinton seemed to think about it for a few seconds before nodding.

'Yeah, I could do that,' he said.

I stood up and came around the desk, extending my hand.

'Then it looks like we've got ourselves a witness. Many thanks to you, Mr. Clinton.'

We shook hands and then I gestured to Bosch.

'Harry, I should have asked you, did we cover everything?'

Bosch stood up as well.

'I think so. For now. I'll take Mr. Clinton back to his shop.'

'Excellent. Thank you again, Mr. Clinton.'

Clinton stood up.

'Please call me Bill.'

'We will, I promise. We'll call you Bill and we'll call you as a witness.'

Everybody laughed in that phony way and then Bosch shepherded Clinton out of the office. I went back to my desk and sat down.

'So tell me about the hat,' I said to Maggie.

'It's a good connection,' she said. 'When we interviewed Sarah she remembered that Kloster radioed from the bedroom down to the street and had them make Jessup take off his hat. That was when she made the ID. Harry then looked through the case file and found a property list from Jessup's arrest. The Dodgers hat was on there. We're still trying to track his property—hard to do after twenty-four years. But it might have gone up to San Quentin. Either way, if we don't have the hat, we have the list.'

I nodded. This was good on a number of levels. It showed witnesses independently corroborating each other, put a crack in any sort of defense contention that memories cannot be trusted after so many years and, last but not least, showed state of mind of the defendant. Jessup knew he was somehow in danger of being identified. Someone had seen him abduct the girl.

'All right, good,' I said. 'What do you think about the initial stuff, about how there was competition between them and somebody was going to get laid off? Maybe two of them.'

'Again, it's good state-of-mind material. Jessup was under pressure and he acted out. Maybe this whole thing was about that. Maybe we should put a shrink on the witness list.'

I nodded.

'Did you tell Bosch to find and interview Clinton?'

She shook her head.

'He did it on his own. He's good at this.'

'I know. I just wish he'd tell me a little more about what he's up to.'

18

Thursday, February 25, 11:00 A.M.

Rachel Walling wanted to meet at an office in one of the glass towers in downtown. Bosch went to the address and took the elevator up to the thirty-fourth floor. The door to the offices of Franco, Becerra & Itzuris, attorneys-at-law, was locked and he had to knock. Rachel answered promptly and invited him into a luxurious suite of offices that was empty of lawyers, clerks and anybody else. She led him to the firm's board-room, where he saw the box and files he had given her the week before on a large oval table. They entered and he walked over to the floor-to-ceiling windows that looked out over downtown.

Bosch couldn't remember being up so high in down-town. He could see all the way to Dodger Stadium and beyond. He checked out the civic center and saw the glass-sided PAB sitting next to the *Los Angeles Times* building. His eyes then scanned toward Echo Park and he remembered a day there with Rachel Walling. They had been a team then, in more ways than one. But now that seemed so long ago.

'What is this place?' he said, still staring out and with his back to her. 'Where is everybody?'

'There isn't anybody. We just used this in a money-laundering sting. So it's been empty. Half of this building is empty. The economy. This was a real law office but it went out of business. So we just sort of borrowed it. The management was happy for the government subsidy.'

'They were washing money from drugs? Guns?'

'You know I can't say, Harry. I am sure you'll read about it in a few months. You'll put it together then.'

Bosch nodded as he remembered the firm's name on the door. Franco, Becerra & Itzuris: FBI. Clever.

'I wonder if management will tell the next tenants that this place was used by the bureau to take down some bad people. Friends of those bad people could come looking.'

She didn't respond to that. She just invited him to sit down at the table. He did, taking a good look at her as she sat across from him. Her hair was down, which was unusual. He had seen her that way before but not while she was on duty. The dark ringlets framed her face and helped direct attention to her dark eyes.

'The firm's refrigerator is empty or I'd offer you something to drink.'

'I'm fine.'

She opened the box and started taking out the files he had given her.

'Rachel, I really appreciate this,' Bosch said. 'I hope it didn't disrupt your life too much.'

'The work, no. I enjoyed it. But you, Harry, you coming back into my life was a disruption.'

Bosch wasn't expecting that.

'What do you mean?'

'I'm in a relationship and I'd told him about you. About the single-bullet theory, all of that. So he wasn't happy that I've been spending my nights off working this up for you.'

Bosch wasn't sure about how to respond. Rachel Walling always hid deeper messages in the things she said. He wasn't sure if there was more to be considered than what she had just said out loud.

'I'm sorry,' he finally said. 'Did you tell him it was only work, that I just wanted your professional opinion? That I went to you because I can trust you and you're the best at this?'

'He knows I'm the best at it, but it doesn't matter. Let's just do this.'

She opened a file.

'My ex-wife is dead,' he said. 'She was killed last year in Hong Kong.'

He wasn't sure why he'd blurted it out like that. She looked up at him sharply and he knew she hadn't known.

'Oh my God, I'm so sorry.'

Bosch just nodded, deciding not to tell her the details.

'What about your daughter?'

'She lives with me now. She's doing okay but it's been pretty tough on her. It's only been four months.'

She nodded and then seemed to lose her grounding as she took in what had just been said.

'What about you? I assume it's been rough for you, too.'

He nodded but couldn't think of the right words. He had his daughter fully in his life now, but at a terrible cost. He realized that he had brought the subject up but couldn't talk about it.

'Look,' he said, 'that was weird. I don't know why I just laid that on you. You mentioned the single bullet and I remember I told you about her. We can talk about it some other time. I mean, if you want. Let's just get to the case now. Is that okay?'

'Yes, sure. I was just thinking about your daughter. To lose her mother and then have to move so far from the place she knows. I mean, I know living with you will be fine, but it's... quite an adjustment.'

'Yeah, but they say kids are resilient because they actually are. She's got a lot of friends already and is doing well in school. It's been a major adjustment for both of us but I think she'll come out okay.'

'And how will you come out?'

Bosch held her eyes for a moment before answering.

'I've already come out ahead. I have my daughter with me and she's the best thing in my life.'

'That's good, Harry.'

'It is.'

She broke eye contact and finished removing the files and photos from the box. Bosch could see the transformation. She was now all business, an FBI profiler ready to report her findings. He reached into his pocket and pulled out his notebook. It was in a folding leather case with a detective shield embossed on the cover. He opened it and got ready to write.

'I want to start with the photos,' she said.

'Fine.'

She spread out four photos of Melissa Landy's body in the Dumpster, turning them to face him. She then added two photos from the autopsy in a row above these. Photos of a dead child were never easy to look at for Bosch. But these were particularly difficult. He stared for a long moment before coming to the realization that the clutch in his gut was due to the setting of the body in a Dumpster. For the girl to be disposed of like that seemed almost like a statement about the victim and an added insult to those who loved her.

'The Dumpster,' he said. 'You think that was chosen as a statement?'

Walling paused as if considering it for the first time.

'I'm actually going at it from a different standpoint. I think that it was an almost spontaneous choice. That it wasn't part of a plan. He needed a place to dump the body where he wouldn't be seen and it wouldn't be immediately found. He knew about that Dumpster behind that theater and he used it. It was a convenience, not a statement.'

Bosch nodded. He leaned forward and wrote a note on his pad to remind himself to go back to Clinton and ask about the Dumpster. The El Rey was in the Wilshire corridor the Aardvark drivers worked. It might have been familiar to them.

'Sorry, I didn't mean to start things off in the wrong direction,' he said as he wrote.

'That's okay. The reason I wanted to start with the photos of the girl is that I believe that this crime may have been misunderstood from the very beginning.'

'Misunderstood?'

'Well, it appears that the original investigators took the crime scene at face value and looked at it as the result of the suspect's kill plan. In other words, Jessup grabbed this girl, and his plan was to strangle her and leave her in the Dumpster. This is evidenced by the profile that was drawn up of the crime and submitted to the FBI and the California Department of Justice for comparison to other crimes on record.'

She opened a file and pulled out the lengthy profile and submission forms prepared by Detective Kloster twenty-four years earlier.

'Detective Kloster was looking for similar crimes that he might be able to attach Jessup to. He got zero hits and that was the end of that.'

Bosch had spent several days studying the original case file and knew everything that Walling was telling him. But he let her run with it without interruption because he had a feeling she would take him somewhere new. That was her beauty and art. It didn't matter that the FBI didn't recognize it and use her to the best of her abilities. He always would.

'I think what happened was that this case had a faulty profile from the beginning. Add to that the fact that back then the data banks were obviously not as sophisticated or as inclusive as they are now. This whole angle was misdirected and wrong and so no wonder they hit a dead end with it.'

Bosch nodded and wrote a quick note.

'You tried to rebuild the profile?' he asked.

'As much as I could. And the starting point is right here. The photos. Take a look at her injuries.'

Bosch leaned across the table and over the first row of photographs. He actually didn't see injuries to the girl. She had been dropped haphazardly into the almost full trash bin. There must have been stage building or a renovation project going on inside the theater, because the bin contained mostly construction refuse. Sawdust, paint buckets, small pieces of cut and broken wood. There were small cuts of wallboard and torn plastic sheeting. Melissa Landy was faceup near one of the corners of the Dumpster. Bosch didn't see a drop of blood on her or her dress.

'What injuries are we talking about?' he asked.

Walling stood up in order to lean over. She used the point of a pen to outline the places she wanted Bosch to look on each of the photos. She circled discolorations on the victim's neck.

'Her neck injuries,' she said. 'If you look you see the oval-shaped bruising on the right side of the neck, and on the other side you have a larger corresponding bruise. This evidence makes it clear that she was choked to death with one hand.'

She used the pen to illustrate what she was saying.

'The thumb here on her right side and the four fingers on the left. One-handed. Now, why one-handed?'

She sat back down and Bosch leaned back away from the photos himself. The idea that Melissa had been strangled with one hand was not new to Bosch. It was in Kloster's original profile of the murder.

'Twenty-four years ago, it was suggested that Jessup strangled the girl with his right hand while he masturbated with his left. This theory was built on one thing—the semen collected from the victim's dress. It was deposited by someone with the same blood type as Jessup and so it was assumed to have come from him. You follow all of this?'

'I'm with you.'

'Okay, so the problem is, we now know that the semen didn't come from Jessup and so the basic profile or theory of the crime in nineteen eighty-six is wrong. It is further demonstrated as being wrong because Jessup is right-handed according to a sample of his writing in the files, and studies have shown that with right-handers masturbation is almost always carried out by the dominant hand.'

'They've done studies on that?'

'You'd be surprised. I sure was when I went online to look for this.'

'I knew there was something wrong with the Internet.'

She smiled but was not a bit embarrassed by the subject matter of their discussion. It was all in a day's work.

'They've done studies on everything, including which hand people use to wipe their butts. I actually found it to be fascinating reading. But the point here is that they had this wrong from the beginning. This murder did not occur during a sex act. Now let me show you a few other photos.'

She reached across the table and slid all of the photos together in one stack and then put them to the side. She then spread out photos taken of the inside of the tow truck Jessup was driving on the day of the murder. The truck actually had a name, which was stenciled on the dashboard.

'Okay, so on the day in question, Jessup was driving Matilda,' Walling said.

Bosch studied the three photos she had spread out. The cab of the tow truck was in neat order. Thomas Brothers maps—no GPS back then—were neatly stacked on top of the dashboard and a small stuffed animal that Bosch presumed was an aardvark hung from the rearview mirror. A cup holder on the center console held a Big Gulp from 7-Eleven and a sticker on the glove compartment door read *Grass or Ass—Nobody Rides for Free.*

With her trusty pen, Walling circled a spot on one of the photos. It was a police scanner mounted under the dashboard.

'Did anybody consider what this means?'

Bosch shrugged.

'Back then, I don't know. What's it mean now?'

'Okay, Jessup worked for Aardvark, which was a towing company licensed by the city. However, it wasn't the only one. There was competition among tow companies. The drivers listened to scanners, picking up police calls about accidents and parking infractions. It gave them the jump on the competition, right? Except that every tow truck had a scanner and everybody was listening and trying to get the jump on everyone else.'

'Right. So what's it mean?'

'Well, let's look at the abduction first. It is pretty clear from the witness testimony and everything else that this was not a crime of great planning and patience. This was an impulse crime. That much they've had right from the beginning. We can talk about the motivating factors at length in a little while, but suffice it to say, something caused Jessup to act out in an almost uncontrollable way.'

'I think I might have motivating factors covered,' Bosch said.

'Good, I'm eager to hear about it. But for now, we will assume that some sort of internal pressure led Jessup to act on an undeniable impulse and he grabbed the girl. He took her back to the truck and took off. He obviously didn't know about the sister hiding in the bushes and that she would sound the alarm. So he completes the abduction and drives away, but within minutes he hears the report about the abduction on the police scanner he has in the truck. That brings home to him the reality of what he's done and what his predicament is. He never imagined things would move so fast. He more or less comes to his senses. He realizes he must abandon his plan now and move into preservation mode. He needs to kill the girl to eliminate her as a witness and then hide her body in order to prevent his arrest.'

Bosch nodded as he understood her theory.

'So what you're saying is, the crime that occurred was not the crime that he intended.'

'Correct. He abandoned the true plan.'

'So when Kloster went to the bureau looking for similars, he was looking for the wrong thing.'

'Right again.'

'But could there actually have been a plan? You just said yourself that it was a crime of compulsion. He saw an opportunity and within a few seconds acted on it. What plan could there have been?'

'Actually, it is more than likely that he had a complex and complete plan. Killers like these have a paraphilia — a set construct of the perfect psychosexual experience. They fantasize about it in great detail. And as you can expect, it often involves torture and murder. The paraphilia is part of their daily fantasy life and it builds to the point where the desire becomes the urge which eventually becomes a compulsion to act out. When they do cross that line and act out, the abduction of the victim may be completely unplanned and improvisational, but the killing sequence is not. The victim is unfortunately dropped into a set construct that has played over and over in the killer's mind.'

Bosch looked at his notebook and realized he had stopped taking notes.

'Okay, but you're saying that didn't happen here,' he said. 'He abandoned the plan. He heard the abduction report on the scanner, and that took him from fantasy to reality. He realized that they could be closing in on him. He killed her and dumped her, hoping to avoid detection.'

'Exactly. And therefore, as you just noted, when

investigators attempted to compare elements of this murder to others', they were comparing apples and oranges. They found nothing that matched and believed that this was a onetime crime of opportunity and compulsion. I don't think it was.'

Bosch looked up from the photos to Rachel's eyes.

'You think he did this before.'

'I think the idea that he had acted out before in this way is compelling. It would not surprise me if you were to find that he was involved in other abductions.'

'You're talking about more than twenty-four years ago.'

'I know. And since there was no linking of Jessup to known unsolved murders, we are probably talking about missing children and runaways. Cases where there was never a crime scene established. The girls were never found.'

Bosch thought of Jessup's middle-of-the-night visits to the parks along Mulholland Drive. He thought he might now know why Jessup would light a candle at the base of a tree.

Then a more stunning and scary thought pushed through.

'Do you think a guy like this would use those crimes from so long ago to feed his fantasy now?'

'Of course he would. He's been in prison, what other choice did he have?'

Bosch felt an urgency take hold inside. An urgency that came with the growing certainty that they weren't dealing with an isolated instance of murder. If Walling's theory was correct, and he had no reason to doubt it, Jessup was a repeater. And though he had been on ice for twenty-four years, he was now roaming the city freely. It would not be long now before he became vulnerable to the pressures and urges that had driven him to deadly action before.

Bosch came to a fast resolve. The next time Jessup was seized by the pressures of his life and overcome by the compulsion to kill, Bosch was going to be there to destroy him.

His eyes refocused and he realized Rachel was looking at him oddly.

'Thank you for all of this, Rachel,' he said. 'I think I need to go.'

19

Thursday, March 4, 9:00 A.M.

It was only a hearing on pretrial motions but the courtroom was packed. Lots of courthouse gadflies and
media, and a fair number of trial lawyers were sitting
in as well. I sat at the prosecution table with Maggie
and we were going over our arguments once again. All
issues before Judge Breitman had already been argued
and submitted on paper. This would be when the judge
could ask further questions and then announce her rulings. I had a growing sense of anxiety. The motions
submitted by Clive Royce were all pretty routine and
Maggie and I had submitted solid responses. We were
also ready with oral arguments to back them, but a
hearing like this was also a time for the unexpected.
On more than one occasion I had sandbagged the prosecution in a pretrial hearing. And sometimes the case
is won or lost before the trial begins with a ruling in
one of these hearings.

I leaned back and looked behind us and then took a
quick glance around the courtroom. I gave a phony
smile and nod to a lawyer I saw in the spectator section,
then turned back to Maggie.

'Where's Bosch?' I asked.

'I don't think he's going to be here.'

'Why not? He's completely disappeared in the last week.'

'He's been working on something. He called yesterday and asked if he had to be here for this and I said he didn't.'

'He'd better be working on something related to Jessup.'

'He tells me it is and that he's going to bring it to us soon.'

'That's nice of him. The trial starts in four weeks.'

I wondered why Bosch had chosen to call her instead of me, the lead prosecutor. I realized that this made me upset with Maggie as well as Bosch.

'Listen, I don't know what happened between you two on your little trip to Port Townsend, but he should be calling me.'

Maggie shook her head as if dealing with a petulant child.

'Look, you don't have to worry. He knows you're the lead prosecutor. He probably figures you are too busy for the day-to-day updates on what he's doing. And I'm going to forget what you said about Port Townsend. This one time. You make another insinuation like that and you and I are going to have a real problem.'

'Okay, I'm sorry. It's just that—'

My attention was drawn across the aisle to Jessup, who was sitting at the defense table with Royce. He was staring at me with a smirk on his face and I realized he had been watching Maggie and me, maybe even listening.

'Excuse me a second,' I said.

I got up and walked over to the defense table. I leaned over him.

'Can I help you with something, Jessup?'

Before Jessup could say a word his lawyer cut in.

'Don't talk to my client, Mick,' Royce said. 'If you want to ask him something, then you ask me.'

Now Jessup smiled again, emboldened by his attorney's defensive move.

'Just go sit down,' Jessup said. 'I got nothing to say to you.'

Royce held his hand up to quiet him.

'I'll handle this. You be quiet.'

'He threatened me. You should complain to the judge.'

'I said be quiet and that I would handle this.'

Jessup folded his arms and leaned back in his chair.

'Mick, is there a problem here?' Royce asked.

'No, no problem. I just don't like him staring at me.'

I walked back to the prosecution table, annoyed with myself for losing my calm. I sat down and looked at the pool camera set up in the jury box. Judge Breitman had approved the filming of the trial and the various hearings leading up to it, but only through the use of a pool camera, which would provide a universal feed that all channels and networks could use.

A few minutes later the judge took the bench and called the hearing to order. One by one we went through the defense motions, and the rulings mostly fell our way without much further argument. The most important one was the routine motion to dismiss for lack of evidence, which the judge rejected with little comment. When Royce asked to be heard, she said that it wasn't necessary to discuss the issue further. It was a solid rebuke and I loved it even though outwardly I acted as though it were routine and boring.

The only ruling the judge wanted to discuss in detail was the oddball request by Royce to allow his client to use makeup during trial to cover the tattoos on his neck and fingers. Royce had argued in his motion that the tattoos were all prison tattoos applied while he was falsely incarcerated for twenty-four years. He said the tattoos could be prejudicial when noticed by jurors. His client intended to cover these with skin-tone makeup and he wanted to bar the prosecution from addressing it in front of the jury.

'I have to admit I have not had a motion like this come before me,' the judge said. 'I'm inclined to allow it and hold the prosecution from drawing attention to it but I see the prosecution has objected to the motion, saying that it contains insufficient information about the content and history of these tattoos. Can you shed some light on the subject, Mr. Royce?'

Royce stood and addressed the court from his place at the defense table. I looked over and my eyes were drawn to Jessup's hands. I knew the tattoos across his knuckles were Royce's chief concern. The neck markings could largely be covered with a collared shirt, which he would wear with a suit at trial. But the hands were difficult to hide. Across the four digits of each hand he had inked the sentiment FUCK THIS and Royce knew that I would make sure it was seen by jurors. That sentiment was probably the chief impediment to having Jessup testify in his defense, because Royce knew I would find a way either casually or specifically to make sure the jury got his message.

'Your Honor, it is the defense's position that these tattoos were administered to Mr. Jessup's body while he was falsely imprisoned and are a product of that harrowing experience. Prison is a dangerous place, Judge, and inmates take measures to protect themselves. Sometimes it is through tattooing that is designed to be intimidating or to show an association the prisoner might not actually have or believe in. It would certainly be prejudicial for the jury to see, and therefore we ask for relief. This, I might add, is merely a tactic by the prosecution to delay the trial, and the defense firmly stands by its decision to not delay justice in this case.'

Maggie stood up quickly. She had handled this motion on paper and therefore it was hers to handle in court.

'Your Honor, may I be heard on the defense's accusation?'

'One moment, Ms. McPherson, I want to be heard myself. Mr. Royce, can you explain your last statement?'

Royce bowed politely.

'Yes, of course, Judge Breitman. The defendant has begun to go through a tattoo removal process. But this takes time and will not be completed by trial. By objecting to our simple request to use makeup, the prosecution is trying to push the trial back until this removal process is completed. It's an effort to subvert the speedy trial statute which since day one the defense, to the prosecution's consternation, has refused to waive.'

The judge turned her gaze to Maggie McFierce. It was her turn.

'Your Honor, this is simply a defense fabrication. The state has not once asked for a delay or opposed the defense's request for a speedy trial. In fact, the prosecution is ready for trial. So this statement is outlandish and objectionable. The true objection on the part of the prosecution to this motion is to the idea of the defendant being allowed to disguise himself. A trial is a search for truth, and allowing him to use makeup to cover up who he really is would be an affront to the search for truth. Thank you, Your Honor.'

'Judge, may I respond?' Royce, still standing, said immediately.

Breitman paused for a moment while she wrote a few notes from Maggie's brief.

'That won't be necessary, Mr. Royce,' she finally said. 'I'm going to make a ruling on this and I will allow Mr. Jessup to cover his tattoos. If he chooses to testify on his behalf, the prosecution will not address this issue with him in front of the jury.'

'Thank you, Your Honor,' Maggie said.

She sat down without showing any outward sign of disappointment. It was just one ruling among many others and most had gone the prosecution's way. This loss was minor at worst.

'Okay,' the judge said. 'I think we have covered everything. Anything else from counsel at this time?'

'Yes, Your Honor,' Royce said as he stood again. 'Defense has a new motion we would like to submit.'

He stepped away from the defense table and brought copies of the new motion first to the judge and then to us, giving Maggie and me individual copies of a one-page motion. Maggie was a fast reader, a skill she had genetically passed on to our daughter, who was reading two books a week on top of her homework.

'This is bullshit,' she whispered before I had even finished reading the title of the document.

But I caught up quickly. Royce was adding a new lawyer to the defense team and the motion was to disqualify Maggie from the prosecution because of a conflict of interest. The new lawyer's name was David Bell.

Maggie quickly turned around to scan the spectator seats. My eyes followed and there was David Bell, sitting at the end of the second row. I knew him on sight because I had seen him with Maggie in the months after our marriage had ended. One time I had come to her apartment to pick up my daughter and Bell had opened the door.

Maggie turned back and started to stand to address the court but I put my hand on her shoulder and held her in place.

'I'm taking this,' I said.

'No, wait,' she whispered urgently. 'Ask for a ten-minute recess. We need to talk about this.'

'Exactly what I was going to do.'

I stood and addressed the judge.

'Your Honor, like you, we just got this. We can take it with us and submit but we would rather argue it right now. If the court could indulge us with a brief recess, I think we would be ready to respond.'

'Fifteen minutes, Mr. Haller? I have another matter holding. I could handle it and come back to you.'

'Thank you, Your Honor.'

This meant we had to leave the table while another prosecutor handled his business before the judge. We pushed our files and Maggie's laptop to the back of the table to make room, then got up and walked toward the back door of the courtroom. As we passed Bell he raised a hand to get Maggie's attention but she ignored him and walked by.

'You want to go upstairs?' Maggie asked as we came through the double doors. She was suggesting that we go up to the DA's office.

'There isn't time to wait for an elevator.'

'We could take the stairs. It's only three flights.'

We walked through the door into the building's enclosed stairwell but then I grabbed her arm.

'This is good enough right here,' I said. 'Tell me what we do about Bell.'

'That piece of shit. He's never defended a criminal case, let alone a murder, in his life.'

'Yeah, you wouldn't have made the same mistake twice.'

She looked pointedly at me.

'What's that supposed to mean?'

'Never mind, bad joke. Let's just stay on point.'

She had her arms folded tightly against her chest.

'This is the most underhanded thing I've ever seen. Royce wants me off the case so he goes to Bell. And Bell...I can't believe he would do something like this to me.'

'Yeah, well, he's probably in it for a dip into the pot of gold at the end of the rainbow. We probably should have seen something like this coming.'

It was a defense tactic I had used myself before, but not with such obviousness. If you didn't like the judge or the prosecutor, one way of getting them off the case was to bring someone onto your team who has a conflict of interest with them. Since the defendant is constitutionally guaranteed the defense counsel of his choice, it is usually the judge or prosecutor who must be disqualified from the trial. It was a shrewd move by Royce.

'You see what he's doing, right?' Maggie said. 'He is trying to isolate you. He knows I'm the one person you would trust as second chair and he's trying to take that away from you. He knows that without me you are going to lose.'

'Thanks for your confidence in me.'

'You know what I mean. You've never prosecuted a case. I'm there to help you through it. If he gets me kicked off the table, then who are you going to have? Who would you trust?'

I nodded. She was right.

'Okay, give me the facts. How long were you with Bell?'

'With him? I wasn't. We went out briefly seven years ago. No more than two months and if he says differently he's a liar.'

'Is the conflict that you had the relationship or is there something else, something you did or said, something he has knowledge of that creates the conflict?'

'There's nothing. We went out and it just didn't take.'

'Who dropped who?'

She paused and looked down at the floor.

'He did.'

I nodded.

'Then there's the conflict. He can claim you carry a grudge.'

'A woman scorned, is that it? This is such bullshit. You men are—'

'Hold on, Maggie. Hold on. I'm saying that is their argument. I am not agreeing. In fact, I want—'

The door to the stairwell opened and the prosecutor who took our places when we had gotten up for the recess entered and started up the steps. I checked my watch. Only eight minutes had gone by.

'She went back into chambers,' he said as he passed. 'You guys are fine.'

'Thanks.'

I waited until I heard his steps on the next landing before continuing in a quiet tone with Maggie.

'Okay, how do I fight this?'

'You tell the judge that this is an obvious attempt to sabotage the prosecution. They've hired an attorney for the sole reason that he had a relationship with me, not because of any skill he brings to the table.'

I nodded.

'Okay. What else?'

'I don't know. I can't think...it was remote in time, no strong emotional attachment, no effect on professional judgment or conduct.'

'Yeah, yeah, yeah...and what about Bell? Does he have something or know something I have to watch out for?'

She looked at me like I was some sort of traitor.

'Maggie, I need to know so there's no surprise on top of the surprise, okay?'

'Fine, there's nothing. He must really be hard up if he's taking a fee just to knock me off the case.'

'Don't worry, two can play this game. Let's go.'

We went back into the courtroom and as we went through the gate I nodded to the clerk so she could call the judge back from chambers. Instead of going to the prosecution table, I diverted to the defense side where Royce was sitting next to his client. David Bell was now seated at the table on the other side of Jessup. I leaned over Royce's shoulder and whispered just loud enough that his client would hear.

'Clive, when the judge comes out, I'll give you the chance to withdraw this motion. If you don't, number one, I'm going to embarrass you in front of the camera and it will be digitally preserved forever. And number two, the release-and-remuneration offer I made to your client last week is withdrawn. Permanently.'

I watched Jessup's eyebrows rise a few centimeters. He hadn't heard anything about an offer involving money and freedom. This was because I hadn't made one. But now it would be up to Royce to convince his client that he had not withheld anything from him. Good luck with that.

Royce smiled like he was pleased with my comeback. He leaned back casually and tossed his pen on his legal pad. It was a Montblanc with gold trim and that was no way to treat it.

'This is really going to get good, yes, Mick?' he said. 'Well, I'll tell you. I'm not withdrawing the motion and I think if you had made me an offer involving release and remuneration I would've remembered it.'

So he had called my bluff. He'd still have to convince his client. I saw the judge step out from the door of her chambers and start up the three steps to the bench. I took one more whispered shot at Royce.

'Whatever you paid Bell you wasted.'

I stepped over to the prosecution table and remained standing. The judge brought the courtroom to order.

'Okay, back on the record in *California versus Jessup*. Mr. Haller, do you want to respond to the defendant's latest motion or take it on submission.'

'Your Honor, the prosecution wishes to respond right now to... this motion.'

'Go right ahead, then.'

I tried to build a good tone of outrage into my voice.

'Judge, I am as cynical as the next guy but I have to say I am surprised by the defense's tactics here with this motion. In fact, this isn't a motion. This is very plainly an attempt to subvert the trial system by denying the People of Cal—'

'Your Honor,' Royce interjected, jumping to his feet, 'I strenuously object to the character assassination Mr. Haller is putting on the record and before the media. This is nothing more than grand—'

'Mr. Royce, you will have an opportunity to respond *after* Mr. Haller responds to your motion. Please be seated.'

'Yes, Your Honor.'

Royce sat down and I tried to remember where I was.

'Go ahead, Mr. Haller.'

'Yes, Your Honor, as you know, the prosecution turned over all discovery materials to the defense on Tuesday. What you have before you now is a very disingenuous motion spawned by Mr. Royce's realization of what he will be up against at trial. He thought the state was going to roll over on this case. He now knows that it is not going to do so.'

'But what does this have to do with the motion at hand, Mr. Haller?' the judge asked impatiently.

'Everything,' I said. 'You've heard of judge shopping? Well, Mr. Royce is prosecutor shopping. He knows through his examination of discovery materials that Margaret McPherson is perhaps the most important part of the prosecution team. Rather than take on the evidence at trial, he is attempting to undercut the prosecution by splintering the team that has assembled that evidence. Here we are, just four weeks before trial and he makes a move against my second chair. He has hired an attorney with little to no experience in criminal defense, not to mention defending a murder case. Why would he do that, Judge, other than for the purpose of concocting this supposed conflict of interest?'

'Your Honor?'

Royce was on his feet again.

'Mr. Royce,' the judge said, 'I told you, you will have your chance.'

The warning was very clear in her voice.

'But, Your Honor, I can't—'

'*Sit down.*'

Royce sat down and the judge put her attention back on me.

'Judge, this is a cynical move made by a desperate defense. I would hope that you would not allow him to subvert the intentions of the Constitution.'

Like two men on a seesaw, I went down and Royce immediately popped up.

'One moment, Mr. Royce,' the judge said, holding up her hand and signaling him back down to his seat. 'I want to talk to Mr. Bell.'

Now it was Bell's turn to stand up. He was a well-dressed man with sandy hair and a ruddy complexion, but I could see the apprehension in his eyes. Whether he had come to Royce or Royce had come to him, it was clear that he had not anticipated having to stand in front of a judge and explain himself.

'Mr. Bell, I have not had the pleasure of seeing you

practice in my courtroom. Do you handle criminal defense, sir?'

'Uh, no, ma'am, not ordinarily. I am a trial attorney and I have been lead counsel in more than thirty trials. I do know my way around a courtroom, Your Honor.'

'Well, good for you. How many of those trials were murder trials?'

I felt total exhilaration as I watched what I had set in motion take on its own momentum. Royce looked mortified as he watched his plan shatter like an expensive vase.

'None of them were murder trials per se. But several were wrongful death cases.'

'Not the same thing. How many criminal trials do you have under your belt, Mr. Bell?'

'Again, Judge, none were criminal cases.'

'What do you bring to the defense of Mr. Jessup?'

'Your Honor, I bring a wealth of trial experience but I don't think that my résumé is on point here. Mr. Jessup is entitled to counsel of his choice and—'

'What exactly is the conflict you have with Ms. McPherson?'

Bell looked perplexed.

'Did you understand the question?' the judge asked.

'Yes, Your Honor, the conflict is that we had an intimate relationship and now we would be opposing each other at trial.'

'Were you married?'

'No, Your Honor.'

'When was this intimate relationship and how long did it last?'

'It was seven years ago and it lasted about three months.'

'Have you had contact with her since then?'

Bell raised his eyes to the ceiling as if looking for an answer. Maggie leaned over and whispered in my ear.

'No, Your Honor,' Bell said.

I stood up.

'Your Honor, in the interest of full disclosure, Mr. Bell has sent Ms. McPherson a Christmas card for the past seven years. She has not responded likewise.'

There was a murmur of laughter in the courtroom. The judge ignored it and looked down at something in front of her. She looked like she had heard enough.

'Where is the conflict you are worried about, Mr. Bell?'

'Uh, Judge, this is a bit difficult to speak of in open court but I was the one who ended the relationship with Ms. McPherson and my concern is that there could be some lingering animosity there. And that's the conflict.'

The judge wasn't buying this and everyone in the courtroom knew it. It was becoming uncomfortable even to watch.

'Ms. McPherson,' the judge said.

Maggie pushed back her chair and stood.

'Do you hold any lingering animosity toward Mr. Bell?'

'No, Your Honor, at least not before today. I moved on to better things.'

I could hear another low rumble from the seats behind me as Maggie's spear struck home.

'Thank you, Ms. McPherson,' the judge said. 'You can sit. And so can you, Mr. Bell.'

Bell thankfully dropped into his chair. The judge leaned forward and spoke matter-of-factly into the bench's microphone.

'The motion is denied.'

Royce stood up immediately.

'Your Honor, I was not heard before the ruling.'

'It was your motion, Mr. Royce.'

'But I would like to respond to some of the things Mr. Haller said about—'

'Mr. Royce, I've made my ruling on it. I don't see the need for further discussion. Do you?'

Royce realized his defeat could get even worse. He cut his losses.

'Thank you, Your Honor.'

He sat down. The judge then ended the hearing and we packed up and headed toward the rear doors. But not as quickly as Royce. He and his client and supposed co-counsel split the courtroom like men who had to catch the last train on a Friday night. And this time Royce didn't bother stopping outside the courtroom to chat with the media.

'Thanks for sticking up for me,' Maggie said when we got to the elevators.

I shrugged.

'You stuck up for yourself. Did you really mean that, what you said about moving on from Bell to better things?'

'From him, yes. Definitely.'

I looked at her but couldn't read her beyond the spoken line. The elevator doors opened, and there was Harry Bosch waiting to step off.

20

Bosch stepped off the elevator and almost walked right into Haller and McPherson.

'Is it over?' he asked.

'You missed it,' Haller said.

Bosch quickly turned and hit one of the bumpers on the elevator doors before it could close.

'Are you going down?'

'That's the plan,' Haller said in a tone that didn't hide his annoyance with Bosch. 'I thought you weren't coming to the hearing.'

'I wasn't. I was coming to get you two.'

They rode the elevator down and Bosch convinced them to walk with him a block over to the Police Administration Building. He signed them in as visitors and they went up to the fifth floor, where Robbery-Homicide Division was located.

'This is the first time I've been here,' McPherson said. 'It's as quiet as an insurance office.'

'Yeah, I guess we lost a lot of the charm when we moved,' Bosch replied.

The PAB had been in operation for only six months.

It had a quiet and sterile quality about it. Most of the building's denizens, including Bosch, missed the old headquarters, Parker Center, even though it was beyond decrepit.

'I've got a private room over here,' he said, pointing to a door on the far side of the squad room.

He used a key to unlock the door and they walked into a large space with a boardroom-style table at center. One wall was glass that looked out on the squad room but Bosch had lowered and closed the blinds for privacy. On the opposite wall was a large whiteboard with a row of photos across the top margin and numerous notes written beneath each shot. The photos were of young girls.

'I've been working on this nonstop for a week,' Bosch said. 'You probably have been wondering where I disappeared to so I figured it was time to show you what I've got.'

McPherson stopped just a few steps inside the door and stared, squinting her eyes and revealing to Bosch her vanity. She needed glasses but he'd never seen her wearing them.

Haller stepped over to the table, where there were several archival case boxes gathered. He slowly pulled out a chair to sit down.

'Maggie,' Bosch prompted. 'Why don't you sit down?'

McPherson finally broke from her stare and took the chair at the end of the table.

'Is this what I think it is?' she asked. 'They all look like Melissa Landy.'

'Well,' Bosch said. 'Let me just go over it and you'll draw your own conclusions.'

Bosch stayed on his feet. He moved around the table to the whiteboard. With his back to the board he started to tell the story.

'Okay, I have a friend. She's a former profiler. I've never —'

'For whom?' Haller asked.

'The FBI, but does it matter? What I'm saying is that I've never known anybody who was better at it. So, shortly after I came into this I asked her informally to take a look at the case files and she did. Her conclusions were that back in 'eighty-six this case was read all wrong. And where the original investigators saw a crime of impulse and opportunity, she saw something different. To keep it short, she saw indications that the person who killed Melissa Landy may have killed before.'

'Here we go,' Haller said.

'Look, man, I don't know why you're giving me the attitude,' Bosch said. 'You pulled me in as investigator on this thing and I'm investigating. Why don't you just let me tell you what I know? Then you can do with it whatever you want. You think it's legit, then run with it. You don't, then shitcan it. I will have done my job by bringing it to you.'

'I'm not giving you any attitude, Harry. I'm just thinking out loud. Thinking about all the things that can complicate a trial. Complicate discovery. You realize that everything you are telling us has to be turned over to Royce now?'

'Only if you intend to use it.'

'What?'

'I thought you'd know the rules of discovery better than me.'

'I know the rules. Why did you bring us here for this dog and pony show if you don't think we should use it?'

'Why don't you just let him tell the story,' McPherson said. 'And then maybe we'll understand.'

'Then, go ahead,' Haller said. 'Anyway, all I said was "Here we go," which I think is a pretty common phrase indicating surprise and change of direction. That's all. Continue, Harry. Please.'

Bosch glanced back at the board for a moment and then turned back to his audience of two and continued.

'So my friend the profiler thinks Jason Jessup killed before he killed Melissa Landy, and most likely was successful in hiding his involvement in these previous crimes.'

'So you went looking,' McPherson said.

'I did. Now, remember our original investigator, Kloster, was no slouch. He went looking, too. Only problem was he was using the wrong profile. They had semen on the dress, strangulation and a body dump in an accessible location. That was the profile, so that is what he went looking for and he found no similars, or at least no cases that connected. End of story, end of search. They believed Jessup acted out this one time, was exceedingly disorganized and sloppy, and got caught.'

Harry turned and gestured to the row of photographs on the whiteboard behind him.

'So I went a different way. I went looking for girls who were reported missing and never showed up again. Girls reported as runaways as well as possible abductions. Jessup is from Riverside County so I expanded the search to include Riverside and L.A. counties. Since Jessup was twenty-four when he was arrested I went back to when he was eighteen, putting the search limits from nineteen eighty to 'eighty-six. As far as victim profile, I went Caucasian aged twelve to eighteen.'

'Why did you go as old as eighteen?' McPherson asked. 'Our victim was twelve.'

'Rachel said—I mean, the profiler said that sometimes starting out, these people pick from their own peer group. They learn how to kill and then they start to define their targets according to their paraphilias. A paraphilia is—'

'I know what it is,' McPherson said. 'You did all of this work yourself? Or did this Rachel help you?'

'No, she just worked up the profile. I had some help from my partner pulling all of this together. But it was tough because not all the records are complete, especially on cases that never got above runaway status, and a lot was cleared out. Most of the runaway files from back then are gone.'

'They didn't digitize?' McPherson asked.

Bosch shook his head.

'Not in L.A. County. They prioritized when they switched over to computerized records and went back and captured records for major crimes. No runaway cases unless there was the possibility of abduction involved. Riverside County was different. Fewer cases out there so they archived everything digitally. Anyway, for that time period in these two counties, we came up with twenty-nine cases over the six-year period we're looking at. Again, these were unresolved cases. In each the girl disappeared and never came home. We pulled what records we could find and most didn't fit because of witness statements or other issues. But I couldn't rule out these eight.'

Bosch turned to the board and looked at the photos of eight smiling girls. All of them long gone over time.

'I'm not saying that Jessup had anything to do with any of these girls dropping off the face of the earth, but he could have. As Maggie already noticed, they all have a resemblance to one another and to Melissa Landy. And by the way, the resemblance extends to body type as well. They're all within ten pounds and two inches of one another and our victim.'

Bosch turned back to his audience and saw McPherson and Haller transfixed by the photographs.

'Beneath each photo I've put the particulars,' he said. 'Physical descriptors, date and location of disappearance, the basic stuff.'

'Did Jessup know any of them?' Haller asked. 'Is he connected in any way to any of them?'

That was the bottom line, Bosch knew.

'Nothing really solid—I mean, not that I've found so far,' he said. 'The best connection that we have is this girl.'

He turned and pointed to the first photo on the left.

'The first girl. Valerie Schlicter. She disappeared in nineteen eighty-one from the same neighborhood in Riverside that Jessup grew up in. He would've been nineteen and she was seventeen. They both went to Riverside High but because he dropped out early, it doesn't look like they were there at the same time. Anyway, she was counted as a runaway because there were problems in her home. It was a single-parent home. She lived with her mother and a brother and then one day about a month after graduating from high school, she split. The investigation never rose above a missing persons case, largely because of her age. She turned eighteen a month after she disappeared. In fact, I wouldn't even call it an investigation. They more or less waited to see if she'd come home. She didn't.'

'Nothing else?'

Bosch turned back and looked at Haller.

'So far that's it.'

'Then discovery is not an issue. There's nothing here. There's no connection between Jessup and any of these girls. The closest one you have is this Riverside girl and she was five years older than Melissa Landy. This whole thing seems like a stretch.'

Bosch thought he detected a note of relief in Haller's voice.

'Well,' he said, 'there's still another part to all of this.'

He stepped over to the case boxes at the end of the table and picked up a file. He walked it down and put it in front of McPherson.

213

'As you know, we've had Jessup under surveillance since he was released.'

McPherson opened the file and saw the stack of 8 × 10 surveillance shots of Jessup.

'With Jessup they've learned that there is no routine schedule, so they stick with him twenty-four/seven. And what they're documenting is that he has two remarkably different lives. The public one, which is carried in the media as his so-called journey to freedom. Everything from smiling for the cameras and eating hamburgers to surfing Venice Beach to the talk-show circuit.'

'Yes, we're well aware,' Haller said. 'And most of it orchestrated by his attorney.'

'And then there's the private side,' Bosch said. 'The bar crawls, the late-night cruising and the middle-of-the-night visits.'

'Visits where?' McPherson asked.

Bosch went to his last visual aid, a map of the Santa Monica Mountains. He unfolded it on the table in front of them.

'Nine different times since his release Jessup has left the apartment where he stays in Venice and in the middle of the night driven up to Mulholland on top of the mountains. From there he has visited one or two of the canyon parks up there per night. Franklin Canyon is his favorite. He's been there six times. But he also has hit Stone Canyon, Runyon Canyon and the overlook at Fryman Canyon a few times each.'

'What's he doing at these places?' McPherson asked.

'Well, first of all, these are public parks that are closed at dusk,' Bosch replied. 'So he's sneaking in. We're talking two, three o'clock in the morning. He goes in and he just sort of sits. He communes. He lit candles a couple times. Always the same spots in each of the parks. Usually on a trail or by a tree. We don't have photos because it's too dark and we can't risk getting in close. I've gone out with the SIS a couple times this week and watched. It looks like he just sort of meditates.'

Bosch circled the four parks on the map. Each was off Mulholland and close to the others.

'Have you talked to your profiler about all this?' Haller asked.

'Yeah, I did, and she was thinking what I was thinking. That he's visiting graves. Communing with the dead...his victims.'

'Oh, man...' Haller said.

'Yeah,' Bosch said.

There was a long pause as Haller and McPherson considered the implications of Bosch's investigation.

'Harry, has anybody done any digging in any of these spots?' McPherson asked.

'No, not yet. We didn't want to go too crazy with the shovels, because he keeps coming back. He'd know something was up and we don't want that yet.'

'Right. What about—'

'Cadaver dogs. Yeah, we brought them out there undercover yesterday. We—'

'How do you make a dog go undercover?' Haller asked.

Bosch started to laugh and it eased some of the tension in the room.

'What I mean is, there were two dogs and they weren't brought out in official vehicles and handled by people in uniforms. We tried to make it look like somebody walking their dog, but even that was a problem because the park doesn't allow dogs on these trails. Anyway, we did the best we could and got in and got out. I checked with SIS to make sure Jessup wasn't anywhere near Mulholland when we went in. He was surfing.'

'And?' McPherson asked impatiently.

'These dogs are the type that just lie down on the ground when they pick up the scent of human decay. Supposedly they can pick it up through the ground after even a hundred years. Anyway, at three of the four places Jessup's gone in these parks, the dogs didn't react. But at one spot one of the two dogs did.'

Bosch watched McPherson swivel in her seat and look at Haller. He looked back at her and there was some sort of silent communication there.

'It should also be noted that this particular dog has a history of being wrong—that is, giving a false positive—about a third of the time,' Bosch said. 'The other dog didn't react to the same spot.'

'Great,' Haller said. 'So what does that tell us?'

'Well, that's why I invited you over,' Bosch said. 'We've reached the point where maybe we should start digging. At least in that one spot. But if we do, we run the risk that Jessup will find out and he'll know we've been following him. And if we dig and we find human remains, do we have enough here to charge Jessup?'

McPherson leaned forward while Haller leaned back, clearly deferring to his second chair.

'Well, I see no legal embargo on digging,' she finally said. 'It's public property and there is nothing that would stop you legally. No need for a search warrant. But do you want to dig right now based on this one dog with what seems like a high false-positive rate, or do we wait until after the trial?'

'Or maybe even during the trial,' Haller said.

'The second question is the more difficult,' McPherson said. 'For the sake of argument, let's say there are remains buried in one or even all of those spots. Yes, Jessup's activities seem to form an awareness of what is below the earth in the places he visits in the middle of the night. But does that prove he's responsible? Hardly. We could charge him, yes, but he could mount a number of defenses based on what we know right now. You agree, Michael?'

Haller leaned forward and nodded.

'Suppose you dig and you find the remains of one of these girls. Even if you can confirm the ID—and that's going to be a big if—you still don't have any evidence connecting her death to Jessup. All you have is his guilty knowledge of the burial spot. That is very significant but is it enough to go into court with? I don't know. I think I'd rather be defense counsel than prosecutor on that one. I think Maggie's right, there are any number of defenses that he could employ to explain his knowledge of the burial sites. He could invent a straw man—

somebody else who did the killings and told him about them or forced him to take part in the burials. Jessup's spent twenty-four years in prison. How many other convicts has he been exposed to? Thousands? Tens of thousands? How many of them were murderers? He could lay this whole thing on one of them, say that he heard in prison about these burial spots and he decided to come and pray for the souls of the victims. He could make up anything.'

He shook his head again.

'The bottom line is, there are a lot of ways to go with a defense like this. Without any sort of physical evidence connecting him or a witness, I think you would have a problem.'

'Maybe there is physical evidence in the graves that connects him,' Bosch offered.

'Maybe, but what if there isn't?' Haller shot right back. 'You never know, you could also pull a confession out of Jessup. But I doubt that, too.'

McPherson took it from there.

'Michael mentioned the big if, the remains. Can they be IDed? Will we be able to establish how long they were in the ground? Remember, Jessup has an ironclad alibi for the last twenty-four years. If you pull up a set of bones and we can't say for sure that they've been down there since at least 'eighty-six, then Jessup would walk.'

Haller got up and went to the whiteboard, grabbing a marker off the ledge. In a clear spot he drew two circles side by side.

'Here's what we've got so far. One is our case and one is this whole new thing you've come up with. They're separate. We have the case with the trial about to go and then we have your new investigation. When they're separate like this we're fine. Your investigation has no bearing on our trial, so we can keep the two circles separate. Understand?'

'Sure,' Bosch said.

Haller grabbed the eraser off the ledge and wiped the two circles off the board. He then drew two new circles, but this time they overlapped.

'Now if you go out there and start digging and you find bones? This is what happens. Our two circles become connected. And that's when your thing becomes our thing and we have to reveal this to the defense and the whole wide world.'

McPherson nodded in agreement.

'So then, what do we do?' Bosch asked. 'Drop it?'

'No, we don't drop it,' Haller said. 'We just be careful and we keep them separate. You know what is universally held as the best trial strategy? Keep it simple, stupid. So let's not complicate things. Let's keep our circles separate and go to trial and get this guy for killing Melissa Landy. And when we're done that, we go up to Mulholland with shovels.'

'Done *with*.'

'What?'

'When we're done *with* that.'

'Whatever, Professor.'

Bosch's eyes moved from Haller's connected circles

on the board to the row of faces. All his instincts told him that at least some of those girls did not get any older than they were in the photos. They were in the ground and had been buried there by Jason Jessup. He hated the idea of them spending another day in the dirt but knew that they would have to wait a little longer.

'Okay,' he said. 'I'll keep working it on the side. For now. But there's also one other thing from the profiler that you should know.'

'The other shoe drops,' McPherson said. 'What?'

Haller had returned to his seat. Bosch pulled out a chair and sat down himself.

'She said a killer like Jessup doesn't reform in prison. The dark matter inside doesn't go away. It stays. It waits. It's like a cancer. And it reacts to outside pressures.'

'He'll kill again,' McPherson said.

Bosch slowly nodded.

'He can visit the graves of his past victims for only so long before he'll feel the need for . . . fresh inspiration. And if he feels under pressure, the chances are good he'll move in that direction even sooner.'

'Then we'd better be ready,' Haller said. 'I'm the guy who let him out. If you have any doubts about him being covered, then I want to hear them.'

'No doubts,' Bosch said. 'If Jessup makes a move, we'll be on him.'

'When are you planning on going out with the SIS again?' McPherson asked.

'Whenever I can. But I've got my daughter, so it's

whenever she's on a sleepover or I can get somebody to come in.'

'I want to go once.'

'Why?'

'I want to see the real Jessup. Not the one in the papers and on TV.'

'Well...'

'What?'

'Well, there are no women on the team and they're constantly moving with this guy. There won't be any bathroom breaks. They piss in bottles.'

'Don't worry, Harry, I think I can handle it.'

'Then I'll set it up.'

21

I checked my watch when I heard Maggie say hello to Lorna in the reception room. She entered the office and dropped her case on her desk. It was one of those slim and stylish Italian leather laptop totes that she never would have bought for herself. Too expensive and too red. I wanted to know who gave it to her like I wanted to know a lot of things she would never tell me.

But the origin of her red briefcase was the least of my worries. In thirteen days we would start picking jurors in the Jessup case and Clive Royce had finally landed his best pretrial punch. It was an inch thick and sat in front of me on my desk.

'Where have you been?' I said with a clear note of annoyance in my voice. 'I called your cell and got no answer.'

She came over to my desk, dragging the extra chair with her.

'More like, where were you?'

I glanced at my calendar blotter and saw nothing in the day's square.

'What are you talking about?'

'My phone was turned off because I was at Hayley's

222

honors assembly. They don't like cell phones ringing when they are calling the kids up to get their pins.'

'Ah, shit!'

She had told me and copied me on the e-mail. I printed it out and put it on the refrigerator. But not on my desk blotter or into my phone's calendar. I blew it.

'You should've been there, Haller. You would've been proud.'

'I know, I know. I messed up.'

'It's all right. You'll get other chances. To mess up or stand up.'

That hurt. It would've been better if she had chewed my ass out like she used to. But the passive-aggressive approach always got deeper under the skin. And she probably knew that.

'I'll be at the next one,' I said. 'That's a promise.'

She didn't sarcastically say *Sure, Haller,* or *I've heard that one before.* And somehow that made it worse. Instead, she just got down to business.

'What is that?'

She nodded at the document in front of me.

'This is Clive Royce's last best stand. It's a motion to exclude the testimony of Sarah Ann Gleason.'

'And of course he drops it off on a Friday afternoon three weeks before trial.'

'More like seventeen days.'

'My mistake. What's he say?'

I turned the document around and slid it across the desk to her. It was held together with a large black clip.

'He's been working on this one since the start because

223

he knows the case comes down to her. She's our primary witness and without her none of the other evidence matters. Even the hair in the truck is circumstantial. If he takes out Sarah he takes out our case.'

'I get that. But how's he trying to get rid of her?'

She started flipping through the pages.

'It was delivered at nine and is eighty-six pages long so I haven't had the time to completely digest it. But it's a two-pronged effort. He's attacking her original identification from when she was a kid. Says the setup was prejudicial. And he—'

'That was already argued, accepted by the trial court and it held up on appeal. He's wasting the court's time.'

'He's got a new angle this time. Remember, Kloster's got Alzheimer's and is no good as a witness. He can't tell us about the investigation and he can't defend himself. So this time out Royce alleges that Kloster told Sarah which man to identify. He pointed Jessup out for her.'

'And what is his backup? Supposedly only Sarah and Kloster were in the room.'

'I don't know. There's no backup but my guess is he's riffing on the radio call Kloster made telling them to make Jessup take off his hat.'

'It doesn't matter. The lineup was put together to see if Sarah could identify Derek Wilbern, the other driver. Any argument that he then told her to put the finger on Jessup is ridiculous. That ID came quite unexpectedly but naturally and convincingly. This is nothing to get worked up about. Even without Kloster we'll tear this one up.'

I knew she was right but the first attack wasn't really what I was most worried about.

'That's just his opening salvo,' I said. 'That's nothing compared with part two. He also seeks to exclude her entire testimony based on unreliable memory. He's got her whole drug history laid out in the motion, seemingly down to every chip of meth she ever smoked. He's got arrest records, jail records, witnesses who detail her consumption of drugs, multiple-partner sex and what they term her belief in out-of-body experiences—I guess she forgot to mention that part up in Port Townsend. And to top it all off, he's got experts on memory loss and false memory creation as a by-product of meth addiction. So in all, you know what he's got? He's got us fucked coming and going.'

Maggie didn't respond as she was scanning the summary pages at the end of Royce's motion.

'He's got investigators here and up in San Francisco,' I added. 'It's thorough and exhaustive, Mags. And you know what? It doesn't even look like he's gone up to Port Townsend to interview her yet. He says he doesn't have to because it doesn't matter what she says now. It can't be relied upon.'

'He'll have his experts and we'll have ours on rebuttal,' she said calmly. 'We expected this part and I've already been lining ours up. At worst, we can turn this into a wash. You know that.'

'The experts are only a small part of it.'

'We'll be fine,' she insisted. 'And look at these witnesses. Her ex-husbands and boyfriends. I see Royce conveniently didn't bother to include their own arrest records here. They're all tweakers themselves. We'll make them look like pimps and pedophiles with grudges against her because she left them in the dust when she got straight. She married the first one when she was eighteen and he was twenty-nine. She told us. I'd love to get him in the chair in front of the judge. I really think you are overreacting to this, Haller. We can argue this. We can make him put some of these so-called witnesses in front of the judge and we can knock every one of them out of the box. You're right about one thing, though. This is Royce's last best stand. It's just not going to be good enough.'

I shook my head. She was seeing only what was on paper and what could be blocked or parried with our own swords. Not what was not written.

'Look, this is about Sarah. He knows the judge is not going to want to chop our main witness. He knows we'll get by this. But he's putting the judge on notice that this is what he is going to put Sarah through if she takes the stand. Her whole life, every sordid detail, every pipe and dick she ever smoked, she's going to have to sit up there and take it. Then he'll trot out some PhD who'll put pictures of a melted brain on the screen and say this is what meth does. Do we want that for her? Is she strong enough to take it? Maybe we have to go to Royce, offer a deal for time served and some kind of payout from the city. Something everybody can live with.'

Maggie flopped the motion onto the desk.

'Are you kidding me? You're running scared because of this?'

'I'm not running scared. I'm being realistic. I didn't go up to Washington. I have no feel for this woman. I don't know if she can stand up to this or not. Besides, we can always take a second bite of the apple with those cases Bosch has been working.'

Maggie leaned back in her chair.

'There's no guarantee that anything will come out of those other cases. We have to put everything we have into this one, Haller. I could go back up there and hold Sarah's hand a little bit. Tell her more about what to expect. Get her ready. She already understood it wasn't going to be pretty.'

'To put it mildly.'

'I think she's strong enough. I think in some weird way she might need it. You know, get it all out there, expiate her sins. It's about redemption with her, Michael. You know about that.'

We held each other's eyes for a long moment.

'Anyway, I think she'll be more than strong and the jury will see it,' she said. 'She's a survivor and everybody likes a survivor.'

I nodded.

'You have a way of convincing people, Mags. It's a gift. We both know you should be lead on this, not me.'

'Thank you for saying that.'

'All right, go up there and get her prepped for this. Next week, maybe. By then we should have a witness schedule and you can tell her when we'll be bringing her down.'

'Okay,' she said.

'Meantime, how's your weekend looking? We have to put together an answer to this.'

I pointed at the defense motion on the desk.

'Well, Harry finally got me a ride-along with the SIS tomorrow night. He's going, too—I think his daughter has a sleepover. Other than that, I'm around.'

'Why are you going to spend all that time watching Jessup? The police have that covered.'

'Like I said before, I want to see Jessup out there when he doesn't think anyone is watching. I would suggest that you come, too, but you've got Hayley.'

'I wouldn't waste the time. But when you see Bosch, can you give him a copy of this motion? We're going to need him to run down some of these witnesses and statements. Not all of them were in Royce's discovery package.'

'Yeah, he played it smart. He keeps them off his witness list until they show up here. If the judge shoots down the motion, saying Gleason's credibility is a jury question, he'll come back with an amended witness list, saying, okay, I need to put these people in front of the jury in regard to credibility.'

'And she'll allow it or she'll be contradicting her own ruling. Clever Clive. He knows what he's doing.'

'Anyway, I'll get a copy to Harry, but I think he's still chasing those old cases.'

'Doesn't matter. The trial is the priority. We need complete backgrounds on these people. You want to deal with him or do you want me to?'

In our divvying up of pretrial duties I had given Maggie

the responsibility of prepping for defense witnesses. All except Jessup. If he testified, he was still mine.

'I'll talk to him,' she said.

She furrowed her brow. It was a habit I'd seen before.

'What?'

'Nothing. I'm just thinking about how to attack this. I think we throw in a motion *in limine,* seeking to limit Royce on the impeachable stuff. We argue that the events of her life in between are not relevant to credibility if her identification of Jessup now matches her identification back then.'

I shook my head.

'I would argue that you're infringing on my client's sixth amendment right to cross-examine his accuser. The judge might limit some of this stuff if it's repetitive, but don't count on her disallowing it.'

She pursed her lips as she recognized that I was right.

'It's still worth a try,' I said. 'Everything is worth a try. In fact, I want to drown Royce in paper. Let's hit him back with a phonebook to wade through.'

She looked at me and smiled.

'What?'

'I like it when you get all angry and righteous.'

'You haven't seen anything yet.'

She looked away before it went a step further.

'Where do you want to set up shop this weekend?' she asked. 'Remember, you have Hayley. She's not going to like it if we work the entire weekend.'

I had to think about that for a moment. Hayley loved museums. To the point that I was tired of going to the same museums over and over. She also loved movies. I would need to check and see if a new movie was out.

'Bring her to my house in the morning and be prepared to work on our response. We can maybe trade off. I'll take her to a movie or something in the afternoon and then you go on and do your thing with the SIS. We'll make it work.'

'Okay, that's a deal.'

'Or...'

'Or what?'

'You could bring her over tonight and we could have a little dinner celebrating our kid making second honors. And we might even get a little work on this done.'

'And I stay over, is that what you mean?'

'Sure, if you want.'

'You wish, Haller.'

'I do.'

'By the way, it was first honors. You better have it right when you see her tonight.'

I smiled.

'Tonight? You mean that?'

'I think so.'

'Then don't worry. I'll have everything right.'

22

Because Bosch had mentioned that a prosecutor wanted to join the SIS surveillance, Lieutenant Wright arranged his schedule to work Saturday night and be the driver of the car the visitors were assigned to. The pickup point was in Venice at a public parking lot six blocks off the beach. Bosch met McPherson there and then he put a radio call in to Wright, saying they were ready and waiting. Fifteen minutes later a white SUV entered the lot and drove up to them. Bosch gave McPherson the front seat and he climbed into the back. He wasn't being chivalrous. The long bench seat would allow him to stretch out during the long night of surveillance.

'Steve Wright,' the lieutenant said, offering McPherson his hand.

'Maggie McPherson. Thanks for letting me come along.'

'No sweat. We always like it when the District Attorney's Office takes an interest. Let's hope tonight is worth your while.'

'Where's Jessup now?'

'When I left he was at the Brig on Abbot Kinney. He

likes crowded places, which works in our favor. I have a couple guys inside and a few more on the street. We're kind of used to his rhythm now. He hits a place, waits to be recognized and for people to start buying him drinks, then he moves on—quickly if he isn't recognized.'

'I guess I'm more interested in his late-night travels than his drinking habits.'

'It's good that he's out drinking,' Bosch said from the backseat. 'There's a causal relationship. The nights he takes in alcohol are usually the nights he goes up to Mulholland.'

Wright nodded in agreement and headed the SUV out of the lot. He was a perfect surveillance man because he didn't look like a cop. In his late fifties with glasses, a thinning hairline and always two or three pens in his shirt pocket, he looked more like an accountant. But he had been with the SIS for more than two decades and had been in on several of the squad's kills. Every five years or so the *Times* did a story on the SIS, usually analyzing its kill record. In the last exposé Bosch remembered reading, the paper had labeled Wright 'SIS's unlikely chief gunslinger.' While the reporters and editors behind the story probably viewed that as an editorial putdown, Wright wore it like a badge of honor. He had the sobriquet printed below his name on his business card. In quotes, of course.

Wright drove down Abbot Kinney Boulevard and past the Brig, which was located in a two-story building on the east side of the street. He went two blocks down and made a U-turn. He came back up the street and pulled to the curb in front of a fire hydrant a half block from the bar.

The lighted sign outside the Brig depicted a boxer in a ring, his red gloves up and ready. It was an image that seemed at odds with the name of the bar, but Bosch knew the story behind it. As a much younger man he had lived in the neighborhood. He knew the sign with the boxer was put up by a former owner who had bought out the original owners. The new man was a retired fighter and had decorated the interior with a boxing motif. He also put the sign up out front. There was still a mural on the side of the building that depicted the fighter and his wife, but they were long gone now.

'This is Five,' Wright said. 'What's our status?'

He was talking to the microphone clipped to the sun visor over his head. Bosch knew there was a foot button on the floor that engaged it. The return speaker was under the dash. The radio setup in the cars allowed the surveillance cops to keep their hands free while driving and, more important, helped them maintain their cover. Talking into a handheld rover was a dead give-away. The SIS was too good for that.

'Three,' a voice said over the radio. 'Retro is still in the location along with One and Two.'

'Roger that,' Wright said.

'Retro?' McPherson said.

'Our name for him,' Wright said. 'Our freqs are pretty far down the bandwidth and on the FCC registry they're listed as DWP channels, but you never know who might be listening. We don't use the names of people or locations on the air.'

'Got it.'

It wasn't even nine yet. Bosch wasn't expecting Jessup to leave anytime soon, especially if people were buying him drinks. As they settled in, Wright seemed to like McPherson and liked informing her about procedures and the art of high-level surveillance. She might have been bored with it but she never let on.

'See, once we establish a subject's rhythms and routines we can react much better. Take this place, for example. The Brig is one of three or four places Retro hits sort of regularly. We've assigned different guys to different bars so they can go in while he's in the location and be like regulars. The two guys I've got right now in the Brig are the same two guys that always go in there. And two other guys would go into Townhouse when he's there and two others have James Beach. It goes like that. If Retro notices them he'll think it's because he's seen them in there before and they're regulars in the place. Now if he saw the same guy at two different places, he'd start getting suspicious.'

'I understand, Lieutenant. Sounds like the smart way to do it.'

'Call me Steve.'

'Okay, Steve. Can your people inside communicate?'

'Yes, but they're deaf.'

'Deaf?'

'We've all got body mikes. You know, like the Secret Service? But we don't put in the earpieces when we're in play inside a place like a bar. Too obvious. So they call in their positions when possible but they don't hear anything coming back unless they pull the receiver up from under their collar and put it in. Unfortunately, it's not like TV where they just put the bean in their ear and there's no wire.'

'I see. And do your men actually drink while in a bar on a surveillance?'

'A guy in a place like that ordering a Coke or a glass of water is going to stand out as suspicious. So they order booze. But then they nurse it. Luckily, Retro likes to go to crowded places. Makes it easier to maintain cover.'

While the small talk continued in the front seat, Bosch pulled his phone and started what some would consider a conversation of small talk himself. He texted his daughter. Though he knew there were several sets of eyes on the Brig and even inside on Jessup, he looked up and checked the door of the bar every few seconds.

Howzit going? Having fun?

Madeline was staying overnight at her friend Aurora Smith's house. It was only a few blocks from home but Bosch would not be nearby if she needed him. It was several minutes before she grudgingly answered the text. But they had a deal. She must answer his calls and texts, or her freedom—what she called her leash— would be shortened.

Everything's fine. You don't have to check on me.

And that was it. A child's shorthand in a shorthand relationship. Bosch knew he needed help. There was so much he didn't know. At times they seemed fine and everything appeared to be perfect. Other times he was sure she was going to sneak out the door and run away. Living with his daughter had resulted in his love for her growing more than he thought was possible. Thoughts of her safety as well as hopes for her happy future invaded his mind at all times. His longing to make her life better and take her far past her own history had at times become a physical ache in his chest. Still, he couldn't seem to reach across the aisle. The plane was bouncing and he kept missing.

He put his phone away and checked the front of the Brig again. There was a crowd of smokers standing outside. Just then a voice and the sharp crack of billiard balls colliding in the background came over the radio speaker.

'Coming out. Retro is coming out.'

'This seems early,' Wright said.

'Does he smoke?' McPherson asked. 'Maybe he's just—'

'Not that we've seen.'

Bosch kept his eyes on the door and soon it pushed open. A man he recognized even from a distance as Jessup stepped out and headed along the sidewalk. Abbot Kinney slashed in a northwesterly direction across Venice. He was heading that way.

'Where did he park?' Bosch asked.

'He didn't,' Wright said. 'He only lives a few blocks from here. He walked over.'

They watched in silence after that. Jessup walked two blocks on Abbot Kinney, passing a variety of restaurants, coffee shops and galleries. The sidewalk was busy. Almost every place was still open for Saturday-night business. He stepped into a coffee shop called Abbot's Habit. Wright got on the radio and assigned one of his men to enter it but before that could happen, Jessup stepped back out, coffee in hand, and proceeded on foot again.

Wright started the SUV and pulled into traffic going the opposite direction. He made a U-turn when he was two blocks further down and away from Jessup's view, should he happen to turn around. All the while he maintained constant radio contact with the other followers. Jessup had an invisible net around him. Even if he knew it was there he couldn't lose it.

'He's heading home,' a radio voice reported. 'Might be an early night.'

Abbot Kinney, named for the man who built Venice more than a century earlier, became Brooks Avenue, which then intersected with Main Street. Jessup crossed Main and headed down one of the walk streets where automobiles could not travel. Wright was ready for this and directed two of the tail cars over to Pacific Avenue so they could pick him up when he came through.

Wright pulled to a stop at Brooks and Main and waited for the report that Jessup had passed through and was on Pacific. After two minutes he started to get anxious and went to the radio.

'Where is he, people?'

There was no response. No one had Jessup. Wright quickly sent somebody in.

'Two, you go in. Use the twenty-three.'

'Got it.'

McPherson looked over the seatback at Bosch and then at Wright.

'The twenty-three?'

'We have a variety of tactics we use. We don't describe them on the air.'

He pointed through the windshield.

'That's the twenty-three.'

Bosch saw a man wearing a red windbreaker and carrying an insulated pizza bag cut across Main and into the walk street named Breeze Avenue. They waited and finally the radio burst to life.

'I'm not seeing him. I walked all the way through and he's not—'

The transmission cut off. Wright said nothing. They waited and then the same voice came back in a whisper.

'I almost walked into him. He came out between two houses. He was pulling up his zipper.'

'Okay, did he make you?' Wright asked.

'That's a negative. I asked for directions to Breeze Court and he said this was Breeze Avenue. We're cool. He should be coming through now.'

'This is Four. We got him. He's heading toward San Juan.'

The fourth car was one of the vehicles Wright had put on Pacific. Jessup was living in an apartment on San Juan Avenue between Speedway and the beach.

Bosch felt the momentary tension in his gut start to ease. Surveillance work was sometimes tough to take. Jessup had ducked between two houses to take a leak and it had caused a near panic.

Wright redirected the teams to the area around San Juan Avenue between Pacific and Speedway. Jessup used a key to enter the second-floor apartment where he was staying and the teams quickly moved into place. It was time to wait again.

Bosch knew from past surveillance gigs that the main attribute a good watcher needed was a comfort with silence. Some people are compelled to fill the void. Harry never was and he doubted anyone in the SIS was. He was curious to see how McPherson would do, now that the surveillance 101 lesson from Wright was over and there was nothing left but to wait and watch.

Bosch pulled his phone to see if he had missed a text from his daughter but it was clear. He decided not to pester her with another check-in and put the phone away. The genius of his giving McPherson the front seat now came into play. He turned and put his legs up and across the seat, stretching himself into a lounging position with his back against the door. McPherson glanced back and smiled in the darkness of the car.

'I thought you were being a gentleman,' she said. 'You just wanted to stretch out.'

Bosch smiled.

'You got me.'

Everyone was silent after that. Bosch thought about what McPherson had said while they had waited in the parking lot to be picked up by Wright. First she handed him a copy of the latest defense motion, which he locked in the trunk of his car. She told him he needed to start vetting the witnesses and their statements, looking for ways to turn their threats to the case into advantages for the prosecution. She said she and Haller had worked all day crafting a response to the attempt to disqualify Sarah Ann Gleason from testifying. The judge's ruling on the issue could decide the outcome of the trial.

It always bothered Bosch when he saw justice and the law being manipulated by smart lawyers. His part in the process was pure. He started at a crime scene and followed the evidence to a killer. There were rules along the way but at least the route was clear most of the time. But once things moved into the courthouse, they took on a different shape. Lawyers argued over inter-pretations and theories and procedures. Nothing seemed to move in a straight line. Justice became a labyrinth.

How could it be, he wondered, that an eyewitness to a horrible crime would not be allowed to testify in court against the accused? He had been a cop more than thirty-five years and he still could not explain how the system worked.

'This is Three. Retro's on the move.'

Bosch was jarred out of his thoughts. A few seconds went by and the next report came from another voice.

'He's driving.'

Wright took over.

'Okay, we get ready for an auto tail. One, get out to Main and Rose, Two, go down to Pacific and Venice. Everybody else, sit tight until we have his direction.'

A few minutes later they had their answer.

'North on Main. Same as usual.'

Wright redirected his units and the carefully orchestrated mobile surveillance began moving with Jessup as he took Main Street to Pico and then made his way to the entrance of the 10 Freeway.

Jessup headed east and then merged onto the northbound 405, which was crowded with cars even at the late hour. As expected, he was heading toward the Santa Monica Mountains. The surveillance vehicles ranged from Wright's SUV to a black Mercedes convertible to a Volvo station wagon with two bikes on a rear rack to a pair of generic Japanese sedans. The only thing missing for a surveillance in the Hollywood Hills was a hybrid. The teams employed a surveillance procedure called the *floating box*. Two outriders on either side of the target car, another car up front and one behind, all moving in a choreographed rotation. Wright's SUV was the floater, running backup behind the box.

The whole way Jessup stayed at or below the speed limit. As the freeway rose to the crest of the mountains Bosch looked out his window and saw the Getty Museum rising in the mist at the top like a castle, the sky black behind it.

Anticipating that Jessup was heading to his usual

destinations on Mulholland Drive, Wright told two teams to break off from the box and move ahead. He wanted them already up and on Mulholland ahead of Jessup. He wanted a ground team with night vision goggles in Franklin Canyon Park before Jessup went in.

True to form, Jessup took the Mulholland exit and was soon heading east on the winding, two-lane snake that runs the spine of the mountain chain. Wright explained that this was when the surveillance was most vulnerable to exposure.

'You need a bee to properly do this up here but that's not in the budget,' he said.

'A bee?' McPherson asked.

'Part of our code. Means helicopter. We could sure use one.'

The first surprise of the night came five minutes later when Jessup drove by Franklin Canyon Park without stopping. Wright quickly recalled his ground team from the park as Jessup continued east.

Jessup passed Coldwater Canyon Boulevard without slowing and next drove by the overlook above Fryman Canyon. When he passed through the intersection of Mulholland and Laurel Canyon Boulevard he was taking the surveillance team into new territory.

'What are the chances he's made us?' Bosch asked.

'None,' Wright said. 'We're too good. He's got something new on his mind.'

For the next ten minutes the follow continued east toward the Cahuenga Pass. The command car was well behind the surveillance, and Wright and his two passengers had to rely on radio reports to know what was happening.

One car was moving in front of Jessup while all the rest were behind. The rear cars followed a continual rotation of turning off and moving up so the headlight configurations would keep changing in Jessup's rearview. Finally, a radio report came in that made Bosch move forward in his seat, as if closer proximity to the source of the information would make things clearer.

'There's a stop sign up here and Retro turned north. It's too dark to see the street sign but I had to stay on Mulholland. Too risky. Next up turn left at the stop.'

'Roger that. We got the left.'

'Wait!' Bosch said urgently. 'Tell him to wait.'

Wright checked him in the mirror.

'What do you have in mind?' he asked.

'There's only one stop on Mulholland. Woodrow Wilson Drive. I know it. It winds down and reconnects with Mulholland at the light down at Highland. The lead car can pick him up there. But Woodrow Wilson is too tight. If you send a car down there he may know he's being followed.'

'You sure?'

'I'm sure. I live on Woodrow Wilson.'

Wright thought for a moment and then went on the radio.

'Cancel that left. Where's the Volvo?'

'We're holding up until further command.'

'Okay, go on up and make the left on the two wheelers. Watch for oncoming. And watch for our guy.'

'Roger that.'

Soon Wright's SUV got to the intersection. Bosch saw the Volvo pulled off to the side. The bike rack was empty. Wright pulled over to wait, checking the teams on the radio.

'One, are you in position?'

'That's a roger. We're at the light at the bottom. No sign of Retro yet.'

'Three, you up?'

There was no response.

'Okay, everybody hold till we hear.'

'What do you mean?' Bosch asked. 'What about the bikes?'

'They must've gone down deaf. We'll hear when they—'

'This is Three,' a voice said in a whisper. 'We came up on him. He'd closed his eyes and went to sleep.'

Wright translated for his passengers.

'He killed his lights and stopped moving.'

Bosch felt his chest start to tighten.

'Are they sure he's in the car?'

Wright communicated the question over the radio.

'Yeah, we can see him. He's got a candle burning on the dashboard.'

'Where exactly are you, Three?'

'About halfway down. We can hear the freeway.'

Bosch leaned all the way forward between the two front seats.

'Ask him if he can pick a number off the curb,' he said. 'Get me an address.'

Wright relayed the request and almost a minute went by before the whisper came back.

'It's too dark to see the curbs here without using a flash. But we got a light next to the door of the house he's parked in front of. It's one of those cantilever jobs hanging its ass out over the pass. From here it looks like seventy-two-oh-three.'

Bosch slid back and leaned heavily against the seat. McPherson turned to look at him. Wright used the mirror to look back.

'You know that address?' Wright asked.

Bosch nodded in the darkness.

'Yeah,' he said. 'It's my house.'

23

My daughter liked to sleep in on Sundays. Normally I hated losing the time with her. I only had her every other weekend and Wednesdays. But this Sunday was different. I was happy to let her sleep while I got up early to go back to work on the motion to save my chief witness's testimony. I was in the kitchen pouring the first cup of coffee of the day when I heard knocking on my front door. It was still dark out. I checked the peep before opening it and was relieved to see it was my ex-wife with Harry Bosch standing right behind her.

But that relief was short-lived. The moment I turned the knob they pushed in and I could immediately feel a bad energy enter with them.

'We've got a problem,' Maggie said.

'What's wrong?' I asked.

'What's wrong is that Jessup camped outside my house this morning,' Bosch said. 'And I want to know how he found it and what the hell he's doing.'

He came up too close to me when he said it. I didn't know which was worse, his breath or the accusatory tone of his words. I wasn't sure what he was thinking but I realized all the bad energy was coming from him.

I stepped back from him.

'Hayley's still asleep. Let me just go close her bed-room door. There's fresh decaf in the kitchen and I can brew some fully leaded if you need it.'

I went down the hall and checked on my daughter. She was still down. I closed the door and hoped the voices that were bound to get loud would not wake her.

My two visitors were still standing when I got back to the living room. Neither had gone for coffee. Bosch was silhouetted by the big picture window that looked out upon the city—the view that made me buy the house. I could see streaks of light entering the sky behind his shoulders.

'No coffee?'

They just stared at me.

'Okay, let's sit down and talk about this.'

I gestured toward the couch and chairs but Bosch seemed frozen in his stance.

'Come on, let's figure it out.'

I walked past them and sat down in the chair by the window. Finally, Bosch started to move. He sat down on the couch next to Hayley's school backpack. Maggie took the other chair. She spoke first.

'I've been trying to convince Harry that we didn't put his home address on the witness list.'

'Absolutely not. We gave no personal addresses in discovery. For you, I listed two addresses. Your office and mine. I even gave the general number for the PAB.

Didn't even give a direct line.'

'Then how did he find my house?' Bosch asked, the accusatory tone still in his voice.

'Look, Harry, you're blaming me for something I had nothing to do with. I don't know how he found your house but it couldn't have been that hard. I mean, come on. Anybody can find anybody on the Internet. You own your house, right? You pay property taxes, have utility accounts, and I bet you're even registered to vote—Republican, I'm sure.'

'Independent.'

'Fine. The point is, people can find you if they want. Added to that, you have a singular name. All anybody would have to do is punch in—'

'You gave them my full name?'

'I had to. It's what's required and what's been given in discovery for every trial you've ever testified in. It doesn't matter. All Jessup needed was access to the Internet and he could've—'

'Jessup's been in prison for twenty-four years. He knows less about the Internet than I do. He had to have help and I'm betting it came from Royce.'

'Look, we don't know that.'

Bosch looked pointedly at me, a darkness crossing his eyes.

'You're defending *him* now?'

'No, I'm not defending anybody. I'm just saying we shouldn't rush to any conclusions here. Jessup's got a roommate and is a minor celebrity. Celebrities get people to do things for them, okay? So why don't you calm down and let's back up a little bit. Tell me what happened at your house.'

Bosch seemed to take it down a notch but he was still anything but calm. I half expected him to get up and take a swing at a lamp or punch a hole in a wall. Thankfully, Maggie was the one who told the story.

'We were with the SIS, watching him. We thought he was going to go up to one of the parks he's been visiting. Instead, he drove right by them all and kept going on Mulholland. When we got to Harry's street we had to hang back so he wouldn't see us. The SIS has a bike car. Two of them saddled up and rode down. They found Jessup sitting in his car in front of Harry's house.'

'Goddamn it!' Bosch said. 'I have my daughter living with me. If this prick is—'

'Harry, not so loud and watch what you say,' I said. 'My daughter's on the other side of that wall. Now, please, go back to the story. What did Jessup do?'

Bosch hesitated. Maggie didn't.

'He just sat there,' Maggie said. 'For about a half hour. And he lit a candle.'

'A candle? In the car?'

'Yeah, on the dashboard.'

'What the hell does that mean?'

'Who knows?'

Bosch couldn't remain sitting. He jumped up from the couch and started pacing.

'And after a half hour he drove off and went home,' Maggie said. 'That was it. We just came from Venice.'

Now I stood up and started to pace, but in a pattern clear of Bosch's orbit.

'Okay, let's think about this. Let's think about what he was doing.'

'No shit, Sherlock,' Bosch said. 'That's the question.'

I nodded. I had that coming.

'Is there any reason to think that he knows or suspects he's being followed?' I asked.

'No, no way,' Bosch said immediately.

'Wait a minute, not so fast on that,' Maggie said. 'I've been thinking about it. There was a near-miss earlier in the night. You remember, Harry? On Breeze Avenue?'

Bosch nodded. Maggie explained it to me.

'They thought they lost him on a walk street in Venice. The lieutenant sent a guy in with a pizza box. Jessup came out from between two houses after taking a leak. It was a close call.'

I spread my hands.

'Well, maybe that was it. Maybe that planted suspicion and he decided to see if he was being followed. You show up outside the lead investigator's house and it's a good way to draw out the flies if you've got them on you.'

'You mean like a test?' Bosch asked.

'Exactly. Nobody approached him out there, right?'

'No, we left him alone,' Maggie said. 'If he had gotten out of his car I think it would've been a different story.'

I nodded.

'Okay, so it was either a test or he's got something planned. In that case, it would've been a reconnaissance mission. He wanted to see where you live.'

Bosch stopped and stared out the window. The sky was fully lit now.

'But one thing you have to keep in mind is that what he did was not illegal,' I said. 'It's a public street and the OR put no restrictions on travel within Los Angeles County. So no matter what he was up to, it's a good thing you didn't stop him and reveal yourself.'

Bosch stayed at the window, his back to us. I didn't know what he was thinking.

'Harry,' I said. 'I know your concerns and I agree with them. But we can't let this be a distraction. The trial is coming up quick and we have work to do. If we convict this guy, he goes away forever and it won't matter if he knows where you live.'

'So what do I do till then, sit on my front porch every night with a shotgun?'

'The SIS is on him twenty-four/seven, right?' Maggie said. 'Do you trust them?'

Bosch didn't answer for a long moment.

'They won't lose him,' he finally said.

Maggie looked at me and I could see the concern in her eyes. Each of us had a daughter. It would be hard to put your trust in anybody else, even an elite surveillance squad. I thought for a moment about something I had been considering since the conversation began.

'What about you moving in here? With your daughter. She can use Hayley's room because Hayley's going back to her mother's today. And you can use the office. It's got a sleeper sofa that I've spent more than a few nights on. It's actually comfortable.'

Bosch turned from the window and looked at me.

'What, stay here through the whole trial?'

'Why not? Our daughters will finally get a chance to meet when Hayley comes over.'

'It's a good idea,' Maggie said.

I didn't know if she was referring to the daughters meeting or the idea of Bosch and child staying with me.

'And look, I'm here every night,' I said. 'If you have to go out with the SIS, I got you covered with your daughter, especially when Hayley's here.'

Bosch thought about it for a few moments but then shook his head.

'I can't do that,' he said.

'Why not?' I asked.

'Because it's my house. My home. I'm not going to run from this guy. He's going to run from me.'

'What about your daughter?' Maggie asked.

'I'll take care of my daughter.'

'Harry, think about it,' she said. 'Think about your daughter. You don't want her in harm's way.'

'Look, if Jessup has my address, then he probably has this address, too. Moving in here isn't the answer. It's just...just running from him. Maybe that's his test—to see what I do. So I'm not doing anything. I'm not moving. I've got the SIS, and if he comes back and so much as crosses the curb out front, I'll be waiting for him.'

'I don't like this,' Maggie said.

I thought about what Bosch had said about Jessup having my address.

'Neither do I,' I said.

24

Bosch didn't need to be in court. In fact, he wouldn't be needed until after jury selection and the actual trial began. But he wanted to get a close look at the man he had been shadowing from a distance with the SIS. He wanted to see if Jessup would show any reaction to seeing him in return. It had been a month and a half since they had spent the long day in the car driving down from San Quentin. Bosch felt the need to get closer than the surveillance allowed him to. It would help him keep the fire burning.

It was billed as a status conference. The judge wanted to deal with all final motions and issues before beginning jury selection the next day and then moving seamlessly into the trial. There were scheduling and jury issues to discuss and each side's list of exhibits were to be handed in as well.

The prosecution team was locked and loaded. In the last two weeks Haller and McPherson had sharpened and streamlined the case, run through mock witness examinations and reconsidered every piece of evidence. They had carefully choreographed the ways in which they would bring the twenty-four-year-old evidence forward. They were ready. The bow had been pulled taut and the arrow was ready to fly.

Even the decision on the death penalty had been made—or rather, announced. Haller had officially withdrawn it, even though Bosch assumed all along that his use of it to threaten Jessup had merely been a pose. He was a defense attorney by nature, and there was no getting him across that line. A conviction on the charges would bring Jessup a sentence of life in prison without the possibility of parole, and that would have to be enough justice for Melissa Landy.

Bosch was ready as well. He had diligently reinvestigated the case and located the witnesses who would be called to testify. All the while, he was still out riding with the SIS as often as possible—nights that his daughter stayed at the homes of friends or with Sue Bambrough, the assistant principal. He was prepared for his part and had helped Haller and McPherson get ready for theirs. Confidence was high and that was another reason for Bosch to be in the courtroom. He wanted to see this thing get started.

Judge Breitman entered and the courtroom was brought to order at a few minutes after nine. Bosch was in a chair against the railing directly behind the prosecution table where Haller and McPherson sat side by side. They had told him to pull the chair up to the table but Harry wanted to hang back. He wanted to be able to watch Jessup from behind, and besides, there was too much anxiety coming from the two prosecutors. The judge was going to make a ruling on whether Sarah

Ann Gleason would be allowed to testify against Jessup. As Haller had said the night before, nothing else mattered. If they lost Sarah as a witness, they would surely lose the case.

'On the record with *California versus Jessup* again,' the judge said upon taking the bench. 'Good morning to all.'

After a chorus of good mornings fired back to her, the judge got right down to business.

'Tomorrow we begin jury selection in this case and then we proceed to trial. Therefore today is the day that we're going to clean out the garage, so to speak, so that we can finally bring the car in. Any last motions, any pending motions, anything anybody wants to talk about in regard to exhibits or evidence or anything else, now is the time. We have a number of motions pending and I will get to them first. The prosecution's request to redress the issue of the defendant's use of makeup to cover certain body tattoos is dismissed. We argued that at length already and I do not see the need to go at it further.'

Bosch checked Jessup. He was at a sharp angle to him, so he could not see the defendant's face. But he did see Jessup nod his head in approval of the judge's first ruling of the day.

Breitman then went through a housekeeping list of minor motions from both sides. She seemed to want to accommodate all so neither side emerged as a clear favorite. Bosch saw that McPherson was meticulously keeping notes on each decision on a yellow legal pad.

It was all part of the buildup to the ruling of the day. Since Sarah was to be McPherson's witness to question during trial, she had handled the oral arguments on the defense motion two days earlier. Though Bosch had not attended that hearing, Haller had told him that Maggie had held forth for nearly an hour in a well-prepared response to the motion to disqualify. She had then backed it with an eighteen-page written response. The prosecution team was confident in the argument but neither member of the team knew Breitman well enough to be confident in how she would rule.

'Now,' the judge said, 'we come to the defense motion to disqualify Sarah Ann Gleason as a witness for the prosecution. The question has been argued and submitted by both sides and the court is ready to make a ruling.'

'Your Honor, could I be heard?' Royce said, standing up at the defense table.

'Mr. Royce,' the judge said, 'I don't see the need for further argument. You made the motion and I allowed you to respond to the prosecution's submission. What more needs to be said?'

'Yes, Your Honor.'

Royce sat back down, leaving whatever he was going to add to his attack on Sarah Gleason a secret.

'The defense's motion is dismissed,' the judge said immediately. 'I will be allowing the defense wide latitude in its examination of the prosecution's witness as well as in the production of its own witnesses to address Ms. Gleason's credibility before the jury. But I believe that this witness's credibility and reliability is indeed something that jurors will need to decide.'

A momentary silence enveloped the courtroom, as if everyone collectively had drawn in a breath. No response followed from either the prosecution or defense table. It was another down-the-middle ruling, Bosch knew, and both sides were probably pleased to have gotten something. Gleason would be allowed to testify, so the prosecution's case was secured, but the judge was going to let Royce go after her with all he had. It would come down to whether Sarah was strong enough to take it.

'Now, I would like to move on,' the judge said. 'Let's talk about jury selection and scheduling first, and then we'll get to the exhibits.'

The judge proceeded to outline how she wanted voir dire to proceed. Though each side would be allowed to question prospective jurors, she said she would strictly limit the time for each side. She wanted to start a momentum that would carry into the trial. She also limited each side to only twelve peremptory challenges—juror rejections without cause—and said she wanted to pick six alternates because it was her practice to be quick with the hook on jurors who misbehaved, were chronically late or had the audacity to fall asleep during testimony.

'I like a good supply of alternates because we usually need them,' she said.

The low number of peremptory challenges and the high number of alternates brought objections from both the prosecution and the defense. The judge grudgingly gave each side two more challenges but warned that she would not allow voir dire to get bogged down.

'I want jury selection completed by the end of the day Friday. If you slow me down, then I will slow you down. I will hold the panel and every lawyer in here until Friday night if I have to. I want opening statements first thing Monday. Any objection to that?'

Both sides seemed properly cowed by the judge. She was clearly exerting command of her own courtroom. She next outlined the trial schedule, stating that testimony would begin each morning at nine sharp and continue until five with a ninety-minute lunch and morning and afternoon breaks of fifteen minutes each.

'That leaves a solid six hours a day of testimony,' she said. 'Any more and I find the jurors start losing interest. So I keep it to six a day. It will be up to you to be in here and ready to go each morning when I step through the door at nine. Any questions?'

There were none. Breitman then asked each side for estimates on how long their case would take to present. Haller said he would need no more than four days, depending on the length of the cross-examinations of his witnesses. This was already a shot directed at Royce and his plans to attack Sarah Ann Gleason.

For his part, Royce said he needed only two days. The judge then did her own math, adding four and two and coming up with five.

'Well, I'm thinking an hour each for opening statements on Monday morning. I think that means we'll finish Friday afternoon and go right to closing arguments the following Monday.'

Neither side objected to her math. The point was clear. Keep it moving. Find ways to cut time. Of course a trial was a fluid thing and there were many unknowns. Neither side would be held to what was said at this hearing, but each lawyer knew that there might be consequences from the judge if they didn't keep a continuous velocity to their presentations.

'Finally, we come to exhibits and electronics,' Breitman said. 'I trust that everyone has looked over each other's lists. Any objections to these?'

Both Haller and Royce stood up. The judge nodded at Royce.

'You first, Mr. Royce.'

'Yes, Judge, the defense has an objection to the prosecution's plans to project numerous images of Melissa Landy's body on the courtroom's overhead screens. This practice is not only barbaric but exploitative and prejudicial.'

The judge swiveled in her seat and looked at Haller, who was still standing.

'Your Honor, it is the prosecution's duty to produce the body. To show the crime that brings us here. The last thing we want to do is be exploitative or prejudicial. I will grant Mr. Royce that it is a fine line, but we do not plan to step across it.'

Royce came back with one more shot.

'This case is twenty-four years old. In nineteen eighty-six there were no overhead screens, none of this Hollywood stuff. I think it infringes on my client's right to a fair trial.'

Haller was ready with his own comeback.

'The age of the case has nothing to do with this issue, but the defense is perfectly willing to present these exhibits the way they would've—'

McPherson had grabbed his sleeve to interrupt him. He bent down and she whispered in his ear. He then quickly straightened up.

'Excuse me, Your Honor, I misspoke. The *prosecution* is more than willing to present these exhibits in the manner they would have been presented to the jury in nineteen eighty-six. We would be happy to hand out color photographs to the jurors. But in earlier conversation the court indicated that she did not like this practice.'

'Yes, I find handing these sorts of photos directly to the jurors to be possibly more exploitative and prejudicial,' Breitman said. 'Is that what you wish, Mr. Royce?'

Royce had walked himself into a jam.

'No, Judge, I would agree with the court on this point. The defense was simply trying to limit the scope and use of these photographs. Mr. Haller lists more than thirty photographs that he wants to put on the big screen. It seems over-the-top. That is all.'

'Judge Breitman, these are photographs of the body in the place it was found as well as during autopsy. Each one is—'

'Mr. Haller,' the judge intoned, 'let me just stop you right there. Crime scene photographs are acceptable, as long as they come with appropriate foundation and testimony. But I see no need to show our jurors this poor girl's autopsy shots. We're not going to do that.'

'Yes, Your Honor,' Haller said.

He remained standing while Royce sat down with his partial victory. Breitman spoke while writing something.

'And you have an objection to Mr. Royce's exhibit list, Mr. Haller?'

'Yes, Your Honor, the defense has a variety of drug paraphernalia alleged to have once been owned by Ms. Gleason on its exhibit list. It also lists photos and videos of Ms. Gleason. The prosecution has not been given the opportunity to examine these materials but we believe they only go to the point that we will be conceding at trial and eliciting in direct examination of this witness. That is that at one time in her life she used drugs on a regular basis. We do not see the need to show photos of her using drugs or the pipes through which she ingested drugs. It's inflammatory and pre-judicial. It is not needed based on the concessions of the prosecution.'

Royce stood back up and was ready to go. The judge gave him the floor.

'Judge, these exhibits are vitally important to the defense case. The prosecution of Mr. Jessup hinges on the testimony of a longtime drug addict who cannot be relied upon to remember the truth, let alone tell it. These exhibits will help the jury understand the depth and breadth of this witness's use of illegal substances over a lengthy period of time.'

Royce was finished but the judge was silent as she studied the defense exhibit list.

'All right,' she finally said, putting the document aside. 'You both make cogent arguments. So what we are going to do is take these exhibits one at a time. When the defense would like to proffer an exhibit, we will discuss it first out of earshot of the jury. I'll make a decision then.'

The lawyers sat down. Bosch almost shook his head but didn't want to draw the judge's attention. Still, it burned him that she had not slapped the defense down on this one. Twenty-four years after seeing her little sister abducted from the front yard, Sarah Ann Gleason was willing to testify about the awful, nightmarish moment that had changed her life forever. And for her sacrifice and efforts, the judge was actually going to entertain the defense's request to attack her with the glass pipes and accoutrements she had once used to escape what she had been through. It didn't seem fair to Bosch. It didn't seem like anything that approached justice.

The hearing ended soon after that and all parties packed their briefcases and moved through the doors of the courtroom en masse. Bosch hung back and then insinuated himself into the group right behind Jessup. He said nothing but Jessup soon enough felt the presence behind him and turned around.

He smirked when he saw it was Bosch.

'Well, Detective Bosch, are you following me?'

'Should I be?'

'Oh, you never know. How's your investigation going?'

'You'll find out soon enough.'

'Yes, I can't—'

'Don't talk to him!'

It was Royce. He had turned and noticed.

'And don't *you* talk to him,' he added, pointing a finger at Bosch. 'If you continue to harass him, I'll complain to the judge.'

Bosch held his hands out in a no-touching gesture.

'We're cool, Counselor. Just making small talk.'

'There is no such thing when it comes to the police.'

He reached out and put his hand on Jessup's shoulder and shepherded him away from Bosch.

In the hallway outside they moved directly to the waiting huddle of reporters and cameras. Bosch moved past but looked back in time to see Jessup's face change. His eyes went from the steely glare of a predator to the wounded look of a victim.

The reporters quickly gathered around him.

PART THREE
–To Seek a True and Just Verdict

25

I watched the jury file in and take their assigned seats in the box. I watched them closely, keying on their eyes mostly. Checking for how they looked at the defendant. You can learn a lot from that; a furtive glance or a strong judgmental stare.

Jury selection had gone as scheduled. We went through the first panel of ninety prospective jurors in a day but had sat only eleven after most were eliminated because of their media knowledge of the case. The second panel was just as difficult to choose from and it wasn't until Friday evening at five-forty that we had our final eighteen.

I had my jury chart in front of me, and my eyes were jumping between the faces in the box and the names on my Post-its, trying to memorize who was who. I already had a good handle on most of them but I wanted the names to become second nature to me. I wanted to be able to look at them and address them as if they were friends and neighbors.

The judge was on the bench and ready to go at nine sharp. She first asked the attorneys if there was any new or unfinished business to address. Upon learning there was not, she called in the jurors.

'Okay, we are all here,' she said. 'I want to thank all of the jurors and other parties for being on time. We begin the trial with opening statements from the attorneys. These are not to be construed as evidence but merely—'

The judge stopped, her eyes fixed on the back row of the jury box. A woman had timidly raised her hand. The judge stared for a long moment and then checked her own seating chart before responding.

'Ms. Tucci? Do you have a question?'

I checked my chart. Number ten, Carla Tucci. She was one of the jurors I had not yet committed to memory. A mousy brunette from East Hollywood. She was thirty-two years old, unmarried and she worked as a receptionist at a medical clinic. According to my color-coded chart, I had her down as a juror who could be swayed by stronger personalities on the panel. This was not a bad thing. It just depended on whether those personalities were for a guilty verdict or not.

'I think I saw something I wasn't supposed to see,' she said in a frightened voice.

Judge Breitman hung her head for a moment and I knew why. She couldn't get the wheels out of the mud. We were ready to go and now the trial would be delayed before opening statements were even in the record.

'Okay, let's try to take care of this quickly. I want the jury to stay in place. Everyone else stay in place and Ms. Tucci and the attorneys and I will go quickly back to chambers to find out what this is about.'

As we got up I checked my jury chart. There were six alternates. I had three of them pegged as pro-prosecution, two in the middle and one siding with the defense. If Tucci was ejected for whatever misconduct she was about to reveal, her replacement would be chosen randomly from the alternates. This meant that I had a better-than-even chance of seeing her replaced with a juror who was partial to the prosecution and only a one in six chance of getting a juror who was pro-defense. As I followed the entourage into chambers I decided that I liked my chances and I would do what I could to have Tucci ejected from the panel.

In chambers, the judge didn't even go behind her desk, perhaps hoping this was only going to be a minor question and delay. We stood in a group in the middle of her office. All except the court reporter, who sat on the edge of a side chair so she could type.

'Okay, on the record,' the judge said. 'Ms. Tucci, please tell us what you saw and what is bothering you.'

The juror looked down at the ground and held her hands in front of her.

'I was riding on the Metro this morning and the man sitting across from me was reading the newspaper. He was holding it up and I saw the front page. I didn't mean to look but I saw a photo of the man on trial and I saw the headline.'

The judge nodded.

'You are talking about Jason Jessup, correct?'

'Yes.'

'What newspaper?'

'I think it was the *Times*.'

'What did the headline say, Ms. Tucci?'

'New trial, old evidence for Jessup.'

I hadn't seen the actual *L.A. Times* that morning but had read the story online. Citing an unnamed source close to the prosecution, the story said the case against Jason Jessup was expected to be comprised entirely of evidence from the first trial and leaning heavily on the identification provided by the victim's sister. Kate Salters had the byline on it.

'Did you read the story, Ms. Tucci?' Breitman asked.

'No, Judge, I just saw it for a second and when I saw his picture I looked away. You told us not to read anything about the case. It just kind of popped up in front of me.'

The judge nodded thoughtfully.

'Okay, Ms. Tucci, can you step back into the hallway for a moment?'

The juror stepped out and the judge closed the door.

'The headline tells the story, doesn't it?' she said.

She looked at Royce and then me, seeing if either of us was going to make a motion or a suggestion. Royce said nothing. My guess was that he had juror number ten pegged the same way that I did. But he might not have considered the leanings of the six alternates.

'I think the damage is done here, Judge,' I said. 'She knows there was a previous trial. Anybody with any basic knowledge of the court system knows they don't retry you if you get a not-guilty. So she'll know Jessup went down on a guilty before. As much as that prejudices things in the prosecution's favor, I think to be fair she has to go.'

Breitman nodded.

'Mr. Royce?'

'I would agree with Mr. Haller's assessment of the prejudice, not his so-called desire to be fair. He simply wants her off the jury and one of those churchgoing alternates on it.'

I smiled and shook my head.

'I won't dignify that with a response. You don't want to kick her off, that's fine with me.'

'But it's not counsel's choice,' the judge said.

She opened the door and invited the juror back in.

'Ms. Tucci, thank you for your honesty. You can go back to the jury room and gather your things. You are dismissed and can report back to the juror assembly room to check with them.'

Tucci hesitated.

'Does that mean—?'

'Yes, unfortunately, you are dismissed. That headline gives you knowledge of the case you should not have. For you to know that Mr. Jessup was previously tried for these crimes is prejudicial. Therefore, I cannot keep you on the jury. You may go now.'

'I'm sorry, Judge.'

'Yes, so am I.'

Tucci left the chambers with her shoulders slumped and with the hesitant walk of someone who has been accused of a crime. After the door closed, the judge looked at us.

'If nothing else, this will send the right message to the rest of the jury. We're now down to five alternates and we haven't even started. But we now clearly see how the media can impact our trial. I have not read this story but I will. And if I see anyone in this room quoted in it I am going to be very disappointed. There are usually consequences for those who disappoint me.'

'Judge,' Royce said. 'I read the story this morning and no one here is quoted by name but it does attribute information to a source close to the prosecution. I was planning to bring this to your attention.'

I shook my head.

'And that's the oldest defense trick in the book. Cut a deal with a reporter to hide behind the story. A source close to the prosecution? He's sitting four feet across the aisle from me. That was probably close enough for the reporter.'

'Your Honor!' Royce blurted. 'I had nothing to —'

'We're holding up the trial,' Breitman said, cutting him off. 'Let's get back to court.'

We trudged back. As we went back into the courtroom I scanned the gallery and saw Salters, the reporter, in the second row. I quickly looked away, hoping my brief eye contact had not revealed anything. I had been her source. My goal was to manipulate the story — the *scene setter,* as the reporter had called it — into being something that gave the defense false confidence. I hadn't intended it as a means of changing the makeup of the jury.

Back on the bench, the judge wrote something on a

pad and then turned and addressed the jury, once again warning the panelists about reading the newspaper or watching television news programs. She then turned to her clerk.

'Audrey, the candy bowl, please.'

The clerk then took the bowl of individually wrapped sourballs off the counter in front of her desk, dumped the candy into a drawer, and took the bowl to the judge. The judge tore a page from her notebook, tore it again into six pieces and wrote on each piece.

'I have written the numbers one through six on pieces of paper and I will now randomly select an alternate to take juror number ten's seat on the panel.'

She folded the pieces of paper and dropped them into the bowl. She then swirled the bowl in her hand and raised it over her head. With her other hand she withdrew one piece of paper, unfolded it and read it out loud.

'Alternate number six,' Breitman said. 'Would you please move with any belongings you might have to seat number ten in the jury box. Thank you.'

I could do nothing but sit and watch. The new juror number ten was a thirty-six-year-old film and television extra named Philip Kirns. Being an extra probably meant that he was an actor who had not yet been successful. He took jobs as a background extra to make ends meet. That meant that every day, he went to work and stood around and watched those who had made it. This put him on the bitter side of the gulf between the haves and have-nots. And this would make him partial to the defense—the underdog facing off against the Man. I had him down as a red juror and now I was stuck with him.

Maggie whispered into my ear at the prosecution table as we watched Kirns take his new seat.

'I hope you didn't have anything to do with that story, Haller. Because I think we just lost a vote.'

I raised my hands in a *not me* gesture but it didn't look like she was buying it.

The judge turned her chair fully toward the jury.

'Finally, I believe we are ready to start,' she said. 'We begin with the opening statements from the attorneys. These statements are not to be taken as evidence. These statements are merely an opportunity for the prosecution and defense to tell the jury what they expect the evidence will show. It is an outline of what you can expect to see and hear during the trial. And it is incumbent upon counsel to then present evidence and testimony that you will later weigh during deliberations. We start with the prosecution statement. Mr. Haller?'

I stood up and went to the lectern that was positioned between the prosecution table and the jury box. I took no legal pad, 3 × 5 cards or anything else with me. I believed that it was important first to sell myself to the jury, then my case. To do that I could not look away from them. I needed to be direct, open and honest the whole time. Besides, my statement was going to be brief and to the point. I didn't need notes.

I started by introducing myself and then Maggie. I next pointed to Harry Bosch who was seated against the rail behind the prosecution table and introduced him as the case investigator. Then I got down to business.

'We are here today about one thing. To speak for someone who can no longer speak for herself. Twelve-year-old Melissa Landy was abducted from her front yard in nineteen eighty-six. Her body was found just a few hours later, discarded in a Dumpster like a bag of trash. She had been strangled. The man accused of this horrible crime sits there at the defense table.'

I pointed the finger of accusation at Jessup, just as I had seen prosecutor after prosecutor point it at my clients over the years. It felt falsely righteous of me to point a finger at anyone, even a murderer. But that didn't stop me. Not only did I point at Jessup but I pointed again and again as I summarized the case, telling the jury of the witnesses I would call and what they would say and show. I moved along quickly, making sure to mention the eyewitness who identified Melissa's abductor and the finding of the victim's hair in Jessup's tow truck. I then brought it around to a big finish.

'Jason Jessup took the life of Melissa Landy,' I said. 'He grabbed her in the front yard and took her away from her family and this world forever. He put his hand around this beautiful little girl's throat and choked the life out of her. He robbed her of her past and of her future. He robbed her of everything. And the state will prove this to you beyond a reasonable doubt.'

I nodded once to underline the promise and then returned to my seat. The judge had told us the day before to be brief in our openers, but even she seemed surprised by my brevity. It took her a moment to realize I was finished. She then told Royce he was up.

As I expected he would, Royce deferred to the second half, meaning he reserved his opening statement until the start of the defense's case. That put the judge's focus back on me.

'Very well, then. Mr. Haller, call your first witness.'

I went back to the lectern, this time carrying notes and printouts. I had spent most of the previous week before jury selection preparing the questions I would ask my witnesses. As a defense attorney I am used to cross-examining the state's witnesses and picking at the testimony brought forward by the prosecutor. It's a task quite different from direct examination and building the foundation for the introduction of evidence and exhibits. I fully acknowledge that it is easier to knock something down than to build it in the first place. But in this case I would be the builder and I came prepared.

'The People call William Johnson.'

I turned to the back of the courtroom. As I had gone to the lectern Bosch had left the courtroom to retrieve Johnson from a witness waiting room. He now returned with the man in tow. Johnson was small and thin with a dark mahogany complexion. He was fifty-nine but his pure white hair made him look older. Bosch walked him through the gate and then pointed him in the direction of the witness stand. He was quickly sworn in by the court clerk.

I had to admit to myself that I was nervous. I felt what Maggie had tried to describe to me on more than one occasion when we were married. She always called it the *burden of proof*. Not the legal burden. But the psychic burden of knowing that you stood as representative of all the people. I had always dismissed her explanations as self-serving. The prosecutor was always the overdog. The Man. There was no burden in that, at least nothing compared to the burden of the defense attorney, who stands all alone and holds someone's freedom in his hands. I never understood what she was trying to tell me.

Until now.

Now I got it. I felt it. I was about to question my first witness in front of the jury and I was as nervous as I had been at my first trial out of law school.

'Good morning, Mr. Johnson,' I said. 'How are you, sir?'

'I am good, yes.'

'That's good. Can you tell me, sir, what you do for a living?'

'Yes, sir. I am head of operations for the El Rey Theatre on Wilshire Boulevard.'

'"Head of operations," what does that mean?'

'I make sure everything works right and runs—from the stage lights to the toilets, it's all part of my job. Mind you, I have electricians work on the lights and plumbers work on the toilets.'

His answer was greeted with polite smiles and modest laughter. He spoke with a slight Caribbean accent but his words were clear and understandable.

'How long have you worked at the El Rey, Mr. Johnson?'

'For going on thirty-six years now. I started in nineteen seventy-four.'

'Wow, that's an achievement. Congratulations. Have you been head of operations for all that time?'

'No, I worked my way up. I started as a janitor.'

'I would like to draw your attention back to nineteen eighty-six. You were working there then, correct?'

'Yes, sir. I was a janitor back then.'

'Okay, and do you remember the date of February sixteenth of that year in particular?'

'Yes, I do.'

'It was a Sunday.'

'Yes, I remember.'

'Can you tell the court why?'

'That was the day I found the body of a little girl in the trash bin out back of the El Rey. That was a terrible day.'

I checked the jury. All eyes were on my witness. So far so good.

'I can imagine that being a terrible day, Mr. Johnson. Now, can you tell us what it was that brought you to discover the body of the little girl?'

'We were working on a project in the theater. We were putting new drywall into the ladies' room on account of a leak. So I took a wheelbarrow full of the stuff we had demoed—the old wall and some rotting wood and such—and wheeled it out to put in the Dumpster. I opened the top and there this poor little girl was.'

'She was on top of the debris already in the trash bin?'

'That's right.'

'Was she covered at all with any trash or debris?'

'No, sir, not at all.'

'As if whoever threw her in there had been in a hurry and didn't have time to cover—'

'Objection!'

Royce had jumped to his feet. I knew he would object. But I had almost gotten the whole sentence—and its suggestion—to the jury.

'Mr. Haller is leading the witness and asking for conclusions for which he would have no expertise,' Royce said.

I withdrew the question before the judge could sustain the objection. There was no sense in having the judge side with the defense in front of the jury.

'Mr. Johnson, was that the first trip you had made to the trash bin that day?'

'No, sir. I had been out there two times before.'

'Before the trip during which you found the body, when had you last been to the trash bin?'

'About ninety minutes before.'

'Did you see a body on top of the trash in the bin that time?'

'No, there was no body there.'

'So it had to have been placed in that bin in the ninety minutes prior to you finding it, correct?'

'Yes, that's right.'

'Okay, Mr. Johnson, if I could draw your attention to the screen.'

The courtroom was equipped with two large flat-screen monitors mounted high on the wall opposite the jury box. One screen was slightly angled toward the gallery to allow courtroom observers to see the digital presentations as well. Maggie controlled what appeared on the screens through a PowerPoint program on her laptop computer. She had constructed the presentation over the last two weeks and weekends as we choreographed the prosecution's case. All of the old photos from the case files had been scanned and loaded into the program. She now put up the trial's first photo exhibit. A shot of the trash bin Melissa Landy's body had been found in.

'Does that look like the trash bin in which you found the little girl's body, Mr. Johnson?'

'That's it.'

'What makes you so sure, sir?'

'The address—fifty-five fifteen—spray-painted on the side like that. I did that. That's the address. And I can tell that's the back of the El Rey. I've worked there a long time.'

'Okay, and is this what you saw when you raised the top and looked inside?'

Maggie moved to the next photo. The courtroom was already quiet but it seemed to me that it grew absolutely silent when the photo of Melissa Landy's body in the trash bin went up on the screens. Under the existing rules of evidence as carved by a recent ruling by the Ninth District, I had to find ways of bringing old evidence and exhibits to the present jury. I could not rely on investigative records. I had to find people who were bridges to the past and Johnson was the first bridge.

Johnson didn't answer my question at first. He just stared like everyone else in the courtroom. Then, unexpectedly, a tear rolled down his dark cheek. It was perfect. If I had been at the defense table I would have viewed it with cynicism. But I knew Johnson's response was heartfelt and it was why I had made him my first witness.

'That's her,' he finally said. 'That's what I saw.'

I nodded as Johnson blessed himself.

'And what did you do when you saw her?'

'We didn't have no cell phones back then, you see. So I ran back inside and I called nine-one-one on the stage phone.'

'And the police came quickly?'

'They came real quick, like they were already looking for her.'

'One final question, Mr. Johnson. Could you see that trash bin from Wilshire Boulevard?'

Johnson shook his head emphatically.

'No, it was behind the theater and you could only see it if you drove back there and down the little alley.'

I hesitated here. I had more to bring out from this witness. Information not presented in the first trial but gathered by Bosch during his reinvestigation. It was information that Royce might not be aware of. I could just ask the question that would draw it out or I could roll the dice and see if the defense opened a door on cross-examination. The information would be the same either way, but it would have greater weight if the jury believed the defense had tried to hide it.

'Thank you, Mr. Johnson,' I finally said. 'I have no further questions.'

The witness was turned over to Royce, who went to the lectern as I sat down.

'Just a few questions,' he said. 'Did you see who put the victim's body in the bin?'

'No, I did not,' Johnson said.

'So when you called nine-one-one you had no idea who did it, is that correct?'

'Correct.'

'Before that day, had you ever seen the defendant before?'

'No, I don't think so.'

'Thank you.'

And that was it. Royce had performed a typical cross of a witness who had little value to the defense. Johnson couldn't identify the murderer, so Royce got that on the record. But he should have just let Johnson pass. By asking if Johnson had ever seen Jessup before the murder, he opened a door. I stood back up so I could go through it.

'Redirect, Mr. Haller?' the judge asked.

'Briefly, Your Honor. Mr. Johnson, back during this period that we're talking about, did you often work on Sundays?'

'No, it was my day off usually. But if we had some special projects I would be told to come in.'

Royce objected on the grounds that I was opening up a line of questioning that was outside the scope of his cross-examination. I promised the judge that it was within the scope and that it would become apparent soon. She indulged me and overruled the objection. I went back to Mr. Johnson. I had hoped Royce would object because in a few moments it would look like he had been trying to stop me from getting to information damaging to Jessup.

'You mentioned that the trash bin where you found the body was at the end of an alley. Is there no parking lot behind the El Rey Theatre?'

'There is a parking lot but it does not belong to the El Rey Theatre. We have the alley that gives us access to the back doors and the bins.'

'Who does the parking lot belong to?'

'A company that has lots all over the city. It's called City Park.'

'Is there a wall or a fence separating this parking lot from the alley?'

Royce stood again.

'Your Honor, this is going on and on and it has nothing to do with what I asked Mr. Johnson.'

'Your Honor,' I said. 'I will get there in two more questions.'

'You may answer, Mr. Johnson,' Breitman said.

'There is a fence,' Johnson said.

'So,' I said, 'from the El Rey's alley and the location of its trash bin, you can see into the adjoining parking lot, and anyone in the adjoining parking lot could see the trash bin, correct?'

'Yes.'

'And prior to the day you discovered the body, did

you have occasion to be at work on a Sunday and to notice that the parking lot behind the theater was being used?'

'Yes, like a month previously, I came to work and in the back there were many cars and I saw tow trucks towing them in.'

I couldn't help myself. I had to glance over at Royce and Jessup to see if they were squirming yet. I was about to draw the first blood of the trial. They thought Johnson was going to be a noncritical witness, meaning he would establish the murder and its location and nothing else.

They were wrong.

'Did you inquire as to what was going on?' I asked.

'Yes,' Johnson said. 'I asked what they were doing and one of the drivers said that they were towing cars from the neighborhood down the street and holding them there so people could come and pay and get their cars.'

'So it was being used like a temporary holding lot, is that what you mean?'

'Yes.'

'And did you know what the name of the towing company was?'

'It was on the trucks. It was called Aardvark Towing.'

'You said trucks. You saw more than one truck there?'

'Yeah, there were two or three trucks when I saw them.'

'What did you tell them after you were informed what they were doing there?'

'I told my boss and he called City Park to see if they knew about it. He thought there could be an insurance concern, especially with people being mad about being towed and all. And it turned out Aardvark wasn't supposed to be there. It wasn't authorized.'

'What happened?'

'They had to stop using the lot and my boss told me to keep an eye out if I worked on weekends to see if they kept using it.'

'So they stopped using the lot behind the theater?'

'That's right.'

'And this was the same lot from which you could see the trash bin in which you would later find the body of Melissa Landy?'

'Yes, sir.'

'When Mr. Royce asked you if you had ever seen the defendant before the day of the murder, you answered that you didn't think so, correct?'

'Correct.'

'You don't think so? Why are you not sure?'

'Because I think he could've been one of the Aardvark drivers I saw using that lot. So I can't be sure I didn't see him before.'

'Thank you, Mr. Johnson. I have no further questions.'

26

Monday, April 5, 10:20 A.M.

For the first time since he had been brought into the case Bosch felt as though Melissa Landy was in good hands. He had just watched Mickey Haller score the first points of the trial. He had taken a small piece of the puzzle Bosch had come up with and used it to land the first punch. It wasn't a knockout by any means but it had connected solidly. It was the first step down the path of proving Jason Jessup's familiarity with the parking lot and trash bin behind the El Rey Theatre. Before the trial would end, its importance would be made clear to the jury. But what was even more significant to Bosch at the moment was the way Haller had used the information Harry had provided. He had hung it on the defense, made it look as though it had been their attempt to obfuscate the facts of the case that drew the information out. It was a smooth move and it gave Bosch a big boost in his confidence in Haller as a prosecutor.

He met Johnson at the gate and walked him out of the courtroom to the hallway, where he shook his hand.

'You did real good in there, Mr. Johnson. We can't thank you enough.'

'You already have. Convicting that man of killing that little girl.'

'Well, we're not quite there yet but that's the plan. Except most people who read the paper think we're going after an innocent man.'

'No, you got the right man. I can tell.'

Bosch nodded and felt awkward.

'You take care, Mr. Johnson.'

'Detective, your music is jazz, right?'

Bosch had already turned to go back to the courtroom. Now he looked back at Johnson.

'How'd you know that?'

'Just a guess. We got jazz acts that come through. New Orleans jazz. You ever want tickets to a show at the El Rey, you look me up.'

'Yeah, I'll do that. Thanks.'

Bosch pushed through the doors leading back into the courtroom. He was smiling, thinking about Johnson's guess about his music. If he was right about that, then maybe he would be right about the jury convicting Jessup. As he moved down the aisle, he heard the judge telling Haller to call his next witness.

'The state calls Regina Landy.'

Bosch knew he was on. This part had been choreographed a week earlier by the judge and over the objection of the defense. Regina Landy was unavailable to testify because she was dead, but she had testified in the first trial and the judge had ruled that her testimony could be read to the current jurors.

Breitman now turned to the jurors to offer the explanation, guarding against revealing any hint that there had been an earlier trial.

'Ladies and gentlemen, the state has called a witness who is no longer available to testify. However, previously she gave sworn testimony that we will read to you today. You are not to consider why this witness is unable to testify or where this previous sworn testimony is from. Your concern is the testimony itself. I should add that I have decided to allow this over the objection of the defense. The U.S. Constitution holds that the accused is entitled to question his accusers. However, as you will see, this witness was indeed questioned by an attorney who previously represented Mr. Jessup.'

She turned back to the court.

'You may proceed, Mr. Haller.'

Haller called Bosch to the stand. He was sworn in and then took the seat, pulling the microphone into position. He opened the blue binder he had carried with him and Haller began.

'Detective Bosch, can you tell us a little bit about your experience as a law enforcement officer?'

Bosch turned toward the jury box and moved his eyes over the faces of the jurors as he answered. He did not leave the alternates out.

'I have been a sworn officer for thirty-six years. I have spent more than twenty-five of those years working homicides. I have been the lead investigator in more than two hundred murder investigations in that time.'

'And you are the lead investigator on this case?'

'Yes, I am now. I did not take part in the original investigation, however. I came into this case in February of this year.'

'Thank you, Detective. We will be talking about your investigation later in the trial. Are you prepared to read the sworn testimony of Regina Landy taken on October seventh, nineteen eighty-six?'

'I am.'

'Okay, I will read the questions that were posed at the time by Deputy District Attorney Gary Lintz and defense counsel Charles Barnard and you will read the responses from the witness. We start with direct examination from Mr. Lintz.'

Haller paused and studied the transcript in front of him. Bosch wondered if there would be any confusion from his reading the responses of a woman. In deciding to allow the testimony the week before, the judge had disallowed any reference to emotions described as having been exhibited by Regina Landy. Bosch knew from the transcript that she was crying throughout her testimony. But he would not be able to communicate that to the present jurors.

'Here we go,' Haller said. 'Mrs. Landy, can you please describe your relationship with the victim, Melissa Landy.'

' "I am her mother," ' Bosch read. ' "She was my daughter…until she was taken away from me." '

27

The reading of Regina Landy's testimony from the first trial took us right up to lunch. The testimony was needed to establish who the victim was and who had identified her. But without the incumbent emotion of a parent's testimony, the reading by Bosch was largely procedural, and while the first witness of the day brought reason to be hopeful, the second witness was about as anticlimactic as a voice from the grave could possibly be. I imagined that Bosch's reading of Regina Landy's words was confusing to the jurors when they were not provided with any explanation for her absence from the trial of her daughter's alleged killer.

The prosecution team had lunch at Duffy's, which was close enough to the CCB to be convenient but far enough away that we wouldn't have to worry about jurors finding the same place to eat. Nobody was ecstatic about the start of the trial but that was to be expected. I had planned the presentation of evidence like the unfolding of *Scheherazade,* the symphonic suite that starts slow and quiet and builds to an all-encompassing crescendo of sound and music and emotion.

The first day was about the proof of facts. I had to bring forward the body. I had to establish that there was a victim, that she had been taken from her home and later found dead and that she had been murdered. I had hit two of those facts with the first witnesses, and now the afternoon witness, the medical examiner, would complete the proof. The prosecution's case would then shift toward the accused and the evidence that tied him to the crime. That would be when my case would really come to life.

Only Bosch and I came back from lunch. Maggie had gone over to the Checkers Hotel to spend the afternoon with our star witness, Sarah Ann Gleason. Bosch had gone up to Washington on Saturday and flown down with her Sunday morning. She wasn't scheduled to testify until Wednesday morning but I had wanted her close and I had wanted Maggie to spend as much time as possible prepping her for her part in the trial. Maggie had already been up to Washington twice to spend time with her but I believed that any time they could spend together would continue to promote the bond I wanted them to have and the jury to see.

Maggie left us reluctantly. She was concerned that I would make a misstep in court without her there watching over me as my second. I assured her that I could handle the direct examination of a medical examiner and would call her if I ran into trouble. Little did I know how important this witness's testimony would come to be.

The afternoon session got off to a late start while we

waited ten minutes for a juror who did not return from lunch on time. Once the panel was assembled and returned to court, Judge Breitman lectured the jurors again on timeliness and ordered them to eat as a group for the remainder of the trial. She also ordered the courtroom deputy to escort them to lunch. This way no one would stray from the pack and no one would be late.

Finished with the lunch business, the judge gruffly ordered me to call my next witness. I nodded to Bosch and he headed to the witness room to retrieve David Eisenbach.

The judge grew impatient as we waited but it took Eisenbach a few minutes longer than most witnesses to make his way into the courtroom and to the witness stand. Eisenbach was seventy-nine years old and walked with a cane. He also carried a pillow with a handle on it, as if he were going to a USC football game at the Coliseum. After being sworn in he placed the pillow on the hard wood of the witness chair and then sat down.

'Dr. Eisenbach,' I began, 'can you tell the jury what you do for a living?'

'Currently I am semiretired and derive an income from being an autopsy consultant. A *gun for hire,* you lawyers like to call it. I review autopsies for a living and then tell lawyers and juries what the medical examiner did right and did wrong.'

'And before you were semiretired, what did you do?'

'I was assistant medical examiner for the county of Los Angeles. Had that job for thirty years.'

'As such you conducted autopsies?'

'Yes, sir, I did. In thirty years I conducted over twenty thousand autopsies. That's a lot of dead people.'

'That is a lot, Dr. Eisenbach. Do you remember them all?'

'Of course not. I remember a handful off the top of my head. The rest of them I would need my notes to remember.'

After receiving permission from the judge I approached the witness stand and put down a forty-page document.

'I draw your attention to the document I have placed before you. Can you identify it?'

'Yes, it's an autopsy protocol dated February eighteenth, nineteen eighty-six. The deceased is listed as Melissa Theresa Landy. My name is also on it. It is one of mine.'

'Meaning you conducted the autopsy?'

'Yes, that is what I said.'

I followed this with a series of questions that established the autopsy procedures and the general health of the victim prior to death. Royce objected several times to what he termed leading questions. Few of these were sustained by the judge but that was not the point. Royce had adopted the tactic of attempting to get me out of rhythm by incessantly interrupting, whether such interruptions were valid or not.

Working around these interruptions, Eisenbach was able to testify that Melissa Landy was in perfect health until the moment of her violent death. He said she had not been sexually attacked in any determinable way. He said there was no indication of prior sexual activity—she was a virgin. He said the cause of her death was asphyxiation. He said the evidence of crushed bones in her neck and throat indicated she had been choked by a powerful force—a man's single hand.

Using a laser pointer to mark locations on photographs of the body taken at autopsy, Eisenbach identified a bruise pattern on the victim's neck that was indicative of a one-handed choke hold. With the laser point he delineated a thumb mark on the right side of the girl's neck and the larger, four-finger mark on the left side.

'Doctor, did you make a determination of which hand the killer used to choke the victim to death?'

'Yes, it was quite simple to determine the killer had used the right hand to choke this girl to death.'

'Just one hand?'

'That is correct.'

'Was there any determination of how this was done? Had the girl been suspended while she was choked?'

'No, the injuries, particularly the crushed bones, indicated that the killer put his hand on her neck and pressed her against a surface that offered resistance.'

'Could that have been the seat of a vehicle?'

'Yes.'

'How about a man's leg?'

Royce objected, saying the question called for pure speculation. The judge agreed and told me to move on.

'Doctor, you mentioned twenty thousand autopsies.

I assume that many of these were homicides involving asphyxiation. Was it unusual to come across a case where only one hand was used to choke a victim to death?'

Royce objected again, this time saying the question asked for an answer outside the witness's expertise. But the judge went my way.

'The man has conducted twenty thousand autopsies,' she said. 'I'm inclined to think that gives him a lot of expertise. I'm going to allow the question.'

'You can answer, Doctor,' I said. 'Was this unusual?'

'Not necessarily. Many homicides occur during struggles and other circumstances. I've seen it before. If one hand is otherwise occupied, the other must suffice. We are talking about a twelve-year-old girl who weighed ninety-one pounds. She could have been subdued with one hand if the killer needed the left hand for something else.'

'Would driving a vehicle fall into that category?'

'Objection,' Royce said. 'Same argument.'

'And same ruling,' Breitman said. 'You may answer, Doctor.'

'Yes,' Eisenbach said. 'If one hand was being used to maintain control of a vehicle the other hand could be used to choke the victim. That is one possibility.'

At this point I believed I had gotten all that there was to get from Eisenbach. I ended direct examination and handed the witness over to Royce. Unfortunately for me, Eisenbach was a witness who had something for everybody. And Royce went after it.

'"One possibility," is that what you called it, Dr. Eisenbach?'

'Excuse me?'

'You said the scenario Mr. Haller described—one hand on the wheel, one hand on the neck—was one possibility. Is that correct?'

'Yes, that is a possibility.'

'But you weren't there, so you can't know for sure. Isn't that right, Doctor?'

'Yes, that is right.'

'You said one possibility. What are some of the other possibilities?'

'Well…I wouldn't know. I was responding to the question from the prosecutor.'

'How about a cigarette?'

'What?'

'Could the killer have been holding a cigarette in his left hand while he choked the girl with his right?'

'Yes, I suppose so. Yes.'

'And how about his penis?'

'His…'

'His penis, Doctor. Could the killer have choked this girl with his right hand while holding his penis with his left?'

'I would have to…yes, that is a possibility, too.'

'He could have been masturbating with one hand while he choked her with the other, correct, Doctor?'

'Anything is possible but there is no indication in the autopsy report that supports this.'

'What about what is not in the file, Doctor?'

'I'm not aware of anything.'

'Is this what you meant about being a hired gun, Doctor? You take the prosecution's side no matter what the facts are?'

'I don't always work for prosecutors.'

'I'm happy for you.'

I stood up.

'Your Honor, he's badgering the witness with—'

'Mr. Royce,' the judge said. 'Please keep it civil. And on point.'

'Yes, Your Honor. Doctor, of the twenty thousand autopsies you have performed, how many of them were on victims of sexually motivated violence?'

Eisenbach looked across the floor to me, but there was nothing I could do for him. Bosch had taken Maggie's place at the prosecution table. He leaned over to me and whispered.

'What's he doing? Trying to make our case?'

I held up my hand so I would not be distracted from the back-and-forth between Royce and Eisenbach.

'No, he's making their case,' I whispered back.

Eisenbach still hadn't answered.

'Doctor,' the judge said, 'please answer the question.'

'I don't have a count but many of them were sexually motivated crimes.'

'Was this one?'

'Based on the autopsy findings I could not make that conclusion. But whenever you have a young child, particularly a female, and there is a stranger abduction, then you are almost always—'

'Move to strike the answer as nonresponsive,' Royce said, cutting the witness off. 'The witness is assuming facts not in evidence.'

The judge considered the objection. I stood up, ready to respond but said nothing.

'Doctor, please answer only the question you are asked,' the judge said.

'I thought I was,' Eisenbach said.

'Then let me be more specific,' Royce said. 'You found no indications of sexual assault or abuse on the body of Melissa Landy, is that correct, Doctor?'

'That is correct.'

'What about on the victim's clothing?'

'The body is my jurisdiction. The clothing is analyzed by forensics.'

'Of course.'

Royce hesitated and looked down at his notes. I could tell he was trying to decide how far to take something. It was a case of 'so far, so good—do I risk going further?'

Finally, he decided.

'Now, Doctor, a moment ago when I objected to your answer, you called this a stranger abduction. What evidence from the autopsy supported that claim?'

Eisenbach thought for a long moment and even looked down at the autopsy report in front of him.

'Doctor?'

'Uh, there is nothing I recall from the autopsy alone that supports this.'

'Actually, the autopsy supports a conclusion quite the opposite, doesn't it?'

Eisenbach looked genuinely confused.

'I am not sure what you mean.'

'Can I draw your attention to page eight of the autopsy protocol? The preliminary examination of the body.'

Royce waited a moment until Eisenbach turned to the page. I did as well but didn't need to. I knew where Royce was going and couldn't stop him. I just needed to be ready to object at the right moment.

'Doctor, the report states that scrapings of the victim's fingernails were negative for blood and tissue. Do you see that on page eight?'

'Yes, I scraped her nails but they were clean.'

'This indicates she did not scratch her attacker, her killer. Correct?'

'That would be the indication, yes.'

'And this would also indicate that she knew her attack–'

'Objection!'

I was on my feet but not quick enough. Royce had gotten the suggestion out and to the jury.

'Assumes facts not in evidence,' I said. 'Your Honor, defense counsel is clearly attempting to plant seeds with the jury that do not exist.'

'Sustained. Mr. Royce, a warning.'

'Yes, Your Honor. The defense has no further questions for this prosecution witness.'

28

Bosch knocked on the door of room 804 and looked directly at the peephole. The door was quickly opened by McPherson, who was checking her watch as she stood back to let him enter.

'Why aren't you in court with Mickey?' she asked.

Bosch entered. The room was a suite with a decent view of Grand Avenue and the back of the Biltmore. There was a couch and two chairs, one of them occupied by Sarah Ann Gleason. Bosch nodded his hello.

'Because he doesn't need me there. I'm needed here.'

'What's going on?'

'Royce tipped his hand on the defense's case. I need to talk to Sarah about it.'

He started toward the couch but McPherson put her hand on his arm and stopped him.

'Wait a minute. Before you talk to Sarah you talk to me. What's going on?'

Bosch nodded. She was right. He looked around but there was no place for private conversation in the suite.

'Let's take a walk.'

McPherson went to the coffee table and grabbed a key card.

'We'll be right back, Sarah. Do you need anything?'

'No, I'm fine. I'll be here.'

She held up a sketchpad. It would keep her company.

Bosch and McPherson left the room and took the elevator down to the lobby. There was a bar crowded with pre-happy hour drinkers but they found a private spot in a sitting area by the front door.

'Okay, how did Royce tip his hand?' McPherson asked.

'When he was cross-examining Eisenbach, he riffed off of Mickey's question about the killer using only his right hand to choke her.'

'Right, while he was driving. He panicked when he heard the call on the police radio and killed her.'

'Right, that's the prosecution theory. Well, Royce is already setting up a defense theory. On cross he asked whether it was possible that the killer was choking her with one hand while masturbating with the other.'

She was silent as she computed this.

'This is the old prosecution theory,' she said. 'From the first trial. That it was murder in the commission of a sex act. Mickey and I sort of figured that once Royce got all the discovery material and learned that the DNA came from the stepfather, the defense would play it this way. They're setting up the stepfather as the straw man. They'll say he killed her and the DNA proves it.'

McPherson folded her arms as she worked it out further.

'It's good but there are two things wrong with it. Sarah and the hair evidence. So we're missing something.

Royce has got to have something or someone who discredits Sarah's ID.'

'That's why I'm here. I brought Royce's witness list. These people have been playing hide-and-seek with me and I haven't run them all down. Sarah's got to look at this list and tell me which one I need to focus on.'

'How the hell will she know?'

'She's got to. These are her people. Boyfriends, husbands, fellow tweakers. All of them have records. They're the people she hung out with before she got straight. Every address is a last-known and worthless. Royce has got to be hiding them.'

McPherson nodded.

'That's why they call him Clever Clive. Okay, let's talk to her. Let me try first, okay?'

She stood up.

'Wait a minute,' Bosch said.

She looked at him.

'What is it?'

'What if the defense theory is the right one?'

'Are you kidding me?'

He didn't answer and she didn't wait long. She headed back toward the elevator. He got up and followed.

They went back to the room. Bosch noticed that Gleason had sketched a tulip on her pad while they had been gone. He sat down on the couch across from her, and McPherson took the chair right next to her.

'Sarah,' McPherson said. 'We need to talk. We think that somebody you used to know during those lost years we were talking about is going to try to help the defense. We need to figure out who it is and what they are going to say.'

'I don't understand,' Sarah said. 'But I was thirteen years old when this happened to us. What does it matter who my friends were after?'

'It matters because they can testify about things you might have done. Or said.'

'What things?'

McPherson shook her head.

'That's what is so frustrating. We don't really know. We only know that today in court the defense made it clear that they are going to try to put the blame for your sister's death on your stepfather.'

Sarah raised her hands as if warding off a blow.

'That's crazy. I was there. I saw that man take her!'

'We know that, Sarah. But it's a matter of what is conveyed to the jury and what and who the jurors believe. Now, Detective Bosch has a list of the defense's witnesses. I want you to take a look at it and tell us what the names mean to you.'

Bosch pulled the list from his briefcase. He handed it to McPherson, who handed it to Sarah.

'Sorry, all those notes are things I added,' Bosch said, 'when I was trying to track them down. Just look at the names.'

Bosch watched her lips move slightly as she started to read. Then they stopped moving and she just stared at the paper. He saw tears in her eyes.

'Sarah?' McPherson prompted.

'These people,' Gleason said in a whisper. 'I thought I'd never see them again.'

'You may never see them again,' McPherson said. 'Just because they're on that list, it doesn't mean they'll be called. They pull names out of the records and load up the list to confuse us, Sarah. It's called *haystacking*. They hide the real witnesses, and our investigator— Detective Bosch—wastes his time checking out the wrong people. But there's got to be at least one name on there that counts. Who is it, Sarah? Help us.'

She stared at the list without responding.

'Someone who will be able to say you two were close. Who you spent time with and told secrets to.'

'I thought a husband couldn't testify against a wife.'

'One spouse can't be forced to testify against the other. But what are you talking about, Sarah?'

'This one.'

She pointed to a name on the list. Bosch leaned over to read it. Edward Roman. Bosch had traced him to a lockdown rehab center in North Hollywood where Sarah had spent nine months after her last incarceration. The only thing Bosch had guessed was that they'd had contact in group therapy. The last known address provided by Royce was a motel in Van Nuys but Roman was long gone from there. Bosch had gotten no further with it and had dismissed the name as part of Royce's haystack.

'Roman,' he said. 'You were with him in rehab, right?'

'Yes,' Gleason said. 'Then we got married.'

'When?' McPherson said. 'We have no record of that marriage.'

'After we got out. He knew a minister. We got married on the beach. But it didn't last very long.'

'Did you get divorced?' McPherson asked.

'No...I never really cared. Then when I got straight I just didn't want to go back there. It was one of those things you block out. Like it didn't happen.'

McPherson looked at Bosch.

'It might not have been a legal marriage,' he said. 'There's nothing in the county records.'

'Doesn't matter if it was a legal marriage or not,' she said. 'He is obviously a volunteer witness, so he can testify against her. What matters is what his testimony is going to be. What's he going to say, Sarah?'

Sarah slowly shook her head.

'I don't know.'

'Well, what did you tell him about your sister and your stepfather?'

'I don't know. Those years...I can hardly remember anything from back then.'

There was a silence and then McPherson asked Sarah to look at the rest of the names on the list. She did and shook her head.

'I don't know who some of these people are. Some people in the life, I just knew them by street names.'

'But Edward Roman you know?'

'Yes. We were together.'

'How long?'

Gleason shook her head in embarrassment.

'Not long. Inside rehab we thought we were made for each other. Once we were out, it didn't work. It lasted maybe three months. I got arrested again and when I got out of jail, he was gone.'

'Is it possible that it wasn't a legitimate marriage?'

Gleason thought for a moment and halfheartedly shrugged.

'Anything is possible, I guess.'

'Okay, Sarah, I'm going to step out with Detective Bosch again for a few minutes. I want you to think about Edward Roman. Anything you can remember will be helpful. I'll be right back.'

McPherson took the witness list from her and handed it back to Bosch. They left the room but just took a few paces down the hallway before stopping and talking in whispers.

'I guess you'd better find him,' she said.

'It won't matter,' Bosch said. 'If he's Royce's star witness he won't talk to me.'

'Then find out everything you can about him. So when the time comes we can destroy him.'

'Got it.'

Bosch turned and headed down the hall toward the elevators. McPherson called after him. He stopped and looked back.

'Did you mean it?' McPherson asked.

'Mean what?'

'What you said down in the lobby. What you asked. You think twenty-four years ago she made it all up?'

Bosch looked at her for a long moment, then shrugged.

'I don't know.'

'Well, what about the hair in the truck? Doesn't that tie her story in?'

Bosch held a hand up empty.

'It's circumstantial. And I wasn't there when they found it.'

'What's that supposed to mean?'

'It means sometimes things happen when the victim is a child. And that I wasn't there when they found it.'

'Boy, maybe you should be working for the defense.'

Bosch dropped his hand to his side.

'I'm sure they've thought of all of this already.'

He turned back toward the elevators and headed down the hallway.

29

Sometimes the wheels of justice roll smoothly. The second day of trial started exactly as scheduled. The full jury was in the box, the judge was on the bench and Jason Jessup and his attorney were seated at the defense table. I stood and called my first witness of what I hoped would be a productive day for the prosecution. Harry Bosch even had Izzy Gordon in the courtroom ready to go. By five minutes after the hour, she was sworn in and seated. She was a small woman with black-framed glasses that magnified her eyes. My records said she was fifty years old but she looked older.

'Ms. Gordon, can you tell the jury what you do for a living?'

'Yes. I am a forensic technician and crime scene supervisor for the Los Angeles Police Department. I have been so employed in the forensics unit since nineteen eighty-six.'

'Were you so employed on February sixteenth of that year?'

'Yes, I was. It was my first day of work.'

'And what was your assignment on that day?'

'My job was to learn. I was assigned to a crime scene

308

supervisor and I was to get on-the-job training.'

Izzy Gordon was a major find for the prosecution. Two technicians and a supervisor had worked the three separate crime scenes relating to the Melissa Landy case—the home on Windsor, the trash bin behind the El Rey and the tow truck driven by Jessup. Gordon had been assigned to be at the supervisor's side and therefore had been in attendance at all three crime scenes. The supervisor was long since dead and the other techs were retired and unable to offer testimony about all three locations. Finding Gordon allowed me to stream-line the introduction of crime scene evidence.

'Who was that supervisor?'

'That was Art Donovan.'

'And you got a call out with him that day?'

'Yes, we did. An abduction that turned into a homi-cide. We ended up going from scene to scene to scene that day. Three related locations.'

'Okay, let's take those scenes one at a time.'

Over the next ninety minutes I walked Gordon through her Sunday tour of crime scenes on February 16, 1986. Using her as the conduit, I could deliver crime scene photographs, videos and evidence reports. Royce continued his tack of objecting at will in an effort to prevent the unimpeded flow of information to the jury. But he was scoreless and getting under the judge's skin. I could tell, and so I did not complain. I wanted that annoyance to fester. It might come in handy later.

Gordon's testimony was fairly pedestrian as she first discussed the unsuccessful efforts to find shoe prints and other trace evidence on the front lawn of the Landy's house. It turned more dramatic when she recalled being urgently called to a new crime scene—the trash bin behind the El Rey.

'We were called when they found the body. It was handled in whispers because the family was there in the house and we did not want to upset them until it was confirmed that there was a body and that it was the little girl.'

'You and Donovan went to the El Rey Theatre?'

'Yes, along with Detective Kloster. We met the assistant medical examiner there. We now had a homicide, so more technicians were called in, too.'

The El Rey portion of Gordon's testimony was largely an opportunity for me to show more video footage and photographs of the victim on the overhead screens. If nothing else, I wanted every juror in the box to be incensed by what they saw. I wanted to light the fire of one of the basic instincts. Vengeance.

I counted on Royce to object and he did, but by then he had exhausted his welcome with the judge, and his argument that the images were graphic and cumulatively excessive fell on deaf ears. They were allowed.

Finally, Izzy Gordon brought us to the last crime scene—the tow truck—and she described how she had spotted three long hairs caught in the crack that split the bench seat and pointed them out to Donovan for collection.

'What happened to those hairs?' I asked.

'They were individually bagged and tagged and then

taken to the Scientific Investigation Division for comparison and analysis.'

Gordon's testimony was smooth and efficient. When I turned her over to the defense, Royce did the best he could. He did not bother to assail the collection of evidence but merely attempted once again to gain a foothold for the defense theory. In doing so he skipped the first two crime scenes and zeroed in on the tow truck.

'Ms. Gordon, when you got to the Aardvark towing yard, were there police officers already there?'

'Yes, of course.'

'How many?'

'I didn't count but there were several.'

'What about detectives?'

'Yes, there were detectives conducting a search of the whole business under the authority of a search warrant.'

'And were these detectives you had seen earlier at the previous crime scenes?'

'I think so, yes. I would assume so but I do not remember specifically.'

'But you seem to remember other things specifically. Why don't you remember which detectives you were working with?'

'There were several people working this case. Detective Kloster was the lead investigator but he was dealing with three different locations as well as the girl who was the witness. I don't remember if he was at the tow yard when I first arrived but he was there at some point. I think that if you refer to the crime scene attendance logs, you will be able to determine who was at what scene and when.'

'Ah, then we shall do just that.'

Royce approached the witness stand and gave Gordon three documents and a pencil. He then returned to the lectern.

'What are those three documents, Ms. Gordon?'

'These are crime scene attendance logs.'

'And which scenes are they from?'

'The three I worked in regard to the Landy case.'

'Can you please take a moment to study those logs and use the pencil I have given you to circle any name that appears on all three lists.'

It took Gordon less than a minute to complete the task.

'Finished?' Royce asked.

'Yes, there are four names.'

'Can you tell us?'

'Yes, myself and my supervisor, Art Donovan, and then Detective Kloster and his partner, Chad Steiner.'

'You were the only four who were at all three crime scenes that day, correct?'

'That is correct.'

Maggie leaned into me and whispered.

'Cross-scene contamination.'

I shook my head slightly and whispered back.

'That suggests accidental contamination. I think he's going for intentional planting of evidence.'

Maggie nodded and leaned away. Royce asked his next question.

'Being one of only four who were at all three scenes, you had a keen understanding of this crime and what it meant, isn't that correct?'

'I'm not sure what you mean.'

'Among police personnel, were emotions high at these crime scenes?'

'Well, everyone was very professional.'

'You mean nobody cared that this was a twelve-year-old girl?'

'No, we cared and you could say things were at least tense at the first two scenes. We had the family at one and the dead little girl at the other. I don't really remember things being emotional at the tow yard.'

Wrong answer, I thought. She had opened a door for the defense.

'Okay,' Royce said, 'but you are saying that at the first two scenes the emotions were high, correct?'

I stood up, just to give Royce a dose of his own medicine.

'Objection. Asked and answered already, Your Honor.'

'Sustained.'

Royce was undaunted.

'Then how did these emotions display themselves?' he asked.

'Well, we talked. Art Donovan told me to keep professional detachment. He said we had to do our best work because this had been just a little girl.'

'What about detectives Kloster and Steiner?'

'They said the same thing. That we couldn't leave any stone unturned, that we had to do it for Melissa.'

'He called the victim by her name?'

'Yes, I remember that.'

'How angry and upset would you say Detective Kloster was?'

I stood and objected.

'Assumes facts not in evidence or testimony.'

The judge sustained it and told Royce to move on.

'Ms. Gordon, can you refer to the crime scene attendance logs still in front of you and tell us if the arrival and departure of law enforcement personnel is kept by time?'

'Yes, it is. There are arrival and departure times listed after each name.'

'You have previously stated that detectives Kloster and Steiner were the only two investigators besides yourself and your supervisor to appear at all three scenes.'

'Yes, they were the lead investigators on the case.'

'Did they arrive at each of the scenes before you and Mr. Donovan?'

It took Gordon a moment to confirm the information on the lists.

'Yes, they did.'

'So they would have had access to the victim's body before you ever arrived at the El Rey Theatre, correct?'

'I don't know what you mean by "access" but, yes, they were on scene first.'

'And so they would have also had access to the tow truck before you got there and saw the three strands of hair conveniently caught in the seat crack, correct?'

I objected, saying the question required the witness to speculate on things she would not have witnessed and was argumentative because of the use of the word 'conveniently.' Royce was obviously playing to the jury. The judge told Royce to rephrase the question without taking editorial license.

'The detectives would have had access to the tow truck before you got there and before you were the first to see the three strands of hair lodged in the seat crack, correct?'

Gordon took the hint from my objection and answered the way I wanted her to.

'I don't know because I wasn't there.'

Still, Royce had gotten his point across to the jury. He had also gotten the point of his case across to me. It was now fair to assume that the defense would put forth the theory that the police—in the person of Kloster and/or his partner, Steiner—had planted the hair evidence to secure a conviction of Jessup after he had been identified by the thirteen-year-old Sarah. Further to this, the defense would posit that Sarah's wrongful identification of Jessup was intentional and part of the Landy family's effort to hide the fact that Melissa had died either accidentally or intentionally at the hands of her stepfather.

It would be a tough road to take. To be successful it would take at least one person on the jury buying into what amounted to two conspiracies working independently of one another and yet in concert. But I could think of only two defense attorneys in town who could pull it off, and Royce was one of them. I had to be prepared.

'What happened after you noticed the hair on the tow truck's seat, do you remember?' Royce asked the witness.

'I pointed it out to Art because he was doing the actual collection of evidence. I was just there to observe and gather experience.'

'Were detectives Kloster and Steiner called over to take a look?'

'Yes, I believe so.'

'Do you recall what if anything they did then?'

'I don't recall them doing anything in relation to the hair evidence. It was their case and so they were notified of the evidence find and that was it.'

'Were you happy with yourself?'

'I don't think I understand.'

'It was your first day on the job — your first case. Were you pleased with yourself after spotting the hair evidence? Were you proud?'

Gordon hesitated before answering, as if trying to figure out if the question was a trap.

'I was pleased that I had contributed, yes.'

'And did you ever wonder why you, the rookie, spotted the hair in the seat crack before your supervisor or the two lead investigators?'

Gordon hesitated again and then said no. Royce said he had no further questions. It had been an excellent cross, planting multiple seeds that could later bloom into something larger in the defense case.

I did what I could on redirect, asking Gordon to recite the names of the six uniformed police officers and two other detectives who were listed as arriving ahead of Kloster and Steiner on the crime scene attendance log kept at the location where Melissa Landy's body was found.

'So, hypothetically, if Detective Kloster or Steiner had wanted to take hair from the victim to plant elsewhere, they would have had to do it under the noses of eight other officers or enlist them in allowing them to do it. Is that correct?'

'Yes, it would seem so.'

I thanked the witness and sat down. Royce then went back to the lectern for recross.

'Also hypothetically, if Kloster or Steiner wanted to plant hair from the victim at the third crime scene, it would not have been necessary to take it directly from the victim's head if there were other sources for it, correct?'

'I guess not if there were other sources.'

'For example, a hairbrush in the victim's home could have provided hair to them, correct?'

'I guess so.'

'They were in the victim's home, weren't they?'

'Yes, that was one of the locations where they signed in.'

'Nothing further.'

Royce had nailed me and I decided not to pursue this any further. Royce would have a comeback no matter what I brought forward from the witness.

Gordon was dismissed and the judge broke for lunch. I told Bosch that he would be on the stand after the break, reading Kloster's testimony into the record. I asked if he wanted to grab lunch together to talk about the defense's theory but he said he couldn't, that he had something to do.

Maggie was heading over to the hotel to have lunch with Sarah Ann Gleason, so that left me on my own.

Or so I thought.

As I headed down the center aisle to the rear door of the courtroom, an attractive woman stepped out of the back row in front of me. She smiled and stepped up to me.

'Mr. Haller, I'm Rachel Walling with the FBI.'

At first it didn't compute but then the name caught on a memory prompt somewhere inside.

'Yes, the profiler. You distracted my investigator with your theory that Jason Jessup is a serial killer.'

'Well, I hope it was more help than distraction.'

'I guess that remains to be seen. What can I do for you, Agent Walling?'

'I was going to ask if you might have time for lunch. But since you consider me a distraction, then maybe I should just...'

'Guess what, Agent Walling. You're in luck. I'm free. Let's have lunch.'

I pointed to the door and we headed out.

30

This time it was the judge who was late returning to court. The prosecution and defense teams were seated at the appointed time and ready to go but there was no sign of Breitman. And there had been no indication from the clerk as to whether the delay was because of personal business or some sort of trial issue. Bosch got up from his seat at the railing and approached Haller, tapping him on the back.

'Harry, we're about to start. You ready?'

'I'm ready, but we need to talk.'

'What's wrong?'

Bosch turned his body so his back was to the defense table and lowered his voice into a barely audible whisper.

'I went to see the SIS guys at lunch. They showed me some stuff you need to know about.'

He was being overly cryptic. But the photos Lieutenant Wright had showed him from the surveillance the night before were troubling. Jessup was up to something and whatever it might be, it was going to go down soon.

Before Haller could respond, the background hubbub of the courtroom ceased as the judge took the bench.

'After court,' Haller whispered.

He then turned back to the front of the courtroom and Bosch returned to his seat at the railing. The judge told the deputy to seat the jury and soon everyone was in place.

'I want to apologize,' Breitman said. 'This delay was my responsibility. I had a personal matter come up and it took far longer than I expected it would. Mr. Haller, please call your next witness.'

Haller stood and called for Doral Kloster. Bosch stood and headed for the witness stand while the judge once again explained to the jury that the witness called by the prosecution was unavailable and that prior sworn testimony would be read by Bosch and Haller. Though all of this had been worked out in a pretrial hearing and over the objection of the defense, Royce stood once again and objected.

'Mr. Royce, we've already argued this issue,' the judge responded.

'I would ask that the court reconsider its ruling as this form of testimony entirely undercuts Mr. Jessup's Constitutional right to confront his accusers. Detective Kloster was not asked the questions I would want to ask him based on the defense's current view of the case.'

'Again, Mr. Royce, this issue has been settled and I do not wish to rehash it in front of the jury.'

'But, *Your Honor,* I am being inhibited from presenting a full defense.'

'Mr. Royce, I have been very generous in allowing

you to posture in front of the jury. My patience is now growing thin. You may sit down.'

Royce stared the judge down. Bosch knew what he was doing. Playing to the jury. He wanted them to see him and Jessup as the underdogs. He wanted them to understand that it was not just the prosecution against Jessup but the judge as well. When he had drawn out the stare as long as he dared, he spoke again.

'Judge, I cannot sit down when my client's freedom is at stake. This is an egregious—'

Breitman angrily slammed her hand down, making a sound as loud as a shot.

'We're not going to do this in front of the jury, Mr. Royce. Will the jurors please return to the assembly room.'

Wide-eyed and alert to the tension that had engulfed the courtroom, the jurors filed out, to a person glancing back over their shoulders to check the action behind them. The whole time, Royce held his glare on the judge. And Bosch knew it was mostly an act. This was exactly what Royce wanted, for the jury to see him being persecuted and prevented from bringing his case forward. It didn't matter that they would be sequestered in the jury room. They all knew that Royce was about to get slapped down hard by the judge.

Once the door to the jury assembly room was closed, the judge turned back to Royce. In the thirty seconds it had taken the jury to leave the courtroom, she had obviously calmed down.

'Mr. Royce, at the end of the trial we will be holding

a contempt hearing during which your actions today will be examined and penalized. Until then, if I ever order you to sit down and you refuse that order, I will have the courtroom deputy forcibly place you in your seat. And it will not matter to me if the jury is present or not. Do you understand?'

'Yes, Your Honor. And I would like to apologize for allowing the emotions of the moment to get the best of me.'

'Very well, Mr. Royce. You will now sit down and we'll bring the jury back in.'

They held each other's eyes for a long moment until Royce finally and slowly sat down. The judge then told the courtroom deputy to retrieve the jury.

Bosch glanced at the jurors as they returned. They all had their eyes on Royce, and Harry could see the defense attorney's gambit had worked. He saw sympathy in their eyes, as if they all knew that at any moment they might cross the judge and be similarly rebuked. They didn't know what happened while they were behind the closed door, but Royce was like the kid who had been sent to the principal's office and had returned to tell everyone about it at recess.

The judge addressed the jury before continuing the trial.

'I want the members of the jury to understand that in a trial of this nature emotions sometimes run high. Mr. Royce and I have discussed the issue and it is resolved. You are to pay it no mind. So, let's proceed with the reading of prior sworn testimony. Mr. Haller?'

'Yes, Your Honor.'

Haller stood and went to the lectern with his printout of Doral Kloster's testimony.

'Detective Bosch, you are still under oath. Do you have the transcript of sworn testimony provided by Detective Doral Kloster on October eighth, nineteen eighty-six?'

'Yes, I do.'

Bosch placed the transcript on the stand and took a pair of reading glasses out of his jacket's inside pocket.

'Okay, then once again I will read the questions that were posed to Detective Kloster under oath by Deputy District Attorney Gary Lintz, and you will read the responses from the witness.'

After a series of questions used to elicit basic information about Kloster, the testimony moved quickly into the investigation of the murder of Melissa Landy.

' "Now, Detective, you are assigned to the detective squad at Wilshire Division, correct?" '

' "Yes, I am on the Homicide and Major Crimes table." '

' "And this case did not start out as a homicide." '

' "No, it did not. My partner and I were called in from home after patrol units were dispatched to the Landy house and a preliminary investigation determined that it appeared to be a stranger abduction. That made it a major crime and we were called out." '

' "What happened when you got to the Landy house?" '

' "We initially separated the individuals there—the mother, father and Sarah, the sister—and conducted interviews. We then brought the family together and conducted a joint interview. It often works best that way and it did this time. In the joint interview we found our investigative direction." '

' "Tell us about that. How did you find this direction?" '

' "In the individual interview, Sarah revealed that the girls had been playing a hide-and-seek game and that she was hiding behind some bushes at the front corner of her house. These bushes blocked her view of the street. She said she heard a trash truck and saw a trashman cross the yard and grab her sister. These events occurred on a Sunday, so we knew there was no city trash pickup. But when I had Sarah recount this story in front of her parents, her father quickly said that on Sunday mornings several tow trucks patrol the neighborhood and that the drivers wear overalls like the city sanitation workers do. And that became our first lead." '

' "And how did you follow that lead?" '

' "We were able to obtain a list of city-licensed tow truck companies that operated in the Wilshire District. By this time I had called in more detectives and we split the list up. There were only three companies that were operating on that day. Each pair of detectives took one. My partner and I went to a tow yard on La Brea Boulevard that was operated by a business called Aardvark Towing." '

' "And what happened when you got there?" '

' "We found that they were about to shut down for

the day because they essentially worked no-parking zones around churches. By noon they were done. There were three drivers and they were securing things and about to head out when we got there. They all voluntarily agreed to identify themselves and answer our questions. While my partner asked preliminary questions I went back to our car and called their names into central dispatch so they could check them for criminal records." '

' "Who were these men, Detective Kloster?" '

' "Their names were William Clinton, Jason Jessup and Derek Wilbern." '

' "And what was the result of your records search?" '

' "Only Wilbern had an arrest record. It was an attempted rape with no conviction. The case, as I recall, was four years old." '

' "Did this make him a suspect in the Melissa Landy abduction?" '

' "Yes, it did. He generally fit the description we had gotten from Sarah. He drove a large truck and wore overalls. And he had an arrest record involving a sex crime. That made him a strong suspect in my mind." '

' "What did you do next?" '

' "I returned to my partner and he was still interviewing the men in a group setting. I knew that time was of the essence. This little girl was still missing. She was still out there somewhere and usually in a case like this, the longer the individual is missing, the less chance you have of a good ending." '

' "So you made some decisions, didn't you?" '

' "Yes, I decided that Sarah Landy ought to see Derek Wilbern to see if she could identify him as the abductor." '

' "So did you set up a lineup for her to view?" '

' "No, I didn't." '

' "No?" '

' "No. I didn't feel there was time. I had to keep things moving. We had to try to find that girl. So what I did was ask if the three men would agree to go to a separate location where we could continue the interview. They each said yes." '

' "No hesitation?" '

' "No, none. They agreed." '

' "By the way, what happened when the other detectives visited the other towing companies that worked in the Wilshire District?" '

' "They did not find or interview anyone who rose to the level of suspect." '

' "You mean no one with a criminal record?" '

' "No criminal records and no flags came up during interviews." '

' "So you were concentrating on Derek Wilbern?" '

' "That's right." '

' "So when Wilbern and the other two men agreed to be interviewed at another location, what did you do?" '

' "We called for a couple of patrol cruisers and we put Jessup and Clinton in the back of one car and Wilbern in the back of the other. We then closed and locked the Aardvark tow yard and drove ahead in our car." '

' "So you got back to the Landy house first?" '

' "By design. We had told the patrol officers to take a circuitous route to the Landy house on Windsor so we could get there first. When we arrived back at the house I took Sarah upstairs to her bedroom, which was located at the front and was overlooking the front yard and street. I closed the blinds and had her look through just a crack so she would not be visibly exposed to the tow truck drivers." '

' "What happened next?" '

' "My partner had stayed out front. When the patrol cruisers arrived, I had him take the three men out of the cars and have them stand together on the sidewalk. I asked Sarah if she recognized any of them." '

' "Did she?" '

' "Not at first. But one of the men—Jessup—was wearing a baseball hat and he was looking down, using the brim to guard his face." '

Bosch flipped over two pages of the testimony at this point. The pages had been X-ed out. They contained several questions about Jessup's demeanor and attempt to use his hat to hide his face. These questions were objected to by Jessup's then-defense counsel, sustained by the trial judge, then resculpted and reasked, and objected to again. In the pretrial hearing, Breitman had agreed with Royce's contention that the current jury should not even hear them. It was one of the only points Royce had won.

Haller picked up the reading at the point the skirmish had ended.

' "Okay, Detective, why don't you tell the jury what happened next?" '

' "Sarah asked me if I could ask the man with the hat to remove it. I radioed my partner and he told Jessup to take off the hat. Almost immediately, Sarah said it was him." '

' "The man who abducted her sister?" '

' "Yes." '

' "Wait a minute. You said Derek Wilbern was your suspect." '

' "Yes, based on his having a record of a prior arrest for a sex crime, I thought he was the most likely suspect." '

' "Was Sarah sure of her identification?" '

' "I asked her several times to confirm the identification. She did." '

' "What did you do next?" '

' "I left Sarah in her room and went back downstairs. When I got outside I placed Jason Jessup under arrest, handcuffed him and put him in the back of a patrol car. I told other officers to put Wilbern and Clinton in another car and take them down to Wilshire Division for questioning." '

' "Did you question Jason Jessup at this point?" '

' "Yes, I did. Again, time was of the essence. I didn't feel that I had the time to take him to Wilshire Division and set up a formal interview. Instead, I got in the car with him, read him the Miranda warning and asked if he would talk to me. He said yes." '

' "Did you record this?" '

' "No, I did not. Frankly, I forgot. Things were moving

so quickly and all I could think about was finding that little girl. I had a recorder in my pocket but I forgot to record this conversation." '

' "Okay, so you questioned Jessup anyway?" '

' "I asked questions but he gave very few answers. He denied any involvement in the abduction. He acknowledged that he had been on tow patrol in the neighborhood that morning and could have driven by the Landy house but that he did not remember specifically driving on Windsor. I asked him if he remembered seeing the Hollywood sign, because if you are on Windsor you have a straight view of it up the street and on top of the hill. He said he didn't remember seeing the Hollywood sign." '

' "How long did this questioning go on?" '

' "Not long. Maybe five minutes. We were interrupted." '

' "By what, Detective?" '

' "My partner knocked on the car's window and I could tell by his face that whatever he had was important. I got out of the car and that's when he told me. They had found her. A girl's body had been found in a Dumpster down on Wilshire." '

' "That changed everything?" '

' "Yes, everything. I had Jessup transported downtown and booked while I proceeded to the location of the body." '

' "What did you discover when you got there?" '

' "There was a body of a girl approximately twelve or thirteen years old discarded in the Dumpster. She was unidentified at that time but she appeared to be

Melissa Landy. I had her photograph. I was pretty sure it was her." '

' "And you moved the focus of your investigation to this location?" '

' "Absolutely. My partner and I started conducting interviews while the crime scene people and coroner's people dealt with the body. We soon learned that the parking lot adjacent to the rear yard of the theater had previously been used as a temporary auto storage point by a towing company. We learned that company was Aardvark Towing." '

' "What did that mean to you?" '

' "To me it meant there was now a second connection between the murder of this girl and Aardvark. We had the lone witness, Sarah Landy, identifying one of the Aardvark drivers as the abductor, and now we had the victim found in a Dumpster next to a parking lot used by Aardvark drivers. To me the case was coming together." '

' "What was your next step?" '

' "At that point my partner and I split up. He stayed with the crime scene and I went back to Wilshire Division to work on search warrants." '

' "Search warrants for what?" '

' "One for the entire premises at Aardvark Towing. One for the tow truck Jessup was driving that day. And two more for Jessup's home and personal car." '

' "And did you receive these search warrants?" '

' "Yes, I did. Judge Richard Pittman was on call and he happened to be playing golf at Wilshire Country Club. I brought him the warrants and he signed them on the ninth hole. We then began the searches, starting at Aardvark." '

' "Were you present at this search?" '

' "Yes, I was. My partner and I were in charge of it." '

' "And at some point did you become aware of any particular evidence being found that you deemed important to the case?" '

' "Yes. At one point the forensics team leader, a man named Art Donovan, informed me that they had recovered three hairs that were brown in color and over a foot in length each from the tow truck that Jason Jessup was driving that day." '

' "Did Donovan tell you specifically where in the truck these hair specimens were found?" '

' "Yes, he said they were caught in the crack between the lower and upper parts of the truck's bench seat." '

Bosch closed the transcript there. Kloster's testimony continued but they had reached the point where Haller had said he would stop because he would have all he needed on the record.

The judge then asked Royce if he wished to have any of the defense's cross-examination read into the record. Royce stood to respond, holding two paper-clipped documents in his hand.

'For the record, I am reluctant to participate in a procedure I object to but since the court is calling the game, I shall play along. I have two brief read-backs of Detective Kloster's cross-examination. May I give a highlighted printout to Detective Bosch? I think it will make this much easier.'

'Very well,' the judge said.

The courtroom deputy took one of the documents from Royce and delivered it to Bosch, who quickly scanned it. It was only two pages of testimony transcriptions. Two exchanges were highlighted in yellow. As Bosch read them over, the judge explained to the jury that Royce would read questions posed by Jessup's previous defense attorney, Charles Barnard, while Bosch would continue to read the responses of Detective Doral Kloster.

'You may proceed, Mr. Royce.'

'Thank you, Your Honor. Now reading from the transcript, "Detective, how long was it from when you closed and locked Aardvark Towing and took the three drivers over to Windsor, and returned with the search warrant?" '

' "May I refer to the case chronology?" '

' "You may." '

' "It was about two hours and thirty-five minutes." '

' "And when you left Aardvark Towing, how did you secure those premises?" '

' "We closed the garages, and one of the drivers—I believe, Mr. Clinton—had a key to the door. I borrowed it to lock the door." '

' "Did you return the key to him after?" '

' "No, I asked if I could keep it for the time being and he said that was okay." '

' "So when you went back with the signed search warrant, you had the key and you simply unlocked the door to enter." '

' "That is correct." '

Royce flipped the page on his copy and told Bosch to do likewise.

'Okay, now reading from another point in the cross-examination. "Detective Kloster, what did you conclude when you were told about the hair specimens found in the tow truck Mr. Jessup had been driving that day?" '

' "Nothing. The specimens had not been identified yet." '

' "At what later point were they identified?" '

' "Two days later I got a call from SID. A hair-and-fiber tech told me that the hairs had been examined and that they closely matched samples taken from the victim. She said that she could not exclude the victim as a source." '

' "So then what did that tell you?" '

' "That it was likely that Melissa Landy had been in that tow truck." '

' "What other evidence in that truck linked the victim to it or Mr. Jessup to the victim?" '

' "There was no other evidence." '

' "No blood or other bodily fluids?" '

' "No." '

' "No fibers from the victim's dress?" '

' "No." '

' "Nothing else?" '

' "Nothing." '

' "With the lack of other corroborating evidence in the truck, did you ever consider that the hair evidence was planted in the truck?" '

' "Well, I considered it in the way I considered all aspects of the case. But I dismissed it because the witness to the abduction had identified Jessup, and that was the truck he was driving. I didn't think the evidence was planted. I mean, by who? No one was trying to set him up. He was identified by the victim's sister." '

That ended the read-back. Bosch glanced over at the jury box and saw that it appeared that everyone had remained attentive during what was most likely the most boring stage of the trial.

'Anything further, Mr. Royce?' the judge asked.

'Nothing further, Judge,' Royce responded.

'Very well,' Breitman said. 'I think this brings us to our afternoon break. I will see everyone back in place— and I will admonish myself to be on time—in fifteen minutes.'

The courtroom started to clear and Bosch stepped down from the witness stand. He went directly to Haller, who was huddled with McPherson. Bosch butted into their whispered conversation.

'Atwater, right?'

Haller looked up at him.

'Yes, right. Have her ready in fifteen minutes.'

'And you have time to talk after court?'

'I'll make time. I had an interesting conversation at lunch, as well. I need to tell you.'

Bosch left them and headed out to the hall. He knew the line at the coffee urn in the little concession stand near the elevators would be long and full of jurors from the case. He decided he would hit the stairwell and find coffee on another floor. But first he ducked into the restroom.

As he entered he saw Jessup at one of the sinks. He was leaning over and washing his hands. His eyes were below the mirror line and he didn't realize Bosch was behind him.

Bosch stood still and waited for the moment, thinking about what he would say when he and Jessup locked eyes.

But just as Jessup raised his head and saw Bosch in the mirror, the door to a stall to the left opened and juror number ten stepped out. It was an awkward moment as all three men said nothing.

Finally, Jessup grabbed a paper towel out of the dispenser, dried his hands and tossed it into the wastebasket. He headed to the door while the juror took his place at the sink. Bosch moved silently to a urinal but looked back at Jessup as he was pushing through the door.

Bosch shot him in the back with his finger. Jessup never saw it coming.

31

During the break I checked on my next witness and made sure she was good to go. I had a few spare minutes, so I tracked Bosch down in the line at the coffee concession one floor down. Juror number six was two spots in front of him. I took Bosch by the elbow and led him away.

'You can get your coffee later. There's no time to drink it anyway. I wanted you to know that I had lunch with your girlfriend from the bureau.'

'What? Who?'

'Agent Walling.'

'She's not my girlfriend. Why did she have lunch with you?'

I led him to the stairwell and we headed back upstairs as we talked.

'Well, I think she wanted to have lunch with you but you split out of here too fast so she settled for me. She wanted to give us a warning. She said she's been watching and reading the reports on the trial and she thinks if Jessup is going to blow, it's going to be soon. She said he reacts to pressure and he's probably never been under more than he is right now.'

336

Bosch nodded.

'That's sort of what I wanted to talk to you about before.'

He looked around to make sure that no one was in earshot.

'The SIS says Jessup's nighttime activities have increased since the start of the trial. He's going out every night now.'

'Has he gone down your street?'

'No, he hasn't been back there or to any of the other spots off Mulholland in a week. But over the last two nights he's done things that are new.'

'Like what, Harry?'

'Like on Sunday they followed him down the beach from Venice and he went into the old storage area under the Santa Monica Pier.'

'What storage area? What's this mean?'

'It's an old city storage facility but it got flooded by high tides so many times it's locked up and abandoned. Jessup dug underneath one of the old wood sidings and crawled in.'

'Why?'

'Who knows? They couldn't go in or they would risk exposing the surveillance. But that's not the real news. The real news is, last night he met with a couple of guys at the Townhouse in Venice and then went out to a car in one of the beach lots. One of the guys took something wrapped in a towel out of the trunk and gave it to him.'

'A gun?'

Bosch shrugged.

'Whatever it was, they never saw, but through the car's plates they IDed one of the two guys. Marshall Daniels. He was in San Quentin in the nineties—same time as Jessup.'

I was now catching some of the tension and urgency that was coming off Bosch.

'They could've known each other. What was Daniels up there for?'

'Drugs and weapons.'

I checked my watch. I needed to be back in court.

'Then we have to assume Jessup has a weapon. We could violate his OR right now for associating with a convicted felon. Do they have pictures of Jessup and Daniels together?'

'They have photos but I am not sure we want to do that.'

'If he's got a gun...Do you trust the SIS to stop him before he makes a move or does some damage?'

'I do, but it would help if we knew what the move was.'

We stepped out into the hallway and saw no sign of any jurors or anyone else from the trial. Everybody was back in court but me.

'We'll talk about this later. I have to get back into court or the judge will jump on my ass next. I'm not like Royce. I can't afford a contempt hearing just to make a point with the jury. Go get Atwater and bring her in.'

I hurried back to Department 112 and rudely pushed

around a couple of the courthouse gadflies who were moving slowly through the door. Judge Breitman had not waited for me. I saw everyone but me in place and the jury was being seated. I moved up the aisle and through the gate and slipped into the seat next to Maggie.

'That was close,' she whispered. 'I think the judge was hoping to even things up by holding *you* in contempt.'

'Yeah, well, she may still.'

The judge turned away from the jurors and noticed me at the prosecution table.

'Well, thank you for joining us this afternoon, Mr. Haller. Did you have a nice excursion?'

I stood.

'My apologies, Your Honor. I had a personal matter come up and it took far longer than I expected it would.'

She opened her mouth to deliver a rebuke but then paused as she realized I had thrown her words from the morning's delay — her delay — right back at her.

'Just call your next witness, Counselor,' she said curtly.

I called Lisa Atwater to the stand and glanced to the back of the courtroom to see Bosch leading the DNA lab technician down the aisle to the gate. I checked the clock up on the rear wall. My goal was to use up the rest of the day with Atwater's testimony, bringing her to the nuts and bolts just before we recessed for the day. That might give Royce a whole night to prepare his cross-examination, but I would happily trade that for what I would get out of the deal — every juror going home with knowledge of the unimpeachable evidence that linked Jason Jessup to the murder of Melissa Landy.

As I had asked her to, Atwater had kept her lab coat on when she walked over from the LAPD lab. The light blue jacket gave her a look of competence and professionalism that the rest of her didn't convey. Atwater was very young—only thirty-one—and had blond hair with a pink stripe down one side, modeling her look after a supercool lab tech on one of the TV crime shows. After meeting her for the first time, I tried to get her to think about losing the pink, but she told me she wouldn't give up her individuality. The jurors, she said, would have to accept her for who and what she was.

At least the lab coat wasn't pink.

Atwater identified herself and was sworn in. After she took the witness seat I started asking questions about her educational pedigree and work experience. I spent at least ten more minutes on this than I normally would have, but I kept seeing that ribbon of pink hair and thought I had to do all I could to turn it into a badge of professionalism and accomplishment.

Finally, I got to the crux of her testimony. With me carefully asking the questions, she testified that she had conducted DNA typing and comparison on two completely different evidence samples from the Landy case. I went with the more problematic analysis first.

'Ms. Atwater, can you describe the first DNA assignment you received on the Landy case?'

'Yes, on February fourth I was given a swatch of

fabric that had been cut from the dress that the victim had been wearing at the time of her murder.'

'Where did you receive this from?'

'It came from the LAPD's Property Division, where it had been kept in controlled evidence storage.'

Her answers were carefully rehearsed. She could give no indication that there had been a previous trial in the case or that Jessup had been in prison for the past twenty-four years. To do so would create prejudice against Jessup and trigger a mistrial.

'Why were you sent this swatch of fabric?'

'There was a stain on the fabric that twenty-four years ago had been identified by the LAPD forensics unit as semen. My assignment was to extract DNA and identify it if possible.'

'When you examined this swatch, was there any degradation of the genetic material on it?'

'No, sir. It had been properly preserved.'

'Okay, so you got this swatch of material from Melissa Landy's dress and you extracted DNA from it. Do I have that right so far?'

'That's right.'

'What did you do next?'

'I turned the DNA profile into a code and entered it into the CODIS database.'

'What is CODIS?'

'It's the FBI's Combined DNA Index System. Think of it as a national clearinghouse of DNA records. All DNA signatures gathered by law enforcement end up here and are available for comparison.'

'So you entered the DNA signature obtained from semen on the dress Melissa Landy wore on the day she was murdered, correct?'

'Correct.'

'Did you get a hit?'

'I did. The profile belonged to her stepfather, Kensington Landy.'

A courtroom is a big space. There is always a low-level current of sound and energy. You can feel it even if you can't really hear it. People whisper in the gallery, the clerk and deputy handle phone calls, the court reporter touches the keys on her steno machine. But the sound and air went completely out of Department 112 after Lisa Atwater said what she said. I let it ride for a few moments. I knew this would be the lowest point of the case. With that one answer I had, in fact, revealed Jason Jessup's case. But from this point on, it would all be my case. And Melissa Landy's case. I wouldn't forget about her.

'Why was Kensington Landy's DNA in the CODIS database?' I asked.

'Because California has a law that requires all felony arrest suspects to submit a DNA sample. In two thousand four Mr. Landy was arrested for a hit-and-run accident causing injury. Though he eventually pleaded to lesser charges, it was originally charged as a felony, thus triggering the DNA law upon his booking. His DNA was entered into the system.'

'Okay. Now getting back to the victim's dress and the semen that was on it. How did you determine that the semen was deposited on the day that Melissa Landy was murdered?'

Atwater seemed confused by the question at first. It was a skilled act.

'I didn't,' she said. 'It is impossible to know exactly when that deposit was made.'

'You mean it could have been on the dress for a week before her death?'

'Yes. There's no way of knowing.'

'What about a month?'

'It's possible because there is—'

'What about a year?'

'Again, it is—'

'Objection!'

Royce stood. About time, I thought.

'Your Honor, how long does this have to go on past the point?'

'Withdrawn, Judge. Mr. Royce is right. We're well past the point.'

I paused for a moment to underline that Atwater and I would now be moving in a new direction.

'Ms. Atwater, you recently handled a second DNA analysis in regard to the Melissa Landy case, correct?'

'Yes, I did.'

'Can you describe what that entailed?'

Before answering she secured the pink band of hair behind her ear.

'Yes, it was a DNA extraction and comparison of hair specimens. Hair from the victim, Melissa Landy, which was contained in a kit taken at the time of her autopsy and hair recovered from a tow truck operated by the defendant, Jason Jessup.'

'How many hair specimens are we talking about?'

'Ultimately, one of each. Our objective was to extract nuclear DNA, which is available only in the root of a hair sample. Of the specimens we had, there was only one suitable extraction from the hairs recovered from the tow truck. So we compared DNA from the root of that hair to DNA from a hair sample taken from the autopsy kit.'

I walked her through the process, trying to keep the explanations as simple as possible. Just enough to get by, like on TV. I kept one eye on my witness and one on the jury box, making sure everybody was staying plugged in and happy.

Finally, we came out the other end of the techno-genetic tunnel and arrived at Lisa Atwater's conclusions. She put several color-coded charts and graphs up on the screens and thoroughly explained them. But the bottom line was always the same thing; to feel it, jurors had to hear it. The most important thing a witness brings into a courtroom is her word. After all the charts were displayed, it came down to Atwater's words.

I turned and looked back at the clock. I was right on schedule. In less than twenty minutes the judge would recess for the evening. I turned back and moved in for the kill.

'Ms. Atwater, do you have any hesitation or doubt at all about the genetic match you have just testified about?'

'No, none whatsoever.'

'Do you believe beyond a doubt that the hair from Melissa Landy is a unique match to the hair specimen obtained from the tow truck the defendant was operating on February sixteenth, nineteen eighty-six?'

'Yes, I do.'

'Is there a quantifiable way of illustrating this match?'

'Yes, as I illustrated earlier, we matched nine out of the thirteen genetic markers in the CODIS protocol. The combination of these nine particular genetic markers occurs in one in one-point-six trillion individuals.'

'Are you saying it is a one-in-one-point-six-trillion chance that the hair found in the tow truck operated by the defendant belonged to someone other than Melissa Landy?'

'You could say it that way, yes.'

'Ms. Atwater, do you happen to know the current population of the world?'

'It's approaching seven billion.'

'Thank you, Ms. Atwater. I have no further questions at this time.'

I moved to my seat and sat down. Immediately I started stacking files and documents, getting it all ready for the briefcase and the ride home. This day was in the books and I had a long night ahead of me preparing for the next one. The judge didn't seem to begrudge me finishing ten minutes early. She was shutting down herself and sending the jury home.

'We will continue with the cross-examination of this witness tomorrow. I would like to thank all of you for paying such close attention to today's testimony. We will be adjourned until nine o'clock sharp tomorrow morning and I once again admonish you not to watch any news program or—'

'Your Honor?'

I looked up from the files. Royce was on his feet.

'Yes, Mr. Royce?'

'My apologies, Judge Breitman, for interrupting. But by my watch, it is only four-fifty and I know that you prefer to get as much testimony as possible in each day. I would like to cross-examine this witness now.'

The judge looked at Atwater, who was still on the witness stand, and then back to Royce.

'Mr. Royce, I would rather you begin your cross tomorrow morning rather than start and then interrupt it after only ten minutes. We don't go past five o'clock with the jury. That is a rule I will not break.'

'I understand, Judge. But I am not planning to interrupt it. I will be finished with this witness by five o'clock and then she will not be required to return tomorrow.'

The judge stared at Royce for a long moment, a disbelieving look on her face.

'Mr. Royce, Ms. Atwater is one of the prosecution's key witnesses. Are you telling me you only need five minutes for cross-examination?'

'Well, of course it depends on the length of her answers, but I have only a few questions, Your Honor.'

'Very well, then. You may proceed. Ms. Atwater, you remain under oath.'

Royce moved to the lectern and I was as confused as

the judge about the defense's maneuver. I had expected Royce to take most of the next morning on cross. This had to be a trick. He had a DNA expert on his own witness list but I would never give up a shot at the prosecution's witness.

'Ms. Atwater,' Royce said, 'did all of the testing and typing and extracting you conducted on the hair specimen from the tow truck tell you how the specimen got inside that truck?'

To buy time Atwater asked Royce to repeat the question. But even upon hearing it a second time, she did not answer until the judge intervened.

'Ms. Atwater, can you answer the question?' Breitman asked.

'Uh, yes, I'm sorry. My answer is no, the lab work I conducted had nothing to do with determining how the hair specimen found its way into the tow truck. That was not my responsibility.'

'Thank you,' Royce said. 'So to make it crystal clear, you cannot tell the jury how that hair—which you have capably identified as belonging to the victim—got inside the truck or who put it there, isn't that right?'

I stood.

'Objection. Assumes facts not in evidence.'

'Sustained. Would you like to rephrase, Mr. Royce?'

'Thank you, Your Honor. Ms. Atwater, you have no idea—other than what you were perhaps told—how the hair you tested found its way into the tow truck, correct?'

'That would be correct, yes.'

'So you can identify the hair as Melissa Landy's but you cannot testify with the same sureness as to how it ended up in the tow truck, correct?'

I stood up again.

'Objection,' I said. 'Asked and answered.'

'I think I will let the witness answer,' Breitman said. 'Ms. Atwater?'

'Yes, that is correct,' Atwater said. 'I cannot testify about anything regarding how the hair happened to end up in the truck.'

'Then I have no further questions. Thank you.'

I turned back and looked at the clock. I had two minutes. If I wanted to get the jury back on track I had to think of something quick.

'Any redirect, Mr. Haller?' the judge asked.

'One moment, Your Honor.'

I turned and leaned toward Maggie to whisper.

'What do I do?'

'Nothing,' she whispered back. 'Let it go or you might make it worse. You made your points. He made his. Yours are more important—you put Melissa inside his truck. Leave it there.'

Something told me not to leave it as is but my mind was a blank. I couldn't think of a question derived from Royce's cross that would get the jury off his point and back onto mine.

'Mr. Haller?' the judge said impatiently.

I gave it up.

'No further questions at this time, Your Honor.'

'Very well, then, we will adjourn for the day. Court

will reconvene at nine A.M. tomorrow and I admonish the jurors not to read newspaper accounts about this trial or view television reports or talk to family or friends about the case. I hope everyone has a good night.'

With that the jury stood and began to file out of the box. I casually glanced over at the defense table and saw Royce being congratulated by Jessup. They were all smiles. I felt a hollow in my stomach the size of a baseball. It was as though I had played it to near perfection all day long—for almost six hours of testimony—and then in the last five minutes managed to let the last out in the ninth go right between my legs.

I sat still and waited until Royce and Jessup and everybody else had left the courtroom.

'You coming?' Maggie said from behind me.

'In a minute. How about I meet you back at the office?'

'Let's walk back together.'

'I'm not good company, Mags.'

'Haller, get over it. You had a great day. *We* had a great day. He was good for five minutes and the jury knows that.'

'Okay. I'll meet you there in a little bit.'

She gave up and I heard her leave. After a few minutes I reached over to the top file on the stack in front of me and opened it up halfway. A school photo of Melissa Landy was clipped inside the folder. Smiling at the camera. She looked nothing like my daughter but she made me think of Hayley.

I made a silent vow not to let Royce outsmart me again.

A few moments later, someone turned out the lights.

32

Bosch stood by the swing set planted in the sand a quarter mile south of the Santa Monica Pier. The black water of the Pacific to his left was alive with the dancing reflection of light and color from the Ferris wheel at the end of the boardwalk. The amusement park had closed fifteen minutes earlier but the light show would go on through the night, an electronic display of ever-changing patterns on the big wheel that was mesmerizing in the cold darkness.

Harry raised his phone and called the SIS dispatcher. He had checked in earlier and set things up.

'It's Bosch again. How's our boy?'

'He appears to be tucked in for the night. You must've worn him out in court today, Bosch. On the way home from the CCB he went to Ralphs to pick up some groceries and then straight home, where he's been ever since. First night in five he hasn't been out and about at this time.'

'Yeah, well, don't count on it staying that way. They've got the back door covered, right?'

'And the windows and the car and the bicycle. We got him, Detective. Don't worry.'

'Then I won't. You've got my number. Call me if he moves.'

'Will do.'

Bosch put the phone away and headed toward the pier. The wind was strong off the water and a fine mist of sand stung his face and eyes as he approached the huge structure. The pier was like a beached aircraft carrier. It was long and wide. It had a large parking lot and an assortment of restaurants and souvenir shops on top. At its midpoint it had a full amusement park with a roller coaster and the signature Ferris wheel. And at its furthest extension into the sea it was a traditional fishing pier with a bait shop, management office and yet another restaurant. All of it was supported on a thick forest of wood pilings that started landside and carried seven hundred feet out beyond the wave break and to the cold depths.

Landside, the pilings were enclosed with a wooden siding that created a semi-secure storage facility for the city of Santa Monica. Only semi-secure for two reasons: The storage area was vulnerable to extreme high tides, which came on rare occasion during offshore earthquakes. Also, the pier spanned a hundred yards of beach, which entailed anchoring the wood siding in moist sand. The wood was always in the process of rotting and was easily compromised. The result was that the storage facility had become an unofficial homeless shelter that had to be periodically cleared out by the city.

The SIS observers had reported that Jason Jessup

had slipped underneath the south wall the night before and had spent thirty-one minutes inside the storage area.

Bosch reached the pier and started walking its length, looking for the spot in the wood siding where Jessup had crawled under. He carried a mini Maglite and quickly found a depression where the sand had been dug out at the wall's base and partially filled back in. He crouched down, put the light into the hole and determined that it was too small for him to fit through. He put the light down to the side, reached down and started digging like a dog trying to escape the yard.

Soon the hole seemed big enough and he crawled through. He was dressed for the effort. Old black jeans and work boots, and a long-sleeved T-shirt beneath a plastic raid jacket he wore inside out to hide the luminescent yellow LAPD across the front and back.

He came up inside to a dark, cavernous space with slashes of light filtering down between the planks of the parking lot above. He stood up and brushed the sand off his clothes, then swept the area with the flashlight. It had been made for close-in work, so its beam did little to illuminate the far reaches of the space.

There was a damp smell and the sound of waves crashing through the pilings only twenty-five yards away echoed loudly in the enclosed space. Bosch pointed the light up and saw fungus caked on the pier's crossbeams. He moved forward into the gloom and quickly came upon a boat covered by a tarp. He lifted up a loose end and saw that it was an old lifeguard boat. He moved on and came upon stacks of buoys and then stacks of traffic barricades and mobile barriers, all of them stenciled with CITY OF SANTA MONICA.

He next came to three stacks of scaffolding used for paint and repair projects on the pier. They looked long untouched and were slowly sinking in the sand.

Across the rear was a line of enclosed storage rooms, but the wood sidings had cracked and split over time, making storage in them porous at best.

The doors were unlocked and Bosch went down the line, finding each one empty until the second to the last. Here the door was secured with a shiny new padlock. He put the beam of his light into one of the cracks between the planks of the siding and tried to look in. He saw what appeared to be the edge of a blanket but that was all.

Bosch moved back to the door and knelt down in front of the lock. He held the light with his mouth and extracted two lock picks from his wallet. He went to work on the padlock and quickly determined that it had only four tumblers. He got it open in less than five minutes.

He entered the storage corral and found it largely empty. There was a folded blanket on the ground with a pillow on top of it. Nothing else. The SIS surveillance report had said that the night before, Jessup had walked down the beach carrying a blanket. It did not say that he had left it behind under the pier, and there had been nothing in the report about a pillow.

Harry wasn't even sure he was in the same spot that Jessup had come to. He moved the light over the wall and then up to the underside of the pier, where he held it. He could clearly see the outline of a door. A trapdoor. It was locked from underneath with another new padlock.

Bosch was pretty sure that he was standing beneath the pier's parking lot. He had occasionally heard the sound of vehicles up above as the pier crowd went home. He guessed that the trapdoor had been used as some sort of loading door for materials to be stored. He knew he could grab one of the scaffolds and climb up to examine the second lock but decided not to bother. He retreated from the corral.

As he was relocking the door with the padlock he felt his phone begin to vibrate in his pocket. He quickly pulled it out, expecting to learn from SIS dispatch that Jessup was on the move. But the caller ID told him the call was from his daughter. He opened the phone.

'Hey, Maddie.'

'Dad? Are you there?'

Her voice was low and the sound of crashing waves was loud. Bosch yelled.

'I'm here. What's wrong?'

'Well, when are you coming home?'

'Soon, baby. I've got a little bit more work to do.'

She dropped her voice even lower and Bosch had to clamp a hand over his other ear to hear her. In the background he could hear the freeway on her end. He knew she was on the rear deck.

'Dad, she's making me do homework that isn't even due until next week.'

Bosch had once again left her with Sue Bambrough, the assistant principal.

'So next week you'll be thanking her when everybody else is doing it and you'll be all done.'

'Dad, I've been doing homework all night!'

'You want me to tell her to let you take a break?'

His daughter didn't respond and Bosch understood. She had called because she wanted him to know the misery she was suffering. But she didn't want him to do anything about it.

'I'll tell you what,' he said. 'When I get back I will remind Mrs. Bambrough that you are not in school when you are at home and you don't need to be working the whole time. Okay?'

'I guess. Why can't I just stay at Rory's? This isn't fair.'

'Maybe next time. I need to get back to work, Mads. Can we talk about it tomorrow? I want you in bed by the time I get home.'

'Whatever.'

'Good night, Madeline. Make sure all the doors are locked, including on the deck, and I'll see you tomorrow.'

'Good night.'

The disapproval in her voice was hard to miss. She disconnected the call ahead of Bosch. He closed his phone and just as he slid it into his pocket he heard a noise, like a banging of metal parts, coming from the direction of the hole he had slid through into the storage area. He immediately killed his flashlight and moved toward the tarp that covered the boat.

Crouching behind the boat, he saw a human figure

stand up by the wall and start moving in the darkness without a flashlight. The figure moved without hesitation toward the storage corral with the new lock on it.

There were streetlights over the parking lot above. They sent slivers of illumination down through the cracks formed by retreating planks in the boardwalk. As the figure moved through these, Bosch saw that it was Jessup.

Harry dropped lower and instinctively reached his hand to his belt just to make sure his gun was there. With his other hand he pulled his phone and hit the mute button. He didn't want the SIS dispatcher to suddenly remember to call him to alert him that Jessup was moving.

Bosch noticed that Jessup was carrying a bag that appeared to be heavily weighted. He went directly to the locked storage room and soon swung the door open. He obviously had a key to the padlock.

Jessup stepped back and Bosch saw a slash of light cross his face as he turned and scanned the entire storage area, making sure he was alone. He then went inside the room.

For several seconds, there was no sound or movement, then Jessup reappeared in the doorway. He stepped out and closed the door, relocking it. He then stepped back into the light and did a 180-degree scan of the larger storage area. Bosch lowered his body even further. He guessed that Jessup was suspicious because he had found the hole under the wall freshly dug out.

'*Who's there?*' he called out.

Bosch didn't move. He didn't even breathe.

'Show yourself!'

Bosch snaked his hand under the raid jacket and closed his hand on his gun's grips. He knew the indications were that Jessup had obtained a weapon. If he made even a feint in Bosch's direction, Harry was going to pull his own weapon and be ready to fire first.

But it never happened. Jessup started moving quickly back to the entrance hole and soon he disappeared in the darkness. Bosch listened but all he could hear was the crashing of the waves. He waited another thirty seconds and then started moving toward the opening in the wall. He didn't turn on the light. He wasn't sure Jessup had actually left.

As he moved around the stack of scaffolding frames, he banged his shin hard on a metal pipe that was extending out from the pile. It sent a sudden burst of pain up his left leg and shifted the balance of metal frames. The top two loudly slid off stack, clattering to the sand. Bosch threw himself to the sand next to the pile and waited.

But Jessup didn't appear. He was gone.

Bosch slowly got up. He was in pain and he was angry. He pulled his phone and called SIS dispatch.

'You were supposed to call me when Jessup moved!' he whispered angrily.

'I know that,' said the dispatcher. 'He hasn't moved.'

'What? Are you—patch me through to whoever's in charge out there.'

'I'm sorry, Detective, but that's not how—'

'Look, shithead, Jessup is not *tucked in* for the night. I just saw him. And it almost turned bad. Now let me talk to somebody out there or my next call is to Lieutenant Wright at home.'

While he waited Bosch moved to the sidewall so he could get out of the storage area. His leg hurt badly and he was walking with a limp.

In the darkness he couldn't find the spot where he could slip under the wall. Finally, he put the light on, holding it low to the ground. He found the spot but saw that Jessup had pushed sand into the hole, just as he had the night before.

A voice finally came to him over the phone.

'Bosch? This is Jacquez. You claim you just saw our subject?'

'I don't claim I saw him. I did see him. Where are your people?'

'We're sitting on his zero, man. He hasn't left.'

Zero was a surveillance subject's home location.

'Bullshit, I just saw him under the Santa Monica Pier. Get your people up here. Now.'

'We got his zero down tight, Bosch. There's no—'

'Listen, Jackass, Jessup is my case. I know him and he almost just crawled up my ass. Now call your men and find out which one went off post because—'

'I'll get back to you,' Jacquez said curtly and the line went dead.

Bosch turned the phone's ringer back on and put it in his pocket. Once again he dropped to his knees and quickly dug out the hole, using his hands as a scoop.

He then pushed his body through, half expecting Jessup to be waiting for him when he came up on the other side.

But there was no sign of him. Bosch got up, gazed south down the beach in the direction of Venice and saw no one in the light from the Ferris wheel. He then turned and looked up toward the hotels and apartment buildings that ran along the beach. Several people were on the beach walk that fronted the buildings but he didn't recognize any of the figures as Jessup.

Twenty-five yards up the pier was a set of stairs leading topside and directly to the pier's parking lot. Bosch headed that way, still limping badly. He was halfway up the stairs when his phone rang. It was Jacquez.

'All right, where is he? We're on our way.'

'That's the thing. I lost him. I had to hide and I thought you people were on him. I'm going to the top of the pier now. What the hell happened, Jacquez?'

'We had a guy step out to drop a deuce. Said his stomach was giving him trouble. I don't think he'll be in the unit after tonight.'

'Jesus Christ!'

Bosch got to the top of the steps and walked out onto the empty parking lot. There was no sign of Jessup.

'Okay, I'm up on the pier. I don't see him. He's in the wind.'

'Okay, Bosch, we're two minutes out. We're going to spread. We'll find him. He didn't take the car or the bike, so he's on foot.'

'He could've grabbed a cab at any one of the hotels

over here. The bottom line is we don't know where—'

Bosch suddenly realized something.

'I gotta go. Call me as soon as you have him, Jacquez. You got that?'

'Got it.'

Bosch ended the call and then immediately called his home on the speed dial. He checked his watch and expected Sue Bambrough to answer, since it was after eleven.

But his daughter picked up the call.

'Dad?'

'Hey, baby, why are you still up?'

'Because I had to do all that homework. I wanted a little break before I went to sleep.'

'That's fine. Listen, can you put Mrs. Bambrough on the line?'

'Dad, I'm in my bedroom and I'm in my pajamas.'

'That's okay. Just go to the door and tell her to pick up the phone in the kitchen. I need to talk to her. And meantime, you have to get dressed. You're leaving the house.'

'What? Dad, I have—'

'Madeline, listen to me. This is important. I am going to tell Mrs. Bambrough to take you to her house until I can get there. I want you out of the house.'

'Why?'

'You don't need to know that. You just need to do what I ask. Now, please, get Mrs. Bambrough on the phone.'

She didn't respond but he heard the door of her room

open. Then he heard his daughter say, 'It's for you.'

A few moments later the extension was picked up in the kitchen.

'Hello?'

'Sue, it's Harry. I need you to do something. I need you to take Maddie to your house. Right now. I will be there in less than an hour to get her.'

'I don't understand.'

'Sue, listen, we've been watching a guy tonight who knows where I live. And we lost him. Now, there is no reason to panic or to believe he is heading that way but I want to take all precautions. So I want you to take Maddie and get out of the house. Right now. Go to your place and I will see you there. Can you do this, Sue?'

'We're leaving right now.'

He liked the strength in her voice and realized it probably came with the territory of being a teacher and assistant principal in the public school system.

'Okay, I'm on my way. Call me back as soon as you get to your place.'

But Bosch wasn't really on his way. After the call, he put the phone away and went back down the steps to the beach. He returned to the hole he had dug under the storage area wall. He crawled back under and this time used his flashlight to find his way to the locked storage room. He used his picks again on the padlock and the whole time he worked he was distracted by thoughts of Jessup's escape from the surveillance. Had it just been a coincidence that he had left his apartment at the same time the SIS watcher had left his post, or was he aware of the surveillance and did he break free when he saw the opportunity?

At the moment, there was no way to know.

Finally, he got the lock open, taking longer than he had the first time. He entered the storage room and moved the light to the blanket and pillow on the ground. The bag Jessup had carried was there. It said *Ralphs* on its side. Bosch dropped to his knees and was about to open it when his phone buzzed. It was Jacquez.

'We got him. He's on Nielson at Ocean Park. It looks like he's walking home.'

'Then try not to lose him this time, Jacquez. I gotta go.'

He disconnected before Jacquez could reply. He quickly called his daughter's cell. She was in the car with Sue Bambrough. Bosch told her they could turn around and go back home. This news was not received with a thankful release of tension. His daughter was left upset and angry over the scare. Bosch couldn't blame her but he couldn't stay on the line.

'I'll be home in less than an hour. We can talk about it then if you're still awake. I'll see you soon.'

He disconnected the call and focused on the bag. He opened it without moving it from its spot next to the blanket.

The bag contained a dozen single-serving-size cans of fruit. There were diced peaches in heavy syrup, chopped pineapple and something called fruit medley. Also in the bag was a package of plastic spoons. Bosch stared at the contents for a long moment and then his eyes moved up the wall to the crossbeams and the locked trapdoor above.

'Who are you bringing here, Jessup?' he whispered.

33

All eyes were on the back of the courtroom. It was time
for the main event, and while I had ringside seats, I was
still going to be just a spectator like everybody else.
That didn't sit very well with me but it was a choice I
could live with and trust. The door opened and Harry
Bosch led our main witness into the courtroom. Sarah
Ann Gleason told us she didn't own any dresses and
didn't want to buy one to testify in. She wore black
jeans and a purple silk blouse. She looked pretty and
she looked confident. We didn't need a dress.

Bosch stayed on her right side and when opening the
gate for her positioned his body between her and Jessup, who sat at the defense table, turned like everybody
else toward his main accuser's entrance.

Bosch let her go the rest of the way by herself. Maggie
McFierce was already at the lectern and she smiled
warmly at her witness as she went by. This was Maggie's
moment, too, and I read her smile as one of hope for
both women.

We'd had a good morning, with testimony from Bill
Clinton, the former tow truck driver, and then Bosch

taking the case through to lunch. Clinton told his story about the day of the murder and Jessup borrowing his Dodgers cap just before they became part of the impromptu lineup outside the house on Windsor Boulevard. He also testified to the Aardvark drivers' frequent use of and familiarity with the parking lot behind the El Rey Theatre, and Jessup's claim to Windsor Boulevard on the morning of the murder. These were good, solid points for the prosecution, and Clinton gave no quarter to Royce on cross.

Then Bosch took the stand for a third time in the trial. Rather than read previous testimony, this time he testified about his own recent investigation of the case and produced the Dodgers cap—with the initials *BC* under the brim—from property that had been seized from Jessup during his arrest twenty-four years earlier. We were forced to dance around the fact that the hat as well as Jessup's other belongings had been in the property room at San Quentin for the past twenty-four years. To bring that information out would be to reveal that Jessup had previously been convicted of Melissa Landy's murder.

And now Sarah Gleason would be the prosecution's final witness. Through her the case would come together in the emotional crescendo I was counting on. One sister standing for a long-lost sister. I leaned back in my seat to watch my ex-wife—the best prosecutor I had ever encountered—take us home.

Gleason was sworn in and then took her seat on the stand. She was small and required the microphone to be lowered by the courtroom deputy. Maggie cleared her voice and began.

'Good morning, Ms. Gleason. How are you today?'

'I'm doing pretty good.'

'Can you please tell the jury a little bit about yourself?'

'Um, I'm thirty-seven years old. Not married. I live in Port Townsend, Washington, and I've been there about seven years now.'

'What do you do for a living?'

'I'm a glass artist.'

'And what was your relationship to Melissa Landy?'

'She was my younger sister.'

'How much younger was she than you?'

'Thirteen months.'

Maggie put a photograph of the two sisters up on the overhead screen as a prosecution exhibit. It showed two smiling girls standing in front of a Christmas tree.

'Can you identify this photo?'

'That was me and Melissa at the last Christmas. Right before she was taken.'

'So that would be Christmas nineteen eighty-five?'

'Yes.'

'I notice that she and you are about the same size.'

'Yes, she wasn't really my little sister anymore. She had caught up to me.'

'Did you share the same clothes?'

'We shared some things but we also had our favorite things that we didn't share. That could cause a fight.'

She smiled and Maggie nodded that she understood.

'Now, you said she was taken. Were you referring to February sixteenth of the following year, the date of your sister's abduction and murder?'

'Yes, I was.'

'Okay, Sarah, I know it will be difficult for you but I would like you to tell the jury what you saw and did on that day.'

Gleason nodded as if steeling herself for what was ahead. I checked the jury and saw every eye holding on her. I then turned and glanced at the defense table and locked eyes with Jessup. I did not look away. I held his defiant stare and tried to send back my own message. That two women—one asking the questions, the other answering them—were going to take him down.

Finally, it was Jessup who looked away.

'Well, it was a Sunday,' Gleason said. 'We were going to go to church. My whole family. Melissa and I were in our dresses so my mother told us to go out front.'

'Why couldn't you use the backyard?'

'My stepfather was building a pool and there was a lot of mud in the back and a big hole. My mother was worried we might fall down and get our dresses dirty.'

'So you went out to the front yard.'

'Yes.'

'And where were your parents at this time, Sarah?'

'My mother was still upstairs getting ready and my stepfather was in the TV room. He was watching sports.'

'Where was the TV room in the house?'

'In the back next to the kitchen.'

'Okay, Sarah, I am going to show you a photo called

"People's prosecution exhibit eleven." Is this the front of the house where you lived on Windsor Boulevard?'

All eyes went to the overhead screen. The yellow-brick house spread across the screen. It was a long shot from the street, showing a deep front yard with ten-foot hedges running down both sides. There was a front porch that ran the width of the house and that was largely hidden behind ornamental vegetation. There was a paved walkway extending from the sidewalk, across the lawn and to the steps of the front porch. I had reviewed our photo exhibits several times in preparation for the trial. But for the first time, I noticed that the walkway had a crack running down the center of its entire length from sidewalk to front steps. It somehow seemed appropriate, considering what had happened at the home.

'Yes, that was our house.'

'Tell us what happened that day in the front yard, Sarah.'

'Well, we decided to play hide-and-seek while we waited for our parents. I was It first and I found Melissa hiding behind that bush on the right side of the porch.'

She pointed to the exhibit photo that was still on the screen. I realized we had forgotten to give Gleason the laser pointer we had prepared her testimony with. I quickly opened Maggie's briefcase and found it. I stood and handed it to her. With the judge's permission, she gave it to the witness.

'Okay, Sarah, could you use the laser to show us?' Maggie asked.

Gleason moved the red laser dot in a circle around a thick bush at the north corner of the front porch.

'So she hid there and you found her?'

'Yes, and then when it was her turn to be It, I decided to hide in the same spot because I didn't think she would look there at first. When she was finished counting she came down the steps and stood in the middle of the yard.'

'You could see her from your hiding place?'

'Yes, through the bush I could see her. She was sort of turning in a half circle, looking for me.'

'Then what happened?'

'Well, first I heard a truck go by and—'

'Let me just stop you right there, Sarah. You say you heard a truck. You didn't see it?'

'No, not from where I was hiding.'

'How do you know that it was a truck?'

'It was very loud and heavy. I could feel it in the ground, like a little earthquake.'

'Okay, what happened after you heard the truck?'

'Suddenly I saw a man in the yard...and he went right up to my sister and grabbed her by her wrist.'

Gleason cast her eyes down and held her hands together on the dais in front of her seat.

'Sarah, did you know this man?'

'No, I did not.'

'Had you ever seen him before?'

'No, I had not.'

'Did he say anything?'

'Yes, I heard him say, "You have to come with me."'

And my sister said...she said, "Are you sure?" And that was it. I think he said something else but I didn't hear it. He led her away. To the street.'

'And you stayed in hiding?'

'Yes, I couldn't...for some reason I couldn't move. I couldn't call for help, I couldn't do anything. I was very scared.'

It was one of those solemn moments in the court-room when there was absolute silence except for the voices of the prosecutor and the witness.

'Did you see or hear anything else, Sarah?'

'I heard a door close and then I heard the truck drive away.'

I saw the tears on Sarah Gleason's cheeks. I thought the courtroom deputy had noticed as well because he took a box of tissues from a drawer in his desk and crossed the courtroom with them. But instead of taking them to Sarah he handed the box to juror number two, who had tears on her cheeks as well. This was okay with me. I wanted the tears to stay on Sarah's face.

'Sarah, how long was it before you came out from behind the bush where you were hiding and told your parents that your sister had been taken?'

'I think it was less than a minute but it was too late. She was gone.'

The silence that followed that statement was the kind of void that lives can disappear into. Forever.

Maggie spent the next half hour walking Gleason through her memory of what came after. Her stepfather's desperate 9-1-1 call to the police, the interview she gave to the detectives, and then the lineup she viewed from her bedroom window and her identifying Jason Jessup as the man she saw lead her sister away.

Maggie had to be very careful here. We had used sworn testimony of witnesses from the first trial. The record of that entire trial was available to Royce as well, and I knew without a doubt that he had his assistant counsel, who was sitting on the other side of Jessup, comparing everything Sarah Gleason was saying now with the testimony she gave at the first trial. If she changed one nuance of her story, Royce would be all over her on it during his cross-examination, using the discrepancy to try to cast her as a liar.

To me the testimony came off as fresh and not rehearsed. This was a testament to the prep work of the two women. Maggie smoothly and efficiently brought her witness to the vital moment when Sarah reconfirmed her identification of Jessup.

'Was there any doubt at all in your mind when you identified Jason Jessup in nineteen eighty-six as the man who took your sister?'

'No, none at all.'

'It has been a long time, Sarah, but I ask you to look around the courtroom and tell the jury whether you see the man who abducted your sister on February sixteenth, nineteen eighty-six?'

'Yes, him.'

She spoke without hesitation and pointed her finger at Jessup.

'Would you tell us where he is seated and describe an article of clothing he is wearing?'

'He's sitting next to Mr. Royce and he has a dark blue tie and a light blue shirt.'

Maggie paused and looked at Judge Breitman.

'Let the record show that the witness has identified the defendant,' she said.

Maggie went right back to Sarah.

'After all these years, do you have any doubt that he is the man who took your sister?'

'None at all.'

Maggie turned and looked at the judge.

'Your Honor, it may be a bit early but I think now would be a good time to take the afternoon break. I am going to go in a different direction with this witness at this point.'

'Very well,' Breitman said. 'We will adjourn for fifteen minutes and I will expect to see everyone back here at two-thirty-five. Thank you.'

Sarah said she wanted to use the restroom and left the courtroom with Bosch running interference and making sure she would not cross paths with Jessup in the hallway. Maggie sat down at the defense table and we huddled.

'You have 'em, Maggie. This is what they've been waiting all week to hear and it's better than they thought it was going to be.'

She knew I was talking about the jury. She didn't need my approval or encouragement but I had to give it.

'Now comes the hard part,' she said. 'I hope she holds up.'

'She's doing great. And I'm sure Harry's telling her that right now.'

Maggie didn't respond. She started flipping through the legal pad that had her notes and the rough script of the examination. Soon she was immersed in the next hour's work.

34

Bosch had to shoo away the reporters when Sarah Gleason came out of the restroom. Using his body as a shield against the cameras he walked her back to the courtroom.

'Sarah, you're doing really well,' he said. 'You keep it up and this guy's going right back to where he belongs.'

'Thanks, but that was the easy part. It's going to get hard now.'

'Don't kid yourself, Sarah. There is no easy part. Just keep thinking about your sister, Melissa. Somebody has to stand up for her. And right now that's you.'

As they got to the courtroom door, he realized that she had smoked a cigarette in the restroom. He could smell it on her.

Inside, he walked her down the center aisle and delivered her to Maggie McFierce, who was waiting at the gate. Bosch gave the prosecutor the nod. She was doing really well herself.

'Finish the job,' he said.

'We will,' Maggie said.

After passing the witness off, Bosch doubled back up

375

the center aisle to the sixth row. He had spotted Rachel Walling sitting in the middle of the row. He now squeezed around several reporters and observers to get to her. The space next to her was open and he sat down.

'Harry.'

'Rachel.'

'I think the man who was in that space was planning on coming back.'

'That's okay. Once court starts, I have to move back up. You should've told me you were coming. Mickey said you were here the other day.'

'When I have some time I like to come by. It's a fascinating case so far.'

'Well, let's hope the jury thinks it's more than fascinating. I want this guy back in San Quentin so bad I can taste it.'

'Mickey told me Jessup was moonlighting. Is that still—'

She lowered her voice to a whisper when she saw Jessup walking down the aisle and back to his seat at the defense table.

'–happening?'

Bosch matched her whisper.

'Yeah, and last night it almost went completely south on us. The SIS lost him.'

'Oh, no.'

The judge's door opened and she stepped out and headed up to the bench. Everyone stood. Bosch knew he had to get back to the prosecution table in case he was needed.

'But I found him,' he whispered. 'I have to go, but are you sticking around this afternoon?'

'No, I have to go back to the office. I'm just on a break right now.'

'Okay, Rachel, thanks for coming by. I'll talk to you.'

As people started sitting back down he worked his way out of the row and then quickly went back down the aisle and through the gate to take a seat in the row of chairs directly behind the prosecution table.

McPherson continued her direct examination of Sarah Ann Gleason. Bosch thought that both prosecutor and witness had been doing an exceptional job so far, but he also knew that they were moving into new territory now and soon everything said before wouldn't matter if what was said now wasn't delivered in a believable and unassailable fashion.

'Sarah,' McPherson began, 'when did your mother marry Kensington Landy?'

'When I was six.'

'Did you like Ken Landy?'

'No, not really. At first things were okay but then everything changed.'

'You, in fact, attempted to run away from home just a few months before your sister's death, isn't that right?'

'Yes.'

'I show you People's exhibit twelve, a police report dated November thirtieth, nineteen eighty-five. Can you tell the jury what that is?'

McPherson delivered copies of the report to the witness, the judge and the defense table. Bosch had found the report during his record search on the case. It had been a lucky break.

'It's a missing persons report,' Gleason said. 'My mother reported me missing.'

'And did the police find you?'

'No, I just came home. I didn't have anyplace to go.'

'Why did you run away, Sarah?'

'Because my stepfather...was having sex with me.'

McPherson nodded and let the answer hang out there in the courtroom for a long moment. Three days ago Bosch would have expected Royce to jump all over this part of the testimony but now he knew that this played to the defense's case as well. Kensington Landy was the straw man and any testimony that supported that would be welcomed.

'When did this start?' McPherson finally asked.

'The summer before I ran away,' Gleason responded. 'The summer before Melissa got taken.'

'Sarah, I am sorry to put you through these bad memories. You testified earlier that you and Melissa shared some of each other's clothes, correct?'

'Yes.'

'The dress she wore on the day she was taken, that was your dress, wasn't it?'

'Yes.'

McPherson then introduced the dress as the state's next exhibit and Bosch set it up for display to the jury on a headless manikin he placed in front of the jury box.

'Is this the dress, Sarah?'

'Yes, it is.'

'Now, you notice that there is a square of material removed from the bottom front hem of the dress. You see that, Sarah?'

'Yes.'

'Do you know why that was removed?'

'Yes, because they found semen on the dress there.'

'You mean forensic investigators?'

'Yes.'

'Now, is this something you knew back at the time of your sister's death?'

'I know it now. I wasn't told about it back then.'

'Do you know who the semen was genetically identified as belonging to?'

'Yes, I was told it came from my stepfather.'

'Did that surprise you?'

'No, unfortunately.'

'Do you have any explanation for how it could have gotten on your dress?'

Now Royce objected, saying that the question called for speculation. It also called for the witness to diverge from the defense theory, but he didn't mention that. Breitman sustained the objection and McPherson had to find another way of getting there.

'Sarah, prior to your sister borrowing your dress on the morning she was abducted, when was the last time you wore it?'

Royce stood and objected again.

'Same objection. We're speculating about events twenty-four years old and when this witness was only thirteen years old.'

'Your Honor,' McPherson rejoined, 'Mr. Royce was fine with this so-called speculation when it fit with the defense's scheme of things. But now he objects as we get to the heart of the matter. This is not speculation. Ms. Gleason is testifying truthfully about the darkest, saddest days of her life and I don't think—'

'Objection overruled,' Breitman said. 'The witness may answer.'

'Thank you, Your Honor.'

As McPherson repeated the question Bosch studied the jury. He wanted to see if they saw what he saw— a defense attorney attempting to stop the forward progression of truth. Bosch had found Sarah Gleason's testimony to be fully convincing up to this point. He wanted to hear what she had to say and his hope was that the jury was in the same boat and would look unkindly upon defense efforts to stop her.

'I wore it two nights before,' Gleason said.

'That would have been Friday night, the fourteenth. Valentine's Day.'

'Yes.'

'Why did you wear the dress?'

'My mother was making a nice dinner for Valentine's Day and my stepfather said we should get dressed up for it.'

Gleason was looking down again, losing all eye contact with the jurors.

'Did your stepfather engage in a sexual act with you on that night?'

'Yes.'

'Were you wearing the dress at the time?'

'Yes.'

'Sarah, do you know if your father ejac—'

'He wasn't my father!'

She yelled it and her voice echoed in the courtroom, reverberating around a hundred people who now knew her darkest secret. Bosch looked at McPherson and saw her checking out the jury's reaction. It was then Bosch knew that the mistake had been intentional.

'I am sorry, Sarah. I meant your stepfather. Do you know, did he ejaculate in the course of this moment with you?'

'Yes, and some of it got on my dress.'

McPherson studied her notes, flipping over several pages of her yellow pad. She wanted that last answer to hang out there as long as possible.

'Sarah, who did the laundry at your house?'

'A lady came. Her name was Abby.'

'After that Valentine's Day, did you put your dress in the laundry?'

'No, I didn't.'

'Why not?'

'Because I was afraid Abby would find it and know what happened. I thought she might tell my mother or call the police.'

'Why would that have been a bad thing, Sarah?'

'I... my mother was happy and I didn't want to ruin things for her.'

'So what did you do with the dress that night?'

'I cleaned off the spot and hung it in my closet. I

didn't know my sister was going to wear it.'

'So two days later when she wanted to put it on, what did you say?'

'She already had it on when I saw her. I told her that I wanted to wear it but she said it was too late because it wasn't on my list of clothes I didn't share with her.'

'Could you see the stain on the dress?'

'No, I looked and because it was down at the hem I didn't see any stain.'

McPherson paused again. Bosch knew from the prep work that she had covered all the points she wanted to in this line of questioning. She had sufficiently explained the DNA that was the cause of everyone's being here. She now had to take Gleason further down the road of her dark journey. Because if she didn't, Royce certainly would.

'Sarah, did your relationship with your stepfather change after your sister's death?'

'Yes.'

'How so?'

'He never touched me again.'

'Do you know why? Did you talk to him about it?'

'I don't know why. I never talked to him about it. It just never happened again and he tried to act like it had never happened in the first place.'

'But for you, all of this—your stepfather, your sister's death—it took a toll, didn't it?'

'Yes.'

'In what way, Sarah?'

'Uh, well, I started getting into drugs and I ran away again. I ran away a lot, actually. I didn't care about sex.

It was something I used to get what I needed.'

'And were you ever arrested?'

'Yes, a bunch of times.'

'For what?'

'Drugs mostly. I got arrested once for soliciting an undercover, too. And for stealing.'

'You were arrested six times as a juvenile and five more times as an adult, is that correct?'

'I didn't keep count.'

'What drugs were you taking?'

'Crystal meth mostly. But if there was something else available, I would probably take it. That was the way I was.'

'Did you ever receive counseling and rehabilitation?'

'A lot of times. It didn't work at first and then it did. I got clean.'

'When was that?'

'About seven years ago. When I was thirty.'

'You've been clean for seven years?'

'Yes, totally. My life is different now.'

'I want to show you People's exhibit thirteen, which is an intake and evaluation form from a private rehab center in Los Angeles called the Pines. Do you remember going there?'

'Yes, my mother sent me there when I was sixteen.'

'Was that when you first started getting into trouble?'

'Yes.'

McPherson distributed copies of the evaluation form to the judge, clerk and defense table.

'Okay, Sarah, I want to draw your attention to the

paragraph I have outlined in yellow in the evaluation section of the intake form. Can you please read it out loud to the jury?'

'Candidate reports PTSD in regard to the murder of her younger sister three years ago. Suffers unresolved guilt associated with murder and also evinces behavior typical of sexual abuse. Full psych and physical evaluation is recommended.'

'Thank you, Sarah. Do you know what PTSD means?'

'Posttraumatic stress disorder.'

'Did you undergo these recommended evaluations at the Pines?'

'Yes.'

'Did discussion of your stepfather's sexual abuse come up?'

'No, because I lied.'

'How so?'

'By then I'd had sex with other men, so I never mentioned my stepfather.'

'Before revealing what you have today in court, did you ever talk about your stepfather and his having sex with you with anyone?'

'Just you and Detective Bosch. Nobody else.'

'Have you been married?'

'Yes.'

'More than once?'

'Yes.'

'And you didn't even tell your husbands about this?'

'No. It's not the kind of thing you want to tell anybody. You keep it to yourself.'

'Thank you, Sarah. I have no further questions.'

McPherson took her pad and returned to her seat, where she was greeted with a squeeze on the arm by Haller. It was a gesture designed for the jury to see but by then all eyes were on Royce. It was his turn and Bosch's measure of the room was that Sarah Gleason had everybody riding with her. Any effort by Royce to destroy her ran the strong risk of backfiring against his client.

Royce did the smart thing. He decided to let emotions cool for a night. He stood and told the judge that he reserved the right to recall Gleason as a witness during the defense phase of the trial. In effect he put off her cross-examination. He then retook his seat.

Bosch checked his watch. It was four-fifteen. The judge told Haller to call his next witness but Bosch knew there were no more witnesses. Haller looked at McPherson and in unison they nodded. Haller then stood up.

'Your Honor,' he said. 'The People rest.'

35

The prosecution team convened for dinner at Casa Haller. I made a thick Bolognese using a store-bought sauce for a base and boiled a box of bow tie pasta. Maggie chipped in with her own recipe for Caesar salad that I had always loved when we were married but hadn't had in years. Bosch and his daughter were the last to arrive, as Harry first took Sarah Ann Gleason back to her hotel room following court and made sure she was secure for the night.

Our daughters were shy upon meeting and embarrassed by how obvious their parents were about watching the long-awaited moment. They instinctively knew to move away from us and convened in the back office, ostensibly to do their homework. Pretty soon after, we started to hear laughter from down the hall.

I put the pasta and sauce into a big bowl and mixed it all together. I then called the girls out first to serve themselves and take their dishes back to the office.

'How's it going back there, anyway?' I asked them while they were making their plates. 'Any homework getting done?'

'Dad,' Hayley said dismissively, as if my question were a great invasion of privacy.

So I tried the cousin.

'Maddie?'

'Um, I'm almost finished with mine.'

Both girls looked at each other and laughed, as if either the question or its answer were cause for great glee. They scurried out of the kitchen then and back to the office.

I put everything out on the table, where the adults were sitting. The last thing I did was make sure the door to the office was closed so the girls would not hear our conversation and we would not hear theirs.

'Well,' I said as I passed the pasta to Bosch. 'We're finished with our part. Now comes the hard part.'

'The defense,' Maggie said. 'What do we think they have in store for Sarah?'

I thought for a moment before answering and tried my first bow tie. It was good. I was proud of my dish.

'We know they'll throw everything they can at her,' I finally said. 'She's the case.'

Bosch reached inside his jacket and brought out a folded piece of paper. He opened it on the table. I could see that it was the defense's witness list.

'At the end of court today Royce told the judge he would complete the defense's case in one day,' he said. 'He said he's calling only four witnesses but he's got twenty-three listed on here.'

'Well, we knew all along that most of that list was subterfuge,' Maggie said. 'He was hiding his case.'

'Okay, so we have Sarah coming back,' I said, holding up one finger. 'Then we have Jessup himself. My guess is that Royce knows he has to put him on. That's two. Who else?'

Maggie waited until she finished a mouthful of food before speaking.

'Hey, this is good, Haller. When did you learn to make this?'

'It's a little thing I like to call Newman's Own.'

'No, you added to it. You made it better. How come you never cooked like this when we were married?'

'I guess it came out of necessity. Being a single father. What about you, Harry? What do you cook?'

Bosch looked at us both like we were crazy.

'I can fry an egg,' he said. 'That's about it.'

'Let's get back to the trial,' Maggie said. 'I think Royce has got Jessup and Sarah. Then I think he's got the secret witness we haven't found. The guy from the last rehab center.'

'Edward Roman,' Bosch said.

'Right. Roman. That makes three and the fourth one could be his investigator or maybe his meth expert but is probably just bullshit. There is no fourth. So much of what Royce does is misdirection. He doesn't want anybody's eyes on the prize. Wants them looking anywhere but right at the truth.'

'What about Roman?' I said. 'We haven't found him, but have we figured out his testimony?'

'Not by a long shot,' Maggie said. 'I've gone over and over this with Sarah and she has no idea what he's going to say. She couldn't remember ever talking about her sister with him.'

'The summary Royce provided in discovery says he will testify about Sarah's "revelations" about her childhood,' Bosch said. 'Nothing more specific than that and, of course, Royce claims he didn't take any notes during the interview.'

'Look,' I said, 'we have his record and we know exactly what kind of guy we're dealing with here. He's going to say whatever Royce wants him to say. It's that simple. Whatever works for the defense. So we should be less concerned by what he says—because we know it will be lies—and more concerned with knocking him out of the box. What do we have that can help us there?'

Maggie and I both looked at Bosch and he was ready for us.

'I think I might have something. I'm going to go see somebody tonight. If it pans out we'll have it in the morning. I'll tell you then.'

My frustrations with Bosch's methods of investigation and communication boiled over at that point.

'Harry, come on. We're part of a team here. This secret agent stuff doesn't really work when we're in that courtroom every day with our asses on the line.'

Bosch looked down at his plate and I saw the slow burn. His face grew as dark as the sauce.

'*Your* asses on the line?' he said. 'I didn't see anywhere in the surveillance reports that Jessup was hanging around outside your house, Haller, so don't tell me about your ass being on the line. Your job is in that courtroom. It's nice and safe and sometimes you win and sometimes you lose. But no matter what happens, you're back in court the next day. You want your ass on the line, try working out there.'

He pointed out the window toward the view of the city.

'Hey, guys, let's just calm down here,' Maggie said quickly. 'Harry, what's the matter? Has Jessup gone back to Woodrow Wilson? Maybe we should just revoke this guy and put him back in lockup.'

Bosch shook his head.

'Not to my street. He hasn't been back there since that first night and he hasn't been up to Mulholland in more than a week.'

'Then what is it?'

Bosch put his fork down and pushed his plate back.

'We already know there's a good chance that Jessup has a gun from that meeting the SIS saw him have with a convicted gun dealer. They didn't see what he got from the guy, but since it came wrapped in a towel, it doesn't take a lot to figure it out. And then, you want to know what happened last night? Some bright guy on the surveillance decides to leave his post to use the john without telling anybody and Jessup walked right out of the net.'

'They lost him?' Maggie asked.

'Yeah, until I found him right before he found me, which might not have turned out so well. And you know what he's up to? He's building a dungeon for somebody and for all I know—'

He leaned forward over the table and finished in an urgent whisper.

'–might be for my kid!'

'Whoa, wait, Harry,' Maggie said. 'Back up. He's building a dungeon? Where?'

'Under the pier. There's like a storage room. He put a lock on the door and dropped canned food off there last night. Like he's getting it ready for somebody.'

'Okay, that's scary,' Maggie said. 'But your daughter? We don't know that. You said he went by your place only the one time. What makes you think—?'

'Because I can't afford not to think it. You understand?'

She nodded.

'Yes, I do. Then I come back to what I just said. We violate him for associating with a known criminal—the gun dealer—and pull his OR release. There's only a few days left in the trial and he obviously didn't act out or make the mistake we thought he would. Let's be safe and put him back inside until this is over.'

'And what if we don't get the conviction?' Bosch said. 'What happens then? This guy walks and that'll also be the end of the surveillance. He'll be out there without any eyes on him.'

That brought a silence to the table. I stared at Bosch and understood the pressure he was under. The case, the threat to his daughter, and no wife or ex-wife to help him out at home.

Bosch finally broke the uneasy silence.

'Maggie, are you taking Hayley home with you to-night?'

Maggie nodded.

'Yes, when we're finished here.'

'Can Maddie stay with you two tonight? She brought a change of clothes in her backpack. I'd come by in the morning in time to take her to school.'

The request seemed to take Maggie by surprise, especially since the girls had just met. Bosch pressed her.

'I need to meet somebody tonight and I don't know where it will take me,' Bosch said. 'It might even lead to Roman. I need to be able to move without worrying about Maddie.'

She nodded.

'Okay, that's fine. It sounds like they're becoming fast friends. I just hope they don't stay up all night.'

'Thank you, Maggie.'

About thirty seconds of silence went by before I spoke.

'Tell us about this dungeon, Harry.'

'I was standing in it last night.'

'Why the Santa Monica Pier?'

'My guess is that it's because of the proximity to what's on top of the pier.'

'Prey.'

Bosch nodded.

'But what about noise? You're saying this place is directly below the pier?'

'There are ways of controlling human sound. And last night the sound of waves crashing against the pilings under there was so loud you could've screamed all night and nobody would've heard you. You probably wouldn't even hear a gunshot from down there.'

Bosch spoke with a certain authority of the dark places of the world and the evil they held. I lost my appetite then and pushed my plate away. I felt dread come inside me.

Dread for Melissa Landy and all the other victims in the world.

36

Gilbert and Sullivan were waiting for him in a car parked on Lankershim Boulevard near its northern terminus at San Fernando Road. It was a blighted area populated primarily with used-car lots and repair shops. In the midst of all of this low-rent industry was a run-down motel advertising rooms for fifty dollars a week. The motel had no name on display. Just the lighted sign that said MOTEL.

Gilbert and Sullivan were Gilberto Reyes and John Sullivan, a pair of narcs assigned to the Valley Enforcement Team, a street-level drug unit. When Bosch was looking for Edward Roman he put the word out in all such units in the department. His assumption from Roman's record was that he had never gotten away from the life as Sarah Gleason had. There had to be somebody in the department's narco units with a line on him.

It paid off with a call from Reyes. He and his partner didn't have a bead on Roman but they knew him from past interactions on the street and knew where his current trick partner was holed up and apparently awaiting his return. Long-term drug addicts often partnered with a prostitute, offering her protection in exchange for a share of the drugs her earnings bought.

Bosch pulled his car up behind the narcs' UC car and parked. He got out and moved up to their car, getting in the back after checking the seat to make sure it was clean of vomit and any other detritus from the people they had transported lately.

'Detective Bosch, I presume?' said the driver, whom Bosch guessed was Reyes.

'Yeah, how are you guys?'

He offered his fist over the seat and they both gave him a bump while identifying themselves. Bosch had it wrong. The one who looked to be of Latin origin was Sullivan and the one who looked like a bag of white bread was Reyes.

'Gilbert and Sullivan, huh?'

'That's what they called us when we got partnered,' Sullivan said. 'Kind of stuck.'

Bosch nodded. That was enough for the meet-and-greet. Everybody had a nickname and a story to go with it. These guys together didn't add up to how old Bosch was and they probably had no clue who Gilbert and Sullivan were, anyway.

'So you know Eddie Roman?'

'We've had the pleasure,' Reyes said. 'Just another piece of human shit that floats around out here.'

'But like I told you on the phone, we ain't seen him in a month or so,' Sullivan added. 'So we got you his next best thing. His onion. She's over there in room three.'

'What's her name?'

Sullivan laughed and Bosch didn't get it.

'Her name is Sonia Reyes,' said Reyes. 'No relation.'

'That he knows of,' Sullivan added.

He burst into laughter, which Bosch ignored.

'Spell it for me,' he said.

He took out his notebook and wrote it down.

'And you're sure she's in the room?'

'We're sure,' Reyes said.

'Okay, anything else I should know before I go in?'

'No,' Reyes said, 'but we were planning on goin' in with you. She might get squirrelly with you.'

Bosch reached forward and clapped him on the shoulder.

'No, I got this. I don't want a crowd in the room.'

Reyes nodded. Message delivered. Bosch did not want any witnesses to what he might need to do here.

'But thanks for the help. It will be noted.'

'An important case, huh?' Sullivan said.

Bosch opened the door and got out.

'They all are,' he said.

He closed the door, slapped the roof twice and walked away.

The motel had an eight-foot security fence around it. Bosch had to press a buzzer and hold his badge up to a camera. He was buzzed into the compound but walked right by the office and down a breezeway leading to the rooms.

'Hey!' a voice called from behind.

Bosch turned and saw a man with an unbuttoned shirt leaning out the door of the motel's office.

'Where the fuck you goin', dude?'

'Go back inside and shut the door. This is police business.'

'Don't matter, man. I let you in but this is private property. You can't just come through the—'

Bosch started quickly moving back up the breezeway toward the man. The man took his measure and backed down without Bosch saying a word.

'Never mind, man. You're good.'

He quickly stepped back inside and closed the door. Bosch turned back and found room three without a further problem. He leaned close to the jamb to see if he could pick up any sound. He heard nothing.

There was a peephole. He put his finger over it and knocked. He waited and then knocked again.

'Sonia, open up. Eddie sent me.'

'Who are you?'

The voice was female, ragged and suspicious. Bosch used the universal pass code.

'Doesn't matter. Eddie sent me with somethin' to hold you over till he's done.'

No response.

'Okay, Sonia, I'll tell him you weren't interested. I've got someone else who wants it.'

He took his finger off the peep and started walking away. Almost immediately the door opened behind him.

'Wait.'

Bosch turned back. The door was open six inches. He saw a set of hollow eyes looking out at him, a dim light behind them.

'Let me see.'

Bosch looked around.

'What, out here?' he said. 'They got cameras all over the place.'

'Eddie tol' me not to open the door for strangers. You look like a cop to me.'

'Well, maybe I am, but that doesn't change that Eddie sent me.'

Bosch started to turn again.

'Like I said, I'll tell him I tried. Have a nice night.'

'Okay, okay. You can come in but only to make the drop. Nothing else.'

Bosch walked back toward the door. She moved behind it and opened it. He entered and turned to her and saw the gun. It was an old revolver and he saw no bullets in the exposed chambers. Bosch raised his hands chest high. He could tell she was hurting. She'd been waiting too long for somebody, putting blind junkie trust in something that wouldn't pay off.

'That's not necessary, Sonia. Besides, I don't think Eddie left you with any bullets.'

'I got one left. You want to try it?'

Probably the one she was saving for herself. She was skin and bones and close to the end of the line. No junkie went the distance.

'Give it to me,' she ordered. 'Now.'

'Okay, take it easy. I have it right here.'

He reached his right hand into his coat pocket and pulled out a balled piece of aluminum foil he had taken from a roll in Mickey Haller's kitchen. He held it out to the right of his body and he knew her desperate eyes would follow it. He shot his left hand out and snatched the gun out of her hand. He then stepped forward and roughly shoved her onto the bed.

'Shut up and don't move,' he commanded.

'What is—?'

'I said shut up!'

He popped the gun's barrel out and checked it. She had been right. There was one bullet left. He slid it out into his palm and then put it in his pocket. He hooked the gun into his belt. Then he pulled his badge wallet and opened it for her to see.

'You had that right,' he said.

'What do you want?'

'We'll get to that.'

Bosch moved around the bed, looking about the threadbare room. It smelled like cigarettes and body odor. There were several plastic grocery bags on the floor containing her belongings. Shoes in one, clothing in a few others. On the bed's lone side table was an overloaded ashtray and a glass pipe.

'What are you hurting for, Sonia. Crack? Heroin? Or is it meth?'

She didn't answer.

'I can help you better if I know what you need.'

'I don't want your help.'

Bosch turned and looked at her. So far things were going exactly as he predicted they would.

'Really?' he said. 'Don't need my help? You think Eddie Roman is going to come back for you?'

'He's coming back.'

'I got news for you. He's already gone. I'm guessing they got him cleaned up nice and neat and he won't be coming back up here once he does what they want him to do. He'll take the paycheck and when that runs out he'll just find himself a new trick partner.'

He paused and looked at her.

'Somebody who still has something somebody would want to buy.'

Her eyes took on the distant look of someone who knows the truth when she hears it.

'Leave me alone,' she said in a hoarse whisper.

'I know I'm not telling you anything you don't already know. You've been waiting for Eddie longer than you thought you would, huh? How many days you have left on the room?'

He read the answer in her eyes.

'Already past, huh? Probably giving the guy in the office blowjobs to let you stay. How long's that going to last? Pretty soon he'll just want the money.'

'I said go away.'

'I will. But you come with me, Sonia. Right now.'

'What do you want?'

'I want to know everything you know about Eddie Roman.'

PART FOUR
–The Silent Witness

37

Thursday, April 8, 9:01 A.M.

Before the judge called for the jury, Clive Royce stood
and asked the court for a directed verdict of acquittal.
He argued that the state had failed to live up to its duty
in carrying the burden of proof. He said that the evidence presented by the prosecutors failed to cross the
threshold of guilt beyond a reasonable doubt. I was
ready to stand to argue the state's side, but the judge
held up her hand to signal me to stay in place. She then
quickly dispensed with Royce's motion.

'Motion denied,' Breitman said. 'The court holds
that the evidence presented by the prosecution is suffi-
cient for the jury to consider. Mr. Royce, are you ready
to proceed with the defense?'

'I am, Your Honor.'

'Okay, sir, then we will recall the jury now. Will you
have an opening statement?'

'A brief one, Your Honor.'

'Very well, I am going to hold you to that.'

The jurors filed in and took their assigned places. On
many of them I saw expressions of anticipation. I took
this as a good sign, as if they were wondering how in
the hell the defense would be able to dig its way out of

all the evidence the state had dumped on it. It was probably all wishful thinking on my part, but I had been studying juries for most of my adult life and I liked what I saw.

After welcoming the jury back, the judge turned the courtroom over to Royce, reminded the jurors that this was an opening statement, not a listing of facts unless backed up later with testimony and evidence. Royce strode with full confidence to the lectern without a note or file in his hand. I knew he had the same philosophy as I did when it came to making opening statements. Look them in the eyes and don't flinch and don't back down from your theory, no matter how far-fetched or unbelievable. Sell it. If they don't think you believe it, they never will.

His strategy of deferring his opener until the start of the defense's case would now pay dividends. He would begin the day and his case by delivering to the jury a statement that didn't have to be true, that could be as outlandish as anything ever heard in the courtroom. As long as he kept the jury riding along, nothing else really mattered.

'Ladies and gentlemen of the jury, good morning. Today begins a new phase of the trial. The defense phase. This is when we start to tell you our side of the story, and believe me, we have another side to almost everything the prosecution has offered you over the past three days.

'I am not going to take a lot of your time here because I am very eager, and Jason Jessup is very eager, to get to the evidence that the prosecution has either failed to find or chosen not to present to you. It doesn't matter which, at this point; the only things that matter are that you hear it and that it allows you to see the full picture of what transpired on Windsor Boulevard on February sixteenth, nineteen eighty-six. I urge you to listen closely, to watch closely. If you do that, you will see the truth emerge.'

I looked over at the legal pad on which Maggie had been doodling while Royce spoke. In large letters she had written *WINDBAG!* I thought, She hasn't seen anything yet.

'This case,' Royce continued, 'is about one thing. A family's darkest secrets. You got only a glimpse of them during the prosecution's presentation. You got the tip of the iceberg from the prosecution, but today you will get the whole iceberg. Today you will get the cold hard truth. That being that Jason Jessup is the true victim here today. The victim of a family's desire to hide their darkest secret.'

Maggie leaned toward me and whispered, 'Brace yourself.'

I nodded. I knew exactly where we were going.

'This trial is about a monster who killed a child. A monster who defiled one young girl and was going to move on to the next when something went wrong and he killed that child. This trial is about the family that was so fearful of that monster that they went along with the plan to cover up the crime and point the finger elsewhere. At an innocent man.'

Royce pointed righteously at Jessup as he said this last line. Maggie shook her head in disgust, a calculated move for the jury.

'Jason, would you please stand up?' Royce said.

His client did as instructed and turned fully to the jury, his eyes boldly scanning from face to face, not flinching or looking away.

'Jason Jessup is an innocent man,' Royce said with the requisite outrage in his voice. 'He was the fall guy. An innocent man caught in an impromptu plan to cover up the worst kind of crime, the taking of a child's life.'

Jessup sat down and Royce paused so his words would burn into every juror's conscience. It was highly theatrical and planned that way.

'There are two victims here,' he finally said. 'Melissa Landy is a victim. She lost her life. Jason Jessup is also a victim because they are trying to take his life. The family conspired against him and then the police followed their lead. They ignored the evidence and planted their own. And now after twenty-four years, after witnesses are gone and memories have dimmed, they've come calling for him...'

Royce cast his head down as if tremendously burdened by the truth. I knew he would now wrap things up.

'Ladies and gentlemen of the jury, we are here for only one reason. To seek the truth. Before the end of this day, you will know the truth about Windsor Boulevard. You will know that Jason Jessup is an innocent man.'

Royce paused again, then thanked the jury and moved back to his seat. In what I was sure was a well-rehearsed moment, Jessup put his arm around his lawyer's shoulders, gave him a squeeze and thanked him.

But the judge gave Royce little time to savor the moment or the slick delivery of his opening statement. She told him to call his first witness. I turned in my seat and saw Bosch standing in the back of the courtroom. He gave me the nod. I had sent him to get Sarah Ann Gleason from the hotel as soon as Royce had informed me upon arriving at court that she would be his first witness.

'The *defense* calls Sarah Ann Gleason to the stand,' Royce said, putting the accent on defense in a way that suggested that this was an unexpected turnabout.

Bosch stepped out of the courtroom and quickly returned with Gleason. He walked her down the aisle and through the gate. She went the rest of the way on her own. She again was dressed for court informally, wearing a white peasant blouse and a pair of jeans.

Gleason was reminded by the judge that she was still under oath and turned over to Royce. This time when he went to the lectern he carried a thick file and a legal pad. Probably most of it—the file, at least—was just an attempt to intimidate Gleason, to make her think he had a big fat file on everything she had ever done wrong in life.

'Good morning, Ms. Gleason.'

'Good morning.'

'Now, you testified yesterday that you were the

victim of sexual abuse at the hands of your stepfather, Kensington Landy, is that correct?'

'Yes.'

With the first word of her testimony I detected trepidation. She hadn't been allowed to hear Royce's opening statement but we had prepared Gleason for the way we thought the defense case would go. She was exhibiting fear already and this never played well with the jury. There was little Maggie and I could do. Sarah was up there on her own.

'At what point in your life did this abuse start?'

'When I was twelve.'

'And it ended when?'

'When I was thirteen. Right after my sister's death.'

'I notice you didn't call it your sister's murder. You called it her death. Is there a reason for that?'

'I'm not sure what you mean.'

'Well, your sister was murdered, correct? It wasn't an accident, was it?'

'No, it was murder.'

'Then why did you refer to it as her death just a moment ago?'

'I'm not sure.'

'Are you confused about what happened to your sister?'

Maggie was on her feet objecting before Gleason could answer.

'Counsel is badgering the witness,' she said. 'He's more interested in eliciting an emotional response than an answer.'

'Your Honor, I simply am trying to learn how and why this witness views this crime the way she does. It goes to state of mind of the witness. I am not interested in eliciting anything other than an answer to the question I asked.'

The judge weighed things for a moment before ruling.

'I'm going to allow it. The witness may answer the question.'

'I'll repeat it,' Royce said. 'Ms. Gleason, are you confused about what happened to your sister?'

During the exchange between lawyers and the judge, Gleason had found some resolve. She answered forcefully while hitting Royce with a hard stare of defiance.

'No, I'm not confused about what happened. I was there. She was kidnapped by your client and after that I never saw her again. There is no confusion about that at all.'

I wanted to stand and clap. Instead, I just nodded to myself. It was a fine, fine answer. But Royce moved on, acting as though he had not been hit with the tomato.

'There have been times in your life when you were confused, however, correct?'

'About my sister and what happened and who took her? Never.'

'I'm talking about times you were incarcerated in mental health facilities and the psych wards of jails and prisons.'

Gleason lowered her head in full realization that she would not escape this trial without a full airing of the lost years of her life. I just had to hope she would respond in the way Maggie had told her to.

'After the murder of my sister, many things went wrong in my life,' she said.

She then looked up directly at Royce as she continued.

'Yes, I spent some time in those kinds of places. I think, and my counselors agreed, that it was because of what happened to Melissa.'

Good answer, I thought. She was fighting.

'We'll get back into that later on,' Royce said. 'But getting back to your sister, she was twelve at the time of her murder, correct?'

'That's right.'

'This would have been the same age you were when your stepfather began to sexually abuse you. Am I right?'

'About the same, yes.'

'Did you warn your sister about him?'

There was a long pause as Gleason considered her answer. This was because there was no good answer.

'Ms. Gleason?' the judge prompted. 'Please answer the question.'

'No, I didn't warn her. I was afraid to.'

'Afraid of what?' Royce asked.

'Him. As you've already pointed out, I've been through a lot of therapy in my life. I know that it is not unusual for a child to be unable to tell anyone. You get trapped in the behavior. Trapped by fear. I've been told that many times.'

'In other words, you go along to get along.'

'Sort of. But that is a simplification. It was more—'

'But you did live with a lot of fear in your life back then?'

'Yes, I—'

'Did your stepfather tell you not to tell anyone about what he was doing to you?'

'Yes, he said—'

'Did he threaten you?'

'He said that if I told anyone I would be taken away from my mother and sister. He said he would make sure that the state would think my mother knew about it and they would consider her unfit. They would take Melissa and me away. Then we would get split up because foster homes couldn't always take two at a time.'

'Did you believe him?'

'Yes, I was twelve. I believed him.'

'And it scared you, didn't it?'

'Yes. I wanted to stay with my fam—'

'Wasn't it that same fear and control that your step-father had over you that made you go along to get along after he killed your sister?'

Again Maggie jumped up to object, stating that the question was leading and assumed facts not in evidence. The judge agreed and sustained the objection.

Undeterred, Royce went at Gleason relentlessly.

'Isn't it true that you and your mother did and said exactly what your stepfather told you to in the cover-up of Melissa's murder?'

'No, that's not—'

'He told you to say it was a tow truck driver and that

you were to pick one of the men the police brought to the house.'

'No! He didn't—'

'Objection!'

'There was no hide-and-seek game outside the house, was there? Your sister was murdered inside the house by Kensington Landy. Isn't that true?'

'Your Honor!'

Maggie was now shouting.

'Counsel is badgering the witness with these leading questions. He doesn't want her answers. He just wants to deliver his lies to the jury!'

The judge looked from Maggie to Royce.

'All right, everyone just calm down. The objection is sustained. Mr. Royce, ask the witness one question at a time and allow her the time to answer. And you will not ask leading questions. Need I remind you, you called her as a witness. If you wanted to lead her you should've conducted a cross-examination when you had the opportunity.'

Royce put on his best look of contrition. It must've been difficult.

'I apologize for getting carried away, Your Honor,' he said. 'It won't happen again.'

It didn't matter if it happened again. Royce had already gotten his point across. His purpose was not to get an admission from Gleason. In fact, he expected none. His purpose was to get his alternate theory to the jury. In that, he was being very successful.

'Okay, let's move on,' Royce said. 'You mentioned

earlier that you spent a considerable part of your adult life in counseling and drug rehab, not to mention incarceration. Is that correct?'

'To a point,' Gleason said. 'I have been clean and sober and a—'

'Just answer the question that was asked,' Royce quickly interjected.

'Objection,' Maggie said. 'She is trying to answer the question he asked, but Mr. Royce doesn't like the full answer and is trying to cut her off.'

'Let her answer the question, Mr. Royce,' Breitman said tiredly. 'Go ahead, Ms. Gleason.'

'I was just saying that I have been clean for seven years and a productive member of society.'

'Thank you, Ms. Gleason.'

Royce then led her through a tragic and sordid history, literally going arrest by arrest and revealing all the details of the depravity Sarah wallowed in for so long. Maggie objected often, arguing that it had little to do with Sarah's identification of Jessup, but Breitman allowed most of the questioning to continue.

Finally, Royce wrapped up his examination by setting up his next witness.

'Getting back to the rehabilitation center in North Hollywood, you were there for five months in nineteen ninety-nine, correct?'

'I don't remember exactly when or for how long. You obviously have the records there.'

'But you do remember meeting another client, named Edward Roman, known as Eddie?'

'Yes, I do.'

'And you got to know him well?'

'Yes.'

'How did you meet him?'

'We were in group counseling together.'

'How would you describe the relationship you had with Eddie Roman back then?'

'Well, in counseling we sort of realized that we knew some of the same people and liked doing the same things—meaning drugs. So we started hanging out and it continued after we were both released.'

'Was this a romantic relationship?'

Gleason laughed in a way that was not supposed to impart humor.

'What passed for romance between two drug addicts,' she said. 'I think the term is *enablers*. By being together we were enabling each other. But *romance* is not a word I would use. We had sex on occasion—when he was able to. But there was no romance, Mr. Royce.'

'But didn't you in fact believe at one point that you two were married?'

'Eddie set something up on the beach with a man he said was a minister. But it wasn't real. It wasn't legal.'

'But at the time you thought it was, didn't you?'

'Yes.'

'So were you in love with him?'

'No, I wasn't in love with him. I just thought he could protect me.'

'So you were married, or at least thought you were. Did you live together?'

'Yes.'

'Where?'

'In different motels in the Valley.'

'All this time you were together, you must've confided in Eddie, yes?'

'About some things, yes.'

'Did you ever confide in him about your sister's murder?'

'I am sure I did. I didn't keep it a secret. I would have talked about it in group therapy in North Hollywood and he was sitting right there.'

'Did you ever tell him that your stepfather killed your sister?'

'No, because that didn't happen.'

'So if Eddie Roman were to come to this courtroom and testify that you did indeed tell him that, then he would be lying.'

'Yes.'

'But you have already testified yesterday and today that you have lied to counselors and police. You have stolen and committed many crimes in your life. But you're not lying here. Is that what we are to believe?'

'I'm not lying. You are talking about a period of my life when I did those things. I don't deny that. I was human trash, okay? But I am past that now and have been past it for a long time. I'm not lying now.'

'Okay, Ms. Gleason, no further questions.'

As Royce returned to his seat, Maggie and I put our heads together and whispered.

'She held up really well,' Maggie said. 'I think we

should let it stand and I'll just hit a couple high notes.'

'Sounds good.'

'Ms. McPherson?' the judge prompted.

Maggie stood.

'Yes, Your Honor. Just a few questions.'

She went to the lectern with her trusty legal pad. She skipped the buildup and got right to the matters she wanted to cover.

'Sarah, this man Eddie Roman and the phony marriage—whose idea was it to get married?'

'Eddie asked me to get married. He said we would work together as a team and share everything, that he would protect me and that we could never be forced to testify against each other if we got arrested.'

'And what did working together as a team mean in that circumstance?'

'Well, I...he wanted me to sell myself so we would have money to buy drugs and to have a motel room.'

'Did you do that for Eddie?'

'For a little bit of time. And then I got arrested.'

'Did Eddie bail you out?'

'No.'

'Did he come to court?'

'No.'

'Your record shows you pleaded guilty to soliciting and were sentenced to time served, is that correct?'

'Yes.'

'How long was that?'

'I think it was thirteen days.'

'And was Eddie there waiting when you got out of jail?'

'No.'

'Did you ever see him again?'

'No, I didn't.'

Maggie checked her notes, flipped up a couple pages and found what she was looking for.

'Okay, Sarah, you mentioned several times during your testimony earlier today that you did not remember specific dates and occurrences that Mr. Royce asked you about during the time you were a drug user. Is that a fair characterization?'

'Yes, that's true.'

'During all of those years of drug abuse and counseling and incarceration, were you ever able to forget what happened to your sister, Melissa?'

'No, never. I thought about it every day. I still do.'

'Were you ever able to forget about the man who crossed your front yard and grabbed your sister while you watched from the bushes?'

'No, never. I thought about him every day and still do.'

'Have you ever had a moment of doubt about the man you identified as your sister's abductor?'

'No.'

Maggie turned and pointedly looked at Jessup, who was looking down at a legal pad and writing what were probably meaningless notes. Her eyes held on him and she waited. Just as Jessup looked up to see what was holding up the testimony she asked her last question.

'Never a single doubt, Sarah?'

'No, never.'

'Thank you, Sarah. No further questions.'

38

The judge followed Sarah Gleason's testimony by announcing the midmorning break. Bosch waited in his seat at the railing until Royce and Jessup got up and started to file out. He then stood and moved against the grain to get to his witness. As he passed by Jessup he clapped him hard on the arm.

'I think your makeup's starting to run, Jason.'

He said it with a smile as he went by.

Jessup stopped and turned and was about to respond to the taunt when Royce grabbed him by the other arm and kept him going.

Bosch moved forward to collect Gleason from the witness stand. After parts of two days on the stand, she looked like she was both emotionally and physically drained. Like she might need help just getting up from the chair.

'Sarah, you did great,' he told her.

'Thank you. I couldn't tell if anybody believed me.'

'They all did, Sarah. They all did.'

He walked her back to the prosecution table, where Haller and McPherson had similar reviews of her testimony. McPherson got up out of her seat and hugged her.

'You stood up to Jessup and you stood up for your sister,' she said. 'You can be proud of that for the rest of your life.'

Gleason suddenly burst into tears and held her hand over her eyes. McPherson quickly pulled her back into the hug.

'I know, I know. You've held it together and stayed strong. It's okay to let it go now.'

Bosch walked over to the jury box and grabbed the box of tissues. He brought them to Gleason and she wiped away her tears.

'You're almost done,' Haller said to her. 'You've totally finished testifying so now all we want you to do is sit in court and observe the trial. We want you to sit up here in the front row when Eddie Roman testifies. After that, we can put you on a plane home this afternoon.'

'Okay, but why?'

'Because he's going to tell lies about you. And if he is going to do that, then he's going to have to tell them to your face.'

'I don't think he's going to have a problem with that. He never did.'

'Well, then, the jury will want to see how you react. And how he'll react. And don't worry, we've got something else cooking that'll make Eddie feel some heat.'

At that, Haller turned to Bosch.

'You ready with this?'

'Just give me the sign.'

'Can I ask something?' Gleason said.

'Sure,' Haller said.

'What if I don't want to get on a plane today? What if I want to be here for the verdict? For my sister.'

'We would love that, Sarah,' Maggie said. 'You are welcome and can stay as long as you like.'

Bosch stood in the hallway outside the courtroom. He had his phone out and was slowly typing a text to his daughter with one finger. His efforts were interrupted when he received a text. It was from Haller and was only one word.

NOW

He put his phone away and walked to the witness waiting room. Sonia Reyes was slumped in a chair with her head down, two empty coffee cups on the table in front of her.

'Okay, Sonia, rise and shine. We're going to go do this. You okay? You ready?'

She looked up at him with tired eyes.

'That's too many questions, po-liceman.'

'Okay, I'll settle for one. How're you feeling?'

'About how I look. You got any more of that stuff they gave me at the clinic?'

'That was it. But I'm going to have someone take you right back there as soon as we're finished here.'

'Whatever you say, policeman. I don't think I've been up this early since the last time I was in county lockup.'

'Yeah, well, it's not that early. Let's go.'

He helped her up and they headed toward Department 112. Reyes was what they called a *silent witness*.

She wouldn't be testifying in the trial. She was in no condition to. But by walking her down the aisle and putting her in the front row, Bosch would make sure she would be noticed by Edward Roman. The hope was that she'd knock Roman off his game, maybe even make him change it up. They were banking on his not knowing the rules of evidence and therefore not understanding that her appearance in the gallery precluded her from testifying at the trial and exposing his lies.

Harry hit the door with a fist as he pushed it open because he knew it would draw attention inside the court. He then ushered Reyes in and walked her down the aisle. Edward Roman was already on the stand, sworn in and testifying. He wore an ill-fitting suit borrowed from Royce's client closet and was clean-shaven with short, neat hair. He stumbled verbally when he saw Sonia in the courtroom.

'We had group counseling twice...'

'Only twice?' Royce asked, unaware of the distraction in the aisle behind him.

'What?'

'You said you only had group counseling with Sarah Gleason twice?'

'Nah, man, I meant twice a day.'

Bosch escorted Reyes to a seat with a reserved sign on it. He then sat down next to her.

'And approximately how long did this last?' Royce asked.

'Each one was fifty minutes, I think,' Roman answered, his eyes holding on Reyes in the audience.

'I mean how long were you both in counseling? A month, a year, how long?'

'Oh, it was for five months.'

'And did you become lovers while you were in the center?'

Roman lowered his eyes.

'Uh . . . yeah, that's right.'

'How did you manage that? I assume there are rules against that.'

'Well, if there's a will, there's always a way, you know? We found time. We found places.'

'Did this relationship continue after you two were released from the center?'

'Yes. She got out a couple weeks ahead of me. Then I got out and we hooked up.'

'Did you live together?'

'Uh-huh.'

'Is that a yes?'

'Yes. Can I ask a question?'

Royce paused. He hadn't expected this.

'No, Mr. Roman,' the judge said. 'You can't ask a question. You are a witness in these proceedings.'

'But how can they bring her in here like that?'

'Who, Mr. Roman?'

Roman pointed out to the gallery and right at Reyes. 'Her.'

The judge looked at Reyes and then at Bosch sitting next to her. A look of deep suspicion crossed her face.

'I'm going to ask the jury to step back into the jury room for a few moments. This should not take long.'

The jurors filed back into the jury room. The moment the last one in closed the door, the judge zeroed in on Bosch.

'Detective Bosch.'

Harry stood up.

'Who is the woman sitting to your left?'

'Your Honor,' Haller said. 'Can I answer that question?'

'Please do.'

'Detective Bosch is sitting with Sonia Reyes, who has agreed to help the prosecution as a witness consultant.'

The judge looked from Haller to Reyes and back to Haller.

'You want to run that by me again, Mr. Haller?'

'Judge, Ms. Reyes is acquainted with the witness. Because the defense did not make Mr. Roman available to us prior to his testimony here, we have asked Ms. Reyes to give us advice on how to proceed with our cross-examination.'

Haller's explanation had done nothing to change the look of suspicion on Breitman's face.

'Are you paying her for this advice?'

'We have agreed to help her get into a clinic.'

'I should hope so.'

'Your Honor,' Royce said. 'May I be heard?'

'Go ahead, Mr. Royce.'

'I think it is quite obvious that the prosecution is attempting to intimidate Mr. Roman. This is a gangster move, Judge. Not something I would expect to see from the District Attorney's Office.'

'Well, I strongly object to that characterization,' Haller said. 'It is perfectly acceptable within the canon of courtroom procedure and ethics to hire and use consultants. Mr. Royce employed a jury consultant last week and that was perfectly acceptable. But now that the prosecution has a consultant that he knows will help expose his witness as a liar and someone who preys on women, he objects. With all due respect, I would call that the gangster move.'

'Okay, we're not going to debate this now,' Breitman said. 'I find that the prosecution is certainly within bounds in using Ms. Reyes as a consultant. Let's bring the jury back.'

'Thank you, Judge,' Haller said as he sat down.

As the jurors filed back into the box, Haller turned and looked back at Bosch. He gave a slight nod and Bosch knew that he was happy. The exchange with the judge could not have worked better in delivering a message to Roman. The message being that we know your game, and come our turn to ask the questions, so will the jury. Roman now had a choice. He could stick with the defense or start playing for the prosecution.

Testimony continued once the jury was back in place. Royce quickly established through Roman that he and Sarah Gleason had a relationship that lasted nearly a year and involved the sharing of personal stories as well as drugs. But when it came to revealing those personal stories, Roman did a cut and run, leaving Royce hanging in the wind.

'Now, did there come a time when she spoke about her sister's murder?'

'A time? There were lots of times. She talked about it a lot, man.'

'And did she ever tell you in detail what she called the "real story"?'

'Yes, she did.'

'Can you tell the court what she told you?'

Roman hesitated and scratched his chin before answering. Bosch knew this was the moment that his work either paid off or went for naught.

'She told me that they were playing hide-and-seek in the yard and a guy came and grabbed her sister and that she saw the whole thing.'

Bosch's eyes made a circuit of the room. First he checked the jurors and it seemed that even they had been expecting Roman to say something else. Then the prosecution table. He saw that McPherson had grabbed Haller by the back of his arm and was squeezing it. And lastly Royce, who was now the one hesitating. He stood at the lectern looking down at his notes, one arm cocked with his fist on his hip like a frustrated teacher who could not draw the correct answer from a student.

'That is the story you heard Sarah Gleason tell in group counseling at the rehabilitation center, correct?' he finally asked.

'That's right.'

'But isn't it true that she told you a different version of events—what she called the "real story"—when you were in more private settings?'

'Uh, no. She pretty much stuck to the same story all the time.'

Bosch saw McPherson squeeze Haller's arm again. This was the whole case right here.

Royce was like a man left behind in the water by a dive boat. He was treading water but he was in the open sea and it was only a matter of time before he went down. He tried to do what he could.

'Now, Mr. Roman, on March second of this year, did you not contact my office and offer your services as a witness for the defense?'

'I don't know about the date but I called there, yeah.'

'And did you speak to my investigator, Karen Revelle?'

'I spoke to a woman but I can't remember her name.'

'And didn't you tell her a story that is quite different from the one you just recounted?'

'But I wasn't under oath or nothin' then.'

'That's right, sir, but you did tell Karen a different story, true?'

'I might've. I can't remember.'

'Didn't you tell Karen at that time that Ms. Gleason had told you that her stepfather had killed her sister?'

Haller was up with the objection, arguing that not only was Royce leading the witness but that there was no foundation for the question and that counsel was trying to get testimony to the jury that the witness was not willing to give. The judge sustained the objection.

'Your Honor,' Royce said, 'the defense would like to request a short break to confer with its witness.'

Before Haller could object the judge denied the request.

'By this witness's own testimony this morning, you have had since March second to prepare for this moment. We go to lunch in thirty-five minutes. You can confer with him then, Mr. Royce. Ask your next question.'

'Thank you, Your Honor.'

Royce looked down at his legal pad. From Bosch's angle he could tell he was looking at a blank page.

'Mr. Royce?' the judge prompted.

'Yes, Your Honor, just rechecking a date. Mr. Roman, why did you call my office on March second?'

'Well, I seen something about the case on the TV. In fact, it was you. I seen you talking about it. And I knew something about it from knowing Sarah like I did. So I called up to see if I was needed.'

'And then you came to my offices, correct?'

'Yeah, that's right. You sent that lady to pick me up.'

'And when you came to my office, you told me a different story than you are telling the jury now, isn't that right?'

'Like I said, I don't remember exactly what I said then. I'm a drug addict, sir. I say a lot of things I don't remember and don't really mean. All I remember is that the woman who came said she'd put me up in a nicer hotel and I had no money for a place at that time. So I sort of said what she told me to say.'

Bosch made a fist and bounced it once on his thigh. This was an unmitigated disaster for the defense. He looked over at Jessup to see if he realized how bad things had just turned for him. And Jessup seemed to sense it. He turned and looked back at Bosch, his eyes dark with growing anger and realization. Bosch leaned forward and slowly raised a finger. He dragged it across his throat.

Jessup turned away.

39

Thursday, April 8, 11:30 A.M.

I have had many good moments in court. I've stood next to men at the moment they knew that they were going free because of my good work. I have stood in the well in front of a jury and felt the tingle of truth and righteousness roll down my spine. And I have destroyed liars without mercy on the witness stand. These are the moments I live for in my professional life. But few of them measured up to the moment I watched Jason Jessup's defense unravel with the testimony of Edward Roman.

As Roman crashed and burned on the stand, my ex-wife and prosecution partner squeezed my arm to the point of pain. She couldn't help it. She knew it, too. This was not something Royce was going to recover from. A key part of what was already going to be a fragile defense was crumbling before his eyes. It wasn't so much that his witness had pulled a one-eighty on him. It was the jury seeing a defense that was now obviously built upon a liar. The jury would not forgive this. It was over and I believed everyone in the courtroom — from the judge to the gadflies in the back row of the gallery — knew it. Jessup was going down.

I turned and looked back to share the moment with Bosch. After all, the silent witness maneuver had been his idea. And I caught him giving Jessup the throat slash—the internationally recognized sign that it was over.

I looked back to the front of the court.

'Mr. Royce,' the judge said. 'Are you continuing with this witness?'

'A moment, Your Honor,' Royce said.

It was a valid question. Royce had few ways with which to go with Roman at this point. He could cut his losses and simply end the questioning. Or he could ask the judge to declare Roman to be a hostile witness—a move that was always professionally embarrassing when the hostile witness is one you called to the stand. But it was a move that would allow Royce more latitude in asking leading questions that explored what Roman had initially said to the defense investigator and why he was dissembling now. But this was fraught with danger, especially since this initial interview had not been recorded or documented in an effort to hide Roman during the discovery process.

'Mr. Royce!' the judge barked. 'I consider the court's time quite valuable. Please ask your next question or I will turn the witness over to Mr. Haller for cross-examination.'

Royce nodded to himself as he came to a decision.

'I'm sorry, Your Honor. But no further questions at this time.'

Royce walked dejectedly back to his seat and a waiting client who was visibly upset with the turnabout. I stood up and started moving to the lectern even before the judge turned the witness over to me.

'Mr. Roman,' I said, 'your testimony has been somewhat confusing to me. So let me get this straight. Are you telling this jury that Sarah Ann Gleason did or did not tell you that her stepfather murdered her sister?'

'She didn't. That's just what they wanted me to say.'

'Who is "they," sir?'

'The defense. The lady investigator and Royce.'

'Besides a hotel room, were you to receive anything else if you testified to such a story today?'

'They just said they'd take care of me. That a lot of money was at—'

'Objection!' Royce yelled.

He jumped to his feet.

'Your Honor, the witness is clearly hostile and acting out a vindictive fantasy.'

'He's your witness, Mr. Royce. He can answer the question. Go ahead, sir.'

'They said there was a lot of money at stake and they would take care of me,' Roman said.

It just kept getting better for me and worse for Jessup. But I had to make sure I didn't come off to the jury as gleeful or vindictive myself. I recalibrated and focused on what was important.

'What was the story that Sarah told you all those years ago, Mr. Roman?'

'Like I said, that she was in the yard and she was hiding and she saw the guy who grabbed her sister.'

'Did she ever tell you she identified the wrong man?'

'No.'

'Did she ever tell you that the police told her who to identify?'

'No.'

'Did she ever once tell you that the wrong man was charged with her sister's murder?'

'No.'

'No further questions.'

I checked the clock as I returned to my seat. We still had twenty minutes before the lunch break. Rather than break early, the judge asked Royce to call his next witness. He called his investigator, Karen Revelle. I knew what he was doing and I was going to be ready.

Revelle was a mannish-looking woman who wore slacks and a sport jacket. She had ex-cop written all over her dour expression. After she was sworn in, Royce got right to the point, probably hoping to stem the flow of blood from his case before the jurors went to lunch.

'What do you do for a living, Ms. Revelle?'

'I am an investigator for the law firm of Royce and Associates.'

'You work for me, correct?'

'That is correct.'

'On March second of this year, did you conduct a telephone interview with an individual named Edward Roman?'

'I did.'

'What did he tell you in that call?'

I stood and objected. I asked the judge if I could discuss my objection at a sidebar conference.

'Come on up,' she said.

Maggie and I followed Royce to the side of the bench. The judge told me to state my objection.

'My first objection is that anything this witness states about a conversation with Roman is clearly hearsay and not allowed. But the larger objection is to Mr. Royce trying to impeach his own witness. He's going to use Revelle to impeach Roman, and you can't do that, Judge. It's damn near suborning perjury on Mr. Royce's part, because one of these two people is lying under oath and he called them both!'

'I strongly object to Mr. Haller's last characterization,' Royce said, leaning over the sidebar and moving in closer to the judge. 'Suborning perjury? I have been practicing law for more than—'

'First of all, back up, Mr. Royce, you're in my space,' Breitman said sternly. 'And second, you can save your self-serving objection for some other time. Mr. Haller is correct on all counts. If I allow this witness to continue her testimony, you are not only going to go into hearsay but we will have a situation where one of your witnesses has lied under oath. You can't have it both ways and you can't put a liar on the stand. So this is what we're going to do. You are going to get your investigator off the stand, Mr. Haller is going to make a motion to strike what little testimony she has already given and I will agree to that motion. Then we're going to lunch. During that time, you and your client can get together and decide what to do next. But it's looking to me like your options got really limited in the last half hour. That's all.'

She didn't wait for any of us to respond. She simply rolled her chair away from the sidebar.

Royce followed the judge's advice and ended his questioning of Revelle. I moved to strike and that was that. A half hour later I was sitting with Maggie and Sarah Gleason at a table at the Water Grill, the place where the case had started for me. We had decided to go high-end because we were celebrating what appeared to be the beginning of the end for Jason Jessup's case, and because the Water Grill was just across the street from Sarah's hotel. The only one missing at the table was Bosch, and he was on his way after dropping our silent witness, Sonia Reyes, at the drug rehab facility at County-USC Medical Center.

'Wow,' I said after the three of us were seated. 'I don't think I've ever seen anything like that before in a courtroom.'

'Me, neither,' Maggie said.

'Well, I've been in a few courtrooms but I don't know enough to know what it all means,' said Gleason.

'It means the end is near,' Maggie said.

'It means the entire defense imploded,' I added. 'See, the defense's case was sort of simple. Stepfather killed the girl and the family concocted a cover-up. They came up with the story about hide-and-seek and the man on the lawn to throw the authorities off of stepdad. Then sister—that's you—made a false identification of Jessup.

'Just sort of randomly set him up for a murder he did not commit.'

'But what about Melissa's hair in the tow truck?' Gleason asked.

'The defense claims it was planted,' I said. 'Either in conspiracy or independent of the family's cover-up. The police realized they didn't have much of a case. They had a thirteen-year-old girl's ID of a suspect and almost nothing else. So they took hair from the body or a hairbrush and planted it in the tow truck. After lunch—if Royce is foolish enough to continue this—he will present investigative chronology reports and time logs that will show Detective Kloster had enough access and time to make the plant in the tow truck before a search warrant was obtained and forensics opened the truck.'

'But that's crazy,' Gleason said.

'Maybe so,' Maggie said, 'but that was their case and Eddie Roman was the linchpin because he was supposed to testify that you told him your stepfather did it. He was supposed to plant the seed of doubt. That's all it takes, Sarah. One little doubt. Only he took one look at who was in the audience—namely Sonia Reyes—and thought he was in trouble. You see Eddie did the same thing with Sonia as he did with you. Met her, got close and turned her out to keep him in meth. When he saw her in court, he knew he was in trouble. Because he knew if Sonia got on the stand and told the same story about him as you did, then the jury would know what he was—a liar and predator—and wouldn't trust a single thing he said. He also had no idea what Sonia might have told us about crimes they committed together. So he decided up there that his best out was the truth. To screw the defense and make the prosecution happy. He changed his story.'

Gleason nodded as she began to understand.

'Do you think Mr. Royce really told him what to say and was going to pay him off for his lies?'

'Of course,' Maggie said.

'I don't know,' I said quickly. 'I've known Clive a long time. I don't think that's how he operates.'

'What?' Maggie said. 'You think Eddie Roman just made it all up on his own?'

'No, but he spoke to the investigator before he ever got to Clive.'

'Plausible denial. You're just being charitable, Haller. They don't call him Clever Clive for no reason.'

Sarah seemed to sense that she had pushed us into a zone of contention that had existed long before this trial. She tried to move us on.

'Do you really think it's over?' she asked.

I thought for a moment about it and then nodded.

'I think if I was Clever Clive I'd be thinking of what's best for my client and that would be not to let this go to a verdict. I'd start thinking about a deal. Maybe he'll even call during lunch.'

I pulled my phone out and put it down on the table, as if being ready for Royce's call would make it happen. Just as I did so, Bosch showed up and took the seat next to Maggie. I grabbed my water glass and raised it to him.

436

'Cheers, Harry. Smooth move today. I think Jessup's house of cards is falling down.'

Bosch raised a water glass and clinked it off mine.

'Royce was right, you know,' he said. 'It was a gangster move. Saw it in one of the *Godfather* movies way back.'

He then held his water glass up to the two women.

'Anyway, cheers,' he said. 'You two are the real stars. Great work yesterday and today.'

We all clinked glasses but Sarah hesitated.

'What's wrong, Sarah?' I asked. 'Don't tell me you're afraid of clinking glass.'

I smiled, proud of my own humor.

'It's nothing,' she said. 'I think it's supposed to be bad luck to toast with water.'

'Well,' I said, quickly recovering, 'it's going to take more than bad luck to change things now.'

Bosch switched subjects.

'What happens next?' he asked.

'I was just telling Sarah that I don't think this will go to a jury. Clive has to be thinking disposition. They really don't have any other choice.'

Bosch turned serious.

'I know there's money on the line and your boss probably thinks that's the priority,' he said, 'but this guy has got to go back to prison.'

'Absolutely,' Maggie said.

'Of course,' I added. 'And after what happened this morning, we have all the leverage. Jessup has to take what we offer or we—'

My phone started to buzz. The ID screen said un-known.

'Speak of the devil,' Maggie said.

I looked at Sarah.

'You might be on that plane home tonight after all.'

I opened the phone and said my name.

'Mickey, District Attorney Williams here. How are you?'

I shook my head at the others. It wasn't Royce.

'I'm doing fine, Gabe. How are you?'

My informality didn't seem to faze him.

'I'm hearing good things out of court this morning.'

His statement confirmed what I had thought all along. While Williams had never once showed his face in the courtroom, he had a plant in the gallery watching.

'Well, I hope so. I think we'll know more about which way this will go after lunch.'

'Are you considering a disposition?'

'Well, not yet. I haven't heard from opposing counsel, but I assume that we may soon enter into discussions. He's probably talking to his client about it right now. I would be if I were him.'

'Well, keep me in the loop on that before you sign off on anything.'

I paused as I weighed this last statement. I saw Bosch put his hand inside his jacket and pull out his own phone to take a call.

'Tell you what, Gabe. As independent counsel I prefer to stay independent. I'll inform you of a disposition if and when I have an agreement.'

'I want to be part of that conversation,' Williams insisted.

I saw some sort of darkness move into Bosch's eyes. Instinctively, I knew it was time to get off my call.

'I'll get back to you on that, Mr. District Attorney. I've got another call coming in here. It could be Clive Royce.'

I closed the phone just as Bosch closed his and started to stand up.

'What is it?' Maggie asked.

Bosch's face looked ashen.

'There's been a shooting over at Royce's office. There's four on the floor over there.'

'Is Jessup one of them?' I asked.

'No... Jessup's gone.'

40

Bosch drove and McPherson insisted on riding with him. Haller had split off with Gleason to head back to court. Bosch pulled a card out of his wallet and got Lieutenant Stephen Wright's number off it. He handed the card and his phone to McPherson and told her to punch in the number.

'It's ringing,' she said.

He took the phone and got it to his ear just as Wright answered.

'It's Bosch. Tell me your people are on Jessup.'

'I wish.'

'Damn it! What the hell happened? Why wasn't SIS on him?'

'Hold your horses, Bosch. We *were* on him. That's one of my people on the floor in Royce's office.'

That hit like a punch. Bosch hadn't realized a cop was one of the victims.

'Where are you?' he asked Wright.

'On my way there. I'm three minutes out.'

'What do you know so far?'

'Not a hell of a lot. We had a light tail on him during court hours. You knew that. One team during court and full coverage before and after. Today they followed him from the courthouse to Royce's office at lunchtime. Jessup and Royce's team walked over. After they were in there a few minutes my guys heard gunshots. They called it in and then went in. One was knocked down, the other pinned down. Jessup went out the back and my guy stayed to try CPR on his partner. He had to let Jessup go.'

Bosch shook his head. The thought of his daughter pushed through everything. She was at school for the next ninety minutes. He felt that she would be safe. For now.

'Who else was hit?' he asked.

'As far as I know,' Wright said, 'it was Royce and his investigator and then another lawyer. A female. They were lucky it was lunchtime. Everybody else in the office was gone.'

Bosch didn't see much that was lucky about a quad-ruple murder and Jessup out there somewhere with a gun. Wright kept talking.

'I'm not going to shed a tear over a couple of defense lawyers but my guy on the floor in there's got two little kids at home, Bosch. This is not a good goddamn thing at all.'

Bosch turned onto First, and up ahead he could see the flashing lights. Royce's office was in a storefront on a dead-end street that ran behind the Kyoto Grand Hotel on the edge of Japantown. Easy walking distance to the courthouse.

'Did you get Jessup's car out on a broadcast?'

441

'Yes, everybody has it. Somebody will see it.'

'Where's the rest of your crew?'

'Everybody's heading to the scene.'

'No, send them out looking for Jessup. At all the places he's been. The parks, everywhere, even my house. There's no use for them at the scene.'

'We'll meet there and I'll send them out.'

'You're wasting time, Lieutenant.'

'You think I can stop them from coming to the scene first?'

Bosch understood the impossibility of Wright's situation.

'I'm pulling up now,' he said. 'I'll see you when you get here.'

'Two minutes.'

Bosch closed the phone. McPherson asked him what Wright had said and he quickly filled her in as he pulled the car to a stop behind a patrol car.

Bosch badged his way under the yellow tape and McPherson did the same. Because the shooting had occurred only twenty-five minutes earlier, the crime scene was largely inhabited by uniformed officers—the first responders—and was chaotic. Bosch found a patrol sergeant issuing orders regarding crime scene protection and went to him.

'Sergeant, Harry Bosch, RHD. Who is taking this investigation?'

'Isn't it you?'

'No, I'm on a related case. But this one won't be mine.'

'Then I don't know, Bosch. I was told RHD will handle.'

'Okay, then they're still on their way. Who's inside?'

'Couple guys from Central Division. Roche and Stout.'

Babysitters, Bosch thought. As soon as RHD moved in, they would be moved out. He pulled his phone and called his lieutenant.

'Gandle.'

'Lieutenant, who's taking the four on the floor by the Kyoto?'

'Bosch? Where are you?'

'At the scene. It was my guy from the trial. Jessup.'

'Shit, what went wrong?'

'I don't know. Who are you sending and where the hell are they?'

'I'm sending four. Penzler, Kirshbaum, Krikorian and Russell. But they were all at lunch up at Birds. I'm coming over, too, but you don't have to be there, Harry.'

'I know. I'm not staying long.'

Bosch closed the phone and looked around for McPherson. He had lost her in the confusion of the crime scene. He spotted her crouching down next to a man sitting on the sidewalk curb in front of the bail-bonds shop next door to Royce's office. Bosch recognized him from the night he and McPherson rode on the surveillance of Jessup. There was blood on his hands and shirt from his efforts to save his partner. Bosch went to them.

'...he went to his car when they got back here. For just a minute. Got in and then got out. He then went into the office. Right away we heard shots. We moved and Manny got hit as soon as we opened the door. I got off a couple rounds but I had to try to help Manny...'

'So Jessup must've gotten the gun from his car, right?'

'Must've. They've got the metal detectors at the courthouse. He didn't have it in court today.'

'But you never saw it?'

'No, never saw the weapon. If we had seen it, we would've done something.'

Bosch left them there and went to the door of Royce and Associates. He got there just as Lieutenant Wright did. Together they entered.

'Oh, my God,' Wright said when he saw his man on the floor just inside the front door.

'What was his name?' Bosch asked.

'Manuel Branson. He's got two kids and I have to go tell his wife.'

Branson was on his back. He had bullet entry wounds on the left side of his neck and upper left cheek. There had been a lot of blood. The neck shot appeared to have sliced through the carotid artery.

Bosch left Wright there and moved past a reception desk and down a hallway on the right side. There was a wall of glass that looked into a boardroom with doors on both ends. The rest of the victims were in here, along with two detectives who wore gloves and booties and were taking notes on clipboards. Roche and Stout. Bosch stood in the first doorway of the room but did not enter. The two detectives looked at him.

'Who are you?' one asked.

'Bosch, RHD.'

'You taking this?'

'Not exactly. I'm on something related. The others are coming.'

'Christ, we're only two blocks from the PAB.'

'They weren't there. They were at lunch up in Hollywood. But don't worry, they'll get here. It's not like these people are going anywhere.'

Bosch looked at the bodies. Clive Royce sat dead in a chair at the head of a long board table. His head was snapped back as if he were looking at the ceiling. There was a bloodless bullet hole in the center of his forehead. Blood from the exit wound at the back of his head had poured down the back of his jacket and chair.

The investigator, Karen Revelle, was on the floor on the other side of the room near the other door. It appeared that she had tried to make a run for it before being hit by gunfire. She was facedown and Bosch could not see where or how many times she had been hit.

Royce's pretty associate counsel, whose name Bosch could not remember, was no longer pretty. Her body was in a seat diagonal to Royce, her upper body down on the table, an entry wound at the back of her head. The bullet had exited below her right eye and destroyed her face. There was always more damage coming out than going in.

'What do you think?' asked one of the Central guys.

'Looks like he came in shooting. Hit these two first

and then tagged the other as she made a run for the door. Then backed into the hall and opened up on the SIS guys as they came in.'

'Yeah. Looks that way.'

'I'm going to check the rest of the place out.'

Bosch continued down the hall and looked through open doors into empty offices. There were nameplates on the wall outside the doors and he was reminded that Royce's associate was named Denise Graydon.

The hallway ended at a break room, where there was a kitchenette with a refrigerator and a microwave. There was another communal table here. And an exit door that was three inches ajar.

Bosch used his elbow to push the door open. He stepped into an alley lined with trash bins. He looked both ways and saw a pay parking lot a half block down to his right. He assumed it was the lot where Jessup had parked his car and had gone to retrieve the gun.

He went back inside and this time took a longer look in each of the offices. He knew from experience that he was treading in a gray area here. This was a law office, and whether the lawyers were dead or not, their clients were still entitled to privacy and attorney-client privilege. Bosch touched nothing and opened no drawer or file. He simply moved his eyes over the surface of things, seeing and reading what was in plain sight.

When he was in Revelle's office he was joined by McPherson.

'What are you doing?'

'Just looking.'

'We might have a problem going into any of their offices. As an officer of the court I can't—'

'Then wait outside. Like I said, I'm just looking. I am making sure the premises are secure.'

'Whatever. I'll be out front. The media's all over the place out there now. It's a circus.'

Bosch was leaning over Revelle's desk. He didn't look up.

'Good for them.'

McPherson left the room at the same moment Bosch read something off a legal pad that was on top of a stack of files on the side of the desk near the phone.

'Maggie? Come back here.'

She returned.

'Take a look at this.'

McPherson came around the desk and bent over to read the notes on the top page of the pad. The page was covered with what looked like random notes, phone numbers and names. Some were circled, others scratched out. It looked like a pad Revelle jotted on while on the phone.

'What?' McPherson asked.

Without touching the pad, Bosch pointed to a notation in the bottom right corner. All it said was *Checkers—804.* But that was enough.

'Shit!' McPherson said. 'Sarah isn't even registered under her name. How did Revelle get this?'

'She must've followed us back after court, paid somebody for the room number. We have to assume that Jessup has this information.'

Bosch pulled his phone and called Mickey Haller on speed dial.

'It's Bosch. You still have Sarah with you?'

'Yes, she's here in court. We're waiting for the judge.'

'Look, don't scare her but she can't go back to the hotel.'

'All right. How come?'

'Because there's an indication here that Jessup has that location. We'll be setting up on it.'

'What do I do, then?'

'I'll be sending a protection team to the court—for both of you. They'll know what to do.'

'They can cover her. I don't need it.'

'That'll be your choice. My advice is you take it.'

He closed the phone and looked at McPherson.

'I gotta get a protection team over there. I want you to take my car and get my daughter and your daughter and go somewhere safe. You call me then and I'll send a team to you, too.'

'My car's two blocks from here. I can just—'

'That'll waste too much time. Take mine and go now. I'll call the school and tell them you're coming for Maddie.'

'Okay.'

'Thank you. Call me when you have—'

They heard shouting from the front of the office suite. Angry male voices. Bosch knew they came from the friends of Manny Branson. They were seeing their fallen comrade on the floor and getting fueled with outrage and the scent of blood for the hunt.

'Let's go,' he said.

They moved back through the suite to the front. Bosch saw Wright standing just outside the front door, consoling two SIS men with angry, tear-streaked faces. Bosch made his way around Branson's body and out the door. He tapped Wright on the elbow.

'I need a moment, Lieutenant.'

Wright broke away from his two men and followed. Bosch walked a few yards to where they could speak privately. But he need not have worried about being overheard. In the sky above, there were at least four media choppers circling over the crime scene and laying down a layer of camouflage sound that would make any conversation on the block private.

'I need two of your best men,' Bosch said, leaning toward Wright's ear.

'Okay. What do you have going?'

'There's a note on the desk of one of the victims. It's the hotel and room number of our prime witness. We have to assume our shooter has that information. The slaughter inside there indicates he's taking out the people associated with the trial. The people he thinks did him wrong. That's a long list but I think our witness would be at the top of it.'

'Got it. You want to set up at the hotel.'

Bosch nodded.

'Yeah. One man outside, one inside and me in the room. We wait and see if he shows.'

Wright shook his head.

'We use four. Two inside and two outside. But forget

waiting in the room, because Jessup will never get by the surveillance. Instead, you and I find a viewpoint up high and set up the command post. That's the right way to do it.'

Bosch nodded.

'Okay, let's go.'

'Except there's one thing.'

'What's that?'

'If I bring you in on this, then you stay back. My people take him down.'

Bosch studied him for a moment, trying to read everything hidden in what he was saying.

'There are questions,' Bosch said. 'About Franklin Canyon and the other places. I need to talk to Jessup.'

Wright looked over Bosch's shoulder and back toward the front door of Royce and Associates.

'Detective, one of my best people is dead on the floor in there. I'm not guaranteeing you anything. You understand?'

Bosch paused and then nodded.

'I understand.'

41

There was more media in the courtroom than there had been at any other point of the trial. The first two rows of the gallery were shoulder-to-shoulder with reporters and cameramen. The rest of the rows were filled with courthouse personnel and lawyers who had heard what had happened to Clive Royce.

Sarah Gleason sat in a row by the courtroom deputy's desk. It was marked as reserved for law enforcement officers but the deputy put her there so the reporters couldn't get to her. Meantime, I sat at the prosecution table waiting for the judge like a man on a desert island. No Maggie. No Bosch. Nobody at the defense table. I was alone.

'Mickey,' someone whispered from behind me.

I turned to see Kate Salters from the *Times* leaning across the railing.

'I can't talk now. I have to figure out what to say here.'

'But do you think your total destruction of this morning's witness is what could have—?'

I was saved by the judge. Breitman entered the courtroom and bounded up to the bench and took her seat.

Salters took hers and the question I wanted to avoid for the rest of my life remained unasked—at least for the moment.

'We are back on the record in *California versus Jessup*. Michael Haller is present for the People. But the jury is not present, nor is defense counsel or the defendant. I am aware through unconfirmed media reports of what has transpired in the last ninety minutes at Mr. Royce's office. Can you add anything to what I have seen and heard on television, Mr. Haller?'

I stood up to address the court.

'Your Honor, I don't know what they are putting out to the media at the moment, but I can confirm that Mr. Royce and his cocounsel on this case, Ms. Graydon, were shot and killed in their offices at lunchtime. Karen Revelle is also dead, as well as a police officer who responded to the shooting. The suspect in the shooting has been identified as Jason Jessup. He remains at large.'

Judging by the murmur from the gallery behind me, those basic facts had probably been speculated upon but not yet confirmed to the media.

'This is, indeed, very sad news,' Breitman said.

'Yes, Your Honor,' I said. 'Very sad.'

'But I think at this moment we need to put aside our emotions and act carefully here. The issue is, how do we proceed with this case? I am pretty sure I know the answer to that question but am willing to listen to counsel before ruling. Do you wish to be heard, Mr. Haller?'

'Yes, I do, Judge. I ask the court to recess the trial for the remainder of the day and sequester the jury

452

while we await further information. I also ask that you revoke Mr. Jessup's pretrial release and issue a capias for his arrest.'

The judge considered these requests for a long moment before responding.

'I will grant the motion revoking the defendant's release and issue the capias. But I don't see the need to sequester the jury. Regrettably, I see no alternative to a mistrial here, Mr. Haller.'

I knew that would be her first thought. I had been considering my response since the moment I had returned to the courthouse.

'The People object to a mistrial, Judge. The law is clear that Mr. Jessup waives his right to be present at these proceedings by voluntarily absenting himself from them. According to what the defense represented earlier, he was scheduled to be the last witness today. But he has obviously decided not to testify. So, taking all of this into—'

'Mr. Haller, I am going to have to stop you right there. I think you are missing one part of the equation and I am afraid the horse is already out of the barn. You may recall that Deputy Solantz was assigned lunch duty with our jurors after we had the issue of tardiness on Monday.'

'Yes.'

'Well, lunch for eighteen in downtown Los Angeles is a tall order. Deputy Solantz arranged for the group to travel by bus together and eat each day at Clifton's Cafeteria. There are TVs in the restaurant but Deputy

Solantz always keeps them off the local channels. Unfortunately, one TV was on CNN today when the network chose to go live with what was occurring at Mr. Royce's office. Several jurors saw the live report and got the gist of what was happening before Deputy Solantz managed to kill the feed. As you can imagine, Deputy Solantz is not very happy with himself at the moment, and neither am I.'

I turned and looked over at the courtroom deputy's desk. Solantz had his eyes down in humiliation. I looked back at the judge and I knew I was dead in the water.

'Needless to say, your suggestion of sequestering the jury was a good one, just a little late. Therefore, and after taking all things into consideration, I find that the jury in this trial has been prejudiced by events which have occurred outside of the court. I intend to declare a mistrial and continue this case until such time as Mr. Jessup has been brought again before this court.'

She paused for a moment to see if I had an objection but I had nothing. I knew what she was doing was right and inevitable.

'Let's bring in the jury now,' she said.

Soon the jurors were filing into the box, many of them glancing over at the empty defense table.

When everyone was in place, the judge went on the record and turned her chair directly to the jurors. In a subdued tone she addressed them.

'Ladies and gentlemen of the jury, I must inform you that because of factors that are not fully clear to you but will soon become so, I have declared a mistrial in the case of *California versus Jason Jessup*. I do this with great regret because all of us here have invested a great deal of time and effort in these proceedings.'

She paused and studied the confused faces in front of her.

'No one likes to invest so much time without seeing the case through to a result. I am sorry for this. But I do thank you for your duty. You were all dependable and for the most part on time every day. I also watched you closely during the testimony and you were all attentive. The court cannot thank you enough. You are dismissed now from this courtroom and discharged from jury duty. You may all go home.'

The jurors slowly filed back into the jury room, many taking a last look back at the courtroom. Once they were gone the judge turned back to me.

'Mr. Haller, for what it's worth, I thought you acquitted yourself quite well as a prosecutor. I am sorry it ended this way but you are welcome back to this court anytime and on either side of the aisle.'

'Thank you, Judge. I appreciate that. I had a lot of help.'

'Then I commend your whole team as well.'

With that, the judge stood and left the bench. I sat there for a long time, listening to the gallery clear out behind me and thinking about what Breitman had said at the end. I wondered how and why such a good job in court had resulted in such a horrible thing happening in Clive Royce's office.

'Mr. Haller?'

I turned, expecting it to be a reporter. But it was two uniformed police officers.

'Detective Bosch sent us. We are here to take you and Ms. Gleason into protective custody.'

'Only Ms. Gleason and she's right here.'

Sarah was waiting on the bench next to Deputy Solantz's desk.

'Sarah, these officers are going to take care of you until Jason Jessup is in custody or...'

I didn't need to finish. Sarah got up and walked over to us.

'So there's no more trial?' she asked.

'Right. The judge declared a mistrial. That means if Jessup is caught, we would have to start over. With a new jury.'

She nodded and looked a little dumbfounded. I had seen the look on the faces of many people who venture naively into the justice system. They leave the court-house wondering what just happened. Sarah Gleason would be no different.

'You should go with these men now, Sarah. We'll be in touch as soon as we know what happens next.'

She just nodded and they headed for the door.

I waited a while, alone in the courtroom, and then headed out to the hallway myself. I saw several of the jurors being interviewed by the reporters. I could've watched but at the moment I wasn't interested in what anybody had to say about the case. Not anymore.

Kate Salters saw me and broke away from one of the clusters.

'Mickey, can we talk now?'

'I don't feel like talking. Call me tomorrow.'

'The story's today, Mick.'

'I don't care.'

I pushed by her in the direction of the elevators.

'Where are you going?'

I didn't answer. I got to the elevators and jumped through the open doors of a waiting car. I moved into the rear corner and saw a woman standing by the panel. She asked me the same question as Salters.

'Where are you going?'

'Home,' I said.

She pushed the button marked G and we went down.

PART FIVE
– The Takedown

42

Bosch was stationed with Wright in a borrowed office across the street from the Checkers Hotel. It was the command post, and although no one thought Jessup would be stupid enough to walk in the front door of the hotel, the position gave them a good view of the entire property as well as two of the other surveillance positions.

'I don't know,' Wright said, staring out the window. 'This guy is smart, right?'

'I guess so,' Bosch said.

'Then I don't see him making this move, you know? He'd have already been here if he was. He's probably halfway to Mexico by now and we're sitting here watching a hotel.'

'Maybe.'

'If I were him, I'd get down there and lie low. Try to spend as many days on the beach as I could before they found me and put me back in the Q.'

Bosch's phone began to buzz and he saw that it was his daughter.

'I'm going to step out to take this,' he said to Wright. 'You got it covered here?'

'I've got it.'

Bosch answered the phone as he left the office for the hallway.

'Hey, Mads. Everything all right?'

'There's a police car outside now.'

'Yeah, I know. I sent it there. Just an added precaution.'

They had talked an hour earlier after Maggie McPherson had gotten them safely to a friend's home in Porter Ranch. He had told his daughter about Jessup being out there and what had happened at Royce's office. She didn't know about Jessup's nocturnal visit to their house two weeks earlier.

'So they didn't catch that guy yet?'

'We're working on it and I'm in the middle of stuff here. Stay close to Aunt Maggie and stay safe. I'll come get you as soon as this is over.'

'Okay. Here, Aunt Maggie wants to talk to you.'

McPherson took the phone.

'Harry, what's the latest?'

'Same as before. We're out looking for him and sitting on all the known locations. I'm with Wright at Sarah's hotel.'

'Be careful.'

'Speaking of that, where's Mickey? He turned down protection.'

'He's at home right now but said he's coming up here.'

'Okay, sounds good. I'll talk to you later.'

'Keep us posted.'

'I will.'

Bosch closed the phone and went back into the office. Wright was still at the window.

'I think we're wasting our time and should shut this down,' he said.

'Why? What's going on?'

'Just came over the radio. They found the car Jessup was using. In Venice. He's nowhere near here, Bosch.'

Bosch knew that dumping the car in Venice could merely be a misdirection. Drive out to the beach, leave the car and then double back in a cab to downtown. Nonetheless, he found himself reluctantly agreeing with Wright. They were spinning their wheels here.

'Damn it,' he said.

'Don't worry. We'll get him. I'm keeping one team here and one on your house. Everybody else I'm moving down into Venice.'

'And the Santa Monica Pier?'

'Already covered. Got a couple teams on the beach and nobody's gone in or out of that location.'

Wright went on the SIS band on the radio and started redeploying his men. As Bosch listened he paced the room, trying to figure Jessup out. After a while he stepped back out to the hallway so as not to disturb Wright's radio choreography and called Larry Gandle, his boss at RHD.

'It's Bosch. Just checking in.'

'You still at the hotel?'

'Yeah, but we're about to clear and head to the beach. I guess you heard they found the car.'

'Yeah, I was just there.'

Bosch was surprised. With four victims at Royce's office, he thought Gandle would still be at the murder scene.

'The car's clean,' Gandle said. 'Jessup still has the weapon.'

'Where are you now?' Bosch asked.

'On Speedway,' Gandle said. 'We just hit the room Jessup was using. Took a while to get the search warrant.'

'Anything there?'

'Not so far. This fucking guy, you see him in court wearing a suit and you think...I don't know what you think, but the reality was, he was living like an animal.'

'What do you mean?'

'There are empty cans all over the place, food still rotting in them. Food rotting on the counter, trash everywhere. He hung blankets over the windows to black it out like a cave. He made it like a prison cell. He was even writing on the walls.'

All at once it hit him. Bosch knew who Jessup had prepared the dungeon under the pier for.

'What kind of food?' he asked.

'What?' Gandle asked.

'The canned food. What kind of food?'

'I don't know, fruits and peaches—all kinds of stuff you can get fresh in any store you walk into. But he had it in cans. Like prison.'

'Thanks, Lieutenant.'

Bosch closed the phone and walked quickly back into the office. Wright was off the radio now.

'Did your people go under the pier and check the storage room or just set up surveillance?'

'It's a loose surveillance.'

'Meaning they didn't check it out?'

'They checked the perimeter. There was no sign that anybody went under the wall. So they backed out and set up.'

'Jessup's there. They missed him.'

'How do you know?'

'I just know. Let's go.'

43

Thursday, April 8, 6:35 P.M.

I stood at the picture window at the end of my living room and looked out at the city with the sun dropping behind it. Jessup was out there someplace. Like a rabid animal he would be hunted, cornered and, I had no doubt, put down. It was the inevitable conclusion to his play.

Jessup was legally to blame but I couldn't help but think about my own culpability in these dark matters. Not in any legal sense, but in a private, internal sense. I had to question whether consciously or not I had set all of this in motion on the day I sat with Gabriel Williams and agreed to cross a line in the courtroom as well as within myself. Maybe by allowing Jessup his freedom I had determined his fate as well as that of Royce and the others. I was a defense attorney, not a prosecutor. I stood for the underdog, not for the state. Maybe I had taken the steps and made the maneuvers so that there would never be a verdict and I would not have to live with it on my record and conscience.

Such were the musings of a guilty man. But they didn't last long. My phone buzzed and I pulled it from my pocket without looking away from my view of the city.

'Haller.'

'It's me. I thought you were coming up here.'

Maggie McFierce.

'Soon. I'm just finishing up here. Everything all right?'

'For me, yes. But probably not for Jessup. Are you watching the TV news?'

'No, what are they showing?'

'They've evacuated the Santa Monica Pier. Channel Five has a chopper over it. They're not confirming that it's related to Jessup but they said that LAPD's SIS unit sought an okay from SMPD to conduct a fugitive apprehension. They're on the beach moving in.'

'The dungeon? Did Jessup grab somebody?'

'If he did, they're not saying.'

'Did you call Harry?'

'I just tried but he didn't pick up. I think he's probably down there on the beach.'

I broke away from the window and grabbed the television remote off the coffee table. I snapped on the TV and punched in Channel 5.

'I have it on here,' I told Maggie.

On the screen was an aerial view of the pier and the surrounding beach. It looked like there were men on the beach and they were advancing on the pier's underside from both the north and south.

'I think you're right,' I said. 'It's gotta be him. The dungeon he made down there was actually for himself. Like a safe house he could run to.'

'Like the prison cell he was used to. I wonder if he

knows they're coming in on him. Maybe he hears the helicopters.'

'Harry said the waves under there are so loud you couldn't even hear a gunshot.'

'Well, we might be about to find that out.'

We watched in silence for a few moments before I spoke.

'Maggie, are the girls watching this?'

'God, no! They're playing video games in the other room.'

'Good.'

They watched in silence. The newscaster's voice echoing over the line as he inanely described what was on the screen. After a while Maggie asked the question that had probably been on her mind all afternoon.

'Did you think it would come to this, Haller?'

'No, did you?'

'No, never. I guess I thought everything would sort of be contained in the courtroom. Like it always is.'

'Yeah.'

'At least Jessup saved us the indignity of the verdict.'

'What do you mean? We had him and he knew it.'

'You didn't watch any of the juror interviews, did you?'

'What, on TV?'

'Yeah, juror number ten is on every channel saying he would've voted not guilty.'

'You mean Kirns?'

'Yeah, the alternate that got moved into the box. Everybody else interviewed said guilty, guilty, guilty.

But Kirns said not guilty, that we hadn't convinced him. He would've hung the jury, Haller, and you know Williams wouldn't have signed on for round two. Jessup would've walked.'

I considered this and could only shake my head. Everything was for nothing. All it took was one juror with a grudge against society, and Jessup would've walked. I looked up from the TV screen and out toward the western horizon to the distance, where I knew Santa Monica hugged the edge of the Pacific. I thought I could see the media choppers circling.

'I wonder if Jessup will ever know that,' I said.

44

The sun was dropping low over the Pacific and burning a brilliant green path across the surface. Bosch stood close to Wright on the beach, a hundred yards south of the pier. They were both looking down at the 5 × 5 video screen contained in a front pack strapped to Wright's chest. He was commanding the SIS takedown of Jason Jessup. On the screen was a murky image of the dimly lit storage facility under the pier. Bosch had been given ears but no mike. He could hear the operation's communications but could not contribute to them. Anything he had to say would have to go through Wright.

The voices over the com were hard to hear because of the background sound of waves crashing beneath the pier.

'This is Five, we're in.'

'Steady the visual,' Wright commanded.

The focus on the video tightened and Bosch could see that the camera was aimed at the individual storage rooms at the rear of the pier facility.

'This one.'

He pointed to the door he had seen Jessup go through.

'Okay,' Wright said. 'Our target is the second door

470

from the right. Repeat, second door from the right. Move in and take positions.'

The video moved in a herky-jerky fashion to a new position. Now the camera was even closer.

'Three and Four are—'

The rest was wiped out by the sound of a crashing wave.

'Three and Four, say again,' Wright said.

'Three, Four in position.'

'Hold until my go. Topside, you ready?'

'Topside ready.'

On the upper level of the evacuated pier there was another team, which had placed small explosives at the corners of the trapdoor above the storage corral where they believed Jessup was holed up. On Wright's command the SIS teams would blow the trapdoor and move in from above and below.

Wright wrapped his hand around the mike that ran along his jawline and looked at Bosch.

'You ready for this?'

'Ready.'

Wright released his grip and gave the command to his teams.

'Okay, let's give him a chance,' he said. 'Three, you have the speaker up?'

'That's a go on the speaker. You're hot in three, two...one.'

Wright spoke, trying to convince a man hidden in a dark room a hundred yards away to give himself up.

'Jason Jessup. This is Lieutenant Stephen Wright of

the Los Angeles Police Department. Your position is surrounded top and bottom. Step out with your hands behind your head, fingers laced. Move forward to the waiting officers. If you deviate from this order you will be shot.'

Bosch pulled his earplugs out and listened. He could hear the muffled sound of Wright's words coming from under the pier. There was no doubt that Jessup could hear the order if he was under there.

'You have one minute,' Wright said as his final communication to Jessup.

The lieutenant checked his watch and they waited. At the thirty-second mark Wright checked with his men under the pier.

'Anything?'

'This is Three. I got nothing.'

'Four, clear.'

Wright gave Bosch a wishful look, like he had hoped it wouldn't come to this.

'Okay, on my mark we go. Keep tight and no crossfire. Topside, if you shoot, you make sure you know who you—'

There was movement on the video screen. A door to one of the storage corrals flung open, but not the door they were focused on. The camera made a jerking motion left as it redirected its aim. Bosch saw Jessup emerge from the darkness behind the open door. His arms came up and together as he dropped into a combat pose.

'Gun!' Wright yelled.

The barrage of gunfire that followed lasted no more

than ten seconds. But in that time at least four officers under the pier emptied their weapons. The crescendo was punctuated by the unneeded detonation from the topside. By then Bosch had already seen Jessup go down in the gunfire. Like a man in front of a firing squad, his body seemed at first to be held upright by the force of multiple impacts from multiple angles. Then gravity set in and he fell to the sand.

After a few moments of silence, Wright was back on the com.

'Everybody safe? Count off.'

All officers under and on top of the pier reported in safe.

'Check the suspect.'

In the video Bosch saw two officers approach Jessup's body. One checked for a pulse while the other held his aim on the dead man.

'He's ten-seven.'

'Secure the weapon.'

'Got it.'

Wright killed the video and looked at Bosch.

'And that's that,' he said.

'Yeah.'

'I'm sorry you didn't get your answers.'

'Me, too.'

They started walking up the beach to the pier. Wright checked his watch and went on the com, announcing the official time of the shooting as 7:18 P.M.

Bosch looked off across the ocean to his left. The sun was now gone.

PART SIX
−All That Remains

PART SIX
An Introduction to

45

Harry Bosch and I sat on opposite sides of a picnic table, watching the ME's disinterment team dig. They were on the third excavation, working beneath the tree where Jason Jessup had lit a candle in Franklin Canyon.

I didn't have to be there but wanted to be. I was hoping for further evidence of Jason Jessup's villainy, as though that might make it easier to accept what had happened.

But so far, in three excavations, they had found nothing. The team moved slowly, stripping away the dirt one inch at a time and sifting and analyzing every ounce of soil they removed. We had been here all morning and my hope had waned into a cold cynicism about what Jessup had been doing up here on the nights he was followed.

A white canvas sheet had been strung from the tree to two poles planted outside the search zone. This shielded the diggers from the sun as well as from the view of the media helicopters above. Someone had leaked word of the search.

Bosch had the stack of files from the missing persons cases on the table. He was ready to go with records and descriptors of the missing girls should any human remains be found. I had simply come armed with the morning's newspaper and I read the front-page story now for a second time. The report on the events of the day before was the lead story in the *Times* and was accompanied by a color photo of two SIS officers pointing their weapons into the open trapdoor on the Santa Monica Pier. The story was also accompanied by a front-page sidebar story on the SIS. Headline: ANOTHER CASE, ANOTHER SHOOTING, SIS's BLOODY HISTORY.

I had the feeling this would be a story with legs. So far, no one in the media had found out that the SIS knew Jessup had obtained a gun. When that got out—and I was sure it would—there would no doubt be a firestorm of controversy, further investigations and police commission inquiries. The chief question being: Once it was established that it was likely that this man had a weapon, why was he allowed to remain free?

It all made me glad I was no longer even temporarily in the employ of the state. In the bureaucratic arena, those kinds of questions and their answers have the tendency to separate people from their jobs.

I needed not worry about the outcome of such inquiries for my livelihood. I would be returning to my office—the backseat of my Lincoln Town Car. I was going back to being private counsel for the defense. The lines were cleaner there, the mission clearer.

'Is Maggie McFierce coming?' Bosch asked.

I put the paper down on the table.

'No, Williams sent her back to Van Nuys. Her part in the case is over.'

'Why isn't Williams moving her downtown?'

'The deal was that we had to get a conviction for her to get downtown. We didn't.'

I gestured to the newspaper.

'And we weren't going to get one. This one holdout juror is telling anybody who'll listen that he would've voted not guilty. So I guess you can say Gabriel Williams is a man who keeps his word. Maggie's going nowhere fast.'

That's how it worked in the nexus of politics and jurisprudence. And that's why I couldn't wait to go back to defending the damned.

We sat in silence for a while after that and I thought about my ex-wife and how my efforts to help her and promote her had failed so miserably. I wondered if she would begrudge me the effort. I surely hoped not. It would be hard for me to live in a world where Maggie McFierce despised me.

'They found something,' Bosch said.

I looked up from my thoughts and focused. One of the diggers was using a pair of tweezers to put something from the dirt into a plastic evidence bag. Soon she stood up and headed toward us with the bag. She was Kathy Kohl, the ME's forensic archaeologist.

She handed Bosch the bag and he held it up to look. I could see that it contained a silver bracelet.

'No bones,' Kohl said. 'Just that. We're at thirty-two inches down and it's rare that you find a murder interment much further down than that. So this one's looking like the other two. You want us to keep digging?'

Bosch glanced at the bracelet in the bag and looked up at Kohl.

'How about another foot? That going to be a problem?'

'A day in the field beats a day in the lab anytime. You want us to keep digging, we'll keep digging.'

'Thanks, Doc.'

'You got it.'

She went back to the excavation pit and Bosch handed the evidence bag to me to examine. It contained a charm bracelet. There were clots of dirt in the links and its charms. I could make out a tennis racket and an airplane.

'Do you recognize it?' I asked. 'From one of the missing girls?'

He gestured to the stack of files on the table.

'No. I don't remember anything about a charm bracelet in the lists.'

'It could've just been lost up here by somebody.'

'Thirty-two inches down in the dirt?'

'So you think Jessup buried it, then?'

'Maybe. I'd hate to come away from this empty-handed. The guy had to have come up here for a reason. If he didn't bury them here, then maybe this was the kill spot. I don't know.'

I handed the bag back to him.

'I think you're being too optimistic, Harry. That's not like you.'

'Well, then what the hell do you think Jessup was doing up here all those nights?'

'I think he and Royce were playing us.'

'Royce? What are you talking about?'

'We were had, Harry. Face it.'

Bosch held the evidence bag up again and shook it to loosen the dirt.

'It was a classic misdirection,' I said. 'The first rule of a good defense is a good offense. You attack your own case before you ever get to court. You find its weaknesses and if you can't fix them, then you find ways of deflecting attention away from them.'

'Okay.'

'The biggest weakness to the defense's case was Eddie Roman. Royce was going to put a liar and a drug addict on the stand. He knew that given enough time, you would either find Roman or find out things about him or both. He needed to deflect. Keep you occupied with things outside the case at hand.'

'You're saying he knew we were following Jessup?'

'He could've easily guessed it. I put up no real opposition to his request for an OR release. That was unusual and probably got Royce thinking. So he sent Jessup out at night to see if there was a tail. As we already considered before, he probably even sent Jessup to your house to see if he would engage a response and confirm surveillance. When it didn't, when it got no response, Royce probably thought he was wrong and dropped it. After that, Jessup stopped coming up here at night.'

'And he probably thought he was in the clear to go build his dungeon under the pier.'

'It makes sense. Doesn't it?'

Bosch took a long time to answer. He put his hand on top of the stack of files.

'So what about all these missing girls?' he asked. 'It's all just coincidence?'

'I don't know,' I said. 'We may never know now. All we know is that they're still missing and if Jessup was involved, then that secret probably died with him yesterday.'

Bosch stood up, a troubled look on his face. He was still holding the evidence bag.

'I'm sorry, Harry.'

'Yeah, me, too.'

'Where do you go from here?'

Bosch shrugged.

'The next case. My name goes back into the rotation. What about you?'

I splayed my hands and smiled.

'You know what I do.'

'You sure about that? You made a damn good prosecutor.'

'Yeah, well, thanks for that, but you gotta do what you gotta do. Besides, they'd never let me back on that side of the aisle. Not after this.'

'What do you mean?'

'They're going to need somebody to blame for all of this and it's going to be me. I was the one who let Jessup out. You watch. The cops, the *Times,* even Gabriel

Williams will eventually bring it around to me. But that's okay, as long as they leave Maggie alone. I know my place in the world and I'm going to go back to it.'

Bosch nodded because there was nothing else to say. He shook the bag with the charm bracelet again and worked it with his fingers, removing more dirt from its surfaces. He then held it up to study closely and I could tell he saw something.

'What is it?'

His face changed. He was keying on one of the charms, rubbing dirt off it through the plastic bag. He then handed it to me.

'Take a look. What is that?'

The charm was still tarnished and dirty. It was a square piece of silver less than a half inch wide. On one side there was a tiny swivel at center and on the other what looked like a bowl or a cup.

'Looks like a teacup on a square plate,' I suggested. 'I don't know.'

'No, turn it over. That's the bottom.'

I did and I saw what he saw.

'It's one of those...a mortarboard. A graduation cap and this swivel on the top was for the tassel.'

'Yeah. The tassel's missing, probably still in the dirt.'

'Okay, so what's it mean?'

Bosch sat back down and quickly started looking through the files.

'You don't remember? The first girl I showed you and Maggie. Valerie Schlicter. She disappeared a month after graduating from Riverside High.'

'Okay, so you think...'

Bosch found the file and opened it. It was thin. There were three photos of Valerie Schlicter, including one of her in her graduation cap and gown. He quickly scanned the few documents that were in the file.

'Nothing here about a charm bracelet,' he said.

'Because it probably wasn't hers,' I said. 'This is a long shot, don't you think?'

He acted as though I had said nothing, his mind shutting out any opposing response.

'I'm going to have to go out there. She had a mother and a brother. See who's still around and can look at this thing.'

'Harry, you sure you—'

'You think I have a choice?'

He stood back up, took the evidence bag back from me and gathered up the files. I could almost hear the adrenaline buzzing through his veins. A dog with a bone. It was time for Bosch to go. He had a long shot in his hand but it was better than no shot. It would keep him moving.

I got up, too, and followed him to the excavation. He told Kohl that he had to go check out the bracelet. He told her to call him if anything else was found in the hole.

We moved to the gravel parking lot, Bosch walking quickly and not looking back to see if I was still with him. We had driven separately to the dig.

'Hey,' I called to him. 'Wait up!'

He stopped in the middle of the lot.

484

'What?'

'Technically, I'm still the prosecutor assigned to Jessup. So before you go rushing off, tell me what the thinking is here. He buried the bracelet here but not her? Does that even make sense?'

'Nothing makes sense until I ID the bracelet. If somebody tells me it was hers, then we try to figure it out. Remember, when Jessup was up here, we couldn't get close to him. It was too risky. So we don't know exactly what he was doing. He could've been looking for this.'

'Okay, I can maybe see that.'

'I gotta go.'

He continued on to his car. It was parked next to my Lincoln. I called after him.

'Let me know, okay?'

He looked back at me when he got to his car.

'Yeah,' he said. 'I will.'

He then dropped into the car and I heard it roar to life. Bosch drove like he walked, pulling out quickly and throwing dust and gravel into the air. A man on a mission. I got in the Lincoln and followed him out of the park and up to Mulholland Drive. After that, I lost him on the curving road ahead.

Acknowledgments

The author wishes to thank several people for their help in the research and writing of this book. They include Asya Muchnick, Michael Pietsch, Pamela Marshall, Bill Massey, Jane Davis, Shannon Byrne, Daniel Daly, Roger Mills, Rick Jackson, Tim Marcia, David Lambkin, Dennis Wojciechowski, John Houghton, Judge Judith Champagne, Terrill Lee Lankford, John Lewin, Jay Stein, Philip Spitzer, and Linda Connelly.

The author also greatly benefited from reading *Defending the Damned: Inside a Dark Corner of the Criminal Justice System* by Kevin Davis.

Bosch is back.

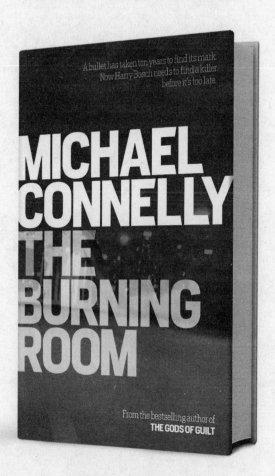

A bullet has taken ten years to find its mark.
Now Harry Bosch needs to find a killer.
before it's too late.

MICHAEL
CONNELLY
THE
BURNING
ROOM

From the bestselling author of
THE GODS OF GUILT

Out Now

The next case begins over the page . . .

1

It seemed to Bosch to be a form of torture heaped upon torture. Corazon was hunched over the steel table, her bloody and gloved hands deep inside the gutted torso, working with forceps and a long bladed instrument she called the butter knife. Corazon was not tall and she stood on her tiptoes to be able to reach down and in with her tools. She braced her hip against the side of the autopsy table to gain leverage.

What bothered Bosch about the grisly tableau was that the body had already been so violated for so long. Both legs gone, one arm taken at the shoulder, the surgical scars old but somehow raw and red. The man's mouth was open in a silent scream. His eyes were directed upward as if beseeching his God for mercy. Deep down Bosch knew that the dead were the dead and they no longer suffered the cruelties of life, but even so, he felt like saying, *Enough is enough*. Asking, When does it stop? Shouldn't death be the relief from the tortures of life?

But he didn't say anything. He stood mute and just watched like he had hundreds of times before. More important than his outrage and the desire to speak out against the continuing atrocity inflicted on Orlando Merced was Bosch's need for the bullet Corazon was trying to pry loose from the dead man's spine.

Corazon dropped back on her heels to rest. She blew out her breath and temporarily fogged her spatter shield. She glanced at Bosch through the steamed plastic.

"Almost there," she said. "And I'll tell you what, they were right not to try to take it out back then. They would have had to saw entirely through T-twelve."

Bosch just nodded, knowing she was referring to one of the vertebrae.

She turned to the table, where her instruments were spread out.

"I need something else..." she said.

She put the butter knife in a stainless-steel sink, where a running faucet kept the water level to the overflow drain. She then moved her hand to the left of the sink and across the display of sterilized tools until she chose a long, slender pick. She went back to work with her hands in the hollow of the victim's torso. All the organs and intestines had been removed, weighed, and bagged, leaving just the husk formed by the upturned ribs. She went up on her toes again and used her upper-body strength and the steel pick to finally pop the bullet loose from the spinal column. Bosch heard it rattle loose inside the rib cage.

"Got it!"

She pulled her arms out of the hollow, put down the pick, and sprayed the forceps with the hose attached to the table. She then held the instrument up to examine her find. She tapped the floor button for the recorder with her foot and went on the record.

"A projectile appearing to be a large-caliber bullet was removed from the anterior T-twelve vertebrae. It is in damaged condition with severe flattening. I will mark with my initials and turn over to Detective Hieronymus Bosch with the Open-Unsolved Unit of the Los Angeles Police Department."

She tapped the recorder button with her foot again and they were off the record. She smiled at him through her plastic screen.

"Sorry, Harry, you know me, a stickler for formalities."

"I didn't think you'd even remember."

He and Corazon had once had a brief romance but that was a long time ago and very few people knew his real full name.

"Of course I would," she said in mock protest.

There was almost an aura of humility about Teresa Corazon that had not been there in the past. She had been a climber and had eventually gotten what she wanted—the chief medical examiner's post and all of its trappings, including a reality television show. But when one reaches the top of a public agency, one becomes a politician, and politicians fall out of favor. Teresa eventually fell hard and now she was back where she started, a deputy coroner with a caseload like anyone else in the office. At least they had let her keep her private autopsy suite. For now.

She took the bullet over to the counter, where she marked it with an indelible black pen. Bosch was ready with a small plastic evidence bag and she dropped it in. He then marked the bag with both of their initials, a chain-of-custody routine. He noted the heft of the slug. He believed it had come from a rifle. If so, that would be a significant new piece of information in the case.

"Will you stay for the rest, or was that all you wanted?"

She asked it as if there were something else going on between them. He held up the evidence bag.

"I think I should probably get this going. We've got a lot of eyes on this case."

"Right. Well, then, I'll just finish up by myself. What happened to your partner anyway? Wasn't she here with you in the hall?"

"She had to make a call."

"Oh, I thought maybe she wanted us to have some

alone time. Did you tell her about us?"

She smiled and batted her eyes and Bosch looked away awkwardly.

"No, Teresa. You know I don't talk about stuff like that."

She nodded.

"You never did. You're a man who keeps his secrets."

He looked back at her.

"I try," he said. "Besides, that was a long time ago."

"And the flame's gone out, hasn't it?"

He pushed things back on subject.

"On the cause. You're not seeing anything different from what the hospital is reporting, right?"

Corazon shook her head, able to move back as well.

"No, nothing different here. Sepsis. Blood poisoning, to use the more common phrase. Put that in your press release."

"And you have no trouble linking this back to the shooting? You could testify to that?"

She was nodding before Bosch was finished speaking.

"Mr. Merced died because of blood poisoning, but I am listing cause of death as homicide. This was a nine-year murder, Harry, and I will gladly testify to that. I hope that bullet helps you find the killer."

Bosch nodded and closed his hand around the plastic bag containing the bullet.

"I hope so too," he said.

2

Bosch took the elevator up to the ground floor. In the past few years the county had spent thirty million dollars renovating the coroner's office but the elevators moved just as slowly as ever. He found Lucia Soto on the back loading dock, leaning against an empty gurney and looking at her phone. She glanced up as Bosch approached and then stood up hurriedly like a kid who'd been caught doing something wrong.

"Got it," Bosch said.

He held up the evidence bag containing the bullet. Soto took it and studied the bullet through the plastic for a moment. A couple of body movers came up behind her and pulled the empty gurney toward the door of what was known as the Big Crypt. It was a new addition to the complex, a refrigerated space the size of a Mayfair Market where all of the bodies that came in were staged before being scheduled for autopsy.

"It's big," Soto said.

Bosch nodded.

"I'm thinking we're looking for a rifle," he said.

"It looks like it's in pretty bad shape," Soto said. "Mushroomed."

She handed the bag back and Bosch put it in his coat pocket.

"There's enough there for a comparison, I think," he said. "Enough for us to get lucky."

The men behind Soto opened the door of the Big Crypt to wheel the gurney in. Cold air carrying a disagreeable chemical scent blasted across the loading dock. Soto turned in time to see a glimpse of the giant refrigerated room. Row after row of bodies stacked four high on a stainless-steel scaffolding system. The dead were wrapped in opaque plastic sheeting, their feet exposed, toe tags flapping in the breeze from the refrigeration vents.

Soto quickly turned away, her naturally brown face turning white.

"You okay?" Bosch asked.

"Yes, fine," she said quickly. "That just grosses me out."

"It's actually a big improvement. The bodies used to be lined up in the hallways. Sometimes stacked on top of one another after a busy weekend. It got pretty ripe around here."

She held a hand up to stop him from further description.

"Please, are we done?"

"We're done."

He started moving and Soto followed, falling in a step behind him. She tended to walk behind Bosch, and he didn't know if it was some sort of deferential thing to his age and rank or something else, like a confidence issue. He headed to the steps at the end of the dock. It was a shortcut to the visitor parking lot.

"Where do we go?" she asked.

"We get the slug over to firearms," Bosch said. "Speaking of getting lucky—it's walk-in Wednesday. Then we go pick up the murder book and evidence at Hollenbeck. We take it from there."

"Okay."

They went down the steps and started crossing the employee parking lot. The visitor lot was on the side of the building.

"Did you make your call?" Bosch asked.

"What?" Soto asked, confused.

"You said you had to make a call."

"Oh, yes, I did. Sorry about that."

"No problem. You get what you need?"

"Yes, thanks."

Bosch was guessing that there had been no call. He suspected that Soto wanted to skip out on the autopsy because she had never seen a human body hollowed out before. Soto was new not only to the Open-Unsolved Unit but to homicide work as well. This was the third case she had worked with Bosch and the only one with a death fresh enough for an autopsy. Soto probably hadn't been counting on live autopsies when she signed up to work cold cases.

In recent years the crime rate in Los Angeles had decreased markedly across the board, including and most dramatically in the number of homicides. This had spurred a shift within the LAPD's investigative philosophy and practice. With fewer active murder cases, the department increased its emphasis on clearing cold cases. With more than five thousand unsolved murders on the books in the past fifty years, there was plenty of work to go around. The Open-Unsolved Unit had nearly tripled in size over the course of the previous year and now had its own command staff, including a captain and two lieutenants. Many seasoned detectives were brought in from Homicide Special and other elite units within the Robbery-Homicide Division. Also a class of young detectives with little if any investigative experience was brought in. The philosophy and edict handed down from the tenth-floor OCP—Office of the Chief of Police—was that it was a new world out there, with new technologies and new ways to look at things. While nothing beats investigative experience, there is nothing wrong with combining it with new viewpoints and different life experiences.

These new detectives—the "Mod Squad," as they were derisively called by some—got the choice assignment to the Open-Unsolved Unit for a variety of reasons ranging from political connections to particular acumen and skills to rewards for heroism in the line of duty. One of the new detectives had worked in IT for a hospital chain before becoming a cop and was instrumental in solving the murder of a patient through a computerized prescription delivery system. Another had studied chemistry as a Rhodes Scholar. There was even a detective who was formerly an investigator with the Haitian National Police.

Soto was only twenty-eight years old and had been on the force fewer than five years. She made the jump from a one-stripe patrol officer to detective by being a twofer. She was second-generation Mexican-American and spoke both English and Spanish fluently. That fit nicely with the new philosophy of the OCP. But she also punched a more traditional ticket to the detective ranks when she became an overnight media sensation after a deadly shoot-out with armed robbers at a check-cashing store in Pico-Union. She and her partner engaged four gunmen. Her partner was fatally shot but Soto took down two of the robbers and held the second pair pinned in an alley until SWAT arrived and finished the capture. The gunmen were members of 13th Street, one of the most violent gangs operating in the city, and Soto's heroics were splashed across newspapers, websites, and television screens. She was later awarded the department's Medal of Valor. Her partner received the award as well, posthumously.

Captain Greg Malins, the new commander of the Open-Unsolved Unit, decided the best way to handle the influx of new blood into the unit was to split up all the existing partnerships and pair every detective who had OU experience with a new detective who had none. Bosch was the oldest man in the unit and had the most years on the job. As such he was paired with the youngest—Soto.

"Harry, you're the old pro," Malins had explained. "I want you watching over the rookie."

While Bosch didn't particularly care to be reminded of his age and standing, he was nonetheless happy with the assignment. He was entering what would be his last year with the department, as the clock was ticking on his DROP contract. To him, every day he had left on the job was golden. The hours were like diamonds—as valuable as anything on earth. He thought that it might be a good way to finish things, training an inexperienced detective and passing on whatever it was he had to pass on. When Malins told him his new partner would be Lucia Soto, Bosch was pleased. Like everybody else in the department, he had heard of Soto's exploits in the shoot-out. Bosch knew what it was like to kill someone in the line of duty, as well as to lose a partner. He understood the mixture of grief and guilt that would afflict Soto. He thought that he and Soto could work well together and that he might train her to be a solid investigator.

There was also a nice bonus for Bosch in being teamed with Soto. Because she was a female, he would not have to share a hotel room when on the road on a case. They would get their own rooms. This was a big thing. The travel component to a job on the cold case squad was high. Oftentimes those who think they have gotten away with murder leave town, hoping that by putting physical distance between themselves and their crimes, they are also outdistancing the reach of the police. Now Bosch looked forward to finishing his time in the department without having to share a bathroom or put up with the snoring or other emissions from a partner in a cramped double at a Holiday Inn.

Soto might not have been hesitant when pulling her gun while outnumbered in a barrio alley, but watching a live autopsy was something different. Soto had seemed reluctant that morning when Bosch told her they had caught a live one and had to go to the ME's office for an autopsy. Soto's first question was whether it was required that both partners in an investigative team attend the dissection of the body. With most cold cases, the body was long in the ground and the only dissection involved was the analysis of old records and evidence. Open-Unsolved allowed Soto to work the most important cases—murders—without having to view a live autopsy, or for that matter, a homicide scene.

Or so it seemed until that morning, when Bosch got the call at home from Malins.

The captain asked Bosch if he had read the *Los Angeles Times* that morning and Bosch said he didn't get the paper. This was in keeping with the long-standing tradition of disdain that existed between the two institutions of law enforcement and the media.

The captain then proceeded to tell him about a story on the front page that morning that was the origin of a new assignment for Bosch and Soto. As Bosch listened, he opened his laptop and went to the newspaper's website, where the story was similarly receiving a lot of play.

The newspaper was reporting that Orlando Merced had died. Nine years earlier, Merced became famous in Los Angeles as a victim—the unintended target of a shooting at Mariachi Plaza in Boyle Heights. The bullet that struck Merced in the abdomen had traveled across the plaza from the vicinity of Pleasant Avenue and was thought to have been a stray shot from a gang confrontation.

The shooting occurred at 4 p.m. on a Saturday. Merced was thirty-one years old at the time and a member of a mariachi band for which he played the *vihuela*, the five-string guitarlike instrument that is the mainstay of the traditional Mexican folk sound. He and his three bandmates were among several mariachis waiting in the plaza for jobs—a restaurant gig or a *quinceañera* party or maybe a last-minute wedding. Merced was a large man, thick in the middle, and the bullet that seemingly came from nowhere splintered the mahogany facing of his instrument and then tore through his gut before lodging in his anterior spine.

Merced would have become just another victim in a city where the media hits and runs—a thirty-second story on the English news channels, a four-paragraph report in the *Times*, a little more longevity in the Spanish media.

But a simple twist of fate changed that. Merced and his band, *Los Reyes Jalisco*, had performed three months earlier at the wedding of city councilman Armando Zeyas, and Zeyas was now ramping up a campaign for the mayor's office.

Merced lived. The bullet damaged his spine and rendered him both a paraplegic and a cause. As the mayoral campaign took shape, Zeyas rolled him out in his wheelchair at all of his political rallies and speeches. He used Merced as the symbol of neglect suffered by the communities of East Los Angeles. Crime was high, and police attention low—they had yet to catch Merced's shooter. Gang violence was unchecked, basic city services and long-planned projects like the extension of the Metro Gold Line were long delayed. Zeyas promised to be the mayor who would change that, and he used Merced and East L.A. to forge a base and strategy that separated him from a crowded pack of contenders. He made it to the runoff and then easily took the election. All the way, Merced was by his side, sitting in the wheelchair, clad in his *charro* suit and sometimes even wearing the bloodstained blouse he wore on the day of the shooting.

Zeyas served two terms. East L.A. got new attention from the city and the police. Crime went down. The Gold Line went through—even including an underground stop at Mariachi Plaza—and the mayor basked in the glow of his successes. But the person who shot Orlando Merced was never caught, and over time the bullet took a steady toll on his body. Infections led to numerous hospitalizations and surgeries. First he lost one leg, then the other. Adding insult to injury, the arm that once strummed the instrument that produced the rhythms of Mexican folk music was taken.

And, finally, Orlando Merced had died.

"The ball's in our court now," Malins had said to Bosch. "I don't care what the goddamn newspaper says, *we* have to decide if this is a homicide. If his death can be attributed medically to that shooting nine years ago, then we make a case and you and Lucky Lucy go back into it."

"Got it."

"The autopsy's gotta say homicide or this whole thing dies with Merced. No matter what the fucking *Times* says about it."

"Got it."

KA͟ ͟ ͟LER is t͟h͟e ͟a͟u͟t͟h͟o͟r ͟of three st͟o͟r͟y coll͟e͟c͟t͟i͟o͟ns ͟a͟n͟d͟ novels, one a national bestseller, another a PEN/Faulkner winner, and all *New York Times* Notable Books. She lives in Santa Cruz, California.

Praise for *Sister Noon*

"In *Sister Noon*, Karen Joy Fowler re-creates a lost world so thrillingly, with such intelligence, trickery, and art, that when you at last put the book down and look up from the page it all seems to linger, shimmering, around you, like the residue of a marvelous dream" Michael Chabon, Pulitzer Prize-winning author of *The Amazing Adventures of Kavalier & Clay*

"Fowler's prose is full of shimmering melancholy, and a ruminative irony that brings her characters and their world alive in the most unexpected ways—reading *Sister Noon* is like staring at early portrait photographs until the eyes begin to shine and your head is filled with voices that urge you to recall that these vanished lives, and your own, are stranger than you allow. A dazzling book" Jonathan Lethem, bestselling author of *Motherless Brooklyn*

"A playful literary mystery" *The Atlanta Journal-Constitution*

"Fowler has a voice like no other, lyrical, shrewd, and addictive, with a quiet deadpan humor that underlies almost every sentence" *Newsday*

"Fowler's lyrical prose and deft use of historical fact are a joy to read. She also exhibits a sly sense of humor ... A strange and enchanting novel" *The Oregonian*

Praise for *We Are All Completely Beside Ourselves*

"There have been many books written about sibling love and rivalry but few, I'm sure, can rend the heart and bore beneath the skin quite like this one … prepare to be charmed and traumatised" Carol Midgley, *The Times*

"[An] achingly funny, deeply serious heart-breaker…This is amoral comedy to shout about from the treetops" Liz Jensen, *Guardian*

"Karen Joy Fowler's smart, witty take on what constitutes a family, and the part the individual ingredients play in the whole, is a beautifully skewed look at domestic relationships" John Harding, *Daily Mail*

"Very good indeed … nothing less than a full-on exploration of what makes human beings human" *Reader's Digest*

"A novel so readably juicy and surreptitiously smart, it deserves all the attention it can get" Barbara Kingsolver, *New York Times Book Review*

"A dark cautionary tale hanging out, incognito-style, in what at first seems a traditional family narrative … deliciously jaunty in tone and disturbing in material" Alice Sebold

"One of the best twists in years makes this novel unique, captivating and so moving it will stay with you for a long time" *Stylist*

"It's been years since I've felt so passionate about a book.When I finished at 3 a.m., I wept, then I woke up the next morning, reread the ending, and cried all over again" Ruth Ozeki

"Utterly beguiling … combines a precise Austenian sensitivity to emotional nuance with the discomforted perception of a narrator who feels herself an alien … has an unforgettable, tender ferocity" Jane Shilling, *New Statesman*

"Reading *We Are All Completely Beside Ourselves* is both a delight and a provocation. I turned the last page nearly breathless with admiration" Valerie Martin

"If you're anything like me, you'll finish this novel with tears in your eyes and want to turn right back to the beginning. Wonderful" *DIVA*

"No contemporary writer creates characters more appealing, or examines them with greater acuity and forgiveness, than she does" Michael Chabon

"*We Are All Completely Beside Ourselves* is that rare thing, a comic novel that wrestles seriously with serious moral questions" *Salon*

"Anyone with an interest in animals—human or otherwise—will love this book" Henry Nicholls, *Guardian*

"This amazing and sad-yet-witty story begins in the middle and goes back to the start twice—with a huge twist along the way" *Company*

"A novel that is both one giant moral compass and a harrowing depiction of a family's implosion, the prose of which zings on the pages … deserves to be acclaimed for the right reasons" Lucy Scholes, *Observer*

"An unsettling, emotionally complex story that plumbs the mystery of our strange relationship with the animal kingdom—relatives included" Ron Charles, *Washington Post*

"Karen Joy Fowler has written the book she's always had in her to write" Ursula K. Le Guin

"Rosemary's voice hooked me in, making it impossible to put down this thought-provoking, moving and entertaining novel" *Woman & Home*

"Smart, funny, moving" *Marie Claire*

"One of the greatest pleasures I take in reading is being able to hand over the books that thrill me, which this summer would be Karen Joy Fowler's *We Are All Completely Beside Ourselves*" Ann Patchett, *Wall Street Journal*

"A gripping and surreptitiously intelligent book about a family's falling apart after a young daughter is sent away ... The book is far deeper and more ambitious, however, than its central conceit would lead one to think" Khaled Hosseini

"Intelligent and forces the reader to question what we owe our fellow creatures" Elizabeth George

"This novel is weighty, yet written with a lightness of touch ... It charts a profound philosophic journey, mixing wit with scientific rigour. The result might be Fowler's most important work yet" *Sydney Morning Herald*

"A masterful novel, painful and memorable, and, like all the best novels, it will stay with you long afterwards" *Psychologies*

SISTER NOON

Karen Joy Fowler

First published in the USA in 2001 by Penguin Putnam Inc., New York

First published in the UK in this edition in 2015 by Serpent's Tail,
an imprint of Profile Books Ltd
3 Holford Yard
Bevin Way
London
WC1X 9HD
www.serpentstail.com

Trade paperback ISBN 978 1 78125 549 0
Export paperback ISBN 978 1 78125 556 8
eISBN 978 1 78283 208 9

Designed and typeset in Fournier by MacGuru Ltd
info@macguru.org.uk

Printed and bound in Great Britain by CPI Group (UK) Ltd, Croydon CRO 4YY

3 5 7 9 10 8 6 4 2

For Marian and Wendy,
East Coast angels

Words were invented so that lies could be told.

MARY ELLEN PLEASANT

PRELUDE

IN 1894, MRS. PUTNAM took Lizzie Hayes to the Midwinter Exhibition in San Francisco's Golden Gate Park, where they both used a telephone for the very first time. They stood behind curtains at opposite ends of a great hall, with only their shoes showing from the outside. "Isn't this a wonder?" Mrs. Putnam asked. Her voice was high and tight, as if it had been stretched to reach. "And someday you'll be able to call the afterlife, just as easy. Now that we've taken this first step."

There was a droning in Lizzie's ear as if, indeed, a multitude of distant voices were also speaking to her. But that was merely the thought Mrs. Putnam had put in her mind. Lizzie might just as easily have heard the ocean or the ceaseless insectile buzz that underlies the material world.

It made little practical difference. The dead are terrible gossips. They don't remember, or they don't care to say, or, if they do talk, then they all talk at once. They can't be questioned. They won't change a word, no matter how preposterous. The truth might look like a story. A lie might outlast a fact. You must remember that, for everything that follows, we have only the word of someone long dead.

*

In 1852, while on his way from Valparaiso to San Francisco aboard the steamship *Oregon*, a clerk named Thomas Bell met a woman named Madame Christophe. Mr. Bell was an underling at Bolton, Barron, and Company, a firm specializing in cotton, mining, and double deals. Madame Christophe was the most beautiful woman he had ever seen, very tall, with clouds of dark hair and rosy, satiny skin. Her most remarkable feature was her eyes, for they didn't match. One was blue and one was brown, and yet the difference was subtle and likely to be noticed only on a close and careful inspection and only when she was looking right at you. She did this often.

One night they stood together at the rail. The stars were as thick and yellow as grapes. There was a silver road of moonlight on the black surface of the ocean. Thomas Bell was asking questions. Where had she come from? Madame Christophe told him she was a widow from New Orleans. Where was she going? Who was she? Whom did she know in San Francisco?

She turned her eyes on him, which made him catch his breath. "Why do you look at me like that?" he asked.

"Why do you ask so many questions?" Her voice was full of slow vowels, soft stops. "Words were invented so that lies could be told. If you want to know someone, don't listen to what they say. Look at them. Look at me," she said. "Look closely." Her voice dropped to a whisper. "What does that tell you?"

Mr. Bell couldn't look closely. His vision was clouded by his ardor. But he saw her shiver. He rushed to his cabin for a wrap to lend her, a green and black tartan shawl.

They debarked in San Francisco. In the crush of people, she got into a carriage, and he lost sight of her.

She should have been easy to find. There were so few women in San Francisco. Fewer still were beautiful. He sent inquiries to all the hotels. None had a Madame Christophe registered. He asked everyone he knew, he spoke of her everywhere, but could say only that she was a widow from New Orleans, that her eyes didn't match, and that she had his shawl. He was forced to depart for Mexico, where he would conduct negotiations concerning the New Almaden mine, without seeing her again.

In the 1850s, most of the people who made up San Francisco's society had once been or still were distinctly disreputable. In 1855, when Belle Cora, a popular madame, inadvertently caused the murder of a United States marshal simply by assuming she could sit in that part of the theater occupied by respectably married women, it was not always so easy to explain why one person was top-hole and another was not.

But Mrs. Nora Radford's case was simple. Her husband had died owing everyone money. Her conversation, she overheard young Mrs. Putnam say, was interesting enough, only there was too much of it. This observation was as hurtful as it was inaccurate. She had always been considered rather witty. Mrs. Putnam and everybody else knew that she was more surprised than anyone by her husband's debts.

She refused to blame him for any of it. In fact, she was impressed. How clever he must have been to have fooled them all.

And she was touched. How hard he must have worked to give her such a sense of security. Much harder than if he'd actually had money. Forty years of marriage and he'd never once let it slip. She moved into rooms and missed her husband hourly.

Her new home was in the country, overlooking a graveyard. This was not as dismal as it might sound. She had a curtained bed and a carved dressing table. The cemetery was filled with flowers. On a warm day, the scent came in on the sunshine. The boardinghouse was called Geneva Cottage.

Her landlady was a tireless southern woman named Mrs. Ellen Smith. Mrs. Smith took in laundry and worked as housekeeper for Selim Woodworth, a wealthy San Francisco businessman. It was Mr. Woodworth who had suggested the arrangement to Mrs. Radford. Mr. Woodworth was a prominent philanthropist, a kind and thoughtful man whose marked attentions to her after her husband's death, in contrast to the disregard of others, vouched for his quality. "My Mrs. Smith," he said warmly. "She works hard and makes canny investments. I don't know why she continues on as my housekeeper. Perhaps her fortunes have been so vagarious, she can never be secure. But she is a wonderful woman, as devoted to helping the unfortunate as she is to making a living in the world. That's where her money goes." He tipped his hat, continued his way down the little muddy track that was Market Street. Mrs. Radford hoisted her heavy skirts, their hems weighted with bird shot as a precaution against the wind, and picked her way through the mud. She took his advice immediately.

Mrs. Radford's initial impression of her landlady was that she was about thirty years old. In fact, this fell somewhat short of the mark. But also that she was beautiful, which was accurate. The first time Mrs. Radford saw her, she was sitting in a sunlit pool on the faded brocade of the parlor sofa. In Mrs. Radford's mind she always retained that golden glow.

"You'll find me here when the sun is shining," Mrs. Smith told her. "I never will get used to the cold."

"It seems to get colder every year," Mrs. Radford agreed. The words came out too serious, too sad. There was an embarrassing element of self-pity she hadn't intended.

Mrs. Smith smiled. "I hope we can make you feel at home here." She looked straight at Mrs. Radford. Her eyes didn't match. There was a shawl of green and black plaid on the sofa.

Mrs. Radford thought of her friend Mr. Bell. She couldn't remember the name of his vanished shipmate, but she was sure it wasn't Ellen Smith. Something foreign, something Latin. Mrs. Smith's beauty was darkly Mediterranean.

She stood and was surprisingly tall, a whole head above Mrs. Radford. "Take a cup of tea with me."

The kitchen was an elegant place of astral lamps and oil chandeliers. There were golden cupids in the wallpaper, and a young Negro man who swept the floor and washed the dishes while they talked. Mrs. Smith filled her cup half with cream, heaped it with sugar. She stirred it and stirred it.

"I can't quite place your accent," Mrs. Radford said.

"Oh, it's a mix, all right. I've lived a great many places." Mrs. Smith stared into her clouded tea. She lifted the cup and blew on it.

"I lived on the hill," Mrs. Radford said, coaxing her into confidences by offering her own. "Until my husband died. I'm quite come down in the world."

"You'll rise again. I started with nothing."

Mrs. Radford had often been embarrassed at how much beauty meant to her. At the age when Mrs. Radford might have been beautiful herself, she suffered badly from acne. It pitted her skin, and her lovely hair was little compensation. At the time, she'd thought her life was over. But then she'd made such a happy marriage and it had hardly seemed to matter. God had granted her a great love. And yet she had never stopped wishing she were beautiful, had apparently learned nothing from her own life. She would have been the first to admit this. It would have hurt her to have had ugly children, and this was a painful thing to know about herself. As it turned out, she had no children at all. "You had beauty," she said.

Mrs. Smith raised her extraordinary eyes. "I suppose I did." The day was clouding. The sun went off and on again, like a blink. Mrs. Smith turned her head. "My mother was beautiful. It did her no particular good. I lost her early. She used to fret so over me—what would happen to me, who would take care of me. She told me to go out to the road and stand where I would be seen. That was the last thing she said to me."

It had been just a little back lane, without much traffic. The fence was falling into ruins; she stepped over it easily. She could see to the end of the road, shimmering in the distance like a dream. There was an apple tree over her head, blossoming into pink and filled with the sound of bees. She stood and waited all morning, crying from time to time about her mother, until she was sleepy from the sun and the buzzing and the crying, and no one came by.

Finally, in the early afternoon, when the sun had started to slant past her, she heard a horse in the distance. The sound grew louder. She raised her hand to shade her eyes. The horse was black. The man was as old as her grandfather, who was also her father, truth be told.

He almost went by her. He was half asleep on the slow-moving horse, but when she moved, a breath only, he stopped so suddenly that saliva dripped from the silver bit onto the road. He looked her over and removed his hat. "What's your name?" he asked. She said nothing. He reached out a hand. "Well, I'm not fussy," he told her. "How would you like to go to New Orleans?" And that was how she moved up in the world, by putting her foot in the stirrup.

"I was ten years old."

"Oh, my dear." Mrs. Radford was shocked and distressed.

Mrs. Smith put her hand on Mrs. Radford's arm. Mrs. Radford had rarely been touched by anyone since her husband died. Sometimes her skin ached for it, all over her body. Where did an old woman with no children go to be touched? Mrs. Smith's hand was warm. "It wasn't the way you're thinking. He turned out very kind," she said.

Mrs. Radford adjusted to country living as well as could be expected. The laundry was a busy place. The cemetery was not. She especially enjoyed her evenings. She would join Mrs. Smith. The parlor would be brightened by a lively fire. They would drink a soothing concoction Mrs. Smith called "balm tea." "Just a splash of rum," Mrs. Smith assured her, but it went straight to Mrs. Radford's head. In these convivial surroundings, she told Mrs. Smith how she had planned once to teach.

"I had a train ticket to Minneapolis. I had a job. I'd only known Alexander a week. But he came to the station and asked me to marry him. 'I want to see the world before I get married,' I told him. 'See it after,' he said. 'See it with me.'"

"And did you?"

His actual language had been much more passionate—things Mrs. Radford could hardly repeat, but would never forget. His voice remained with her more vividly than his face; over the years it had changed less. It pleased her to speak of him; she was grateful to Mrs. Smith for listening. "I saw my corner of it. It was a very happy corner."

In her turn, Mrs. Radford heard that Mrs. Smith's original benefactor, a Mr. Price, had taken her to a convent school in New Orleans. She spent a year there, learning to read and write. Then he sent her to Cincinnati. She lived with some friends of his named Williams. "I was to go to school for four more years and also to help Mrs. Williams with the children. She made quite a pet of me, at first.

"But then Mr. Price died. I know he'd already paid the Williamses for my schooling, but they pretended he hadn't. They sent me to Nantucket as a bonded servant."

The weathered wood and sand of Nantucket was a new landscape for her. Her mistress was the Quaker woman who owned the island's general store. She came from a line of whalers—very wealthy. She invited Ellen to the Friends meeting house, where they sat in the darkness on hard wooden benches and waited for the Spirit. "It didn't take with me, I'm afraid," said Mrs. Smith, fingering the locket she wore at her throat. "I'm too fond of nice things. But she was also very kind. I called her Grandma and worked for her until she died, quite suddenly, and then again there were no provisions made for me. By now I was sixteen or so. I sold off some of her stock and got to Boston. Her real granddaughter lived there and I thought she might take me in, but she didn't." It was there that Ellen met James Smith, a wealthy and prominent businessman. They were married. He died. "It's been my pattern," Mrs. Smith conceded. "Life is loss."

Mrs. Radford could see that Mrs. Smith had not loved her husband. It was nothing she said; it appeared on her face when she spoke of him.

Mrs. Radford had not decided what to do about Thomas Bell. He'd been back from Mexico for almost a year now. He was an old friend, so she owed him some loyalty, although he hadn't, in fact, been to see her since his return. Served him right, really; if he'd come to call, to express his condolences, he might have seen the woman. Virtue provided its rewards.

And what of her loyalty to her new friend? Mr. Bell was not the sort of man who married. There were rumors that he had been seen going into a house of assignation on Washington Street.

Before her husband's death, Mrs. Radford would only have

had to write the invitations and San Francisco's most eligible men would have gathered. Sometimes she let herself imagine the dinner. Alexander pouring wine. The gold-rimmed china. The sensation of the beautiful Mrs. Smith.

But Mr. Bell had been so desperate. Mrs. Radford was a great believer in love. She longed to do her little bit to help it along. Marriage was the happy ending to Mrs. Smith's hard and blameless life. The right man had only to see her, and it still might be Thomas Bell, who already had.

The most enjoyable parts of a social occasion are often the solitary pleasures of anticipation and recollection. But it is sadly true that one cannot relish these without having had an invitation to the party itself.

The MacElroys, who were special friends of Thomas Bell's, had announced the engagement of their middle daughter. There was to be a fabulous ball. Although Mrs. Radford had, with her husband, been a guest at the party celebrating the engagement of their first daughter and also at the marriage of their youngest daughter, there was no certainty that she would be included now.

It was only a party. Only a fabulous ball. She did not mind for herself, not so much, really, although she had always enjoyed a party. But it would be just the setting for Mrs. Smith. With this in mind, Mrs. Radford finally called on Thomas Bell. He was living in the bachelor club on Grove. He apologized for the cigar smoke, which did not bother her, but not for the fact that he had never come to see her, which did. His blond hair had receded over the years, giving him a high, wide forehead. He had always been a handsome man; now he'd attained a dignity he had lacked before. He looked marriageable. "Did you ever find your lovely shipmate?" she asked him, quite directly, with no cunning preamble.

"Madame Christophe?" he said immediately. "No. I looked everywhere."

"In the servants' quarters?"

He responded with some heat. "She was a queen."

"And if she was not?" Mrs. Radford watched his face closely. She was looking for true love. She thought she saw it.

And also rising comprehension. "You know where she is." Mr. Bell reached excitedly for her arm. "Take me to her at once."

"No. But if she were invited to the MacElroys' ball, I would deliver the invitation. Then you could take your turn with every other eligible man in San Francisco." She meant this quite literally, but she allowed a familiar, teasing tone to come into her voice to hide it.

"Dear Mrs. Radford," he said.

"She is a working woman," Mrs. Radford warned him. "With a different name."

"She is a queen," Mr. Bell repeated. "Whatever she does, whatever she calls herself. Blood will tell."

Mrs. Radford was in black. Mrs. Smith wore a gown of pink silk. It was fitted at the bodice, but blossomed at the hips with puffings and petals. The hem was larger still, and laced with ribbons. The MacElroys' drawing room had been cleared for dancing, and she entered it like a rose floating on water. Couples were just assembling for the grand march. Every head turned. Mr. Bell made a spectacle of himself in his effort to get to her first. He was slightly shorter than she was.

"Mrs. Radford," he said politely. "How lovely to see you here.

And Madame Christophe. I mustn't imagine that you remember me, simply because I remember you."

"Though I do," she said. She glanced at Mrs. Radford and then looked back to Mr. Bell. "And my name is not Madame Christophe. I owe you an explanation." There was a pause. Mr. Bell rushed to fill it.

"All you owe me is a dance," he assured her. He was eager, nervous. He drew her away from Mrs. Radford, who went to sit with the older women and the married ones. The music began. She watched Mr. Bell bend in to Mrs. Smith to speak. She watched the pink skirt swinging over the polished floor, the occasional glimpse of the soft toes of Mrs. Smith's shoes. She attended to the music and the lovely, old sense of being involved in things.

Some of the men seemed to know Mrs. Smith already. Young Mr. Ralston engaged her for the redowa, and everyone knew he never danced. Mr. Sharon took the lancers, his head barely reaching her shoulder. Mr. Hayes chose her for the waltz, leaving his wife without a partner. And Mr. Bell danced with no one else, spent the time while she danced with others pacing and watching for the moment she came free.

In her own small way, Mrs. Radford also triumphed. People approached who hadn't spoken to her since her husband's death. Innocuous pleasantries, but she could no longer take such attentions for granted. Eventually every conversation arrived at Mrs. Smith.

"That lovely woman you came with?" said Mrs. Putnam. "I've not seen her before."

"She's an old friend," Mrs. Radford answered contentedly. "A widow from New Orleans." She said nothing else, although it was clearly insufficient. Let Mrs. Putnam remember how she had accused Mrs. Radford of talking too much!

At the end of the evening, Mr. Bell went to find their cloaks. "I so enjoyed that party," Mrs. Smith told Mrs. Radford.

"You'll have many nights like this now. Many invitations. You were such a success."

Mrs. Smith had a gray velvet cloak. Mr. Bell returned with it, settled it slowly over her shoulders. He was reluctant to release her. "About my name," she said. They were walking outside, Mrs. Smith in the middle, the women's skirts crushed one against the next, like blossoms in a bouquet. On the steps, they joined a crowd waiting for carriages. To the right were the Mills family and that peevish, gossipy attorney, Henry Halleck. "I had a need to change my name to get out of New Orleans. I was born into slavery in Georgia," Mrs. Smith said. Everyone could hear her. "I became a white woman to escape. Ellen Smith isn't my real name, either."

And then Mrs. Smith and Mrs. Radford were alone in their carriage. The ride to the country was a long one. Mrs. Radford's feelings were too tender to bear examination. It seemed as though Mrs. Smith had deliberately humiliated her. "Is it true?" Mrs. Radford asked.

"Everything I've told you is true."

"Why pick that moment to say it?"

"It was time. I've been a white woman for so many years. And I didn't want what that was bringing me. It wasn't aimed at you. Or your ideas about love and beauty."

The horse hooves clapped. The carriage rocked. "You don't want to be the same person your whole life, do you?" Mrs. Smith asked. The carriage wheel hit a stone. It threw Mrs. Radford against Mrs. Smith. Mrs. Smith caught her by the arm. She was wearing gloves, so they didn't actually touch.

This was the last party Mrs. Radford would attend in San Francisco. One month later she left on a boat filled with missionaries going to Hawaii. One year later she was one of only seven white women in Edo, Japan. From there she sailed to Russia; from there she made her way to Peking. She died somewhere near Chungking at the age of seventy-four.

In 1883, many years after her death, Selim Woodworth received a message from her. It was a bedraggled note, crumpled, carried in a pocket, trod upon, lost, left out in the rain. Even the stamps were indecipherable. "The mountains here!" was the only legible bit, and it wasn't even clear where, exactly, Mrs. Radford had been when she wrote those words. It didn't matter. Selim Woodworth had been dead himself for more than thirteen years.

Visits

1

BY THE 1890s, San Francisco was an entirely different city from the one Mrs. Radford had left behind. The streets were paved. The sand was landscaped. Cable cars ran up and down Nob Hill. The Railroad Kings were old or dead, and also the Bonanza Kings, and also the Lawyer Kings. Society had arrived and settled, its standards strictly maintained by Ned "I would rather see my sister dead than waltzing" Greenway. Fashionable women belonged to the Conservative Set, the Fast Set, the Smart Set, the Serious Set, the Very Late at Night Set, or the highly respectable Dead Slow Set.

There were still many more men than women in the city. This imbalance resulted in a high percentage of unrequited passions. Afflicted men consoled themselves with horse racing, graft, and most frequently, liquor. Any woman whose nerves did not compel her to depend on Lydia Pinkham's Vegetable Compound (alcohol, dandelion, chamomile, and licorice) or Jayne's Carminative Balm (alcohol and opium) or Dover's Powder (opium and ipecac) could count on the advantage of sobriety in her dealings with men. The destabilizing effects of widespread heartache combined with widespread drunkenness were somewhat alleviated by the rigging of local elections.

The city was propelled in equal parts by drunken abuse and sober recompense. In those days every steamer that docked in San Francisco Bay was fitted with a large box. Each box was the same—pinewood, a sizable slot edged with brass, and the words "Give to the Ladies' Relief and Protection Society Home" burned in a circle about it. After the wreck of the SS *Rio de Janeiro*, one of these boxes was found floating past Alcatraz Island, and miraculously, the money was still inside. When levered open, the box contained rubles and yen, lire and pesos, all shuffled together like cards.

Successive treasurers for the Society counted out coins stamped with the profiles of queens they couldn't name and birds they'd never seen. Some of the coins were worn so thin there was no picture at all, just a polished disk with no clue remaining as to its history or origin. Occasionally during rough seas someone would donate a holy medallion, usually Saint Christopher. One box held a single amethyst earring with a small drop pearl.

It was still charity, it was still begging, but it bore the semblance of adventure.

Lizzie Hayes wore one of the more puzzling coins on a chain around her neck, so whenever they looked at her, the people of San Francisco would be reminded that she needed their money. The coin was imprinted with a mermaid curled into a circle, her hair so wide and wild it netted the tip of her own tail. If anyone asked, Lizzie said it was the currency of Atlantis.

Lizzie Hayes had been a volunteer for the Ladies' Relief Home for almost ten years, its treasurer for three. She had few intimate friends, but attended two churches, Grace Church and St. Luke's Episcopal, which was good for her soul and also for fund-raising. In 1890 she was a spinster who had just seen her fortieth birthday.

She was working in the cupola one day in January, sorting

through a box of donated books, when one of the older girls came to tell her Mrs. Mary E. Pleasant was at the door. "The front door," the girl said. "She'd like to speak to you."

Culling books was surprisingly dirty work, and Lizzie could feel a layer of grit on her hands and face. She wiped herself with her apron and went downstairs at once. She'd never spoken with Mrs. Pleasant, never been in the same room with her, although two years earlier she'd waited on an overloaded streetcar while the driver made an unscheduled stop so that Mrs. Pleasant could ride. Mrs. Pleasant walked the half-block to the car, and it seemed to Lizzie that she had walked as slowly as possible. She had given the driver an enormous, showy tip.

Lizzie had also seen Mrs. Pleasant on occasion in her opulent Brewster buggy with its matched horses from the Stanford stables. Mrs. Pleasant dressed like a servant, but she had her own driver in green livery and a top hat, and also her own footman to attend her.

If she hadn't ever seen her, Lizzie would still have recognized Mrs. Pleasant's face. It was one of the most famous in the city, appearing often in editorial cartoons, particularly in the *Wasp*. (Although actually the last drawing had not used her face. Instead, a black crow had peered out from underneath Mrs. Pleasant's habitual bonnet.)

"Now, I never cared a feather's weight for public opinion," Mrs. Pleasant had been once quoted as saying, "for it's the ghostliest thing I ever did see." It was fortunate she thought so. Here are just a few of the things people said about Mary Ellen Pleasant:

She'd buried three husbands before she turned forty, and in her sixties had still been the secret mistress of prominent and powerful men. At seventy years of age, she'd looked no older than fifty.

She had a small green snake tattooed in a curl around one breast.

She could restore the luster to pearls by wearing them.

Although she worked as Thomas Bell's housekeeper, she was as rich as a railroad magnate's widow. Some of the city's wealthiest men came to her for financial advice. Thomas Bell owed his entire fortune to her.

She was an angel of charity. She had donated five thousand dollars of her own money to aid the victims of yellow fever during the epidemic in New Orleans. When she got to heaven, she would soon have the blessed organized and sending cups of cool water to the sinners below.

She practiced voodoo and had once sunk a boat full of silver with a curse.

She was a voodoo queen and the colored in San Francisco both worshipped and feared her. She could start and stop pregnancies; she would, for a price, make a man die of love.

She trafficked in prostitution and had a number of special white protegees with whom her relationships were irregular, intimate, and possibly sapphic. She was responsible for all of poor Sarah Althea Hill Sharon Terry's mischiefs and misfortunes.

She ran a home for unwed mothers and secretly sold the infant girls to the Chinese tongs.

She was the best cook in San Francisco.

Here is what people said about Lizzie Hayes:

She would have married William Fletcher if she could have got him.

No one had asked Mrs. Pleasant into the parlor. Lizzie found her standing just inside the heavy oak door under the portrait of philanthropist Horace Hawes, with his brooding Lincolnesque looks. No one had offered to take her wrap, a bright purple shawl, which she nevertheless had removed and carried over one arm.

Lizzie Hayes had not kept Mrs. Pleasant waiting, but neither had she taken off her work apron. Mrs. Pleasant was better dressed. She wore a skirt of polished black alpaca, a shirtwaist with a white collar, gold gypsy hoops through her ears, and her usual outdated Quaker bonnet, purple with a wide brim. She noticed the apron at once; Lizzie saw her famous mismated eyes, one blue, one brown, flicker over it, but her facial expression did not change. Her skin was finely wrinkled, like crushed silk, and she smelled of lavender.

There were no courteous preliminaries. "I've brought you a girl," Mrs. Pleasant said. She'd come to California forty years earlier with the miners, but never lost the southern syrup of her vowels. "Named Jenny Ijub. She's just off a boat from Panama. Her mother took sick on the voyage and was buried at sea. When I ask how old she is, she holds up all five fingers. Quiet little thing. She doesn't seem to know her father."

One of her hands rested on the little girl's hair. Mrs. Pleasant dipped her head as she talked, so her face was hidden by the bonnet brim. "I have my friends at the docks. I'm known to care for such cases." As her face vanished, her voice grew softer, more confiding. She knew how to make white people comfortable.

She knew how to make them uncomfortable. Where had she really gotten the child? Lizzie felt the contrast between them. Mrs. Pleasant was tall, elegant, and spotless. Lizzie was short, dusty, fat as a toad. She was a person who rumpled, and not a person who rumpled attractively.

She cleared her throat. "We have a waiting list." Lizzie would have said this to anyone. It was the simple truth. So many in need. "And I'd have to be certain of her age. She's quite small. We don't take children under four years."

"I'll have to find somewhere else, then." Mrs. Pleasant smiled down at Lizzie. It was an understanding smile. Seventy-some years old and Mrs. Pleasant still had all her own splendid teeth. She stooped a little and aimed her smile farther down. "Don't you worry, Jenny. We'll find someone who wants you."

Lizzie looked for the first time at the girl. She was dark-haired and sallow-skinned. She had sand on her shoes and stockings, it was impossible to get to the Home without picking up sand, but was otherwise as clean as could be. Neatly and simply dressed. Hatless, though someone— Mrs. Pleasant?—had woven a bright bit of red ribbon into her hair. Her cheeks were flushed as if she were too warm, or embarrassed. She did not look up, but Lizzie imagined that if she could see the girl's eyes they would be large and tragic. She held her back stiffly; you could deduce the eyes from that.

Lizzie hated saying no to anyone about anything. Saying no, however you disguised it, was a confession of your own limitations. Not only was it unhelpful, it was galling. She reached out and touched Jenny's arm. "I have some discretion. Since she really has no one. We'll find a bed somehow. Would you like to stay with us, Jenny?"

Jenny made no response. Her eyes were still lowered; she had one knuckle firmly hooked behind her front teeth, and her spare hand wrapped around the cloth of Mrs. Pleasant's skirt. When Mrs. Pleasant was ready to leave, Jenny's fingers would have to be pried apart.

"That's lovely, then," said Mrs. Pleasant. "Now I know she'll have the best of care."

"We might even find a family to take her. Be better if she had a bit of sparkle. Don't put your fingers in your mouth, dear," Lizzie said. She reached into her apron pocket and pulled out a silver bell. "This is how we call Matron," she told Jenny. She rang the bell twice. "We have two Jennys already, but they are both much older than you. So we must call you Little Jenny. Shall we do that?"

The bell sounded very loud. Jenny's fingers twisted inside Mrs. Pleasant's skirt. Mrs. Pleasant knelt. She pulled a violet-hemmed handkerchief from her sleeve and wiped Jenny's mouth with it. She had the face of a grandmother. "Listen," she said. "You must be brave now. Remember that I'm your friend. I'll send you a present soon so you'll see I don't forget you, either." Mrs. Pleasant said these things quietly, intimately. It was not for the matron to hear, but she arrived just in time to do so.

"I hope your present is something that can be shared," the matron told Jenny as she took her away. "If you have things the others don't, you can't expect them not to mind."

The matron was a fifty-year-old woman named Nell Harris. She had come to the Home as a charity case; she had stayed on as an employee. She had soft-cooked features and a shifting seascape for a body. Her bosom lay on the swell of her stomach, rising and falling dramatically with her breath. Her most defining characteristic was that no one had ever made a good first impression on her.

She took Jenny down to the kitchen and offered her a large slice of wholesome bread. "Mrs. Pleasant gave me cake," Jenny told her. The kitchen counters were piled with dishes, half clean, half not. Two girls in aprons were washing; another was drying. That one smiled at Jenny and flicked her dishrag. The air was wet and warm and smelled of pork grease.

"And that's all it takes to make you think she's nice as pie. She gave you away pretty fast, didn't she?" Nell said.

2

LIZZIE HAYES went back upstairs to the cupola. Out the window was an unbroken view of sand dunes, loosely strewn with scrub, chaparral, and bunches of beach grass. A storm was coming. Far to the west, the clouds were black and piled solidly against one another like rocks in a cairn.

Straight beneath Lizzie the prow of Mrs. Pleasant's bonnet cut through the wind toward her carriage. Her purple wrap was around her shoulders and the ends of her bonnet ribbons whipped about her head. Mrs. Pleasant walked away quickly, like someone who had someplace to go.

The foghorn blew in the distance. Gulls streamed inland, shrieking, and the wind spun the ghosts of sand castles into the air. Lizzie returned to her box of donated books. Suddenly, unjustly, she found herself resenting them. What did such donations do but make more work for the staff? Nothing arrived in good shape; everything needed to be sorted and cleaned and mended.

She blew the dust off *The Good Child's Picture Book*. The author had the improbable name of Mrs. Lovechild. Lizzie opened to a woodcut of two girls picnicking together in an English garden. One of them had dark hair, the other light. They wore sun hats, which circled their heads like the auras of medieval saints, but tied in bows on the side. The flowers were as large as the girls' faces.

Lizzie brought the picture closer. The book had an odd smell, like fermented fruit. The title page had been torn out, but a hand-written message on the flyleaf remained. "To my darlingest Mitzy," it read. "On the occasion of her fourth birthday. Hope you feel better soon! Your Uncle Beau." The book was probably filled with infectious germs.

Lizzie Hayes was an easy person to underestimate. Slow to act, she often appeared indecisive, but once she'd fixed on a course, it was fixed. She was hard to dissuade and hard to intimidate.

As a child she'd been passive and biddable. "So dependable. Quite beyond her years," her mother had said on those frequent occasions when Lizzie did as she'd been told. But just beneath this tractable surface lay romance and rebellion. She loved to read, engaging books with such intensity that her parents had allowed only the dullest of them, and then curtailed the time she spent with those. Her mother was quick to spot the symptoms of overstimulation, and Lizzie had spent many hours lying in bed, sentenced to absolute inactivity until she could be calm again.

It was an ill-conceived punishment. With everything but her imagination forbidden to her, Lizzie's reveries grew ever more fevered. She could lie without moving for hours in the semblance of obedience, and all the while an unacceptable cascade of pirates, prophets, and Indians pounded through her mind.

She was not trusted with fairy tales until she was sixteen years old; they were so full of murder and mayhem. She was not trusted with poetry at all, not since, at the age of six, she had wept bitterly while listening to Sir Walter Scott's "Proud Maisie." She had made it only as far as the second stanza.

"Tell me, thou bonny bird,
When shall I marry me?"
"When six braw gentlemen
Kirkward shall carry ye."

Sermons could have the same effect. When the Reverend Paul Clarkson came to luncheon, her mother was forced, over a nice lobster bisque, to suggest a little less exaltation on Sundays. "For a woman, religion should be a steadying thing," she'd suggested, and the reverend, who had just burned his mouth on his soup and was taking great gulps of cold water medicinally, had not disagreed.

In adolescence, Lizzie had been prone to the type of satisfying melancholia that expresses itself in diets and music. "I'm not raising any saints," her mother had said one morning when Lizzie was irritating her by fasting. She stood at the doorway to Lizzie's bedroom, carrying a breakfast of steak and peas, and then stayed to watch each bite. In our modern age, she informed Lizzie, extravagant holiness is ill mannered as well as ill advised. "The world is as the world is," she was fond of saying. "And just as God made it. You're ungrateful to Him when you wish it otherwise."

Lizzie's mother knew that she hated peas. Lizzie ate them all silently, offered them to God, one by one, as a form of fleshly mortification.

As she'd aged Lizzie's inner and outer aspects grew increasingly ill matched. Her breathless, romantic imagination, charming in a young woman, and delightful in a beautiful young woman, was entirely ridiculous in someone short, fat, and well past her middle age. Lizzie was sharp enough to know this, and since there was no way to keep the outer woman private, she generally kept the inner woman so.

The outer woman: Often when she'd misbehaved, her mother would march her to the dressing room mirror to look at herself. "That's what a bad girl looks like!" her mother would say, her own sagging eyes floating behind the bad girl's head, as if the mere sight of Lizzie's face was a punishment. (As a consequence, Lizzie didn't like mirrors much. When she was finally allowed to read the story of Snow White, she'd instantly understood that the mirror was the real villain of the piece. "Why, I couldn't possibly choose between two such beautiful women," is what the mirror would have said if it hadn't been bent on blood.)

"You have only the beauty of youth," her father had told her when her refusal to marry his good friend, Dr. Beecher, had made him angry enough to be honest. "I'm not a fussy man," Paul Burbank had said on the occasion of her second proposal. "*You* won't be expecting romance," Christopher Ludlow had said on the occasion of her third.

Lizzie remembered these things partly because they'd hurt, but mainly because for most of her life her appearance had been so rarely commented on.

The inner woman: And yet, as far back as Lizzie could remember, she had suffered from a kind of self-importance that expressed itself as the conviction that every move she made was watched. This made a certain sense among ladies out in society, where the mere whisper of eccentricity could cost a reputation, and among the religious, since God was interested, exacting, and everywhere. Lizzie was both out and devout.

Even so, her conviction was pronounced. Add to society and God that special circumstance familiar to every passionate reader: An unseen narrator hovered somewhere behind Lizzie, marking her every move.

And *then* add the fact that for most of her life Lizzie had been haunted by a photograph of an angel in a christening gown. Her mother had made the picture frame herself, an intricate, heartbroken oval of ribbon roses and wax lilies encircling the likeness of Lizzie's brother, Edward. Lizzie was five years old when Edward was born. He'd lived less than three weeks and died, sinless, of inanition. Lizzie hardly remembered him alive.

Dead, he'd been inescapable. His picture hung first in the nursery and later in her bedroom. "To watch over you," Lizzie's mother had said. It was the sort of misunderstanding Lizzie and her mother were likely to have. Eventually Lizzie knew the difference between watching someone and watching over someone. Eventually she understood that her mother had intended this as a comfort. But by the time she'd made the distinction, Edward was a pale, palpable, disapproving presence who could be neither banished nor appeased.

Nell Harris appeared, startling Lizzie with her large pudding face rising over the top edge of the book. "She's in the kitchen, having a bite now," Nell said. "I'm afraid she looks to be a fussy eater. So I'm to squeeze a bed in for her somewhere?" Everything about her tone and posture expressed reproach. We have a waiting list, she might as well have said. We have no beds. We have no money. We have standards. Deciding who we take in is not your job.

"She's a friendless child," said Lizzie. "With a father somewhere. And unless I miss my guess, a wealthy father. Out of wedlock, of course. But quite, quite wealthy. Mrs. Pleasant wouldn't bother, otherwise."

"So you don't think that the child might be colored?" Nell asked.

The idea had been so far from Lizzie's thoughts as to shock her now. She responded slowly. "There's nothing of the colored in her face."

"You can't go by that. Mammy Pleasant herself fooled a lot of people for a long time, if the stories are true. Though I never credited them myself. You saw, she's black as a Mussulman. But if this child comes out of the Home, if she's adopted somewhere, no one is going to question her. They'll just take her as white. It will be as if we've said so."

Lizzie set the book down and wiped her hands on her apron while she thought this through. Lizzie Hayes believed it was better to be white than colored, believed it so absolutely that this was not the part she thought about. But within these confines, she was a well-intentioned woman. She genuinely didn't care what or who Jenny was. Lizzie wanted to be an influence for good in the world. If she could take in a motherless colored girl and turn her out white and adopted, she would count it a good day's work.

Still, many of their most generous donors would no doubt feel differently. The Ladies' Relief Home had no savings, no margin for error. Even a small drop in donations could mean ruin. Wasn't Lizzie's first obligation to protect the wards already there? Could she set them all at risk for the sake of one child?

The next book was a *Robinson Crusoe* someone had evidently dropped in the bathtub. Lizzie picked it up and tried to flatten the crusty cover with her hand. What she admired most about Crusoe was his calm sequentiality. He found himself in an overwhelming situation and survived simply by dealing with each task in its turn. The mere sight of the book was clarifying.

These are the things Lizzie thought, and in this order:

Today's task was to take care of Jenny. Possible repercussions were not today's task.

Besides, she had often noticed that charity made misers of donor and recipient both. She had always sworn that it wouldn't work this way on her.

Plus, she genuinely thought it likely Jenny had a wealthy father. What might such a man not do in gratitude for the preservation of his daughter? Lizzie was in charge of the Ladies' Relief Home finances, and in her professional opinion the financial risk was easily outweighed by the possible benefit.

And then Mrs. Pleasant was no one to trifle with. Lizzie would do nothing wrong to please her, but if she did the right thing and it pleased Mrs. Pleasant as well, wasn't that a bit of luck?

And who would not be moved by little Jenny's situation?

"You're not to say this to anyone else," Lizzie told Nell. "Once you've said it, it won't be unsaid, no matter how untrue. And it is untrue. Mrs. Pleasant cares about money. She doesn't care about the colored. You mark me, she'll be back within the month with a wealthy father in tow." Her voice began friendly, but sharpened as she spoke.

"What kind of a name is Ijub?" Nell Harris asked, and since Lizzie didn't know the answer, she said nothing, but she said it to good effect. It shut Nell up entirely.

Two weeks later a box arrived for Jenny. Lizzie Hayes was there to open it. It contained a doll, wrapped in tissue, and a note. "I have noticed that many young girls are more interested in their needle-work if they have a friend to sew for," Mrs. Pleasant wrote. "This is a doll that needs just such a friend." Her penmanship was as twisty as wrought iron. The note was signed "Mrs. Mary E. Pleasant."

Lizzie unwrapped the doll. Her head was made of china, her hair was paint. She had a sweet, pouting face. She wore a necklace with a tiny coin, and a work apron over her dress. She fell out of Lizzie's hand and her head broke into several curved pieces. On one piece Lizzie could see a little heart-shaped mouth.

Mary Ellen Pleasant was a voodoo queen and Lizzie Hayes was an Episcopalian. They had had a very cordial exchange. There was no reason for Mrs. Pleasant to be angry. Except that Lizzie hadn't removed her work apron. Such a small thing, a careless thing, an oversight, honestly, when the big thing, Jenny's care, had all gone exactly as Mrs. Pleasant wished. Lizzie told herself that Mrs. Pleasant would not send a doll to curse her, and reminded herself that she couldn't be cursed by a doll even if Mrs. Pleasant had.

In fact, Lizzie had parts of this right. Mrs. Pleasant was angry about the apron, but the doll was just a bit of a joke, a bit of misdirection. There was no need to curse Lizzie with a doll. Not when she'd been given Jenny Ijub.

No one ever mentioned the doll to Jenny. It would have been pointlessly cruel, since she was already broken.

3

THE LADIES' RELIEF and Protection Society Home occupied a lot on the corner of Geary and Franklin. There wasn't a tree on the property, just scrub and sand, so storms hit hard. The Home was familiarly called the Brown Ark. Though blocks from the ocean, it had a shipwrecked, random air, like something the tides had left. In this respect, it matched the fortunes of most of its residents. During the year of 1890, the Ark housed a total of two hundred thirty-nine women and children, many only on a temporary, emergency basis.

The motif of randomness was carried up from the basement, with its kitchen, laundry, and schoolrooms, all the way to the bell-tower cupola. The furnishings had been donated, and represented the worst taste of several decades. The parlor, into which Mrs. Pleasant had not been asked, contained a clock face painted with clouds and trapped under a bell jar, a handmade mantelpiece decoration of gangrenous velvet, pinned into tufts with brass studs, and an old set of stuffed chairs that crouched before the fireplace like large, balding cats. The effect was little offset by the posting of embroidered quotations intended to uplift and edify. "He who loves a friend is too rich to know what poverty and misery are." And "Some flowers give out no odor until crushed." And "The true perfection of mankind lies not in what man has, but in what man is."

The last had been gleaned from the deplorable Oscar Wilde. In 1882, Wilde made a visit to the city and was absolutely undone by the vulgarity of it. He said so in public lectures addressed to the badly dressed perpetrators themselves. "Too, too utter," he said, though they all felt this described him far better than them. His observation on the parlor wall of the Ladies' Relief and Protection Society Home was unattributed.

The Bell place was only a few blocks away, on the corner of Octavia and Bush. It was known throughout San Francisco as the House of Mystery, although there was a second House of Mystery, out on the beach at Land's End, owned by the Alexander Russells. Mrs. Russell, despite her increasingly vehement denials, was widely believed to be the center of an Oriental cult whose disciples all called her Mother. Soon there would be a third House of Mystery, the Winchester house, but that would be down by San Jose.

The Bell House of Mystery was the occasional home of Thomas Bell, his reclusive wife, Teresa, an indeterminate but large number of children, servants, and Mrs. Mary Ellen Pleasant. Mrs. Pleasant was the housekeeper, although everyone knew she was too rich and too old and too famous to be a servant. This was part of the mystery. In the 1890 census she listed her occupation as "capitalist."

Mr. Bell had another house on Bush Street where he sometimes stayed. Mrs. Bell had a house in Oakland. Mrs. Pleasant had a house called Geneva Cottage on the San Jose Road, and properties on Washington Street and in Berkeley and Oakland. She was currently thinking of buying a large country ranch in the Valley of the Moon.

The Octavia place was a thirty-room mansion shadowed by blue gum trees. It had a red mansard roof, a southern mood. The interior was stuffed with hidden passageways, spiral staircases, statuary, and gold-veined mirrors. Rock-crystal chandeliers dripped from the ceilings. Every Saturday, even in winter, cut roses were arranged in vases with ferns and peacock feathers. The rooms smelled faintly of old bouquets. Mrs. Pleasant had chosen the decorations, many of which were imported from Italy. She had a fondness for vaulted ceilings and also for the gilt cupids that were so liked by everyone.

Lizzie Hayes was seriously considering walking from the Brown Ark to the House of Mystery. The distance between the two was not best measured in blocks; the Bell home was simply not a place one visited. Lizzie had never even passed by it. But she'd recently suffered a series of devastating headaches. Though she'd had headaches before, had them all her life, these were particularly rough going. The night after she dropped Jenny's doll, she'd had a vivid dream in which both her hands were encased in a block of ice. She tried to free herself by raising the ice and dashing it against a stone. Her hands broke off at the wrists instead. She could see them dimly through the scarred surface, floating, with the fingers widely separated and streaming off like jellyfish tentacles. She woke terrified, and although the feeling subsided, it did not disappear. The next day, the headaches began in earnest.

It occurred to her that nothing would be more natural than to go to Mrs. Pleasant and offer a report on Jenny's settling in. Dress with care and behave with the same. It would be a courteous attention and would show Mrs. Pleasant that Lizzie was a good-hearted, respectable woman.

Part of her recoiled from her own plan. She did not believe in voodoo and would not be governed by superstition. Good-hearted, respectable women did not visit Teresa Bell in the House of Mystery, much less Mrs. Pleasant. "How does Jenny like her doll?" Mrs. Pleasant was bound to ask, and then what would Lizzie say? Plus there was the matter of Lizzie's card. This wouldn't be a social call, but it would take place in Mrs. Pleasant's home. Would Mrs. Pleasant expect her to leave her card? If she did, would Mrs. Pleasant feel compelled to return the visit? If she didn't, mightn't this merely compound the original rudeness?

Besides, Lizzie didn't really know how Jenny was settling in. With sixty-two children now in residence, she could scarcely be expected to keep track of them all.

She rang the bell for Nell Harris. Nell took some time arriving and appeared impatient when she did so. "Yes?" she said.

"Little Jenny. Jenny Ijub. How does she get on?"

"Well enough."

"Has she settled? Does she eat heartily?"

"She's not much of an eater, I'm afraid. I believe I told you as much the first day."

"Does she get on with the other children?"

"She's not entirely truthful. The other children naturally resent it. And the dress she came in. It was turned. I don't think she's as wealthy as you hoped."

"Has she said anything about her home and family?"

"Not a whisper. She claims to remember nothing about it. But then, she's not a truthful child."

"But she seems content?"

"She thrashes at night. Her bedclothes are a rat's nest by morning. Miss Hayes, I'm dishing supper. If there's nothing further ..."

Lizzie had a sudden memory of her own dining room table many years before. Her mother at one end. Her father at the other. And she between them, balanced unsteadily on two cushions, her legs dangling. No one was allowed to speak at meals, so she could hear her father swallowing his soup, her mother rustling a napkin under the table, out of sight.

It must have been a special occasion—she was never permitted to eat with her parents. It might have been her birthday. Lemon ices were to be served. But then Effie had been summoned to carry her off. "I simply cannot have you thrashing about," her mother told her. Lizzie could still feel the bewildered humiliation of it. She would have said she was sitting still as stone.

"Thank you," said Lizzie to Nell.

It was not the report she had wanted. But was it, after all, such a bad one? An imaginative little sprite, Lizzie could still say to Mrs. Pleasant. She so entertains the other children with her fanciful tales. An active, spirited girl.

BEFORE SHE'D MADE UP her mind about the visit, something occurred to necessitate it. Jenny was taken with several of the other children to Layman's German castle on Telegraph Hill, as a treat for learning her Bible verses. The middle school children were reading *Ivanhoe*, and there was to be a special exhibition of armor and swordfighting. Mrs. Lake, a postman's widow who taught the middles, had been assured that the thrusts and parries would be accurately medieval. There were rumors of actual tilting, and she assumed this meant horses. Tilting afoot would be a sad spectacle even for orphans.

The children were sorted into pairs, an older child with each younger. Jenny Ijub was partnered with Minna Graham, a pretty ten-year-old with fat black braids, and front teeth that folded toward each other like an opened book. The two girls held hands on the cable car. Mrs. Lake was getting a cold, and she sneezed until her nose swelled.

A large crowd had gathered at the castle, whose Gothic turrets and parapets had been decked from top to bottom with banners. At noon the copper time-ball fell through its glass shaft. A group of strolling musicians sang madrigals. Minna Graham was not musical, but she was entranced by the women's costumes. She wished that she, too, wore dunce caps with feathers and veils, velvet bodices with brocade inserts, high waistlines and yards of skirt. She followed the singers a few steps only, fell behind the other children. When the first combat began, people pressed forward to see it.

Mrs. Lake complained to Lizzie later that little chivalry was shown to her and her pupils. There were several moments of confusion in the crush. But they all heard Jenny scream.

By the time Mrs. Lake got there, Jenny was being held and petted by a fat, handsome man in a yellow waistcoat. He said that Jenny had been frightened by the appearance of the black knight. The black knight wore a facemask that looked like the back of a shovel, with a row of stiff bristles over the top of his head. The bristles appeared to Mrs. Lake to be cut by machine and therefore not something that would have been available to Ivanhoe, although the metal part might well have been old enough.

In any case, Jenny denied being frightened of the knight. She said instead that a man had tried to snatch her, a man in green trousers. It was the only description they were able to get. He had clutched her by the neck, one hand over her mouth. She bit him and screamed as he dropped her. Then he'd disappeared into the crowd. Mrs. Lake could find no one who had seen any of this.

She lost control of the children. The older boys abandoned their partners and dashed off to look for green trousers. Mrs. Lake was unable to stop them. She used her energies to keep the little ones huddled together. This was not hard; many of them were frightened. Others, especially Minna Graham, were clearly envious. Minna was one of those children who liked to turn attention to herself whenever possible. She did so on this occasion by fainting.

Minna's head hit the pavement with a crack they could all hear. Blood seeped into her hair, and Mrs. Lake found a large lump on the scalp. The lump was as soft as a cooked carrot and gave slightly when poked. Minna was too dizzy to walk. Mrs. Lake, who was planning on confronting Minna with her failure to watch over Jenny, instead saw her carried from the castle to the cable car on the back of the black knight's horse, the crowd cheering as she passed. "She actually waved to everyone," Mrs. Lake told Lizzie and Nell, "as if she were Queen of the May."

All in all, the children were judged to be overexcited, and when Mrs. Lake collected them again, she brought them straight back. As a result, she couldn't know about the tilting.

She gave Lizzie and Nell an aggrieved report, blowing her nose into her handkerchief frequently but silently. She then went home to rest. Nell stayed with Lizzie a few moments more, to give her own version of events, events to which she was not a witness. Nell had no time for knights; it amazed her that anyone did. And she had three particular points to make. The first was that Mrs. Lake was the kind of woman who lived a life of high drama in which nothing ever actually happened. The second was that *Ivanhoe* was likely to overexcite, even when it wasn't combined with unnecessary outings. It was a swoony sort of book, and she wondered at Mrs. Lake for encouraging the children to read it. The third was that it was time to know more about Jenny Ijub. Where had she come from? Had they put themselves and the other children in danger by taking her in? Someone needed to go to Mammy Pleasant and ask some hard questions.

Lizzie guessed that Nell was right on all counts.

Ivanhoe: Swoony indeed—why, Lizzie had only to think in the most glancing way about the licentiousness of Norman nobles to feel a flush coming up her neck and into her cheeks. How many nights she'd drifted to sleep imagining herself struggling futilely, imprisoned for love by the swarthy, ardent Bois-Gilbert!

Mrs. Lake: Mrs. Lake was a neat, pretty, red-haired woman of thirty and could still carry on about knights and steeds and beheaded queens (how that woman loved the Stuarts!) without looking the fool, but her day was coming. Since Lizzie secretly shared all of Mrs. Lake's shortcomings, she was quick to find Mrs. Lake silly and sentimental. It was a form of protective coloration. Nell's veins ran with a heavier ore.

Questions about Jenny: The staff was busy and Lizzie was the only member of the board at hand, so these were bound to fall to her. She fixed her hair with combs, fixed her hat with pins, fixed her face in a smile, and walked to Octavia Street. By the time she reached the Bells' front porch, she had worked herself into such a state over occult rituals and blood sacrifices she could hardly knock on the door.

5

LIZZIE WAS NOT THE SORT TO RETREAT, not when she'd made up her mind to call, and especially not with the elderly gardener watching her. He stood staring, scary in his very ordinariness, armed with a shining set of pruning shears and the thorny stems of a dozen dead roses. Lizzie picked up her skirts and climbed the steps to the front doors. These were of carved cherry wood, inset with a high pane of beveled glass. The knocker was a roaring lion with a ring in his mouth.

A white girl, very pretty and dressed in a green uniform, answered Lizzie's knock, took her hat and gloves, and showed her into a white-and-gold drawing room. She was told to sit, but went instead to examine a set of statues of women, white marble on black onyx bases. They held various poses of resignation and supplication. They were women who wanted something they would not get. And they were quite naked. There was a slight shadow of dust in the marble crevices. Lizzie could imagine a housemaid too embarrassed to clean more thoroughly. Lizzie herself did not much like them. She didn't mind the lack of clothing; she knew about art. She was no prig. But a lady shouldn't need to beg.

A gold-and-white woman entered the room. She wore pearls in

her ears and gold on her wrists. Her hair was brown with a little meander of gold; her eyes were like trout ponds. A complicated fragile white dress gathered and spilled over her. She seemed about Lizzie's own age, though much more beautiful. "I'm Mrs. Bell," she said. Lizzie had expected Mrs. Bell to be younger.

"Miss Hayes. Of the Ladies' Relief and Protection Society Home."

"I suppose Mr. Bell has made contributions." Her tone was distant and uninterested.

Lizzie had no recollection of this, and since she kept the books, she should know. But it would be an awkward thing to contradict.

Mrs. Bell was already sweeping Lizzie back toward the door. "Perhaps we could do a mite more. I'm not the one to ask. I'm not the one to know when we have money and when we don't."

"I didn't come to ask for money. I'm here about a child."

"I love children," said Mrs. Bell. "Mr. Bell and me have our six. The oldest grown. I think Fred might be in San Jose. Or maybe Mexico. Somewhere south."

"This is a girl. She's only been with us a few weeks. Her mother passed away."

"I hardly knew my mother." Mrs. Bell's voice retained its formal-tea tone. "I had two older brothers who both died right after birth. When I was three months old my mother stripped me to the skin and set me on a windowsill in a thunderstorm. My father found me and he gave me to another family to raise."

"I'm very sorry," Lizzie responded uneasily.

"A three-month baby left soaking in the rain." Still, Mrs. Bell's composure was perfect; she might have been discussing the new fashion in women's sleeves or expressing hopes for a mild winter. "A pretty little thing, too, with a head of silky hair. Before it was even born, she hated it. Wouldn't nurse it. I refuse to think on her much. What might I do for your motherless girl?"

"Mrs. Pleasant brought her to us. Actually, it was Mrs. Pleasant I was hoping to see."

Mrs. Bell's poise proved as diaphanous as her dress. It slipped from her face like smoke. Lizzie watched this happen, and then looked away, since clearly it was something she shouldn't have seen. "Don't do that," said Mrs. Bell. "Just go. I won't say you been here. I won't say anything." There was the sound of brisk footsteps in the corridor. "See how fast she walks?" Mrs. Bell whispered. "She comes on you in a moment."

Mrs. Pleasant entered the room. "Teresa," she said. She spoke as quickly as she moved. "You've met Miss Hayes, then. I'm delighted. She's a woman of good works." She didn't look delighted. She didn't look surprised. Her face was gracious, but this could have been an illusion created by age, by the texture of her skin, like a crumpled handkerchief. Her hair was white about her face, but still, even now, when she was in her seventies, mostly black. She'd gathered it into a knot with bits curled tightly around her temples. Her eyes were sharp; they seemed to take much in while giving nothing away.

"Really?" said Mrs. Bell. "Now, she didn't say. I'm rather a creature of ideals, myself."

"Would you take a cup of tea?"

Lizzie did not want to stay long enough to drink a cup of tea. She didn't wish to make a social call. She didn't wish to conduct her business in front of the peculiar Mrs. Bell. She couldn't think of a courteous way to send Mrs. Bell from her own drawing room. "Tea would be lovely," she said. "Aren't you kind."

She took a seat on the couch. Mrs. Pleasant vanished. Mrs. Bell sat beside her, sliding her hand into Lizzie's, giving it the ghost of a squeeze. Her hand was cold, limp, corpselike. Lizzie could feel her own warmth draining out of her. Yet courtesy prevented her from withdrawing.

"Don't eat or drink nothing," Mrs. Bell warned Lizzie. Her tone suggested they were old friends now, co-conspirators. There was an odd footstep in the hall. "I'm not talking to you, Miss Viola." Mrs. Bell's voice grew louder. "You just run along," and a girl, dark-eyed and unnaturally pale, of perhaps sixteen or seventeen years, passed slowly by the doorway. She walked with some difficulty, her left foot twisted inward. "Not everything in this house is your business." Mrs. Bell turned back to Lizzie. "Viola is queen of the keyhole." She did not lower her voice, though Lizzie was sitting right there beside her.

Something exploded in Lizzie's peripheral vision. She turned to look out an arched window and saw a burst of silver light, as if a fairy were coming into the room. The fairy spun over the sill, darted into the corners and up to the vaulted ceiling, where it hung for a moment like a star. Then it dropped again, touched the roses, the statues, Teresa Bell's brown hair. Everything it touched remained under a silvery film, as if seen by moonshine and through ruffled water. The sight filled Lizzie with dread.

The first time Lizzie had seen such colors, she'd thought a Christmas angel was visiting. She'd cried, it was that beautiful. Later she imagined it was Baby Edward giving her the silver taste of his unhappiness, angry not to be the one alive when everybody would have preferred him.

She heard a noise deep in her own throat without understanding that she had made it. She hardly noticed Mrs. Bell's hand sliding away, Mrs. Bell herself leaving the room.

"Are you all right, Miss Hayes?" Mrs. Pleasant asked. Her voice moved at the wrong speed and was pitched in the wrong key.

"I must get home," Lizzie said. She took a great, unladylike gulp of air, pressed her hands into her temples to try to block the pain before it arrived. "Please. I don't believe I can walk so far. If I might have the loan of your buggy ..."

"Your head aches?"

"Not yet." The blood was beginning to beat in her ears. She curled into her own lap, the corset cutting upward into the bottom of her breasts. "But I must go home."

There was no answer. She was alone in the room again, with the silent, pleading, naked silvery statues. She tried to rise, but her legs shook beneath her. She heard a clock sounding the hour with a slow, sobering tune. She heard a tapping in the hall, footsteps entering the room, each louder than the previous and all of them too loud.

"I've made you something. Drink it up, but slow. You'll feel better."

Lizzie raised her head. Mrs. Pleasant stood before her, and behind Mrs. Pleasant, Mrs. Bell. Mrs. Bell's eyes flashed like silver coins.

Mrs. Pleasant guided her fingers around a china cup in which Lizzie smelled a foul sort of tea. Bay leaves, wet moss, blackberries, and rum. She allowed Mrs. Pleasant to lift her hand, tip the cup into her mouth. She was sluggish from apprehension, too limp to resist. The drink was bitter enough to sting, dribbling down her throat in a thin stream, leaving behind a runnel of heat. She drank more. With every sip, she felt the impending headache recede, the warmth spreading until it reached even her frozen fingers. "There," said Mrs. Pleasant. "See how that helps." This might have been a question. It might have been a command. Followed by a command. "Keep drinking."

As she emptied the cup, Lizzie felt as if she were waking, finally, from a long dream. The dream was her whole life until now. The silver light leached from the room. The tables and flowers flattened into ordinariness and further, better even, to detachment.

Sometime after Lizzie finished her tea, Mrs. Pleasant asked if she was happy with her life. She should have said yes. She rarely felt unhappy. Daily association with the downtrodden kept her keenly aware of her advantages. She knew the pleasure of doing good. She knew moments of great joy, often in church during the high notes of particular hymns. She would open her mouth to sing them, and her heart would leap with her voice up to where the sunlight filtered through the colored glass, igniting the motes of dust above her head. So many pleasures. The sight of red tulips. The little buzz of life in the grass. A letter with her name and foreign stamps. The smell of rain. The taste of pomegranate jelly. Reading novels in the afternoon, with no corset and her shoes off and her feet on a chair.

And at the moment of the question, she was feeling nothing at all. It had seemed to Lizzie that as the room returned to normal around her, she herself shrank away like Alice in Wonderland in the "Drink Me" episode. Her concerns, her alarms, became tiny and laughable. She remembered how lovely it was to be small and cared for. She remembered a fever from many years before, not a high fever, just high enough to be exhilarating. She remembered Effie sitting on the edge of the bed and feeding her sips of a salty broth with one of her mother's special apostle spoons.

And yet she answered that she was not. In direct contradiction, she then went on at length about the gratifications of her work. She couldn't seem to stop herself. Somehow she mentioned that her mother had once said she played the piano as if she had hooves instead of hands. She felt no distress over this, and yet her eyes filled with tears. She pulled her handkerchief from her bodice and wiped her nose. The handkerchief was hot, and stiff with soap.

"My mother left me naked out in the pouring rain," Mrs. Bell said. Lizzie had already managed to forget this.

"My mother was sold off." Mrs. Pleasant sat with her arms crossed and her hands showing. Her fingernails were like white pearls against her dark skin. "The overseer was frightened of her eyes. He couldn't bear the way she looked at him. He sickened and died soon after."

Lizzie felt outdone. She was tempted to say something of her father—there were things she could say! But one look at Mrs. Pleasant made her see that she would not win this, either.

And she didn't really mind being bested. She was finding, to her surprise, that she was quite relaxed in the company of notorious women. Teresa Bell was said to have been a prostitute. Mary Ellen Pleasant was rumored to sell babies to Chinamen. Lizzie felt that she could say anything; how could mere words lower her here? "I've never been in love," someone said, and most likely it was Lizzie herself, although she very much hoped not. She put her handkerchief away, tucked it to the side of her breast and felt her heart beat as she did so. Her pulse was rapid and skimmed over the surface of her skin, delicate as a bird's. She could hear it, washing through her ears, loud and then soft and then loud again. She was so involved in these observations that she forgot the unseemly topic of love had been raised.

"Anyone who wants love can have it," Mrs. Pleasant said. "There are ways."

"Charms," explained Mrs. Bell.

"You can do anything you want. You don't have to be the same person your whole life. As to love, you're better off without. That's about all I know about that!"

"Mr. Bell and I are very much in love," said Mrs. Bell. There was an odd pause. "With each other." She was seated by Lizzie again; she tapped on Lizzie's arm. "Mrs. Pleasant reads tea leaves," she said. "If you want to know your future. Not that it's always such a good idea."

"Miss Hayes doesn't believe in that sort of thing," Mrs. Pleasant observed, and rightly so, but Mrs. Bell's warning aside, who wouldn't want her tea leaves read?

"Please," said Lizzie.

She watched as Mrs. Pleasant peered into her cup, dumped the dregs onto a saucer, let them settle, looked again, and finally smashed them with the back of her spoon in a gesture that could only disturb. The clock struck and still Mrs. Pleasant contemplated the ruins of Lizzie's tea. She looked for so long that Lizzie suspected she was seeing something bad.

But when Mrs. Pleasant spoke it was all bland bits of other fortunes. "You've come to a magical juncture," she said, which was nice, since Lizzie had been feeling old and used up. Nice to think she was at the beginning of something. "A critical turning. You could lose your way." This was less nice.

"You must watch out for three signs. This is the order of them: a blue-eyed man, a white dog, and the number twelve. When you've seen them all, you'll have a choice to make." She looked straight at Lizzie's face and didn't look away. Lizzie hated being looked at.

"Your impulses are good," Mrs. Pleasant said finally, "but you don't trust them. You fret overly about appearances and say things you don't really think. Put all that away when you make this choice, or you'll blunder."

And that was it. "I see," Lizzie replied. "That's helpful, then," which was not what she really thought. And nothing at all about falling in love, which she'd thought was the whole point. She would have liked to ask, but having already introduced the matter once, she felt it would be nagging.

At just that moment a large Negro in a black top hat entered the room. He whispered something to Mrs. Pleasant, who rose. "The carriage is hitched," she said. "I'll get you to it."

She took Lizzie's arm, which was quite unnecessary. Lizzie felt a small piece of paper pressed into her hand, a wave of lavender perfume. "Here's where to buy that tea. You just tell the druggist I sent you, he'll take special care. Sam, please see Miss Hayes safely back."

Lizzie's arm was transferred to Sam. "I'm perfectly well able to walk," she said crossly, and then looked up to see the crippled girl, Viola, who wasn't. "So sorry," she offered, vaguely aware that an apology would only make matters worse.

IN LATER YEARS the *San Francisco Chronicle* would refer to the residents of the House of Mystery as the strangest bunch ever to live in the city. The Bell household had a predilection for assumed names and fanciful histories. The 1890 census showed several of them lying about their ages as well.

To have seen the inside, as Lizzie had just done, to have your tea leaves read by Mrs. Pleasant herself, was rare enough to be worth the telling of it. Yet Lizzie found she was reluctant to do so. Her own role was an ambiguous one; she had made herself too much at home.

In fact, Nell Harris told Mrs. Lake that Lizzie had returned to the Brown Ark in a disgraceful state of intoxication. The children all witnessed it, Nell said—Lizzie, with her hair tipped off the side of her head like a melting pudding, setting her feet down with such deliberation and laughing like a crazy woman about it. She had asked Nell if Nell thought she was happy. As if a person could think she was happy, but really not be. As if Nell had time to worry about such things!

And then, when pressed, Lizzie admitted to having learnt absolutely nothing further about Jenny Ijub. Oh, Nell could see poor Lizzie had been as clay in the hands of the cunning Mrs. Pleasant.

While Lizzie had been off tippling, a sparrow had flown into the basement of the Brown Ark. Before Nell could sweep it out the door with the broom, the orange cat had gotten it. This information reduced Lizzie to shockingly voluble sobs—"Poor bright little spirit!" she said in a trembly voice—and then she went upstairs to the tower room and fell asleep at once on the scratchy settee.

If Nell and Lizzie had been a generation older, if they'd read the *Pacific Appeal,* the paper that came from the Negro community, instead of the *Wasp,* the things they thought they knew about Mrs. Pleasant might have been quite different. As it was, their familiarity with her was based almost entirely on the coverage of a sensational and long-running court case commonly called the Sharon business.

A lady's name, Lizzie's mother had always told her, appears in the paper only twice, once when she's married and once when she's buried. Yet there Mrs. Pleasant was, often as not, on page six, or page twelve, a few paragraphs down, or in the very headline itself. On one side of the Sharon case was a red-haired beauty from Missouri named Sarah Althea (Allie) Hill. On the other was William Sharon, ex-U.S. senator and executive of the Bank of California. Sharon was *a San Francisco millionaire,* a title reserved for those whose fortunes exceeded thirty million.

Sharon and Hill were either married or they weren't when she sued him for divorce on grounds of adultery. She had a letter from him attesting to the marriage, a letter Sharon claimed was a forgery.

In 1885, with the trial ongoing, William Sharon had died, leaving Allie widowed or not, disgraced or unimaginably wealthy, or some combination of the above. It took four years for the courts to rule finally against her.

Mrs. Pleasant was rumored to have paid all Allie's legal costs. She spent many days in court at Allie's side for no reason anyone could see, except to fix the judge with the evil eye.

The witnesses for William Sharon included an endless succession of star, palm, and tea-leaf readers, spirit mediums and charm workers, all of whom claimed that, under Mrs. Pleasant's guidance, Allie had fed the ex-senator love potions, placed items of power in fresh graves, pierced the dried heart of a pigeon with nine pins and worn it in a red silk bag about her neck. These were not seen to be the actions of a wife, and Allie had denied them.

The testimony that followed concerned previous lovers, suicide attempts, even the details of carnal intimacies, right there in the press, where any innocent child might read them. It was the sort of case that exposed no end of human frailties and, Lizzie thought sadly, no one's more than her own. It was so like a good novel, except for the being-real part. Real embarrassments, real heartbreak, real death. She was ashamed of how avidly she'd followed it. Her mother would have canceled the paper first.

So there Lizzie was, only three signs shy of a magical juncture and too ashamed to tell anyone. She spoke only to Nell about the visit and was as brief as could be. In this way she hoped to conceal her intense interest.

It was an interest widely shared. How did a colored woman, an ex-slave, come to have so much money and influence, San Francisco asked itself, and gave itself three possible answers.

Visitations

1

PROPOSITION ONE: Mary E. Pleasant rose to power and prominence in San Francisco through her cooking.

A better case can be made for this than one might imagine. When Mrs. Pleasant arrived in 1852, San Francisco was little more than a mining camp. Streets were made by sinking emptied whiskey bottles into the mud; shacks were made by dismantling boats and wagons. The food was revolting.

Mrs. Pleasant was already in possession of a sizable inheritance from her first husband when she went to work as housekeeper at an elegant bachelor club on Washington Street.

Among those who sat at her table in the early years were:

The Woodworth brothers—Fred, part owner of the fabulous Ophir mine, and Selim, acting consul for China and a commodore in the U.S. Navy.

Newton Booth, who would go on to be governor and a U.S. senator.

Those kings of the Comstock, William Ralston, who ran the Bank of California and built the Palace Hotel, and William Sharon, senator from Nevada, who inherited the Palace after Ralston drowned.

Senator David S. Broderick and California Supreme Court justice David S. Terry, before the latter killed the former in a dubiously conducted duel and had to flee the state.

And Representative Milton Latham, a lawyer, financier, and railroad engineer.

Here were some of the wealthiest men in San Francisco, most of them quite fond of her. Stock tips, management concerns, and investment strategies were passed about the table as readily as salt and pepper.

Mrs. Pleasant was sharp, well funded, and well informed. By 1880 she owned a stable, a saloon, a dairy farm, a brothel, two board-inghouses, several residences, and considerable amounts of unde-veloped land in Oakland and Berkeley. She'd invested in railroads, mining, and ranching, and managed to dodge the crash of 1873 and the crookedness of 1879.

No other explanation of her wealth is necessary. No explanation of power besides wealth is needed.

Many of her recipes survive. Some call for ingredients in propor-tions large enough to serve more than a hundred diners.

PROPOSITION TWO: Mary E. Pleasant rose to power and prominence in San Francisco through a system of carefully managed secrets.

At that same table, Mrs. Pleasant must have heard a great many things besides stock tips. She was widely known as a superior cook, but equally widely as someone who would keep a secret.

She was a woman for women to turn to in a scrape. She found hospitals for girls in trouble, homes for unwanted children; Teresa Bell's diaries connect her to one Dr. Monser, who ran a foundling hospital (and later died in San Quentin while serving sentence for a botched abortion). Both black women and white women depended on her; she made no distinctions.

Before the war, Mary Ellen Pleasant had taken enormous personal risks on behalf of slaves. She carried money to John Brown and participated in the Franchise League. She went to court to oppose those laws that penalized free blacks.

After the war, people began to refer to her as the Black City Hall. She loaned money to new businesses. She donated to black churches. She found domestic positions for new arrivals in the hotels and in the households of her wealthy white friends.

Any servant sees things, and some of these servants had been trained by slavery to be observant on penalty of death. If an unmarried daughter seemed tired in the mornings, if a married man had unusual appetites or an extra wife back East, if there were gambling debts or domestic violence or alcoholic madness, this information was likely to reach Mrs. Pleasant.

A favor can be freely extended out of gratitude for a secret kept. A favor can be extorted in return for the promise of secrecy. From the outside it may be hard to distinguish the former from the latter. But Teresa Bell was not the only one to call it blackmail.

PROPOSITION THREE: Mary E. Pleasant rose to a position of power and prominence in San Francisco through Vodoun.

Mrs. Pleasant sometimes said that her mother had been a Vodoun priestess killed by slave owners frightened of her power. (Sometimes she said other things.) Sometimes she said that she herself had used her Vodoun power to escape slavery.

She was related through her second marriage to the famous Marie LaVeau and had been a guest of that house before sailing to California. In New Orleans, LaVeau created a political base through domestic spies, blackmail, and matchmaking. Mrs. Pleasant appears to have adapted these same methods to San Francisco.

She enjoyed close friendships with several white women for whom she'd found, if not husbands, then near-equivalents to husbands. She introduced Selim Woodworth to his wife, and Governor Booth to a woman whom he felt unable to marry for political reasons, but with whom he had a long relationship as well as a child. She introduced Thomas and Teresa Bell.

A few years before her death, the *Chronicle* ran an article on Mrs. Pleasant entitled "Queen of the Voodoos." It was a very unpleasant article, and one of the things it accused her of was genuine belief.

From an item in the *Examiner,* October 13, 1895:
Safely locked in her loyal breast are the secret histories of many of the prominent families of the coast. She has supplied the ladder upon which more than one proud woman and ambitious man have climbed to wealth and social position. Her purse—for she has been for years a wealthy woman—has ever been open to aid the needy and unfortunate.... Neither creed, color, sex nor condition in life ever had meaning for her when her interest had been once awakened. Her deeds of charity are as numerous as the gray hairs in her proud old head.

An acquaintance, as quoted in the *Call,* May 7, 1899:
"She has not a spark of affection, nor an atom of conscience. She is the smoothest talker and the shrewdest woman in San Francisco. She is childish in her vanities, diabolical in her schemings, a woman to whom the feeling of power is the breath of life, and one who realizes that it is money that gives power. An intellectual giant, but a moral idiot."

2

ON THE NIGHT FOLLOWING her visit to the House of Mystery, Lizzie awoke sometime after dark. It took her a moment to know where she was, since she was not in her bed, where she ought to be. She couldn't imagine why she hadn't told Sam to take her home. A fat moon floated just outside the tower window, one small, dark cloud patting its face like a powder puff. There was a tatted antimacassar under her cheek; when she raised her head, she could feel its web indented into her skin.

She was still dressed, even to her shoes. She still had Mrs. Pleasant's slip of paper balled in her hand. The gaslights had been long ago put out. She took the paper to the window. She could see the halo of lights over the downtown, too far away to be useful. There was also Mrs. Pleasant's elaborate script to contend with. Plus the ink had smeared from the heat of Lizzie's fingers. But she thought the address was in Chinatown.

She'd not eaten since breakfast. She made her way, partly by sight, partly by touch, partly by memory to the basement and the kitchen. The Brown Ark groaned from her weight on the stairs. The parlor clock chimed a quarter-hour. She groped through the dark pantry for an apple. When she bit down, it became a potato instead.

After her initial disappointment, she thought it tasty enough. She was very hungry!

What might Mrs. Pleasant and Mrs. Bell have eaten for dinner? Lizzie wondered whether Mr. Bell would have joined them; somehow she thought not. Lizzie pictured the two women at the table together, Teresa and Mary Ellen, both of them elegantly gowned, necklaces flickering in the candlelight, the murmur of their voices. Laughter. She herself might have been spoken of, though she couldn't imagine what would be said. It was strangely exciting to think of being talked of by two women so often talked of. Ordinarily Lizzie hated the idea of being a topic for conversation.

She took another bite of potato, less pleased with the taste this time. Then she heard someone who shouldn't have been there coming soft and halting down the stairs.

During this period, an eleven-year-old girl named Maud Gurry also lived as a ward at the Brown Ark. Maud was a thin child, with white-blond hair that coiled down her neck so thickly it was kept cut short, to prevent the abundance from sapping her strength. Maud's mother was consumptive and had been separated from her daughter for the child's own health. Her father had owned a small dry-goods store, but it had been embezzled away by his bookkeeper. Unable to bear presenting his darling, ailing wife with bankruptcy and failure, he brought Maud one morning to the Ark, kissed her, told her he would return for her in a day or so, and disappeared. He was by nature a cheerful, hearty man, and he had never given any outward sign of distress.

It might have been easier on Maud if he hadn't dissembled so persuasively. As she saw the days pass and his promises turn to lies, she began to suspect his every emotion: Had he ever been happy with her and her mother? Had he ever intended to stay? Had he ever loved them?

Her mother's health was not improved by her father's desertion. She sent Maud many tender letters, but often they were not even in her own hand and she did not pretend that Maud was coming home soon.

After the initial shock, Maud's unhappiness settled so deep inside her she was rarely aware of it. She was her father's daughter. She made a place for herself among the other wards as someone who was ready for anything. "Maud is a sport," the boys said admiringly. "Maud will stop at nothing."

At least she had a mother and a father. At the Brown Ark, that counted for something. It was the first question they asked when a new child arrived. They'd asked it of Jenny Ijub. Did she have a mother? A father? Anybody?

Jenny Ijub was not settling in. She was small, but without the ingratiating manner that might have turned this to her advantage. She refused to be dressed and carried about like a doll, though this would have vastly improved her popularity. Lizzie believed her to be four years old, but she was, in fact, five. She had told the other children that her friend, Mrs. Pleasant, was sending her a special gift, loved her dearly, would be coming to take her away soon. This was what she had made of Mrs. Pleasant's promises.

Maud had once said something too much like this herself, had even believed it. She'd been made to look a fool. By the time of Jenny's arrival, Maud had lived at the Ark for almost a year. Jenny's assertions were preposterous. Jenny was trying to make fools of them all. Maud held Jenny's nose and mouth closed until she confessed as much. She pinched Jenny's nose hard enough to leave fingerprints.

"She sleepwalks," Maud told the matron when questioned about the bruising. "And she's such a liar! If there's one thing I can't bear, it's a liar."

She'd heard the matron say this herself often enough to know it would find its mark. "So a friend is coming to fetch you?" Nell asked Jenny. "And what friend would that be? You'll find no friends here, missy, if you can't learn to be truthful."

The warning had no apparent effect. Maud told the other children that Jenny boasted she'd owned a pony, a parrot, a silver cup with her initials, dresses, and dolls. Her mother had allowed her lemon sticks whenever she liked, had kept a vase full of them on a low table within Jenny's reach. Her lies grew more and more fanciful. Her father had been as rich as a sultan. She believed in fairies, because she had actually seen them. She'd seen ghosts and angels, too. She didn't believe in God. Before a week had passed, everyone at the Brown Ark knew you couldn't trust a thing Jenny said.

Even Jenny was persuaded. Her memories tangled into the things Maud reported. Jenny thought there had been a pony, dresses, and candies, but apparently these were lies. And more confusing, she didn't remember telling Maud anything. She vowed to say nothing about herself to anyone—she already hated them all—but in the midst of her rigorous silence, her lies carried on without her.

Once her untruthfulness was known, she became an easy target for pranks. Cups of sand were poured into her shoes at night, followed by cups of water. Imogene Reed caught a fat black spider and saved it in a glass, to be dropped onto Jenny's face as she slept. The cores of several apples were stuffed into her pillowcase.

The food at the Brown Ark was not what Jenny was used to. The discipline was also a hardship. She'd never before been expected to stay voluntarily in her chair, with its terrible spindled back, for hours at a time. She had never been asked to envision God's disappointment in her. She had not been told to keep so clean. She reacted against confinement like a wild animal. She paced in her cage.

It was Jenny, then, whom Lizzie heard on the stairs. When Lizzie turned around, there she was, her eyes brooding, her hair wild as a nest of sticks. She had been unable to do up the laces at the back of her dress, but was otherwise fully clothed.

"Jenny Ijub," Lizzie said. "Little Jenny. You frightened me. You should be in bed."

"I know." Jenny began to back upstairs, her legs so short each step was a difficulty. Lizzie caught her by the arm. What a twig it was! Lizzie's fingers wrapped about it and squeezed, and she could feel right down to the bone.

"Where were you going?"

"Nowhere."

"All dressed up to go nowhere? It won't do, miss. I know you're fond of deceits. I'll have the truth from you now."

"I wanted the cat," Jenny said. "The stripe cat."

"The cats don't come inside."

"I didn't know."

Jenny's voice was unconvincing, but she met Lizzie's eyes steadily. The look on her face surprised Lizzie. It was an altogether adult look. It was anger.

"You know this very well, Jenny. Someone let the orange cat in today and it killed a lovely little bird. Jesus hates to hear a child lie."

"I can't sleep," Jenny said, her chin coming up and her mouth setting. "I want to go out."

Lizzie turned Jenny away, intending to march her smartly upstairs. Instead she fastened up the back of Jenny's dress. She smoothed her own hair with one hand. "Get your coat. I won't have you catching a chill. Matron has enough to do without nursing you."

She fetched her own coat, too. Complying with Jenny's wishes made no sense, but this seemed to be exactly the part that appealed to Lizzie. You don't have to be the same person your whole life, she told herself. She was excited to see that she could be impulsive, unpredictable. They don't expect that from me, she thought. She would show them. She had no idea at all who they were.

3

NOTHING COULD HAVE BEEN more familiar than the walk in and out of the Brown Ark, but Lizzie had seldom done it at night. She was disoriented, exhilarated by the darkness and her own strange behavior. Everything common, the garbage and ash barrels, the cellar door, the dunes, was transformed into something she'd never seen before. She could be underwater, or in another century.

It was a clear, dry winter night. No streetlights lit this part of the city yet, and the moon had receded higher and smaller and dimmer in the sky. There were a preposterous number of stars. Who could ever need so many? Lizzie raised her chin to look at them all, strung like beads along the telegraph wires, scattered in handfuls across the netted void.

The cold air made a mist of her breath. A scratchy wind came over the dunes and into the sleeves of her coat. The orange cat was lurking by the door. It took off into the scrub, then turned to watch them. "You're a bad one," she told it, softly, but she knew it heard. Lizzie could see the unearthly jewels of its eyes.

What now? It was too late to get the buggy. Jenny was too small to walk more than a few blocks. Lizzie had gotten this far on momentum, but now she had to invent something. Now she had to have a plan.

"Where are we going?" Jenny asked.

"Where would you like to go?"

"The ducks."

Lizzie had no idea where that might be, but since they weren't going there, it hardly mattered. "The ducks are asleep."

"Wake them," suggested Jenny.

There was really only one destination that Lizzie could think of within walking distance. She took Jenny's hand and started off. She wasn't sure exactly how late it was. There were still lights far away in the city, but no one else seemed to be abroad.

The streets were unpaved and full of obstacles, stones and dips and horse droppings. Lizzie was not used to walking with a child. People credited her with maternal instincts simply because she volunteered at the Brown Ark, but as treasurer, she worked solely with adults and accounts. She was actually quite awkward around the young wards. Jenny's steps were so small. She labored on the uphill slope to Sutter Street. Lizzie recalculated how long the few blocks would take, and then leaned over and hoisted Jenny. "You're a bigger girl than I thought," she said, trying to keep the disapproval out of her voice. She could smell Jenny's hair, a stale-molasses smell, not entirely pleasant. If she were mine, Lizzie thought, I would keep her as clean as a kitten.

Jenny refused to put her arms around Lizzie, which would have helped balance her. "Where are we going?" she asked again.

"Do you want to go back?"

"No."

Lizzie turned left at the thorny rose garden of Trinity Church. The wind picked up considerably. A man walked ahead of them, going their same direction on Bush Street. She put Jenny down, glad for a reason to fall farther behind him.

"Will we ever go back?" asked Jenny.

"Yes, of course. Soon. We're just taking the air."

The man had heard them. He turned, but only briefly. Lizzie wondered who he imagined they were, what he imagined they were doing. A woman evinced her class in a variety of ways; Lizzie was good at reading the clues herself and assumed that she was also good at sending them. An unescorted woman could always be misunderstood, but surely the presence of a child conferred respectability. In any case, the man appeared uninterested.

It was very cold. Lizzie began to wish she'd sent Jenny straight back to bed. Why in the world hadn't she? She wished for a different place to go. She wished for lights and more people, or absolute dark and fewer.

"When I was just a little girl like you, you'd hear coyotes out here at night," Lizzie said. "The city hadn't come this far yet. I saw a horse race near this very spot with those big golden horses the Spanish had. It was Diego Estenegas's sixteenth birthday. We had *cascarones*. Do you know what *cascarones* are?"

"No."

"Eggshells filled with perfume and tinsel and flour. You break them over people's heads. Even my father came home streaked with flour."

"Why?"

"My father did business with the Estenegas family. He brokered their beef to local hotels. They were kind enough to include me in the invitation. It was a party."

Jenny sat down in the dirt. "Something's in my shoe," she said. She removed it.

Lizzie was forced to squat beside her. She took Jenny's shoe, shook out a thin stream of sand, like the drift in an hourglass. Lizzie had been to few enough parties as a child. Perhaps that was why this one remained so vivid. How could it be so long ago? She could see her mother, her hair falling from its pins, brandishing an eggshell, but that couldn't have happened, it must have been someone else's mother.

The Spanish women had been beautiful, with their bright dresses and diamond haircombs. Though some had married American husbands, few of the men had taken American wives. Were there really so many fewer Spanish families now, which was the way it seemed, or had the city simply filled in around them with Italians and Irish and Chinese? Diego Estenegas was like a prince and smiled once at Lizzie so she always remembered it.

Her father would have been furious with her if he'd known she was waiting for a Spanish prince. Her mother would have sent her to bed until she got over the idea. Because she'd managed to keep it a secret, she never had gotten over it.

"You might be Spanish, Jenny," Lizzie said, "what with your dark eyes and hair. ¿Hablas español?"

Jenny didn't answer. Lizzie replaced her shoe and picked her up. The man was gone. The ground was level again.

The sidewalk began on Octavia Street and ran beneath the blue-gum eucalyptus trees. Mary Ellen Pleasant had planted these herself, only a few years before, but they had grown quickly and were already tall by San Francisco standards. Mrs. Pleasant was rumored to use the bark and the seeds in her brews. Lizzie looked up the trunk to where the leaves hung, clustered and limp as Japanese wind chimes. The trees gave off the smell of unripened lemons.

Lizzie set Jenny down. The House of Mystery was dark, except for one window on the second floor. Its curtains were drawn, and glowed faintly with a backlight of gold. A dog barked in the distance;

Lizzie couldn't tell whether it was inside the house or out. "Have you ever been here?" Lizzie asked.

"No."

"I've been to tea here. You can't imagine how beautiful it is. You can't tell from the outside."

"Like a palace?" Jenny asked.

Lizzie had never been to a palace. "Inside, yes. Exactly like."

Suddenly, all around the quiet mansion with its homey golden window was the illusion of tumult. Clouds flew across the sky like enormous birds, making the moonlight blink on and off so the whole landscape flickered. The shadows of the trees scudded over the ground; the wind rattled the leaves.

In all that movement there was no person. Lizzie wouldn't have been surprised if there had been. Reporters sometimes flocked outside the House of Mystery, pigeons pecking for crumbs. Occasionally someone sneaked into the yard to dig for the diamond necklaces Mrs. Pleasant was rumored to have buried there.

Quite inexplicably, everything combined to unnerve Lizzie—the lack of people, the flying clouds, the witches'-brew smell, the single lit window, the Wilkie Collins book at home that she was halfway through. The string of women who'd been murdered on the streets of Whitechapel a year or so ago.

There was a thought Lizzie wished she hadn't had! She tried desperately to unthink it. Diego Estenegas smiling at her.

No good! The women were fed with poisoned grapes. Golden horses! Diamond haircombs! Diamond necklaces! Their hearts cut out as if they were voodoo chickens! Lizzie's breath was shallow and fast.

Jenny yawned and shivered. Lizzie picked her up and started back to the Ark, moving now as quickly as she could. On Bush Street they passed a pair of young men walking arm in arm. Lizzie heard their footsteps first and was relieved to see that there were two of them, and both apparently sober.

The men had almost passed before one of them spoke. "Are you an idiot?" he asked, in a tone no one had used with her since her father died. She turned to make sure he was addressing her and not his companion, and this allowed him to come too close. "Out here after dark with a child?" He was shaking his head. "What kind of a mother are you?"

The other man spoke next. "What kind of woman walks the streets at night? Is that what you want men to think?"

They were at least twenty years younger than she, and not so nicely dressed. She would not be chastised by boys. "How does it concern you?"

"We're compelled to see you safely home. It wasn't our plan for the evening."

"Nor is it my plan now."

"We don't want you," said Jenny.

"Go away," said Lizzie. She used her public-speaking voice and she expected to be obeyed. "You must see I wouldn't be here without a compelling reason. You must see that I wouldn't have brought this child out into the cold and dark, in the dead of winter, on a whim." There was an uneven place in the road. Lizzie stumbled.

One man offered his arm. One man offered to take Jenny.

Lizzie refused both offers. She carried Jenny without stopping, all the way to the edge of the Brown Ark's sandy yard, though her arms and back ached as a result. The men strolled beside her, smoking cigars and continuing a private conversation about a friend named Darby who'd recently fallen down a flight of stairs and yet was planning a balloon ascension. Lizzie tried twice more to send them off, but they were enjoying her embarrassment too much. It was highly likely that one, at least, had blue eyes, but Lizzie refused to permit either of them the dignity of being portentous. There'd be plenty more blue-eyed men to choose from, men she liked better. "When she turned in at the Ark, they finally left her, tipping their hats and congratulating themselves, no doubt, on their fine manners.

Lizzie was so angry her jaw hurt. She paused outside to remove Jenny's shoes and brush the sand from her stockings. "Let's not tell," she suggested. "Can you keep a secret?"

"Yes," said Jenny. Lizzie suspected she excelled at it.

"Of course, if they ask us right out, did you walk to Mrs. Pleasant's last night, we won't lie," Lizzie added. "You must never tell a lie, Jenny."

She led Jenny up the stairs to her cot, helped her undress and get into her nightgown. There was no movement or sound; the abandoned girls slept like princesses, each with a scuffed pair of shoes waiting by the bed.

Lizzie returned to the cupola, wishing for her bed at home. She could not get comfortable; she was not tired enough. Cold, anger, and the itchy settee kept her awake. Her first escapade, and nothing had come of it but her own ridiculous panic and the insults of chivalrous men. She had been laughed at in the public streets.

But by the morning she saw things quite differently. She had gotten away with it completely. Surely her impulsiveness could only improve. It just wanted practice.

4

BY MORNING LIZZIE was finally tired. She went home for a restorative nap. On the breakfast table, she found an invitation from the Putnams. "I'll watch over Lizzie until the day she weds," Mrs. Putnam had once promised Lizzie's mother, and she'd been as good as her word. Lizzie's mother was on her deathbed at the time, so the promise was a binding one. So many people watching over Lizzie! Of course, no one had imagined Lizzie's wedding day to be quite so far off as it was proving.

She slit the Putnams' invitation open with her father's marble-handled letter knife and read that she was to be included in an evening of inquiry, in Suite 540 at the Palace. Dr. Ellinwood, a medium visiting from Philadelphia, would host an informal discussion of spiritism and its compatibility with the tenets of Christianity. If the aspects were favorable, if the guests then desired it, Dr. Ellinwood was prepared to contact the dead. "Such an obliging man," Mrs. Putnam wrote, "for you can't imagine how exhausting Contact is."

And yet Lizzie could imagine this perfectly well. Lizzie didn't really want to talk to the dead. It was a difficult thing to say to the Putnams. It was a difficult thing to acknowledge even to herself. Her parents had loved her. They were entitled to be deeply missed. Lizzie didn't want to be present when they came back and discovered they were not.

Besides, she had gone to séances before, heard many a table rapped, been a link in many a magnetic chain. In her experience, the dead had surprisingly little of interest to say. It seemed to be all me, me, me, after you died.

And on the other hand, the Palace! Eight hundred rooms, seven floors, and an enormous amber skylight topping the whole. The opulent hotel had been built with the profits of the Comstock Lode supplemented by the embezzlement of the Bank of California. Leland Stanford was the first name on its guestbook, Charles Crocker the first to enter its dining room.

Only recently the gaslamps in the restaurant had been replaced with three hundred twenty electric lights. In the suites themselves, major improvements were rumored to have been made in the bathrooms. If a ladylike opportunity presented itself, Lizzie would like to see one of those bathrooms.

Plus, the Putnams were rich and charitable and would invite more of the same. Contact with the dead would put all present in mind of their immortal souls. It was the best possible setting in which to ask for money. The Brown Ark needed more beds, the children coats and shoes. In point of fact, Lizzie had a clear duty to attend.

The evening of inquiry took place on the very next Saturday. Outside, a chilly rain fell, and the Putnams had kindly offered their carriage. Lizzie paused to remove her gloves and pet Roscoe, the closest of the horses. She had driven Roscoe herself as a girl. Blind in one eye, so you had to use a single rein or he wandered to the wrong side of the road, but utterly unprovocable, with a gait like cream. The rain left shiny streaks on his coat. His neck was warm and wet on Lizzie's hand, and he steamed like a teakettle in the cold.

She climbed into the carriage and the comfortable heat of Mrs. Putnam. Mrs. Putnam was an ample woman, dressed against the cold in a fashionable sealskin sacque and a new black straw hat. "Erma's had her fourth. A little boy," Mrs. Putnam told Lizzie straight off, hugging her so tightly she left the scent of almond soap on her sleeves. Erma was the Putnams' only child, and everyone imagined Lizzie was fond of her. Certainly they'd played together often as children. But since Erma had married and moved to Sacramento more than fifteen years before, Lizzie had hardly seen her.

"Six and a half pounds. Little Charlie John. The mother blooming. Father bursting with pride."

"Never you mind, now, Lizzie," Mr. Putnam said, when Lizzie didn't mind in the least. Any marriage that necessitated a move to Sacramento was nothing to envy.

Mrs. Mullin was seated opposite Lizzie. She was a gaunt woman with dark, deep-set eyes; it was hard to look at her face without imagining her skull. Her hat was more opulent but less smart than Mrs. Putnam's. Emerald wings spread over the crown as if her hair were a nest on which a headless bird brooded. "We'll see you with your own babies yet," she told Lizzie.

"I have sixty-two babies at present." Lizzie kept her tone light.

"That's the way to look at it," Mr. Putnam said. He turned to his wife. "Our Lizzie has sixty-two babies!"

Lizzie didn't often mind not being married. She'd had offers. Few women in San Francisco went entirely uncourted, and none of those had yellow hair and financial prospects. Dr. Beecher, a friend of her father's, had taken a fancy to her when she was just a girl. Strange how people would think better of her now if she'd only accepted him then, and him a man with a coarse manner, who smelled of brine, but dirty, and who stared at her as though she were something to be killed and eaten. Cats fled when Dr. Beecher entered a room.

Even now, her father's fury over her refusal was an awful thing to remember. She'd spent five whole weeks confined to her bedroom under Baby Edward's reproachful eyes, and she suspected her mother had sent her there for protection as much as punishment. In the ten years between her mother's death and her father's, Lizzie learnt what a shield her mother had been.

But even in the midst of his rage, Lizzie had never reconsidered. And she hadn't known about copulation then; she'd merely wished to avoid dining at one end of a table with Dr. Beecher at the other. He was still alive, and some girl even younger than Lizzie had married him. She couldn't bear to think of it.

When she was in her thirties, Lizzie's body had developed a pronounced restlessness, a physical ache that was bone-deep and could manifest at any moment, from any cause. This was unsettling, but it wasn't her, of course, only her body. She didn't even know what was wanted; it might have nothing at all to do with men. When the feeling hit too hard, she dosed herself with baths and novels. She was in love with the men in books and particularly with the men in books written by women. She liked to describe herself as a passionate reader, knowing no one would take her full meaning.

The only thing she minded about not being married was how everyone knew. If she could have passed as widowed, there would have been little else to regret. She was not pitied by her friends so much as criticized. In San Francisco, demographics being what they were, an unmarried woman was looked upon as the most selfish of creatures.

Lizzie disliked being thought selfish, mainly because it was so likely true. She lacked the gift for intimacy. "The real woman regards all men, be they older or younger than herself, not as possible lovers, but as sort of stepsons toward whom her heart goes out in motherly tenderness," Lizzie had recently read. Where in the world was her own motherly tenderness? All spent on the characters in books.

"What if none of us married!" her mother had said in a voice like scratched glass at the time of Lizzie's second refusal. The new suitor was Paul Burbank, a quiet, clean law clerk whose main demerits were that saliva puddled whitely at the corners of his mouth when he talked and that he didn't seem actually to like Lizzie. She'd found him at the other end of her tangled string during the cobweb ball marking Erma Putnam's debut. She'd seen his face as she wound her way toward him, seen the moment he realized she was his partner for the evening, and he hadn't been pleased. Even when he'd proposed, he'd acted as though he had no choice in the matter. "What if we all thought only of ourselves and our own pleasures?" her mother asked.

This sentiment was echoed often enough in the daily press. A generation before, America's sons had perished in inconceivable numbers, in inconceivable agony, on the battlefields of the Civil War. Such a contrast to America's spoiled, selfish daughters. And them wanting the vote, some of them, likely the very ones with no children wanting it the loudest of all!

"I wash my hands of you," her father said at the time of her third refusal—Christopher Ludlow, an irritable flautist—but it turned out he'd washed more than that.

After her father's death, Mr. Griswold, the family solicitor, was too embarrassed to read his will aloud to Lizzie. They sat in her father's office with the smell of bourbon and cigars still hanging in the air. "There's a monthly allowance," Mr. Griswold said merely.

"With stipulations. I want you to know I strongly advised against them." He passed the pages to her.

"I fear my estate," her father had written, "will make my daughter the target of fortune hunters. Elizabeth wouldn't marry while I was alive and wished it. I won't have her marrying on her own authority after my death.

"Old women are even more foolish than young ones. Let her live to be a hundred, these conditions will not change. On her wedding day all monies to her instantly cease."

"I'm willing to contest the terms," Mr. Griswold offered, "should an attractive offer of marriage ever be made." Lizzie was at this time already thirty-seven years old, and his tone suggested the unlikeliness of further proposals. She agreed that no legal redress was necessary. Contesting the will might suggest she wished to be married; it would make her publicly ridiculous. She'd told herself that she didn't even want money given so grudgingly, which made her feel very high-minded, like the heroine of a romance, but now she often thought it would have also been romantic to be wealthy. She would have made her own donations to the running of the Ark instead of having constantly to beg them from others.

The carriage rocked. The sounds of the horses' hooves and the rain were wonderfully steadying. Lizzie's necklace danced in the space between her breasts; she caught it in her hand. No one raised money for charity by sulking, she reminded herself. She contrived to brighten her voice. "Sixty-two babies is more beds than the Home can offer. The need always grows so much faster than the treasury. . . ."

No one was listening. "Little Charlie John"—Mrs. Mullin threaded her knobby fingers together—"I long to see him!" while Mr. Putnam fussed aloud that the weather might worsen during the evening. "I mind for the sake of the horses," he said. "I fear for poor old Roscoe's footing."

Lizzie did not press. She sat quietly, biding her time, bouncing when the carriage bounced and listening to talk of late rains in earlier years and how the roses and heliotrope had not been pruned as they should be in the fall, so there would be the very devil to pay for it soon, and that six and a half pounds was neither so very large for a baby nor so very small, but was, in fact, just right, until the driver turned into the circular driveway of the Palace.

The courtyard was heated by enormous bronze braziers and covered with the dome of the amber skylight seven floors above them. Every balcony was lit; the hotel glowed like a birthday cake.

A huge hydraulic elevator took them to the fifth floor. From there they looked down on the Grand Court, with its splendor of Persian rugs, purple tablecloths, the flickering rose and gold of women's fans, the sharp black of men's evening coats, the bronze of the spittoons.

"San Francisco will not be civilized until the men stop spitting indoors," someone famous had said, but Lizzie didn't remember who. In any case, he was surely mistaken, because tonight the spittoons were dazzling in the hot civilized glare of electricity.

Lizzie had only the vaguest notion what electricity was. Lightning, she thought, collected and tamed somehow, broken to harness and spread throughout the room as evenly as melted butter. But there was something about the view that was not quite right tonight; something besides the lighting was different, only Lizzie couldn't determine what it was. She gave up trying and followed the Putnams down the corridor.

Suite 540 had high ceilings, bay windows, and Louis XV chairs. On one wall was a landscape of Yosemite, Half Dome at sunrise,

with a tiny party of mules at its base. Dr. Ellinwood stood at the door
to greet them.

He was a small man, smooth-faced, pink-skinned. His hair was
the color of goose feathers, and something of the same consistency.
His ears were large and round. His eyes, Lizzie noted, were brown.
"I'm so glad you could join us in our little adventure," he said. "Mrs.
Mullin, what a stunning hat!"

Lizzie was sorry to see Myrtle Rolphe across the room. Miss
Rolphe ran a Christian school in Chinatown and was universally
admired for it. Undoubtedly she also was there for money.

Sure enough, Miss Rolphe addressed the Putnam party first thing.
"May I talk to you about one of my boys?" Her hands clasped and
unclasped with charming earnestness as she spoke, and her voice had
a throaty sweetness. Such an unfair advantage! If Lizzie could have
duplicated it, she would have. "Eleven years old," said Miss Rolphe.
"The brightest, sweetest child you'll ever see. And so eager to come
to Jesus. His name is Ti Wong."

"He's lucky to have you," Mr. Putnam said encouragingly. "This
young Mr. Ti. Whatever you're up against, you'll win through." Mr.
Putnam was the sort of gentleman who felt obliged to flirt with any
woman, but Myrtle Rolphe was especially flirtable—young, given to
blushes, with a neck as white as a meringue.

"The forces arrayed against me are all of China!" she answered,
her throat quivering like a wren's. "Wong is an orphan who lives
with his aunt and uncle. He first came to us four years ago. I never
saw a child so young so determined to belong to Jesus. His eyes when
he sings! Then all of a sudden his uncle withdrew him. He told me he
wanted no Jesus boy in the house."

Dr. Ellinwood was requesting their attention. Miss Rolphe
acknowledged this by lowering her voice. "Last week I happened to

see Ti Wong again. He's very troubled. His uncle demands that he participate in ancestor worship. If we don't find a way to remove him from the company of other Chinese, Jesus will lose him forever."

"Please!" said Dr. Ellinwood. His voice was loud and firm, though he was smiling good-naturedly. "Please come and sit."

"Do you think he might work at the Brown Ark?" Miss Rolphe asked Lizzie. "He so needs to be with other Christians."

"I'd have to ask," said Lizzie, fully aware that Nell would say no. "Eleven years old, but he works like an adult."

"Let's not keep the dead waiting, ladies!" Dr. Ellinwood said pleadingly, when surely, of all people, the dead had time.

The chairs were arranged in a semicircle, at whose mouth stood a large cabinet with a glass door. This cabinet was open at the top and bottom, like a sentry box on wheels. A curtain of black velvet fell behind the glass. Dr. Ellinwood draped a cloak, also black velvet, over his shoulders. The cloak was lined with purple silk and had the signs of the zodiac embroidered in gold. The effect of this on Dr. Ellinwood was comical, a Christmas elf on All Hallows' Eve.

He then led a discussion on the compatibility of religion and science. Lizzie had no qualms herself on this score. She had a great interest in the Higher Criticism, through which the sources of biblical narratives were scientifically examined. She felt that such activities could only strengthen one's faith, by demonstrating the reliability of its origins; to object, as many in the church did, seemed to Lizzie to suggest a troubling doubt as to the findings. The God that Lizzie believed in was not the sort to set such traps for the faithful.

This evening's discussion came quickly to the same conclusion— although spiritism had had early, unfortunate associations with free love, it had long before outgrown and discarded them. A scientifi-cally conducted dialogue with the dead could only, ultimately, reflect the Glory of God. Dr. Ellinwood invoked the name of Eilley Orrum several times during the discussion; apparently he was personally acquainted with the celebrated Washoe seeress. He contrived to give the impression that she wholeheartedly endorsed him as a fellow traveler in the realm of the occult. The whole thing took less than an hour, and then they were free to proceed.

Mrs. Putnam read aloud from Elizabeth Stuart Phelps's *Songs of the Silent World:*

> *"Death is a mood of life. It is no whim*
> *By which life's Giver mocks a broken heart.*
> *Death is life's reticence. Still audible to Him*
> *the hushed voice, happy, speaketh on apart…"*

while Dr. Ellinwood invited Myrtle Rolphe to tie his hands. He took a seat in the cabinet and allowed Mrs. Putnam to tie his ankles. "If everyone will please take the hand of the person next," the fettered Dr. Ellinwood then said, "right hands on left wrists, all around the circle."

He sent one of his agents to draw the curtains and put out the lights. The room vanished into utter black.

Miss Rolphe held Lizzie's wrist, and Lizzie held Mrs. Mullin's. Miss Rolphe's fingers were soft. Mrs. Mullin's wrist was cold and dry as wood, but pulsed forcefully. "I need everyone's absolute concentration now," Dr. Ellinwood told them. "Please shut out everything else." Lizzie heard the cabinet door open and close.

She expected an artful period of prolonged tension, but Dr. Ellinwood sacrificed drama for efficiency. The knocking began almost at once. Then an unfamiliar voice whispered into the silence. "Who has come here tonight? Who wishes something from someone on the other side?" Miss Rolphe's fingers fluttered over Lizzie's wrist.

The voice did not sound like Dr. Ellinwood, but Lizzie had no doubt that was who it was. Why else put the lights out? She couldn't even see the shapes of the women on either side of her, although she could hear each time Mrs. Mullin exhaled. The wind sent the rain against the window with a sound like the tapping of fingernails. Ordinarily such a sound would have made Lizzie feel warm, cozy, sheltered. Tonight it made her skin inch up the back of her neck. Mrs. Mullin's pulse throbbed against her fingertips as if trapped there.

"Please," said the voice. "I've come such a long way. Someone must need to communicate."

"Is my Aunt Rose there?" Miss Rolphe asked quietly. "I'd love to speak to Rose Schubert."

Rose was indeed present. She told them how peaceful it was to be dead. "Like sleeping in your mother's arms again." She and Miss Rolphe exchanged some family gossip; she told Miss Rolphe to be especially careful on the night of the nineteenth. More departed relatives were called. There were mysterious footsteps. A strong scent of roses. The usual rappings. The sleep-inducing darkness and the whispers of the dead.

Lizzie's attention began to stray. She suddenly realized what was wrong with the view of the Grand Court. All the waiters in the restaurant were white. The Palace was famous for its Negro waiters. She heard her parents' names.

"Harriet?" Mrs. Putnam was asking. "Harriet or Wellington Hayes? Are you there, my dears?"

Lizzie supposed Dr. Ellinwood had spent the afternoon cadging information about the Hayes family from the unsuspecting Putnams. The idea annoyed her. She dropped Mrs. Mullin's hand, deliberately breaking the magnetic chain, but Mrs. Mullin's sharp fingers closed over hers like a cat's paw on a bird's wing.

"We have your Lizzie here," said Mrs. Mullin. Her words resounded loudly in the absolute darkness. "Harriet?"

"Lizzie?" A tiny, sleepy, faraway voice came from behind. "Is it Lizzie?"

"Speak up, dear." Mrs. Mullin squeezed Lizzie's hand. "Your mother is asking for you."

"Yes, Mother," said Lizzie. Mrs. Mullin's nails dug into her skin. "I'm sitting right here."

"Oh, Lizzie. Your father says to tell you we miss you. And our darling Edward. He loves you very much."

"I love you, too."

"We're all watching over you now!"

Lizzie had never doubted it. "Thank you, Mother." She thought to provide a distraction. "Mrs. Mullin is here."

"But Lizzie, you have us so anxious."

"And the Putnams. Your dear, dear friends."

"Why do you put us through this worry? You were always so dependable. What's come over you?" The voice was beginning to sound like her mother's, after all. It had her mother's disappointed, unsurprised tone. It came closer, spoke in her ear. Lizzie thought she could have touched it, if Mrs. Mullin and Miss Rolphe weren't holding her hands so resolutely. Everything Miss Rolphe did was resolutely done. There was no reason for Lizzie to find this irritating. Miss Rolphe was a thoroughly admirable young woman.

Lizzie's corset was cutting off her air. Mrs. Mullin's grip was cutting off her circulation. Lizzie's fingertips began to throb. "Mother, I'm the treasurer for a charitable home. I'm quite good at it. I have sixty-two wards at present." The wind whined outside. Something scraped against the window.

"You're our only living child. We should be at peace. You never used to behave this way."

"What way? What have I done?" This was rash, and Lizzie immediately wished she could retract it. She was letting the mere semblance of her mother get to her, and in front of everyone, too. But even as she told herself to calm down, she felt her agitation growing.

"Stay away from Mammy Pleasant."

Lizzie shook abruptly free of Myrtle. "Don't tell me what to do, Mother!" she said. Her voice was loud and angry and unlike her voice.

Never before had she spoken that way to her mother in public. There was a stunned pause and then a shaft of light, as if someone had opened the door into the corridor. A gust hit the window like an explosion. The glass of the cabinet shivered and cracked into a spider web of fissures. Through the glass, a multitude of green hands and staring faces could be seen. They seemed to slide through the cracks, evaporating immediately, flattened and bleached, into the material world.

5

IT TOOK AN ENTIRE GLASS of sour wine to calm Lizzie down. Everyone was looking at her, and she hated this above all things. Her corset was sawing her in half. She had the ghosts of ghosts burning in orange afterimages under her eyelids, which could easily bring on a headache, and she would blame Dr. Ellinwood if she got one, for all the good that would do.

Dr. Ellinwood hovered, rubbing his wrists where the bonds had been, to emphasize their tightness. "Obviously I unleashed something I couldn't control," he told the group. "I blame myself. Galling the dead is not a party game." He apologized to them all, just as if he hadn't orchestrated the entire catastrophe.

Which, of course, he had. From the other side of the wine, Lizzie could see that her mother had not come back, certainly not. Was Lizzie the only one who'd read that Margaret Fox, the most famous of the American table-rappers, had admitted to fraud? Lizzie didn't know how Dr. Ellinwood performed his illusions, but that was no reason to credit them. Surely the dead led lives of more dignity than this feeble, grasping, greenish manifesting.

Mrs. Mullin raised her voice. "Dr. Ellinwood? Do you think the dead can still tell lies?"

"They can indeed," he assured her. "But they have no reason to."
Which was, Lizzie thought, practically an admission of guilt.

She herself regretted nothing. She wished only that she'd been
louder and ruder. In the category of small mercies, at least there'd
been no ectoplasm.

Half an hour later Lizzie was safely back in the carriage and clattering
out of the Palace courtyard. The rain was falling harder and colder.
The streetlamps shone in the damp, soft and rainbowed like bubbles.
On Mrs. Putnam's instructions, the driver was urging the horses to
hurry—at Roscoe's age! with the road so wet!—and Lizzie couldn't
help feeling guilty about this. Roscoe himself could scarcely believe
it. He would take a quick pace or two, then slow until whipped, then
take another quick pace, then slow again. His obstinacy was affecting
the other horse. The carriage rocked like a train, bumped like a boat.

Rain was too ordinary in San Francisco to spoil a Saturday night.
The streets were brightly lit. Sheltered under canopies and alcoves,
bands played bravely along their route—ecstatic polkas and somber
Salvation Army hymns. The carriage passed phrenologists and
shooting galleries and the Snake Drugstore, with rattlers coiled in its
windows. Revolutionaries shouted from the steps of jewelry stores,
salesmen offered the afflicted the revivifying powers of aconite,
tiger fat, and belts stuffed with cayenne pepper. The *nymphes du
pavé* beckoned from beneath umbrellas, their smiles wet, scarlet, and
practiced.

Mrs. Putnam was not speaking to her. Lizzie was clearly meant
to feel guilty about this as well, but the impact was lessened by
Mr. Putnam's need to fill any silence with labored gallantries. He
was a naturally garrulous man; now he also appeared to be drunk.

Mr. Putnam noted that Mrs. Mullin's shawl was as good as Italian, that Lizzie's color was attractively up. He observed his own good fortune in being the only man among three such elegant ladies. He informed them that the king of Hawaii, Kalakaua, was staying at the Palace. The livery boy had said so when he brought the carriage around. "They say he is very ill." Mr. Putnam's voice was serious and subdued. "Might die." Rain plonked on the fabric roof of the carriage, slid down the glass windows.

"Surely not," Lizzie answered politely, although how did she know? She imagined the stretched green dead people dispersing throughout the Palace, inhaled out of one room and exhaled into another through the pneumatic tubes. She couldn't imagine this would improve the king's chances.

"Death comes to king and commoner alike," Mr. Putnam intoned. He shook his head sadly.

And what if it didn't? People always said things like that as if it were such a shame, but how much more of a shame would it be if death were selective? A brougham crossed them on the left. The driver sat, hunched in a thick wool coat, rain dripping from the brim of his hat onto his hands. A gray horse shook rainwater from its mane. The brougham's windows were draped, but twitched briefly as they passed. Lizzie had a quick glimpse of a woman's eyes in a veiled face.

"In Hawaii, they admire a dark skin," Mrs. Mullin said. "They see it as a mark of royal blood. The king is very dark."

"In Hawaii they admire a stout figure," Mr. Putnam said. "Not merely stout. Actually fat." Mr. Putnam was himself a remarkably thin man.

"I just this moment remembered." Mrs. Mullin was seated next to Lizzie, opposite Mrs. Putnam. She leaned forward as the carriage wheel hit a hole, and the broody, headless wings on her hat jumped in an unpleasant parody of flight. "You were there at the ball the night Mammy Pleasant turned colored."

Mrs. Putnam nodded once, a sharp, brief nod. Her face was turned away toward the street. The hair around her ears bobbed gently; the feather in her hat shook. In fact, she was atremble from head to toe. It was the carriage making her so. That, and the angry stiffness of her spine, a forced rigidity adding much to her bouncing.

The real cause, of course, was Lizzie's insulting behavior. Mrs. Putnam believed that mothers and the dead should be treated with the utmost deference. Rudeness to one's mother when she was also dead was beyond the beyond.

"Oh, yes," said Mr. Putnam. "Yes, indeed. Everyone was there. Mr. Ralston. Senator Sharon. Mr. Bell. Of course, they were young men, they were no one important yet. They were just like us. And all of them lining up to dance with her. She was a looker. No one called her Mammy that night."

"And her not nearly as young as everyone thought, neither," Mrs. Mullin noted.

Mrs. Putnam directed herself strictly to Mrs. Mullin; Lizzie was still only getting the profile. "And out of the blue, she just says it. I'm a colored woman, she says. I thought it was a joke, when I first heard about it. More and more people from the South were arriving then, with the war coming, so she must have known she'd be exposed. People from the South, they know what to look for."

"Once you were told, it was obvious," said Mr. Putnam. "She was dark. We all knew she was Spanish or something. But Ralston, Sharon, Bell, and her, they were great friends even after. They all got rich together."

"Nothing more needs be said on the subject." Mrs. Putnam shook her head, then continued. "There were so few respectable women in the city back then. No one maintaining standards. Vigilantes and hoodlums roaming the streets, vying with each other to see who could make the most misery for the most people. But those days are past and in the past may stay."

Roscoe had settled back into his usual pace with his usual roll. The ride had smoothed accordingly. The sounds of the rain on the fabric roof, of hooves and wheels on pavement, the warmth of the Putnams' lap robes, the smell of perfume and horsehair, and the wine she had taken medicinally combined to make Lizzie sleepy. She closed her eyes and let the conversation float over her. She'd heard about rough San Francisco all her life; she even remembered a bit of it. This and the sleepiness made her feel young as a girl.

"And then there was that business with Mrs. Bell," said Mrs. Putnam. Lizzie opened her eyes. "People have all but forgot about that. He's living on Bush Street, like a bachelor. She's over on Sutter with two of his children and calling herself Mrs. Percy. One minute the papers say they're married, the next, not. She vanishes for months, and Mrs. Pleasant hires the Pinks to track her down. And then Mrs. Pleasant up and invites everyone to a wedding party as if all is right as rain. With Thomas Bell still denying he's a married man."

"Were you invited to that as well?" asked Mrs. Mullin.

"I wouldn't have gone," said Mrs. Putnam, and no doubt she wouldn't have, though this clearly meant no.

The carriage swung slightly, following the curve of Mission Street. They were leaving the lamps of the downtown, heading into darkness. Lizzie covered a yawn with her hand. "What happened to the Palace's Negro waiters?" she asked.

"Fired," Mrs. Mullin told her. "Just this week. One of them was caught filching food from the kitchen, so Morgan fired the lot of them. You see how old and toothless Mrs. Pleasant has become since the Sharon business. No one would have dared do that to the colored when she was younger. She's always been a great one for the courts."

"Oh, Lizzie." Mrs. Putnam turned and seized Lizzie's hands, shaking her fully awake. Her face shone in the carriage, dim and yellowed by the black hat and deeply creased, pocked as the moon. She was a decade younger than Mrs. Pleasant, but she looked a decade older. "I have nothing against the hardworking colored. You know I believe in judging people by their hearts. But you don't know how treacherous she can be. Will you promise me not to see her? For your dear, dear mother's sake?"

When Lizzie was fifty instead of forty, she would still be a child to the Putnams. She didn't mind; it was one of the things she loved about them. Nobody else could make her feel young now that she so definitely wasn't.

One afternoon when Lizzie was twelve, and Erma seven, they'd begged to eat their supper on the Putnams' back lawn. They were playing castaways, they were playing Robinson Crusoe—Lizzie's idea, of course; this was a book she'd been allowed to read early, all except for the chapter with the pirates. "You'll break a dish," Mrs. Putnam protested, and they promised to be ever so careful.

"We'll make maps," Lizzie said, getting overexcited as usual, and then, racing into the house for pencils, she stepped on the pink rosebuds of her dirty plate, heard it crack, and ran home without another word to anyone, before Erma even knew. An hour or so later, Mrs. Putnam appeared in her room. "I hope the day never comes when I care more for a dish than for a little girl," Mrs. Putnam said. She didn't even tell Lizzie's mother. How could Lizzie ever bear to refuse her anything?

She opened her mouth to accede. In that moment she saw,

through her left eye, the tiny disturbance in the air, the silver flash that presaged a headache. The emerald wings on Mrs. Mullin's hat hung like a hawk. There was a gummy silence within the carriage; without it, the mounting drumbeat of rain and hooves. She closed her mouth in a panic. Her vision improved immediately.

"Do you know what voodoo is?" Mrs. Mullin swayed in the carriage and her voice became a whisper. "What it *really* is? Black arts aimed at the destruction of the white race.

"You don't believe in magic, do you, Mrs. Mullin? Hocus-pocus? Habeas corpus?" Mr. Putnam shifted in his seat so as to engage Lizzie's eyes, involve her in the joke.

"I believe in malice. As if you or I or poor, fanciful, inconsequential little Lizzie could ever do Mammy Pleasant a speck of harm."

Lizzie's eyesight had normalized, but her breathing had not. Her voice was oddly tilted. "She came to the Brown Ark on business," she told Mrs. Putnam. "I don't expect her back, but I can't promise not to see her on business. I have to do whatever's best for the children." She touched her hands together to reassure herself that they were both warm. She pressed her fingers to her forehead.

"Her business is just what I want you kept out of," Mrs. Putnam said.

Lizzie lowered her hands and saw Mrs. Mullin patting Mrs. Putnam's knee. "Lizzie's not her usual type," Mrs. Mullin said. Mrs. Pleasant's usual type was a fragile beauty like Mrs. Bell.

"Lizzie is being very obstinate," Mrs. Putnam complained.

"Lizzie looks very handsome this evening," Mr. Putnam observed without looking at her. "I have spent the evening with three very handsome ladies."

"Are you getting one of your headaches, dear?" Mrs. Putnam asked.

"No," Lizzie said cautiously. It appeared not. She began to feel the charged, sweet heat of relief rising inside her.

"She was the most wonderful cook," Mr. Putnam said. All three women turned to look at him. He raised his hands in protest. "I was never at her table, myself. But everyone says. Cajun crab cakes and candied figs. Wine jellies. Caraway cheese. Dishes from the South."

And then Roscoe stopped, because Lizzie was home. She looked through the rain to her dark, cold house. A woman who had just released a quantity of dead people, including her own angry mother, into the city should probably not sleep alone. E.D.E.N. Southworth's *The Hidden Hand* lay on her bedstead, a popular, feverish book, and she was just up to the chapter where robbers hid themselves under little Capitola's bed.

Mr. Putnam prepared to help her down. Outside the carriage she heard Roscoe shake himself. She did the mental equivalent. Nonsense, she told herself firmly.

There was no room under her bed for a pack of robbers.

The green people were a fraud and an illusion.

And anyway, her mother's spirit, if it was loose at all, was at the Palace Hotel and surely happy. The Palace would be her mother's idea of heaven, especially if there was also a king dying there.

Teresa Bell

1

WHATEVER COMPLAINTS LIZZIE may have had concerning her mother were slight compared with Teresa Bell's complaints regarding hers. Teresa Bell was obsessed. She referred to her mother often in conversation and, late in her life, wrote two similar accounts of their relationship. One of these she sent to the physician who attended her in her final years. The other formed the heart of her Last Will and Testament. Teresa Bell died in 1923.

Her maternal grandfather was one Colonel Nathaniel Tibbals. Colonel Tibbals distinguished himself during the Revolutionary War and was given, for his services, a parcel of land in Auburn, New York. He married Sarah Lydia Ward, one of a family of celebrated Kentucky beauties, and together they raised four healthy children.

The youngest was the youngest by far, and her father, rather an elderly man by the time she was born, doted most upon her. She had her own harp, her own pony, and she knew her own mind. Her name was Elmina Caroline, and her father would hear nothing against her. He died when she was only eleven.

Some years later Elmina married Wessel Harris. She brought six hundred acres of farmland to the marriage, as well as her own considerable beauty; he thought himself the luckiest man in the world. He kissed his bride and commenced his living happily ever after.

But in the next years he faced the inexplicable loss of his first two children. Both of them boys, they were full-weight, pink-cheeked, active babies. Labor and births unremarkable. Yet neither lived to see four months. When a third child was born, a pretty girl who favored her mother, with eyes like cornflowers and hair like cornsilk, Elmina refused even to hold her. Before the child was three months old, her father came home to find her stripped to the skin and set outside on a windowsill, sobbing her heart out in the soaking rain.

Wessel wrapped the baby warmly in an old, soft undershirt, tucked her inside his coat, and walked off in the storm. Five miles away lived the family of a bricklayer named John Clingan. The Clingans had recently lost their middle daughter, Matilda. Wessel Harris gave his baby to the Clingan family, and she remained with them for many years.

She was visited often by her grandmother Tibbals, her father, and even occasionally by her mother. One day her mother arrived alone. She took the child to play in a creek that ran through the Clingans' lot. The girl made a pile of wet silvery rocks. Elmina removed her own shoes and stockings and tucked up her skirt. She knelt and splashed her face with water while her hair tumbled down. She looked like a wild creature, a doe, a naiad.

"Come here," she told her daughter. "Come see the crawdad hiding in this pool here."

"I hear voices in the wind," the little girl confessed. She went to meet her mother's outstretched hand.

"What do the voices tell you?" Elmina asked.

The little girl didn't like to say, since the voices were telling her to run away. She felt her mother's damp fingers moving down her cheek to her shoulder. "Just my name," the little girl said. She really did hear her name.

"Kneel down here so you can look." Her mother's hand moved from her shoulder to the back of her neck. "Lean forward."

The little girl knelt with her face nearly touching the water. She saw how the surface twitched with waterbugs, how big and shivery the rocks looked. She thought she saw the crawdad's claws under one of those rocks. "Run while you can," the wind whispered. "Run away, Teresa. Teresa."

"Teresa! There you are!" her grandmother Tibbals said. She was out of breath and gulping like a fish. She came down the bank, sliding in her haste, losing her footing. "You're wanted back at the house." She pulled the child from Elmina's hands.

"Yes," Elmina said. She gathered her dripping hair together, twisted it so the water streamed down her arms. "You run along now, dear, since Mrs. Clingan needs you so immediately."

The Clingans may have been a hasty choice. Mrs. Clingan was a drunken, abusive mother. Mr. Clingan was a cardplayer who lost more than he won. There were two daughters in the family already— Mary Jane, who was six years older than Teresa, and Kate, who was four years older. "I know why you live with us," Kate said one day when Teresa was seven years old. Kate had light brown hair and a fat face.

"She's not to say." Mary Jane shook her head. "You're not to say," she told Kate.

"I didn't say I'd tell. I just said I know." Kate leaned toward Teresa, her lips pinched together so the words wouldn't pop out inadvertently.

Mary Jane dropped a hint. "It's the same reason your mother can't visit you alone."

"It's because she wants to kill you," Kate said. "Just like she killed your brothers."

This was instantly plausible. Wasn't Mrs. Clingan always saying, I'll kill you if you can't be quiet? I'll kill you if those dishes aren't washed when I get home? "Just like *your* mother," Teresa said, understanding, and the two girls looked at her with suddenly angry mouths and waspish little eyes.

"No," they told her.

"It's not anything at all like," said Kate.

In Teresa's will she refers to the Clingans as a bogus crew who may try to claim a blood relationship to her. She singles out Kate in particular as one of the vilest characters on earth, who once "even tried to claim that my father Wessel Harris begot me with the aid of her mother. Wessel was my father and her mother was my mother, so she said."

"Well, someone needs to tell you," Kate finished. "Because now your mother's run off and no one knows where she is or what she's up to. I'd be plenty scared if I was you."

The wind told Teresa to leave the horrible Clingans, to run away to the creek, but now she could hear that it spoke in her mother's voice, and she was too frightened to obey it ever again. She didn't leave the house for several days, and she didn't see Elmina for many years.

Mr. Clingan died. A neighbor turned the family in to the county and they were all shipped off to the county farm. Teresa went, too, her father and grandmother apparently unable or unwilling to intervene. From the farm the children were fostered out to separate homes. Teresa was now twelve.

"That I live is a wonder," Teresa wrote later in a letter to her doctor. "But that my soul lives is a still greater wonder." Describing herself at age twelve, she says she was "proud, sensitive, and refined clear beyond her years," with a delicacy of perception and a purity of soul. These things she attributed entirely to her father, Wessel Harris. Blood will tell, she often liked to say. We cannot know which of these qualities—the delicacy or the purity—first attracted the attention of a young man like James Percy.

Mr. Percy came calling when she was seventeen. He sat with Teresa in the parlor of a shabby boardinghouse that catered mostly to immigrants. The most intimate business could be conducted in that parlor, and if the conversation was in English, one's privacy was complete. James Percy's business with Teresa was of the most intimate sort. "I want to tell you everything I see in your eyes," he was saying. "I can read your fortune in them if you'll only look at me."

And then he suddenly stood. Teresa turned to see why, and there was Elmina, faintly reflected in the cracked glass of the parlor doors, in an expensive lilac dress. She didn't seem to have aged a minute, but then the parlor was a dim room, no good for sewing or reading whatever the time of day. Elmina entered and sat on a dirty chair, her skirt billowing in a lilac froth about her legs. "Aren't you pretty?" she said to Teresa. "Could I have just a moment alone with you, dear? If the gentleman will kindly excuse us?"

Teresa caught James's hand. "Don't go," she said, and he sat again.

"Which of us is the prettier, do you think?" Elmina asked him. She was flirting, in her costly dress, with her hair coiled about her head like a snake. Teresa might have been in rags by comparison.

"I couldn't possibly choose," James said, "when faced with two such beautiful women."

"Now you're teasing me. Though there are those think I've held up rather well for such an old lady, I won't deny it. But beauty can't last forever. That's why a woman wants children. So her beauty will survive her. It pleases a beautiful woman to have a beautiful daughter."

"You must be very pleased."

"Teresa is my only living child," Elmina said. "Naturally I'm proud of her."

It wasn't until Elmina left that Teresa realized she was still allowing James to hold her hand. He tried to kiss her then, because that was the idea her fingers had given him. That night Teresa blocked her door with a chair and kept her window closed.

The next day Kate Clingan drove by. She was a swollen tick of a woman but, even so, already married, and really her name now was Kate Gray. "Your father has died," she said. She didn't even get out of the wagon to say this. "He left six hundred acres of land and he left it to you instead of your mother. It only goes to Elmina if you die before she does. I thought you should know. I thought you should know she was there when they read the will and she said it was her land from her father, not your land from yours."

Teresa left New York hastily at the age of seventeen and in the company of James Percy. She arrived in San Francisco when she was twenty-three. She was calling herself Mrs. Percy in 1870 when Mary Ellen Pleasant first met her, although James was by then in San Quentin. He'd been caught robbing drunken farmboys in the bars of the Barbary Coast.

Teresa had asked the Bank of California for a loan to see her past this drop in income. On the application was a space for her maiden name, in which she wrote "Clingan," and a space for her mother's name, in which she wrote simply the word "mother."

Mary Ellen Pleasant thought her very lovely and very sad. "I own six hundred acres in New York," Teresa told her coolly. She was wearing a patched dress, a glass brooch, and shoes that didn't quite fit.

It must be noted that extensive rebuttal for all the above was supplied over the years in which Teresa Bell's estate was contested. Both Mary Jane and Kate testified that Teresa was their sister, the youngest daughter of John and Bridget Clingan. Their contention was supported by baptismal records.

Their mother was a drunk, but had never tried to kill anyone, they said. Teresa went to live with Wessel Harris and his wife, Elmina, when she was fostered off the county farm. He was no blood relation and he never did adopt her. Any land he might have owned was certainly not left to her.

> *Perhaps in some one great heroic act*
> *The soul its own redemption may attract*
> *And thus from sin and shame swift fly*
> *Made fit and ready to meet the Eternal eye*
> *Ah, to live until all is dead within us*
> *But ambition and that live to mock us!* *

---

* Opening to Teresa Bell's Last Will and Testament.

2

ACCORDING TO OFFICIAL POLICY, abandoned girls could remain as wards at the Ladies' Relief and Protection Society Home until they were sixteen or, in special cases, even older, but boys weren't kept much past their twelfth birthdays. After this age, the danger of hoodlumism was seen to increase sharply.

In the winter of 1890, truancy was all the fashion; the boys had to be continually hunted down and punished. Lizzie had never seen such a season for starvation and isolation and paddlings, but no penalty proved a deterrent. The draw was the Presidio and the sight of soldiers marching back and forth on Van Ness.

"It's worth the licking any lady can hand out," twelve-year-old Tom Branan told Lizzie confidentially, just before he left the Home to work on a farm south of San Jose. "You all don't hit hard enough to stop us." He was standing in Lizzie's entryway on the Monday after the séance, with a red runny nose and a thickly inked note from Nell.

"Your friend Mammy Pleasant has just sent over a basket of food," Nell had written, pressing hard enough to tear the paper. "Including several chickens it will take a whole morning to pluck. Please join us for lunch." And to make the prospect as uninviting as possible—"Boxty will also be served."

Lizzie ate only rarely at the Ark, and only when invited. She would have liked to dine there more often, as food tasted so much better when taken with conversation. She fully enjoyed the company of the teachers—warm, impassioned Mrs. Lake, who taught the middles, and tiny, practical Miss Stevens, who taught the littles.

Miss Stevens had red hair, freckled skin thin as paper, and eyes the same green as Chinese tea. Her particular enthusiasm was nature studies. She was a woman who took the world as she found it, and did so with great interest if not actual approval. She had no problem showing small children a praying mantis devouring its mate, a rabbit eating its young, a large crab ripping the leg off another, smaller crab. She delighted in pulling the petals from flowers and, in this context, could talk about pistils and stamens, could even say the word "ovary" to an entire class with a great loud "O" to begin it and no sign of hesitation. In her spare time, for dissipation, she dissected.

She ran the littles with an organizational genius that bordered on military, but was actually, she told Lizzie, adapted from the habits of migratory geese. When she took the children out, they walked behind her in a V formation, only somewhat narrowed so they all stayed out of the street.

She'd recently joined a ladies' debating society. Mrs. Lake had complained to Lizzie that the discourse at table was increasingly competitive as a result. Lizzie sometimes wondered about the educational progression that sent children from the strict empiricism of Miss Stevens into the classroom of the sentimental Mrs. Lake. Fortunately, educational policy was not her concern.

But Lizzie liked picking over issues: the morality of hunting as sport, voting rights for women, the Hawaii question, separate schools for the city's Chinese children. She guessed she would enjoy those dinner-table debates.

Yet she could not impose. The staff would suspect her of suspecting them; they would think her a spy. "We take the same meals as the wards," Nell told Lizzie often when they were discussing expenditures, and of course, Lizzie had never thought otherwise. Nell periodically asked board members to lunch just to show there was nothing to hide, and she was already plenty offended to be doing so.

Apparently it was Lizzie's turn to enjoy this hospitality again. She arrived early at the Ark and found the children huddled in the yard. The cause was a stray dog—some sort of terrier, with coarse gray fur and a white belly, ludicrous white tufts like fishing lures at its cheeks, and a lively, intelligent face. The children told her the dog had belonged to a little boy who'd lived on Nob Hill until he died of influenza.

Lizzie couldn't imagine how they could know this unless the dog himself had talked, but before she could say so, Mrs. Lake supplied even more details. The dog collapsed on the boy's grave, she reported to Lizzie tremulously, refusing all food and consolation and howling until the neighbors threatened to shoot it as a mercy to everyone involved. By the time it arrived at the Home it was half starved, and covered with fleas. Mrs. Lake's eyes ran with sympathetic tears. She went to give it another pat.

"Essence of Lake," Nell said sniffily to Lizzie. "Don't look half starved to me. Don't look one-quarter starved. But I'll grant you the fleas."

Lizzie nodded, as she was too distraught now to speak. She averted her eyes so Nell wouldn't see them. Dogs were just too good for this wicked world!

But she had to concede she saw no signs of noble grief. She watched the dog provoking the orange cat into stiff, furious poses, tangling among the children's legs as they played in the cold, nosing in their pockets for scraps from breakfast. Lizzie didn't want some stray eating the bread that the Swain bakery donated for the children. Yet as treasurer she made no objection to its remaining, even said it could come inside, sandy and germy as it was, whenever the pound man was sighted in the neighborhood. How could she do otherwise? Weren't the children all strays themselves?

She noted the coincidence of a dog's showing up when Mrs. Pleasant had predicted a dog. She didn't really believe in omens, but she couldn't help looking for them. This dog struck her as mostly gray, but there were those bits of white. "What color do you think it is?" she asked Nell, who answered that it was so grimy even the white was gray.

Lizzie saw little Jenny standing alone in the sand, but they didn't speak and Lizzie was relieved to see Jenny ignore her. The secret of their nighttime excursion seemed to be safe. Lizzie was also the tiniest bit hurt. This was a preposterous feeling, and she disregarded it.

She was not currently inclined to credit the medieval festival kidnapping attempt. It was too overheated, too much like something Lizzie herself would make up, springing into her head from the pages of a book. Such things didn't happen, not in modern-day San Francisco.

She was also less and less sure of the wealthy father. No secretly wealthy child had sheltered with them yet. How could sullen little Jenny be the first? In short, there was really no reason to think much more upon her, and Lizzie didn't plan to do so. "Come with me," Nell said, and Lizzie followed her inside.

On the way downstairs Lizzie raised the question of hiring a devout, hardworking Christian boy from Chinatown. Nell said it was not to be thought of, Lizzie knew their budget as well as Nell did. Better! Did he even speak English? Nell asked, and was annoyed when Lizzie did not know. Nell did not have the time to be forever pointing and gesturing when she needed a thing done.

3

ON THE KITCHEN COUNTER, surrounded by baskets of onions, lemons, jars of jelly, and an extravagant amount of spilt flour, a note had been caught under a teacup. Nell stood with her round fists on her round hips while Lizzie read it. "For Miss Hayes, to distribute as she sees fit," Mrs. Pleasant had written in her twisty hand, and also a recipe for the chicken.

Lizzie was both pleased and discomfited to have been so singled out. Mostly she was surprised. "How kind," she said uncertainly. *Don't eat or drink anything,* Mrs. Bell had told her.

Nell's eyes were sharp as pins. "The two of you are such chums now," she said. "Had such a gay time together. She's also sent you rosehip wine. Now there's all we need, to see poor blind Mrs. Wright in her cups."

The unspoken point here, the message in Nell's careless tone and rigid mouth and pinprick eyes, was Lizzie's drunken return from the House of Mystery. Lizzie refused to defend herself. Instead, as demonstration of her own clear conscience, she took the wine and two glasses and went immediately up to Mrs. Wright's first-floor apartment. *I can be anyone I like,* she thought to herself. *I care nothing for appearances. If it all results in generous donations of food to orphans, where's the harm?*

Mrs. Wright was more than eighty years old, a lonely soul who had survived most of her friends and the whole of her family. She'd lost her money in the rigged market of 1879, was one of those women who'd clustered each morning on Leidesdorff Street, hoping to see her shares of Sierra Nevada Mining turn to silver again. Such women were known in San Francisco as mud hens. On each new day, as the stock market opened, they were a little muddier, mothier, and more insane.

The Ladies' Relief and Protection Society Home had gathered Mrs. Wright in when she went blind as well as broke. Although she now kept herself clean as could be, the room smelled of camphor and the insides of old shoes. There was another smell, too, which Lizzie identified simply as age.

"We have Mrs. Mary E. Pleasant to thank for the wine," Lizzie told her. She turned her glass and watched the liquid in it spin. "It's a lovely color, a pale gold. Did you ever meet Mrs. Pleasant?"

"I recollect her calling on the Barclays once when I was there." Mrs. Wright's dentures were too large; they filled her *s*'s with spit. She'd chosen them deliberately, since the larger were the same price as the smaller. Value for money. "Their girl had just married and they must have invited her, people always used to, never expecting her to come, you understand. But she did, and she knew her mistake right away. So she just took a tray from one of the servants and began to pass it. I remember thinking that was clever. She was quick as they make 'em. Avoided the awkwardness, and half the guests didn't even guess. Nobody looks at the servants, don't you know."

This didn't match up with the woman who was so proud Lizzie's apron had insulted her. Lizzie couldn't imagine *that* woman passing a tray. "Did you ever see her as a white woman?"

"I know some people say so, but I don't recollect it," said Mrs. Wright. "I don't see how it could be true. She was a famous cook before she even arrived. Men met her at the docks to bid for her services. 'No washing up!' she said. She drove a bargain.

"And she was always proud of how far she'd come. She fought the Fugitive Slave Act, and she sued the trolleys for refusing her a ride. You wouldn't do that if you were passing.

"Did she win?'"

"My word, it was so long ago. I don't remember, dear. But she was all for the colored in those early days. When they took John Brown, he had a letter from our Mrs. Pleasant right in his pocket. She was a big part of all that."

Mrs. Wright was giddy with wine and conversation. Lizzie poured her a second glass, because she could see Mrs. Wright wanted one but wouldn't ask. Lizzie reproached herself for not visiting more often. She then suffered through a long story, which floated in and out of the past, a story in which many people Mrs. Wright had once known came to no good. There were mine cave-ins and ships lost at sea and deaths attributed to disease but so unexpected they might easily have been poisonings, and there were people who profited from these deaths. Even Lizzie, who could fill in the blanks in someone's story like nobody's business, was having trouble following.

She was rescued by Minna Graham. Come to fetch them to lunch, Lizzie assumed, but no, Minna said, the chickens weren't cooked yet, still running blood from the joints, but there was a man in the parlor Matron wanted her to deal with.

Only, Matron wanted specifically to see Lizzie first; she had something most urgent to say. "She does think he's here to adopt," Minna added, and Lizzie thought that, whatever his business, Minna should not have been informed of it. So when Lizzie returned to the kitchen, she also had things to say to Nell.

4

ALTHOUGH NELL HAD TAKEN an instant dislike to the man— "A Mr. Finney, or so it suits him to have us believe. I couldn't see one of our girls going home with him," she had said—Lizzie's own first impression was most approving. He rose eagerly at her entrance. He should have been relieved of his coat and hat, yet like Mrs. Pleasant, he still had them. Lizzie wished Mrs. Pleasant could see this. It was nothing personal. The wards were just ill mannered. Abetted by Nell, who never wanted company anyway.

The coat was stained and the hat needed blocking. Mr. Finney's shirt was worn clear through at the cuffs. But his hair, face, and hands were clean. Lizzie appreciated the effort he had made. He was a young man, fine-looking, with a trim moustache and gold-edged spectacles. One of his teeth, the right incisor, was thin as a nail. His eyes were blue, but gray enough for argument.

He stood beneath the embroidery that read, "Never too late to mend." "Miss Hayes," he said. "It's good of you to see me." His accent was Irish, his voice melodious. "Isn't it a grand morning? Auspicious." There was a nervousness about him that appealed to Lizzie. She liked the way he met her gaze, as if this was difficult but he was determined to do it. She imagined him as naturally shy. He'd spread a handkerchief over the old, bald chair before seating himself, and she thought it was gracious of him to pretend the furniture was worth such care. He set his hat on his knee.

With some prompting, he told Lizzie that he owned his own hack and drove it for hire, though his real job was speculations. Investments. Futures. "I'm a man who takes the long view," he said, which Lizzie supposed meant he'd no ready cash in the here and now. "I'm a man who thinks several steps ahead."

His wife had recently given birth. "A boy," he said, "a delight to all," which made her think of the new Putnam grandchild. But his wife was "as little as a fairy," and the demands of the baby were wearing on her. She wished for a girl to help with the housework.

Then Mr. Finney said he feared he was giving Lizzie the wrong idea. They were not looking for a maid so much as a daughter. "What's wanted is a girl young enough to come to feel part of the family. Mrs. Finney thought of a miss about the age of five or so."

Lizzie had noted that parents often had preposterous expectations of children only a bit older than their own. A mother would excuse the behavior of her neighbor's three-year-old, having a three-year-old herself and knowing him quite a baby still. But she would expect her neighbor's seven-year-old to behave with adult patience and charity. What might the parents of a new infant expect of a little girl of five? "I'm afraid a child that young would only make more work for your wife," she informed Mr. Finney. "I'd recommend a girl of at least ten, perhaps even older."

"It's not help Mrs. Finney is after so much as company. She's an affectionate woman, a little girl would suit her down to the ground. I don't know how to explain it to you," Mr. Finney said. He turned his hat in his hands; his head was bent watching this.

The sun had just reached the parlor window. A pale wand of

light turned Mr. Finney's hair the red of an autumn leaf. He looked up, smiling at her nervously, and tiny clouds reflected through the window onto his glasses. "She's always wanted a child. She was so happy during her confinement. But she seems surprised that the baby can't be played with, read to. 'He doesn't even have eyebrows!' she says to me. I tell her it only needs a little time and baby grows up and she's got the child she wants. But she won't wait."

"I see," said Lizzie. In fact she didn't see, and Mr. Finney knew she didn't. It all sounded a bit whimsical. New mothers were often prey to disappointments and frivolities. You didn't adopt a child in a mood.

"Perhaps her heart was set on a girl," Mr. Finney offered. "Not that she'd ever said."

Lizzie decided to let the point pass. "Still, you would want someone dependable," she said. "Sturdy."

"Ah, you can't go by that. Mrs. Finney is the littlest bit of a thing herself, but placid as a cow." Mr. Finney sat back. "If you could just let me have a look at what you've got. I'll know what I want when I see it."

As if they were a kennel. And quick as that, Lizzie stopped liking him. It was unfair of her, unfair that good manners, which everyone understood to contain an element of artifice, should cease to be good manners the moment the artifice showed. But there it is.

The older children were taking exercise in the yard between the Brown Ark and the barn. Their voices flowed into the parlor on the sunshine, and Lizzie could distinguish no words, but the emotions carried clearly. She had no illusions about the sort of people they would grow into. She never told herself she might be helping to harbor a future president, or even a poet, much as she would have loved to think so.

But it didn't matter, because they were children. Lizzie didn't even like children particularly, but they went to her heart, just the idea of them. "I can't release a child to you without references," she said, which was only the truth and had nothing to do with her change of feelings. "And members of the board would want to meet with Mrs. Finney. I'm only the treasurer. Adoptions aren't really my concern."

"Look, now." Mr. Finney's charming voice took on an edge. The sun brightened suddenly, revealing all the disreputable aspects of the parlor, the tufts of velvet over the mantelpiece, the thready chairs. "I should think you'd want one of your orphans set up in a loving home."

"That's exactly what we do want," Lizzie said.

They stared at each other. "Perhaps I could just have a look at the little ones." His voice smoothed out. "If you've not got a miss to suit, then there's no need to trouble either of us further."

His insistence on seeing their littlest girls was beginning to disturb Lizzie. She had an irrational conviction that he had come for Jenny Ijub. His trousers were old and faded, but in the sunlight now, she might have called them green. If he had come for Jenny, if he was the same man who had tried to grab her at Layman's German castle, sending him away would not suffice. He must be made to believe that Jenny was no longer with them. "Very well," she said. "Currently we have only a few girls so young. Several have left us for loving homes only quite recently."

There followed a number of hasty and awkward arrangements. Lizzie contrived to remove Jenny from her class and settle her in the sewing room with a picture book. The nice thing about Jenny was that she asked for no explanations. Less nice was the sullenness of her submission.

Lizzie then asked Nell to take Mr. Finney to the sheltered yard where the babies took the air. She knew that Nell would discourage him in any way possible. Nell told Lizzie later that he expressed disappointment in their "selection." Nell's own opinion was that he wanted a child on whom he and his wife could practice being parents, a child to serve as a buffer between their inexperienced blunders and their own dear baby. "And then discard like a worn sock," she said. "Having served her purpose."

The gray mongrel had barked at him. Nell saw this as evidence of a canine shrewdness quite uncanny. She did not expect to see Mr. Finney again. "And a good riddance to the bad," she concluded.

Lizzie stood at the sewing room window until she saw him drive off. She called Jenny over. "Have you ever seen that man?" she asked, but already he was too far away, a very commonplace figure, and Jenny said she couldn't know.

Lizzie lacked Nell's conviction. Now that the interview was over, it seemed more than possible that she had given in to an unwarranted suspicion. The feeling nagged at her. She wondered whether it was worth trying to track Mr. Finney down, to visit him in his home, interview his little fairy wife. She pictured Mrs. Finney's disappointment; she saw the two of them holding hands over the kitchen table, tears on Mrs. Finney's tiny radish-red cheeks.

Perhaps his eyes *had been* blue. But San Francisco was full of blue-eyed men. How was Lizzie supposed to determine the right one? Why was she even looking? She was too distracted to enjoy the lunch. Miss Stevens proposed the Chicago anarchists as a topic, and Lizzie had strong opinions regarding them—the mere thought of handsome August Spies, the hood over his face, his own death only moments away, saying without tremor, "The time will come when our silence will be more powerful than the voices you strangle today," was enough to send her heart straight up to her throat—but she found she didn't like the rules of debate. They transformed a disagreement between two or more people into an etiquette designed to obstruct rather than reveal the truth. The key was to misrepresent your opponent's position and then attack your own misrepresentation. It was all about strategies and generally invoked just as Lizzie was making her main point.

She went home in a pet and managed not to think about Mr. Finney again until the next morning, when she was awakened at six by Jack, a stable boy at the Brown Ark, who told her Matron wanted her at once, as Jenny Ijub had vanished in the night. The new dog, the dog who was definitely gray and not white, was also missing.

5

AT THAT HOUR, the city lay drowning in a cold, dense fog that tasted faintly of salt. It sat like a tongue against Lizzie's cheeks, licked the hair at her temples into waves. Jack drove Lizzie to the Brown Ark, and she was glad not to be the one driving, she couldn't see the street at all. She couldn't even see the mule clearly, only its long ears sticking up, flicking to the left and to the right when other buggies passed. A dozen kidnapped girls could have been bundled by and she wouldn't have known. The harness broke and delayed them many minutes. The sounds of wheels and hooves continued about them, phantom carriages, audible but invisible. By the time she arrived at the Home, she was rigid from the damp cold and from fear.

It was something of a relief to hear that, among the staff, Jenny was assumed to have run away. There had been an incident in the night. Nell was not immediately forthcoming, but apparently there had been an upset. Apparently it was not the first, though possibly the loudest.

According to Nell, Jenny was a troubled sleeper, making frequent complaints about the girls in her room. Last night had been once too often. Since Jenny couldn't manage to sleep nicely with other girls, Nell had told her, she must sleep alone. She was removed to the settee in the cupola room.

As Jenny was taken up the stairs, however, she grew more agitated. She begged to be allowed to return to her bed; she begged not to be left alone in the dark. This was distressing for Nell. She'd not intended the punishment to be a severe one, but there was no going back; it would not do for discipline in general if she was seen to retreat. She had to carry Jenny the final steps.

By now Jenny was hysterical, ungovernable, like an animal, Nell said. She was forced to stand at the door, holding it shut, while Jenny screamed and pulled at the handle and threw herself against it. Fully an hour passed in this manner, an hour at least; Nell had heard the clock. Finally Jenny quieted. Nell had waited, assuring herself the girl was asleep before tiptoeing down the stairs and back to her own bed. She had then spent a sleepless night herself, yet heard nothing more. "It didn't occur to me she might leave," she told Lizzie. "I never even thought. Seeing as she's got nowhere to go."

Nell was apologetic, but she had given Lizzie her first hopeful moment. Lizzie was afraid to share it, afraid someone would take it away again, show her that such a little girl could not walk so far alone in the dark. She put her coat and gloves back on, commandeered the mule, and told the staff only that she was going out to look for Jenny. She dismissed Jack; she wanted no witnesses. She drove herself to Octavia Street, stopped at the trees, which she could barely see, in front of the house, which she could not. Fog ran down the eucalyptus leaves and onto her straw hat with the gentle popping sound of rain. She secured the mule and made her way through the gate and up the brick walk. Sure enough, the dog came off the porch to meet her, the white tufts of its whiskers dripping with fog, its gums showing pink, its tongue limp with the pleasure of seeing her. This was a pleasure she fully returned.

Teresa Bell answered the door herself, in a silver dressing gown.

She nodded politely and for a moment too long. It was clear she didn't remember Lizzie's name. "I'm looking for a little girl," Lizzie told her. "I'm Miss Hayes?"

"She's yours? I couldn't think what to do with her. Another hour I'd have sent for the police."

Lizzie began to cry. This was the final result of her mother's impatience with tears, that after a dry-eyed childhood, she was likely to cry at almost anything, and especially at the wrong times, her weeping matched forever to the wrong emotions—joy, relief, exultation. Mrs. Bell pretended not to notice.

"You'll come in, then." She gestured vaguely, brilliantly; in Lizzie's liquid gaze Mrs. Bell's rings flickered like tiny darting fish. "I thought she was one of Mrs. Pleasant's. So she said. Butter wouldn't melt."

Lizzie wiped her nose, leaving a wet smear on the back of one gloved hand, removed her hat, and let Mrs. Bell lead her into a dark paneled library. A chandelier of rock crystal dripped from the ceiling, though the light was poor. On the floor by the sofa was a metal bird, a canary with painted feathers and a green hinged beak. It was a music box, turned with a key, and Lizzie guessed the beak would open and shut when it played. The bird's eyes were inset rather than painted. Obsidian beads, they had the dead, dull depth of taxidermy.

She looked about for Jenny, but there was no one else in the room. She remembered how beautiful she'd thought the house before. Now it seemed cavernous, poorly lit, a place of whispers and echoes. She had never seen a library with so few books.

"Join me in a cordial," Mrs. Bell suggested. There was a decanter on a table by the door. "To settle your nerves."

"Where is the little girl?" Lizzie asked.

"Sleeping."

"Will you take me to her?"

"I had such a time getting her to sleep, I couldn't bear to wake her just yet. Let's uncurl here with a glass."

"Is Mrs. Pleasant at home?"

"The whole house has fled to the country." She nodded in a reassuring way. "We're *quite* alone." She gave the word a disquieting emphasis. Lizzie was not at all sure she wished to be quite alone in the House of Mystery with Teresa Bell, and certainly not *quite* alone.

Teresa Bell was rarely seen outside. She belonged to no church, held no at-homes. Some thought she was frightened of something. Some said Mary Ellen Pleasant allowed her no friends. Some said it was Thomas Bell. Some of the latter said Thomas Bell valued his wife's innocence so highly that he kept her shut away from the contamination of society. Others said he could never trust her, she being no better than a whore when they met. Still others thought she had tricked him into marriage and he'd retaliated by going into society without her, as if she didn't exist, for more than a decade.

Lizzie hoped that Mrs. Bell was merely shy. She wished to demand to be taken to Jenny at once, but saw how rude this would be. She removed her gloves, accepted a cordial. It was far too early for one, really—and wine just yesterday!—but she'd had such a fright. She took a seat on the sofa. Mrs. Bell sat next to her.

There was a long and uncomfortable silence. The cordial was in a tulip glass and tasted of fermented raspberries. The fog pressed against the windows to Lizzie's right, where she could see, dimly, the reflection of her own face. She watched a drop of water fatten until it was too heavy and then stretch thin as it fell. Just for fun, she repositioned her face until a teary trail ran down her reflected cheek. She glanced at a clock on the wall. It had stopped at three forty-three.

There was no evidence of a servant anywhere. But surely Mrs. Bell's hair was too elaborate for her to have done it herself.

"Such a quiet house," Lizzie said, trying to make it sound a compliment. She set down her glass. "Your servants ..."

"All of them drunk," Mrs. Bell said. "Or I miss my guess." Lizzie made a noise she intended as sympathetic but feared came out startled. She reminded herself that it was a scandalous household and Mrs. Bell a scandalous woman. Lizzie had not minded the last time she was here. She'd rather enjoyed it. She tried to find the mood of her last visit, the sense of waking up, the hope of her life taking a magical turn. What was missing now was the tea, the sun, and Mary Ellen Pleasant. "I'm sorry not to see Mrs. Pleasant," she offered. "She's in the country, you said?"

"Well, one never knows." Mrs. Bell's voice dropped confidingly. "But I've searched the house."

She put her cordial aside, the red liquid shivering in the glass, and reached for Lizzie's hands. Her own were as cold and soft as Lizzie recollected; the fingernails so icy they made the back of Lizzie's neck twitch, tightened the skin over her skull. Mrs. Bell continued to stroke Lizzie's hands, and Lizzie forced herself not to withdraw. She touched Lizzie's wrists, rubbed them with her thumbs. She seemed to be warming her hands on Lizzie like a cat. It occurred to Lizzie that Mrs. Bell might be drunk herself. Or drugged. Hadn't Mrs. Pleasant's tea come from Chinatown?

Lizzie wondered exactly how old Mrs. Bell was. Her skin was so translucent the shadows under her eyes were blue. Her gold-brown hair caught the lamplight and glowed like amber. When she smiled, tiny wrinkles opened like fans at the edges of her mouth and eyes. If she didn't smile, there were no lines in her face at all. Her shoulder touched Lizzie's, and Lizzie smelled milkweed powder.

"You should stay away from Mrs. Pleasant," Mrs. Bell whispered. "She don't like fine white women." She nodded for emphasis, then straightened. "She wasn't always that way. She was good to me at first, she introduced me to Mr. Bell. We married in this very house."

"Weddings are such lovely occasions," Lizzie said. Actually she thought they lacked spontaneity, but as an unmarried woman she could hardly say so. In books they were interrupted, protested, prevented. They were the scenes of great drama. Jane Eyre's wedding, for example, the one that had not taken place—you couldn't call it a lovely occasion, but so much passion! As a young lady, whenever Lizzie had imagined her own wedding, she'd imagined it not taking place the way Jane Eyre's had not taken place. (And not ever the way it had actually not taken place.)

"Ours was private. I left next day on my wedding trip. Mr. Bell stayed back."

This was interesting, and Lizzie would have liked to know more about it. "How sad for you both," she said encouragingly.

But Mrs. Bell waved the point past. "He's a businessman. Business prevented him."

6

ON HER RETURN from her wedding trip, Mrs. Bell told Lizzie, Mrs. Pleasant felt there had been insufficient ceremony to mark the occasion. She insisted on a party. It was winter. Mrs. Bell wore a gown of green *crêpe de Chine* shot with silver thread, and her wedding gift from Mrs. Pleasant, a diamond choker. The mansion was strung with lamps, filled with flowers, and the food was extraordinary. Seven courses were served, smoked and fresh meats, out-of-season vegetables, pâtés and wines from France, fruits glazed with liqueurs; there were jewelry boxes containing teas from China for the guests to take home. "Mrs. Pleasant puffs herself a bit on her table," said Mrs. Bell. "She used to cook for Governor Booth when he came to town."

Mrs. Bell was not a good storyteller. Her affect was too even, her chronology unusual, her vocabulary common. But Lizzie loved stories with *crêpe de Chine* and strings of lamps and out-of-season vegetables. She was a passionate reader. She was more than able to supply whatever details Mrs. Bell omitted.

Only the men had attended. One by one they arrived, without their wives. They made unconvincing, embarrassed excuses, agues and toothaches and unexpected family obligations; a few of one, a few of the other, as if it had been orchestrated. That's what angered Mrs. Pleasant most, the sense of collusion. She insisted on seating the men at the tables as set, with every other chair left empty. The men began to drink and, when drunk, to make discourteous comments. Teresa Bell was admired, but in an intimate, insulting way, not befitting a married woman. Ribald toasts were made to Mrs. Pleasant as well. Eventually Mrs. Pleasant told Mrs. Bell to leave, and she did so, fleeing up the stairs.

"Wasn't the insult to me?" Mrs. Bell asked Lizzie. Her voice was plaintive. "I was the bride." But Mrs. Pleasant insisted on appropriating it. Years before Mrs. Bell had even arrived in San Francisco, Mrs. Pleasant had tried to host a dinner for society's finest. The result had been the same. The result would always be the same.

Although at the time of their marriage she lived with Mr. and Mrs. Bell, Mrs. Pleasant still owned Geneva Cottage on the San Jose Road. She began to redecorate it. She put in oriel windows, reddened the wood floors with stains, bought gold-veined mirrors, marble basins, and fountains. She hung curtains of lace patterned with orchids. The gardens were replanted to make a large, lush greensward surrounded by groves and private trysting grottoes. There were cool shaded places where ferns and violets could grow, patches of sunny grass perfumed by hidden herbs. When she was finished, she sent out invitations again.

This time she invited only men, some of the most powerful in the city and all of them married to the women who had snubbed her. The invitations were delivered in secret by Negro messengers. Two of the men were bankers; there were a railroad millionaire, three mine owners, and a newspaper baron. There were a blind ward boss and a judge from the state supreme court.

"She never told me the guest list," said Mrs. Bell. "She does keep her secrets. But anyone could guess that much."

Mrs. Pleasant promised the men a special evening in the country without their wives. The invitations were written on heavy red paper; the ink was silver. Only one man declined.

The story moved briefly south. When Mrs. Pleasant had left New Orleans, under the name of Madame Christophe, she was only a step ahead of the hangman. She had been stealing slaves, connecting them with the Underground Railroad, and the plantation owners were closing in. She escaped through the help and intervention of Marie LaVeau.

"You've heard of LaVeau?" Mrs. Bell asked.

Lizzie hadn't, but Mrs. Bell did not elaborate further except to say that Mrs. LaVeau had taught Mrs. Pleasant many things and that one of them was how to give a party.

There was little to eat and much to drink. They called the drink champagne, but it was really something far more lethal. Mrs. Pleasant had put it down herself from strawberries she'd grown in special barrels. "The entertainment tonight is voodoo," she told the men. There were ten beautiful young women, dressed like princesses, but with the skin of slaves, to sit with the men while they smoked and to dance the calinda with them after. There were drums. There were ritual incantations. The ballroom grew hot from the dancing and the liquor; the drumming quickened.

One of the women was a sixteen-year-old named Malina Paillet. She wore yellow roses on her wrist and yellow silk on her shoulders. She caught the attention of one of the men, perhaps a banker, perhaps a mine owner. What appealed to him most was her shyness. She couldn't answer his questions, couldn't smile at his jokes. Her movements during the dance were slight, but this, he thought, made them even more suggestive. He drank and she didn't. When he put his hand on her skirt, groped through the petticoat to squeeze the leg beneath, she froze suddenly, awkwardly, and asked another of the women to change places with her. There was a silence in the room. When the dancing began again, the man had a different partner.

Mrs. Pleasant could see that he was angry and very drunk. She took Malina aside and told her she was a fool to be rude to a rich man. Mrs. Pleasant wanted the men entangled, wanted the women installed as mistresses, draining whatever time and money they could from the men's wives.

But this was not New Orleans. Malina refused to listen. "I hate him," she said, and it was loud enough to be heard throughout the room. She was sobbing, salty tears that would ruin the yellow silk, an expensive dress that belonged, Mrs. Bell noted, to Mrs. Pleasant and not to Malina.

Lizzie had begun to wonder whether this was a story she should be hearing. Mrs. Bell's manner was so tranquil there was no anticipating the things that came from her mouth. And yet Lizzie was far too engrossed to stop her. It was like a story by Conan Doyle, but with voodoo instead of Mormons. The Palace Hotel hired pretty young mulatto girls as maids. Lizzie could easily picture one of them in a floating silk, tears falling like diamonds from her eyes.

Malina ran from the room and the man went after her. She ran through the pink-and-white parlor, into the courtyard, and into the trees. The man followed. There was silence, and then a single scream. It might have been the peacocks Mrs. Pleasant had purchased to patrol the grounds.

When Mrs. Pleasant and the others reached the yard, Malina was returning. Her hair was loose about her face and she was not wearing her roses or her shoes. She stumbled between the two fountains with their statues—"statues of women," said Mrs. Bell, in a tone that Lizzie understood immediately to mean they had no clothes on—her head at a strange angle. She fell in the courtyard. Her throat had been cut.

"I'll take care of this," Mrs. Pleasant told the men. The other women had fled. "You can rely on my discretion." She removed her housekeeping apron and covered Malina's face. "No one will ever know you were here tonight. Your wives need never know."

Teresa Bell's hands reached for Lizzie's neck. Lizzie gasped and pulled away, but Mrs. Bell had caught hold of the chain of her necklace and held her fast. "Such a strange coin." Her face was very close to Lizzie's. Lizzie could feel the heat of her breath, could see the raspberry stain like blood on her tongue, the pores of her skin clotted with powder. "Is it very old? I never saw its like," she said.

"I really must be going." Lizzie opened Mrs. Bell's icy fingers by force and stood. Won't you promise to stay away from Mrs. Pleasant, Mrs. Putnam had begged her, and if the question were put to her again, put to her just now, she would return quite a different answer. Despite every effort, her words came out with a tremble. "I must get back. Everyone is so worried about little Jenny. Please take me to her at once."

"Did I scare you? I apologize."

"Not at all." Lizzie managed to govern her voice, though not her legs. They shook and she sat again. "Why do you keep her on?"

"Keep her on?" Mrs. Bell smiled so her teeth showed. They were small and perfectly graduated, like strung pearls. "You don't understand a thing, do you? Old Mrs. Pleasant does what she likes. And Mr. Bell, if he has a fault, it's loyalty. He'd never turn on her."

"Who was the murderer?"

"She never said. Mr. Bell knows, of course, seeing as he was there."

"Why have you told me this?" Lizzie asked.

"Because you're a white woman. And so am I."

"Then why won't you take me to Jenny?"

"I will, of course. Are you worried about her? She's just upstairs, asleep."

Lizzie felt her heart rattling against the cage of her ribs. Mrs. Bell's face was too composed; her tone of voice too even. It had all been a performance, and Lizzie had been taken in. "You're lying, then. She's frightened to sleep by herself. What have you done with her?" She remembered Mrs. Bell's face the first time they had met, her courteous, placid voice. My mother set me out on the windowsill in a thunderstorm, she'd said.

Now Mrs. Bell's face showed annoyance, perhaps— surprise, at least. Something swam through the bright glass surface of her eyes. She picked up the painted canary, wound its key. "We played with this music box here until she dozed off. I lugged her upstairs. I see my word isn't enough. I'm happy to show you."

There was a sequence of tinny chirping, then a strangled cry. The automaton froze into place, its beak open in silent alarm.

Lizzie followed Mrs. Bell to the back of the house, where a spiral staircase coiled its way from the basement to the third floor. A glass dome capped the staircase; as a result, the house was slightly brighter here. The light fell directly on a newel post that supported a statue of a woman carved of dark wood, and holding up a lamp. Of course, she was insufficiently clothed. Lizzie would have been surprised to find her otherwise.

They started to climb. The spiral of the stairs formed a murky well at its center. Lizzie watched the well deepen as she rose; it gave her a vague vertigo.

The gas was not lit on the second floor, and the curtains throughout were drawn, so once they left the skylight it was darker than ever. Mrs. Bell fetched a lantern, then opened a small door, too small to lead to a room; Lizzie would have guessed it led to a closet. "The whole house is stuffed with passageways and peepholes," Mrs. Bell said. "There's not a room you can know yourself safe from spying eyes. Mrs. Pleasant designed it. This is the shortest route." She stepped inside.

Lizzie forced herself to follow. The space was low at the entry, but opened at the back into a narrow, windowless corridor. The air was still and smelled of dust. Lizzie saw Mrs. Bell's light receding in front of her. Mrs. Bell made a turn and the light went out. The space was narrow enough for Lizzie to hold the walls on either side. She imagined they were narrowing further. She made the turn herself and could just see Mrs. Bell's light again. She hurried forward. The light went out.

Lizzie listened for Mrs. Bell's footsteps but heard nothing. She groped forward and hit another wall. No one knew she had come here. She and Mrs. Bell were apparently alone in the house except for the drunken servants. Quite alone. No one would ever come to look for her.

"Mrs. Bell," she called. "Mrs. Bell!" She hit the wall in front of her with her fists. The knocking echoed about her. "Mrs. Bell!"

She decided to go back. They had made only one turn. They had left an open door. It was hard to set her feet on a floor she could not see. She was moving slowly, far more slowly than when she'd had the light. She told herself that this was why it took so long to get back to the turn. Eventually she was forced to acknowledge that she had missed it. She turned back again.

Her eyes were beginning to adjust, but the beating of her heart made the corridor seem to pulse about her, as if with each heartbeat she were being squeezed. In the distance she thought she saw a tiny orange pin of light, like an afterimage of sun. Shadows now appeared, impossible without light, and therefore illusions. She held one hand across her face to protect her eyes and groped forward with the other toward the tiny mirage of brightness. Before entering this corridor she would have said the house was silent; now her straining ears heard no end of creaks, paddings, scuttlings, and shiftings, the worst of which were her own footsteps. Her hip hit something on the wall to her right, something round and cold, which she shrank from at first, and then realized was a doorknob. She twisted it and fell into a room. In the dim light she could make out heavy velvet curtains. She ran to these and wrenched them open. The fog was still too thick to see out, but she could now see inside.

She was in a bedchamber, all done in reds. On a stone pillar by the window was a statue of a woman on a horse. She carried a bow and wore only a quiver of arrows, the strap of which fell between her breasts. There was a vase with raised figures of men and women. Lizzie had to bend close to see. They were riding each other in positions she found hard to credit. She made herself look away.

A picture hung on the wall to her left. It showed a dark woman in a white dress. She lay on a grassy hill, one hand tucked into her own bodice, the other lifting an apple toward her mouth. Her shoulders were carelessly bare, her skirt had fallen away from her ankles; clearly she thought she was alone. But the shadow of a cloaked man stretched across the grass beside her. His legs were elongated in the manner of shadows. He stood watching her, just a step outside the gilded frame. It was a dreamy scene, but full of foreboding.

Another picture showed an older, fattish woman in modern dress. Her hair was in disarray, but not seductively so. There was something about her so out of place that Lizzie moved to look more closely. The woman in the picture took a step toward her. Lizzie's throat closed over and then opened. It was a mirror, of course, enormous, nine or ten feet across, with grapevines carved into the frame and painted in red, gold, and green. "You're such an idiot!" she told her reflection, who seemed unsurprised to hear it.

The bed itself was piled with cushions, puffy coverlets, and knitted shawls in such chaotic profusion that Lizzie couldn't immediately tell whether it was occupied or vacant. The bedding lay in mounds and curves. She put a hand hesitantly onto one such drift; it collapsed when pushed. If she had touched someone in the bed this would have finished her. She would have screamed or fainted or died. It was a narrow escape, but the bed was empty.

The knob on the door to the outer hallway was made of white china and painted with a woman's eyes and apple-red lips. Lizzie walked across a carpet whose edges were embroidered with roses, and turned the knob.

Mrs. Bell was waiting in the hallway with her lamp.

"Right through here," she said, as if she and Lizzie had never been separated.

Lizzie wanted nothing more than to run for the staircase, the mule, the Ark. But a person who has freely chosen to spend her days asking rich people for money is no coward. She governed her spirited imagination and followed Mrs. Bell down the hall, down a second hall, and into a room at the very end.

THE ROOM AT THE END of the hall was a nursery, although not just now in use. There was the smell of trapped air, and sheeted forms that suggested chairs, chests, rocking horses, phantasms. There had been some testimony about the Bell children at the William Sharon-Allie Hill divorce trial. Lizzie couldn't quite recall it and couldn't imagine how it had been relevant. She did remember a cartoon from the *Wasp* at about that time—Mrs. Pleasant, dressed like Gilbert and Sullivan's Buttercup, but with a basket of babies. "In my youth when I was young and charming, I practiced baby farming," the caption had read. She remembered Mrs. Bell telling her there were six children, but some of them grown.

In one corner was a small bed. Mrs. Bell stepped toward it and her light fell on Jenny Ijub, lying on her back under a tumbling-blocks quilt. The bedding had been pulled over her, but incompletely, so that Lizzie could see the brown shoulders of her dress, the dirty toes of one stocking. She had a finger in her mouth and there was a high flush on her cheeks.

She was asleep. For the second time in as many hours, Lizzie felt relief shoot through her. She knelt on the floor and touched Jenny's face, drawing a finger along the brow of one closed eye. Beneath the lid, the eye flickered, then stilled. Lizzie shook her shoulder gently and then less gently. "Jenny. Jenny Ijub. I've come for you."

The little girl didn't move. "I gave her something to help her sleep," Mrs. Bell said. "She was so agitated. It wasn't healthy." Dust spun about Mrs. Bell's lamp, swirled across her powdered face.

Lizzie leaned in and smelled camphor on Jenny's breath. She shook Jenny harder. Was it possible to come into the House of Mystery and not go away drugged? *Don't eat or drink anything.* She herself shouldn't have had the cordial. She felt fine, but it had been incautious. She wedged her arms under Jenny and pulled her closer.

Jenny came awake all at once, kicking and striking out till Lizzie released her. Her body relaxed then, but her features remained pinched and her voice was strung with tears. "I won't go back," she said. "You're not the mother of me."

Lizzie didn't want a quarrel in front of Mrs. Bell, with whom she was still angrier than she could say. She didn't want to take the time to overcome Jenny with reason and gentleness. Neither did she want to carry her forcibly from the house. She had a happy inspiration. "I'll take you to the ducks, then."

Jenny regarded her, suspicious but sleepy. Her pupils were black points in the brown eyes. Her hair was wild and blown about her head. One ear stuck out. Lizzie smoothed the hair to cover it.

Jenny indicated Mrs. Bell. "Can she go, too?"

"May she go," said Lizzie. "No, we've taken too much of Mrs. Bell's time already."

"All right," Jenny said. She fell asleep again.

Mrs. Bell stood above her, half lit by the lamp she held and half in shadow. She didn't look at Lizzie and she didn't say a word. On a shelf behind her, a row of expensive dolls stared into the middle distance of the room, seven painted skulls, seven tiny Cupid's-bow mouths. This made Lizzie think, inevitably and guiltily, of Jenny's broken doll.

Lizzie couldn't see that these dolls had ever been played with. She'd had three dolls herself as a child and never played with any of them, not liking their compulsive smiles, their lumpy bodies, the emptiness of their lives. Without her to pick them up, move their arms, and speak their voices, they were nothing. It was too much to ask. And then they had stared, of course, much like Baby Edward. Their eyes had never closed.

"You lie there until you calm down," she'd said to them sometimes, to justify her neglect. ("Lizzie keeps her dolls just like new," her mother told people, with obvious approval.)

Lizzie searched the floor for Jenny's shoes. She took them in one hand and lifted Jenny into her arms. She recognized the smell of Jenny's hair, sweet but spoiled, like stale cake or those candies in Chinatown that came in a thin wrapping of rice paper that you ate along with the sweet. "We're most grateful for your kindness," she told Mrs. Bell stiffly.

"My pleasure." Mrs. Bell's voice matched Lizzie's, note for impeccable note. Her face was as vacant and unused as the dolls'. "Do call again."

Jenny was an awkward load. The steps seemed steeper descending, the bottom of the well a terrifying distance away now that Lizzie had no hand free for the banister.

There was a portrait on the wall next to Lizzie where she paused to rest. She assumed this was the likeness of Mr. Bell. If so, he was a balding, handsome man with a sharp nose and white side-whiskers. His eyes were very, very blue. Mrs. Bell's portrait hung next to him, life-sized and wearing fewer clothes than you might expect of a mother of six. In her arms she held a tiny white dog with a smashed flat face. Its color was incontrovertible.

Behind Mrs. Bell and the dog was the grandfather clock from the entryway. The time in the picture was just past two, an artful reference to Mrs. Bell's age at the time of the sitting, or so Lizzie supposed. The longer hand was just past twelve. XII, in fact, but what difference did that make?

If Lizzie had seen these things on the way up, her magical juncture might have begun in wandering lost and frightened in the dark. This would have been an awful way to start the rest of her life.

Of course, if she'd seen her signs on the way up, they would have come in the wrong order.

Lizzie shifted Jenny in her arms and continued down the stairs. At the bottom she paused to look up. Mrs. Bell stood with her lamp in the darkness of the floor above. The lamp lit her face from below, gave her a ghoulish tint. It occurred to Lizzie that she really should have asked Mrs. Bell to thank Mrs. Pleasant for the chickens, but it seemed unbearably awkward to do so now. She passed the real grandfather clock and went out the door.

8

THE NOT-WHITE TERRIER was delighted at the chance to ride in the buggy. Lizzie knew she should go straight back to the Brown Ark, where everyone was worried most to death. Jenny was asleep and could hardly appreciate an outing. But Lizzie had promised her one.

Besides, Lizzie thought she could use a little time to compose herself before facing her magical juncture, not that she believed in such things, not that the appearance of the clues hadn't been all too neatly arranged in the House of Mystery. It didn't feel like the hand of fate; it felt like the hand of Mrs. Pleasant. Still, Lizzie was tense and nervy; the morning had been too much.

So she turned right instead of left and drove out to Golden Gate Park, letting the mule pick the pace, giving the hacks for hire a wide berth, so as not to risk a meeting with Mr. Finney. A road to Ocean Beach was being constructed. South Drive swarmed with laborers. The fog was burning away, exposing a watery sun, reluctant and cold.

If Jenny had been awake, Lizzie would have taken her to the new Children's Quarters and maybe bought her a ride on the merry-go-round. She would have stood with the mothers, watching from the balcony of the Sharon building. Lizzie had not seen it yet herself, but the orphans at the Ark had been guests there twice and come back talking of painted horses and maypoles.

The original plan for the William Sharon bequest had been a huge marble gate with the senator's name cut into it. As if he'd donated the entire park instead of merely an unnecessary portal, the outraged papers had said. The park commissioner had persuaded the estate into the Children's Quarters instead—croquet sets, tricycles, ice cream fountains, donkeys, and goat carts. A happy memorial, then, but a curious consequence, to turn Senator William Sharon into Saint Nicholas when his case hadn't even been settled yet. Allie Hill had accused him of adultery, and his spirited public defense was that he'd paid her five hundred dollars a month to share his bed and never once considered marrying her.

Lizzie stopped the buggy at Alvord Lake, where a tribe of mallards had settled the past autumn. She was sorry not to have bread. She'd noticed how children who themselves had nothing enjoyed the chance to be generous. She'd seen dreadful bullies who, when given a handful of stale biscuits and a mob of ducks, suddenly developed a fine sense of justice. It was wonderful to see them trying to feed every duck, no duck more than the others, taking special pains to see that the littlest got a share. That would have been worth waking Jenny. That would have been a treat. "We're here," Lizzie said, shaking Jenny until her eyes opened.

She could not find one of Jenny's shoes, so she carried her to a park bench and held her there in the pale sunlight, listening to the mild griping of the mallards. The dog dashed about on the lawn, where, when next Lizzie looked, it had found something nasty to roll in.

It was not yet eleven in the morning and Lizzie was already exhausted. Each duck cut a small wake in the water, V-shaped, spreading open like a wing. The sun struck these waves so that the surface of the water was crossed with brief veins of gold. At the lake edges, the reflections of trees floated and undulated. It was all so beautiful. She shook Jenny again. "Ducks," she said.

Jenny scarcely opened her eyes. "Not those ducks," she answered. Even asleep, even drugged, she was not relaxed. She lay in Lizzie's lap, curled up tightly, and one elbow dug into Lizzie's thigh.

Lizzie had so many things to think about. She tried to impose some order on the recurring images of fog and red wallpaper, the spiral staircase, black passageways, a murdered girl in a yellow dress. She'd had an adventure, no doubt about it, and it hadn't been pleasant. Ever since her first visit to the House of Mystery she'd chafed at her usual life. She'd been impulsive, discontented. She'd drunk daytime wine and been rude to dead people. She'd been the object of occult concern, and honestly, it was time to admit she'd enjoyed it.

But this morning she'd been frightened. She couldn't think of Malina Paillet without distress and she couldn't think of Mrs. Pleasant with pleasure. The party was over, and all Lizzie wanted was her same old corner in the cinders. You can be anyone you want, Mrs. Pleasant had said, and what luck! Lizzie wanted to be her old, unintrusive self. Her magical juncture must be made to take her right back home.

She was done with Jenny. She was done with the House of Mystery. She had no curiosity over Mr. Finney. She was merely the treasurer, merely involved in donations, and these other matters would be well handled by other people.

Jenny's breath was fragrantly medicinal, wet and warm on Lizzie's neck as they returned to the buggy. Lizzie had never said they wouldn't be going back to the Brown Ark eventually. Obviously there was no choice for it. She'd honored her part of the bargain by producing ducks. As she clicked her tongue at the mule she told herself that it was cruel to keep the staff in suspense when Jenny had been safely found. Besides, she was tired of staggering about Golden Gate Park with a drugged child in her arms.

Back at the Ark, their appearance was greeted with great relief, quickly mastered. Jenny was carried, still sleeping, to her bed. Dr. Kearney was sent for, to confirm that she'd taken no lasting harm from the adventure.

Nell remained with Lizzie to ask many questions. In the face of Lizzie's evasions, Nell was persistent. She couldn't understand how Jenny would have known the way to the House of Mystery, or how Lizzie had known to look for her there. She couldn't understand how Lizzie could have been so careless as to lose one of Jenny's shoes. "It doesn't matter that only one has been lost," she pointed out. "Two will have to be purchased." She took exception to the impulse to take Jenny to the park instead of bringing her back to begin her punishment. Truancy was not tolerated at the Brown Ark, and most runaways were not treated to outings. It wouldn't help Jenny's popularity when the other children heard. Lizzie had no children herself and no sense of how often a firm hand was required. It was easy to be too sympathetic; more mothers had ruined their children with indulgence than with neglect.

And while Lizzie was out larking, the Chinese boy had arrived. He could not be run off. He responded to any attempt to dislodge him by falling to his knees and praying loudly. It appeared to be the Lord's Prayer, Nell was able to pick out a word here and there, but aside from that he seemed to speak no English. She did allow that he was very clean, still he must be sent back at once, and they were all depending on Lizzie to manage this, since it was Lizzie who'd encouraged him to come in the first place.

None of the scolding offended Lizzie; she imagined it was mostly on the mark. It made her miss her mother. She'd been far too hard on her mother recently. Lizzie was so lucky to have belonged somewhere and to someone. Sleeping in one's own bed was one of the most agreeable sensations she knew. Sad to think how foreign it was to the wards.

She imagined Jenny, waking up this afternoon, or this evening, or sometime in the night, to find herself back in the Ark, and resolutely erased the image. Would Jenny even remember having seen the ducks? "I won't be going to the House of Mystery ever again," she told Nell, who hadn't asked and was, of course, made even more suspicious by the declaration.

"Well, goodness, why should you?" Nell agreed. "Why would anyone?"

9

JENNY CONTINUED TO SLEEP. In her dreams she heard Maud Curry's voice. "They found her in a Chinese opium den," Maud was explaining authoritatively. "Kidnapped and drugged. At least that's what she says. But who'd want to kidnap her? Me, I don't believe a word of it."

Jenny held very still. She kept her eyes closed. If she was going to wake up back at the Brown Ark, then she would just not wake up at all. She was curiously contented. She told herself she was still in the house with the woman so sad and so beautiful she was almost a princess. They were waiting there together for Mrs. Pleasant. You'll see I don't forget you, either, Mrs. Pleasant had promised.

The day passed, and every time Jenny opened her eyes enough to see where she was, she shut them immediately. A bowl of potato soup was left for her, but she didn't wake up to eat. Night came again and Maud was beside her on the bed, pinching her, shaking her hard. Her voice was so close Jenny could smell it, a boiled-egg and licorice smell. "You listen to me," Maud whispered fiercely. "Little Jenny Ijub. Are you listening?"

She shook Jenny again. "I know where you really went. You ran away to old Mrs. Pleasant. And she didn't want you any more than we do. Do you hear me?" She took the lobe of Jenny's ear between her fingers and squeezed. "Say it," she told Jenny. "Say out loud that nobody loves you."

Jenny tried not to wake up, but Maud's fingernails were cutting into her ear. At first it was an ache she could ignore, but it quickly grew sharper and more painful. The pain hooked Jenny like a fish, hauled her out of her secret contentment, gasping, into the open air.

Ti Wong

1

LIZZIE HAD LOOKED in on Jenny that afternoon while Dr. Kearney was at her bedside. Dr. Kearney was a thin man, unusually tall, with almost no hair on his face. His shoulders were hunched, his spine permanently curved from years of leaning down to talk to people. He was considerably younger than Lizzie, but he was a man and a professional, so she never felt the advantage of it. Yet she was quite fond of him. For all his nervous energy and towering height, he was soft with the children. He read widely and with great enthusiasm, though never novels.

"No damage," he assured Lizzie. "All serene." He spoke past her. "Let the child sleep as long as she likes." Lizzie turned to see Nell behind her in the doorway.

"The Chinese boy is in the kitchen," Nell said. Dr. Kearney was still talking, so Lizzie could pretend not to have heard. "When she wakes, don't be surprised if she has no memory of this adventure at all," Dr. Kearney was saying. "Don't be alarmed."

"*This* one has no memory of any adventure," Nell said. "Or so she claims."

"And entirely plausibly." Dr. Kearney began to put his instruments back into his bag. "A German doctor has published a series of investigations on memory. I was just reading about it. A Dr. Ebbing-haus. He set himself the task of learning four hundred and twenty sets of sixteen-syllable lines. Unrelated syllables. *Vollig sinnloses Material.* A fatiguing investigation. All marvelously scientific."

"I'm sure," said Nell. She disappeared from the doorway. Conversations of this sort about studies of this sort were no doubt a very fine thing for those with nothing to do, she'd told Lizzie often enough on similar occasions. This was, of course, the category into which Lizzie fell.

"How interesting," Lizzie said. She accompanied Dr. Kearney out of the room, inviting him to continue. It did interest her, but mostly she was using him for cover. She wished to escape from Nell without confronting the Chinese boy, since she saw no reason he couldn't stay if he wished to.

And she certainly had no desire to communicate his unwelcomeness in some sort of extended charade.

Besides, Lillie Langtry had just adopted a small Chinese boy; they were all the rage in the more fashionable homes.

Most important, Nell would not manage to send him away herself. She was more softhearted than she sounded, and better able to delegate unkindness than to deliver it. If Lizzie could avoid her now, then Nell would simply wait until the next time she saw her. If that didn't happen for a week or two, if it could be delayed until Ti Wong was no longer making his first unfavorable impression, then Nell would be just as content to keep him. Lizzie had only to lie low, keep her head down and wait for this happy result. The first step was escaping the Brown Ark unnoticed.

"Dr. Ebbinghaus found that he could impose a rhythm on his syllables as a memory aid," Dr. Kearney was telling her. "Actors learn the words of many plays over the course of their careers. I've seen mention of monks in the Dark Ages who couldn't read, but could recite the entire Bible. I don't think it was uncommon. I myself could recite poetry by the bushelful when I was a boy. 'In Xanadu did Kubla Khan a stately pleasure-dome decree.'"

"'Where Alph, the sacred river, ran,'" said Lizzie encouragingly. They were approaching the front door. "'Through caverns measureless to man.'"

"'Down to a sunless sea.'"

It was her father's favorite poem. Perhaps her father had also imagined himself inside Xanadu; perhaps he responded only to the music. He had a sentimental side, little as Lizzie had seen of it. But now the words reminded her of her own recent wander through the darkness. Less grand in the flesh. Less grand when it didn't rhyme, didn't sing that song with the vowels. Less grand when cut to fit *her*.

Lizzie wished Dr. Kearney would keep his voice down, but his enthusiasm for Ebbinghaus was growing with every sentence. He reached for the doorknob. "'Obliviscence' is Dr. Ebbinghaus's term for forgetting," Dr. Kearney said heartily. "Don't you find that's often the more interesting topic? Isn't 'obliviscence' a lovely, drowsy word?" and then they were finally outside, walking through the sand, with only steps to go.

He untied his horse, gave Lizzie a lift in his rig to the streetcar. "How I do carry on!" he cried in apology as they parted, but she assured him she wouldn't have him any other way. She caught the streetcar home and slept all afternoon. She spent the next few days calling on donors, determined not to return to the Ark until she was sure the Chinese boy was well settled in.

2

THAT WEDNESDAY, Lizzie called at the Putnams'. Odd Wednesdays were Mrs. Putnam's regular at-home days and Lizzie was resuming her regular, pre-magical-juncture life down to the tiniest particular. Erma was visiting from Sacramento with the new baby, and Mrs. Mullin, like Lizzie, was obligated to attend. Lizzie was eager to show everyone her same old self, boring as ever, and keeping quiet about her real thoughts, just the way they liked her best.

She sat in the Putnams' conservatory, a fashionable room with a terracotta tile floor and curtains of dotted muslin. A fern grew in a bronze planter at the end of the sofa next to Lizzie. It was so large that one frond tapped her shoulder whenever she moved her head.

Outside, the sky darkened. A light rain flicked against the windows, giving the room a contrasting coziness. The baby fussed. Mrs. Putnam took him from Erma, bounced him on her thighs, floated him on her fat, rustling skirts until he quieted. "Isn't he precious?" she asked, and Lizzie supposed that another time he was bound to be. He hiccoughed, his heavy eyelids flying open, startled, with each spasm. "Isn't he the precious man?"

"He is just so precious," Mrs. Mullin said. "Erma, he's a little rosebud!" Mrs. Mullin was wearing a dress of gray wool, with a white collar that sprang up around her thin neck. From certain angles her head seemed suspended above it like an impossibly balanced egg.

Blythe appeared, pushing a cart with their afternoon tea. Blythe was a widow with two adult sons who'd worked for the Putnams fifteen years now. When she left the room, Mrs. Putnam would say that they thought of Blythe as one of the family. Mrs. Mullin would add what a charity it was to keep her on, when a Chinaman could be got for so much less. Cheap Chinese help was one reason wives in San Francisco society were considered so spoiled.

Lizzie's own contributions were equally unvarying. "How are the boys, Blythe?" Lizzie asked, just as she always did, as if they weren't, in fact, grown men.

"I've no complaints, Miss Hayes," Blythe said, but in her absence, Mrs. Putnam would know better. The boys were badly behaved, shockingly extravagant. They would be the ruin of poor Blythe if not the actual death of her.

Blythe brought Lizzie the tea tray. On it were biscuits with almonds pressed into the tops and arranged like petals, and buttered toast with lime marmalade. Lizzie circled the spoon in her cup so it made a rough music against the china, like the tongue of a crude bell. She turned to Erma. "Think how many times you and I played at this. Tea parties with water for tea and wooden blocks for tea cakes. In this very house. Why are children in such a hurry to grow up?"

"Babies," said Erma complacently, "are God's very best idea." And that quickly the coziness was gone. Lizzie felt excluded from the sentiment, as though she were still playing make-believe while everyone else had gone on and done the real thing. She would never have a baby, nor would she be anyone's baby ever again. She had a tactile memory of her mother's hand on the back of her head, following the brushstroke down her hair, and was overcome with self-pity when it turned out to be the fern. Poor Lizzie had no one of her very own. She sat back and the fern frond groped at her bosom.

Outside the melancholy ticking of rain, inside the murmur of women's voices. Blythe was one of the family, but ever so much more expensive than a Chinaman would be. Children were God's very best idea, except for Blythe's, who would be the death of her. Mrs. Mullin had met a Mr. and Mrs. Derry while attending a lecture on the customs of Japan. "In Japan, they consider it impolite to finish the food on your plate!"

"Not really! Do you hear, Lizzie?"

"They won't take a gift unless it's offered three times! The first two are considered mere politeness."

Lizzie helped herself to another biscuit. What a nightmare fund-raising must be in Japan!

According to Mrs. Mullin, the Japanese were an exceptionally clean, respectable race, who only looked like the Chinese. The way you could tell the difference was that the Japanese were extremely sensitive to beauty. Sunrises and waterfalls and the like, they couldn't get enough of them. The Chinese didn't care so much for nature, which is why they were so good underground.

But the Derrys were a nice, refined sort of people, and they lived on Octavia, close to the Bell mansion. They'd told Mrs. Mullin that in the days before the Sharon trial had made Mrs. Pleasant such a public figure, large groups of Negroes used to gather at the House of Mystery for voodoo ceremonies. This would happen only on stormy nights and when Thomas Bell was away. "How those women carried on in his absence! They counted on the noise of the wind to cover the drums, but it didn't hardly do the job," Mrs. Mullin noted. "As if thunder rolls in rhythm!"

Mrs. Putnam's teacup floated to her mouth. She spoke from

behind it. "I hope you've kept your promise and not seen that woman again." Everyone turned to look at Lizzie. "I'm forced to tell you there's been talk." Her voice *sounded* forced. It sounded tired, upset. "Ever since the séance your name has been linked to hers. A strong public disavowal right then and there would have settled the matter."

"I'll make one here and now. I'll have nothing more to do with her," Lizzie said. The room was warm with tea and approval. Poor Malina Paillet, who never got to be warm again. Drums and the moon and a young dead girl about whom no one cared. Red rooms and painted mouths. Statues of naked, pleading women. Goodbye to all of that, and not the tiniest touch of headache.

In fact, after her declaration, things got even better. As a reward for being the same old Lizzie, Mrs. Putnam invited her to join them for the Saturday-evening promenade. Not this week, when they had a dinner to go to, but weather permitting, the next. Happy Lizzie! She loved the Saturday-night Market Street parade. Saturday afternoon was for women and fashion. Lizzie could go to that alone, but she had no interest. Saturday night required an escort.

And then things got better yet. The baby made a series of gaseous noises and began to smell. The nursemaid was hovering nearby. She was thin and drained-looking, a woman whose hands, when empty, drooped exhausted from her wrists. Mrs. Putnam handed little Charles to her. His odor receded down the hall, up the stairs, and behind the nursery doors. There was no further talk of what a rosebud he was. Lizzie drank her tea in utter contentment.

3

THEN, AFTER ALL that stalwart normalcy, that very Sunday, as she was leaving St. Luke's, she met Mr. Finney out with his hack. He tipped his hat, exclaimed unconvincingly on the coincidence, and offered her a free ride to the Ark or her home, wherever she was headed. In full sunlight, his eyes, behind his glasses, were bluer, but mottled as pebbles.

As part of being her same old self, Lizzie had determined never to see Mr. Finney again. Someone else could deal with the mystery of Jenny Ijub, though it had seduced her initially by being so like a story, with its medieval jousting and Irish wives as tiny as fairies. But she was resolved to leave it now unfinished, had never found Jenny an agreeable little girl. If there were a wealthy father, someone else would have to produce him.

Lizzie's mood of the moment was elevated. She'd just heard an improving sermon with many particulars worth considering at her leisure. "Making a home for Christ in your heart" had been the basic text, and she'd planned to spend the afternoon examining and redoubling her efforts to do so.

Instead, Mr. Finney. After the first shock, she was not frightened of him. It was daylight; there were plenty of people on the streets.

He made the offer so courteously. There was a nasty, gritty wind, and a ride, even in an open hack, would be nicer than walking. She could see that the only way out was through. She asked to be taken to the Brown Ark, since there was no reason he should learn where she lived and she very much doubted the ride would be free.

Sure enough, Mr. Finney had a proposition to make. He began by telling her how much he admired her. His opinion of her was exceedingly high. "I see I didn't snow you for a minute," he said. He was relaxed, affable. He really was very good-looking, in a scholarly way, because of the spectacles, but easy in his movements and manner. Lizzie was proud to be seen with such a presentable young man. She rerouted some of her disapproval of him to herself for this ridiculous vanity.

He twisted around in his seat, scarcely tending to the horse, but it seemed to manage without him. "You didn't snow me, either," he continued. "I know you still have the child."

"I don't," Lizzie said, which was a lie on a Sunday and saddened her greatly. The wind boxed her ears. So she quickly tempered it with something true. "I do know where she is." In spite of her resolute uninvolvedness, she found she couldn't stop there. "What do you want with her?" she asked.

There was a suspenseful moment while she waited for the answer. She expected to hear about abandoned women. Romance and betrayal. Summer heat. A child born unwelcomely. *Babies are God's very best idea,* except when they're not. She could practically do the story herself, though the interest would be in the names and details. But a carriage was passing them; Mr. Finney had turned around momentarily to drive.

When he could, he turned back. Why, nothing, he told her. He didn't want the child at all. He was pleased to think of the good care she was getting with the good ladies of the Brown Ark. He gave

Lizzie a gorgeous smile, revealing his tiny incisor like a fang. There was a sudden strong gust of wind, which took the yellow feather from her hat. Lizzie watched it fly away.

Not what the girl was accustomed to, Mr. Finney added darkly. Lizzie turned to look at him again. When he saw she was looking, he shook his head sadly. No, it was her mother wished her returned. Mr. Finney observed that a well-brought-up lady like Miss Hayes would have only the highest opinion of motherhood. Probably Miss Hayes's own mother was a saint. But Miss Hayes mustn't be picturing a natural mother with a natural mother's feelings. "Truly," Mr. Finney finished, "a great shame that God don't deny motherhood to women of cruel and grasping disposition." He seemed to be losing his Irish accent. It faded in and out of his speech now, as if he couldn't decide on his heritage.

It made Lizzie wonder whether he needed the glasses. At just that moment he took them off. He pulled a handkerchief from his pocket; it snapped like a flag.

"But the child's mother could take her at any time," she pointed out. "I don't understand what she needs you for. I don't understand the need for lies and subterfuges."

The horse wandered to the side of Gough Street and stopped. In the resulting silence, Mr. Finney muted his voice. "Ah, but then there's Mammy Pleasant. She paid the mother good money for the child. She mustn't know the child's been taken back."

"She bought the child?" Lizzie asked. How would that happen? Was the child for sale to anyone, or had Mrs. Pleasant simply made an irresistible offer? She imagined Mrs. Pleasant coolly covering the face of a murdered girl with her housekeeping apron. What wouldn't the woman do? She resolved yet again not to play any part in Mrs. Pleasant's machinations.

"I imagine it pleased her to buy a little white girl." Mr. Finney's voice was prim. He wiped one eye with his handkerchief, dabbed at it. "I'm afraid some sand has blown into my eye," he said. "Might I impose upon you, Miss Hayes, to look?" There was nothing of Ireland in his accent now, but there might have been a whisper of Australia. "Please. I can feel a stone the size of a goose egg rolling about in there."

Lizzie could see no way to refuse him, not with his eye so obviously streaked with red. He leaned down to her and she leaned forward. The brim of her hat touched his face. They were almost close enough to kiss.

The eye he held open was swimming with tears. Through them Lizzie could see a pinpoint of dust. She took his handkerchief and touched it away. Inside her leather gloves, her fingers shivered. "I thank you," he told her. "You're a lady who doesn't shrink from a rough task. Many would have fainted."

He blinked several times, then returned to the topic under discussion. He didn't know what the bill of sale had been, he said, but he'd been offered thirty dollars for the quiet restoration of child to mother. Now, for that same thirty dollars, he would tell the mother he'd been unable to locate the child. He would pretend that Lizzie's trick had fooled him, as it might, after all, have done. He asked for no additional sum, because it sat so much better with his conscience to leave the girl where she was. He would have the thirty dollars he'd already all but earned, and he would have peace of mind as well. Everyone would be happy who deserved to be. He would prefer cash.

The horse urinated loudly. The noise went on and on. It was a sound Lizzie usually found comforting—the same sound as when you poured yourself a hot bath, the lullaby sound of rain on stone. Now it seemed merely coarse. This was an ugly request to come so close after a moment of some intimacy. Could he have dreamt for one instant that she would agree? The particular sum he requested had the touch of Judas in it.

"I have a small independence," Lizzie said coldly. She didn't credit a word he said. "But I'm not a wealthy woman."

The horse stamped its foot. Mr. Finney reached the whip to her shoulder, sketched down her arm with it. It didn't actually touch her, but Lizzie felt her face grow hot. "I begin to see the pattern of our friendship," Mr. Finney said. "And it's you denying me every little thing I ask."

He was flirting with her! "We're not friends," Lizzie said, climbing from the hack to the street. There was nothing flattering about this, she told herself, but she had to make the point sternly. She waited to feel as insulted as she'd been.

Mr. Finney's voice was increasingly soft. "That choice belongs to the lady, of course. But it disappoints me to hear you say so.

"Twenty-five dollars, then." He was clearly a man with a tender heart. "It's worth five dollars to me just to keep Mammy Pleasant out of it."

"I couldn't scrape together more than ten," Lizzie said haughtily. She meant it as a refusal. He took it as an offer. He said he would come to the Brown Ark the next day to get it. He picked up the reins and clattered away, abandoning her on Gough Street like the sharper he was.

Apparently neither age nor position nor blameless respectability protected a woman from the mockery of a man who'd attained none of these. Apparently he thought her so old and neglected that she would respond to any cheap attention. Even worse was the way she had done so. Lizzie stood looking after him, touching her gloved hands to her cheeks. She was angry, but she was also flushed and unsettled. She'd just been blackmailed and it was her very first time.

The wind had grown stronger. It hissed through the lattice of telegraph wires, rattled the ash cans, tossed single sheets of newspaper about like confetti, spit sand into the air. It lifted her dress and breathed on her ankles; loosened her hair from its pins and beat her around the face with it. She clutched her hat to her head.

Rabbi Voorsanger came around the corner. Usually his face was wreathed in his own cigar smoke. Today the wind was carrying the smoke away.

From an upstairs window Lizzie could just hear the chords of an accordion. They resolved themselves into "Santa Lucia." The rabbi's steps were light, and timed to the music. He danced his way down the hill, beard and coat flapping, until he disappeared into a crowd of people.

4

SO INSTEAD OF MAKING A HOME for Christ in her heart, Lizzie spent the afternoon thinking about Mr. Finney. First she thought that she could simply not be at the Brown Ark when he came. Let the matter of the Chinese boy have an extra day to settle itself. Let Nell be the one to send someone to send Mr. Finney off.

Then, having given the matter a troubled night, she'd realized that the right thing, however distasteful, however uncertain in result, the Christian thing, however it prolonged her involvement in the continued, messy saga of Jenny Ijub, would be to return the girl to her mother. She should meet Mr. Finney as planned and she should ask who Jenny's mother was and how to find her.

Perhaps she was not such a bad mother. Lizzie had no evidence beyond Mr. Finney's word that she was, and Mr. Finney's word was clearly insufficient.

There was, of course, the fact that she'd sold her daughter. Could a mother sell a daughter she loved? Lizzie thought that if she asked the Chinese boy this question, he would surely say yes. He would know of wonderful mothers who'd done just that. Apparently the woman cared enough for Jenny to offer thirty dollars for her return. Thirty dollars was probably a fortune to such a woman.

It had begun to rain that night and was raining hard by morning. Lizzie didn't usually go to the Ark in the rain. But when Lizzie made up her mind to something, it was made up. Jenny must be returned to the mother who wanted her back. This meant that Lizzie must first meet with Mr. Finney.

By lunchtime she'd forgotten Mr. Finney even existed.

While she was still dressing and making her plans, the Chinese boy arrived to fetch her. Ti Wong was a round-cheeked child, short and solidly packed, who looked younger than his eleven years. Of course, the Chinese calculated age differently. He told her he was collecting whatever board members he could. Mrs. Hallis, the Ladies' Relief and Protection Society president, and Mrs. Wilson, the ex-president, were already in the buggy. Nell said they were needed at once since some of the wards were ill.

His English turned out to be excellent, a fast, bitten-off staccato, but easy enough to understand and with a good vocabulary. Lizzie learnt later that it had improved wonderfully the minute Nell stopped trying to get someone to run him off.

One boy was especially ill, Meredith Penny, newly arrived from Santa Cruz. Ti Wong had himself helped Nell move Meredith in the night to the sickroom, and he told Lizzie that the boy had been too hot, with a too light, too shallow pulse. "Wood floating on water," he said. And when she didn't answer, added as if in explanation, "a Fu pulse."

The rain turned to a downpour. The mule stared curses at them, its ears set at an outraged angle. Lizzie took the seat in the front of the buggy and tried to hold an umbrella over herself and Ti Wong both. It was more polite than it was effective; he was already drenched. By the time they reached the Brown Ark, Ti Wong's teeth were chattering and his hands trembled the reins over the mule's back.

They drew up beside Dr. Kearney's rig. His bay nickered at them, gleaming wet and miserable. Ti Wong went to stable the mule and change his clothes. Lizzie and the other board members joined Nell and Dr. Kearney in the sickroom.

Meredith Penny was eight years old, Mrs. Lake told Lizzie later. He had plans to be a fireman. "I can't interest you in medicine, then?" Dr. Kearney was asking as Lizzie entered. He was seated by the bed in a chair that was too small for him, his knees high as a grasshopper's. He had his watch out; his hand cupped Meredith's wrist. "You have the look of a doctor to me."

Meredith allowed as how he might be a doctor.

"A doctor meets the nicest people," Dr. Kearney said.

In the parlor he gave the women his diagnosis. Diphtheria. Lizzie's feet were wet and her neck was cold. She didn't know whether the latter was from rain or terror. The storm was painting the parlor windows with water and sand, so that the room grew darker with every gust of wind. "Oh, my Lord," Mrs. Hallis said. Her hands were gripped together and still they shook. "Oh, my Lord."

Dr. Kearney put the Brown Ark under immediate quarantine. Lizzie sent Ti Wong out in his dry clothes into the storm to nail the yellow warning card onto the front door and stable the doctor's horse.

The other children were released from class and told to wait on their beds until Dr. Kearney could see them. By the end of the morning, Jenny Comstock, age fourteen, Ella Louisa Gray, age five, Harry Whinery, age five, and Kate Hanley, age seven, had all been sent to the sickroom. Six days passed and they'd been joined by Tilly Beacon, age twelve, Mansel Bennett, age eleven, Mattie Lorenzen, age seven, Elizabeth Jane Comstock, age fourteen, Alexander

MacPherson, age five, George Maxwell, age nine, and Edward Reed, age twelve.

In later years Lizzie often felt she remembered little of those dreadful days. She had been too tired and too terrified to take it in. Just as often, she felt she could never forget it. One child after another became listless and feverish. Some of them complained of sore throats, more did not. Their cheeks were the color of burnt roses, their lips slowly turned blue. Only the unaffected cried; the sick were too busy breathing.

Every woman on the board with no small children of her own arrived to help. When they slept, they slept on the sofas in the tower room and the parlor and on chairs beside the children's beds. They did manage to contain the disease within the Ark itself; no cases were reported in the rest of the city.

Bartholomew Fitton's father attempted to remove him from the Ark. He stood on the porch, a small, fat, desperate man in a straw hat, shouting at Nell so that all the children could hear. No power on earth would force him to leave his son there to die, he shouted. He tried to shoulder Nell aside, but she would not move. The police took Mr. Fitton away. A gun was found in his breast pocket; the officer then posted at the door told them so. This officer had his own children and wouldn't accept so much as a cup of tea from inside.

Meanwhile, the Comstocks, whose twins were already showing signs of the disease, made a tent for themselves in sight of the sickroom windows. They appeared under these every morning, waiting. Mrs. Lake would open the windows. "All serene," she would call, so they'd know their children had lived through another night.

Meredith Penny was moved again, this time into a private room. Lizzie sat with him for hours, soaked in the general smell of sickness and the particular smell of this sickness—an unmistakable sort of wet mouse odor. When she'd been without sleep for more than a day, Lizzie had moments that returned her to her mother's deathbed. She stroked her mother's arm. She brushed her mother's hair. Her father's death was much more recent, but sudden and unexpected, a heart attack, and without the awful vigil.

No one had really gotten to know this child. She tried to hold his twitching hands, she talked to him, she sponged his forehead. All the while, his eyes bulged from their sockets; his breath rasped in his throat like a crow cawing.

She ran out of things to say. She didn't know what songs he might like, or what stories. She wanted to talk to him about him, to give him a whole story of himself. This is what you love, she wanted to say. This is what you're good at. These are the foods you like to eat. Here's something you said when you were five. But she didn't know him at all.

On the seventh day he seemed better, and she waited hopefully for Dr. Kearney to tell her this was not her imagination. Dr. Kearney shook his head, leaning down to her softly. "This is the worst for me," he said. "When it's children and there's nothing for me to do." Meredith Penny's fever rose higher and higher, until it carried him away. He died, and Lizzie and Mrs. Hallis and Dr. Kearney and the Reverend Phillips watched him do it.

Later that morning Nell found Lizzie hiding in the cupola. "You need to eat and you need to sleep," Nell said. Grief made her even fiercer than usual. "We're only getting started," she added, because she was not one for the comforting lie.

Lizzie was hungry, but she couldn't make herself go back down-stairs. I'll never sleep, she thought, but she did, though she rose four hours later, unrested. In that same four hours, Lena Heath, age ten, had been sent to the sickroom.

The rain of days before had passed. It would have suited Lizzie better than this calm blue, this high, indifferent sky. She went to the kitchen to make herself some coffee. She turned at the slippery sound of Mrs. Lake's shoes.

"He's with his mother now," Mrs. Lake told her. "That's what I try to hold in my mind. The child falling asleep in his mother's arms. There's rejoicing in heaven today." This surely should have been a great comfort, but Lizzie could not make it so. She was too tired. She had another bit of a cry and then washed her face, combed her hair, and returned to the sickroom.

A week later, the sick included Ella May Howard, age twelve, Franka Haun, age six, May Isabella Miller, age twelve, Dock Franklin Cole, age eight, Bartholomew Fitton, age five, and Harry Ambrose, age eight. Mattie Lorenzen was dead, although Dr. Kearney had performed a tracheotomy to try to save him. So was Ella Louisa Gray, the first child in her class to learn to skip.

On February 22, Nell woke Lizzie from an afternoon nap. "Ti Wong," she said simply, and Lizzie rose to follow her down the stairs to the private room for the dying. Miss Stevens had arrived already and stood by the boy's bed.

His appearance was an enormous shock, just when each of the women would have said she was far past shocking. They'd not thought of him as one of the children. No one had ever asked him how he was feeling. Nell's face was wet and melted at the eyes, soft as dough. "He never complained, the lamb. He did as he was told and he never complained. Just yesterday I sent him to the basement for clean blankets. He must have already been deathly ill. Running up and down those flights of stairs. If only we'd sent him right away as I wished. Just a few weeks with us will be enough to kill him."

Ti Wong did not appear to be conscious. He lay with his fingers opening and closing as if he could catch his breath in his hands. "The policeman's gone for Dr. Kearney," Nell said. "I only hope he can be found."

Lizzie leaned down and tried to speak to Ti Wong. Beneath the thin surface of his lids, his eyes darted about like minnows. She picked up his hand, hot in hers, still grasping spasmodically. She felt his wrist; his pulse was unsteady, intermittent. A Fu pulse, Lizzie remembered he'd said with casual eleven-year-old competence. She was the one who'd let him stay. She was the one to send him out to stable a horse in his last suit of dry clothes. This one would fall to her account.

The other women returned to the other patients. Lizzie sat with Ti Wong. She prayed to God to spare them both. God makes no bargains, her mother had told her often enough, and a woman with a dead child knows this better than anyone. But Lizzie had never gotten out of the habit. In return for Ti Wong she offered God Ti Wong. Give us back this valuable child, she prayed, and I promise to value him. I promise him a valuable life. Not as a servant, but as something requiring education, a minister or a teacher.

She knew this promise would be hard to fulfill. She stood by it. Let the very difficulty of it speak to her desperation. Ti Wong's breath slid in and out of his throat with a sound like sandpaper. He lived on a ribbon of air, which spun down to a thread. His face went from blue to black. His hand went from hot to cold. Two hours passed, and then three.

Then came a long moment when he didn't breathe at all. Lizzie was on her feet, ringing frantically for the other women, when the trough of his chest finally rose.

"He's dying," she told Nell, who arrived first. "If Dr. Kearney's rig isn't already outside, then he's too late."

She couldn't take her eyes off Ti Wong's chest. She was hardly aware of Miss Stevens, arriving with towels, alcohol, a knife, a child's silver whistle, until she spoke. "We'll have to do it ourselves," Miss Stevens said. "I'll do it. I've watched Dr. Kearney three times now."

If she hadn't offered, the procedure might have been discussed. It was possible the terrified women would have talked about it and talked about it until it was too late. Lizzie was overwhelmed with gratitude. Wonderful Miss Stevens with her science projects and her dissections. Her wonderful young eyes and her steady heart. Ti Wong began to convulse. His chest was an empty bowl.

Lizzie held him by the arms. She had to climb onto the bed to do this, hoist her skirts and straddle the boy. Nell took hold of his head. Miss Stevens put the knife to his throat. She paused then, with her eyes closed. "Yea, though I walk through the valley of the shadow of death, I will fear no evil," Lizzie said. She spoke loudly for Ti Wong to hear. Nell joined her. "... for Thou art with me." Miss Stevens made her first cut.

"Hold him still," she cried, because the child had jerked and struggled. Blood flowed from his throat, pooled in the cup of his neck. "I can't see what I'm doing," she said then, sharply. "There wasn't so much blood for Dr. Kearney." Lizzie let go of Ti Wong's arms to towel the blood away with both hands. It came too fast, ran from his neck like water from a spout, seeped into Lizzie's sleeves. Miss Stevens had slit his throat.

Lizzie stopped wiping the blood away and tried to hold it back instead. Miss Stevens pushed her hands aside, made a second blind cut. There, amidst the blood, Lizzie could see a thin white shining reed. Miss Stevens impaled it on the point of her knife, rotated her wrist. With the other hand, she slid the whistle down beside the blade. Ti Wong's chest rose at once, his breath singing a long, high, hysterical note, twice, three times. His face grew pink again and his fists relaxed. He slept while Miss Stevens held the whistle in place with her fingers and Lizzie kept the blood back with soaking towels and her hands.

Five minutes later Dr. Kearney rushed in and found them there, Lizzie still astride Ti Wong, afraid to move. What a picture they must have made, Lizzie thought later. Miss Hayes and Miss Stevens drenched in gore, two Lady Macbeths up to their elbows, their hands inside Ti Wong's neck, and Ti Wong singing in his sleep like a bird. The doctor was impressed all the way to speechlessness by the sight of them.

It was something to remember, something to carry with them out of the horror, that they had behaved with courage and competence. When a thing needed doing, they had done it. Miss Stevens was the heroine, of course, but Lizzie had also come through. Ti Wong survived diphtheria and the Ladies' Relief and Protection Society both, and had the scars to prove it.

The next day Bartholomew Fitton, George Maxwell, and Elizabeth Jane Comstock died within hours of one another. It was a dreadful, unspeakable day.

These proved to be the final diphtheria deaths. Of the fifty-seven children residing in the Brown Ark at the time, twenty contracted the disease and six of those died. The other fourteen recovered their health—"Children are resilient," Dr. Kearney said—but the agony of loss was slow to recede.

5

FOR MANY MONTHS AFTERWARD, every moment of pleasure for Lizzie was quickly followed by feelings of guilt. Where before she'd wished to return to her normal self as a matter of principle, now it was a matter of need. Another magical juncture she must find the strength to refuse. But how would she ever enjoy her dinner, her book, her Saturday ride again? She lost weight, though not to the point of being thin. She couldn't sleep. Ti Wong was the only subject on which she could allow herself to be happy.

What a bright boy he turned out to be. She loved to hear how he'd wheedled Nell into letting him make popcorn or taffy. If any of the other children asked, Nell said it was too much mess. But Ti Wong was her pet, her favorite.

When he was still abed, letting Lizzie read him Sherlock Holmes mysteries and recovering his voice, she had told Nell that they needed to give more thought to his future. Nell was surprisingly agreeable, even to this. "What would you like to be when you grow up?" Lizzie had asked him.

She herself had already decided he'd be a doctor. A Fu pulse, he'd told her. Dr. Kearney could surely be coopted into this project. He would see the value in a doctor who spoke Chinese but was trained in Western medicine, none of that hocus-pocus of spinning needles.

Ti Wong had answered he wanted to be a Pinkerton, but that could be changed. Would have to be changed. The Pinks wouldn't take a Celestial.

And then, just when some routine was finally returning—classes, fights among the boys, quarrels among the girls all resumed—just when it seemed things could, in fact, go on Minna Graham came to the breakfast table, complaining of a headache. The light was dreadful bright, she told them. Her eyes hurt. She asked to go back to bed. Nell was too tired to deal with it. She suggested that Minna, unable to contract diphtheria and largely ignored during the epidemic, now wanted attention. This was agreed to be just like Minna Graham. She went so far as to break out in large red spots.

Measles, Dr. Kearney said. Two weeks later seven of the children, including Jenny Ijub, had rashes. New cases continued to appear throughout the month. Fortunately the strain involved was a light one. The new epidemic recalled the tragedies inevitably to everyone's mind, but didn't repeat them.

6

NEXT CAME AN EPIZOETIC. More than half the horses in the Turf Gallery and the Fashion Stables on Sutter Street contracted distemper, as well as twenty of the horses in the Bill Bridges Stable, thirteen in the Hopkins Stable, and four in Roe Allen's Stable on Market Street. Citywide some three hundred horses were affected. A chloride of lime mixed with carbolic acid was recommended for use about the barn. For horses themselves, potash and licorice root were to be applied in a paste directly onto the swollen glands in the throat.

The symptoms, case by case, were mild, but the aggregate was not; the streetcar companies were all but crippled. Yet under these adverse circumstances Myrtle Rolphe managed to get to Chinatown. Unaccompanied by police or clergy, with the proprietor protesting her every step, Miss Rolphe walked into the bowels of an opium den. With one hand she held a lavender-scented handkerchief over her nose to protect herself from the seductive fumes. With the other she seized one of Jesus' straying lambs by the ear and dragged him to safety. The incident was less than twenty-four hours old, and Lizzie had already heard the story five times at least.

Ti Wong could not hear it often enough. He was so obviously in love with Miss Rolphe. It made Lizzie very sad. Such an open display, such a hopeless object. She thought of Diego Estenagas, her Spanish prince. Only unrequited love lasted forever. Poor Ti Wong would spend his life desiring pretty, charitable white women who liked him only for his faith.

7

ALTHOUGH ALL THE WOMEN at the Brown Ark carried the diphtheria tragedies with them for the rest of their lives, on Mrs. Lake
there was an immediate and peculiar impact. She began to insist that
Ti Wong had brought the disease from Chinatown, even though
Meredith Penny had obviously arrived from Santa Cruz already ill,
even though there'd been no other reported cases in San Francisco
and a deadly plague in Santa Cruz.

Not that it mattered, Mrs. Lake was quick to assert. No one was
blaming anyone. But. Still. Lizzie thought Mrs. Lake was suffering
from not having saved anybody with an emergency tracheotomy.
Miss Stevens was handling herself better.

There was another factor contributing to Mrs. Lake's imbalance.
An unrelenting series of plagues is always bound to carry a biblical
portent. But San Francisco had already been hearing for some time
that Armageddon was coming.

One afternoon back in October, when Lizzie had been eating
a lunch at the Brown Ark, by invitation of course, she'd brought
up the rumors of the appearance in Nevada of an Indian Messiah.
He was reported to be preaching of the coming of a new world,
a world without white people, which was even now floating in the

heavens, drifting eastward from the Pacific toward the plains. When the new world landed, the whites would be destroyed, while all the dead Indians and herds of dead buffalo would be resurrected. The Messiah asked His followers only to be honest, peaceable, and chaste. He was said to perform miracles. This was all, in Lizzie's mind, very Christian, which made it hard to dismiss.

Miss Stevens had responded to Lizzie by telling the table how, in August of 1872, the Indians in Lake County had begun to perform the Misha Dance, prompted by the appearance of a monstrous fish in Blue Lakes. They'd feared the end of the world was at hand, Miss Stevens said. Her tone of voice was amused, as if these fears had, in fact, been demonstrably mistaken.

The real subject of this conversation was Mrs. Maria B. Woodworth. Mrs. Woodworth was an evangelist, called on by God in spite of her sex. She'd arrived in Oakland after a triumphant tour of the Midwest, set up a tent, and begun a series of revivals. Here are just a few of the things people said about her:

"Genuine, old-fashioned Methodist religion" (Dr. Lewis Kern).

"I like it the best of anything I ever saw in the way of a religious meeting" (I. H. Ellis).

"The same low order which characterized the African Voodoo, and the Indian Medicine Man" (Charles Wendt, Unitarian pastor).

"Mental debauchery" *(Tribune* editorial).

Mrs. Woodworth's technique was charismatic to the point of mesmerism. Her followers fell often into ecstatic trances, during which they lay as if dead. These trances could last for hours or days, until those who experienced them came to at last, weeping and seeing angels.

Oakland doctors wrote letters to the papers, expressing concern about the effects of undiluted religion upon the weak-minded. Lizzie had read an article about one Albertson Smith, who, after attending one evening, was convinced he could fly. He leapt from the upper deck of the Oakland ferry, crashed onto the dock, and was taken into police custody.

But Mrs. Lake had actually gone to one of the winter meetings, and brought back a cautiously neutral report. The audience had by then swelled from an initial twenty-three Doom Sealers, as her followers were known, to several thousand. "It was all brimstone and the fiery pit," she'd told Miss Stevens, Lizzie, and Nell. "Babies were crying. Women were screaming. Half the crowd was singing one hymn, the other half another. People of every color there, and all treated exactly alike. Outside, the wind, howling and snapping at the tent. I couldn't hear Mrs. Woodworth at all, I could only just see her, standing at the altar with her arms raised in the air and bodies all around her feet. There must have been twenty of them or more, stiff and lifeless as logs.

"Then, just when I was wishing I hadn't come, just when I was thinking something cynical and worldly, I noticed my hands beginning to shake. They were all atingle, dancing around at the end of my arms, and I couldn't control them. And then it was my legs and I slid to the floor as gently as if I were swimming through water. One of the men cupped his hands through the air above me, as if he saw the water, too, and I were being baptized. 'Now you'll see something beautiful,' he said. Then everything went black except for one light I thought was a star, but it turned out to be the top of the tent." She offered to take Lizzie along next time. "You'll see that she has a power not easily explained," Mrs. Lake said.

But Lizzie thought it didn't sound quite the place for Episcopalians. She was joined in this sentiment by the bishop, who, in November, had issued a general instruction to stay away from women who preached. "Much good can be done by women in a quiet way," he'd said. "There is no need to make a public parade out of praying for the sick."

Privately Nell and Lizzie agreed that Mrs. Lake was among the more susceptible of God's creations and had never had a cynical or worldly thought in her life. "I'd like to see anyone try to make me see angels," said Nell, and Lizzie would have liked to see this, too.

Then Christmas had come and gone, and it was late January when Mrs. Woodworth had her vision. She'd seen a mountain of water rise out of the Pacific and fall on the three cities of Alameda, Oakland, and San Francisco. She'd pleaded with God, asking Him to spare the cities if ten righteous men could be found within them. His answer was that all the righteous should move immediately inland. His judgment on the unrighteous would take the form of a tidal wave.

This vision was shared by several of Mrs. Woodworth's followers, who added their own details. The wave would hit on April 14, 1890, just after Easter. Chicago would be simultaneously destroyed, and also Milwaukee. Europe would be plunged into war. The Doom Sealers petitioned the governor, asking him to read the Book of Jonah, set aside a day for prayer, and remove all prisoners, monies, and securities in the San Francisco area to high ground. They published pamphlets. They quit their jobs, sold their homes and belongings, and left the city.

This was the context in which Mrs. Lake had her pupils praying at all hours, searching their souls for hidden sins as if it were an Easter egg hunt. They were studying the Dark Ages, and she played a dreadful game of tag for which she'd enlisted Ti Wong. She told him to walk up and down the aisles of the room, touching the students— boys and girls both!—at random on the shoulder. Everyone he touched was to go stand at the back of the room. When the game was over, a quarter of the class remained in their seats. The others were dead. It was an aid to understanding the great plagues of Europe. Mrs. Lake claimed she'd asked Ti Wong to participate because the plague came first from China.

Such a cruel lesson, so poorly timed, so unlike gentle Mrs. Lake. The game had given Minna Graham nightmares; she'd been one of the last children touched. In her dreams, a great black bird circled her head and landed on her shoulder. She heard the rustle of its feathers in her ear and awoke crying, saying that it was pecking at her eyes. All the girls in the room with her were in a state. Mrs. Lake was sent off to the spa in Pope Valley to take the waters until she was herself again.

NELL FELT STRONGLY that among the many ill-advised features of this game must be counted the encouragement Ti Wong had been given to touch the girls. She marched him up to the cupola, where Lizzie was sorting through recent donations, so that Lizzie could talk to him about this. Someone had actually donated a used pessary. Lizzie swept it quickly underneath a cotton skirt.

She had no intention of discussing the matter of touching white girls with Ti Wong, but since he was standing before her, waiting, she tried to think of something else to discuss.

"I go somewhere for you?" he asked. "Fetch something?"

"No," Lizzie answered. "I don't need a thing," and then she reconsidered. Somewhere here, on one of the tabletops, she had left the address Mrs. Pleasant had given her for headache medicine. She had tried to go once, but had not been able to communicate with the druggist, was not even sure she'd found the right place. She'd come away with candied ginger, pretending that was what she'd wanted all along, although she had no idea what to do with it, and eventually threw it away even though she could see it would never, ever spoil and maybe she would need it one day. It had represented a failure.

Now she rose and moved the stacks of books, the almost empty bottles of ink, the letter openers, the agate paperweight, the watch face with no innards, and a faded pincushion, filled with sawdust and shaped like a strawberry. Instead of seeds it was studded with glass-topped pins, and underneath was Mrs. Pleasant's scrap of paper. Lizzie read the address aloud. "Could you find this place?" she asked Ti Wong.

"I know this place," he said. "Hall of Joyful Relief."

Myrtle Rolphe had been very clear and quite insistent. Ti Wong would run any errand, she had said, except those that took him into Chinatown. His uncle and aunt were apparently resigned to his Christianity now, and to his new home at the Brown Ark, but they could always change their minds. Any new boat could bring additional relatives, or people who claimed to be additional relatives. Then poor Ti Wong would be taken away and forced to worship idols.

But surely he would be safe enough if he and Lizzie went to Chinatown together. They would take the mule and then walk. Fresh air was always good for growing boys.

For many years a rumor had persisted that Chinatown existed as a false façade over a large underground city. Beneath the streets, the Chinese residents had dug a maze eight stories deep, where opium was smoked, slave girls hidden, gambling and tong wars pursued with Oriental implacability. In these tunnels a new race was feared to be evolving. These new, underground Chinese were said to be even more able to withstand hardship and deprivation than the originals. Someday they would come boiling out of their holes like ants.

There was another persistent rumor—that white women were kidnapped on the streets of Chinatown and kept as slaves in the dark below. Tell the proprietor I sent you, Mrs. Pleasant had said, Mrs. Pleasant about whom it was sometimes whispered that she sold white babies to Chinamen. From Lizzie's point of view there was just enough danger in a trip to Chinatown to make it a pleasure and not so much as to make it an adventure.

The Hall of Joyful Relief was located on Washington Place. The streets were crowded and noisy, dark and narrow. It had rained in the night, the water rushing down California Street to puddle in the alleys and reflect the red and gilt of the balconies above. There was the smell of fish and incense. Ti Wong led Lizzie past a barbershop, where a man bent over a customer, reaching into his ear with a little black pick, then past a grocery, where sugar cane stalks leaned like fishing poles against the walls. Racks of plucked chickens hung by their necks in the windows. On the sidewalk were buckets of live crabs and turtles.

A white man emerged from an alleyway, winked at Lizzie rudely, and walked by. Nothing about him suggested that he was a gentleman. They passed a restaurant whose odors she had never encountered before and could not identify, but made her mouth water anyway. On Dupont, thin, reedy music floated down from an upper story. One huge golden tooth swung from the balcony railing of a building where, presumably, a dentist worked. On the next balcony over, Lizzie saw an old man smoking a pipe and staring back at her. They passed a house flying the dragon flag of China and a large sign in English that read: "Chow Loon, 4 family Parental Tablet Society."

A woman with wooden soles and ankle bracelets walked by, her bracelets ringing, her shoes clapping. She wore rouge in a large red oval that covered her face, and her hair was oiled a shiny black. All San Francisco knew of the sad lives of Chinese slave women. The sight made Lizzie take hold of Ti Wong's sleeve. He turned to look at her. She thought he might imagine she was trying to keep him, instead of her intention, which was to keep him safe. She let go.

In the window of the Hall of Joyful Relief, a row of green bottles caught the sun. Each bottle held a horned toad, pickled and standing on its head. The druggist sat at a table, writing something for another man who stood and dictated in rapid Chinese. When Lizzie and Ti Wong entered, the druggist held up one hand to silence them before they spoke. Lizzie watched him write. He held the brush upright with his thumb and index finger, but moved it down the page with the little finger. After he finished, the two men talked together briefly.

Then the druggist turned to Lizzie. "Tell him," Lizzie said to Ti Wong, "that I want a tea for headache. Tell him Mrs. Pleasant, the colored woman from Octavia Street, said he would know what to give me."

She was embarrassed to have come. The bottles of toads did not look scientific to her. She had no faith in the enigmatic learning of the Orient. If their religion was primitive, wouldn't their medicine be the same? She could just hear the bells of St. Mary's tolling the hour, a reproachful, Christian sound. And yet, as administered by Mrs. Pleasant, the tea had seemed to help. To ignore actual experience was also a form of superstition.

The druggist reached over and took hold of Ti Wong's clipped hair. He rubbed it with his fingers. Lizzie felt his disapproval. He touched the scars on Ti Wong's throat. Next he reached past Ti Wong to Lizzie, grasping her wrist, pressing for her pulse. He spoke extensively in Chinese, then disappeared into the back of the shop, and returned with a paper envelope filled with dried leaves and flowers. He held up four fingers. Four cups of tea? Four cents? Lizzie turned to Ti Wong, who managed the purchase for her.

"What did he say to you?" she asked Ti Wong when they were on the street again.

"That Mrs. Pleasant very smart," said Ti Wong. "That you have many headaches."

It had been a much longer conversation than that, but Lizzie didn't question him further. On the corner of Dupont and Washington, a bearded man sat at a table covered with red cloth on which were placed several painted boxes. He called to Ti Wong, reached into one box, pulled out a paper, and read from it. He laughed, and all trace of expression left Ti Wong's face. They walked on.

"Do you know that man?" Lizzie asked.

"Fortune-teller. Friend of uncle."

"What did he say to you?"

Ti Wong fluttered his fingers along the scars on his neck as if he were playing a flute. Lizzie didn't think he knew he was doing so. She wished it to be a cheerful mannerism, but feared it was a nervous one.

"My fortune," he said. He wouldn't look at her. "That Jesus boys be swimming soon, but Chinese boys stay happy and dry."

9

AFTER LIVING AT THE ARK in quarantine for so many weeks, Lizzie had been surprised by how hard it was to return to her solitary house. She'd thought she couldn't wait for her quiet breakfasts again, with only the newspaper for company, for her own bedroom and her own bed, but sleep eluded her. Or so it seemed, though she must have dozed sometimes, because one morning she remembered a dream. She was in a boat with a blue-eyed man who turned out to be Mr. Finney. He stood. "Save me," he said. He stepped onto the water and sank slowly, as if into mud—up to his knees, up to his waist, up to his shoulders, out of sight.

Lizzie had forgotten about Mr. Finney, and also about Jenny's mother and her own plans regarding them. Currently she had no appetite for schemes of any kind. God would do as God would do. Why meddle? Besides, she'd no way to contact Mr. Finney.

In fact, she could think of nothing worth getting out of bed for. Donations had more than doubled during the epidemics, while the number of wards had significantly dropped. Many of the survivors had been removed at the first chance by relatives. They would not be back until the specter of death faded from everyone's mind. As a consequence there were beds and shoes enough for everyone. The larder was stocked. Lizzie didn't suppose the budget had ever been so healthy.

Take a rest, everyone told Lizzie, take a trip. Just when she hadn't heart enough for either.

She lay one morning, hardly moving, under her mother's quilt, a pattern like a shackle of rings in blue and white. The white was turning to yellow and the fabric was beginning to fray. A large spider web filled the corner of the bedroom window. Lizzie couldn't see the spider, but on the sill beneath the web lay the dry, hollow corpses of two flies. The window and the curtains needed washing. Nothing was as it should be. What kind of world was it that required the deaths of children? What kind of magical juncture was that?

Are you happy with your life? Mrs. Pleasant had asked her on that first afternoon in the House of Mystery, and ever since the question, and only since the question, the answer had become no. How did she used to do it, take such pleasure in small things? How would she ever be able to do so again?

If there had been someone to bring her breakfast, Lizzie wouldn't have gotten up at all. She would have asked for tea, blankets, a fire, a story with dragons in it—a story out of someone else's childhood— or a lullaby from the same. But there was only the constant weight of Baby Edward, watching her lie there as if dead, when anyone could see she was anything but.

Finally she was too hungry. She went to the kitchen without combing her hair and made herself a poached egg on toast. Nothing spoiled food the way eating alone did. Flavors flattened, textures coarsened. Chocolate turned to copper. Chewing became audible and then thunderous. Lizzie looked back on her childhood in this very house, and it seemed to be all solitary meals, brought to her room on trays. She could not recall that she had eaten anything hot more than once or twice in her life before adulthood.

She decided to call on Mrs. Wright, who liked to tell stories and had few chances to do so. Lizzie had grown quite fond of her during their incarceration together. A visit would be an act of charity and, like all the best acts of charity, good for them both.

She found Mrs. Wright sitting in her chair in her bedroom at the Ark, facing the window, the curtains tightly pulled. There was little light in the room, and a cloying, medicinal smell, like fermented cloves. Mrs. Wright spoke before Lizzie had a chance to announce herself. "Did you have a nice time in the country, dear?"

Lizzie had talked of going to the country. "I haven't left yet," she said. She had no energy for holidays.

"You should. Birds and trees. God's poetry. Nature triumphant. Of course, at my age the words bring that bit of a chill. Nature is as nature does."

"Nonsense," said Lizzie. "You're in bloom." After all, Mrs. Wright couldn't see herself. Perhaps she would believe this.

"Nonsense back to you." Mrs. Wright's voice was made of salt.

Lizzie went to open the curtains. The clouds hung low and unbroken. The light was sullen and turned everything it touched green.

She pulled a chair into place beside Mrs. Wright and described the light to her. "I feel that way myself today," Lizzie finished. "Colorless, sunless." It was an intimate revelation. There was no reason for her to trouble Mrs. Wright with it.

"I expect you're just tired. You should buy yourself something. Ask Mr. McCallum at the Bank of California. He'll give you a draft on my account." Mrs. Wright waved her hands as if Lizzie had protested. "You know how I love to see you in something pretty." She felt for Lizzie's lap, patted it, found her hand and squeezed.

She'd drifted again. Lizzie was glad to see that she'd landed in a time when she had money and could be with someone she loved. "I'll do that," Lizzie said. "It's very kind of you."

The orange cat appeared outside. It was stalking something small, a rat perhaps, or a mole. The cat slid along the sand with focused, watery grace. Lizzie, whose heart was all with the world's little victims, could do nothing but refuse to watch. She looked instead at the lowering sky. "The city feels different to me now that I'm out in it again," she said. "It's grown around us so quickly I don't often notice, but I see it fresh just now. Like a scab laid over the past. I remember when this was all sand and chaparral. I remember those gold and silver horses the Spanish used to ride. They were so beautiful. You never see those now. Of course, you remember it better than I."

"Mostly I remember mud," Mrs. Wright said, "with empty whiskey bottles sunk into it like cobblestones to make a sidewalk, and the way the fires kept on coming, one right after another." She sucked on her false teeth with a wet, hissing sound, turned her face to Lizzie, her eyes white and veined as Florentine marble. "The land didn't want us at first. We were the persistent ones, had to be. So bring on your tidal waves. We'll survive them all right."

Well, if nothing more than endurance was required, Lizzie decided she could do it. It occurred to her that probably some Indian woman about her age had once stood in these very sand dunes and thought the same thing. How many white people can there be? How long can they stay? How much can they change?

Still, some things do endure. All around us, all inside us, something ancient manages to survive. The cat had come up empty. It sat, licked at the bottom of one paw, and then turned its head so that Lizzie saw its blunt muzzle outlined against the sand.

The Good Manners Club

MARY ELLEN PLEASANT was called to testify on Allie Hill's behalf six times during the years of the Sharon divorce case and was never cross-examined. Shortly before her death, she gave an interview in which she explained this fact. William Sharon had offered her $500,000 to quit the case. "Take the money," he'd said. "Go away and be Queen of the Niggers."

She'd refused the offer and the insult, but told him she would speak of both if his lawyers ever came after her on the stand.

Mrs. Pleasant was widely believed to be paying Allie Hill's expenses, but what the trial really cost her was her reputation. The main thing Mrs. Pleasant was charged with was baby-farming. This was irrelevant to the Sharon case, but went to character. Mrs. Pleasant had connections with foundling hospitals and prostitutes. She could tell any fun-loving man of influence and property that he'd had a child; he'd have no way of disproving it. She had a reckless unconcern for getting the correct baby into the correct family.

One day Thomas Bell was called to the stand to testify for Allie Hill. On May 1 of 1881, Sharon's lawyers claimed, Allie had been to the graveyard, casting spells and burying socks. Thomas Bell was called to refute. He distinctly recalled that Allie Hill had been at

Octavia Street all that same day, making doll clothes for Viola and Marie.

"How many children do you have?" Sharon's attorney asked on cross-examination.

The question was objected to as irrelevant.

"Thomas Bell claims to remember the exact day of Miss Hill's visit, though it happened three years ago," the lawyer argued. Surely they were entitled to test his memory a bit on other matters.

The question was allowed. Mr. Bell proved unable to answer. It might be six. It might be seven. He was flustered. "Take your time," the attorney said. "Use your fingers."

Mrs. Pleasant's baby-farming, Sharon's lawyers went on to argue, was so pervasive, the House of Mystery itself wasn't safe from her.

In later cases, those concerning the Bell estate, the origins of the Bell children were thoroughly discussed. Friends, tradesmen, physicians, psychics, spurned lovers, and dismissed servants were all called upon to clarify the inner workings of the household, though clarity was never the result of this mass of contradictory testimony.

One servant who did not testify, but was testified about, was a young woman from Panama named Bella Stercus. She'd come to work for the Bell family in 1879. The broad outlines of her story, as told by others, were supported decades later by the testimony given in the Teresa Bell estate case.

Bella Stercus was the oldest of seven children whose father had died and whose mother could no longer manage to feed so many. She came to San Francisco with little money and little English. One of the hands on her boat, pitying her, had told her to find Mrs. Mary

E. Pleasant on Octavia Street and say she needed work. She arrived with only the clothes she was wearing, but she spoke of bringing all six of her siblings to America. Mrs. Pleasant liked her spirit.

"So you've experience with children," Mrs. Pleasant said. Her Spanish was slightly better than Bella's English; between them they managed to understand each other. She engaged Bella to act as nursemaid for Fred Bell, who was now four, and Marie, who was two.

Bella had never seen anything like the House of Mystery. When she first lived there, she walked on tiptoe through the dark halls, the white rooms. The house was as silent and dim as the bottom of a pond, though the lamps and mirrors and bits of glass sent random sparkles into it like flickering fish.

The fact that Bella could hardly talk to anyone made her feel invisible, a ghost from the nursery. The staff was mostly white and she was unused to white people. After a day spent with the two white children, her own face in the mirror seemed murky, strange, all wrong, even to herself.

It was a quiet house, but sometimes she could see that things were going on. Doors and curtains would be closed. A murmur would run through the dark halls. She would take the children onto the lawn and reporters would shout questions she didn't understand through the wrought-iron gate. Once she discovered a man digging in the arbor and had to call Sam from the stables to chase him away. Later she was told that many people thought Mrs. Pleasant had a cache of diamonds buried somewhere in the yard. Sam liked to say that anyone who couldn't get to the Comstock came to dig for treasure on Octavia Street.

Nelson Brady, the colored groundskeeper, did tricks with the shadows of his hands for her. He made wolves, roosters, and angels. "Bella, Bella," he said. He was using her Christian name, or else he was telling her she was beautiful. Either was awfully fresh, but since she didn't know which it was, she didn't take offense.

Fred and Marie were placid and dimpled, easy children to care for, and yet they exhausted Bella as her own siblings never had. She went to bed as soon as the children did, and sank into sleep as if she were drowning. She dreamt of boats with feathered sails, trees that had her mother's eyes. The fog of San Francisco entered her blood, thickened coldly around her heart.

One day Mrs. Pleasant stopped Bella in the hall. She motioned for her to come into the kitchen. There, Mrs. Pleasant fried bread while Bella watched, and gave it to her, sprinkled with sugar and cinnamon. To know that someone had seen her, cared about her, cooked for her and just for her, was the first warm thing to happen to Bella in San Francisco. This was the moment she thought she would survive there. By eating that bread, she ceased to be a ghost.

Nelson Brady walked by the window, and Bella felt herself coloring. "Married," Mrs. Pleasant said. Bella looked at her without expression. Mrs. Pleasant struggled for the word. *"Esposa,"* she said, and Bella found she had understood the first time, after all.

Her English improved. She forced herself to speak it, even to the children, who didn't care. She tried to make sense of the household. The children were alternately petted and ignored. Mrs. Pleasant made all the decisions regarding them and seemed also to handle the finances. When Mrs. Bell needed money, she made the request to Mrs. Pleasant, who spoke to Mr. Bell about it. This seemed odd to Bella, but she assumed it was American.

Mrs. Bell and Mrs. Pleasant were clearly fond of each other, in a stormy, door-slamming sort of way. When Mr. Bell was traveling, which was more often than not, Mrs. Bell trailed Mrs. Pleasant about the house. Mrs. Pleasant was never idle. Bella would hear them in the hall, and the mere sound of women's voices would make her so homesick for her mother she would need to sit down until the fit passed.

But she was better at concealing it. "You're looking well," Mrs. Pleasant said to her one day. "It's good to see you bloom so. Now I know you've settled."

Then a new child arrived, not a baby, but a girl one year older than Fred. Her hair was dark as a shadow, her arms thin where Marie's and Fred's were plump, her eyes brown where theirs were blue, her manner nervous where theirs were steady. Mrs. Pleasant brought her into the nursery and introduced her as their new sister. Her name had been Viola Smith, but now would be Viola Bell. No one suggested that Bella's wages would change with the addition of a third, more difficult child.

Bella often drew pictures for the children to color. She was good with a pencil and favored the birds and flowers of her homeland, which, she told the children, were as bright as spinning tops. She coaxed Viola to the table with paint pots of red and pink.

Two days after Viola's arrival, Mrs. Bell looked in on them. "Up!" Marie said, holding out her little creased arms. "Lift me up!"

"Are we having ice cream, Mama?" Fred asked. Sometimes Mrs. Bell's visits meant special treats.

"Are we having ice cream, Mama?" Viola repeated. Her eyes were wide.

A year later Viola was still there. She was a smart girl, quicker than Fred or Marie, though perhaps merely older. She bossed Marie about, dressed her as if she were a doll, managed her at mealtimes, put her down for her nap. Marie adored her.

One day Bella gave Fred and Viola each a sugar drop for learning a poem and one to Marie for sitting quietly while they recited. Fred's poem was "The Rainbow" by Wordsworth. Viola's poem was "The Fairies" by William Allingham. When they finished, Marie clapped her hands. Then she began to cry.

"She dropped her candy," Viola, who'd already eaten hers, suggested. She knelt. "Pick up your foot, Marie," she said. "Hold on to my shoulder." She ran her fingers along the floor so that they came up dusty. It was quite a performance, and then, at the end of it, Bella found the candy in Viola's pocket.

Bella was disturbed by the incident. On previous occasions she'd also found Viola bossy, deceptive, selfish. And little Marie was thoroughly in her sway. So when Mrs. Bell asked Bella's opinion of Viola, Bella gave it. Viola was a cunning child. Bella was worried about the influence this might have on Marie.

That same afternoon, Mrs. Bell took the children to the back lawn. The sun was high and warm. The children were rosy and glassy-eyed from their naps. Everyone was relaxed and had no reason to be afraid. Mrs. Bell put all three into the hammock together. "Swing me," Fred demanded. He was now six years old. Viola was seven. Marie was four.

"Let me see you holding tight first." Mrs. Bell checked all six hands. "Don't let go," she warned, tugging especially at Marie's fists to make sure she wouldn't. Then she'd given the hammock a push. The children swung out and back. "Higher," said Fred. "Higher, higher!" Mrs. Bell pushed the hammock again. The children were laughing. Marie and Viola knocked heads, but they laughed even harder at that. "Higher," Viola said. They were laughing so hard their mouths were stuck open.

Bella saw Viola's hand lift to her forehead, touching herself where Marie's head had hit. Just then, Mrs. Bell gave another push, harder, her hand under Viola's bottom. Which came first, the shove or Viola's hand on her forehead? Bella remembered it first one way, then the other. They came so close together. She could never settle it in her mind.

The hammock turned over, spilling all three children onto the grass. Viola flew the farthest, but Marie hit the hardest. Bella heard a sound she thought was Marie's arm breaking. She ran to pick her up, wings in her throat. Marie's face had twisted into an expression of shock; her mouth was a sharp, lipless roundness from which no sound came. She stood up, holding both arms out, which was how Bella knew the arms were whole.

Bella picked Marie up and turned to look at the other two children. Fred was still laughing. Viola lay on her back, the color gone from her face. Her eyes stared up at the blue sky, where the hammock swung upside down and empty, into the blue and out and in again.

Viola's hip had cracked and shifted; her leg had been jarred out of place. She was carried to bed, where she stayed more than a month.

After that Viola was given a jump rope and Bella was told to see that she used it. It was a ridiculous request, and Bella didn't understand. Viola could no more jump rope than she could fly. Mrs. Pleasant engaged a piano teacher, and this made more sense. But Viola was no longer treated as a daughter. In spite of her infirmity, she was given many chores and little affection. Mrs. Bell often called her down the steep spiral staircase only to send her back up on some errand. She seemed determined to proceed as if Viola had never been hurt.

A governess was hired for Marie and Fred, but not for Viola. "She's one of Mammy's," Mrs. Bell told the governess in Bella's presence. She suggested that Viola affected the limp. "A real cunning child. Don't you be taken in."

Bella heard her own words coming back at her. She played the scene in the hammock through again, but now she decided Mrs. Bell had purposefully thrown Viola onto the grass. Bella had complained about her, and just that quickly Mrs. Bell had addressed the problem.

Bella had never pitied herself for being in service. She never tried to imagine having a house like the one on Octavia Street, which was more than big enough for her entire family and all their friends as well. She never tried to imagine having servants to cook and fetch for her. She'd heard that Mrs. Pleasant had been born to slavery, and found her rise a wonderful thing, but Mrs. Pleasant was an exceptional woman. Bella herself was saving money to bring her brother Eduardo to San Francisco. If Mrs. Pleasant would only hire him, too, Bella thought, she could be content.

And yet she pitied Viola. Not only crippled, but so fallen from favor as to become a servant in a house where she'd once been a daughter. It was hard to see, horrible to contemplate.

And all Bella's fault. How could she have condemned a child over a piece of candy? She found Mrs. Pleasant on the staircase and forced herself to speak. The portrait of Mrs. Bell watched her from the wall, white diamonds and milky eyes.

Bella was frightened of her own words. She was right to be frightened, because they spun up the staircase to the floor above, where Mrs. Bell heard them. She called down. "My own mother stripped me and set me outside the window to freeze!" Mrs. Bell hovered over the landing like a golden hawk. Her voice was tight and shivered. "I never would hurt a child." She came down to Mrs. Pleasant. "Never. See how everyone conspires against me?" She began to cry.

Mrs. Pleasant embraced her. Her face was half hidden by Mrs. Bell's shoulder, but it did not look friendly. "Mrs. Bell loves children," she said. "How cruel of you. You don't see how she suffers every time she sees Viola. All this time, and you hardly know us."

Bella was dismissed to the nursery. A few days later, she was dismissed for good. Mrs. Pleasant told Bella there was a position open in the house of Mrs. Washington. "Fred and Marie are too old now for a nursemaid," she explained, ignoring the fact that there was a new baby in the nursery, a tiny bald girl named Robina.

A family friend took Viola to Los Angeles, where she stayed more than a year, undergoing a series of unsuccessful operations on her hip. When she came back, Bella was gone. Mrs. Pleasant had given her an excellent reference. But Bella felt she could no longer be trusted with children. She confided the whole guilty tale to Nelson Brady, then used the money saved for Eduardo's passage to return to Panama.

Q: Now, what is it that impresses—is there anything special that impresses your recollection as having been there in the year 1881?

A: Yes: my injury impresses me very clearly.

Q: How did that happen, Miss Bell?

A: Well, I was thrown out of a hammock.

Q: Explain under what circumstances you were thrown out of a hammock, that happened to impress you.

A: Well, Fred, Marie and myself, we were in the hammock—we usually got into the hammock in the evening, because it was a little warm during the day, and my mother was swinging the hammock, and I think she swung a little bit too high, and we were all flung out, and I happened to be swung the furthest and dislocated my hip.

Q: Dislocated your hip?

A: Yes.

Q: And from that injury you have never recovered?

A: No, I have not.*

---

* Transcript from Viola Bell's suit for heirship in the estate of Teresa Bell.

2

WHAT WITH THE PLAGUES and the winter storms and the impending tidal wave, everyone's mind was on charity these days. Mrs. Pleasant sent more baskets of food and also, just for Jenny Ijub, two used dresses and a piano teacher. The dresses were hand-me-downs from the Bell girls. Too fine, really; the staff disliked seeing Jenny dressed so, as if she were at a party instead of living an orphan's life. It was bound to produce envy in the other wards.

But the piano teacher was conceded, however reluctantly, to be a good thing. Someday Jenny would have to support herself. The dental offices were always looking for pianists, and all they needed was someone able to play loudly enough to mask the sounds of screaming. Piano lessons were a very practical plan.

Next, the charity bug bit young Maud Curry, who decided to devote herself to helping Jenny get adopted. Maud had reached a pious age and was bothered, for religious reasons, by Jenny's continual good fortune. She remembered Jenny's stories—lemon sticks, ponies, parents—but had honestly forgotten that she herself was the author. The result of this combination of remembering and forgetting was that Maud thought of Jenny as a dreadful, unrepentant liar.

Why would God dress a dreadful, unrepentant liar like a princess? Maud decided to be an instrument of the Lord. She picked a group of girls—Melody Miller, Tilly Beacon, Ella May Howard, Coral Campbell—and charged them with informing Jenny whenever her manners were wanting, or her appearance, or her attitude. They called themselves the Good Manners Club. Two of these girls had the special status of being diphtheria survivors.

The staff was touched by this display of selfless concern. "I was afraid the other children would be jealous," Mrs. Lake said. "Instead they've made quite a project of her." And from Nell: "She's certainly lucky to have such friends."

Jenny ate her dinner one evening surrounded by well-wishers. "She shouldn't be taking such big bites, should she, Maud?" Tilly Beacon asked.

"No, indeed."

"Don't cut your bread, Jenny. You should break it with your hands," Melody said, when Jenny hadn't even touched her bread yet.

"And everything after the soup is eaten with a fork."

"I know," Jenny said. She wasn't hungry. The chicken she'd just eaten wedged in her throat until she was afraid it was stuck there forever. She took a gulp of milk to try to force it down.

"I'm just making sure." Maud took a prim bite of cheese. Her angel-colored hair was growing out. It curled in lovely rings around her shoulders. Soon Mrs. Lake would cut it back to dandelion fluff, weeping as she did so. "You sound a little conceited. Good manners are spoiled if you're stuck-up about having them."

"We shouldn't be able to hear you drinking," Coral said.

At bedtime the girls gathered around Jenny's bed to discuss her classroom performance. "Your hair was untidy," Melody began. "And you should thank Miss Stevens when she corrects your sums."

"No one else does," Jenny said.

"No one else makes so many mistakes."

"Let me see your hands," Maud instructed. She flipped them from one side to the other. Her own were hot and sticky. "Go wash them again. All the pretty dresses in the world won't help if you don't keep yourself clean."

Jenny went back to the basin. Her feet were bare. She could feel grains of sand beneath them on the wood floor, and there was a sound like buzzing flies in her ears. She poured some water, dipped her hands in. As she rubbed them together she looked out the window. She could see the barn, the wood just turning to silver in the moonlight. Across it lay the long, pointed shadow of the Ark's tower. She took as much time as she could, but whenever she looked back down the row of beds, there was the group of girls on hers, still waiting for her. Jenny had a loose tooth and it was disgusting, they were agreeing, the way she kept poking at it with her tongue. She would have to be made to stop.

The piano teacher was named Miss Viola Bell. She had the largest, darkest eyes Jenny had ever seen, and also a twisted leg. She needed a crutch to lower herself onto the piano bench and to rise. When Jenny sat beside her, Viola's skirts brushed Jenny's legs. They were cold and damp. Matron didn't like her much. Jenny was still deciding.

"I'm forced to wonder about the character of any young woman from that house," Jenny overheard Matron telling Miss Stevens. Jenny could see that Viola was hearing, too, although she pretended not to.

"We always start with middle C." Viola tapped the key quietly, and then louder—*pim, pim, pim, PIM*. They were using the piano in the basement schoolroom while the rest of the children played outside. Matron was in the hall, but the door was open.

"I'm forced to wonder how she'll have the time to practice and still do her chores and her schooling, too," said Matron. "Of course, there's no point if she doesn't practice faithfully. You must tell me at once if she falls behind in her schoolwork."

"Curve your fingers," Viola said. She took Jenny's hand and made it into a claw. She shook it at the wrist. "Relax a little." She showed Jenny how to play a scale.

What she wanted first was even fingering. She wound a metronome to demonstrate. She and Jenny clapped along.

"Don't love any of the notes more than the others," she said. "Every note needs just the same amount of time to breathe."

"I don't love any of them." Jenny didn't mean to speak. It just came out.

"I see," said Viola. She gave Jenny an appraising look. "Don't hate any of the notes more than the others, then."

Jenny had left her with the wrong impression. In fact, Jenny liked the way Viola's hands felt, working her fingers into proper shapes. Viola told Jenny what to do, but not in a bossy way. "Like prancing horses," she said of Jenny's fingers. She pranced her own on the keys in a lively tune. "Two-minute waltz," she said. "You could soft-cook an egg to it.

Jenny could see that, in order to practice, she'd have to come down every day and be by herself. She was happy that Mrs. Pleasant hadn't forgotten her. She thought it was going to be nice, learning to play piano.

3

THE BOARD OF THE LADIES' RELIEF and Protection Society threw a soirée to honor those of its members who'd lived at the Ark and worked so bravely throughout the epidemics. Lizzie's depression had not lifted, but she could hardly refuse to be fêted. The party was at the home of two delightfully ready patrons, Ethel Crosby and Margaret Cole, whom she wouldn't insult for the world. She wore her coin necklace and her apricot silk, but under her corset her heart felt pricked with pins.

The Putnams lent her Roscoe so she could drive over and leave early if the evening proved too much. They continued very pleased with her, as if she'd chosen to stay away from everyone they disapproved of for all those weeks instead of having been put under quarantine. Still, Lizzie had had no plans to do otherwise; her conscience was clear.

As she left her house, an evening fog was beginning to swirl into the streets. The city had a magical, underwater feeling. Horses' hooves echoed in the wet air, and cold currents streamed past her, visible as ghosts.

At Ethel Crosby and Margaret Cole's she listened to any number of fine speeches. The tracheotomy in which she had assisted was repeatedly detailed; she was honored for her patience with Meredith Penny, for the grisly clothes she'd washed, the hands she'd held, the prayers she'd offered. Lizzie didn't suppose she'd ever been the object of so much approval. She felt uncomfortably exposed, yet cautiously pleased. She would never like being noticed, but she *had* done well, so that was the part that pleased her. Everyone had done well.

It was a nasty surprise, then, when she stepped outside for some air, for one moment of privacy, to have Mrs. Hallis follow merely to say something unkind. "I was astonished to learn," Mrs. Hallis began, "that we're sheltering a child for Mammy Pleasant. Your decision, I'm told."

"We had the space," Lizzie said. "In my opinion. The little girl had nowhere to go. She's a nice little girl."

"I'm sure that's all true. I'm sure you were full of good intent. You always are." Somehow Mrs. Hallis managed to make this uncomplimentary. "But none of this falls to your area of concern. And now you've created a situation. What is Mrs. Pleasant most known for? Baby-farming. What do we deal in? Babies. We can't for a moment be seen as one of Mrs. Pleasant's operations. We'd never recover from the scandal. The Ark would close forever."

Mrs. Hallis was a Methodist with the face of a Botticelli. She believed in culpability, which was not the philosophy of most people with such lips. "When we act," Mrs. Hallis had asked the ladies during her installation as president, "why should we not hold ourselves responsible for remote consequences as well as immediate?" This was laudable, but hard.

"I wouldn't have brought it up tonight of all nights," Mrs. Hallis said. "I did plan to wait. But Miss Cole asked about it. If word is already out to the donors, the circumstances are dire."

"The circumstances are imaginary!" Lizzie said. "Mrs. Pleasant came to the Ark only the one time when she brought the child. I don't know her at all, if that's what you're implying."

"I'm relieved to hear you say so. Of course, I believe you, I know you wouldn't lie. And yet, Miss Hayes, we run a charity based on public support. We must consider appearances as well as facts. And my cook, Hop Tung, says it's common knowledge that you run her errands in Chinatown."

Lizzie was so shocked by this she didn't immediately respond. The shock was followed by resentment. She was being watched and talked about. Her neck grew hot, and then her cheeks. Her hands were cold. The image of Mrs. Hallis questioning her Chinese cook about Lizzie's affairs made her first frightened, then humiliated, and then angry. So they'd all only been pretending to admire her all evening, when really she was the object of a campaign of whispers that reached even into their kitchens.

"Am I being dismissed?" she asked. Her voice cracked like ice across the last word.

"Of course not. I only tell you as a friendly warning."

Lizzie couldn't manage another sentence. She left the porch and then the party without a word to anyone, even her hostesses. She woke the next morning with a sickening silver headache on which all the tea in China could have no effect. It had been a great mistake to leave her bed, she decided. She wouldn't make such an error again.

Three days later Mrs. Putnam called. Lizzie roused herself sufficiently to dress, but there was no food in the house, nothing to offer by way of hospitality. The newspapers were piled unread on the parlor settee. There was dust.

Mrs. Putnam took it all in. "How was the party?" she asked. Probably she'd already heard how hastily Lizzie had left. Probably the information was already circulating up in Sacramento through Erma. Soon the governor would know or, at the very least, his Chinese cook.

Lizzie had this bitter succession of thoughts. But Mrs. Putnam's face was too kind. Lizzie chose to confide. When she got to Hop Tung, Mrs. Putnam shook her head. All was unfolding just as Lizzie's mother had feared. If her advice at the séance had only been instantly taken! How disheartening it must be to rouse oneself to Contact only to be ignored.

Not that Mrs. Putnam was ever one to lose herself in regrets. "The past is only useful as a guide to the future," she said briskly. She proposed that Lizzie immediately be seen with respectable people. She proposed the long-promised, long-delayed Saturday-night promenade.

"You can invite that Mrs. Wright you're so taken with," she offered, which made it impossible for Lizzie to refuse. Though she'd lost the taste for it herself, it would be such a treat for poor Mrs. Wright. The Putnams would fetch them both.

The usual Saturday-night route was a loop that could be walked in either direction—Market to Kearny to Bush to Powell or Powell to Bush to Kearny to Market. Whatever the weather, the streets were full of people. The Salvation Army band sang at one end of Market Street, while at the other, groups of young men gathered to smoke cigars and watch the wind lift the ladies' skirts.

You might see anyone in San Francisco on a Saturday night. You could buy stocks or snakes. You could buy a pig or a paste necklace or a paste guaranteed to dissolve warts. The Crockers might be walking in one direction and their servants, off duty, in the other. Fast Irish women passed slow Spanish men. There were sailors from the ships of every country in the world and soldiers from the Presidio. There were sweethearts and zealots and labor agitators and mesmerists; there were black Gilbert Islanders, huge Kanakas, turbaned lascars, tattooed Indians, Chinese with their long hair fiercely loose, Italians in fussy shirts with blue sashes. And the whole scene flooded with so much lamplight it was as if they were all onstage together. The very sidewalks seemed made of light.

Lizzie held Mrs. Wright's arm and tried to describe it aloud. She recognized Mrs. Hallis out promenading with her husband and two married daughters; they nodded briskly to each other. She saw Myrtle Rolphe freezing out a young man with a fast smile and a gold tooth.

Mrs. Putnam began to talk about the phantom fire engine. The story was getting a good deal of press. A Mr. Tomkinson was suing the fire department for damages sustained on Third and Folsom when a recklessly speeding engine had chased his horses. His driver had lost the reins, smashing his buggy into splinters against a telegraph pole. Mr. Tomkinson was asking for one hundred nine dollars and seventy-five cents in compensation. There were more than a dozen credible witnesses.

Only there'd been no fire on this occasion, and none of the city's many engines had been at Third and Folsom. After an investigation so exhaustive that Chief Scannell was forced to retire to the country under a doctor's care, acting Chief Sullivan concluded that Mr. Tomkinson would have to apply for compensation to a supernatural agency. Mrs. Putnam was both pleased and horrified to think there were whole engines of ghosts clattering down the stone pavement on Folsom, carelessly sounding gongs and spooking the horses.

"When you think of all the men who've died fighting fires in San

Francisco," Mr. Putnam noted. "Really, the wonder is there aren't more of these incidents."

Mrs. Putnam was forced to agree. "But what do you think it means?" she asked. "Is the manifestation a random occurrence or is it a warning we should heed? What a time for omens this has been! Can you ever remember another such, Mrs. Wright?"

Mrs. Wright had been squeezing Lizzie's arm for the past few moments. She answered loudly and quickly. "Stuff and nonsense. One of the engines was out and everyone is lying about it to avoid payment. These events can always be readily explained if you remember what liars people are. Especially when money is involved.

"These witnesses you refer to—was there anything supernatural in what they observed? The baying of invisible hounds? The scent of unearthly roses?" Her voice was innocent, but Lizzie could tell Mrs. Wright was goading the Putnams.

Lizzie found Mrs. Wright's rock-solid disbelief extremely comforting. She might shift about from past to present, but Mrs. Wright kept her feet on the ground. It was also slightly rude. Mrs. Wright did not know the Putnams well enough to contradict them so loudly. Nor was her version appealing to them. "That would involve a massive conspiracy to conceal the truth," Mr. Putnam pointed out. His posture was stiff, his tone formal.

"Someone somewhere would be bound to talk." Mrs. Putnam turned to Lizzie. "Don't you think so?"

Lizzie found that she had no opinion on the subject of supernatural fire engines. Naturally, this pleased no one.

The Putnams began to walk faster, and the distance between the two couples increased. This gap was quickly filled with other people. It could not have been the Putnams' intention to abandon her, but suddenly Lizzie couldn't see them anywhere.

A group of Italian sailors walking together, arm in arm, created a phalanx against which Lizzie was forced to give way. A gaunt and rheumy-eyed man staggered drunkenly toward her, only to find his path blocked by a bosomy, theatrical woman with a serious overbite. "Even today, the women of ancient Egypt are remembered for their beauty. What did they have that you don't have?" she asked Lizzie. She extended her hand. In it was a small box, inlaid with an ivory ibis. "Something tiny enough to fit in this box. Would you like to open it?"

Suddenly, inexplicably, the woman and the question filled Lizzie with dread. Why had the woman picked her? Did she look the sort to open a box with no idea as to its contents?

Lizzie tried to walk past without answering, and the woman intercepted her again. "Go ahead. Open it."

Lizzie began to sweat in the cold night air. She moved to the left, pulling Mrs. Wright along so rapidly she careened into a man with a huge black beard and a white top hat. There was the fleshy sound of collision, the smell of whiskey, a small reproachful noise from Mrs. Wright, a large irritated noise from the man.

"What are you afraid of? Only yourself," the woman with the box shouted after Lizzie.

Lizzie saw the opening of a narrow alleyway and guided Mrs. Wright into it and out of the crush. Several moments were spent in apology and explanation. Mrs. Wright's hat had been knocked askew and Lizzie straightened it. They began walking again, forward into the alley. Only then did Lizzie look up. The bright glow of street-lamps was gone, and she found herself in a place she'd never been. She was on Morton Street.

The sounds of the Saturday-night promenade fell away, leaving only their own footsteps. On the left were a dozen small cottages, each with a shallow bay window. In every window a woman sat idly, a smile painted on her lips, and her eyes both staring and unseeing. Instead of dresses, these women wore simple wrappers that would fall away at a touch. Their hair was pinned up in a way that suggested its coming down. The wrappers were in different colors, but otherwise the women looked exactly the same—dark hair, white skin, red mouths.

The dread Lizzie had been feeling doubled, but now she knew what she was afraid of. She feared recognizing a face, some girl they'd sheltered at the Brown Ark. The women were like dolls, waiting for someone to pick them up, move their arms and legs, animate them. She could not take her eyes off them; the women refused to look at her. She thought that what she was seeing was sex, but that it had been made to look like death.

Lines of men drank from flasks and bottles as they waited their turns. In the presence of Lizzie and Mrs. Wright, they fell utterly, eerily silent. A man left one of the cottages, a very young man with barely a beard. When he spotted them he reversed direction and walked ahead so they would see only his back. "Get out of here!" a man who looked to be Lizzie's age snapped at her. "What can you be thinking?"

This late in her life, it was doubtful Lizzie would ever know what physical passion was. She blamed no one for this; there were things she could have done if she'd chosen to do them. As an adolescent she'd conducted her own solitary investigations until somehow her mother knew. There was a period when Effie had been told to tie her hands together every night, but it lasted only a few weeks, only long enough to make the point. "I know you're a good girl," her mother had said, and Lizzie had chosen to be one.

Once, when she was nineteen, Teddy Sprague had pressed against her in the backyard of his house by the large rhododendron. Later she wished she'd pressed back, but at the time she was merely embarrassed. Perhaps if she'd been beautiful, if he'd spoken first, if it had been more like something in a book, she might have behaved differently. Instead she reacted instinctively. It was a revealing instinct, the instinct of no. Lizzie had instantly known that any shared embrace would leave her feeling exposed, observed. The inner woman would not allow the outer woman to look so foolish.

She'd often told herself she didn't really mind; she could do without. Other women seemed to dislike it often as not. There was plenty of excitement to be found in music and in books, even a bodily excitement. And then there were so many other pleasures to be had—water on her skin and in her throat, the taste of crab legs with melted butter, the smell of lemons and horses and the sea, the touch of velvet and satin, hills of poppies, Beethoven, blackberries and olives, sneezing and stretching in the sun. She would not allow these ecstasies to seem any bit less than they were. She loved them. The pleasures of the flesh were a gift from God.

None of this belonged on Morton Street. Lizzie tried to imagine a looking-glass alley where men sat in windows and waited for women with money. She pretended she was entering a door, making a selection, demanding who and what she wanted. Money on the dressing table. The man like a puppet in her arms.

The fantasy was ludicrous. And upsetting. She didn't have a word for the combination of horror and thrill and buffoonery and sadness it gave her. What did men feel when they did such things? Whom did they pretend to do them to? Why must they do them at all?

"What's happening?" Mrs. Wright asked. "Why have you stopped talking? Where are we?"

"Lizzie!" Mr. Putnam's footsteps sounded behind them. "Where do you think you're going?" He seized her by the elbow.

"Mrs. Wright was getting knocked about by all the people," Lizzie said. "I was looking for somewhere less crowded."

"I'll take Mrs. Wright's arm, then," Mr. Putnam said. "Neither of you should be here." He led them back to Kearny Street and Mrs. Putnam.

"What were you thinking, Lizzie?" Mrs. Putnam asked.

It wasn't a question, so Lizzie didn't answer it. Inwardly she was annoyed at the fuss. Wasn't she a grown woman, and perfectly able to look at the realities of life? At the same time her hands were shaking and she couldn't make them stop.

"We were on Morton Street," Mrs. Wright announced to the whole staff the minute Lizzie returned her to the Ark. "Of course, I didn't see a thing."

"How very distressing," Mrs. Lake said.

"How interesting," said Miss Stevens.

Nell fetched them all a glass of wine and a piece of cold apple pie to help them recover. No experience could have brought more ready sympathy. These are real women, Lizzie told herself. This is where I live, with God, first of all, and then these real women in this real world.

4

BECAUSE SHE HAD CONTINUED so listless, because since the quarantine had lifted and she'd learnt that Mrs. Pleasant was a communicable disease, she had spent less and less time at the Brown Ark, Lizzie was not immediately informed of Jenny's piano lessons. She heard of them finally from Ti Wong.

She'd dropped by to give him the new Conan Doyle and was told he was upstairs cleaning the tower room. "I suppose it will be good for his English," Nell said amiably. "Go on up," just as if Nell were happy to see her, were the most agreeable of women. How Ti Wong had charmed her merely by almost dying!

Nell had no way of knowing, of course, that the book Lizzie had brought contained cocaine injections, a wooden-legged convict, and a pair of hideous twins. Even Lizzie hadn't read it yet. Although Doyle's previous stories had garnered little excitement and mixed reviews, this was beginning to change. Lizzie felt that combination of validation and annoyance the early reader feels toward anyone coming later. It dampened her own enthusiasm slightly.

Ti Wong was not cleaning the room at all, but was seated, dreamily looking out the cupola window to the street, when she entered. "I saw you coming," he said. "I saw your tiny, tiny hat."

He smiled when she held out the book. "You read to me?"

"We'll read it together."

"Okay." Yet he showed no inclination to start. Lizzie settled herself on the horsehair couch and opened the book invitingly, but he stayed at the window. "Very high up," he said.

"Yes."

"Ocean far away."

"Yes, indeed. You're not worrying about the prophecy, are you? God doesn't work that way."

"Story of Noah," Ti Wong pointed out. "Story of Red Sea."

"God doesn't work that way *anymore,*" Lizzie told him, but Ti Wong said she was not being as scientific as Mr. Holmes, and even to her own ears it was unconvincing.

Although San Francisco continued largely uninterested, over in Oakland, Mrs. Woodworth's crowds were still growing. When her tent was shredded by high winds and collapsed on the worshippers, it was replaced by a new one, specially made to hold an audience of eight thousand, nine hundred. No evangelist had ever required a space so large before; Mrs. Woodworth asked God's forgiveness for the hubris of it. Her humility was restored by her unfortunate husband, who opened a concession booth and sold lemonade and peanuts to the believers.

Recently the meetings had been attacked by hoodlums and, in consequence, by baton-swinging policemen. The noise of benches being smashed and the hoarse shouts of fighting men were added to the general din. A boy was cured of Saint Vitus's dance. A man was cured of a gambling addiction. Flora Briggs, a fourteen-year-old girl attending a meeting with her four-year-old cousin, fell into a faint and lay on the altar unnoticed for hours. When her uncle tried to fetch her out, he was thrown from the tent by burly men singing hymns. Her doctor told the newspapers he feared the girl's health was permanently weakened by the dampness and the excitement. "If you went to one of Mrs. Woodworth's meetings, you'd see it's just a circus," Lizzie told Ti Wong.

"We go?"

"Certainly not. You'd catch a chill. Or get arrested." But that made it sound too exciting; she was beginning to want to go herself. She tried to stop. "The music is horrid. You're safe here, Ti Wong. I promise. Why would God spare you from diphtheria only to drown you?"

"You think Miss Bell goes to revival?"

"What do you know of Miss Bell?"

Ti Wong pointed down through the window and Lizzie stood to see. There was Viola Bell, papers under one arm and crutch under the other, struggling through the sand up to the Brown Ark door.

"So Mrs. Woodworth can make her walk," Ti Wong explained, just as Lizzie was asking, "What is she doing here?"

Lizzie went downstairs and listened through the open door while Jenny did her scales. When Miss Bell told her to, Jenny walked her fingers on the keys. She marched them, trotted them, galloped them according to Miss Bell's instruction. "Some people play by imposing their will on the instrument," Miss Bell told her. "Others think only of letting the piano sing through them. You must think about what kind of pianist it will suit you best to be."

From outside, Lizzie could just hear Maud's voice.

"Red lion, red lion,
Come out of your den.

Whoever you catch
Will be one of your men."

Nell found Lizzie listening in the basement. "A message arrived for you," she said. "As if we didn't have enough to do without delivering your mail." She handed the note over, and climbed the stairs in a great show of breathlessness.

Lizzie opened the envelope with her fingernails.

"Mr. Finney would be honored if Miss Hayes would consent to meet him in the Grand Court of the Palace at one o'clock Monday, this. He will wait all afternoon in hope."

So, Mr. Finney wanted his money at long last.

Of course, Lizzie courted further scandal by appearing in a public place with a young man who was no relation of hers. The Palace was as public as a place could get—see and be seen. Still, she must endeavor to do what was right. She remembered how Mrs. Pleasant had said she was too concerned with appearances. No doubt it was true. And what seemed right to Lizzie now was that little Jenny be returned to her mother, in spite of Mrs. Pleasant's efforts to separate them. There was surely an irony in this, Lizzie thought. I am no agent of Mrs. Pleasant's, she told an imaginary (and chagrined) Mrs. Hallis. Lizzie was trusting her instincts.

Any remaining doubts were dispelled by Sunday morning's sermon. Like a sign from God, the subject was Abraham and Isaac. Lizzie had never liked this story, and even less the related one of Hagar and Ishmael. Why does Ishmael matter so much less than Isaac? she'd asked once in Sunday school. It was the sort of question bound to occur to a child who feared her parents would rather have lost their five-year-old daughter than their newborn son. Lizzie was probably ten at this time.

God doesn't have favorites, her Sunday-school teacher had answered. And He blessed and protected Ishmael. But His covenant for Isaac was made before either was born.

As if God wouldn't know both were coming. Lizzie was not satisfied, but she let the matter drop. If she quarreled with the Sunday-school teacher, her parents were bound to learn of it. Sunday school is not a place for questions, her mother would say. It was, instead, a training in unquestioning faith.

But what Lizzie had really meant was, Why does Ishmael matter so much less to Abraham? She knew all children were precious to God.

This morning, the Reverend Pilchner reminded them that the sacrifice God suggested to Abraham was the one God would actually make. In fact, the mountain in Moriah where Abraham's son had been spared was very close to the place where Christ was crucified. The sacrifice of a child, then, was something God asked only of Himself. It was beyond man and meant to be so, which interpretation helped Lizzie like the story a great deal better.

The fine weather of the weekend persisted into Monday. Lizzie took the streetcar to the Annie Street entrance with its fine marble walls. She had decided on a two-o'clock arrival as a test of Mr. Finney's patience. She couldn't help hoping he wouldn't pass.

Light spilled into the Grand Court through the dome; sunlight, but sieved softer and more golden by the amber glass. The setting was one of opulence: purple tablecloths, silver sugar dishes, vases of cut crystal. The acoustics of the Grand Court were designed for privacy. Hushed conversations bubbled through the room, indistinct, but various as birdsong. Lizzie was unlikely to enjoy the social aspects of the occasion, so she took a deliberate moment's pleasure in the setting. She didn't often get to the Grand Court, where deals were made and men undone over cocktails.

Mr. Finney was waiting for her. He rose. She had never seen him so nicely dressed. Although his shirt was still a coarse linen, frayed at the cuffs, and his dress coat was thready at the elbows, there was nothing in this to reproach. On the contrary, a gentleman showed good taste by never dressing above his income.

"I'm having champagne," he said. "I'll get you a glass."

Lizzie turned to the waiter, a white man; the colored waiters had never been rehired. "I'll have a cup of tea. And a sandwich, please. Whatever you recommend."

He withdrew at once, and Lizzie and Mr. Finney looked at each other across the table. "Mr. Finney," she said straight off. She wanted no inconsequential pleasantries, nothing that would prolong the meeting. "I need you to tell me the identity of Jenny's mother. And anything else that would help me locate her. I'm determined to see them reunited."

"Right to it." Mr. Finney smiled at her fondly. "You're a businesslike woman. I admire that. I admire you more every time I see you. It's the way you look, Miss Hayes. So proper and churchy, and all the time one of Mrs. Pleasant's own. You do it to a turn."

"Please honor my request," Lizzie said. She struggled with her tone of voice, which somehow settled on lifeless. *One of Mrs. Pleasant's own.* But why argue with such a man? Why argue with anyone? It was only appearances, after all, no truth to it.

He removed his glasses, rubbed them against his sleeve, and replaced them. She remembered leaning toward him to dab the grit from his eye, so close she could feel the intermittent warmth of his breathing.

"Well," he said. "Right to it, then. It embarrasses me mightily to have to begin by admitting that bit about Jenny's mother was a lie. I don't know who she is. Need drove me to it. Debts and creditors. I'm usually quite an honest man."

"I'm sure," said Lizzie. She stood, forcing him to stand as well. "Then we've nothing more to say."

"But I *have* learned the name of the child's father."

They sat again. Mr. Finney was relaxed in his chair. He appeared as comfortable as if he were in his own dining room, sipping his champagne, gesturing with his free hand. "What's that worth to you?"

He appeared to think it worth a lot. He so obviously thought himself in the position of advantage today. Lizzie noted this, and it made her anxious.

Her tea arrived, and her sandwich. She let the waiter withdraw, then took a small bite. Cold tongue. Chewing it helped calm her. She swallowed. "I imagine it's worth a good deal more to the father than to me," she said, casual and self-possessed. "Why not appeal to him?"

"Sadly, he's dead."

"Are there other relatives who might be made to feel their responsibility?"

"There are indeed."

"Then go to them."

"Look here," said Mr. Finney. His aura of sincerity intensified. The air was thick as smoke with it. "I only want a fair cut. My information was hard come by. You were willing to pay me ten dollars just to leave the child alone. How much more valuable is this?" He took a pen from his pocket, called the waiter over and asked for a piece of paper. The hotel stationery was heavy and beautifully monogrammed.

"Now I'm writing the father's name," Mr. Finney said. He folded the paper four times, creased it with his fingernail—his nails were splendidly clean—and set it between them on the purple table. It began to open immediately, like a flower.

Behind him, Lizzie saw Mrs. Hallis enter the Grand Court. She wore a hat all covered with seashells. Very *fin de siècle* and not very Methodist. But what unbelievable, dreadful luck. If Lizzie didn't leave at once, she was about to be seen dining alone with a man, by the last person she would wish. She stood abruptly, forcing Mr. Finney to his feet again.

"I won't pay you a cent," she said. "I was never going to pay you."

"We had an agreement."

"Never."

His face grew troubled. "Just read it, then," he said. "I'll trust to your fairness after. I know you can be trusted."

Lizzie knew she should go. Instead she spoke. There was something here she couldn't make sense of. "If the father was dead, and you didn't know the mother, why did you try to adopt the girl? That first time you came to the Ark?" She didn't have the nerve to ask him about the kidnap attempt. It seemed rude and, anyway, too easily denied.

"I knew Mrs. Pleasant was interested. I figured that meant money somewhere. Mrs. Pleasant is like a dowser when it comes to money.

"But I didn't really plan to get the child. Miss Hayes, I'm a man who takes the long view, a man who thinks several steps ahead. If you can make something seem valuable, then people will pay just to keep it. I came so you'd pay me later to stop coming. It looked an easy scam and I was desperate.

"I'm not so desperate now, and what I've got here is valuable.

Hardly anyone knows about the child's father. So far. If you'll just read it …"

Lizzie looked down. The note had opened entirely, and lay on the table with her father's name, Wellington Hayes, face up for anyone to see.

Lizzie's mind jumped from her body to the mezzanine above them. Her mouth continued to work, but she could hardly hear what she said, being then so far away from her voice. "Is this a joke?" she asked. She might have spoken too loudly. The words arrived to her as if whispered, but two men at a nearby table turned to look. They were young men, and never would have noticed a woman of her age, so she must have been speaking too loudly.

Mr. Finney shook his head. If he'd smiled at her, if he'd patronized her in any way, or pitied her, or mocked her, she would have picked up the sugar bowl and struck him with it, careless of the spectacle.

She fantasized doing so. Clunk, clunk, clunk! His face remained impassive during the attack. His tone was mild. "Perhaps you'll have that champagne, after all."

Her mind reunited with her body; her good sense returned, and all her other faculties with it. They sat again and she whispered to him fiercely. "You'll never make me believe this. First of all, the child could hardly look less like me."

"And you've never seen two sisters, one blond, the other dark before? We even had a name for that when I was growing up—sister noon and sister night, we used to say. Mind you, these were cases when both parents were the same. Or so we judged. The thing is that you can never know about the father for absolute certain. Even your own father, you can never be sure."

"You're not strengthening your case."

"Your mother was dead. Men suffer from loneliness more than women. If you knew what that was like, you'd find it forgivable. You don't strike me as an unforgiving woman." He raised his glass to her and her forgiving nature. The bubbles careened through his champagne.

She was composed enough now to pour her tea without having her hands shake, busied herself with the cream. She did so not because she wanted tea, but to demonstrate how wide of the mark he'd shot. She didn't entertain this preposterous lie for a moment, and showed it by turning to him a face as unperturbed as pond water. That he expected payment for this insult! "Secondly, I just happen to get the care of her. A remarkable coincidence!"

Mr. Finney leaned in. She saw his face reflected in a silver teapot, the nose as big as a potato. When she looked back up to his actual face it was less handsome as well. There was a sheen of oil on his forehead, drops of champagne in his moustache. In the golden light, his eyes were the color of mud. She was amazed she'd ever thought him nice to look at.

"No coincidence," he said. "Mrs. Pleasant brought your sister to you. She knew what she was doing. She was tidying up. I worked for her once, she's a great tidier."

"She's not. Quite the opposite. That's thirdly. Fourthly my father was too old."

"He was old. The—event—didn't proceed smoothly, or so I'm informed. And yet not too old, as it happened."

Lizzie didn't remember that she'd ever been more affronted. This had the brief charm of novelty, and then she'd had more than enough. She left, her tea untasted, her sandwich barely touched, and the bill to fall to Mr. Finney's account. She strode through the tables and past a group of women, which now contained Mrs. Hallis.

Mrs. Hallis stood and Lizzie acknowledged her. She hoped faintly that this marked the first moment she'd been seen. She hoped Mrs. Hallis hadn't watched while Mr. Finney passed his *billet-doux*. But it no longer seemed a large concern.

When she stepped into the white sunlight of Annie Street, she decided to stroll along Market for a while before catching the streetcar. She thought that Mr. Finney might have followed her, but he hadn't, which was too bad, because while she was walking she thought of a fifthly and sixthly she could have delivered, but she felt no temptation to go back.

She passed a street vendor who tried to lure her into a game with cups and a pea, but she'd had quite enough of that sort of thing. He would hide the pea under one of the cups and she would find it or she wouldn't; none of that would be the point. All the while, just like Mr. Finney, he'd be sizing her up: How much did she have, how much would she play, how much could he take? How great a fool was she?

5

A DISCIPLINED IMAGINATION is a useful tool in avoiding unpleasant thoughts. An unbridled imagination carries you straight to them. Lizzie went home and read three novels, one after the other, no daylight between, and no recollection of any of them. She then helped six other ladies dust and scrub St. Luke's in preparation for Easter week. She attended two piano recitals, one in the afternoon and one in the evening. She called on donors. And when she'd finished all this, less than two days had passed since her meeting with Mr. Finney.

The weather turned unusually warm, and Miss Stevens seized her chance to take the littles on a picnic to Ocean Beach to see the rock formations. "Which is strongest," Miss Stevens would ask the littles, "air, water, or stone?" and then show them the smoothly carved pools, caves, and keyholes. This always came as such a surprise to children and could be made to carry some valuable life lessons as well.

She sent Ti Wong to Lizzie with a note. Would Lizzie like to go to the seashore? Miss Stevens needed another adult to chaperone and everyone else was busy. Lizzie was never busy, but Miss Stevens was too polite to say so.

The beach was crowded. There were men in wool swimming costumes, although the water was far too cold for actual swimming. They waded and their feet turned an unappetizingly fishy blue. Women protected themselves from sudden bursts of sun and wind with colored parasols. An Irish couple had made a windbreak of a bedsheet and were charging people a penny apiece to shelter beside it. There was a cart selling chips of ice and bottles of beer. There was a long table on which Charlie the Bird Man had arranged his canary cages. Charlie's canaries walked tightropes, sat in chairs, and fired tiny cannons triggered with strings. One canary flew into the crowd, landing on hats, picking out pigeons for Charlie to pester for money.

Like so many other men in San Francisco, Charlie had been unlucky in love. He'd been robbed on his honeymoon night, as he would tell anyone who'd listen, robbed by his bride. "She took my money, my clothes, my heart," he said, in Lizzie's general direction. His tone was accusing. "All she left me was the birds."

He sent a canary to Lizzie's shoulder. It took hold of her earlobe in a bite so gentle it was almost a kiss. The littles surrounded her, pleading for the bird themselves, reaching out their fingers enticingly, driving it deeper into her hair. It murmured in a way that tingled on the curve of Lizzie's neck. Charlie whistled, and the bird came back to him, just like a dog.

Ti Wong had made the boys a red kite with paste and paint, wood and newsprint. It was shaped vaguely like a falcon, which Charlie said would agitate the canaries, so Miss Stevens sent the boys far down the beach to fly it. They ran along the sand, throwing the kite into the air, but were unable to keep it aloft. Eventually it fell— like Icarus, Miss Stevens pointed out—into the sea and dissolved. When pulled in, only the crossbar remained. The boys threw it back and reeled it in repeatedly, a sort of fishing game, but requiring no patience or experience. They played tag with the waves, dashing in and out, until they were wet to the knees and beyond.

Jenny dropped her sandwich. "Now it's a sandwich," Miss Stevens told her gaily. "Brush it off, dear. A little grit won't hurt." She explained that birds needed just that additional grit as an aid to digestion.

Lizzie had determined to pay Jenny no special attentions. Instead, she found herself aware of Jenny's whereabouts at every moment. Lizzie traded sandwiches with her and ate the sandy one herself. Jenny did not say thank you. If only Maud were there! Maud would coax her into better behavior.

They all went to climb the stairs to the Cliff House. From there they turned to face Seal Rocks. "Actually," Miss Stevens said, "those are sea lions, not seals. You can tell by the ears, which are smaller. And their flippers are larger than a seal's would be." She'd brought opera glasses so the children could see nature close up and detailed. The sea lions lay in the clefts of the rocks. Now and then one would slide languidly into the water, then somersault back onto the rock, its spotted fur newly polished by the water.

"The Costanoan Indians used to tell a story about Seal Rocks," Lizzie told the children standing nearest her. Nobody encouraged her to continue, but nobody moved away, either. "One day a beautiful woman appeared on the beach here to two little girls. She warned them of an attack by sea from another tribe across the bay. To protect them, she gave them three wishes.

"First they wished for a great fog so the boats of the enemy would be lost. Then they wished for a great storm so the boats of the enemy would be destroyed. Then they wished to turn the rival warriors into sea lions. And that's the real reason there are sea lions on the coast here." How many cultures told stories in which everyone was saved through the cunning of little girls? What a shame the Costanoans were gone now, little girls with all the rest of them.

"I would have wished for more wishes," Matthew Burton said, the way children always do, always will. And then, "Wouldn't the third wish have been enough? Why did they need the first two?" Matthew was Miss Stevens's ideal pupil, methodical, logical to a fault.

Jenny passed Lizzie the opera glasses. One of the sea lions yawned. Through the glasses Lizzie could see a fishy flotsam in its throat. The sea lion closed its mouth and turned its head so that it seemed to look right at her. Its eyes were soft as a cow's. Lizzie lowered the glasses and the sea lion didn't turn away.

Out past Seal Rocks, on the horizon, a boat with a white sail floated sleepily. An orange-and-blue hot-air balloon drifted over the water. Sunshine dazzled off the windows of the Cliff House in short, sharp flashes that made Lizzie worry about headache. She looked upward instead, to Sutro Heights and the line of white plaster statues on the bluff.

Without asking permission, the children were already running up the hill and scrambling down to the cove on the far side of the Cliff House. Over the noise of the ocean, the sea lions, the gulls, they could later claim not to have heard anyone calling them back. This left the women with no choice but to follow. The descent was steep.

In spite of a large, enticing peanut stand by the cliff face, it was less crowded here. A dangerous undertow kept people out of the water, and the littles were sternly warned of this. Other children, children who'd come with their parents, were begging for peanuts, but the wards of the Brown Ark knew better than to ask. Lizzie saw Jenny pick up some discarded hulls, look hopefully inside.

The tide had spit seaweed and slivers of wood onto the sand.

Some of the wood was blackened and might well have been all that remained of the *Parallel*, a schooner that had foundered just off Point Lobos a year or so before. The *Parallel* had been loaded with dynamite. They'd heard the explosion way back at the Brown Ark, and it had broken every window in the Cliff House. Miss Stevens explained how a sound could break glass. Like magic!

Lizzie stationed herself between the children and the water. This was a precaution, but it also allowed her a chance to be alone. She wanted to imagine the things the ocean hid, fish with bulbous eyes, forests of coral, clams the size of bathtubs. She wanted a moment in which to feel her life for what it was, an inconsequential bit of noise at the edge of something deep and vast.

She picked her way through a scramble of sand verbena, its leaves thick, flat, and coated with salt. She disturbed several small crabs, sand fleas, and a darkly colored sea gull with a red bill and a black tail. It leapt away, skimmed along the water, rode the updraft just above the foam. Lizzie knelt and pressed her palm into the wet sand. She rose and wiped her hand on her skirt. Water seeped into the pools her fingertips had made. Down the beach she could see Jenny collecting a handful of broken mussel shells.

A young man and woman strolled by arm in arm. "Is she yours?" the woman asked Lizzie. She'd seen how Lizzie watched Jenny.

"No," said Lizzie. Too quickly. "No. She's an orphan."

"How sad," said the man. "Such a sweet little girl."

Close to the waterline the tide had carved a tunnel through the rocky cliffs. This inspired the boys into pirate games. They'd forced the girls inside and were devising tortures, when Miss Stevens caught on and set the prisoners free. Lizzie saw her emerge, a boy's ear in each of her hands.

Miss Stevens called the children together. "Which is strongest, air, water, or stone?" she asked them. The gulls screamed themselves hoarse.

The children returned to the Ark, tired and chapped from the sun and wind. Their clothes were scratchy with salt and sand; the ocean continued to boom distantly in their ears. Jenny had a coiled hermit-crab shell clutched in her fist. She brought it near her face to see how far down into the ink of the coil she could see. She wondered if there was anyone hidden inside. Her fingers smelled of seaweed. She breathed the odor in again and again.

When she went to put the shell into her wardrobe— a box that apples had once arrived in—Maud Curry was sitting on her bed, waiting. "What have you got?" she demanded. "Give it to me. And go wash your hands and smooth your hair. No wonder no one adopts you. You smell."

The Ogre Mother

1

LIZZIE WENT STRAIGHT from her day at the beach to Mrs. Putnam's Wednesday at-home. She cleaned up in the Putnams' bathroom and joined the ladies in the conservatory. Everything was as it should be. Erma had returned to Sacramento with the children—Lizzie was so lucky not to have children! Erma had aged ten years for every child—the sun was shining, the biscuits had raspberry jam fillings, and Mrs. Mullin took the seat under the fern.

A tall vase near Lizzie was stuffed with fresh-cut branches of lilac. They smelled wonderful. Mrs. Putnam had dressed in a harmonious plum. She took her usual chair and told Lizzie she'd met a family whose daughter went to the Sacred Heart Convent in Oakland. This was the same school Marie Bell attended. The prohibition on seeing Mrs. Pleasant apparently would never dampen Mrs. Putnam's need to discuss her.

Mrs. Putnam had learnt that Marie was a taciturn child, but that, in itself, spoke volumes. She was often visited by Mrs. Pleasant, but never by her father or mother. Mrs. Pleasant was also thought to have chosen the school, since she was a practicing Catholic and the Bells were not, though Mrs. Pleasant did occasionally appear also on the donors' list at the African Methodist Episcopal church. Say what you would, that woman took care of her own.

Marie was a pale, plump girl with hair like straw and cheeks like strawberries. "Not the beauty her mother was, I'm told," said Mrs. Putnam, "but that might be all to the good." Beauty was perilous to girls just as often as it was advantageous, and while Mrs. Putnam was not one who liked to pass judgment, it must be remembered that Marie did not have the sort of mother who could guide her to respectability.

Poor Marie was not even lively. "Everyone who knows her can tell," Mrs. Putnam informed Lizzie, "that something is terribly wrong in that house." Meanwhile, she had it on good authority that Fred Bell, the oldest boy, had been sent to military school in the East, but he'd run off with a dancer, or else he'd been expelled for setting a fire. Either way, it was awful, and he was back in San Francisco, but not at the House of Mystery, as his father refused to speak to him.

"There was some testimony about the Bell children during the Sharon trial," Lizzie said. "But I can't quite remember it."

"Oh, I paid no attention to the Sharon trial," Mrs. Putnam said. "No one I know did."

"A degrading business. It reflected so poorly on the city. Why can't the papers publish the nice things people do?" Behind Mrs. Mullin, the fern was a fountain of green feathers rising from her head like the war bonnet of an Indian. "And the way they persisted in printing every sordid detail! As if decent people cared to read such things!"

On the street outside, a man was shouting at his horse or his wife. Mrs. Putnam put down her tea and moved to close the window. She stood between the dotted-muslin curtains in a dazzling cone of sunlight so that Lizzie could hardly see her. This gave her voice an oracular authority. "It was when Mr. Bell was called to the stand," she said. "This was during the first trial. Five, six years ago. Sharon's lawyer—"

"William Barnes, it was then," Mrs. Mullin offered helpfully.

"Mr. Barnes said that one of the Bell twins was actually the daughter of a German Jew working at the Palace as a maid—"

"Until she became the Bell twins' wet nurse."

"She was not a married woman. She gave her baby to Mrs. Pleasant, who promised to find a loving family. But then, Barnes said, Mammy Pleasant palmed Bertha's baby off on Thomas Bell and let Bertha nurse her right in the Bell home. Tricked that old coot into thinking he was the proud father of twins."

"Mrs. Pleasant denied every jot of it, but she refused to say where Bertha's baby had gone. The Bells sued the *Alta* just for publishing the testimony. They said it was libel to the family—"

"Until they dropped the suit," Mrs. Mullin noted. "They didn't want a lot of lawyers poking around the House of Mystery!"

Lizzie remembered it now. "How old would that baby be?" she asked, even though she knew the answer would be too old. Jenny could certainly be Jewish, with her dark hair and dark eyes.

"Oh, goodness, I don't know, dear. Seven or eight, I suppose." Mrs. Putnam returned to her seat so that her voice came again from her mouth and not from a pillar of fire. Inevitably her credibility suffered. "It was Mr. Barnes's contention that Mrs. Pleasant manufactured the whole case against Sharon. Paid every witness. Forged the wedding contract. Coached poor, dim Allie. Hoodwinked Mr. Bell along with everyone else."

"She doesn't feel about family the way we do. No colored person cares about blood."

"How could they?" Mrs. Putnam asked. "In all fairness, it's a matter of history, not race. Sold away from your mother and denied by your father. A white man, let's face that fact. That's why she does that baby-farming, shuffling children into any old family. Why should she care who belongs to whom? Whoever cared for her?" She paused a moment, shaking her head from the pity of it.

"They do say one of the Bell children is colored." Mrs. Mullin's eyes were big and round, and she blinked them slowly. "But no one knows which."

And Lizzie went on saying nothing. She didn't, as was customary, pay with stories of her own. She told no one about the red bedroom, the nursery with its staring dolls, or the murder of Malina Paillet, much as they would have loved it. She didn't mention Jenny Ijub or Mr. Finney's preposterous accusations, much as they would have hated it. She wasn't even sure why she kept silent. In spite of her protestations, her interest in the Bell family had become proprietary; her position, implicated. Listening to these stories made Lizzie feel guilty.

Something had begun to nag at her, something she'd remembered only just now, just here in the Putnams' house. She turned it over and over in her mind, tried to worry or argue it away. It kept resurfacing. Wood floating on water. Lizzie's imagination was tougher than she was, exactly as her mother had always contended.

Blythe came in and Lizzie watched her collect the tea things. The cups were British, gold handles and tiny blue forget-me-nots. The pot was from China, very fat and painted white with blue willow trees, temples, and doves. The tea inside was a black Ceylon. "How are the boys, Blythe?" Lizzie said, forgetting she had already asked.

"I've no complaints," Blythe answered.

Lizzie stood. "I think I'll go say hello to Mr. Putnam."

Invading Mr. Putnam's library was not her usual routine, and she saw it noted, but it was unimpeachable, so she wasn't stopped. He was reading the paper. Some men grew more corpulent as they aged. Mr. Putnam was the sort who shrank. Folds of skin lay across his neck as a result of his slow disappearance.

The curtains were closed here, so it was much darker than the conservatory. Mr. Putnam read by the light of a small bright lamp. Lizzie's father used to do the same. Lizzie's mother had said he kept the curtains closed to fool himself into thinking it was late enough in the day for a drink. A glass of port sat on a mahogany table, close to Mr. Putnam's right hand.

He stood up politely. "Why, Lizzie," he said. "What a pleasant surprise. But you look tired."

Lizzie *was* tired. She sank into a seat across from him. He returned to his chair. The room smelled strongly of books, a smell she loved above all things, and the usual male odors of liquor and old cigars. The same as in her father's study. Many months after her father's death, Lizzie had moved into her mother's bedroom. She changed the rugs, the curtains, the position of the bed (her mother was a great believer in Dr. Crittenton's analysis of magnetic fields and healthful westward orientation during sleep). It was hard at first, but the room was large, with good light, and now it was hers.

In contrast, she'd entered her father's study only once since his death, when she met there with the family's solicitor, Mr. Griswold, and heard the terms of her father's will. There'd been an ashtray on the table with some parings of her father's fingernails in it. Lizzie supposed they'd been thrown out by now, but not by her.

Her heart quickened. She picked up a tasseled cushion, held it in her arms across her chest, against that beating. "Mr. Putnam," she said. She had trouble going on. She started again. "Mr. Putnam."

"Did you wish to see me about something particular?"

In the glow of the lamp Mr. Putnam's face took on a yellowish alarm. Lizzie knew him well. He didn't mind talking to women if he could stick to rehearsed compliments. He fancied himself good at these; he imagined women enjoyed them. An old-fashioned gallant.

But a genuine conversation was sure to tax him. It was unkind to force one on him. She waited while he took a sip from his drink, then spoke quietly. "Some time ago you said that someone had told you the sorts of foods Mrs. Pleasant served at her table. I was wondering who that someone was."

Mr. Putnam's expression intensified into one of trapped horror. Lizzie, who'd merely hoped to set her mind at rest, was surprised. This was a bad result; she shouldn't have come.

Paradoxically, it had a calming effect on her. His reaction was so extreme; it was as if he had taken her anxiousness away and added it to his. She was able to set the pillow back, breathe more evenly. "I was wondering if it was my father," she said. There. She'd thought it, she'd said it. No way to unmake this moment.

He responded with a fit of coughing. Lizzie fetched him water, but he'd already gulped his port, which made him sputter all the more. She waited through this, making small noises of concern and sympathy, the same she would make to a nervous horse. Really, she thought, she had her answer. If this answer hadn't raised other questions she would have taken pity on him and excused herself. He kept sneaking looks at her, hoping she had done so.

But when he finally responded, his voice was nothing but kind. "What brings these questions, my dear?"

Why lie? The Putnams were her parents' oldest friends; she'd known them all her life. "I've been told I have a sister. A half sister. Actually, I think I'm being blackmailed. Please don't tell Mrs. Putnam. She'd be so distressed."

As was he, of course. "Oh, my dear!"

"So you can see I really must know the truth. Sparing me won't spare me now."

Mr. Putnam stared at the empty glass in his hands. He poured himself another two fingers. "May I get you something?" he asked.

"No," said Lizzie. Eventually she would have to rejoin the women. Nothing would rouse their suspicions faster than liquor on her breath. Best to see this straight through straight.

"You must never tell Mrs. Putnam I've said a word." Mr. Putnam shook his head morosely. "I can't tell you how I wish you didn't know. Mind you, I don't believe that part about a sister. I never did. I told your father so.

"What mischief could he get up to, at his age? It was a fleecing, wolves to a lamb. He was a good man, Lizzie, or there'd have been no point. Your mother was already dead. A man—a man is different from a woman. He installed the child in the country, down south where you used to camp summers."

Down by the big trees. Lizzie remembered trunks like houses, a stream that dried by July, pine needles covering the ground so your feet sank when you walked. High, windy cliffs over foam. This all arrived in a moment, a flood of smells and sounds.

"There was a weathervane," she said sadly. "Carved like a flock of flying ducks. It clacked when the wind blew. Every year my father let me repaint it. I used to love doing that." She was so astonished she could feel nothing else besides.

"He made one condition. It was as much to protect you, Lizzie, as himself. The mother was a grasping, mendacious woman, not at all fit to raise a child, and he saw she would only increase her demands once she'd made a start. So he said he'd refuse all support if she ever contacted him again. He swore if she came even once to see the girl, he would cast them both off. After his death, we were forced to do that. Is she the one blackmailing you? She can't prove any of it. You pay her nothing."

"It's not the mother. Do you know where she is now?"

"I don't know anything about her. Which is as much as I wish to know."

"How does Mrs. Pleasant figure in?"

"Mrs. Pleasant helped arrange a nursemaid for the child. Is she the one blackmailing you?"

"No."

"But she's in back of it. Got to be. Who else? That child is not your sister, Lizzie, and no one says she is, excepting a couple of women who were born telling lies. Don't you pay a single cent. Mrs. Pleasant knew your father a long time, since the first days when she cooked at Case and Heiser and he supplied the meat. She made it her business to know the up-and-comers, and she found the way to work him."

"Your mother was a saint. How she suffered!" Mrs. Putnam stood in the doorway. Lizzie didn't know whether she had just arrived or had been standing outside for a while, hearing every word.

She shut the door and came into the room with her wide plum skirt sweeping the floor like a furious pendulum. Lizzie had never seen such a set of high red blotches on her cheeks. "When poor Harriet came all the way back from the grave to warn you! When I learnt that Mrs. Pleasant was making her afterlife a misery as well as her life!"

"Your father was a good man, Lizzie," Mr. Putnam repeated. He looked appealingly at his wife for confirmation, for forgiveness. "Lizzie already knew," he told her. "She came asking."

The color went down in Mrs. Putnam's face. She shifted with visible effort into briskness and efficiency. *"You're* a good man," she said. "Better than I ever deserved, and don't I know it. But you talk too much. This hasn't a thing to do with Lizzie, and it would hurt her mother horribly. I thank God she's dead! The past must bury the past.

"Now." She gave Lizzie a quick nod. "We're all done in here. Mrs. Mullin is waiting in the conservatory, wondering what we've all got up to, and you know what a gossip she is. You just pinch some color into your cheeks and come sit with us, Lizzie, as if nothing has happened. Let poor Mr. Putnam finish his port in peace. Look how you've upset him, but I entirely forgive you and none of this need ever be referred to again."

Mrs. Mullin's suspicions were indeed roused. They expressed themselves as a series of questions as to how Lizzie had found Mr. Putnam. Fortunately they were easily answered. To every delicate probe, Lizzie responded that Mr. Putnam had seemed in good spirits.

Meanwhile she tried to organize her own thoughts and feelings into clear, useful sequentiality. These are the things she thought and in this order:

First, it was a shame she didn't care more for Jenny. She preferred a girl like Maud, someone kind and thoughtful, someone lively, someone you could talk to who'd talk right back. Why couldn't it be Maud? Jenny seemed more Baby Edward's sister than Lizzie's, tight-lipped and disapproving.

And if Jenny really were her sister, wouldn't Lizzie instinctively feel something more for her? Mr. Putnam was quite right to point out that even if her father believed her to be his, she might still very well not be. Novels, even the history books, were littered with women who lied about such things. And for each one caught out, there must be a dozen never doubted.

Jenny had shown up at the Brown Ark, and on Lizzie's day there, too, so Mrs. Pleasant must have arranged it all. But did this make it more or less likely that Jenny was her sister? Lizzie tried to remember whether she'd been specifically asked for, the way Mrs. Pleasant's baskets of food were specifically directed to her. She wasn't sure, but clearly there were schemes within schemes.

And yet Mrs. Pleasant had asked nothing from her beyond Jenny's place at the Ark. She'd left Jenny off and that had been that.

Did it even matter whether Jenny was Lizzie's sister? Her father's acknowledgment certainly attested to the possibility. He had behaved in such a way as to make it possible. Everything else was mere chance. Surely, one's moral responsibilities were not determined by chance. As Mrs. Hallis said, there were immediate consequences to behavior and there were remote ones. Why distinguish between the two?

What moral responsibilities? Lizzie's behavior was not at fault here. Jenny was well cared for at the Ark, where everyone was more than kind to her. She had the prettiest dresses of any ward there. She had piano lessons. She had food and a bed and good friends. Any obligations Lizzie might or might not have were thoroughly discharged.

And what kind of a name *was* Ijub?

And all the while, Lizzie kept up a polite discourse on the weather and Blythe's children and Mr. Putnam's high spirits. It was a bravura performance, supported by Mrs. Putnam, who kept the conversation easy and prompted Lizzie if she ever seemed about to forget her lines.

Outside, two men and a woman strolled by. They'd come up the hill, were laughing and panting, loosening their scarves, unbuttoning their coats. No such thing in San Francisco as going out for a little walk.

The woman wore a soft hat with a black veil folded back. She had a yellow rose pinned to it, not a rosebud, but a full round bloom. It gave Lizzie a start. She actually jerked in response.

"Are you cold, Lizzie?" Mrs. Mullin asked, but Lizzie couldn't answer, because she had just realized that her father must have attended Mrs. Pleasant's Geneva Cottage red-invitation, men-only parties. What else would make her mother such a saint?

Maybe her father was a good man. Mr. Putnam said so, and he would know. Maybe they really had been forced to set Jenny aside, if Jenny's mother was so thoroughly bad. Mr. Putnam had said this, too, though he'd also claimed to know nothing about Jenny's mother. Mr. Finney had said the same thing once and followed it with the same retraction.

In any case, Lizzie had always thought her father a good man. But he was most certainly, most incontrovertibly, a man with a terrible temper.

"What's wrong?" Mrs. Mullin asked.

"She gets those dreadful headaches," Mrs. Putnam said. "Lizzie, I expect you'd better lie down."

But Lizzie had already risen. "I must go," she said. She tried to think of a reason to offer, gave it up. She left the house without her gloves. Blythe had to run after her.

Everywhere Lizzie looked, the color yellow sprang at her. There was so much of it. Sunshine on windows. Buttons on coats. The golden wattles dripping with their fabulous golden spikes of blossoms. It would be a terrible thing to be a young girl dead and missing the springtime.

Lizzie went home and drew the curtains in every room but her father's study, which she didn't enter. A letter from the Brown Ark had been delivered in her absence. She opened it and read:

My dear Lizzie,

I hope this finds you well. My own health is excellent although I'm aware of those wishing otherwise. The vultures gather, but I'll disappoint them as long as I can. I won't tell you their names. Last night's soup had a peculiar taste, but I make nothing of this, I put it down to carelessness in the kitchen. I remember when the food here was always done to a turn. I had a new pair of knitted slippers, but someone seems to have taken them. I won't tell you who or this letter might not be sent.

The dog has disappeared and no one will tell me why. I'm reminded of the day my dear friend Millicent Peterson died. We were told she fell from her horse, but her dog vanished the same hour. Dogs do find ways to tell us things, don't you know? If they're let. I remember how that terrier used to bark at everyone. I always knew when someone was coming through the yard.

I hope you'll think it safe enough to visit when you return,

Sincerely yours, Mrs. Wright

with a postscript from Miss Stevens, serving as secretary:

P.S. The dog is fine and Mrs. Wright petted it only yesterday. She is most unwell, as you can see, and I think it cruel that she must spend her declining days in this endless drama of poisonings and murder. Now she wishes me to add that she has instructed her bank manager to provide you with additional funds should you need them. She believes you've not come to see her because you're on a European tour. It would be a kindness if, when next you speak, you thank her for the money. Otherwise she will worry at us endlessly, convinced she's been robbed. I wonder if her impulses were so generous when she actually had funds, although it is tenderly done; I take nothing away from her genuine benevolence.

At about four o'clock Lizzie heard the foghorn. When she looked outside around dinnertime, she couldn't see across the street. It didn't necessarily follow that no one could see in. She left the curtains drawn.

2

"WAKE UP." Maud's face floated white as paste in the dark, and behind it Melody's face, and behind that, Coral's. When Jenny sat up she saw that Ella May and Tilly were also there. The whole Good Manners Club. Maud's voice was a hiss. "Come with us."

They made Jenny go first up the stairs. "Shhh!" Melody told her once, although she was already making as little noise as an Indian. They went up one flight and then another, until they were in the tower room.

"You're not afraid to be here, are you?" Maud asked.

Outside, the fog was so thick that no lights shone through. "No," said Jenny, with a sense of being trapped. She knew there was no right answer to that question. Maud excelled at questions without right answers.

"You need to toughen up," Maud said. "When you're adopted, you'll probably sleep by yourself. You can't be such a baby about it. None of the rest of us mind the dark."

Jenny thought she didn't mind the dark, either. What she minded was being shut up. But even that was all right, because she knew the door didn't lock. She needed only to wait as long as she could, letting the other girls go back to their beds, and then go out again. She could go anywhere she liked, out to the barn with the dog and the mule, or into the downstairs parlor to sleep. Or out to the street. She often went for walks when she couldn't sleep. As long as you were wherever you were expected when morning came, no one knew. Jenny took a seat on the settee that smelled of dead horses. The door shut with a click.

The room was cold and stank of dust and the bitter Chinese tea Miss Hayes drank. Jenny's breath was coming as fast as if she'd run up the stairs.

She didn't hear the girls, but they would wait for her. She couldn't leave yet. She must stay still as long as she possibly could. The silence pressed against her ears until it turned her pulse into a metronome.

Jenny put her hands on her knees and played scales over them. Two minutes, she told herself. An egg cooking. She kept her hands arched and tried to keep her fingering even. Give every note the same time to breathe. Instead she found herself playing faster and faster, lost track of when the egg was done.

She rose and picked her way through the clutter of charitable donations. There was a stuffed squirrel with its tail raised, and a hat rack with dangerous points on which she scratched her arm. There was a broken music stand, and a large cracked vase for umbrellas. Jenny reached the door and turned the knob.

It spun like a pinwheel. She panicked. She grabbed the doorknob tightly, pulled with both hands. The knob rattled in its socket, could be wiggled this way and that like her loose tooth.

Maud must have known it was broken, or arranged for it to be broken. Generally the boys stayed out of things between the girls, but Duffy Phelps would do anything Maud wanted, and Mrs. Lake said he was a wizard with a hammer, could fix anything. The thought that the boys might have known what Maud had planned was a special humiliation for Jenny.

By now she was gasping for air and unable to speak. No one would hear her, anyway. She stumbled back to the settee and flung herself onto it. Her face was already hot with tears, and now she began to weep with her mouth open, making faces that stretched her cheeks. Whenever she took a breath there was a noise like barking. She wiped her nose on the hem of her nightgown, because she had nothing else, and then fell asleep.

She awoke cold as well as terrified. She found a woman's dress, velvet with the hem kicked out, smelling of mothballs. She pulled its skirt over her as she lay on the settee. The pulse in her ears was deafening and yet she was convinced that something hungry was in the room with her. There'd been a rustle, the tick-tock of claws, only her heart was too loud for her to hear this.

She rose. Whatever was hungry retreated with a scrabble, but it would be back when it saw what a little girl she was. She was exactly what something hungry would want. Jenny had to get out. She crept to the nearest window.

Outside, the world was gone. There were no stars, no scrub, no sand, no city. Nothing above and nothing below. A vast and milky ocean rolled against the glass.

3

THE NEXT AFTERNOON Lizzie heard the front door chime. She was expecting no one. Before she could reach the door, it chimed again. When she opened it, she found Miss Viola Bell standing on the doorstep. She refused to come in. She was wearing a coat of blue wool, pinned at the throat with a large, garish brooch. Inside the coat she looked small and cold. "Do you know what's happened?" she said. "Do you care?"

The fog from the night before had dissipated, but the air was clingy and carried the echoey sounds of horses and wheels. The bit of yard in front of Lizzie's house was trellised. Few blossoms; it still looked wintry, but there was one branch of jasmine, and some sleepy bees.

"How nice to see you, Miss Bell," Lizzie said. "Please come inside. What are you talking of?"

Viola shifted on her crutch and her sheet music fell. Lizzie stooped and retrieved it. "The Mockingbird's Song" was the top sheet, "a piece for Teacher and Student." "I'm talking of Jenny. Who was found this morning, standing on the ledge outside the cupola window. She'd been there all night, in her thin little nightdress, with nothing but yards and yards of air beneath her and the cold, hard ground. If she'd fallen!"

"*Please* come in," Lizzie said again.

Across the way she could see her neighbor's boy in the window, watching. He had his jaw tied up for toothache, and a cat like a shawl on his shoulders.

Again Viola refused. Her voice was thready, her color poor. "Do you see that she could have been killed?"

Lizzie did not. "I don't understand," she said. "Jenny's so happy at the Brown Ark. Happy and safe."

"Happy?" A bead of spit appeared on Viola's lip; she wiped at it with the fingers of her cotton glove. Her dark hair was twisted into her hat, which was of a simple black felt that any shopgirl could have bettered. "How should she be happy? It would be one thing, if she'd never known anything but poverty. But to be petted one minute and cast aside the next. Don't you think that's the cruelest thing can be done to a child?"

It was possible, of course, that Jenny had talked to Viola about her past, but then Jenny didn't talk to anyone about anything. "What do you know about Jenny?" Lizzie asked.

"I know she's not *happy*. I went to the Brown Ark for our lesson. I was told she'd been put to bed and the doctor sent for. I asked the matron for your address and came here. I want you to know I hold you responsible. If she'd died you'd be responsible for that, too." Viola's voice had started low and gotten angrier without getting louder. Her fist gripped the handle of her crutch so tightly that it shook.

"Why am I responsible?" Lizzie asked. She had her own ideas, of course, but she didn't see how Viola could share them. Lizzie had calmed considerably since the day before; another sleepless night avoiding thoughts of her father had spent her. But now Viola was upsetting her again. Lizzie wished Viola would come inside, was afraid the neighbors would see, was afraid she would fall.

Viola tossed her head. The sunlight hit her brooch, making it sparkle threateningly. "Mr. Finney asked me to remind you about his money, if I ever had the chance. We're to be married." She said these last words as if she was aware she shouldn't be saying them but unable to deny herself the pleasure of it.

Now Lizzie wished there were only Jenny to worry about. "I hope you'll be very happy," she said automatically, and then, "I'm afraid he's a dangerous man. I'm sorry, I must say it. You're so very young."

Viola's brooch was a twinkling rose at her throat; her eyes were bright as glass. "I know he's not been a good man," she said. "We tell each other everything. He repents it all."

"You read the Bible together," Lizzie suggested. Your love will save him. She could imagine the potency of that, Mr. Finney, so handsome, so sincere. *Save me.* If he'd offered that aspect to Lizzie, she doubted that even she, twice Viola's age, would have successfully resisted. She had never understood Jane Austen's Fanny Price. "I've seen a different side of him."

It was the wrong thing to say, only confirmed Viola's special intimacy. "I'm sure you have," she said proudly.

Lizzie felt the press of dead air she associated with Baby Edward. The silver color in the corner of her eye, the taste in her mouth, the sickening spin of Viola's brooch. "It was you, then, told Mr. Finney about my father."

"Yes."

"What else did Mrs. Pleasant say about him?" Lizzie closed her eyes and there were tiny fairy lights on the inside of her lids. She pushed the headache firmly away. She couldn't have one now, not with Viola's heart open before her and matters of such delicacy still to be discussed. The usual terror approached, but Lizzie refused it.

"Mrs. Pleasant said nothing. She has a book with names in it, dates, and such like. I saw it last week, just for a moment. I can't show you, but I don't lie. I want the money for Mr. Finney because he has debts to settle before we can marry, but I didn't do it for that. I did it for Jenny. Someone has to watch over her."

Viola's voice had quickened, while Lizzie's mind had slowed. "I believe you," Lizzie said, her words unintelligible. She made a greater effort, achieved a moment's normalcy. Then it was gone again, bees buzzing, lights popping, the silver stain spreading over the world.

But no headache sent by anyone for any reason would stop Lizzie. She was speaking without thinking of it; the pain would come, no doubt, but she'd have what she wanted when it did. "I need to know what else Mrs. Pleasant has in her book about my father." The silver film soaked into Viola's eyes, her hair. Lizzie's hands were made of snow. "Things from long ago. I'll pay you to look again."

"How much?"

"Fifty dollars."

Viola was trembling. She was angry or ill or tired from standing for so long. Lizzie felt the power leaking from her own legs. She couldn't do anything more. She pulled the door shut without waiting for an answer, so that Viola wouldn't see her when the pain hit.

Doggedly her imagination fetched up images of Malina Paillet, but all in silver now. Drops of silver blood fell on silver silk. The sharp slice of a silver moon. Her head falling away from her neck. Silver roses wilting on her wrist. "You have only the beauty of youth," her angry suitor told her. He caught her by the hair.

Lizzie was lying on the marble of the entryway with no recollection of how she'd gotten there. She wondered whether Viola was still waiting outside, but she couldn't lift herself up to go see.

4

LATER LIZZIE MANAGED to reach the sofa in the dayroom, where she spent the rest of the night. She threw up twice, but by morning her headache had receded and she felt it only when she turned her head or sat or stood quickly. She would have liked to stay in bed for the day. But sometime during the ebbing, Viola's initial words had finally penetrated. Little Jenny had spent the night on the cupola ledge in her nightdress, and she might have been killed.

Lizzie washed her face with the coldest water she could stand. She dressed and caught the streetcar on Van Ness and walked the rest of the way to the Ark. The leaves of the silver-dollar eucalyptus were green on one side, silver on the other, so that a breeze made the stands of trees shimmer like water.

Lizzie knew the name of this tree because her father had taught it to her. He'd liked taking her for walks. "You don't complain about the hills," he said approvingly. "You don't chatter on about nothing."

He didn't always talk himself, but she liked it when he did. He was less guarded in what he said than her mother was, not so determined to make a lesson out of everything. Here in San Francisco, where the money grows on trees, he would start off, so that once as a girl she'd asked him which trees the money grew on, and the silver-dollars were the ones he'd named. He'd also said he could remember a time when there were no trees in San Francisco at all, but never, ever a time when there was no money.

He'd liked to tell stories that illustrated the lunacy of the madly rich. He was appalled by them, but proud as well—only in San Francisco.

Mr. Crocker's spite fence.

Layman's medieval castle.

Stanford's mechanical birds.

How many of these men had been at Mrs. Pleasant's parties with him? How many had pretended later not to know her, or one another, either?

Her father had also told her of Dr. Toland, a man who kept his dead wife in a glass-topped coffin in his office. What kind of a story was that to tell a child? Her mother was horrified when she heard. You'll give the child nightmares, she cried, so frightened of Lizzie's unruly imagination. You always underestimate her, Lizzie's father had replied. Lizzie had been so proud to hear him say that.

The story hadn't bothered her a bit. Lizzie asked to be kept under glass herself, which amused her father. But it struck her as a sensible precaution, just in case she wasn't dead after all, to leave a window through which she could get someone's attention.

The dead woman under glass put her in mind of the women on Morton Street. Against all her best efforts, she saw her father waiting in line there, making a selection, the woman like a puppet in his arms. Her mother at home, telling Effie to tie Lizzie's hands at night.

At the Ark, she found Nell in the parlor laying newly crocheted doilies over the backs of the threadbare chairs. The older girls must have been learning to tat. The doilies were round with scalloped edges and in no way improved the appearance of the room. Dubious finery piled on faded finery.

"Still abed," Nell said, without Lizzie's even asking. 'You just missed Dr. Kearney coming by for a second check. He says she's fine. But not talking, not our Jenny. We ask her, Just what were you playing at out on that ledge in the dark, and she won't say a word."

The line of Nell's mouth changed from tight to soft; her cheeks sagged into pockets. "The lamb," she added. "Poor Maudie hasn't left her side since we found her. I thought my heart would stop when I first saw her, her nightdress flying in the wind like a kite, holding on to the window with those tiny fingers. Her hands were so cold I thought they'd crack when we opened them. We were in a state, all right."

Since Jenny wouldn't talk, Ti Wong had taken it upon himself to investigate, Nell added. Nell herself guessed it was simple high jinks of some kind, a game gone wrong. But Ti Wong had been carefully through the tower room, and in his opinion, the door was jiggered. He'd also found a hidden pessary. That had taken some quick talking on Nell's part; she wished Lizzie had been there to see that!

The embroidered wisdom on the wall behind Nell had been changed again. Now it read:

How small, of all that human hearts endure,
That part which laws or kings can cause or cure!

                                          SAMUEL JOHNSON

A square of light fell from the one small window at the end of the room onto the floor. There was a row of empty beds and then one with Jenny in it, awake and sitting up. On the bed past Jenny, Maud lay asleep, facedown across the blankets, her golden curls spilling off the side of the mattress. What a vigil for a young friend to keep! There must be *something* about Jenny to inspire such devotion. Lizzie was determined to find it.

She spoke in a whisper so as not to wake Maud. "Are you all right now, little Jenny?"

"Yes," Jenny said. Her eyelids were swollen as if she'd been crying. Her hair was a tangle that would have to be painfully addressed when she was feeling better.

"I'm glad." Lizzie tried to think what to say next. She had so few ideas she settled on what she was really thinking. "Does it seem to you that we're anything alike?"

Apparently the question was too ridiculous to be worth answering. Jenny looked at her briefly, then looked away.

Lizzie sat on the side of her bed. The headache stabbed once, then stopped. "I like ducks and you like ducks." Lizzie counted on her fingers. "That's one. I used to play the piano when I was a little girl. That's two."

"You're not a little girl." Jenny lay back on her pillow. Now Lizzie saw a bruise on her neck, up by her ear, a scratch on her arm. Her fingernails were torn and must have hurt.

"Not anymore. But I was once. I like stories. Do you like stories?"

"Tell one," Jenny said. She turned her huge dark eyes to Lizzie. She was missing a tooth, right in the front of her mouth. Lizzie saw the gap when Jenny spoke. She would have the smile of a jack-o'-lantern if she ever smiled at all.

Telling a story was the perfect way to have a conversation with someone who refused to talk.

Once upon a time there was a king and a queen, and they had a daughter. They'd wanted a child for many years, and when the baby came she was the answer to their prayers. Her skin was snowy white with just a hint of apples. Her lips were red; her eyes were blue, and bright as stars. She was the most beautiful baby anyone could remember ever seeing.

But one night while the king and queen slept, an ogre took the child from her cradle and replaced her with a child of its own. In the morning the child in the cradle was wrinkled as a walnut, had eyes that crossed, and little pointed teeth. "This is not my child," the queen said, but the king was not so sure. Perhaps the child had fallen ill during the night. He sent for the finest doctors in the kingdom, yet no one could restore the child's beauty.

The ogre child grew every day. It was wicked as well as ugly. When the mother fed it, it bit her and then drank the blood instead of the milk. "This is not my child," the queen said, and when the king again refused to listen, she crept out into the night to find her daughter.

She walked for many days. Her shoes were soft and wore through at the soles. Her feet were soft and began to bleed. She came to a forest and in the forest was a stream and into this stream she put her bloody feet.

She was used to being served and cared for, not fending for herself. She hadn't eaten in quite some time.

So the queen was hungry as well as footsore, and there, beside her toes, trapped in a small pool, was a large silver fish. She picked up a stone to kill the fish, but before she could the fish spoke. "Put me back in the stream," it said, "and if I can ever do you a kindness, I will."

"How can a fish do me a kindness?" the queen asked, but she put it into the stream.

She thrust her feet back in the water and reclined on the bank. Suddenly she noticed an egg near her on the grass. Because she was still so hungry, she picked it up, thinking to crack it open and eat it. To her surprise the egg spoke. "Put me back in the nest," the egg said, "and if I can ever do you a kindness, I will."

"How can an egg do me a kindness?" the queen asked, but she saw the nest on a branch above her and placed the egg inside.

That night she had a dream. In the dream she saw her daughter sleeping in a glass box at the bottom of a lake on top of a mountain. But the mountain was too high to climb and the lake was too deep to swim. The queen woke up weeping.

(Lizzie didn't know why the queen was so certain the dream was true. She hurried on before Jenny could ask about this, in case she, too, found it odd.)

In the nest above the queen's head was a bird. "Take my wings," it said, and as soon as it spoke she felt wings growing from her shoulders. She flew to the top of the mountain and stood at the edge of the lake.

In the lake was the silver fish. "Take my tail," it said, and as soon as it spoke she felt her wings turn to fins and her legs fuse to a tail. She dove into the lake and swam to the very deepest, darkest part and picked her sleeping baby up.

In that instant, she was transported to her own castle, dry, wingless, and tailless. When the ogre child saw her with the baby, it climbed from the cradle and ran into the night and was never heard of again.

"There now, dear," said the king. "I told you it would all come right in the end."

There probably should have been one more animal. Things in fairy tales always came in threes, but Lizzie hadn't been able to think of another. She'd cobbled this story together from bits and pieces of other stories she remembered, but it wasn't a bad effort for all that. She was rather pleased with herself. She'd mastered her intractable imagination and turned it to good use. No dead girls in this story. No dancing, no yellow dresses. Lizzie was having none of those thoughts!

In fact, Lizzie was feeling better about Malina Paillet.

When the headache receded, it took some of her suspicions with it. Maybe her father had attended a party or two, but he wouldn't kill a girl for not liking him. What kind of a daughter would think he might? Yes, he'd had a terrible temper, but he was a good man. A good-hearted man. The only thing Lizzie couldn't quite set aside was the fact that Mrs. Bell had told her about Malina. It was so indiscreet, it seemed the sort of thing that must have a motive.

Maud had awakened. She came and lay next to Jenny, taking her hand. "What happened to the ogre child?" Jenny asked.

Jenny didn't like to be touched. Lizzie remembered that from when she'd fetched her at the House of Mystery; now she saw it with Maud. When Maud took her hand, Jenny jumped as if she'd been pinched. "I don't know," said Lizzie. "I guess she needs a mother, too, doesn't she? She needs an ogre mother."

"But not *that* ogre mother," Jenny said.

Lizzie stood and looked down at the two girls, the blond head and the dark. She felt a sudden lump in her throat over the mother she'd created, the mother who walked so far and risked so much. It occurred to her that the story wasn't really over. The child would grow up and leave. The mother would spend her life remembering the one brief hour when she could fly like a bird, swim like a fish.

ON THE SUBJECT OF VIOLA BELL, Lizzie was utterly ashamed. What excuse could she make? She decided simply to give Viola the fifty dollars next time Jenny had a piano lesson, as recompense for her own appalling behavior. She couldn't believe she'd hired a young girl to snoop for her; Lizzie wasn't the sort to do such a thing.

About Jenny her thoughts were more tentative. If only Jenny seemed contented at the Ark, things could be left as they were. Above all, Lizzie must not pick her up only to set her down again. Viola had that quite right. Lizzie needed to be sure she could see it through before she even began.

And there was still the mother to consider. What if Lizzie adopted Jenny, grew to love her like a sister, and then her mother appeared and took her back? What if her mother was colored? How could Jenny go from white to colored with no preparation? Lizzie remembered the story Mrs. Wright had told—how Mrs. Pleasant had passed a tray at a party to which she'd been invited, pretending to be a servant so that no one would feel awkward about her being there. Jenny was already such a proud little girl. She wouldn't know to do this, and Lizzie didn't want her learning. Lizzie meant to look in next on Mrs. Wright, but before she could do so, Minna Graham appeared in the doorway, clapping her hands. "Sam is here, Miss Hayes!" she said. "He wants to say hello to you!"

Sam had become a great favorite with the girls in the kitchen. He delivered Mrs. Pleasant's baskets with elegance, sweeping his top hat from his head and holding it at his heart. He had a gift for making orphans feel like princesses. It was kinder even than the food he brought. Lizzie excused herself to go see him.

Three of the older girls were still washing up from lunch. An obstinate landscape of creamed potatoes crusted the pots and pans, and the burnt-hair smell of cooked cabbage hung heavily. The kitchen steamed like a greenhouse. Sam stood amidst the dirty dishes, making a pyramid of strawberries. "This here's for you," he told the girls in turn, whenever he came upon a perfect one, passing it over. "This one's a jewel." On the counter, packed in ice, were five large silver fish with popping eyes.

"How are your headaches, Miss Hayes?" he asked, and sympathized over the recent siege. "I'll tell Mrs. Pleasant. She's smart with leaves and pastes. Maybe she'll have something new to try."

"Mrs. Pleasant is so good to remember us." Lizzie said the words around a duplicitous taste in her mouth. Such lovely fruit, such lovely fish. Just when Lizzie had thought to send a spy into the nest.

Sam said Mrs. Pleasant was right as right. Had one of her dizzy spells, her spasmodics as she called them, but bright as a penny now.

"And Mrs. Bell?"

Mrs. Bell was also fine. She didn't always sleep so good, and sometimes she woke the household, screaming they were all being murdered in their beds, but this hadn't happened for a couple of weeks and they were all enjoying the rest.

"And Miss Viola Bell?"

Sam flipped one of the sorrowful, pop-eyed fish over with a slap.

He turned to Lizzie. "Now, there's trouble," he said. He shook his head slowly. "There's a heap of trouble."

Last night, he said, just last night, Miss Viola had been thrown from the house. She didn't get on with Mrs. Bell, and Mrs. Bell was always suspecting Miss Viola snuck around in passageways and spied on people in their bedrooms, as if you couldn't hear her coming a mile with that heavy foot of hers. But last night it was Mrs. Pleasant found her, snooping around in some papers where she'd no business being. The one thing Mrs. Pleasant couldn't forgive was snooping.

Scarce an hour later Miss Viola was packed and gone, living at the home of the Boones now, colored friends of Mrs. Pleasant, since Mrs. Pleasant was not the sort to turn a girl out to the street no matter how angry she was. The servants had all been called together and everyone told she was never to be let back in and her name wasn't Viola Bell anymore, but was Viola Smith, which it always had been, Mrs. Bell said, only they'd all been too nice about it.

Sam was sorrier than he could say, but there were those made better by suffering and those made worse. Miss Viola Bell, Miss Smith, that was, had always been the second, but maybe now she'd be the first. The Boones were nice folks and would be good to her.

In all the horrors of the past few days, this was the worst yet. It demanded an immediate price; Lizzie didn't have to be a Methodist to see her duty, clear and terrible and unavoidable. She must go to the House of Mystery, where she'd sworn never to go again, and take the blame for Viola's disgrace. She must do this at once. She could not allow Mrs. Pleasant to throw Viola out over something Lizzie had put her up to. She could not let Viola suffer through one more night in a strange bed.

She blamed her headache, for she wasn't the sort to snoop and certainly wasn't the sort to pay someone else to snoop when she was in her right mind. Maybe Mrs. Pleasant, who knew about her headaches, would understand. Maybe she wouldn't forgive Lizzie, but would forgive Viola, which was all that mattered. Viola had never needed a mother more than she needed one now with Mr. Finney courting her, repenting day and night.

But Lizzie saw her duty more quickly than she did it. She sat in the parlor while working herself up, and by the time she'd finished, Sam was gone. She got her gloves and hat, and took the same walk she'd once made in the dark with little Jenny. She was glad it wasn't dark. The sun was out, pale as a pearl. The air was damp, and the smell of eucalyptus leaves intense. Lizzie passed beneath, opened the gate, climbed the steps, and knocked with the roaring-lion knocker. She remembered how frightened she'd been the first time she'd done this. Her mind had been a jumble of voodoo curses and headless dolls. She was much more frightened now.

No one came in response to the first knock. She knocked again, with her hand this time. And again. She took off her glove and knocked again.

The door was finally opened, by a blind man in a green butler's uniform. His hair was wild with gray curls, his nose a drunkard's blue. His eyes, pale and filmy, remained fixed on a spot just above Lizzie's right shoulder. No warmth came out through the opened doorway.

"Miss Hayes to see Mrs. Pleasant." The dark entryway yawned before her. There in the corner was the grandfather clock, ticking loudly, and there in the back, on the newel post at the base of the spiral stairs, the black statue of the naked woman. You couldn't see that she was naked from this distance, of course. You had to know the family. "Not in. Are you a reporter?" His words slid up against one another; his accent was Scottish. His "you" was halfway to "ye."

"No. Of course not. I know Mrs. Pleasant. I've been a guest here. And I must speak to her urgently."

"Not in," the butler repeated. "And not often in to uninvited callers even when she is in." He began to close the door.

"Might I see Mrs. Bell?" she asked.

"Not in."

"Sam, then. Might I speak with Sam?"

"Not in," the butler said, shutting the door.

Maybe Mrs. Pleasant and Sam *were* out. But Mrs. Bell was always in. When Lizzie made up her mind to something, it was made up.

She went down the steps. She looked back to check that the butler wasn't watching—instinct only; a moment later she remembered he was blind—and took the path that led around the enormous house to the back.

A white girl came, in answer to her knock on the kitchen door. "I'm looking for Sam," Lizzie said.

"He's not here."

"Or Mrs. Pleasant or Mrs. Bell. Mightn't I speak with Mrs. Bell?"

The girl was uncertain. She stared at Lizzie, biting her lip. "I'm Miss Hayes," Lizzie said encouragingly. "I've called here before. Mrs. Bell knows me. Just go ask her."

"Try the front door."

"No one answers."

"Wait here," the girl said finally.

She let Lizzie into the kitchen. Two men and a woman sat at the table. The men were colored, the woman was white. Someone had been smoking recently. Lizzie could smell it. The stove was out; the room was cold. No one looked at her. They leaned toward one another across the table, murmured a conversation she couldn't hear. The woman laughed. The counters around the dry-sink were covered with dirty dishes, some so crusted Lizzie didn't see how they could ever be scrubbed clean. Over the sink was a line hung with dishrags.

Disorder was meant to be a private thing. Lizzie pretended not to see it. She'd forced herself in here. There was no reason she should be made welcome.

The girl returned. "She's in the drawing room. I'm to take you."

The house was as dim as always, and as quiet. Muted sunlight came through the glass dome and landed on the coiling snake of a staircase; everything around it was dark. As they passed the library, Lizzie caught a glimpse of the blind butler sitting in a chair, helping himself to Mrs. Bell's raspberry wine.

They reached the white-and-gold drawing room. "Miss Hayes," the girl said, and then withdrew.

The curtains were pulled and one lamp lit. "Come, sit with me," Mrs. Bell said, and Lizzie did so.

Mrs. Bell was in blue, her brown hair pinned into curls in the back, her skin dull with powder. She had an embroidery hoop in her lap, with a violet half-stitched into the cloth. Lizzie had seen and heard enough to know there was no point in pleading here on Viola's behalf. Those apologies would have to wait for Mrs. Pleasant.

But she could ask about Malina Paillet—ask why Mrs. Bell had chosen to tell her that story; she could pin down the date as much as possible. Then she could go home and check her father's business ledger. He didn't enter personal information, but there might be something. More important, there might be nothing. This would help Lizzie set Malina completely aside as a sad story, but nothing to do with her. Lizzie turned her head so she wouldn't see the stone statues of the begging women.

None of this went as she'd planned. Mrs. Bell opened with one of her startling conversational gambits; there was no recovery. "There are those wish to kill me," she said, but calmly. "Those who've already tried. No one is to get through the door when Mrs. Pleasant is out. Yet in you waltz."

"Your butler did attempt to stop me," Lizzie confessed. "I was persistent."

"Billy?" Mrs. Bell sighed impatiently. "I said it to Mrs. Pleasant, so now we've a blind man guarding the door. You think a killer won't be persistent? A reporter? My mother? A woman come here once, claimed our Muriel had been kicked in the head by a horse. Near to dying. Slid upstairs, smooth as honey while we were all wringing our hands and carrying on. She was going through my desk when Muriel walked in, fit as ever could be."

"How awful."

"Reporters are lower than lice. I can't offer you coffee. I can ring and ring, without anyone coming. When Mrs. P is out, the servants do as they please. Won't even protect me."

"Do you know when Mrs. Pleasant will be back? I really must talk with her."

Mrs. Bell smiled slyly. The tips of her perfect teeth rested on her full bottom lip. "You better not. You better go before she comes. She don't want surprises."

"It's too important."

As always, Mrs. Bell picked up Lizzie's hands. The room was cold and Mrs. Bell's hands colder. Lizzie's eyes were beginning to adjust to the dark. On the wall was a picture of two cherubs eating sponge cake. It was sweet and sentimental, something Lizzie's mother would have liked. Here, it didn't go with the statuary.

"All Mrs. Pleasant's business is important," Mrs. Bell said.

"She's out on important business now. The city would fall without her."

"Do you remember telling me about one of her parties?" Lizzie began, but Mrs. Bell was still talking and didn't stop to listen.

"I used to have such queer fancies as a child," she said. "Voices in the wind and water. When I was three months old my mother undressed me and put me on a windowsill in an ice storm. She was a tiger-heart. Might still be looking for me, for all I know. She killed my two brothers."

"I have a dead brother, too," Lizzie offered. "He died when he was a baby."

Mrs. Bell dismissed this. She released Lizzie's hands, lifted the embroidery hoop, and began to pick at it with the needle. She worked a purple thread loose, which grew longer and longer while the half-formed violet disappeared. "If your mother didn't kill him, then you don't know what I'm saying."

"But I used to have queer fancies about him," Lizzie insisted. Used to, as if she didn't still, nearly every day. Who was she to think Mrs. Bell odd? She meant to be congenial, but Mrs. Bell didn't like it.

"Do you ever think you're not real?" Now it was a competition.

"Sometimes. Sometimes I'm reading a book and when it ends I believe in the characters more than myself. It doesn't last very long, but I know the sensation."

Mrs. Bell shook her head. "You don't know anything. What I'm saying is, maybe I was supposed to die when I was three months old. That's why I've made no mark. The servants don't notice me. I've nothing that's my own."

"You have a husband and children," Lizzie said. "I wish I had so much as you."

"All I have is six hundred acres in upper New York."

A feeling had been growing over Lizzie during this exchange. It rose from the unvarying at-homes of Mrs. Putnam, the endless circling of Mrs. Wright's memories, but it was strongest with Mrs. Bell in the House of Mystery. These were women under glass. Time had stopped.

Lizzie remembered again, but claustrophobically, her father's story of Dr. Toland's dead wife in her glass-topped coffin. What a good idea, in case you weren't quite dead yet, to leave a window through which you could get someone's attention. "We don't have to be the same person our whole lives," Lizzie said desperately, and then the clock in the hallway struck and the spell was broken.

Mrs. Bell seemed to come to herself, set the embroidery down, patted her hair. "You can probably catch Mrs. Pleasant at the mission," she suggested politely. "She's got another charity case out that way, some family she's feeding. But she likes the mission, she'll probably stop in after. That woman does love a graveyard. She has one of her own, you know. You can imagine how convenient that's been over the years."

They heard the front door open, boots stamping, the voice of a young man calling out. "Mother! Mother!"

Mrs. Bell was on her feet, moving more quickly than Lizzie had thought her capable, and speaking more loudly. "You don't be coming here, Fred! Billy! Billy! Fred's trying to get in!"

Clearly, Lizzie's interview with her had come to an end.

6

ACCORDING TO SOME, Mr. Bell and Mrs. Pleasant were very much in love. They built the House of Mystery to live in together after her husband (and daughter) had died of diseases caused by excessive drink. They mixed assets freely and, after his marriage to Teresa, deeded properties over to her as well. The Bell and Pleasant finances were a Gordian knot no lawyer was ever able to loosen, though for more than thirty years countless numbers of them tried.

In this version of the household, Thomas Bell's marriage to Teresa was something he was tricked into while drunk, "bibulous" being the adjective most frequently assigned him. During the various estate cases, servants testified that the Octavia Street house was a divided one, quite literally. Mrs. Bell was not to enter Mr. Bell's half. He would not enter hers. Nor would he ever speak to her. Any communication was to go through Mrs. Pleasant. Mrs. Pleasant and Mrs. Bell, however, were conceded to be very fond of each other.

Yet there were those eight children (two of them dead). Not a one of them hers, Teresa said. Mr. Bell had paid her fifty thousand dollars a child, so Mrs. Pleasant had produced one whenever the women were short of cash. Thomas Bell died in 1892. Suffering from a flu, he rose in the night, lost his way, and fell into the well of the spiral staircase. "Where am I?" the servants said they heard him cry out.

Mrs. Bell was in Glen Ellen at the time, on the Beltane ranch owned by Mrs. Pleasant. Teresa recorded the death in her diary: "Oct. 16 telegraph from S.F. 10:30 about Mr. Bell. Took two Gal Red Wine to Officer for [word indecipherable] Mrs. Bell [a nephew's wife] and Mrs. Gordon go to town. Telegraph to Mammy 25ck [name indecipherable] I gal wine J Bergman 1 gal wine 2 o'clock Mr. Bell died."

On the day after his death, Mrs. Bell shipped two barrels of apples and one package of cheesecloth, paid some bills, and had some horses shod.

The will was contested by Fred, the oldest boy. He claimed that his mother, the executrix, was incompetent, because she was under the sway of her housekeeper. The court eventually agreed. Judge Coffey ruled that Mrs. Bell and Mrs. Pleasant's relationship was an inappropriate one for a white woman and a colored woman to have. Mrs. Pleasant's influence in the Bell household was unnatural, and illegal as well.

Ironically, the friendship had worsened by this time. In 1902, after a noisy row during which the police were called, Mrs. Bell had Mrs. Pleasant evicted. "She passed out the door after her two trunks snarling like a mad dog," Mrs. Bell wrote in her diary. While Mrs. Pleasant said, "I am glad, very glad to go."

That same year, Mrs. Pleasant published the first chapter of her memoirs. Included was an analysis of her palm—the palmist H. Jerome Fosselli said she showed a "marvelous ability to read motives"—and also the startling assertion that she had never been a slave. She was born in 1814 in Philadelphia. Her father was an importer of silks, a native Kanaka named Louis Alexander Williams. Her mother was a free "full blooded Louisiana negress."

A dispute with the editor prevented the promised second install-ment. Mrs. Pleasant died in 1903.

Teresa Bell died in 1923, leaving an estate whose estimated value was $938,000. Before her death, she'd accused Mary Ellen Pleasant of having murdered an employee named Sam Whittington many years before, and also of killing Thomas Bell by pushing him over the stairs, possibly with Fred Bell's help. She'd accused Fred of murdering two wives. She'd accused Marie Bell's husband, Arthur Holman, of murdering Marie. She'd accused her mother of murdering her brothers. Her estate, which left nothing to either Clingans or Bells, was immediately contested by both families on grounds of insanity.

None of the large San Francisco estates seems to have passed without objection from one generation to the next, but the Bell estate is the standard by which all others are measured. Every case from 1897 to 1926 was as bad as the Bell business or it wasn't. John Bell, Thomas Bell's supposed nephew, made a claim, as did Viola Smith, as did the Clingan sisters. Decisions were made, appealed, reversed. The case went to the state supreme court.

In May of 1926, litigation ended in a compromise. Of the total, $370,000 went to the surviving Bell children, after they had pledged $100,000 to charity and made a settlement to Viola Smith of close to the same.

Maybe:

Fred Bell was the son of May Thompson and a gambler named Bill Thompson.

Marie was the daughter of May Thompson and Dr. Monser, the abortionist who died in San Quentin.

Robina was the child of Sarah Althea Hill and Reuben Lloyd, a prominent city attorney.

Reginald or possibly Muriel was William Sharon's child by Bertha Barnson (or maybe Bonstell), a maid at the Palace.

Eustace was born to "one of the Harris girls."

Or:

They were all, as they themselves claimed, the children of Thomas and Teresa Bell.

Reginald Bell gave the following statement to the *San Francisco Examiner*: "We always called her [Teresa Bell] mother and she was a good mother to us. Mammy Pleasant was a wonderful woman, but there was nothing mysterious about her and there was really no reason why the home should have been called the House of Mystery."

7

BACK IN APRIL 1890, Lizzie waited at the mission. Sunlight came dimly through the yellow glass of the small windows, so the room was lit with a golden daytime dusk, but there was little heat. The sky was a ceiling striped with Indian dyes. The ground was worn tile. At the far end of the adobe room the altar glittered. This place never seemed to change. The city grew in all directions, but here was its eternal, damp, still-beating Spanish Catholic heart.

To Lizzie's New World Episcopalian sensibilities, the room had a thrilling aura of overexcitement. Saint Ann clasped her hands together pleadingly. The Archangel Michael was dressed like a Spanish *grande*. Publicly, Lizzie disapproved of a religion that covered itself in thin gold leaf. It recalled the gorgeous medieval excesses of popery. Privately, if there'd been no one to see her, she would have fallen to her knees.

She sat on the hard pews in the cold cave of the church, wondering how long she would wait. On the wall to her right was a painting of the Last Supper. This suited Lizzie, whose mind was very much on betrayal. The waiting seemed a lenient penance. And better to find Mrs. Pleasant here than have to return again to the still, clogged air of the House of Mystery.

Mrs. Pleasant entered an hour or so later. She did not seem surprised to see Lizzie, though, to Lizzie's chagrin, she did seem pleased. "I didn't know you were Catholic," she said. She crossed herself quickly and gestured for Lizzie to come outside. She wore a purple bonnet with a wide brim, and was wrapped in a purple shawl.

They went to the little graveyard, a garden of blackberries, brambles, and slabs. Mrs. Pleasant stooped over a marker. J Sparrow, whose epitaph was caught in a cage of twisted wrought iron. "There are three vigilante graves around here," Mrs. Pleasant said. "James Sullivan, Charles Cora, and James Casey. Only I can't remember right where. And any number of Indians. No stones for the hundreds of them."

Mrs. Pleasant sighed. "When you get to my age you'll find things that happened forty years ago are more clear than yesterday's doings. Part of my mind is always in those splendid, dreadful years." She shook her head, then straightened, brightened, and began to walk again. "Isn't this a lovely spot, though? Nothing like the company of the dead when you need a bit of peace and quiet."

This had never been Lizzie's experience. "I'm even sorrier, then, to intrude on your peaceful time here," she said.

"Have you ever given thought to your epitaph?"

"No."

"No," repeated Mrs. Pleasant. "Of course, you're far too young. I've picked out mine. Known it for years."

"What will it be?" Lizzie was genuinely curious. How could such a long and tumultuous history be encapsulated on a single stone? "'She was a friend to John Brown,'" Mrs. Pleasant said. "That's what I'd like."

"I have something very difficult to say to you," Lizzie told her.

They'd reached the obelisk of Don Luis Antonio Arguello. Mrs.

Pleasant paused to admire it. "Then just open your mouth and let it come," she suggested.

Lizzie took a breath. Sunlight dappled the leaves, twirled warningly in the wind. Something was corking her throat. She spoke anyway. "It's my fault that Miss Viola was snooping last night. I put her up to it. Please don't hold her responsible, since it's all my fault. I'm more sorry than I can say."

There was a silence. The shards of light, spinning like tops. Lizzie's breath coming through her mouth, thin as thread.

Then, "You astonish me," Mrs. Pleasant said. Her face was shadowed. Lizzie was glad not to see her eyes. *He was frightened of those eyes,* she'd once said, although Lizzie couldn't remember about whom. "I thought you a lady and a friend."

"I meant no harm to you. I certainly meant no harm to Viola. I just got it in my head that my father killed Malina Paillet. I couldn't stop thinking about it. I felt I had to know."

"Who's Malina Paillet?"

Lizzie told herself there was no way to offend Mrs. Pleasant more than she'd already done. No way back, in any case, only forward. "Mrs. Bell told me about Malina. The beautiful young girl in a yellow silk dress. Killed by a white man at one of your parties. Her throat cut."

"There's a Victoria Paillet has a place around the corner from us. Malina, I never heard of."

"But Mrs. Bell said."

Mrs. Pleasant turned. Her face was every bit as angry as Lizzie expected, deserved. The southern vowels hardened and shortened in her mouth. "Mrs. Bell says that she can fly. She floats over the bay to the Oakland estuary. The wind tells her stories. I love her dearly, but I don't credit everything she says."

"Oh," said Lizzie.

"Are you much of a reader, Miss Hayes?"

"Yes."

"I thought so. Now, I've left books alone and studied people. You don't have time for both. A woman like you will always go with the person who tells a story. You should watch out for that."

This was so obviously true. "I'll be more careful," Lizzie said, more and more ashamed. And still she couldn't stop. "Where is Jenny Ijub's mother?"

"Buried in the sea. You society women. You always think everything's about you. You think everyone else is only here to cook your meals or sew your clothes or be grateful for your charity or forgive you."

Lizzie's father had once said that very thing to Lizzie's mother. "You think the poor are only here to provide you with a reason to be charitable," he'd said. "So why *are* the poor here?" her mother had answered.

Had Lizzie's moral position not been so compromised, she might have argued. If it's not all about me, she might have said, why does everyone watch everything I do? Lucky she didn't. Who would complain of this to Mrs. Pleasant, about whom the whispers never hushed? Mary E. Pleasant, who had only to touch a thing to turn it notorious. Mary E. Pleasant, Queen of the Galloping Tongues.

Lizzie tried to believe that Jenny's mother was buried at sea. She owed Mrs. Pleasant at least this much, so she tried her best. Unlikely as it was.

"It does tire me sometimes," Mrs. Pleasant finished, and Lizzie could see why: Lizzie was tired of Lizzie, too.

"I'm going to be different," Lizzie offered, and she meant it; she was determined to be so, but Mrs. Pleasant walked away while she was speaking. Lizzie trailed behind, though there were no more gestures inviting her to do so.

"I have never been given to explaining away lies," Mrs. Pleasant said. "And you can't explain away the truth."

Her voice was tight with hurt. Even so, Lizzie couldn't escape the brief suspicion that everything she'd ever done had been entirely as Mrs. Pleasant wished. Hadn't she produced all those signs out of her very own hallway, forced a magical juncture on Lizzie merely by asserting that she faced one?

An invisible bird sang in the blackberries, a fluttering, descending whistle, which stopped as they approached. They arrived at a large stone. Mrs. Pleasant pointed to the name—James Sullivan. And a prayer with an odd mixture of sentiments:

> *Remember not, O Lord, our offenses, nor those of our parents.*
> *Neither take thou vengeance of our sins—*
> *Thou shalt bring my soul out of Tribulation, and in thy mercy thou*
> *shall destroy mine enemies.*

Lizzie read the epitaph aloud. "'Who died by the hands of the Vigilance Committee.'"

"That was never proved," Mrs. Pleasant said.

The strings of her purple bonnet had come loose. She retied them briskly. Her fingers were long and thin, her creased face set. She did not look saddened or surprised or angry or vengeful. She did not look hurt so much as she looked like a person who could be hurt. She looked old.

"Now our acquaintance is at an end," she said. "Be so good as to leave me here with my friends."

8

ON THE SEVENTH OF APRIL, Maud Curry's mother attended one of Mrs. Woodworth's revival meetings and was instantly cured of her tuberculosis. She came at once to the Brown Ark for Maud, who left in a daze of happiness, hardly able to believe she'd been collected at last.

April 14 approached. Without crediting the prophecy, without mentioning it, possibly without even thinking about it, the Putnams joined a number of residents about the bay who had decided to spend Easter week taking the waters in Napa or Middletown or Calistoga. Some went to confession. Some wrote letters that apologized for old faults, revealed secret loves, and otherwise settled accounts.

Most paid no attention to the Doom Sealers. The press, long bored with it all, gave the story less space than the Sharon trial had routinely taken.

Lizzie dressed in her corset and her apricot silk and went to see her solicitor, Mr. Griswold. It was raining just slightly. Wherever the ground was unpaved it had softened, but not all the way to mud. The air had a lovely laundered smell. Lizzie shook her umbrella off and left it with the doorman.

"I need some money," she told Mr. Griswold. "I was thinking

maybe fifty dollars, but I'm not really sure what would be right. I have to pay off a blackmailer." This wasn't quite true, but avoided a longer explanation.

"How that takes me back!" Mr. Griswold said. "How often your father came to me with those very words!"

Mr. Griswold agreed that fifty was a standard payoff. Low for a man, but very standard for a woman. He thought he could advance Lizzie that much so long as it didn't become a habit. He supposed she'd require cash.

She was planning to give the money to Viola at Jenny's next piano lesson, assuming Viola was still Jenny's piano teacher. Otherwise, Sam would have to tell her where and how to find the Boones. It didn't make up for the trouble Lizzie had caused, of course; she wouldn't pretend that it did.

By the time Lizzie had finished her business, she'd taken up Mr. Griswold's lunchtime. The downtown streets were filled with women at this hour, the men all working in their offices, except for those in the bars. There was a matinee of *Rip Van Winkle* at the Tivoli. Lizzie saw groups of women going inside with their children, their skirts brushing together, the children's voices high and piping like birds'. Edward Bryan would be singing the lead, and his smoldering over-acting was very much to Lizzie's taste. What a treat this would be for the wards. Lizzie determined to suggest it to Mrs. Lake.

A hack stopped beside her and Mr. Finney looked down from it. "May I offer you a lift?" he asked. "Nasty weather to be walking in."

It was nothing of the sort,, a softer rain couldn't be imagined. "I like it." Lizzie went on without stopping.

He jumped down, tied the horses. When Lizzie looked back, he was running after her. He walked a moment by her side, catching his breath, a little water dripping from the brim of his hat. "I hope you've forgiven the messenger, Miss Hayes," he said finally. "I'd be sorry to think I'd lost you as a friend."

"Your interest in me was never social."

"Your interest in *me* was never social," he replied. "You know nothing about my interest in you."

"So you're not here to ask for money? I've quite mistaken things?"

Mr. Finney gave an awkward laugh, made an awkward gesture with his hand. Of course he wished there was nothing financial between them, that they were only a couple of old friends out for a stroll. He hoped someday that would be the case. Nothing would please him more. As to now, he only wanted what was fair. He entirely understood Miss Hayes's reluctance to pay anything before his information had been confirmed. She was a lady with delicate feelings. The things he'd told her were, no doubt, shocking to hear.

But now he had it on good authority that she knew them to be true. Now was the time to determine a fair price for a secret delivered and a secret kept.

Lizzie hauled up her skirts to cross the street. There was a carriage coming, black with glass windows. The driver wore full purple livery except for a large white cowboy hat. Only in San Francisco, her father would have remarked, had he been there to see it. Heaven must be wonderful indeed to make up for all the things you missed by being dead. "You can say whatever you like about my father." Lizzie stepped up onto the far curb. "My father was a good man, and when he was alive he wouldn't have spared a thought for a sharper like you. I don't imagine he cares more now."

Mr. Finney tipped his hat and clucked his tongue in admiration. "I do admire the way you speak your mind. I never met a society lady like you. No pretense, what you think is what you say."

"Only to you." Lizzie was surprised to realize this was true. It made her suddenly, unexpectedly fond of Mr. Finney, in spite of his being such a loathsome man. Hadn't she always stood her ground with him? You couldn't say Lizzie was nobody's fool, but she wasn't Mr. Finney's.

She turned, stopping, and raised her umbrella so that he could slip beneath it, too. He took off his glasses to wipe them dry, and his eyes were that mottled, pebbled blue.

"What about the child?" he said. "There are details, things once said that can't be unsaid." But Lizzie had already reached into her pocket and drawn out the money, and this had nothing at all to do with Jenny. Lizzie was trusting her instincts. She put the fifty dollars into Mr. Finney's hand.

"Here's what I'm buying," she was already saying. "It occurs to me that Miss Viola Bell held an interest for you that Miss Viola Smith might not. For fifty dollars, you look into your heart. If you'll be a good husband to her, then marry her. If you won't be a good husband, then let her alone. The decision is yours. You've come to a magical juncture here, Mr. Finney, but you're a man who takes the long view. I trust you absolutely to do what's right."

He was staring at her, his face close to hers under the single umbrella, the light, intimate tune of the rain hitting the taut cloth and the stone street. The passing horses were polished and the air fragrant. It was a perfect day, one she would often remember. She'd just cursed Mr. Finney with his very own magical juncture. "The person I'm saving here is you," she said.

Then he went forward into his magical juncture and she went backward into hers. She returned to Mr. Griswold for another fifty dollars. He was far less agreeable this time. What an amateur she was at this! If she went on letting just anyone on the street blackmail her this way, her father's estate would be gone before she knew it.

*

When the morning of the fourteenth arrived, it came wrapped in a blue sky and a bright sun. Lizzie woke early and drove to the Brown Ark. "Isn't this a beautiful day?" people asked her as they passed on the street. All over the city people were saying the same thing to one another. "Beautiful day, isn't it? Did you ever see such a beautiful day?"

It was the day after the end of everything. Lizzie had chosen it deliberately as the day on which she would become someone new. She was a notorious woman now; there was no point in continuing to pretend otherwise.

She sent a letter of resignation to Mrs. Hallis. Included in it was her Atlantis-coin necklace and her written decision to remove the offending child from the Brown Ark. On April 14 she took custody of Jenny Ijub.

And then, because she still wasn't sure she liked Jenny all that much, she sweetened the deal by taking Ti Wong, too. Jenny was an obligation of blood, but she and God had a covenant for Ti Wong.

She'd met many times with Mr. Griswold, to discuss her finances. Luckily she had her experience as Ark treasurer to draw on. She knew more about money than some women of her class. Lizzie was going to court to challenge her father's will. It was a frighteningly public thing to do. A lady appears in the papers only twice—on the day she weds and the day she dies, Mrs. Putnam reminded her. The Putnams were, of course, most disapproving. She is *not* your sister, they insisted with some cause, and Lizzie couldn't make them understand that this had simply ceased to matter.

Lizzie hoped for a quick and quiet decision in her favor. She was not, after all, getting married, as her father had absolutely forbidden her to do. If she now had a family to support, there was no one to blame for this but him. She was prepared to say so in open court if it should come to that. She only hoped there'd be no further claimants on the estate, no additional children she knew nothing about.

In any case, it would all take time. Meanwhile she'd packed Baby Edward's picture into a trunk along with many other mementos and removed him to the attic. He protested this. She was burying him all over again. But it was nothing personal, just part of her plan to let her home to a quiet family of four and move with Jenny and Ti Wong down to the Big Trees house for the summer. This was an economy, but would, she hoped, also be a pleasure. Lizzie had every expectation Baby Edward would find a way to come along.

Lizzie arrived at the Ark with her things in a rented wagon. Neither Jenny nor Ti Wong had anything of consequence to add to it. They stood in the sandy lot saying goodbye to everyone. Mrs. Lake was in tears, as was, to Lizzie's surprise, Nell. "You come back and see us," Nell told Jenny, over and over. Her round shoulders shook. She held Ti Wong. "First Maudie and now you!"

Ti Wong hopped from foot to foot, so excited was he not to be drowned this morning. He knew about Lizzie's financial worries and discussed them as he lifted Jenny into the wagon. They could start a detective agency, he suggested. People would pay them to solve cases. "I'm not much good at sneaking around," Lizzie told him, although the ridiculous idea did appeal to her for a moment, she couldn't deny it. Her own detective agency!

Ti Wong argued that he *was* good at sneaking. All he had to do to go unnoticed, he said, was pretend to be Chinese.

His plans were interrupted by Mrs. Wright. She had not spoken a word during Lizzie's goodbye. She'd sat, her eyes stonily turned to the curtained windows as if Lizzie weren't in the room. Then, after Lizzie left, Mrs. Wright had gathered her clothes into her grip and made her way down the stairs alone. "I've decided to join you," she said, "so there will be no need to worry about money. I'll inform Mr. McCallum at my bank."

Lizzie saw her careful budgets disintegrating. She added the grip to the wagon. Then she knelt and hugged the dog so tightly she came away with fleas. Well, why not? she thought, lost for a moment in the heady smell of dog. They could all be different people. Ti Wong could be a detective. Mrs. Wright could be rich. Lizzie would learn to be a mother if she had to grow wings and a tail. She felt an optimism best explained by inexperience and a serious failure of imagination.

"What would you like to be?" she asked Jenny.

"Going," Jenny answered.

Lizzie helped Mrs. Wright climb aboard and scrambled to her own seat. "We're off to see some ducks, then," she said gaily, giving the reins to Ti Wong. He was now the man in the family, so he drove.

The next day all the newspapers were talking about the Doom Sealers. People as far away as Sacramento had scrambled into the capital dome for safety. Believers in Santa Rosa had climbed Taylor Mountain. Noted daredevil Sarah Pike had made a balloon ascension; the morning of April 14 found her aloft over Ocean Beach at just that time, the local papers observed, when the real daredevils were on the ground.

"Mrs. Woodworth All Wet!" the headlines read.

A colored evangelist named Mrs. Simmons had also predicted destruction. The date she'd chosen was 1898, and the method earthquake. Who cared? San Francisco would stand forever. The beautiful weather was compared with the Great Disappointment of '44, when Christ failed once again to appear to the Millerites.

ACKNOWLEDGEMENTS

I had, as always, a lot of help. Thank you, Debbie and Darcy Smith, Clinton Lawrence, Alan Elms, Sara Streich, Carter Scholz, Angus MacDonald, Pat Murphy, Michael Blumlein, Laura Miller, Michael Berry, Richard Russo, Sean Stewart, Nancy Ogle, Jonathan Elkus, and Jeff Walker.

Most particular thanks to Kelly Link. I couldn't have finished without you, Kelly.

Thanks to Helen Holdridge for the Holdridge Collection at the San Francisco Public Library.

And to the MacDowell Colony for time and space.

Marian Wood and Wendy Weil.

Hugh, too.

KAREN JOY FOWLER ON WRITING
SISTER NOON

I began this book with San Francisco. I've spent my adult life circling that city, and though I'm not a city girl, I make that one exception. I like its hills; I like its fog; I like its history. So I took myself to the university library in Davis, found the right shelves, and started looking for my story.

I read about the Palace Hotel, the failure of the Bank of California and subsequent death of its president, William Ralston. I read about the case of Constance Flood and also the Sharon divorce trial. I read about the great diamond hoax, and the diphtheria epidemic at the Ladies Protection and Relief Society Home. I read about Archy Lee, center of a fugitive slave case, and *The Elevator*, a weekly African American Press. I read about Golden Gate Park. I read about Chinatown. And I began to notice something: the name of a woman I'd never heard of, Mary Ellen Pleasant, showed up in everything I read.

She was rarely in the center of the story, more off to the side, but always present, no matter what the topic, no matter what the year. She appeared to be a black woman, very wealthy, who nevertheless worked as a housekeeper. She seemed to know everyone and she seemed to know about everyone. She had published a cookbook.

I thought I would like to write about her. She looked to be the secret at the heart of the city.

The university library had a biography, *Mammy Pleasant*, by Helen Holdredge, published in 1953. *Mammy Pleasant* is a potboiler – voodoo, blackmail, sex, and murder. Great stuff! But I couldn't help but notice that, on the few occasions when Holdredge provided a footnote that I could track to its original source, the original source invariably said something quite different from what Holdredge claimed it said. The book appeared completely unreliable at best. At worst, deliberate character assassination. Plus it was the single source for much of the other material I could find.

But I was still hopeful. The San Francisco History Room had boxes of primary materials – diaries, calendars, letters, interviews. I was confident that by the time I'd made my way through those I'd have a better understanding of who Mary Ellen Pleasant was.

And then I had a very odd research experience. The more I read, the less I knew. A thesis I found began with the assertion that there is not a single fact about Mary Ellen Pleasant not in dispute. Even one of the few photographs of her turned out to actually be of the Hawaiian Queen, Lili'uokalani.

Pleasant was clearly a remarkable, incredibly capable, energetic, brilliant woman. She was also quite a fabulist. She lived for many years in a house on Octavia Street with two other fabulists – Thomas and Teresa Bell. None of them appeared to be using their real names, admitting to their real ages or histories, and the familial organization of the house was a mystery. How many children did the Bells have? Nobody (including Thomas Bell himself) ever knew. Maybe lots. Maybe none. A friend who'd accompanied me to San Francisco to help sort through the boxes threw up her hands. "Well, they're all completely crazy," she said.

Many historians are interested in Mary Ellen Pleasant and the work on her is ongoing. In the years since I wrote this, it's entirely possible much more is known. Not in time for me.

So I gave up on the idea of writing about who Mary Ellen Pleasant was. The best I could manage was to write about the things, the contradictory, unlikely, completely confusing things people said about her. The content of the gossip may be doubtful, but the fact that there was gossip, and plenty of it, is well documented.

I moved my story out of the house of Octavia Street and into the Ladies Protection and Relief Society Home. The first of these (known for years as The House of Mystery) was torn down in 1927, but the second is still standing, repurposed as an assisted living facility. Those characters in my book primarily associated with the House of Mystery are all real, historical figures. The characters in the Ladies Protection and Relief Society Home are all people I made up.

The usual rule regarding my historical fiction applies here: if it appears plausible, I probably made it up. If it seems too strange to be true, I probably didn't.

But maybe someone else did.

TOPICS FOR READING GROUP DISCUSSIONS

The epigraph of *Sister Noon* is a quotation from Mary Ellen Pleasant: "Words were invented so that lies could be told." How does it affect how you read the book? And how does it relate to the book?

Karen Joy Fowler has said that she doesn't say the book is based on truth, because so many facts about Mary Ellen Pleasant and Thomas and Teresa Bell are in dispute, but those characters are based on real people, who went by those names (for at least some of their lives). What is the role of "true stories" in fiction? Would you read a novel differently according to whether or not it has a basis in real life?

Gossip is important to the book in several ways. The characters alternately enjoy it, scorn it (or pretend to), and are victims of it, while the story has as its inspiration gossip about Mary Ellen Pleasant and the Bells, too. As Fowler says of the residents of the House of Mystery, "The content of the gossip may be doubtful, but the fact that there was gossip, and plenty of it, is well documented." What is the role of gossip in Lizzie's transformation through the book? What role does it play in a society that believes itself genteel?

There are said to be six men to every woman in San Francisco, and yet most of the significant characters in the book are women.

What do you think about the interactions between men and women in the book? How do they relate to Lizzie's fantasies about love and romance, and to the reality of her encounters with men, in particular Mr Finney and her father?

There's an important tension in Lizzie's personality between romantic fantasy and hard reality. What effect does Mrs Pleasant's assertion that "You don't have to be the same person all your life" have on Lizzie? And how does the ending express who she is, and who she has decided to be?

The phrase "Sister Night and Sister Noon" is said to describe sisters where one is dark and one fair. But does it have greater significance than that? In what other ways does it relate to Lizzie and Jenny?

San Francisco is a city just establishing itself at the turn of the century. People are trying to preserve old ideas and beliefs, at the same time as being confronted with new possibilities and new ways of living. How does Lizzie's experience through the book relate to the wider backdrop of the city and its inhabitants at that time?

Philanthropy is a central idea in the book – Lizzie's time is mostly spent charitably, raising funds for the Brown Ark, and the Putnams see their behavior towards Lizzie as something of a good deed. Even Mary Ellen Pleasant could be seen as a philanthropist, finding homes for unwanted children. What role does "doing good" play in the book?

The *New York Times* praises Karen Joy Fowler's "willingness to take detours, her unapologetic delight in the odd historical fact, her shadowy humor, and the elegant unruliness of her language". If you have read other books by this author, what do you think they have in common? And how are they different?

Fiction
World literature
Serpent's Tail Classics
Crime

Non-fiction
Politics & Current Affairs
Music
Biography

Serpent's Tail: Books with Bite!

Visit serpentstail.com today to browse our books, learn more about our authors and events, and for exclusive content, downloads and competitions

---

www.serpentstail.com

Latest News

Author Interviews, Biographies and Q&As

Events

Trade & Media News

Sign up to our newsletter today for exclusive content, interviews and competitions: http://bit.ly/STsubscribe

---

More ways to keep in touch

Twitter @serpentstail

Facebook /serpentstailbooks

Pinterest /serpentstail